MICHAEL CONNELLY
Three Great Novels
His Latest Bestsellers

D1439348

Michael Connelly

Three Great Novels: His Latest Bestsellers

A Darkness More Than Night

City of Bones

Chasing the Dime

ORION

A Darkness More Than Night Copyright © 2000 Hieronymus, Inc.
City of Bones Copyright © 2002 Hieronymus, Inc.
Chasing the Dime Copyright © 2002 Hieronymus, Inc.

This omnibus edition first published in Great Britain in 2004 by Orion,
an imprint of the Orion Publishing Group Ltd.

A CIP catalogue record for this book
is available from the British Library.

ISBN 0 75286 733 4 (trade paperback)

Typeset by Deltatype Ltd, Birkenhead, Merseyside
Set in 10.75/12.75pt Minion

Printed in Great Britain by Clays Ltd, St Ives plc

The Orion Publishing Group Ltd
Orion House
5 Upper Saint Martin's Lane
London, WC2H 9EA

Contents

A Darkness More
Than Night

This is for Mary and Jack Lavelle,
who proved there are second acts

Prologue

Bosch looked through the small square of glass and saw that the man was alone in the tank. He took his gun out of its holster and handed it to the watch sergeant. Standard procedure. The steel door was unlocked and slid open. Immediately the smell of sweat and vomit stung Bosch's nostrils.

'How long's he been in here?'

'About three hours,' said the sergeant. 'He blew a one-eight, so I don't know what you're going to get.'

Bosch stepped into the holding tank and kept his eyes on the prone form on the floor.

'All right, you can close it.'

'Let me know.'

The door slid closed with a jarring bang and jolt. The man on the floor groaned and moved only slightly. Bosch walked over and sat down on the bench nearest to him. He took the tape recorder out of his jacket pocket and put it down on the bench. Glancing up at the glass window he saw the sergeant's face move away. He used the toe of his shoe to probe the man's side. The man groaned again.

'Wake up, you piece of shit.'

The man on the floor of the tank slowly rolled his head and then lifted it. Paint flecked his hair and vomit had caked on the front of his shirt and neck. He opened his eyes and immediately closed them against the harsh overhead lighting of the holding tank. His voice came out in a hoarse whisper.

'You again.'

Bosch nodded.

'Yeah. Me.'

'Our little dance.'

A smile cut across the three-day-old whiskers on the drunk's face. Bosch saw that he was missing a tooth he hadn't been missing last time. He reached down and put his hand on the recorder but did not turn it on yet.

'Get up. It's time to talk.'

'Forget it, man. I don't want—'

'You're running out of time. Talk to me.'

'Leave me the fuck alone.'

Bosch looked up at the window. It was clear. He looked back down at the man on the floor.

'Your salvation is in the truth. Now more than ever. I can't help you without the truth.'

'What're you, a priest now? You here to take my confession?'

'You here to give it?'

The man on the floor said nothing. After a while Bosch thought he might have fallen back asleep. He pushed the toe of his shoe into the man's side again, into the kidney. The man erupted in movement, flailing his arms and legs.

'Fuck you!' he yelled. 'I don't want you. I want a lawyer.'

Bosch was silent a moment. He picked up the recorder and slid it back into his pocket. He then leaned forward, elbows on his knees, and clasped his hands together. He looked at the drunk and slowly shook his head.

'Then I guess I can't help you,' he said.

He stood up and knocked on the window for the watch sergeant. He left the man lying on the floor.

1

'Someone's coming.'

Terry McCaleb looked at his wife and then followed her eyes down to the winding road below. He could see the golf cart making its way up the steep and winding road to the house. The driver was obscured by the roof of the cart.

They were sitting on the back deck of the house he and Graciela had rented up on La Mesa Avenue. The view ranged from the narrow winding road below the house to the whole of Avalon and its harbor, and then out across the Santa Monica Bay to the haze of smog that marked overtown. The view was the reason they had chosen this house to make their new home on the island. But at the moment his wife spoke, his gaze had been on the baby in his arms, not the view. He could look no farther than his daughter's wide blue and trusting eyes.

McCaleb saw the rental number on the side of the golf cart passing below. It wasn't a local coming. It was somebody who had probably come from overtown on the *Catalina Express*. Still, he wondered how Graciela knew that the visitor was coming to their house and not any of the others on La Mesa.

He didn't ask about this – she'd had premonitions before. He just waited and soon after the golf cart disappeared from sight, there was a knock at the front door. Graciela went to answer it and soon came back to the deck with a woman McCaleb had not seen in three years.

Sheriff's detective Jaye Winston smiled when she saw the child in his arms. It was genuine, but at the same time it was the distracted smile of someone who wasn't there to admire a new baby. McCaleb knew the thick green binder she carried in one hand and the videocassette in the other meant Winston was there on business. Death business.

'Terry, howya been?' she asked.

'Couldn't be better. You remember Graciela?'

'Of course. And who is this?'

'This is CiCi.'

McCaleb never used the baby's formal name around others. He only liked to call her Cielo when he was alone with her.

'CiCi,' Winston said, and hesitated as if waiting for an explanation of the name. When none came, she said, 'How old?'

'Almost four months. She's big.'

'Wow, yeah, I can see ... And the boy ... where's he?'

'Raymond,' Graciela said. 'He's with some friends today. Terry had a charter and so he went with friends to the park to play softball.'

The conversation was halting and strange. Winston either wasn't really interested or was unused to such banal talk.

'Would you like something to drink?' McCaleb offered as he passed the baby to Graciela.

'No, I'm fine. I had a Coke on the boat.'

As if on cue, or perhaps indignant about being passed from one set of hands to another, the baby started to fuss and Graciela said she would take her inside. She left them standing on the porch. McCaleb pointed to the round table and chairs where they ate most nights while the baby slept.

'Let's sit down.'

He pointed Winston to the chair that would give her the best view of the harbor. She put the green binder, which McCaleb recognized as a murder book, on the table and the video on top of it.

'Beautiful,' she said.

'Yeah, she's amazing. I could watch her all—'

He stopped and smiled when he realized she was talking about the view, not his child. Winston smiled, too.

'She's beautiful, Terry. She really is. You look good, too, so tan and all.'

'I've been going out on the boat.'

'And your health is good?'

'Can't complain about anything other than all the meds they make me take. But I'm three years in now and no problems. I think I'm in the clear, Jaye. I just have to keep taking the damn pills and it should stay that way.'

He smiled and he did appear to be the picture of health. As the sun had turned his skin dark, it had worked to the opposite effect on his hair. Close cropped and neat, it was almost blond now. Working on the boat had also defined the muscles of his arms and shoulders. The only giveaway was hidden under his shirt, the ten-inch scar left by transplantation surgery.

'That's great,' Winston said. 'It looks like you have a wonderful setup here. New family, new home ... away from everything.'

She was silent a moment, turning her head as if to take in all of the view and the island and McCaleb's life at once. McCaleb had always thought Jaye Winston was attractive in a tomboyish way. She had loose sandy-blond hair that she kept shoulder length. She had never worn makeup back when he worked with her. But she had sharp, knowing eyes and an easy and somewhat sad smile, as if she saw the humor and tragedy in everything at once. She wore black jeans and a white T-shirt beneath a black blazer. She looked cool and tough and McCaleb knew from experience that she was.

She had a habit of hooking her hair behind her ear frequently as she spoke. He found that endearing for some unknown reason. He had always thought that if he had not connected with Graciela he might have tried to know Jaye Winston better. He also sensed that Winston intuitively knew that.

'Makes me feel guilty about why I came,' she said. 'Sort of.'

McCaleb nodded at the binder and the tape.

'You came on business. You could have just called, Jaye. Saved some time, probably.'

'No, you didn't send out any change-of-address or phone cards. Like maybe you didn't want people to know where you ended up.'

She hooked her hair behind her left ear and smiled again.

'Not really,' he said. 'I just didn't think people would want to know where I was. So how did you find me?'

'Asked around over at the marina on the mainland.'

'Overtown. They call it overtown here.'

'Overtown, then. They told me in the harbor master's office that you still kept a slip there but you moved the boat over here. I came over and took a water taxi around the harbor until I found it. Your friend was there. He told me how to get up here.'

'Buddy.'

McCaleb looked down into the harbor and picked out *The Following Sea*. It was about a half mile or so away. He could see Buddy Lockridge bent over in the stern. After a few moments he could tell that Buddy was washing off the reels with the hose from the freshwater tank.

'So what's this about, Jaye?' McCaleb said without looking at Winston. 'Must be important for you to go through all of that on your day off. I assume you're off on Sundays.'

'Most of them.'

She pushed the tape aside and opened the binder. Now McCaleb looked over. Although it was upside down to him, he could tell the top page was a standard homicide occurrence report, usually the first page in every murder book he had ever read. It was the starting point. His eyes went to the address box. Even upside down he could make out that it was a West Hollywood case.

'I've got a case here I was hoping you'd take a look at. In your spare time, I mean. I think it might be your sort of thing. I was hoping you'd give me a read, maybe point me someplace I haven't been yet.'

He had known as soon as he saw the binder in her hands that this was what she was going to ask him. But now that it had been asked he felt a confusing rush of sensations. He felt a thrill at the possibility of having a part of his old life again. He also felt guilt over the idea of bringing death into a home so full of new life and happiness. He glanced toward the open slider to see if Graciela was looking out at them. She wasn't.

'My sort of thing?' he said. 'If it's a serial, you shouldn't waste time. Go to the bureau, call Maggie Griffin. She'll—'

'I did all of that, Terry. I still need you.'

'How old is this thing?'

'Two weeks.'

Her eyes looked up from the binder to his.

'New Year's Day?'

She nodded.

'First murder of the year,' she said. 'For L.A. County, at least. Some people think the true millennium didn't start until this year.'

'You think this is a millennium nut?'

'Whoever did this was a nut of some order. I think. That's why I'm here.'

'What did the bureau say? Did you take this to Maggie?'

'You haven't kept up, Terry. Maggie was sent back to Quantico. Things slowed down in the last few years out here and Behavioral Sciences pulled her back. No outpost in L.A. anymore. So, yes, I talked to her. But over the phone at Quantico. She ran it through VICAP and got zilched.'

McCaleb knew she meant the Violent Criminal Apprehension Program computer.

'What about a profile?' he asked.

'I'm on a waiting list. Do you know that across the country there were thirty-four millennium-inspired murders on New Year's Eve and New Year's Day? So they have their hands full at the moment and the bigger departments like us, we're at the end of the line because the bureau figures the smaller departments with less experience and expertise and manpower need their help more.'

She waited a moment while letting McCaleb consider all of this. He understood the bureau's philosophy. It was a form of triage.

'I don't mind waiting a month or so until Maggie or somebody else over there can work something up for me, but my gut on this one tells me time is a consideration, Terry. If it is a serial, a month may be too long to wait. That's why I thought of coming to you. I am banging my head on the wall on this one and you might be our last best hope of coming up with something to move on now. I still remember the Cemetery Man and the Code Killer. I know what you can do with a murder book and some crime scene tape.'

The last few lines were gratuitous and her only false move so far, McCaleb thought. Otherwise he believed she was sincere in the expression of her belief that the killer she was looking for might strike again.

'It's been a long time for me, Jaye,' McCaleb began. 'Other than that thing with Graciela's sister, I haven't been involved in—'

'Come on, Terry, don't bullshit me, okay? You can sit here with a baby in your lap every day of the week and it still won't erase what you were and what you did. I know you. We haven't seen each other or talked in a long time but I know you. And I know that not a day goes by that you don't think about cases. Not a day.'

She paused and stared at him.

'When they took out your heart, they didn't take out what makes you tick, know what I mean?'

McCaleb looked away from her and back down at his boat. Buddy was now sitting in the main fighting chair, his feet up on the transom. McCaleb assumed he had a beer in his hand but it was too far to see that.

'If you're so good at reading people, what do you need me for?'

'I may be good but you're the best I ever knew. Hell, even if they weren't backed up till Easter in Quantico, I'd take you over any of those profilers. I mean that. You were—'

'Okay, Jaye, we don't need a sales pitch, okay? My ego is doing okay without all the—'

'Then what do you need?'

He looked back at her.

'Just some time. I need to think about this.'

'I'm here because my gut says I don't have much time.'

McCaleb got up and walked to the railing. His gaze was out to the sea. A *Catalina Express* ferry was coming in. He knew it would be almost empty. The winter months brought few visitors.

'The boat's coming in,' he said. 'It's the winter schedule, Jaye. You better catch it going back or you'll be here all night.'

'I'll have dispatch send a chopper for me if I have to. Terry, all I need from you is one day at the most. One night, even. Tonight. You sit down, read the book, look at the tape and then call me in the morning, tell me what you see. Maybe it's nothing or at least nothing that's new. But maybe you'll see something we've missed or you'll get an idea we haven't come up with yet. That's all I'm asking. I don't think it's a lot.'

McCaleb looked away from the incoming boat and turned so his back leaned against the rail.

'It doesn't seem like a lot to you because you're in the life. I'm not. I'm out of it, Jaye. Even going back into it for a day is going to change things. I moved out here to start over and to forget all the stuff I was good at. To get good at being something else. At being a father and a husband, for starters.'

Winston got up and walked to the railing. She stood next to him but looked out at the view while he remained facing his home. She spoke in a low voice. If Graciela was listening from somewhere inside, she could not hear this.

'Remember with Graciela's sister what you told me? You told me you got a second shot at life and that there had to be a reason for it. Now you've built this life with her sister and her son and now even your own child. That's wonderful, Terry, I really think so. But that can't be the reason you were looking for. You might think it is but it's not. Deep down you know it. You were good at catching these people. Next to that, what is catching fish?'

McCaleb nodded slightly and was uncomfortable with himself for doing it so readily.

'Leave the stuff,' he said. 'I'll call you when I can.'

On the way to the door Winston looked about for Graciela but didn't see her.

'She's probably in with the baby,' McCaleb said.

'Well, tell her I said good-bye.'

'I will.'

There was an awkward silence the rest of the way to the door. Finally, as McCaleb opened it, Winston spoke.

'So what's it like, Terry? Being a father.'

'It's the best of times, it's the worst of times.'

His stock answer. He then thought a moment and added something he had thought about but never said, not even to Graciela.

'It's like having a gun to your head all the time.'

Winston looked confused and maybe even a little concerned.

'How so?'

'Because I know if anything ever happens to her, anything, then my life is over.'

She nodded.

'I think I can understand that.'

She went through the door. She looked rather silly as she left. A seasoned homicide detective riding away in a golf cart.

2

Sunday dinner with Graciela and Raymond was a quiet affair. They ate white sea bass McCaleb had caught with the charter that morning on the back side of the island near the isthmus. His charters always wanted to keep the fish they caught but then often changed their minds when they got back to the harbor. It was something about the killing instinct in men, McCaleb believed. It wasn't enough just to catch their quarry. They must kill it as well. It meant fish was often served at dinner at the house on La Mesa.

McCaleb had grilled the fish along with corn still in the husks on the porch barbecue. Graciela had made a salad and biscuits. They both had a glass of white wine in front of them. Raymond had milk. The meal was good but the silence wasn't. McCaleb looked over at Raymond and realized the boy had picked up on the vibe passed between the adults and was going along with the tide. McCaleb remembered how he had done the same thing when he was a boy and his parents were throwing silence at each other. Raymond was the son of Graciela's sister, Gloria. His father had never been part of the picture. When Glory died – was murdered – three years before, Raymond had come to live with Graciela. McCaleb met them both when he investigated the case.

'How was softball today?' McCaleb finally asked.

'It was okay, I guess.'

'Get any hits?'

'No.'

'You will. Don't worry. Just keep trying. Keep swinging.'

McCaleb nodded. The boy had wanted to go out on the charter that morning but had not been allowed. The charter was for six men from overtown. With McCaleb and Buddy, that made eight on *The Following Sea* and that was the limit the boat could carry under the rules of safety. McCaleb never broke those rules.

'Well, listen, our next charter isn't until Saturday. Right now it's only four people. In winter season I doubt we'll pick up anybody else. If it stays that way, you can come.'

The boy's dark features seemed to lighten and he nodded vigorously as he worked his fork into the pure white meat of the fish on his plate. The fork looked big in his hand and McCaleb felt a momentary sadness for the boy. He was exceedingly small for a boy of ten. This bothered Raymond a great deal and he often asked McCaleb when he would grow. McCaleb always told him that it would happen soon, though privately he thought the boy would always be small. He knew that his mother had been of average size but Graciela had told McCaleb that Raymond's father had been a very small man – in size and integrity. He had disappeared before Raymond was born.

Always picked last for the team, too small to be competitive with other boys his age, Raymond had gravitated toward pastimes other than team sports. Fishing was his passion and on off days McCaleb usually took him out into the bay to fish for halibut. When he had a charter, the boy always begged to go and when there was room he was allowed to come along as second mate. It was always McCaleb's great pleasure to put a five-dollar bill into an envelope, seal it and hand it to the boy at the end of the day.

'We'll need you in the tower,' McCaleb said. 'This party wants to go down south for marlin. It'll be a long day.'

'Cool!'

McCaleb smiled. Raymond loved being the lookout in the tower, watching for black marlin sleeping or rolling on the surface. And with a pair of binoculars, he was becoming adept at it. McCaleb looked over at Graciela to share the moment but she was looking down at her plate. There was no smile on her face.

In a few more minutes Raymond had finished eating and asked to be excused so he could play on the computer in his room. Graciela told him to keep the sound down so as not to wake the baby. The boy took his plate into the kitchen and then Graciela and McCaleb were alone.

He understood why she was silent. She knew she could not voice her objection to his getting involved in an investigation because her own request that he investigate her sister's death was what had brought them together three years before. Her emotions were caught in this irony.

'Graciela,' McCaleb began. 'I know you don't want me to do this but—'

'I didn't say that.'

'You didn't have to. I know you and I can tell by the look that's been on your face ever since Jaye was here that—'

'I just don't want everything to change, that's all.'

'I understand that. I don't want anything to change either. And it won't. All I'm going to do is look at the file and the tape and tell her what I think.'

'It won't be just that. *I* know *you.* I've seen you do this. You'll get hooked. It's what you are good at.'

'I won't get hooked. I'll just do what she asked and that's it. I'm not even going to do it here. I'm going to take what she gave me and go over to the boat. So it won't even be in the house. Okay? I don't want it in the house.'

He knew he was going to do it with or without her approval but he wanted it from her just the same. Their relationship was still so new that he seemed to always be seeking her approval. He had thought about this and wondered if it was something to do with his second chance. He had fought through a lot of guilt in the past three years but it still came up like a roadblock every few miles. Somehow he felt as though if he could just win this one woman's approval for his existence, then it would all be okay. His cardiologist had called it survivor's guilt. He had lived because someone else had died and must now attain some sense of redemption for it. But McCaleb thought the explanation was not as simple as that.

Graciela frowned but it did not detract from his view of her as beautiful. She had copper skin and dark brown hair that framed a face with eyes so darkly brown that there was almost no demarcation between iris and pupil. Her beauty was another reason he sought her approval of all things. There was something purifying about the light of her smile when it was cast on him.

'Terry, I listened to you two on the porch. After the baby got quiet. I heard what she said about what makes you tick and how a day doesn't go by that you don't think about it, what you used to do. Just tell me this, was she right?'

McCaleb was silent a moment. He looked down at his empty plate and then off across the harbor to the lights in the houses going up the opposite hillside to the inn at the top of Mount Ada. He slowly nodded and then looked back at her.

'Yes, she was right.'

'Then all of this, what we are doing here, the baby, it's all a lie?'

'No. Of course not. This is everything to me and I would protect it with everything I've got. But the answer is yes, I think about what I was and what I did. When I was with the bureau I saved lives, Graciela, plain and simple. And I took evil out of this world. Made it a little less dark out there.'

He raised his hand and gestured toward the harbor.

'Now I have a wonderful life with you and Cielo and Raymond. And I . . . I catch fish for rich people with nothing better to do with their money.'

'So you want both.'

'I don't know what I want. But I know that when she was here I was saying things to her because I knew you were listening. I was saying what I knew you wanted to hear but I knew in my heart it wasn't what I wanted. What I wanted to do was open that book right then and go to work. She was right about me, Gracie. She hadn't seen me in three years but she had me pegged.'

Graciela stood up and came around the table to him. She sat on his lap.

'I'm just scared for you, that's all,' she said.

She pulled him close.

McCaleb took two tall glasses from the cabinet and put them on the counter. He filled the first with bottled water and the second with orange juice. He then began ingesting the twenty-seven pills he had lined up on the counter, intermittently taking swallows of water and orange juice to help them go down. Eating the pills – twice a day – was his ritual and he hated it. Not because of the taste – he was long past that after three years. But because the ritual was a reminder of how dependent he was on exterior concerns for his life. The pills were a leash. He could not live long without them. Much of his world now was built around ensuring that he would always have them. He planned around them. He hoarded them. Sometimes he even dreamed about taking pills.

When he was done, McCaleb went into the living room, where Graciela was reading a magazine. She didn't look up at him when he stepped into the room, another sign that she was unhappy with what was suddenly happening in her home. He stood there waiting for a moment and when things didn't change he went down the hallway into the baby's room.

Cielo was still asleep in her crib. The overhead light was on a dimmer switch and he raised the illumination just enough so that he could see her clearly. McCaleb went to the crib and leaned down so he could listen to her breathe and see her and smell her baby scent. Cielo had her mother's coloring – dark skin and hair – except for her eyes, which were ocean blue. Her tiny hands were balled in fists as if she were showing her readiness to fight for life. McCaleb fell most in love with her when he watched her sleep. He thought about all the preparation they had gone through, the books and classes and advice from Graciela's friends at the hospital who were pediatric nurses. All of it so that they would be ready to care for a fragile life so dependent on them. Nothing had been said or read to prepare him for the opposite: the knowledge that came the first moment he held her, that his own life was now dependent on her.

He reached down to her, the spread of his hand covering her back. She didn't stir. He could feel her tiny heart beating. It seemed quick and desperate, like a whispered prayer. Sometimes he pulled the rocking chair over next to the crib and watched over her until late into the night. This night was different. He had to go. He had work to do. Blood work. He wasn't sure if he was there to simply say good-bye for the night or to somehow gain inspiration or approval from her as well. In his mind it didn't quite make sense. He just knew that he had to watch her and touch her before he went to his work.

McCaleb walked out on the pier and then down the steps to the skiff dock. He found his Zodiac among the other small boats and climbed aboard, careful to put the videotape and the murder book in the shelter of the inflatable's bow so they wouldn't get wet. He pulled the engine cord twice before it started and then headed off down the middle lane of the harbor. There were no docks in Avalon Harbor. The boats were tied to mooring buoys set in lines that followed the concave shape of the natural harbor.

Because it was winter there were few boats in the harbor, but McCaleb didn't cut between the buoys. He followed the fairways, as if driving a car on the streets of a neighborhood. You didn't cut across lawns, you stayed on the roadway.

It was cold on the water and McCaleb zipped up his windbreaker. As he approached *The Following Sea* he could see the glow of the television behind the curtains of the salon. This meant Buddy Lockridge had not finished up in time to catch the last ferry and was staying over.

McCaleb and Lockridge worked the charter business together. While the boat's ownership was in Graciela's name, the marine charter license and all other documentation relating to the business were in Lockridge's name. The two had met more than three years earlier when McCaleb had docked *The Following Sea* at Cabrillo Marina in the Los Angeles Harbor and was living aboard it while restoring it. Buddy was a neighbor, living on a sailboat nearby. They had struck up a friendship that ultimately became a partnership.

During the busy spring and summer season Lockridge stayed most nights on *The Following Sea*. But during the slow times he usually caught a ferry back overtown to his own boat at Cabrillo. He seemed to have greater success finding female companions in the overtown bars than in the handful of places on the island. McCaleb assumed he would be heading back in the morning since they did not have a charter for another five days.

McCaleb bumped the Zodiac into the fantail of *The Following Sea*. He cut the engine and got out with the tape and the binder. He tied the Zodiac off on a stern cleat and headed for the salon door. Buddy was there waiting, having heard the Zodiac or felt its bump on the fantail. He slid the door open, holding a paperback novel down at his side. McCaleb glanced at the television but couldn't tell what it was he had on.

'What's up, Terror?' Lockridge asked.

'Nothing. I just need to do a little work. I'm going to be using the forward bunk, okay?'

He stepped into the salon. It was warm. Lockridge had the space heater fired up.

'Sure, fine. Anything I can do to help?'

'Nah, this isn't about the business.'

'It about that lady who came by? The sheriff's lady?'

McCaleb had forgotten that Winston had come to the boat first and gotten directions from Buddy.

'Yeah.'

'You working a case for her?'

'No,' McCaleb said quickly, hoping to limit Lockridge's interest and involvement. 'I just need to look at some stuff and give her a call back.'

'Very cool, dude.'

'Not really. It's just a favor. What are you watching?'

'Oh, nothing. Just a show about this task force that goes after computer hackers. Why, you seen it?'

'No, but I was wondering if I could borrow the TV for a little while.' McCaleb held up the videotape. Lockridge's eyes lit up.

'Be my guest. Pop that baby in there.'

'Um, not up here, Buddy. This is – Detective Winston asked me to do this in confidence. I'll bring the TV back up as soon as I'm done.'

Lockridge's face registered his disappointment but McCaleb wasn't worried about it. He went over to the counter that separated the galley from the salon and put down the binder and tape. He unplugged the television and removed it from the locking frame that held it in place so it wouldn't fall when the boat encountered high seas. The television had a built-in videocassette player and was heavy. McCaleb lugged it down the narrow stairway and took it to the forward stateroom, which had been partially converted into an office. Two sides of the room had been lined with twin bunk beds. The bottom berth on the left had been changed into a desk and the two top bunks were used by McCaleb to store his old bureau case files – Graciela didn't want them in the house where Raymond might stumble upon them. The only problem was that McCaleb was sure that on occasion Buddy had gone through the boxes and looked at the files. And it bothered him. It was an invasion of some kind. McCaleb had thought about keeping the forward stateroom locked but knew that could be a deadly mistake. The only ceiling hatch on the lower deck was in the forward room and access to it ought not be blocked in case there was ever a need for an emergency evacuation through the bow.

He put the television down on the desk and plugged it in. He turned to go back up to the salon to retrieve the binder and tape when he saw Buddy coming down the stairs, holding the tape and leafing through the binder.

'Hey, Buddy—'

'Looks like a weird one, man.'

McCaleb reached out and closed the binder, then took it and the tape from his fishing partner's hands.

'Just taking a peek.'

'I told you, it's confidential.'

'Yeah, but we work good together. Just like before.'

It was true that by happenstance Lockridge had been a great help when McCaleb had investigated the death of Graciela's sister. But that had been an active street investigation. This was just going to be a review. He didn't need anybody looking over his shoulder.

'This is different, Buddy. This is a one-night stand. I'm just going to take a look at this stuff and then that will be it. Now let me get to work so I'm not here all night.'

Lockridge didn't say anything and McCaleb didn't wait. He closed the door to the forward bunk and then turned to the desk. As he looked down at the murder book in his hands he felt a sharp thrill as well as the familiar rising of dread and guilt.

McCaleb knew it was time to go back to the darkness. To explore it and know it. To find his way through it. He nodded, though he was alone now. It was in acknowledgment that he had waited a long time for this moment.

3

The video was clear and steady, the lighting was good. The technical aspects of crime scene videotaping had vastly improved since McCaleb's days with the bureau. The content had not changed. The tape McCaleb watched showed the starkly lit tableau of murder. McCaleb finally froze the image and studied it. The cabin was silent, the gentle lapping sound of the sea against the boat's hull the only intrusion from outside.

At center focus was the nude body of what appeared to be a man who had been trussed with baling wire, his arms and legs held tightly behind his torso to such an extreme that the body appeared to be in a reverse fetal position. The body was face down on an old and dirty rug. The focus was too tight on the body to determine in what sort of location it had been found. McCaleb judged that the victim was a man solely on the basis of body mass and musculature. For the head of the victim was not visible. A gray plastic mop bucket had been placed entirely over the victim's head. McCaleb could see that a length of the baling wire was stretched taut from the victim's ankles, up his back and between his arms, and beneath the lip of the bucket where it wrapped around his neck. It appeared on first measure to be a ligature strangulation in which the leverage of the legs and feet pulled the wire tight around the victim's neck, causing asphyxia. In effect, the victim had been bound in such a way that he ultimately killed himself when he could no longer hold his legs folded backward in such an extreme position.

McCaleb continued studying the scene. A small amount of blood had poured onto the carpet from the bucket, indicating that some kind of head wound would be found when the vessel was removed.

McCaleb leaned back in his old desk chair and thought about his initial impressions. He had not yet opened the binder, choosing instead to watch the crime scene videotape first and to study the scene as close as possible to the way the investigators had originally seen it. Already he was fascinated by what he was looking at. He felt the implication of ritual in the scene on the television screen. He also felt the trilling of adrenaline in his blood again. He pressed the button on the remote and the video continued.

The focus pulled back as Jaye Winston entered the frame of the video.

McCaleb could see more of the room now and noted that it appeared to be in a small, sparsely furnished house or apartment.

Coincidentally, Winston was wearing the same outfit she had worn when she had come to the house with the murder book and videotape. She had on rubber gloves that she had pulled up over the cuffs of her blazer. Her detective's shield hung on a black shoelace which had been tied around her neck. She took a position on the left side of the dead man while her partner, a detective McCaleb did not recognize, moved to the right side. For the first time there was talking on the video.

'The victim has already been examined by a deputy coroner and released for crime scene investigation,' Winston said. 'The victim has been photographed in situ. We're now going to remove the bucket to make further examination.'

McCaleb knew that she was carefully choosing her words and demeanor with the future in mind, a future that would include a trial for an accused killer in which the crime scene tape would be viewed by a jury. She had to appear professional and objective, completely emotionally removed from what she was encountering. Anything deviating from this could be cause for a defense attorney to seek removal of the tape from evidence.

Winston reached up and hooked her hair behind her ears and then placed both hands on the victim's shoulders. With her partner's help she turned the body on its side, the dead man's back to the camera.

The camera then came in over the victim's shoulder and closed in as Winston gently pulled the bucket handle from under the man's chin and proceeded to carefully lift it off the head.

'Okay,' she said.

She showed the interior of the bucket to the camera – blood had coagulated inside it – and then placed it in an open cardboard box used for evidence storage. She then turned back and gazed down at the victim.

Gray duct tape had been wrapped around the dead man's head to form a tight gag across the mouth. The eyes were open and distended – bugged. The cornea of each eye was rouged with hemorrhage. So was the skin around the eyes.

'CP,' the partner said, pointing to the eyes.

'Kurt,' Winston said. 'We're on sound.'

'Sorry.'

She was telling her partner to keep all observations to himself. Again, she was safeguarding the future. McCaleb knew that what her partner was pointing out was the hemorrhaging, or conjunctive petechiae, which always came with ligature strangulation. However, the observation was one that should be made to a jury by a medical examiner, not a homicide detective.

Blood matted the dead man's medium-length hair and had pooled inside the bucket against the left side of his face. Winston began manipulating the head and combing her fingers through the hair in search of the origin of the blood. She finally found the wound on the crown of the head. She pulled the hair back as much as possible to view it.

'Barney, come in close on this if you can,' she said.

The camera moved in. McCaleb saw a small, round puncture wound that did not appear to penetrate the skull. He knew that the amount of blood evidenced was not always in concert with the gravity of the wound. Even inconsequential wounds to the scalp could produce a lot of blood. He would get a formal and complete description of the wound in the autopsy report.

'Barn, get this,' Winston said, her voice up a notch from the previous monotone. 'We've got writing or something on the tape, on the gag.'

She had noticed it while manipulating the head. The camera moved in. McCaleb could make out lightly marked letters on the tape where it crossed the dead man's mouth. The letters appeared to be written in ink but the message was obliterated by blood. He could make out what appeared to be one word of the message.

'Cave,' he read out loud. 'Cave?'

He then thought maybe it was only a partial word but he couldn't think of any larger word – other than *cavern* – that contained those letters in that order.

McCaleb froze the picture and just looked. He was enthralled. What he was seeing was pulling him backward in time to his days as a profiler, when almost every case he was assigned left him with the same question: *What dark, tortured mind did this come from?*

Words from a killer were always significant and put a case on a higher plane. It most often meant that the killing was a statement, a message transmitted from killer to victim and then from the investigators to the world as well.

McCaleb stood up and reached to the upper bunk. He pulled down one of the old file boxes and let it drop heavily to the floor. Quickly lifting the lid, he began combing through the files for a notebook with some unused pages in it. It had been his ritual with the bureau to start each case he was assigned with a fresh spiral notebook. He finally came across a file with only a BAR form and a notebook in it. With so little paperwork in the file he knew it was a short case and that the notebook should have plenty of blank pages.

McCaleb leafed through the notebook and found it largely unused. He then took out the Bureau Assistance Request form and quickly read the top sheet to see what case it was. He immediately remembered it because he had handled it with one phone call. The request had come from a detective in the small town of White Elk, Minnesota, almost ten years before, when McCaleb still worked out of Quantico. The detective's report said two men had gotten into a drunken brawl in the house they shared, challenged each other to a duel and proceeded to kill each other with simultaneous shots from ten yards apart in the back yard. The detective needed no help with the double homicide case because it was cut and dried. But he was puzzled by something else. In the course of searching the victims' house, investigators had come across something strange in the basement freezer. Pushed into a corner of the freezer cabinet were plastic bags containing dozens and dozens of used tampons. They were of various makes and brands, and preliminary tests on a sampling of the tampons had identified the menstrual blood on them as having come from several different women.

The case detective didn't know what he had but feared the worst. What he wanted from the FBI's Behavioral Sciences Unit was an idea about what these bloody tampons could mean and how to proceed. More specifically, he wanted to know if the tampons could possibly be souvenirs kept by a serial killer or killers who had gone undiscovered until they happened to kill each other.

McCaleb smiled as he remembered the case. He had come across tampons in a freezer before. He called the detective and asked him three questions. What did the two men do for a living? In addition to the firearms used during the duel, were there any long weapons or a hunting license found in the apartment? And, lastly, when did bear hunting season begin in the woods of northern Minnesota?

The detective's answers quickly solved the tampon mystery. Both men worked at the airport in Minneapolis for a subcontractor that provided clean-out crews who prepared commercial airliners for flights. Several hunting rifles were found in the house but no hunting license. And, lastly, bear season was three weeks away.

McCaleb told the detective that it appeared that the men were not serial killers but had probably been collecting the contents from the tampon disposal receptacles in lavatories of the planes they cleaned. They were taking the tampons home and freezing them. When hunting season began they would most likely thaw the tampons and use them to bait bear, which can pick up the scent of blood at a great distance. Most hunters use garbage as bait but nothing is better than blood.

McCaleb remembered that the detective had actually seemed disappointed that he had no serial killer or killers at hand. He had either been embarrassed that an FBI agent sitting at a desk in Quantico had so quickly solved his mystery or he was simply annoyed that there would be no national media ride from his case. He abruptly hung up and McCaleb never heard from him again.

McCaleb tore the few pages of notes from the case out of the notebook, put them in the file with the BAR form and returned the file to its spot. He then put the lid on the box and hoisted it back up onto the shelf that had been the top bunk. He shoved the box back into place and it banged hard on the bulkhead.

Sitting back down, McCaleb glanced at the frozen image on the television screen and then considered the blank page in the notebook. Finally, he took the pen out of his shirt pocket and was about to begin writing when the door to the room suddenly opened and Buddy Lockridge stood there.

'You okay?'

'What?'

'I heard all this banging. The whole boat moved.'

'I'm fine, Buddy, I just—'

'Oh, shit, what the hell is that?'

He was staring at the TV screen. McCaleb immediately raised the remote and killed the picture.

'Buddy, look, I told you this is confidential and I can't—'

'Okay, okay, I know. I was just checking to make sure you didn't keel over or something.'

'Okay, thanks, but I'm fine.'

'I'll be up for a little while if you need something.'

'I won't, but thanks.'

'You know, you're using a lot of juice. You're going to have to run the generator tomorrow after I split.'

'No problem. I'll do it. I'll see you later, Buddy.'

Buddy pointed at the now empty television screen.

'That's a weird one.'

'Good-bye, Buddy,' McCaleb said impatiently.

He got up and closed the door while Lockridge was still standing there. This time he locked it. He returned to the seat and the notebook. He started writing and in a few moments he had constructed a list.

SCENE
1. Ligature
2. Nude
3. Head Wound
4. Tape/Gag – 'Cave'?
5. Bucket?

He studied the list for a few moments, waiting for an idea, but nothing came through. It was too early. Instinctively, he knew the wording on the tape was a key that he wouldn't be able to turn until he had the complete message. He fought the urge to open the murder book and get to it. Instead, he turned the television back on and began running the tape from the spot he had left off. The camera was in and tight on the dead man's mouth and the tape stretched tightly across it.

'We'll leave this for the coroner,' Winston said. 'You got what you can of this, Barn?'

'I got it,' said the unseen videographer.

'Okay, let's pull back and look at these bindings.'

The camera traced the baling wire from the neck to the feet. The wire looped around the neck and passed through a slip knot. It then went down the spine to where it had been wrapped several times around the ankles, which had been pulled so far back that the victim's heels now rested on his buttocks.

The wrists were bound with a separate length of wire that had been wrapped six times around and then pulled into a knot. The bindings had caused deep furrow marks in the skin of the wrists and ankles, indicating that the victim had struggled for a period before finally succumbing.

When the videography of the body was completed, Winston told the unseen man with the camera to make a video inventory of every room in the apartment.

The camera panned away from the body and took in the rest of the living-room/dining-room space. The home seemed to have been furnished out of a secondhand store. There was no uniformity, none of the pieces of furniture matched. The few framed pictures on the walls looked as though they could have come out of a room at a Howard Johnson's ten years before – all orange and aqua pastels. At the far end of the room was a tall china cabinet with no china in it. There were some books on a few of the shelves but most were barren. On top of the cabinet was something McCaleb found curious. It was a two-foot-high owl that looked hand painted. McCaleb had seen many of these before, especially in Avalon Harbor and Cabrillo Marina. Most often the owls were made of hollow plastic and placed at the tops of masts or on the bridges of power boats in a usually unsuccessful attempt to scare gulls and other birds away from the boats. The theory was that the owl would be seen by the other birds as a predator and they would stay clear, thereby leaving the boats unfouled by their droppings.

McCaleb had also seen the owls used on the exteriors of public buildings where pigeons were a nuisance. But what interested him about the plastic owl here was that he had never seen or heard of one being used inside a private home as ornamentation or otherwise. He knew that people collected all manner of things, including owls, but he had so far seen none in the apartment other than the one positioned at center on the cabinet. He quickly opened the binder and found the victim identification report. It listed the victim's occupation as house painter. McCaleb closed the binder and considered for a moment that perhaps the victim had taken the owl from a job or removed it from a structure while prepping it to be painted.

He backed the tape up and watched again as the videographer panned from the body to the cabinet atop which the owl was perched. It appeared to McCaleb that the videographer had made a 180-degree turn, meaning the owl would have been directly facing the victim, looking down upon the scene of the murder.

While there were other possibilities, McCaleb's instinct told him the plastic owl was somehow part of the crime scene. He took up the notebook and made the owl the sixth entry on his list.

The rest of the crime scene videotape fostered little interest in McCaleb. It documented the remaining rooms of the victim's apartment – the bedroom, bathroom and kitchen. He saw no more owls and took no more notes. When he got to the end of the tape he rewound it and watched it all the way through once more. Nothing new caught his attention. He ejected the tape and slid it back into its cardboard slipcase. He then carried the television back up to the salon, where he locked it into its frame on the counter.

Buddy was sprawled on the couch reading his paperback. He didn't say anything and McCaleb could tell he was hurt that McCaleb had closed and locked the door to the office on him. He thought about apologizing but decided to let it go. Buddy was too nosy about McCaleb, past and present. Maybe this rejection would let him know that.

'What are you reading?' he asked instead.

'A book,' Lockridge answered without looking up.

McCaleb smiled to himself. Now he was sure that he had gotten to Buddy.

'Well, there's the TV if you want to watch the news or something.'

'The news is over.'

McCaleb looked at his watch. It was midnight. He had not realized how much time had gone by. This had often been the case with him – while at the bureau it was routine for him to work through lunch or late into the night without realizing it when he became fully engaged in a case.

He left Buddy to sulk and went back down to the office. He closed the door again, loudly, and locked it.

4

After turning to a fresh page in his notebook, McCaleb opened the murder book. He snapped open the rings and pulled the documents out and stacked them neatly on the desk. It was a little quirk but he never liked reviewing cases by turning pages in a book. He liked to hold the individual reports in his hands. He liked squaring off the corners of the whole stack. He put the binder aside and began carefully reading through the investigative summaries in chronological order. Soon he was fully immersed in the investigation.

The homicide report had come in anonymously to the front desk of the West Hollywood substation of the Los Angeles County Sheriff's Department at noon on Monday, January 1. The male caller said there was a man dead in apartment 2B in the Grand Royale Apartments on Sweetzer near Melrose. The caller hung up without giving his name or any other message. Because the call came in on one of the non-emergency lines at the front desk it was not recorded, and there was no caller ID function on the phone.

A pair of patrol deputies were dispatched to the apartment and found the front door slightly ajar. After receiving no answer to their knocks and calls, the deputies entered the apartment and quickly determined that the anonymous caller had given correct information. A man was dead inside. The deputies backed out of the apartment and the homicide squad was called. The case was assigned to partners Jaye Winston and Kurt Mintz, with Winston as lead detective.

The victim was identified in the reports as Edward Gunn, a forty-four-year-old itinerant house painter. He had lived alone in the Sweetzer Avenue apartment for nine years.

A computer search for criminal records or known criminal activity determined that Gunn had a history of convictions for small-time crimes ranging from soliciting for prostitution and loitering to repeated arrests for public intoxication and drunk driving. He had been arrested twice for drunk driving in the three months prior to his death, including the night of December 30. He posted bail on the 31st and was released. Less than twenty-four hours later he was dead. The records also showed an arrest for a serious crime without subsequent conviction. Six years earlier Gunn had been taken into custody by the Los Angeles Police Department and questioned in a homicide. He was later released and no charges were ever filed.

According to the investigative reports Winston and her partner had put into the murder book, there was no apparent robbery of Gunn or his apartment, leaving the motive for his slaying unknown. Other residents in the eight-unit apartment building said that they had heard no disturbances in Gunn's apartment on New Year's Eve. Any sounds that might have emanated from the apartment during the murder were likely camouflaged by the sounds of a party being held by a tenant in the apartment directly below Gunn's. The party had lasted well into the morning of January 1. Gunn, according to several partygoers who were interviewed, had not attended the party or been invited.

A canvass of the neighborhood, which was primarily lined with small apartment buildings similar to the Grand Royale, found no witnesses who remembered seeing Gunn in the days leading up to his death.

All indications were that the murderer had come to Gunn. The lack of damage to doors and windows of the apartment indicated that there had been no break-in and that Gunn might very well have known his killer. To that end, Winston and Mintz interviewed all known coworkers and associates, as well as every tenant and every person who had attended the party at the complex, in an effort to draw out a suspect. They got nothing for their effort.

They also checked all of the victim's financial records for a clue to a possible monetary motivation and found nothing. Gunn had no steady employment. He mostly loitered around a paint and design store on Beverly Boulevard and offered his services to customers on a day-work basis. He lived a hand-to-mouth existence, making just enough to pay for and maintain his apartment and a small pickup truck in which he carried his painting equipment.

Gunn had one living relative, a sister who lived in Long Beach. At the time of his death, he had not seen her in more than a year, though he happened to call her the night before his death from the holding tank of the LAPD's Hollywood Division station. He was being held there following his DUI arrest. The sister reported that she'd told her brother she could no longer keep helping him and bailing him out. She'd hung up. And she could not offer the investigators any useful information in regard to his murder.

The incident in which Gunn had been arrested six years before was fully reviewed. Gunn had killed a prostitute in a Sunset Boulevard motel room. He had stabbed her with her own knife when she attempted to stab and rob him, according to his statement in the report forwarded by the LAPD's Hollywood Division. There were minor inconsistencies between Gunn's original statement to responding patrol officers and the physical evidence but not enough for the district attorney's office to seek charges against him. Ultimately, the case was reluctantly written off as self-defense and dropped.

McCaleb noticed that the lead investigator on the case had been Detective Harry Bosch. Years earlier McCaleb had worked with Bosch on a case, an investigation he still often thought about. Bosch had been abrasive and secretive at times, but still a good cop with excellent investigative skills, intuition and instincts. They had actually bonded in some way over the emotional turmoil the case had caused them both. McCaleb wrote Bosch's name down in the notebook as a reminder to call the detective to see if he had any thoughts on the Gunn case.

He went back to reading the summaries. With Gunn's record of prior engagement with a prostitute in mind, Winston's and Mintz's next step was to comb through the murder victim's phone records as well as check and credit card purchases for indications that he might have continued to use prostitutes. There was nothing. They cruised Sunset Boulevard with an LAPD vice crew for three nights, stopping and interviewing street prostitutes. But none admitted knowing the man in the photos the detectives had borrowed from Gunn's sister.

The detectives scanned the sex want ads in the local alternative papers for an advertisement Gunn might have placed. One more time their efforts hit a wall.

Finally, the detectives took the long shot of tracking the family and associates of the dead prostitute of six years before. Although Gunn had never been charged with the killing, there was still a chance someone believed he had not acted in self-defense – someone who might have sought retribution.

But this, too, was a dead end. The woman's family was from Philadelphia. They had lost contact years before. No family member had even come out to claim the body before it was cremated at county taxpayers' expense. There was no reason for them to seek vengeance for a killing six years old when they had not cared much about the killing in the first place.

The case had hit one investigative dead end after another. A case not solved in the first forty-eight hours had a less than 50 percent chance of being cleared. A case unsolved after two weeks was like an unclaimed body in the morgue – it was going to sit there in the cold and the dark for a long, long time.

And that was why Winston had finally come to McCaleb. He was the last resort on a hopeless case.

Finished with the summaries, McCaleb decided to take a break. He checked his watch and saw it was now almost two. He opened the cabin door and went up to the salon. The lights were off. Buddy had apparently gone to bed in the master cabin without making any noise. McCaleb opened the cold box and looked in. There was a six-pack of beer left over from the charter but he didn't want that. There was a carton of orange juice and some bottled water. He took the water and went out through the salon door to the cockpit. It was always cool on the water but this night seemed crisper than usual. He folded his arms across his chest and looked across the harbor and up the hill to the house where he knew his family slept. A single light shone from the back deck.

A momentary pang of guilt passed through him. He knew that despite his deep love for the woman and two children behind that light, he would rather be on the boat with the murder book than up there in the sleeping house. He tried to push away these thoughts and the questions they raised but could not completely blind himself to the essential conclusion that there was something wrong with him, something missing. It was something that prevented him from fully embracing that which most men seemed to long for.

He went back inside the boat. He knew that immersing himself in the case reports would shut out the guilt.

The autopsy report contained no surprises. The cause of death was as McCaleb had guessed from the video: cerebral hypoxia due to compression of the carotid arteries by ligature strangulation. The time of death was estimated to have been between midnight and 3 A.M. on January 1.

The deputy medical examiner who conducted the autopsy noted that interior damage to the neck was minimal. Neither the hyoid bone nor the thyroid cartilage was broken. This aspect, coupled with multiple ligature furrows on the skin, led the examiner to conclude that Gunn suffocated slowly while desperately struggling to keep his feet behind his torso so that the wire noose was not pulled tight around his neck. The autopsy summation suggested that the victim could have struggled in this position for as long as two hours.

McCaleb thought about this and wondered if the killer had been there in the apartment the whole time, watching the dying man struggle. Or had he set the ligature and left before his victim was dead, possibly to set some kind of alibi scheme into motion – perhaps appearing at a New Year's Eve party so that there would be multiple witnesses able to account for him at the time of the victim's death.

He then remembered the bucket and decided that the killer had stayed. The covering of the victim's face was a frequent occurrence in sexually motivated and rage killings, the attacker covering his victim's face as a means of dehumanizing the victim and avoiding eye contact. McCaleb had worked dozens of cases where he had noted this phenomenon, women who had been raped and murdered with nightgowns or pillowcases covering their faces, children with their heads wrapped in towels. He could write a list of examples that would fill the entire notebook. Instead he wrote one line on the page under Bosch's name.

UNSUB was there the whole time. He watched.

The unknown subject, McCaleb thought. So we meet again.

Before moving on, McCaleb looked through the autopsy report for two other pieces of information. First was the head wound. He found a description of the wound in the examiner's comments. The perimortem laceration was circular and superficial. Its damage was minimal and it was possibly a defensive wound.

McCaleb dismissed the possibility of it being a defensive wound. The only blood on the rug at the crime scene was that spilled from the bucket after it was placed over the victim's head. Plus, the flow of blood from the wound at the point of the crown was forward and over the victim's face. This indicated the head was bowed forward. McCaleb took all of this to mean that Gunn was already bound and on the floor when the blow had been struck to his head and then the bucket placed over it. His instinct told him this might have been a blow delivered with the intention of hurrying the victim's demise; an impact to the head that would weaken the victim and shorten his struggle against the ligature.

He wrote these thoughts down in the notebook and then went back into the autopsy report. He located the findings on the examination of the anus and penis. Swabs indicated no sexual activity had occurred in the time prior to death. McCaleb wrote down *No Sex* in the notebook. Beneath this he wrote the word *Rage* and circled it.

McCaleb realized that many, if not all, of the suspicions and conclusions he was coming up with had probably already been reached by Jaye Winston. But this had always been his routine in analyzing murder scenes. He made his own judgments first, then looked to see how they stacked up next to the primary investigator's conclusions afterward.

After the autopsy he went to the evidence analysis reports. He first looked at the recovered evidence list and noticed that the plastic owl he had seen on the videotape had not been bagged and tagged. He felt sure that it should have been and made a note of it. Also missing from the list was any mention of a weapon recovery. It appeared that whatever had been used to open up the wound on Gunn's scalp had been taken away from the scene by the killer. McCaleb made a note of this as well because it was another piece of information supportive of a profile of the killer as organized, thorough and cautious.

The report on the analysis of the tape used to gag the victim was folded into a separate envelope that McCaleb found in one of the binder's pockets. In addition to a computer printout and an addendum there were several photographs that showed the full length of the tape after it had been cut and peeled away from the victim's face and head. The first set of photos documented the tape front and back as it was found, with a significant amount of coagulated blood obscuring the message written on it. The next set of photos showed the tape front and back after the blood had been removed with a solution of soapy water. McCaleb stared at the message for a long moment even though he knew he would never be able to decipher it on his own.

Cave Cave Dus Videt

He finally put the photos aside and picked up the accompanying reports. The tape was found to be clear of fingerprints but several hairs and microscopic fibers were collected from the underside adhesive. The hair was determined to have belonged to the victim. The fibers were held pending further orders for analysis. McCaleb knew this meant there was a time and cost constraint. The fibers would not be analyzed until the investigation reached a point where there were fibers from a suspect's possessions that also could be analyzed and compared. Otherwise, the costly and time-consuming analysis of the collected fibers would be for nothing. McCaleb had seen this sort of investigative prioritizing before. It was a routine in local law enforcement not to take expensive steps until necessary. But he was a bit surprised that it had not been deemed necessary in this case. He concluded that Gunn's background as a one-time murder suspect might have dropped him into a lower class of victim, one for which the extra step is not taken. Maybe, McCaleb thought, this was why Jaye Winston had come to him. She hadn't said anything about paying him for his time – not that he could accept a monetary payment anyway.

He moved on to an addendum report that had been filed by Winston. She had taken a photograph of the tape and the message to a linguistics professor at UCLA who had identified the words as Latin. She was then referred to a retired Catholic priest who lived in the rectory at St. Catherine's in Hollywood and had taught Latin at the church's school for two decades until it was dropped from the curriculum in the early seventies. He easily translated the message for Winston.

As McCaleb read the translation he felt the feathery run of adrenaline rise up his spine to his neck. His skin tightened and he felt a sensation that came close to lightheadedness.

Cave Cave Dus Videt
Cave Cave D(omin)us Videt
Beware Beware God Sees

'Holy shit,' McCaleb said quietly to himself.

It was not said as an exclamation. Rather, it was the phrase he and fellow bureau profilers had used to informally classify cases in which religious overtures were part of the evidence. When God was discovered to be part of the probable motivation for a crime, it became a 'holy shit' case when spoken of in casual conversation. It also changed things significantly, for God's work was never done. When a killer was out there using His name as part of the imprint of a crime, it often meant there would be more crimes. It was said in the bureau profiling offices that God's killers never stopped of their own volition. They had to be stopped. McCaleb now understood Jaye Winston's apprehension about letting this case gather dust. If Edward Gunn was the first known victim, then somebody else was likely in the sights of the killer right now.

McCaleb scribbled down a translation of the killer's message and some other thoughts. He wrote *Victim Acquisition* and underlined it twice.

He looked back at Winston's report and noticed that at the bottom of the page containing the translation there was a paragraph marked with an asterisk.

*Father Ryan stated that the word 'Dus' as seen on the duct tape was a short form of 'Deus' or 'Dominus' primarily found in medieval Bibles as well as church carvings and other artwork.

McCaleb leaned back in his chair and drank from the water bottle. He found this final paragraph the most interesting of the whole package. The information it contained could be a means by which the killer might be isolated in a small group and then found. Initially the pool of potential suspects was huge – it would essentially include anyone who had had access to Edward Gunn on New Year's Eve. But the information from Father Ryan narrowed it significantly to those who had knowledge of medieval Latin, or someone who had gotten the word *Dus* and possibly the whole message from something he had seen.

Perhaps something in a church.

5

McCaleb was too jazzed by what he had read and seen to think about sleep. It was four-thirty and he knew he would complete this night awake and in the office. It was probably too early in Quantico, Virginia, for anyone to be in the Behavioral Sciences Unit but he decided to make the call anyway. He went up to the salon, got the cell phone out of the charger and punched in the number from memory. When the general operator answered he asked to be transferred to Special Agent Brasilia Doran's desk. There were a lot of people he could have asked for but he had decided on Doran because they had worked well together – and often from long distances – when he had been in the bureau. Doran also specialized in icon identification and symbology.

The call was picked up by a machine and while listening to Doran's outgoing message McCaleb quickly tried to decide whether to leave a message or just call back. Initially, he thought it would be better to hang up and try to catch Doran live later because a personal call is much more difficult to deflect than a taped message. But then he decided to put faith in their former camaraderie, even if he had been out of the bureau for nearly five years.

'Brass, it's Terry McCaleb. Long time no see. Uh, listen, I'm calling because I need a favor. Could you call me back as soon as you get a moment? I'd really appreciate it.'

He gave the number for his cell phone, thanked her and hung up. He could take the phone with him back to the house and wait for the call there but that would mean that Graciela might overhear the conversation with Doran and he didn't want that. He went back down to the forward bunk and started through the murder book documents again. He checked every page again for something that stood out in its inclusion or exclusion. He took a few more notes and made a list of things he still needed to do and know before drawing up a profile. But primarily he was just waiting for Doran. She finally returned his call at five-thirty.

'Long time is right,' she said by way of greeting.

'Too long. How y'doin', Brass?'

'Can't complain because nobody listens.'

'I heard you guys are looking for the Drano over there.'

'You're right about that. We are clogged and flogged. You know last year we sent half the staff to Kosovo to help in the war crimes investigations. On six-week rotations. That just killed us. We are still so far behind it's getting critical.'

McCaleb wondered if she was giving him the woe-is-me pitch so he might not ask the favor he had mentioned on the message. He decided to go ahead with it anyway.

'Well, then you aren't going to like hearing from me,' he said.

'Oh boy, I'm shaking in my boots. What do you need, Terry?'

'I'm doing a favor for a friend out here. Sheriff's homicide squad. Taking a look at a homicide and—'

'Did he already run it through here?'

'It's a she. And, yeah, she ran it on the VICAP box and got blanked. That's all. She got the word on how backed up you guys are on profiling and came to me instead. I sort of owe her one so I said I'd take a look.'

'And now you want to cut in line, right?'

McCaleb smiled and hoped she was smiling as well on the other end of the line.

'Sort of. But I think it's a quickie. It's just one thing I want.'

'Then out with it. What?'

'I need an iconography baseline. I'm following a hunch on something.'

'Okay. Doesn't sound too involving. What's the symbol?'

'An owl.'

'An owl? Just an owl?'

'More specifically, a plastic owl. But an owl just the same. I want to know if it's turned up before and what it means.'

'Well, I remember the owl on the bag of potato chips. What's that brand?'

'Wise. I remember. It's an East Coast brand.'

'Well, there you go. The owl is smart. He is wise.'

'Brass, I was hoping for something a little more—'

'I know, I know. Tell you what, I'll see what I can find. The thing to remember is, symbols change. What means one thing at one time might mean something completely different at another time. You just looking for contemporary uses and examples?'

McCaleb thought for a moment about the message on the duct tape.

'Can you throw in the medieval time period?'

'Sounds like you got a weird one – but ain't they all. Let me guess, a holy shit case?'

'Could be. How'd you know that?'

'Oh, all that medieval Inquisition and church stuff. Seen it before. I've got your number. I'll try to get back today.'

McCaleb thought about asking her to run an analysis of the message from the duct tape but decided not to pile it on. Besides, the message must have been included on the computer run Jaye Winston completed. He thanked her and was about to disconnect when she asked about his health and he told her he was fine.

'You still living on that boat I heard about?'

'Nope. I'm living on an island now. But I still have the boat. I've got a wife and new baby daughter, too.'

'Wow! Is this the Terry "TV Dinner" McCaleb I used to know?'

'Same one, I guess.'

'Well, it sounds like you got your stuff together.'

'I think I finally do.'

'Then be careful with it. What are you doing chasing a case again?'

McCaleb hesitated in his reply.

'I'm not sure.'

'Don't bullshit me. We both know why you're doing it. Tell you what, let me see what I can find out and I'll call you back.'

'Thanks, Brass. I'll be waiting.'

McCaleb went into the master cabin and shook Buddy Lockridge awake. His friend startled and began swinging his arms wildly.

'It's me, it's me!'

Before he calmed down, Buddy clapped McCaleb on the side of the head with a book he had fallen asleep holding.

'What are you doing?' Buddy exclaimed.

'I'm trying to wake you, man.'

'What for? What time is it?'

'It's almost six. I want to take the boat across.'

'Now?'

'Yeah, now. So get up and help me. I'll get the lines.'

'Man, now? We're going to hit the layer. Why don't you wait until it burns off?'

'Because I don't have the time.'

Buddy reached up and turned on the reading lamp that was attached to the cabin wall just above the headboard. McCaleb noticed the book he was reading was called *The Wire in the Blood*.

'Something sure put a wire in your blood, man,' he said as he rubbed his ear where the book had hit him.

'Sorry about that. Why you in such a hurry to cross, anyway? It's that case, isn't it?'

'I'll be on top. Let's get it going.'

McCaleb headed out of the cabin. Buddy called after him as he expected he would.

'You going to need a driver?'

'No, Buddy. You know I've been driving a couple years now.'

'Yeah, but you might need help with the case, man.'

'I'll be all right. Hurry up, Bud, I want to get over there.'

McCaleb took the key off the hook next to the salon door and went out and climbed up into the bridge. The air was still chilled and tendrils of dawn light were working their way through the morning mist. He flicked on the Raytheon radar and started the engines. They turned over immediately – Buddy had taken the boat over to Marina del Rey the week before to have them overhauled.

McCaleb left them idling while he climbed back down and went to the fantail. He untied the stern line and then the Zodiac and led it around to the bow. He tied the Zodiac to the line from the mooring buoy after releasing it from the forward cleat. The boat was free now. He turned in the bow pulpit and looked up at the bridge just as Buddy, his hair a wiry nest from sleep, slid into the pilot seat. McCaleb signaled that the boat was loose. Buddy pushed the throttles forward and *The Following Sea* began to move. McCaleb picked the eight-foot gaff pole up off the deck and used it to keep the buoy off the bow as the boat made the turn into the fairway and slowly headed toward the mouth of the harbor.

McCaleb stayed in the pulpit, leaning back against the railing and watching the island slip away behind the boat. He looked up once again toward his house and saw only the one light still on. It was too early for his family to be awake. He thought about the mistake he had knowingly just made. He should have gone up to the house and told Graciela what he was doing, tried to explain it. But he knew it would lose him a lot of time and that he would never be able to explain it to her satisfaction. He decided to just go. He would call his wife after the crossing and he would deal with the consequences of his decision later.

The cool air of the shark-gray dawn had tightened the skin on his arms and neck. He turned in the bow pulpit and looked forward and across the bay to where he knew overtown lay hidden beneath the marine layer. Not being able to see what he knew to be there gave him an ominous feeling and he looked down. The water the bow cut through was flat and as blue-black as a marlin's skin. McCaleb knew he needed to get up into the bridge to help Buddy. One of them would drive while the other kept an eye on the radar screen to chart a safe course to Los Angeles Harbor. Too bad, he thought, that there would be no radar for him to use once he was on land again and trying to chart his way through the case that now gripped him. A mist of a different kind awaited him there. And these thoughts of trying to see his way through turned his mind to the thing about the case that had hooked him so deeply.

Beware Beware God Sees

The words turned in his head like a newfound mantra. There was someone in the cloaking mist ahead who had written those words. Someone who had acted on them in an extreme capacity at least once and who would likely act on them again. McCaleb was going to find that person. And in doing so, he wondered, whose words would he be acting on? Was there a true God sending him on this journey?

He felt a touch on his shoulder and startled and turned, nearly dropping the gaff pole overboard. It was Buddy.

'Jesus, man, don't do that!'

'You all right?'

'I was till you scared the hell out of me. What are you doing? You should be driving.'

McCaleb glanced over his shoulder to make sure they were clear of the harbor markers and into the open bay.

'I don't know,' Buddy said. 'You looked like Ahab standing out here with that gaff. I thought something was wrong. What are you doing?'

'I was thinking. Do you mind? Don't sneak up on me like that, man.'

'Well, I guess that makes us even then.'

'Just go drive the boat, Buddy. I'll be up in a minute. And check the generator – might as well juice the batteries.'

As Buddy moved away McCaleb felt his heart even out again. He stepped off the pulpit and snapped the gaff back into its clamps on the deck. As he was bent over he felt the boat rise and fall as it went over a three- or four-foot roller. He straightened up and looked around for the origin of the wake. But he saw nothing. It had been a phantom moving across the flat surface of the bay.

6

Harry Bosch raised his briefcase like a shield and used it to push his way through the crowd of reporters and cameras gathered outside the doors of the courtroom.

'Let me through, please, let me through.'

Most of them didn't move until he used the briefcase to lever them out of the way. They were desperately crowding in and reaching tape recorders and cameras toward the center of the human knot where the defense lawyer was holding court.

Bosch finally made it to the door, where a sheriff's deputy was pressed against the handle. He recognized Bosch and stepped sideways so he could open the door.

'You know,' Bosch said to the deputy, 'this is going to happen every day. This guy has more to say outside court than inside. You might want to think about setting up some rules so people can get in and out.'

As Bosch went through the door, he heard the deputy tell him to talk to the judge about it.

Bosch walked down the center aisle and then through the gate to the prosecution table. He was the first to arrive. He pulled the third chair out and sat down. He opened his briefcase on the table, took out the heavy blue binder and put it to the side. He then closed and snapped the briefcase locks and put it down on the floor next to his chair.

Bosch was ready. He leaned forward and folded his arms on top of the binder. The courtroom was still, almost empty except for the judge's clerk and a court reporter who were getting ready for the day. Bosch liked these times. The quiet before the storm. And he knew without a doubt that a storm was surely coming. He nodded to himself. He was ready, ready to dance with the devil once more. He realized that his mission in life was all about moments like these. Moments that should be savored and remembered but that always caused a tight fisting of his guts.

There was a loud metallic clacking sound and the door to the side holding cell opened. Two deputies led a man through the door. He was young and still tanned somehow despite almost three months in lockup. He wore a suit that would easily take the weekly paychecks of the men on either side of him. His hands were cuffed at his sides to a waist chain which looked incongruous with the perfect blue suit. In one hand he clasped an artist's sketch pad. The other held a black felt-tip pen, the only kind of writing instrument allowed in lockdown.

The man was led to the defense table and positioned in front of the middle seat. He smiled and looked forward as the cuffs and the chain were removed. A deputy put a hand on the man's shoulder and pushed him down into the seat. The deputies then moved back and took positions in chairs to the man's rear.

The man immediately leaned forward and opened the sketch pad and went to work with his pen. Bosch watched. He could hear the point of the pen scratching furiously on the paper.

'They don't allow me a charcoal, Bosch. Do you believe that? What threat could a piece of charcoal possibly be?'

He hadn't looked at Bosch as he said it. Bosch didn't reply.

'It's the little things like that that bother me the most,' the man said.

'Better get used to it,' Bosch said.

The man laughed but still did not look at Bosch.

'You know, somehow I knew that was exactly what you were going to say.'

Bosch was quiet.

'You see, you are so predictable Bosch. All of you are.'

The rear courtroom door opened and Bosch turned his eyes away from the defendant. The attorneys were coming in now. They were about to start.

7

By the time McCaleb got to the Farmers' Market he was thirty minutes late for the meeting with Jaye Winston. He and Buddy had made the crossing in an hour and a half and McCaleb had called the sheriff's detective after they tied up at Cabrillo Marina. They arranged to meet but then he found the battery in the Cherokee dead because the car hadn't been used in two weeks. He had to get Buddy to give him a jump from his old Taurus and that had taken up the time.

He walked into Dupar's, the corner restaurant in the market, but didn't see Winston at any of the tables or the counter. He hoped she hadn't come and gone. He chose an unoccupied booth that afforded the most privacy and sat down. He didn't need to look at a menu. They had chosen the Farmer's Market to meet because it was near Edward Gunn's apartment and because McCaleb wanted to eat breakfast at Dupar's. He had told Winston that more than anything else about Los Angeles, he missed the pancakes at Dupar's. Often when he and Graciela and the children made their once-a-month trip overtown to buy clothing and supplies not available on Catalina, they ate a meal at Dupar's. It didn't matter whether it was breakfast, lunch or dinner, McCaleb always ordered pancakes. Raymond did, too. But he was boysenberry while McCaleb was traditional maple.

McCaleb told the waitress he was waiting for another party but ordered a large orange juice and a glass of water. After she brought the two glasses he opened his leather bag and took out the plastic pill box. He kept a week's supply of his pills on the boat and another couple days' worth in the glove box of the Cherokee. He'd prepared the box after docking. Alternating gulps of orange juice and water, he downed the twenty-seven pills that made up his morning dosage. He knew their names by their shapes and colors and tastes; Prilosec, Imuran, digoxin. As he methodically went through the lineup he noticed a woman in a nearby booth watching, her eyebrows arched in wonder.

He would never get rid of the pills. They were as certain for him as the proverbial death and taxes. Over the years some would be changed, some subtracted and new ones added, but he knew he would be swallowing pills and washing away their awful tastes with orange juice for the rest of his life.

'I see you ordered without me.'

He looked up from the last three cyclosporine pills he was about to take as Jaye Winston slid into the opposite side of the booth.

'Sorry, I'm so late. Traffic on the ten was a complete bitch.'

'It's all right. I was late, too. Dead battery.'

'How many of those you take now?'

'Fifty-four a day.'

'Unbelievable.'

'I had to turn a hallway closet into a medicine cabinet. The whole thing.'

'Well, at least you're still here.'

She smiled and McCaleb nodded. The waitress came to the table with a menu for Winston but she said they had better order.

'I'll have what he's having.'

McCaleb ordered a large stack with melted butter. He told the waitress they would share one order of well-done bacon.

'Coffee?' asked the waitress. She looked as though this might have been the one-millionth pancake order she had taken.

'Yes, please,' said Winston. 'Black.'

McCaleb said he was fine with the orange juice.

When they were alone McCaleb looked across the table at Winston.

'So, you get ahold of the manager?'

'He's going to meet us at ten-thirty. The place is still vacant but it has been cleaned. After we released it, the vic's sister came up and went through his things, took what she wanted.'

'Yeah, I was afraid of something like that.'

'The manager didn't think it was very much – the guy didn't have much.'

'What about the owl?'

'He didn't remember the owl. Frankly, I didn't either until you mentioned it this morning.'

'It's just a hunch. I'd like to take a look at it.'

'Well, we'll see if it's there. What else do you want to do? I hope you didn't come all the way across just to look at the guy's apartment.'

'I was thinking about checking out the sister. And maybe Harry Bosch, too.'

Winston was silent but he could tell by her demeanor she was waiting for an explanation.

'In order to profile an unknown subject, it's important to know the victim. His routines, personality, everything. You know the drill. The sister and, to a lesser extent, Bosch can help with that.'

'I only asked you to look at the book and the tape, Terry. You're going to make me start feeling guilty here.'

McCaleb paused while the waitress brought Winston's coffee and put down two small glass pitchers containing boysenberry and maple syrup. After she went away he spoke.

'You knew I'd get hooked, Jayne. "Beware, beware, God sees?" I mean, come on. You're going to tell me you thought I'd look it all over and phone in the report? Besides, I'm not complaining. I'm here because I want to be. If you feel guilty, you can buy the pancakes.'

'What did your wife say about it?'

'Nothing. She knows it's something I have to do. I called her from the dock after I crossed. It was too late for her to really say anything by then anyway. She just told me to pick up a bag of green corn tamales at El Cholo before I headed back. They sell 'em frozen.'

The pancakes came. They stopped talking and McCaleb politely waited for Winston to choose a syrup first but she was using a fork to move her pancakes around on her plate and he finally couldn't wait. He doused his stack with maple syrup and started eating. The waitress came back by and put a check down. Winston quickly grabbed it.

'The sheriff will pay for this.'

'Tell him thanks.'

'You know, I don't know what you expect from Harry Bosch. He told me he'd only had a handful of contacts with Gunn in the six years since the prostitute case.'

'When were those, when he got popped?'

Winston nodded as she poured boysenberry syrup on her pancakes.

'That means he would have seen him the night before he was killed. I didn't see anything about it in the book.'

'I haven't written it up. There's not much to it. The watch sergeant called him and told him Gunn was in the drunk tank on a DUI.'

McCaleb nodded.

'And?'

'And he came in to look at the guy. That was it. He said they didn't even talk because Gunn was too blitzed.'

'Well . . . I still want to talk to Harry. I worked a case with him once. He's a good cop. Intuitive and observant. He might know something I could use.'

'That is, if you can get to talk to him.'

'What do you mean?'

'You don't know? He's riding the prosecution table on the David Storey murder case. Up in Van Nuys. Don't you watch the news?'

'Ah, damn, I forgot about that. I remember reading his name in the newspapers after they took Storey down. That was, what, in October? They're already in trial?'

'They sure are. No delays and they didn't need a prelim because they went through the grand jury. They started jury selection right after the first. Last I heard, they had the panel so openers will probably be this week, maybe even today.'

'Shit.'

'Yeah, good luck getting to Bosch. I'm sure this is just what he'll want to hear about.'

'Are you saying you don't want me to talk to him?'

Winston shrugged her shoulders.

'No, I'm not saying that at all. Do whatever you want to do. I just didn't think you'd be doing so much legwork on this. I can talk to my captain about maybe getting a consulting fee for you but—'

'Don't worry about it. The sheriff's buying breakfast. That's enough.'

'Doesn't seem like it.'

He didn't tell her that he'd work the case for free, just to be back in the life for a few days. And he didn't tell her that he couldn't take any money from her anyway. If he made any 'official' income he would lose his eligibility for the state medical assistance that paid for the fifty-four pills he swallowed every day. The pills were so expensive that if he had to pay for them himself he'd be bankrupt inside six months, unless he happened to be drawing a six-figure salary. It was the ugly secret behind the medical miracle that had saved him. He got a second chance at life, just as long as he didn't use it to try to earn a living. It was the reason the charter business was in Buddy Lockridge's name. Officially, McCaleb was an unpaid deckhand. Buddy simply rented the boat for charter from Graciela, the rent being 60 percent of all charter fees after expenses.

'How are your pancakes?' he asked Winston.

'The best.'

'Damn right.'

8

The Grand Royale was a two-story eyesore, a deteriorating stucco box whose attempt at style began and ended with the modish design of the letters of its name tacked over the entranceway. The streets of West Hollywood and elsewhere in the flats were lined with such banal designs, the high-density apartments that crowded out smaller bungalow courts in the fifties and sixties. They replaced true style with phony ornamental flourishes and names that reflected exactly what they were not.

McCaleb and Winston entered the second-floor apartment that had belonged to Edward Gunn with the building manager, a man named Rohrshak – 'Like the test, only spelled different.'

If he hadn't known where to look, McCaleb would have missed what was left of the bloodstain on the carpet where Gunn had died. The carpet had not been replaced. Instead it had been shampooed, leaving only a small, light brown trace stain that would probably be mistaken by the next renter as the remnant of a soda or coffee spill.

The place had been cleaned and readied for renting. But the furnishings were the same. McCaleb recognized them from the crime scene video.

He looked across the room at the china cabinet but it was empty. There was no plastic owl perched atop it. He looked at Winston.

'It's gone.'

Winston turned to the manager.

'Mr. Rohrshak. The owl that was on top of that cabinet. We think it was important. Are you sure you don't know what happened to it?'

Rohrshak spread his arms wide and then dropped them to his side.

'No, I don't know. You asked before and I thought, "I don't remember any owl." But if you say so . . .'

He shrugged his shoulders and jutted his chin, then nodded as if reluctantly agreeing that there had been an owl on the china cabinet.

McCaleb read his body language and words as the classic mannerisms of a liar. Deny the existence of the object you have stolen and you eliminate the theft. He assumed Winston had picked up on it as well.

'Jaye, you have a phone? Can you call the sister to double-check?'

'I've been holding out until the county buys me one.'

McCaleb had wanted to keep his phone free in case Brass Doran called back but put his leather bag down on an overstuffed couch and dug out his phone and handed it to her.

She had to get the sister's number out of a notebook in her briefcase. While she made the call McCaleb walked slowly around the apartment, taking it all in and trying to get a vibe from the place. In the dining area he stopped in front of the round wooden table with four straight-back chairs placed around it. The crime scene analysis report said that three of the chairs had numerous smears, partials and complete latent fingerprints on them – all of them belonging to the victim, Edward Gunn. The fourth chair, the one found on the north side of the table, was completely devoid of fingerprint evidence in any condition. The chair had been wiped down. Most likely, the killer had done this after handling the chair for some reason.

McCaleb checked his directions and went to the chair on the north side of the table. Careful not to touch the back of it, he hooked his hand under the seat and pulled it away from the table and over to the china cabinet. He positioned it at center and then stepped up onto the seat. He raised his arms as if placing something on top of the cabinet. The chair wobbled on its uneven legs and McCaleb instinctively reached one hand to the top edge of the china cabinet to steady himself. Before he grabbed on he realized something and stopped himself. He braced his forearm across the frame of one of the cabinet's glass doors instead.

'Steady there, Terry.'

He looked down. Winston was standing next to him. His phone was folded closed in her hand.

'I am. So does she have the bird?'

'No, she didn't know what I was talking about.'

McCaleb raised himself on his toes and looked over the top edge of the cabinet.

'She tell you what she did take?'

'Just some clothes and some old photos of them when they were kids. She didn't want anything else.'

McCaleb nodded. He was still looking up and down the top of the cabinet. There was a thick layer of dust on top.

'You say anything about me coming down to talk to her?'

'I forgot. I can call her back.'

'You have a flashlight, Jaye?'

She dug through her purse and then handed up a small penlight. McCaleb flicked it on and held it at a low angle to the top of the cabinet. The light made the surface dust more distinct and now he could clearly see an octagonal-shaped impression that had been left by something that had been put on top of the cabinet and the dust. The base of the owl.

He next moved the light along the edges of the top board, then turned it off and got down off the chair. He handed Jaye the penlight.

'Thanks. You might want to think about getting a print team back out here.'

'How come? The owl's not up there, is it?'

McCaleb glanced at Rohrshak for a moment.

'Nope, it's gone. But whoever put it up there used that chair. When it wobbled they grabbed a hold.'

He took a pen out of his pocket and reached up and tapped the front edge of the cabinet in the area where he had seen finger impressions in the dust.

'It's pretty dusty but there might be prints.'

'What if it was whoever took the owl?'

McCaleb looked pointedly at Rohrshak when he answered.

'Same thing. There might be prints.'

Rohrshak looked away.

'Can I use this again?'

Winston held up his phone.

'Go ahead.'

As Winston called for a print team, McCaleb dragged the chair into the middle of the living room, positioning it a few feet from the bloodstain. He then sat down on it and took in the room. In this position the owl would have looked down on the killer as well as the victim. Some instinct told McCaleb that this was the configuration the killer had wanted. He looked down at the bloodstain and imagined he was looking down at Edward Gunn struggling for his life and slowly losing the battle. The bucket, he thought. Everything fit but the bucket. The killer had set the stage but then couldn't watch the play. He needed the bucket so that he wouldn't see his victim's face. It bothered McCaleb that it didn't fit.

Winston came over and handed him the phone.

'There's a crew just finishing a break-in on Kings. They'll be here in fifteen minutes.'

'That's lucky.'

'Very. What are you doing?'

'Just thinking. I think he sat here and watched but then couldn't take it. He struck the victim on the head, to maybe hurry it up. Then he got the bucket and put it on so he wouldn't have to watch.'

Winston nodded.

'Where'd the bucket come from? There was nothing in the—'

'We think it came from under the sink in the kitchen. There's a ring, a water ring on the shelf that fits the base of the bucket. It's on a supplemental Kurt typed up. He must've forgotten to put it in the book.'

McCaleb nodded and stood up.

'You're going to wait for the print crew, right?'

'Yes, it shouldn't be long.'

'I'm going to take a walk.'

He headed for the open door.

'I will go with you,' Rohrshak said.

McCaleb turned.

'No, Mr. Rohrshak, you need to stay here with Detective Winston. We need an independent witness to monitor what we do in the apartment.'

He glanced over Rohrshak's shoulder at Winston. She winked, telling him she understood the phony story and what he was doing.

'Yes, Mr. Rohrshak. Please stay here, if you don't mind.'

Rohrshak shrugged his shoulders again and raised his hands.

McCaleb went down the stairs to the enclosed courtyard in the center of the apartment building. He turned in a complete circle and his eyes traveled up to the line of the flat roof. He didn't see the owl anywhere and turned and walked out through the entrance hall to the street.

Across Sweetzer was the Braxton Arms, a three-story, L-shaped apartment building with exterior walkways and stairwells. McCaleb crossed and found a six-foot security gate and fence at the entrance. It was more for show than as a deterrent. He took off his windbreaker, folded it and pushed it between two of the gate's bars. He then brought his foot up onto the gate's handle, tested it with his weight, then hoisted himself up to the top of the gate. He dropped down on the other side and looked around to see if anyone was watching him. He was clear. He grabbed his windbreaker and headed for the stairwell.

He walked up to the third level and followed the walkway to the front of the building. His breathing was loud and labored from climbing the gate and then the stairs. When he got to the front he put his hands on the safety railing and leaned forward until he had caught his breath. He then looked across Sweetzer to the flat roof of the apartment building where Edward Gunn had lived. Again, the plastic owl wasn't there.

McCaleb leaned his forearms down on the railing and continued to labor for breath. He listened to the cadence of his heart as it finally settled. He could feel sweat popping on his scalp. He knew it wasn't his heart that was weak. It was his body, weakened by all the drugs he took to keep his heart strong. It frustrated him. He knew that he would never be strong, that he would spend the rest of his life listening to his heart the way a night burglar listens to creaks in the floor.

He looked down when he heard a vehicle and saw a white van with the sheriff's seal on the driver's door pull to a stop in front of the apartment building across the street. The print crew had arrived.

McCaleb glanced at the roof across the street once more and then turned to head back down, defeated. He suddenly stopped. There was the owl. It was perched atop a compressor for a central air-conditioning system on the roof of the L-extension of the building he was in.

He quickly went to the stairs and climbed up to the roof landing. He had to work his way around some furniture that was stacked and stored on the landing but found the door unlocked and hurried across the flat, gravel-strewn roof to the air conditioner.

McCaleb first studied the owl before touching it. It matched his memory of the owl on the crime scene tape. Its base was an octagonal stump. He knew it was the missing owl. He removed the wire that had been wrapped around the base and attached to the intake grill of the air conditioner. He noticed that the grill and metal covering of the unit were covered with old bird droppings. He surmised that the droppings were a maintenance problem and Rohrshak, who apparently managed this building as well as the one across the street, had taken the owl from Gunn's apartment to use to keep the birds away.

McCaleb took the wire and looped it around the owl's neck so that he could carry it without touching it, though he doubted there would be any usable fingerprint or fiber evidence remaining on it. He lifted it off the air conditioner and headed back to the stairs.

When McCaleb stepped back into Edward Gunn's apartment he saw two crime scene techs getting equipment out of a toolbox. A stepladder was standing in front of the china cabinet.

'You might want to start with this,' he said.

He watched Rohrshak's eyes widen as he entered the room and placed the plastic owl on the table.

'You manage the place across the street, don't you, Mr. Rohrshak?'

'Uh . . .'

'It's okay. It's easy enough to find out.'

'Yes, he does,' Winston said, bending down to look at the owl. 'He was over there when we needed him on the day of the murder. He lives there.'

'Any idea how this ended up on the roof?' McCaleb asked.

Rohrshak still didn't answer.

'Guess it just flew over, right?'

Rohrshak couldn't take his eyes off the owl.

'Tell you what, you can go now, Mr. Rohrshak. But stay around your place. If we get a print off the bird or the cabinet, we're going to need to take a set of yours for comparison.'

Now Rohrshak looked at McCaleb and his eyes grew even wider.

'Go on, Mr. Rohrshak.'

The building manager turned and slowly headed out of the apartment.

'And shut the door, please,' McCaleb called after him.

After he was gone and the door was shut Winston almost burst into laughter.

'Terry, you're being so hard on him. He didn't really do anything wrong, you know. We cleared the place, he let the sister take what she wanted and then what was he supposed to do, try to rent the place with this stupid owl up there?'

McCaleb shook his head.

'He lied to us. That was wrong. I almost blew a gasket climbing that building across the street. He could have just told us it was up there.'

'Well, he's properly scared now. I think he learned his lesson.'

'Whatever.'

He stepped back so one of the techs could go to work on the owl while the other climbed the ladder to work on the top of the cabinet.

McCaleb studied the bird as the tech brushed on black fingerprint powder. It appeared that the owl was hand painted. It was dark brown and black on its wings, head and back. Its chest was a lighter brown with some yellow highlighting. Its eyes were a shiny black.

'Has this been outside?' the tech asked.

'Unfortunately,' McCaleb answered, remembering the rains that had swept off the mainland and out to Catalina the week before.

'Well, I'm not getting anything.'

'Figures.'

McCaleb looked at Winston, his eyes portraying renewed anger with Rohrshak.

'Nothing up here, either,' the other tech said. 'Too much dust.'

9.

The trial of David Storey was being held in the Van Nuys courthouse. The crime the case centered on was not remotely connected to Van Nuys or even the San Fernando Valley, but the courthouse had been chosen by schedulers in the district attorney's office because Department N was available and it was the single largest courtroom in the county – constructed out of two courtrooms several years earlier to comfortably hold the two juries as well as the attendant media crush of the Menendez brothers murder case. The Menendezes' slaying of their parents had been one of several Los Angeles court cases in the previous decade to capture the media's and, therefore, the public's attention. When it was over, the DA's office did not bother deconstructing the huge courtroom. Somebody there had the foresight to realize that in L.A. there would always be a case that could fill Department N.

And at the moment it was the David Storey case.

The thirty-eight-year-old film director, known for films that pushed the limits of violence and sexuality within an R rating, was charged with the murder of a young actress he had taken home from the premiere of his most recent film. The twenty-three-year-old woman's body was found the next morning in the small Nichols Canyon bungalow she shared with another would-be actress. The victim had been strangled, her nude body arranged in her bed in a pose investigators believed to be part of a careful plan by her killer to avoid discovery.

The case's elements – power, celebrity, sex and money – and the added Hollywood connection served to bring the case maximum media attention. David Storey worked on the wrong side of the camera to be a fully realized celebrity himself, but his name was known and he wielded the awesome power of a man who had delivered seven box office hits in as many years. The media were drawn to the Storey trial in the way young people are drawn by the dream of Hollywood. The advance coverage clearly delineated the case as a parable on unchecked Hollywood avarice and excess.

The case also had a degree of secrecy not usually seen in criminal trials. The prosecutors assigned to the case took their evidence to a grand jury in order to seek charges against Storey. The move allowed them to bypass a preliminary hearing, where most of the evidence accumulated against a defendant is usually made public. Without that fount of case information, the media were left to mine their sources in both the prosecution and defense camps. Still, little about the case was leaked to the media other than generalities. The evidence the prosecution would use to tie Storey to the murder remained cloaked, and all the more cause for the media frenzy around the trial.

It was just that frenzy that had convinced the district attorney to move the trial to the large Department N courtroom in Van Nuys. The second jury box would be used to accommodate more media members in the courtroom, while the unused deliberation room would be converted into a media room where the video feed could be watched by the second- and third-tier journalists. The move, which would give all media – from the *National Enquirer* to the *New York Times* – full access to the trial and its players, guaranteed the proceedings would become the first full-blooded media circus of the new century.

In the center ring of this circus, sitting at the prosecution table, was Detective Harry Bosch, the lead investigator of the case. All the pretrial media analysis came down to one conclusion: the charges against David Storey would rise and fall with Bosch. All evidence in support of the murder charge was said to be circumstantial; the foundation of the case would come from Bosch. The one solid piece of evidence that had been leaked to the media was that Bosch would testify that in a private moment, with no other witnesses or devices at hand to record the statement, Storey had smugly admitted to him that he had committed the crime and boasted that he would surely get away with it.

McCaleb knew all of this as he walked into the Van Nuys courthouse shortly before noon. He stood in line to go through the metal detector and felt a reminder of all that had changed in his life. When he had been a bureau agent all he needed to do was hold his badge up and walk around the line. Now he was just a citizen. He had to wait.

The fourth-floor hallway was crowded with people milling about. McCaleb noticed that many clutched stacks of eight-by-ten black-and-white glossies of the movie stars they hoped would be attending the trial – either as witnesses or as spectators in support of the defendant. He walked to the double-door entrance to Department N but one of the two sheriff's deputies posted there told him the courtroom was at full capacity. The deputy pointed to a long line of people standing behind a rope. He said it was the line for people waiting to go in. Every time one person left the courtroom another could go in. McCaleb nodded and stepped away from the doors.

He saw that further down the hallway was an open door with people milling about it. He recognized one man as a reporter on a local television news program. He guessed it was the media room and headed that way.

When he got to the open door he could look in and see two large televisions mounted high up in either corner above the room where there were several people crowded around a large jury table. Reporters. They were typing on laptop computers, taking notes on pads, eating sandwiches from to-go bags. The center of the table was crowded with plastic coffee and soda cups.

He looked up at one of the televisions and saw that court was still in session though it was now past noon. The camera focused on a wide angle and he recognized Harry Bosch sitting with a man and a woman at the prosecution table. It did not look as though he was paying attention to the proceedings. A man McCaleb recognized stood at the lectern between the prosecution and defense tables. He was J. Reason Fowkkes, the lead defense attorney. At the table to his left sat the defendant, David Storey.

McCaleb could not hear the audio feed but he knew that Fowkkes was not delivering his opening statement. He was looking up at the judge, not in the direction of the jury box. Most likely last-minute motions were being argued by the attorneys before openers began. The twin television screens switched to a new camera, this angle directly on the judge, who began speaking, apparently delivering his rulings. McCaleb noted the name plate in front of the judge's bench. It said Superior Court Judge John A. Houghton.

'Agent McCaleb?'

McCaleb turned from the television to see a man he recognized but couldn't immediately place standing next to him.

'Just McCaleb. Terry McCaleb.'

The man perceived his difficulty and held out his hand.

'Jack McEvoy. I interviewed you once. It was pretty brief. It was about the Poet investigation.'

'Oh, right, I remember now. That was a while back.'

McCaleb shook his hand. He did remember McEvoy. He had become entwined in the Poet case and then wrote a book about it. McCaleb had had a very peripheral part in the case – when the investigation had shifted to Los Angeles. He never read McEvoy's book but was sure he had not added anything to it and likely wasn't mentioned in it.

'I thought you were from Colorado,' he said, recalling that McEvoy had worked for one of the papers in Denver. 'They sent you out to cover this?'

McEvoy nodded.

'Good memory. I was from there but I live out here now. I work freelance.'

McCaleb nodded, wondering what else there was to say.

'Who are you covering this for?'

'I've been writing a weekly dispatch on it for the *New Times*. Do you read it?'

McCaleb nodded. He was familiar with the *New Times*. It was a weekly tabloid with an anti-authority, muckraking stance. It appeared to subsist mostly on entertainment ads, ranging from movies to the escort services that filled its back pages. It was free and Buddy always seemed to leave issues lying around the boat. McCaleb looked at it from time to time but hadn't noticed McEvoy's name before.

'I'm also doing a general wrap for *Vanity Fair*,' McEvoy said. 'You know, a more discursive, dark-side-of-Hollywood piece. I'm thinking about another book, too. What brings you here? Are you . . . involved with this in some . . .'

'Me, no. I was in the area and I have a friend involved. I was hoping I might be able to get a chance to say hello to him.'

As he told the lie McCaleb looked away from the writer and back through the door to the televisions. The full courtroom camera angle was now being shown. It looked like Bosch was gathering things into a briefcase.

'Harry Bosch?'

McCaleb looked back at him.

'Yeah, Harry. We worked a case together before and . . . uh, what's going on in there now, anyway?'

'Final motions before they start. They started with a closed session and they're just doing some housekeeping. Not worth being in there. Everybody thinks the judge will probably finish before lunch and then give the lawyers the rest of the day to work on openers. They start tomorrow at ten. You think things are crowded here now? Wait till tomorrow.'

McCaleb nodded.

'Oh, well, okay then. Uh, nice seeing you again, Jack. Good luck with the story. And the book, if it comes to that.'

'You know, I would have liked to write your story. You know, with the heart and everything.'

McCaleb nodded.

'Well, I owed Keisha Russell one and she did a good job with it.'

McCaleb noticed people start to push their way out of the media room. Behind them he could see on the television screens that the judge had left the bench. Court was out of session.

'I better go down the hall and see if I can catch Harry. Good to see you again, Jack.'

McCaleb offered his hand and McEvoy shook it. He then followed the other reporters down to the courtroom doors.

The main doors to Department N were opened by the two deputies and out flowed the crowd of lucky citizens who had gotten seats during the session, which had most likely been mind-numbingly boring. Those who had not made it inside pushed up close for a glimpse of a celebrity but they were disappointed. The celebrities wouldn't start showing until the next day. Opening statements were like the opening credits of a film. That's where they would want to be seen.

At the tail end of the crowd came the lawyers and staff. Storey had been returned to lockup but his attorney strode right to the semicircle of reporters and began giving his view of what had transpired inside. A tall man with jet-black hair, a deep tan and ever-shifting green eyes took a position directly behind the lawyer to cover his back. He was striking and McCaleb thought he recognized him but he couldn't think from where. He looked like one of the actors Storey normally put in his films.

The prosecutors came out and soon had their own knot of reporters to deal with. Their answers were shorter than the defense lawyer's. They often declined to comment when asked questions about the evidence they would present.

McCaleb watched for Bosch and finally saw him slip out last. Bosch skirted the crowd by staying close to the wall and headed toward the elevators. One reporter moved in on him but he held up his hand and waved her away. She stopped and moved back like a loose molecule to the pack standing around J. Reason Fowkkes.

McCaleb followed Bosch down the hall and caught him when he stopped to wait for an elevator.

'Hey, Harry Bosch.'

Bosch turned, already putting on his no-comment face, when he saw it was McCaleb.

'Hey ... McCaleb.'

He smiled. The men shook hands.

'Looks like the world's worst eight-by-ten case,' McCaleb said.

'You're telling me. What are you doing here? Don't tell me you're writing a book on this thing.'

'What?'

'All these ex-bureau guys writing books nowadays.'

'Nah, that's not me. Actually, though, I was hoping I could maybe buy you lunch. There's something I wanted to talk to you about.'

Bosch looked at his watch and was deciding something.

'Edward Gunn.'

Bosch looked up at him.

'Jaye Winston?'

McCaleb nodded.

'She asked me to take a look.'

The elevator came and they stepped onto it with a crowd of people who had been in the courtroom. They all seemed to be looking at Bosch while trying not to show it. McCaleb decided not to continue until they were off.

On the first floor they headed toward the exit.

'I told her I'd profile it. A quick one. To do it I need to get a handle on Gunn. I thought maybe you could tell me about that old case and about what kind of guy he was.'

'He was a scumbag. Look, I have about forty-five minutes max. I need to get on the road. I'm running down wits today, making sure everybody's ready to go after openers.'

'I'll take the forty-five if you can spare it. Any place to eat around here?'

'Forget the cafeteria here – it's awful. There's a Cupid's up on Victory.'

'You cops always eat at the best.'

'It's why we do what we do.'

10

They ate their hot dogs at an outdoor table without an umbrella. Though it was a mildly warm winter day, McCaleb found himself sweating. On any given day the Valley could be counted on to be fifteen to twenty degrees warmer than Catalina and he wasn't used to the change. His internal heating and cooling systems had never been normal since the transplant and he was prone to quick chills and sweats.

He began with some small talk about Bosch's current case.

'You ready to become Hollywood Harry with this case?'

'Yeah, no thanks,' Bosch said between bites of what was billed as a Chicago dog. 'I think I'd rather be on midnight shift in the Seventy-seventh.'

'Well, you think you got it together? You got him?'

'Never know. The DA's office hasn't won a big one since disco. I don't know how it will go. The lawyers all say it depends on the jury. I always thought it was the quality of the evidence but I'm just a dumb detective. John Reason brought in O.J.'s jury consultant and they're acting pretty happy with the twelve in the box. Shit, John Reason. See, I'm even calling the guy by the name the reporters use. It shows how good he is at controlling things, sculpting things.'

He shook his head and took another bite of his lunch.

'Who is the big guy I saw him with?' McCaleb asked. 'The guy standing behind him like Lurch.'

'Rudy Valentino, his investigator.'

'That's his name?'

'No, it's Rudy Tafero. He's former LAPD. He worked Hollywood detectives until a few years back. People in the bureau called him Valentino 'cause of his looks. He got off on it. Anyway, he went private. Has a bail bonds license. Don't ask me how but he started getting security contracts with a lot of Hollywood people. He showed up on this one right after we popped Storey. In fact, Rudy brought Storey to Fowkkes. Probably got a nice finder's fee for that.'

'And how about the judge? How's he going to be?'

Bosch nodded as if he had found something good in the conversation.

'Shootin' Houghton. He's no Second Chance Lance. He's no bullshit. He'll slap Fowkkes down if he needs to. At least we have that going for us.'

'Shootin' Houghton?'

'Under that black robe he's usually strapped – or at least most people think so. About five years ago he had a Mexican Mafia case, and when the jury came in guilty a bunch of the defendants' buddies and family in the audience got mad and nearly started a riot in the courtroom. Houghton pulled his Glock and put a round into the ceiling. It quieted things down pretty quick. Ever since he's been reelected by the highest percentage of any incumbent judge in the county. Go in his courtroom and check the ceiling. The bullet hole's still there. He won't let anybody fix it.'

Bosch took another bite and looked at his watch. He changed the subject, talking with his mouth full.

'Nothing personal but I take it they've hit the wall on Gunn if they're going to outside help already.'

McCaleb nodded.

'Something like that.'

He looked down at the chili dog in front of him and wished he had a knife and fork.

'What's wrong? We didn't have to come here.'

'Nothing. I was just thinking. Between pancakes at Dupar's this morning and this, I might need another heart by dinner.'

'You want to stop your heart, next time you go to Dupar's top it off with a stop at Bob's Donuts. Right there in the Farmers' Market. Raised glaze. A couple of those and you'll feel your arteries harden and snap like icicles hanging off a house. They never came up with suspect one, right?'

'Right. Nothing.'

'So what makes you so interested?'

'Same as Jaye. Something about this one. We think whoever it was might be just starting.'

Bosch just nodded. His mouth was full.

McCaleb appraised him. His hair was shorter than McCaleb had remembered it. More gray but that was to be expected. He still had the mustache and the eyes. They reminded him of Graciela's, so dark there was almost no delineation between iris and pupil. But Bosch's eyes were weary and slightly hooded by wrinkles at the corners. Still, they were always moving, observing. He sat leaning slightly forward, as if ready to move. McCaleb remembered that there had always been a spring-loaded feel to Bosch. He felt as though at any moment or for any reason Bosch could put the needle into the red zone.

Bosch reached inside his suit coat and took out a pair of sunglasses and put them on. McCaleb wondered if that had been in response to realizing that McCaleb had been studying him. He bent down, raised up his chili dog and finally took a bite. It tasted delicious and deadly at the same time. He put the dripping mess back on the paper plate and wiped his hand on a napkin.

'So tell me about Gunn. You said he was a scumbag. What else?'

'What else? That's about it. He was a predator. Used women, bought women. He murdered that girl in that motel room, no doubt in my mind.'

'But the DA kicked the case.'

'Yeah. Gunn claimed self-defense. He said some things that didn't add up but not enough to add up to charges. He claimed self-defense and there wasn't going to be enough to go against that in a trial. So they no-billed it, end of story, on to the next case.'

'Did he ever know you didn't believe him?'

'Oh, sure. He knew.'

'Did you try to sweat him at all?'

Bosch gave him a look that McCaleb could read through the sunglasses. The last question went to Bosch's credibility as an investigator.

'I mean,' McCaleb said quickly, 'what happened when you tried to sweat him?'

'Actually, the truth is we never really got the chance. There was a problem. See, we did set it up. We brought him in and put him in one of the rooms. My partner and I were planning to leave him there a while, let him percolate a little and think about things. We were going to do all the paper, put it in the book and then take a run at him, try to break his story. We never got the chance. I mean, to do it right.'

'What happened?'

'Me and Edgar – that's my partner, Jerry Edgar – we went down the hall to get a cup of coffee and talk about how we were going to play it. While we were down there the squad lieutenant sees Gunn sitting in the interview room and doesn't know what the fuck he's doing there. He takes it upon himself to go in and make sure the guy's been properly advised of his rights.'

McCaleb could see the anger working its way into Bosch's face, even six years after the fact.

'You see, Gunn had come in as a witness and ostensibly as the victim of a crime. He said she came at him with the knife and he turned it on her. So we didn't need to advise him. The plan was to go in there, shake his story down and get him to make a mistake. Once we had that, then we were going to advise him. But this dipshit lieutenant didn't know any of this and he just went in and advised the guy. After that, we were dead. He knew we were coming after him. He asked for a lawyer as soon as we walked into the room.'

Bosch shook his head and looked out onto the street. McCaleb followed his eyes. Across Victory Boulevard was a used-car lot with red, white and blue pennants flapping in the wind. To McCaleb, Van Nuys was always synonymous with car lots. They were all over, new and used.

'So what did you say to the lieutenant?' he asked.

'Say? I didn't say anything. I just shoved him through the window of his office. I got a suspension out of it – involuntary stress leave. Jerry Edgar eventually took the case in to the DA and they sat on it a while and then finally kicked it.'

Bosch nodded. His eyes rested on his empty paper plate.

'I sort of blew it,' he said. 'Yeah, I blew it.'

McCaleb waited a moment before speaking. A gust of wind blew Bosch's plate off the table and the detective watched it skitter across the picnic area. He made no move to chase it down.

'You still working for that lieutenant?'

'Nope. He's no longer with us. Not too long after that he went out one night and didn't come home. They found him in his car up in the tunnel in Griffith Park near the Observatory.'

'What, he killed himself?'

'No. Somebody did it for him. It's still open. Technically.'

Bosch looked back at him. McCaleb dropped his eyes and noticed that Bosch's tie tack was a tiny pair of silver handcuffs.

'What else can I tell you?' Bosch said. 'None of this had anything to do with Gunn. He was just a fly in the ointment – the ointment being the bullshit they call the justice system.'

'Doesn't sound like you had time to do much background on him.'

'None, actually. All that I told you took place in the span of eight or nine hours. Afterward, with what happened, I was off the case and the guy walked out the door.'

'But you didn't give up. Jaye told me you visited him in the drunk tank the night before he got himself killed.'

'Yeah, he got popped on a duice while cruising whores on Sunset. He was in the tank and I got a call. I went in to take a look, maybe jerk his chain a little, see if he was ready to talk. But the guy was piss drunk, just lying there on the floor in the puke. So that was it. You could say that we didn't communicate.'

Bosch looked at McCaleb's unfinished chili dog and then his watch.

'Sorry, but that's all I got. You going to eat that or can we go?'

'Couple more bites, couple more questions. Don't you want to have a smoke?'

'I quit a couple years ago. I only smoke on special occasions.'

'Don't tell me, it was the Marlboro-man-gone-impotent sign on Sunset.'

'No, my wife wanted us both to quit. We did.'

'Your wife? Harry, you're full of surprises.'

'Don't get excited. She's come and gone. But at least I don't smoke anymore. I don't know about her.'

McCaleb just nodded, feeling he had stepped too far into the other man's personal world. He got back to the case.

'So any theories on who killed him?'

McCaleb took another bite while Bosch answered.

'My guess is he probably met up with somebody just like himself. Somebody who crossed a line somewhere. Don't get me wrong, I hope you and Jaye get the guy. But so far, whoever he or she is hasn't done anything I'm too upset about. Know what I mean?'

'It's funny you mentioned a "she." You think it could have been a woman?'

'I don't know enough about it. But like I said, he preyed on women. Maybe one of them put a stop to it.'

McCaleb just nodded. He couldn't think of anything else to ask. Bosch had been a long shot anyway. Maybe he'd known it would come to this and he just wanted to reconnect with Bosch for other reasons. He spoke with his eyes down on his paper plate.

'You still think about the girl on the hill, Harry?'

He didn't want to say out loud the name Bosch had given her. Bosch nodded.

'From time to time I do. It sticks with me. They all do, I guess.'

McCaleb nodded.

'Yeah. So nothing ... nobody ever made a claim on her?'

'Nope. And I tried with Seguin one last time, went up to see him at Q last year, about a week before he got the juice. Tried one more time to find out from him but he just smiled at me. It was like he knew it was the last thing he could hold over me or something. He enjoyed it, I could tell. So I got up to leave and I told him to enjoy himself in hell and know what he said to me? He said, "I hear it's a dry heat." '

Bosch shook his head.

'Fucker. I drove up and back on my day off. Twelve hours in the car and the air conditioner didn't work.'

He looked directly at McCaleb and even through the shades McCaleb again felt the bond he had known so long ago with this man.

Before he could say anything he heard his phone begin to chirp from the pocket of his windbreaker, which was folded on the bench next to him. He struggled with the jacket to find the pocket and got to the phone before the caller hung up. It was Brass Doran.

'I have some stuff for you. Not a lot, but maybe a start.'

'You someplace I can call you back in a few minutes?'

'Actually, I'm in the central conference room. We're about to brainstorm a case and I'm the leader. It could be a couple hours before I'm free. You could call me at home tonight if you—'

'No, hold on.'

He held the phone down and looked at Bosch.

'I better take this. I'll talk to you later if anything comes up, okay?'

'Sure.'

Bosch started getting up. He was going to carry his Coke with him.

'Thanks,' McCaleb said, extending his hand. 'Good luck with the trial.'

Bosch shook his hand.

'Thanks. We'll probably need it.'

McCaleb watched him walk out of the picnic area and to the sidewalk leading back to the courthouse. He brought the phone back up then.

'Brass?'

'Here. Okay, you were talking about owls in general, right? You don't know the specific kind or breed, right?'

'Right. It's just a generic owl, I think.'

'What color is it?'

'Uh, it's brown mostly. Like on the back and the wings.'

As he spoke he took a couple of folded pages of notebook paper and a pen out of his pockets. He shoved his half-eaten chili dog out of the way and got ready to take notes.

'Okay, modern iconography is what you'd expect. The owl is the symbol of wisdom and truth, denotes knowledge, the view of the greater picture as opposed to the small detail. The owl sees in the night. In other words, seeing through the darkness is seeing the truth. It is learning the truth, therefore, knowledge. And from knowledge comes wisdom. Okay?'

McCaleb didn't need to take notes. What Doran had said was obvious. But just to keep his head in it he wrote down a line.

Seeing in the dark = Wisdom

He then underlined the last word.

'Okay, fine. What else?'

'That's basically what I have as far as contemporary application. But when I go backward it gets pretty interesting. Our friend the owl has totally rejuvenated his reputation. He used to be a bad guy.'

'Tell me, Brass.'

'Get your pencil out. The owl is seen repeatedly in art and religious iconography from early medieval through late Renaissance periods. It is found often depicted in religious allegorical displays – paintings, church panels and stations of the cross. The owl was—'

'Okay, Brass, but what did it mean?'

'I'm getting to that. Its meaning could be different from depiction to depiction and according to species depicted. But essentially its depiction was the symbol of evil.'

McCaleb wrote the word down.

'Evil. Okay.'

'I thought you'd be more excited.'

'You can't see me. I'm standing on my hands here. What else you have?'

'Let me run down the list of hits. These are taken from the extracts, the critical literature of the art of the period. References to depictions of owls come up as the symbol of – and I quote – doom, the enemy of innocence, the Devil himself, heresy, folly, death and misfortune, the bird of darkness, and finally, the torment of the human soul in its inevitable journey to eternal damnation. Nice, huh? I like that last one. I guess they didn't sell too many bags of potato chips with owls on them back in the fourteen hundreds.'

McCaleb didn't answer. He was busy scribbling down the descriptions she had read to him.

'Read that last one again.'

She did and he wrote it down verbatim.

'Now, there is more,' Doran said. 'There is also some interpretation of the owl as being the symbol of wrath as well as the punishment of evil. So it obviously was something that meant different things at different times *and* to different people.'

'The punishment of evil,' McCaleb said as he wrote it down.

He looked at the list he had written.

'Anything else?'

'Isn't that enough?'

'Probably. Was there anything about books showing some of this stuff or the names of artists or writers who used the so-called "bird of darkness" in their work?'

McCaleb heard some pages turning over the phone and Doran was silent for a few moments.

'I don't have a lot here. No books but I can give you the name of some of the artists mentioned and you could probably get something over the Internet or maybe the library at UCLA.'

'All right.'

'I have to do this quickly. We're about to go here.'

'Give it to me.'

'All right, I have an artist named Bruegel who painted a huge face as the gateway to hell. A brown owl was nesting in the nostril of the face.'

She started laughing.

'Don't ask me,' she said. 'I'm just giving you what I found.'

'Fine,' McCaleb said, writing the description down. 'Go on.'

'Okay, two others noted for using the owl as the symbol of evil were Van Oostanen and Dürer. I don't have specific paintings.'

He heard more pages turning. He asked for spellings of the artists' names and wrote them down.

'Okay, here it is. This last guy's work is supposedly replete with owls all over the place. I can't pronounce his first name. It's spelled H-I-E-R-O-N-Y-M-U-S. He was Netherlandish, part of the Northern Renaissance. I guess owls were big up there.'

McCaleb looked at the paper in front of him. The name she had just spelled seemed familiar to him.

'You forgot his last name. What's his last name?'

'Oh, sorry. It's Bosch. Like the spark plugs.'

McCaleb sat frozen. He didn't move, he didn't breathe. He stared at the name on the page, unable to write the last part that Doran had just given him. Finally, he turned his head and looked out of the picnic area to the spot on the sidewalk where he had last seen Harry Bosch walking away.

'Terry, you there?'

He came out of it.

'Yeah.'

'That's really all I have. And I have to go. We're starting here.'

'Anything else on Bosch?'

'Not really. And I'm out of time.'

'Okay, Brass. Listen, thanks a lot. I owe you one for this.'

'And I'll collect one day. Let me know how it all comes out, okay?'

'You got it.'

'And send me a photo of that little girl.'

'I will.'

She hung up and McCaleb slowly closed his phone. He wrote a note at the bottom of the page reminding him to send Brass a photo of his daughter. It was just an exercise in avoiding the name of the painter he had written down.

'Shit,' he whispered.

He sat with his thoughts for a long time. The coincidence of receiving the eerie information just minutes after eating with Harry Bosch was unsettling. He studied his notes for a few more moments but knew they did not contain the immediate information he needed. He finally reopened the phone and called 213 information. A minute later he called the personnel office of the Los Angeles Police Department. A woman answered after nine rings.

'Yes, I'm calling on behalf of the L.A. County Sheriff's Department and I need to contact a particular LAPD officer. Only I don't know where he works. I only have his name.'

He hoped the woman wouldn't ask what he meant by *on behalf of*. There was what seemed to be a long silence and then he heard the sound of typing on a keyboard.

'Last name?'

'Uh, it's Bosch.'

He spelled it and then looked down at his notes, ready to spell the first name.

'And the first na – never mind, there's only one. Higher – ronny – mus. Is that it? I can't pronounce it, I don't think.'

'Hieronymus. Yes, that's it.'

He spelled the name and asked if it was a match. It was.

'Well, he's a detective third grade and he works in Hollywood Division. Do you need that number?'

McCaleb didn't answer.

'Sir, do you need—'

'No, I have it. Thank you very much.'

He closed the phone, looked at his watch, and then reopened the phone. He called Jaye Winston's direct number and she picked up right away. He asked if she had gotten anything back from the lab on the examination of the plastic owl.

'Not yet. It's only been a couple hours and one of them was lunch. I'm going to give it until tomorrow before I start knocking on their door.'

'Do you have time to make a few calls and do me a favor?'

'What calls?'

He told her about the icon search Brass Doran had conducted but left out any mention of Hieronymus Bosch. He said that he wanted to talk with an expert on Northern Renaissance painting but thought the arrangements could be made more quickly and cooperation would be more forthcoming if the request came from an official homicide detective.

'I'll do it,' Winston said. 'Where should I start?'

'I'd try the Getty. I'm in Van Nuys now. If somebody will see me I could be there in a half hour.'

'I'll see what I can do. You talk to Harry Bosch?'

'Yeah.'

'Anything new?'

'Not really.'

'I didn't think so. Hang tight. I'll call you back.'

McCaleb dumped what was left of his lunch into one of the trash barrels and headed back toward the courthouse, where he had left the Cherokee parked on a side street by the state parole offices. As he walked he thought about how he had lied by omission to Winston. He knew he should have told her about the Bosch connection or coincidence, whichever it was. He tried to understand what it was that made him hold it back. He found no answer.

His phone chirped just as he got to the Cherokee. It was Winston.

'You have an appointment at the Getty at two. Ask for Leigh Alasdair Scott. He's an associate curator of paintings.'

McCaleb got out his notes and wrote the name down, using the front hood of the Cherokee, after asking Winston to spell it.

'That was quick, Jaye. Thanks.'

'We aim to please. I spoke directly to Scott and he said if he couldn't help you he would find someone who could.'

'You mention the owl?'

'No, it's your interview.'

'Right.'

McCaleb knew he had another chance to tell her about Hieronymus Bosch. But again he let it pass.

'I'll call you later, okay?'

'See ya.'

He closed the phone and unlocked the car. He looked over the roof at the parole offices and saw a large white banner with blue lettering hanging across the facade above the building's entrance.

WELCOME BACK THELMA!

He got into the car wondering whether the Thelma being welcomed back was a convict or an employee. He drove off in the direction of Victory Boulevard. He'd take it to the 405 and then head south.

11

As the freeway rose to cross the Santa Monica Mountains in the Sepulveda Pass, McCaleb saw the Getty rise in front of him on the hilltop. The structure of the museum itself was as impressive as any of the great artworks housed within. It looked like a castle sitting atop a medieval hill. He saw one of the double trams slowly working its way up the side of the hill, delivering another group to the altar of history and art.

By the time he parked at the bottom of the hill and caught his own tram ride up, McCaleb was fifteen minutes late for his appointment with Leigh Alasdair Scott. After getting directions from a museum guard, McCaleb hurried across the travertine stone plaza to a security entrance. Having checked in at the counter he waited on a bench until Scott came for him.

Scott was in his early fifties and spoke with an accent McCaleb placed as originating in either Australia or New Zealand. He was friendly and happy to oblige the L.A. County sheriff's office.

'We have had occasion to offer our help and expertise to detectives in the past. Usually in regard to authenticating artwork or offering historical background to specific pieces,' he said as they walked down a long hallway to his office. 'Detective Winston indicated this would be different. You need some general information on the Northern Renaissance?'

He opened a door and ushered McCaleb into a suite of offices. They stepped into the first office past the security counter. It was a small office with a view through a large window across the Sepulveda Pass to the hillside homes of Bel-Air. The office felt crowded because of the bookshelves lining two walls and the cluttered worktable. There was just room for two chairs. Scott pointed McCaleb to one while he took the other.

'Actually, things have changed a bit since Detective Winston spoke to you,' McCaleb said. 'I can be more specific about what I need now. I've been able to narrow down my questions to a specific painter of that period. If you can tell me about him and maybe show me some of his work, that would be a big help.'

'And what is his name?'

'I'll show it to you.'

McCaleb took out his folded notes and showed him. Scott read the name aloud with obvious familiarity. He pronounced the first name Her-ron-i-mus.

'I thought that was how you said it.'

'Rhymes with anonymous. His work is actually quite well known. You are not familiar with it?'

'No. I never did much studying of art. Does the museum have any of his paintings?'

'None of his works are in the Getty collection but there is a descendant piece in the conservation studio. It is undergoing heavy restoration. Most of his verified works are in Europe, the most significant representations in the Prado. Others scattered about. I am not the one you should be talking to, however.'

McCaleb raised his eyebrows in way of a question.

'Since you have narrowed your query to Bosch specifically, there is someone here you would be better advised to talk to. She is a curatorial assistant. She also happens to be working on a catalogue raisonné on Bosch – a rather long-term project for her. A labor of love, perhaps.'

'Is she here? Can I speak to her?'

Scott reached for his phone and pushed the speaker button. He then consulted an extensions list taped to the table next to it and punched in three digits. A woman answered after three rings.

'Lola Walter, can I help you?'

'Lola, it's Mr. Scott. Is Penelope available?'

'She's working on *Hell* this morning.'

'Oh, I see. We'll go to her there.'

Scott hit the speaker button, disconnecting the call, and headed toward the door.

'You're in luck,' he said.

'Hell?' McCaleb asked.

'It's the descendant painting. If you'll come with me please.'

Scott led the way to an elevator and they went down one floor. Along the way Scott explained that the museum had one of the finest conservation studios in the world. Consequently, works of art from other museums and private collections were often shipped to the Getty for repair and restoration. At the moment a painting believed to have come from a student of Bosch's or a painter from his studio was being restored for a private collector. The painting was called *Hell*.

The conservation studio was a huge room partitioned into two main sections. One section was a workshop where frames were restored. The other section was dedicated to the restoration of paintings and was broken into a series of work bays that ran along a glass wall with the same views Scott had in his office.

McCaleb was led to the second bay, where there was a woman standing behind a man seated before a painting attached to a large easel. The man wore an apron over a dress shirt and tie and a pair of what looked like jeweler's magnifying glasses. He was leaning toward the painting and using a paintbrush with a tiny brush head to apply what looked like silver paint to the surface.

Neither the man nor the woman looked at McCaleb and Scott. Scott held his hands up in a *Hold here* gesture while the seated man completed his paint stroke. McCaleb looked at the painting. It was about four feet high and six feet wide. It was a dark landscape depicting a village being burned to the ground in the night while its inhabitants were being tortured and executed by a variety of otherworldly creatures. The upper panels of the painting, primarily depicting the swirling night sky, were spotted with small patches of damage and missing paint. McCaleb's eyes caught on one segment of the painting below this which depicted a nude and blindfolded man being forced up a ladder to a gallows by a group of birdlike creatures with spears.

The man with the brush completed his work and placed the brush on the glass top of the worktable to his left. He then leaned back toward the painting to study his work. Scott cleared his throat. Only the woman turned around.

'Penelope Fitzgerald, this is Detective McCaleb. He is involved in an investigation and needs to ask about Hieronymus Bosch.'

He gestured toward the painting.

'I told him you would be the most appropriate member of staff to speak with.'

McCaleb watched her eyes register surprise and concern, a normal response to a sudden introduction to the police. The seated man did not even turn around. This was not a normal response. Instead he picked up his brush and went back to work on the painting. McCaleb held his hand out to the woman.

'Actually, I'm not officially a detective. I've been asked by the sheriff's department to help out with an investigation.'

They shook hands.

'I don't understand,' she said. 'Has a Bosch painting been stolen?'

'No, nothing like that. This is a Bosch?'

He gestured toward the painting.

'Not quite. It may be a copy of one of his pieces. If so, then the original is lost and this is all we have. The style and design are his. But it's generally agreed to be the work of a student from his workshop. It was probably painted after Bosch was dead.'

As she spoke her eyes never left the painting. They were sharp and friendly eyes that easily betrayed her passion for Bosch. He guessed that she was about sixty and had probably dedicated her life to the study and love of art. She had surprised him. Scott's brief description of her as an assistant working on a catalog of Bosch's work had made McCaleb think she would be a young art student. He silently chastised himself for making the assumption.

The seated man put his brush down again and picked up a clean white cloth off the worktable to wipe his hands. He swiveled in his chair and looked up when he noticed McCaleb and Scott. It was then that McCaleb knew he had made a second error of assumption. The man had not been ignoring them. He just hadn't heard them.

The man flipped the magnifiers up to the top of his head while reaching beneath the apron to his chest and adjusted a hearing aid control.

'I am sorry,' he said. 'I didn't know we had visitors.'

He spoke with a hard German accent.

'Dr. Derek Vosskuhler, this is Mr. McCaleb,' Scott said. 'He's an investigator and he needs to steal Mrs. Fitzgerald away from you for a short while.'

'I understand. This is fine.'

'Dr. Vosskuhler is one of our restoration experts,' Scott volunteered.

Vosskuhler nodded and looked up at McCaleb and studied him in the way he might study a painting. He made no move to extend his hand.

'An investigation? In regard to Hieronymus Bosch, is it?'

'In a peripheral way. I just want to learn what I can about him. I'm told Mrs. Fitzgerald is the expert.'

McCaleb smiled.

'No one is an expert on Bosch,' Vosskuhler said without a smile. 'Tortured soul, tormented genius . . . how will we ever know what is truly in a man's heart?'

McCaleb just nodded. Vosskuhler turned and appraised the painting.

'What do you see, Mr. McCaleb?'

McCaleb looked at the painting and didn't answer for a long moment. 'A lot of pain.'

Vosskuhler nodded approvingly. Then he stood and looked closely at the painting, flipping the glasses down and leaning close to the upper quarter panel, his lenses just inches from the night sky above the burning village.

'Bosch knew all of the demons,' he said without turning from the painting. 'The darkness . . .'

A long moment went by.

'A darkness more than night.'

There was another long moment of silence until Scott abruptly punctuated it by saying he needed to get back to his office. He left then. And after another moment Vosskuhler finally turned from the painting. He didn't bother flipping up the glasses when he looked at McCaleb. He slowly reached into his apron and switched off sound to his ears.

'I, too, must go back to work. Good luck with your investigation, Mr. McCaleb.'

McCaleb nodded as Vosskuhler sat back in his swivel chair and picked up his tiny brush again.

'We can go to my office,' Fitzgerald said. 'I have all the plate books from our library there. I can show you Bosch's work.'

'That would be fine. Thank you.'

She headed toward the door. McCaleb delayed a moment and took one last look at the painting. His eyes were drawn to the upper panels, toward the swirling darkness above the flames.

Penelope Fitzgerald's office was a six-by-six pod in a room shared by several curatorial assistants. She pulled a chair into the tight space from a nearby pod where no one was working and told McCaleb to sit down. Her desk was L-shaped, with a laptop computer set up on the left side and a cluttered work space on the right. There were several books stacked on the desk. McCaleb noticed that behind one stack was a color print of a painting very much in the same style as the painting Vosskuhler was working on. He pushed the books a half foot to the side and bent down to look at the print. It was in three panels, the largest being the centerpiece. Again it was a ramble. Dozens and dozens of figures spread across the panels. Scenes of debauchery and torture.

'Do you recognize it?' Fitzgerald said.

'I don't think so. But it's Bosch, right?'

'His signature piece. The triptych called *The Garden of Earthly Delights*. It's in the Prado in Madrid. I once stood in front of it for four hours. It wasn't enough time to take it all in. Would you like some coffee or some water or anything, Mr. McCaleb?'

'No, I'm fine. Thank you. You can call me Terry if you want.'

'And you can call me Nep.'

McCaleb put a quizzical look on his face.

'Childhood nickname.'

He nodded.

'Now,' she said. 'In these books I can show you every piece of Bosch's identified work. Is it an important investigation?'

McCaleb nodded.

'I think so. It's a homicide.'

'And you are some kind of consultant?'

'I used to work for the FBI here in L.A. The sheriff's detective assigned to the case asked me to look at it and see what I think. It led me here. To Bosch. I am sorry but I can't get into the details of the case and I know that will probably be frustrating to you. I want to ask questions but I can't really answer any from you.'

'Darn.' She smiled. 'It sounds really interesting.'

'Tell you what, if there is ever a point I can tell you about it, I will.'

'Fair enough.'

McCaleb nodded.

'From what Dr. Vosskuhler said, I take it that there isn't a lot known about the man behind the paintings.'

Fitzgerald nodded.

'Hieronymus Bosch is certainly considered an enigma and he probably always will be.'

McCaleb unfolded his notepaper on the table in front of him and started taking notes as she spoke.

'He had one of the most unconventional imaginations of his time. Or any time for that matter. His work is quite extraordinary and still subject these five centuries later to restudy and reinterpretation. However, I think you will find that the majority of the critical analysis to date holds that he was a doomsayer. His work is informed with the portents of doom and hellfire, of warnings of the wages of sin. To put it more succinctly, his paintings primarily carried variations on the same theme: that the folly of humankind leads us all to hell as our ultimate destiny.'

McCaleb was writing quickly, trying to keep up. He wished he had brought a tape recorder.

'Nice guy, huh?' Fitzgerald said.

'Sounds like it.' He nodded to the print of the triptych. 'Must've been fun on a Saturday night.'

She smiled.

'Exactly what I thought when I was in the Prado.'

'Any redeeming qualities? He took in orphans, was nice to dogs, changed flat tires for old ladies, anything?'

'You have to remember his time and place to fully understand what he was doing with his art. While his work is punctuated with violent scenes and depictions of torture and anguish, this was a time when those sorts of things were not unusual. He lived in a violent time; his work clearly reflects that. The paintings also reflect the medieval belief in the existence of demons everywhere. Evil lurks in all of the paintings.'

'The owl?'

She stared blankly at him for a moment.

'Yes, the owl is one symbol he used. I thought you said you were unfamiliar with his work.'

'I *am* unfamiliar with it. It was an owl that brought me here. But I shouldn't go into that and I shouldn't have interrupted you. Please go on.'

'I was just going to add that it is telling when you consider that Bosch was a contemporary of Leonardo, Michelangelo and Raphael. Yet if you were to look at their works side by side you would have to believe Bosch – with all the medieval symbols and doom – was a century behind.'

'But he wasn't.'

She shook her head as though she felt sorry for Bosch.

'He and Leonardo da Vinci were born within a year or two of each other.

By the end of the fifteenth century, da Vinci was creating pieces that were full of hope and celebration of human values and spirituality while Bosch was all gloom and doom.'

'That makes you feel sad, doesn't it?'

She put her hands on the top book in the stack but didn't open it. It was simply labeled BOSCH on the spine and there was no illustration on the black leather binding.

'I can't help but think about what could have been if Bosch had worked side by side with da Vinci or Michelangelo, what could have happened if he had used his skill and imagination in celebration rather than damnation of the world.'

She looked down at the book and then back up at him.

'But that is the beauty of art and why we study and celebrate it. Each painting is a window to the artist's soul and imagination. No matter how dark and disturbing, his vision is what sets him apart and makes his paintings unique. What happens to me with Bosch is that the paintings serve to carry me into the artist's soul and I sense the torment.'

He nodded and she looked down and opened the book.

The world of Hieronymus Bosch was as striking to McCaleb as it was disturbing. The landscapes of misery that unfolded in the pages Penelope Fitzgerald turned were not unlike some of the most horrible crime scenes he had witnessed, but in these painted scenes the players were still alive and in pain. The gnashing of teeth and the ripping of flesh were active and real. His canvases were crowded with the damned, humans being tormented for their sins by visible demons and creatures given image by the hand of a horrible imagination.

At first he studied the color reproductions of the paintings in silence, taking it all in the way he would first observe a crime scene photograph. But then a page was turned and he looked at a painting that depicted three people gathered around a sitting man. One of those standing used what looked like a primitive scalpel to probe a wound on the crown of the sitting man's head. The image was depicted in a circle. There were words painted above and below the circle.

'What is this one?' he asked.

'It's called *The Stone Operation*,' Fitzgerald said. 'It was a common belief at the time that stupidity and deceit could be cured by the removal of a stone from the head of the one suffering the malady.'

McCaleb leaned over her shoulder and looked closely at the painting, specifically at the location of the surgery wound. It was in a location comparable to the wound on Edward Gunn's head.

'Okay, you can go on.'

Owls were everywhere. Fitzgerald did not have to point them out most of the time, their positions were that obvious. She did explain some of the attendant imagery. Most often in the paintings when the owl was depicted in a tree, the branch upon which the symbol of evil perched was leafless and gray – dead.

She turned the page to a three-panel painting.

'This is called *The Last Judgment,* with the left panel subtitled *The Fall of Mankind* and the right panel simply and obviously called *Hell.*'

'He liked painting hell.'

But Nep Fitzgerald didn't smile. Her eyes studied the book.

The left panel of the painting was a Garden of Eden scene with Adam and Eve at center taking the fruit from the serpent in the apple tree. On a dead branch of a nearby tree an owl watched the transaction. On the opposite panel Hell was depicted as a dark place where birdlike creatures disemboweled the damned, cut their bodies up and placed them in frying pans to be slid into fiery ovens.

'All of this came from this guy's head,' McCaleb said. 'I don't . . .'

He didn't finish because he was unsure what he was trying to say.

'A tormented soul,' Fitzgerald said and turned the page.

The next painting was another circular image with seven separate scenes depicted along the outer rim and a portrait of God at center. In a circle of gold surrounding the portrait of God and separating him from the other scenes were four Latin words McCaleb immediately recognized.

'Beware, beware, God sees.'

Fitzgerald looked up at him.

'You obviously have seen this before. Or you just happen to know fifteenth-century Latin. This must be one strange case you are working on.'

'It's getting that way. But I only know the words, not the painting. What is it?'

'It's actually a tabletop, probably created for a church rectory or a holy person's house. It's the eye of God. He is at center and what he sees as he looks down are these images, the seven deadly sins.'

McCaleb nodded. By looking at the distinct scenes he could pick out some of the more obvious of the sins; gluttony, lust and pride.

'And now his masterpiece,' his tour guide said as she turned the page.

She came to the same triptych she had pinned to the wall of the pod. *The Garden of Earthly Delights.* McCaleb studied it closely now. The left panel was a bucolic scene of Adam and Eve being placed in the garden by the creator. An apple tree stood nearby. The center panel, the largest, showed dozens of nudes coupling and dancing in uninhibited lust, riding horses and beautiful birds and wholly imagined creatures from the lake in the foreground. And then the last panel, the dark one, was the payoff. Hell, a place of torment and anguish administered by monster birds and other ugly creatures. The painting was so detailed and enthralling that McCaleb understood how someone might stand before it – the original – for four hours and still not see everything.

'I am sure you are grasping the ideas of Bosch's often repeated themes by now,' Fitzgerald said. 'But this is considered the most coherent of his works as well as the most beautifully imagined and realized.'

McCaleb nodded and pointed to the three panels as he spoke.

'You have Adam and Eve here, the good life until they eat that apple. Then in the center you have what happens after the fall from grace: life without rules. Freedom of choice leads to lust and sin. And where does all of this go? Hell.'

'Very good. And if I could just point out a few specifics that might interest you.'

'Please.'

She started with the first panel.

'The earthly paradise. You are correct in that it depicts Adam and Eve before the Fall. This pool and fountain at center represent the promise of eternal life. You already noted the fruit tree at left center.'

Her finger moved across the plate to the fountain structure, a tower of what looked like flower petals that somehow delivered water in four distinct trickles to the pool below. Then he saw it. Her finger stopped below a small dark entrance at the center of the fountain structure. The face of an owl peered from the darkness.

'You mentioned the owl before. Its image is here. You see all is not right in this paradise. Evil lurks and, as we know, will ultimately win the day. According to Bosch. Then, going to the next panel we see the imagery again and again.'

She pointed out two distinct representations of owls and two other depictions of owl-like creatures. McCaleb's eyes held on one of the images. It showed a large brown owl with shiny black eyes being embraced by a nude man. The owl's coloring and eyes matched that of the plastic bird found in Edward Gunn's apartment.

'Do you see something, Terry?'

He pointed to the owl.

'This one. I can't really go into it with you but this one, it matches up with the reason I am here.'

'A lot of symbols are at work in this panel. That is one of the obvious ones. After the Fall, man's freedom of choice leads him to debauchery, gluttony, folly and avarice, the worst sin of all in Bosch's world being lust. Man wraps his arms around the owl; he embraces evil.'

McCaleb nodded.

'And then he pays for it.'

'Then he pays for it. As you notice in the last panel, this is a depiction of hell without fire. Rather, it is a place of myriad torments and endless pain. Of darkness.'

McCaleb stared silently for a long time, his eyes moving across the landscape of the painting. He remembered what Dr. Vosskuhler had said. *A darkness more than night.*

12

Bosch cupped his hands and held them against the window next to the front door of the apartment. He was looking into the kitchen. The counters were spotless. No mess, no coffee maker, not even a toaster. He started to get a bad feeling. He stepped over to the door and knocked once more. He then paced back and forth waiting. Looking down he saw an outline on the pavement of where a welcome mat had once been.

'Damn,' he said.

He reached into his pocket and took out a small leather pouch. He unzipped it and removed two small steel picks he had made from hacksaw blades. Glancing around he saw no one. He was in a shielded alcove of a large apartment complex in Westwood. Most residents were probably still at work. He stepped up to the door and went to work with the picks on the deadbolt. Ninety seconds later he had the door open and he went inside.

He knew the apartment was vacant as soon as he stepped in but he covered every room anyway. All of them were empty. Hoping for an empty prescription bottle he even checked the bathroom medicine cabinet. There was a used razor made of pink plastic on a shelf, nothing else.

He walked back into the living room and took out his cell phone. He had just put Janis Langwiser's cell phone on the speed dial the day before. She was co-prosecutor on the case and they had worked on Bosch's testimony throughout the weekend. His call found her still in the trial team's temporary office in the Van Nuys courthouse.

'Listen, I don't want to rain on the parade but Annabelle Crowe is gone.'

'What do you mean, gone?'

'I mean gone, baby, gone. I'm standing in what was her apartment. It's empty.'

'Shit! We really need her, Harry. When did she move out?'

'I don't know. I just discovered she was gone.'

'Did you talk to the apartment manager?'

'Not yet. But he's not going to know much more than how long ago she split. If she's running from the trial she wouldn't be leaving any forwarding addresses with the management.'

'Well, when did you talk to her last?'

'Thursday. I called her here. But that line is disconnected today. No forwarding number.'

'Shit!'

'I know. You said that.'

'She got the subpoena, right?'

'Yeah, she got it Thursday. That's why I called. To make sure.'

'Okay, then maybe she'll be here tomorrow.'

Bosch looked around the empty apartment.

'I wouldn't count on it.'

He looked at his watch. It was after five. Because he had been so sure about Annabelle Crowe, she had been the last witness he was going to check on. There had been no hint that she was going to split. Now he knew he would be spending the night trying to run her down.

'What can you do?' Langwiser asked.

'I've got some information on her I can run down. She's got to be in town. She's an actress, where else is she going to go?'

'New York?'

'That's where real actors go. She's a face. She'll stay here.'

'Find her, Harry. We'll need her by next week.'

'I'll try.'

There was a moment of silence while they both considered things.

'You think Storey got to her?' Langwiser finally asked.

'I'm wondering. He could've gotten to her with what she needs – a job, a part, a paycheck. When I find her I'll be asking that.'

'Okay, Harry. Good luck. If you get her tonight, let me know. Otherwise, I'll see you in the morning.'

'Right.'

Bosch closed the phone and put it down on the kitchen counter. From his jacket pocket he took out a thin stack of three-by-five cards. Each card had the name of one of the witnesses he was responsible for vetting and preparing for trial. Home and work addresses as well as phone numbers and pager numbers were noted on the cards. He checked the card assigned to Annabelle Crowe and then punched her pager number into his phone. A recorded message said the pager was no longer in service.

He clapped the phone closed and looked at the card again. The name and number of Annabelle Crowe's agent were listed at the bottom. He decided that the agent might be the one tie she wouldn't sever.

He put the phone and cards back into his pockets. This was one inquiry he was going to make in person.

13

McCaleb made the crossing by himself, *The Following Sea* arriving at Avalon Harbor just as darkness did. Buddy Lockridge had stayed behind at Cabrillo Marina because no new charters had come up and he wouldn't be needed until Saturday. As he arrived at the island McCaleb radioed the harbor master's boat on channel 16 and got help mooring the boat.

The added weight of the two heavy books he had found in the used-books section at Dutton's bookstore in Brentwood plus the smaller cooler filled with frozen tamales made the walk up the hill to his house exhausting. He had to stop twice on the side of the road to rest. Each time he sat down on the cooler and took one of the books out of his leather bag so that he could once more study the dark work of Hieronymus Bosch – even in the shadows of evening.

Since his visit to the Getty, the images in the Bosch paintings were never far from his thoughts. Nep Fitzgerald had said something at the end of the meeting in her office. Just before closing the book on the plates reproducing *The Garden of Earthly Delights* she looked at him with a small smile, as if she had something to say but was hesitant.

'What?' he said.

'Nothing really, just an observation.'

'Go ahead and make it. I'd like to hear it.'

'I was just going to mention that a lot of the critics and scholars who view Bosch's work see corollaries to contemporary times. That's the mark of a great artist – if his work stands the test of time. If it has the power to connect to people and . . . and maybe influence them.'

McCaleb nodded. He knew she wanted him to tell her what he was working on.

'I understand what you are saying. I'm sorry but at the moment I can't tell you about this. Maybe someday I will, or someday you will just know what it was. But thank you. You have helped a lot, I think. I don't know for sure yet.'

Sitting on the cooler now, McCaleb remembered the conversation. Corollaries to contemporary times, he thought. And crimes. He opened the larger of the two books he had bought and opened it to a color illustration of Bosch's masterpiece. He studied the owl with black eyes and all of his instincts told him he was on to something significant. Something very dark and dangerous.

When he got home Graciela took the cooler from him and opened it on the kitchen counter. She took three of the green corn tamales out and put them on a plate for defrosting in the microwave.

'I'm making chili relenos, too,' she said. 'It's a good thing you called from the boat or we would've gone ahead and eaten without you.'

McCaleb let her vent. He knew she was angry about what he was doing. He walked over to the table where Cielo was propped in a bouncing chair. She was staring up at the ceiling fan and moving her hands in front of her, getting used to them. McCaleb bent down and kissed both of them and then her forehead.

'Where's Raymond?'

'In his room. On the computer. Why did you only get ten?'

He looked over at her as he slid into a chair next to Cielo. She was putting the other tamales into a plastic Tupperware container for freezing.

'I took the cooler in and told them to fill it. That's how many fit, I guess.'

She shook her head, annoyed with him.

'We'll have one extra.'

'Then throw it out or invite one of Raymond's friends over for dinner next time. Who cares, Graciela? It's a tamale.'

Graciela turned and looked at him with dark, upset eyes that immediately softened.

'You're sweaty.'

'I just walked up the hill. The shuttle was closed for the night.'

She opened an overhead cabinet and took out a plastic box holding a thermometer. There was a thermometer in every room in the house. She took this one out and shook it and came over to him.

'Open.'

'Let's use the electronic.'

'No, I don't trust them.'

She put the end of the thermometer under his tongue and then used her hand to gently bring his jaw up and close his mouth. Very professional. She had been an emergency room nurse when he met her and was now the school nurse and an office clerk at Catalina Elementary. She had just gone back to work after the Christmas holiday. McCaleb sensed that she wanted to be a full-time mother, but they couldn't afford it so he never brought it up directly. He hoped that in a couple of years the charter service would be more established and they would have the choice then. Sometimes he wished they had kept a share of the money for the book-and-movie deal but he also knew that their decision to honor Graciela's sister by not making money from what happened had been the only choice. They had given half the money to the Make a Wish Foundation and put the other half in a trust fund for Raymond. It would pay for college if he wanted that.

Graciela held his wrist and checked his pulse while he sat silently watching her.

'You're high,' she said, dropping his wrist. 'Open.'

He opened his mouth and she took out the thermometer and read it. She went to the sink and washed it, then returned it to its case and the cabinet. She didn't say anything and McCaleb knew that meant his temperature was normal.

'You wish I had a fever, don't you?'

'Are you crazy?'

'Yes, you do. That way you could tell me to stop this.'

'What do you mean, tell you to stop it? Last night you said it was just going to be last night. Then this morning you said it was just going to be today. What are you telling me now, Terry?'

He looked over at Cielo and held out a finger for her to grasp.

'It's not over.' He now looked back at Graciela. 'Some things came up today.'

'Some *things*? Whatever they are, give them to Detective Winston. It's her job. It's not your job to be doing this.'

'I can't. Not yet. Not until I am sure.'

Graciela turned and walked back to the counter. She put the plate with the tamales on it into the microwave and set it for defrost.

'Will you take her in and change her? It's been a while. And she'll need a bottle while I make dinner.'

McCaleb carefully raised his daughter out of the bouncing seat and put her on his shoulder. She made some fussing noises and he gently patted her back to calm her. He walked over to Graciela's back, put his arm around the front of her and pulled her backward into him. He kissed the top of her head and held his face in her hair.

'It will all be over soon and we'll be back to normal.'

'I hope so.'

She touched his arm, which crossed her body beneath her breasts. The touch of her fingertips was the approval he sought. It told him this was a rough spot but they were okay. He held her tighter, kissed the back of her neck and then let her go.

Cielo watched the slowly moving mobile that hung over the changing table as he put a new diaper on her tiny body. Cardboard stars and half moons hung from threads. Raymond had made it with Graciela as a Christmas present. An air current from somewhere in the house gently turned it and Cielo's dark blue eyes focused on it. McCaleb bent down and kissed her forehead.

After wrapping her in two baby blankets he took her out to the porch and gave her the bottle while gently moving in the rocking chair. Looking down at the harbor he noticed he had left on the instrument lights on *The Following Sea*'s bridge. He knew he could call the harbor master on the pier and whoever was working nights could just motor over and turn them off. But he knew he'd be going back to the boat after dinner. He would get the lights then.

He looked down at Cielo. Her eyes were closed but he knew she was awake. She was working the bottle forcefully. Graciela had stopped full-time breastfeeding when she had gone back to work. Bottle feedings were new and he found them to be perhaps the single most pleasurable moments of being a new father. He often whispered to his daughter during these times. Promises mostly. Promises that he would always love her and be with her. He told her never to be afraid or feel alone. Sometimes when she would suddenly open her eyes and look at him, he sensed that she was communicating the same things back to him. And he felt a kind of love he had never known before.

'Terry.'

He looked up at Graciela's whisper.

'Dinner's ready.'

He checked the bottle and saw it was almost empty.

'I'll be there in a minute,' he whispered.

After Graciela left them he looked down at his daughter. The whispering had made her open her eyes. She stared up at him. He kissed her on the forehead and then just held her gaze.

'I have to do this, baby,' he whispered.

The boat was cold inside. McCaleb turned on the salon lights and then positioned the space heater in the center of the room and turned it on low. He wanted to warm up but not too much, for then he might get sleepy. He was still tired from the exertions of the day.

He was down in the front cabin going through his old files when he heard the cell phone start to chirp from his leather bag up in the salon. He closed the file he was studying and took it with him as he bounded up the stairs to the salon and grabbed the phone out of his bag. It was Jaye Winston.

'So how'd it go at the Getty? I thought you were going to call me back.'

'Oh, well it ran late and I wanted to get back to the boat and get across before dark. I forgot to call.'

'You're back on the island?'

She sounded disappointed.

'Yeah, I told Graciela this morning I'd be back. But don't worry, I'm still working on a few things.'

'What happened at the Getty?'

'Nothing much,' he lied. 'I talked to a couple people and looked at some paintings.'

'You see any owls that match ours?'

She laughed as she asked the question.

'A couple close ones. I got some books I want to look through tonight. I was going to call you, see if maybe we could get together tomorrow.'

'When? I've got a meeting in the morning at ten and another at eleven.'

'I was thinking the afternoon anyway. There's something I have to do in the morning myself.'

He didn't want to tell her that he wanted to watch the opening statements in the Storey trial. He knew they'd be carried live on *Court TV*, which he got up at the house with the satellite dish.

'Well, I could probably get a chopper to take me out there but I'll have to check with aero first.'

'No, I'll be coming back over.'

'You will? Great! You want to come here?'

'No, I was thinking about something more quiet and private.'

'How come?'

'I'll tell you tomorrow.'

'Getting mysterious on me. This isn't a scam to get the sheriff's to pay for pancakes again, is it?'

They both laughed.

'No scam. Any chance you could come out to Cabrillo and meet me at my boat?'

'I'll be there. What time?'

He made the appointment for three o'clock thinking that would give him plenty of time to prepare a profile and figure out how he would tell her what he had to say. It would also give him enough time to be ready for what he hoped she would allow him to do that night.

'Anything on the owl?' he asked once they had the meeting arranged.

'Very little, none of it good. Inside there are manufacturing markings. The plastic mold was made in China. The company ships them to two distributors over here, one in Ohio and one in Tennessee. From there they probably go all over. It's a long shot and a lot of work.'

'So you're going to drop it.'

'No, I didn't say that. It's just not a priority. It's on my partner's plate. He's got calls out. We'll see what he gets from the distributors, evaluate and decide where to go from there.'

McCaleb nodded. Prioritizing investigative leads and even investigations themselves was a necessary evil. But it still bothered him. He was sure the owl was a key and knowing everything about it would be useful.

'Okay, so we're all set?' she asked.

'About tomorrow? Yeah, we're set.'

'We'll see you at three.'

'We?'

'Kurt and I. My partner. You haven't met him yet.'

'Uh, look, tomorrow could it just be me and you? Nothing against your partner but I'd just like to talk to you tomorrow, Jaye.'

There was a moment of silence before she responded.

'Terry, what's going on with you?'

'I just want to talk to you about this. You brought me in, I want to give what I have to you. If you want to bring your partner in on it after, that's fine.'

There was another pause.

'I'm getting a bad vibe from all of this, Terry.'

'I'm sorry, but that's the way I want it. I guess you have to take it or leave it.'

His ultimatum made her go silent even longer this time. He waited for her.

'All right, man,' she finally said. 'It's your show. I'll take it.'

'Thanks, Jaye. I'll see you then.'

They hung up. He looked at the old case file he had pulled and still held in his hand. He put the phone down on the coffee table and leaned back on the couch and opened the file.

14

At first they called it the Little Girl Lost case because the victim had no name. The victim was thought to be about fourteen or fifteen years old; a Latina – probably Mexican – whose body was found in the bushes and among the debris below one of the overlooks off Mulholland Drive. The case belonged to Bosch and his partner at the time, Frankie Sheehan. This was before Bosch worked homicide out of Hollywood Division. He and Sheehan were a Robbery–Homicide team and it had been Bosch who contacted McCaleb at the bureau. McCaleb was newly returned to Los Angeles from Quantico. He was setting up an outpost for the Behavioral Sciences Unit and Violent Criminal Apprehension Program. The Little Girl Lost case was one of the first submitted to him.

Bosch came to him, bringing the file and the crime scene photos to his tiny office on the thirteenth floor of the federal building in Westwood. He came without Sheehan because the partners had disagreed on whether to bring the bureau in on the case. Cross-agency jealousies at work. But Bosch didn't care about all of that. He cared about the case. He had haunted eyes. The case was clearly working on him as much as he worked on it.

The body had been found nude and violated in many ways. The girl had been manually strangled by her killer's gloved hands. No clothes or purse were found on the hillside. Fingerprints matched no computerized records. The girl matched no description on an active missing persons case anywhere in Los Angeles County or on national crime computer systems. An artist's rendering of the victim's face put on the TV news and in the papers brought no calls from a loved one. Sketches faxed to five hundred police agencies across the Southwest and to the State Judicial Police in Mexico drew no response. The victim remained unclaimed and unidentified, her body reposing in the refrigerator at the coroner's office while Bosch and his partner worked the case.

There was no physical evidence found with the body. Aside from being left without her clothes or any identifying property, the victim had apparently been washed with an industrial-strength cleaner before being dumped late at night off Mulholland.

There was only one clue with the body. An impression in the skin of the left hip. Postmortem lividity indicated the blood in the body had settled on the left half, meaning the body had been lying on its left side in the time between the stilling of the heart and the dropping of the body down the hillside where it came to rest face down on a pile of empty beer cans and tequila bottles. The evidence indicated that during the time that the blood settled, the body had been lying on top of the object that left the impression on the hip.

The impression consisted of the number 1, the letter J and part of a third letter that could have been the upper left stem of an H, a K or an L. It was a partial reading of a license plate.

Bosch formed the theory that whoever had killed the girl with no name had hidden the body in the trunk of a car until it was time to dump it. After carefully cleaning the body the killer had put it into the trunk of his car, mistakenly putting it down on part of a license plate that had been taken off the car and also placed in the trunk. Bosch's theory was that the license plate had been removed and possibly replaced with a stolen plate as one more safety measure that would help the killer avoid detection if his car happened to be spotted by a suspicious passerby at the Mulholland overlook.

Though the skin impression gave no indication of what state issued the license plate, Bosch went with the percentages. From the state Department of Motor Vehicles he obtained a list of every car registered in Los Angeles County that carried a plate beginning 1JH, 1JK and 1JL. The list contained over three thousand names of car owners. He and his partner cut 40 percent of it by discounting the female owners. The remaining names were slowly fed into the National Crime Index computer and the detectives came up with a list of forty-six men with criminal records ranging from minor to the extreme.

It was at this point that Bosch came to McCaleb. He wanted a profile of the killer. He wanted to know if he and Sheehan were on the right track in suspecting that the killer had a criminal history, and he wanted to know how to approach and evaluate the forty-six men on the list.

McCaleb considered the case for nearly a week. He looked at each of the crime scene photos twice a day – first thing in the morning and last thing before going to sleep – and studied the reports often. He finally told Bosch that he believed they were on the right course. Using data accumulated from hundreds of similar crimes and analyzed in the bureau's VICAP program, he was able to provide a profile of a man in his late twenties with a history of having committed crimes of an escalating nature and likely including offenses of a sexual nature. The crime scene suggested the work of an exhibitionist – a killer who wanted his crime to be public and to instill horror and fear in the general population. Therefore, the location of the body dump site would have been chosen for these reasons as opposed to reasons of convenience.

In comparing the profile to the list of forty-six names, Bosch narrowed the possibilities to two suspects: a Woodland Hills office building custodian who had a record of arson and public indecency and a stage builder who worked for a studio in Burbank and had been arrested for the attempted rape of a neighbor when he was a teenager. Both men were in their late twenties.

Bosch and Sheehan leaned toward the custodian because of his access to industrial cleaners, like the one that had been used to wash the victim's body. However, McCaleb liked the stage builder as a suspect because the attempted rape of the neighbor in his youth indicated an impulsive action that was more in tune with the profile of the current crime's perpetrator.

Bosch and Sheehan decided to informally interview both men and invited McCaleb along. The FBI agent stressed that the men should be interviewed in their own homes so that he would have the opportunity to study them in their own environment as well as look for clues in their belongings.

The stage builder was first. His name was Victor Seguin. He seemed shell-shocked by seeing the three men at his door and the explanation Bosch gave for their visit. Nevertheless he invited them in. As Bosch and Sheehan calmly asked questions McCaleb sat on a couch and studied the clean and neat furnishings of the apartment. Within five minutes he knew they had the right man and nodded to Bosch – their prearranged signal.

Victor Seguin was informed of his rights and arrested. He was placed in the detectives' car and his small home under the landing zone of Burbank Airport was sealed until a search warrant could be obtained. Two hours later, when they reentered with the search warrant, they found a sixteen-year-old girl bound and gagged but alive in a soundproof coffin-like crawl space constructed by the stage builder beneath a trap door hidden under his bed.

Only after the excitement and adrenaline high of having broken a case and saved a life began to subside did Bosch finally ask McCaleb how he knew they had their man. McCaleb walked the detective over to the living-room bookcase, where he pointed out a well-worn copy of a book called *The Collector,* a novel about a man who abducts several women.

Seguin was charged with the unidentified girl's murder and the kidnapping and rape of the young woman the investigators rescued. He denied any guilt in the murder and pressed for a deal by which he would plead guilty to the kidnapping and rape of the survivor only. The DA's office declined any deal and proceeded to trial with what they had – the survivor's gut-wrenching testimony and the license plate impression on the dead girl's hip.

The jury convicted on all counts after less than four hours' deliberation. The DA's office then floated a possible deal to Seguin: a promise not to go for the death penalty during the second phase of the trial if the killer agreed to tell investigators who his first victim was and from where he had abducted her. To take the deal Seguin would have to drop his pose of innocence. He passed. The DA went for the death penalty and got it. Bosch never learned who the dead girl was and McCaleb knew it haunted him that no one apparently cared enough to come forward.

It haunted McCaleb, too. On the day he came to the penalty phase of the trial to testify, he had lunch with Bosch and noticed that a name had been written on the tabs of his files on the case.

'What's that?' McCaleb asked excitedly. 'You ID'd her?'

Bosch looked down and saw the name on the tabs and turned the files over.

'No, no ID yet.'

'Well, what's that?'

'Just a name. I sort of gave her a name, I guess.'

Bosch looked embarrassed. McCaleb reached over and turned the files back over to read the name.

'Cielo Azul?'

'Yeah, she was Spanish, I gave her a Spanish name.'

'It means blue sky, right?'

'Yeah, blue sky. I, uh . . .'

McCaleb waited. Nothing.

'What?'

'Well . . . I'm not that religious, you know what I mean?'

'Yes.'

'But I sort of figured if nobody down here wanted to claim her, then hopefully . . . maybe there's somebody up there that will.'

Bosch shrugged his shoulders and looked away. McCaleb could see his face turning red in the upper cheeks.

'It's hard to find God's hand in what we do. What we see.'

Bosch just nodded and they didn't speak about the name again.

McCaleb lifted the last page of the file marked Cielo Azul and looked at the inside rear flap of the manila folder. It had become his habit over time at the bureau to jot notes on the back flap, where they would not readily be seen because of the attached file pages. These were notes he made about the investigators who submitted the cases for profiling. McCaleb had come to realize that insights about the investigator were sometimes as important as the information in the case file. For it was through the investigator's eyes that McCaleb first viewed many aspects of the crime.

His case with Bosch had come up more than ten years earlier, before he began his more extensive profiling of the investigators as well as the cases. On this file he had written Bosch's name and just four words beneath it.

Thorough – Smart – M. M. – A. A.

He looked at the last two notations now. It had been part of his routine to use abbreviations and shorthand when making notes that needed to be kept confidential. The last two notations were his reading on what motivated Bosch. He had come to believe that homicide detectives, a breed of cop unto themselves, called upon deep inner emotions and motivations to accept and carry out the always difficult task of their job. They were usually of two kinds, those who saw their jobs as a skill or a craft, and those who saw it as a mission in life. Ten years ago he had put Bosch into the latter class. He was a man on a mission.

This motivation in detectives could then be broken down even further as to what gave them this sense of purpose or mission. To some the job was seen as almost a game; they had some inner deficit that caused them to need to prove they were better, smarter and more cunning than their quarry. Their lives were a constant cycle of validating themselves by, in effect, invalidating the killers they sought by putting them behind bars. Others, while carrying a degree of that same inner deficit, also saw themselves with the additional dimension of being speakers for the dead. There was a sacred bond cast between victim and cop that formed at the crime scene and could not be severed. It was what ultimately pushed them into the chase and enabled them to overcome all obstacles in their path. McCaleb classified these cops as avenging angels. It had been his experience that these cop/angels were the best investigators he ever worked with. He also came to believe that they traveled closest to that unseen edge beneath which lies the abyss.

Ten years before, he had classified Harry Bosch as an avenging angel. He now had to consider whether the detective had stepped too close to that edge. He had to consider that Bosch might have gone over.

He closed the file and pulled the two art books out of his bag. Both were simply titled *Bosch*. The larger one, with full-color reproductions of the paintings, was by R. H. Marijnissen and P. Ruyffelaere. The second book, which appeared to carry more analysis of the paintings than the other, was written by Erik Larsen.

McCaleb started with the smaller book and began scanning through the pages of analysis. He quickly learned that, as Penelope Fitzgerald had said, there were many different and even competing views of Hieronymus Bosch. The Larsen book cited scholars who called Bosch a humanist and even one who believed him to be part of a heretical group that believed the earth was a literal hell ruled over by Satan. There were disputes among the scholars about the intended meanings of some of the paintings, about whether some paintings could actually be attributed to Bosch, about whether the painter had ever traveled to Italy and viewed the work of his Renaissance contemporaries.

Finally, McCaleb closed the book when he realized that, at least for his purposes, the words about Hieronymus Bosch might not be important. If the painter's work was subject to multiple interpretations, then the only interpretation that mattered would be that of the person who killed Edward Gunn. What mattered was what that person saw and took from the paintings of Hieronymus Bosch.

He opened the larger book and began to slowly study the reproductions. His viewing of reproduction plates of the paintings at the Getty had been hurried and encumbered by his not being alone.

He put his notebook on the arm of the couch with the plan to keep a tabulation of the number of owls he saw in the paintings as well as descriptions of each bird. He quickly realized that the paintings were so minutely detailed in the smaller-scale reproductions that he might be missing things of significance. He went down to the forward cabin to find the magnifying glass he had always kept in his desk at the bureau for use while examining crime scene photos.

As he was bent over a box full of office supplies he had cleared out of his desk five years before, McCaleb felt a slight bump against the boat and straightened up. He had tied the Zodiac up on the fantail, so it could not have been his own skiff. He was considering this when he felt the unmistakable up-and-down movement of the boat indicating that someone had just stepped aboard. His mind focused on the salon door. He was sure he had left it unlocked.

He looked down into the box he had just been sorting through and grabbed the letter opener.

As he came up the steps into the galley McCaleb surveyed the salon and saw no one and nothing amiss. It was difficult seeing past the interior reflection on the sliding door but outside in the cockpit, silhouetted by the streetlights on Crescent Street, there was a man. He stood with his back to the salon as if admiring the lights of the town going up the hill.

McCaleb moved quickly to the slider and pulled it open. He held the letter opener at his side but with the point of the blade up. The man standing in the cockpit turned around.

McCaleb lowered his weapon as the man stared at it with wide eyes.

'Mr. McCaleb, I—'

'It's all right, Charlie, I just didn't know who it was.'

Charlie was the night man in the harbor office. McCaleb didn't know his last name. But he knew that he often visited Buddy Lockridge on nights Buddy stayed over. McCaleb guessed that Buddy was a soft touch for a quick beer every now and then on the long nights. That was probably why Charlie had rowed his skiff over from the pier.

'I saw the lights and thought maybe Buddy was here,' he said. 'I was just paying a visit.'

'No, Buddy's overtown tonight. He probably won't be back till Friday.'

'Okay, then. I'll just be going. Everything all right with you? The missus isn't making you sleep on the boat, is she?'

'No, Charlie, everything's fine. Just doing a little work.'

He held up the letter opener as if that explained what he was doing.
'All right then, I'll be heading back.'

'Good night, Charlie. Thanks for checking on me.'

He went back inside and down to the office. He found the magnifying glass, with a light attachment, at the bottom of the box of office supplies.

For the next two hours he went through the paintings. The eerie landscapes of phantasmic demons surrounding human prey enthralled him once again. As he studied each work he marked particular findings such as the owls with yellow Post-its so that he could easily return to them.

McCaleb amassed a list of sixteen direct depictions of owls in the paintings and another dozen portrayals of owl-like creatures or structures. The owls were darkly painted and lurking in all the paintings like sentinels of judgment and doom. He looked at them and couldn't help but think of the analogy of the owl as detective. Both creatures of the night, both watchers and hunters – firsthand observers of the evil and pain humans and animals inflict upon each other.

The single most significant finding McCaleb made during his study of the paintings was not an owl. Rather, it was the human form. He made the discovery as he used the lighted glass to examine the center panel of a painting called *The Last Judgment*. Outside the depiction of hell's oven, where sinners were thrown, there were several bound victims waiting to be dismembered and burned. Among this grouping McCaleb found the image of a nude man bound with his arms and legs behind him. The sinner's extremities had been stretched into a painful reverse fetal position. The image closely reflected what he had seen at center focus in the crime scene videotape and photos of Edward Gunn.

McCaleb marked the finding with a Post-it and closed the book. When the cell phone on the couch next to him chirped just then, he bolted upright with a start. He checked his watch before answering and saw it was exactly midnight.

The caller was Graciela.

'I thought you were coming back tonight.'

'I am. I just finished and I'm on my way.'

'You took the cart down, right?'

'Yeah. So I'll be fine.'

'Okay, see you soon.'

'Yes, you will.'

McCaleb decided to leave everything on the boat, thinking that he needed to clear his mind before the next day. Carrying the files and the heavy books would only remind him of the heavy thoughts he carried within. He locked the boat and took the Zodiac to the skiff dock. At the end of the pier he climbed into the golf cart. He rode through the deserted business district and up the hill toward home. Despite his efforts to deflect them, his thoughts were of the abyss. A place where creatures with sharp beaks and claws and knives tormented the fallen in perpetuity. He knew one thing for sure at this point. The painter Bosch would have made a good profiler. He knew his stuff. He had a handle on the nightmares that rattle around inside most people's minds. As well as those that sometimes get out.

15

Opening statements in the trial of David Storey were delayed while the attorneys argued over final motions behind closed doors with the judge. Bosch sat at the prosecution table and waited. He tried to clear his mind of all extraneous diversions, including his fruitless search for Annabelle Crowe the night before.

Finally, at ten forty-five, the attorneys came into the courtroom and moved to their respective tables. Then the defendant – today wearing a suit that looked like it would cover three deputies' paychecks – was led into court from the holding cell and, at last, Judge Houghton took the bench.

It was time to begin and Bosch felt the tension in the courtroom ratchet up a considerable notch. Los Angeles had raised – or perhaps lowered – the criminal trial to the level of worldwide entertainment, but it was never seen that way by the players in the courtroom. They were playing for keeps and in this trial perhaps more than most there was a palpable sense of the enmity between the two opposing camps.

The judge instructed the deputy sheriff who acted as his bailiff to bring in the jury. Bosch stood with the others and turned and watched the jurors file in silently and take their seats. He thought he could see excitement in some of their faces. They had been waiting through two weeks of jury selection and motions for things to start. Bosch's eyes rose above them to the two cameras mounted on the wall over the jury box. They gave a full view of the courtroom, except for the jury box.

After everyone was seated Houghton cleared his throat and leaned forward to the bench microphone while looking at the jurors.

'Ladies and gentlemen, how are you this morning?'

There was a murmured response and Houghton nodded.

'I apologize for the delay. Please remember that the justice system is in essence run by lawyers. As such it runs slowwwwwwly.'

There was polite laughter in the courtroom. Bosch noticed that the attorneys – prosecution and defense – dutifully joined in, a couple of them overdoing it. It had been his experience that while in open court a judge could not possibly tell a joke that the lawyers did not laugh at.

Bosch glanced to his left, past the defense table, and saw the other jury box was packed with members of the media. He recognized many of the reporters from television newscasts and press conferences in the past.

He scanned the rest of the courtroom and saw the public observation benches were densely packed with citizens, except for the row directly behind the defense table. There sat several people with ample room on either side who looked as if they'd spent the morning in a makeup trailer. Bosch assumed they were celebrities of some sort, but it wasn't a realm he was familiar with and he could not identify any of them. He thought about leaning over to Janis Langwiser and asking but then thought better of it.

'We needed to clean up some last-minute details in my chambers,' the judge continued to the jury. 'But now we're ready to start. We'll begin with opening statements and I need to caution you that these are not statements of fact but rather statements about what each side *thinks* the facts are and what they will endeavor to prove during the course of the trial. These statements are not to be considered by you to contain evidence. All of that comes later on. So listen closely but keep an open mind because a lot is still coming down the pipe. Now we're going to start off with the prosecution and, as always, give the defendant the last word. Mr. Kretzler, you may begin.'

The lead prosecutor stood and moved to the lectern positioned between the two lawyers' tables. He nodded to the jury and identified himself as Roger Kretzler, deputy district attorney assigned to the special crimes section. He was a tall and gaunt prosecutor with a reddish beard beneath short dark hair and rimless glasses. He was at least forty-five years old. Bosch thought of him as not particularly likable but nevertheless very capable at his job. And the fact that he was still in the trenches prosecuting cases when others his age had left for the higher-paying corporate or criminal defense worlds made him all the more admirable. Bosch suspected he had no home life. On nights before the trial when a question about the investigation had come up and Bosch would be paged, the call-back number was always Kretzler's office line – no matter how late it was.

Kretzler identified his co-prosecutor as Janis Langwiser, also of the special crimes unit, and the lead investigator as LAPD detective third grade Harry Bosch.

'I am going to make this short and sweet so all the sooner we will be able to get to the facts, as Judge Houghton has correctly pointed out. Ladies and gentlemen, the case you will hear in this courtroom certainly has the trappings of celebrity. It has event status written all over it. Yes, the defendant, David N. Storey, is a man of power and position in this community, in this celebrity-driven age we live in. But if you strip away the trappings of power and glitter from the facts – as I promise we will do over the next few days – what you have here is something as basic as it is all too common in our society. A simple case of murder.'

Kretzler paused for effect. Bosch checked the jury. All eyes were fastened on the prosecutor.

'The man you see seated at the defense table, David N. Storey, went out with a twenty-three-year-old woman named Jody Krementz on the evening of last October twelfth. And after an evening that included the premiere of his latest film and a reception, he took her to his home in the Hollywood Hills where they engaged in consensual sexual intercourse. I don't believe you will find argument from the defense table about any of this. We are not here about that. But what happened during or after the sex is what brings us here today. On the morning of October thirteenth the body of Jody Krementz was found strangled and in her own bed in the small home she shared with another actress.'

Kretzler flipped up a page of the legal pad on the lectern in front of him even though it seemed clear to Bosch and probably everyone else that his statement was memorized and rehearsed.

'In the course of this trial the State of California will prove beyond a reasonable doubt that it was David Storey who took Jody Krementz's life in a moment of brutal sexual rage. He then moved or caused to be moved the body from his home to the victim's home. He arranged the body in such a way that the death might appear accidental. And following this, he used his power and position in an effort to thwart the investigation of the crime by the Los Angeles Police Department. Mr. Storey, who you will learn has a history of abusive behavior toward women, was so sure that he would walk away untouched from his crime that in a moment of—'

Kretzler chose this moment to turn from the lectern and look down upon the seated defendant with a disdainful look. Storey stared straight ahead unflinchingly and the prosecutor finally turned back to the jury.

'—shall we say candor, he actually boasted to the lead investigator on the case, Detective Bosch, that he would do just that, walk away from his crime.'

Kretzler cleared his throat, a sign he was ready to bring it all home.

'We are here, ladies and gentlemen of the jury, to find justice for Jody Krementz. To make it our business that her murderer not walk away from his crime. The State of California asks, and I personally ask, that you listen carefully during the trial and weigh the evidence fairly. If you do that, we can be sure that justice will be served. For Jody Krementz. For all of us.'

He picked up the pad from the lectern and turned to move back to his seat. But then he stopped, as if a second thought had just occurred to him. Bosch saw it as a well-practiced move. He thought the jury would see it that way as well.

'I was just thinking that we all know it has been part of our recent history here in Los Angeles to see our police department put on trial in these high-profile cases. If you don't like the message, then by all means shoot the messenger. It is a favorite from the defense bar's bag of tricks. I want you all to promise yourselves that you will remain vigilant and keep your eyes on the prize, that prize being truth and justice. Don't be fooled. Don't be misdirected. Trust yourself on the truth and you'll find the way.'

He stepped over to his seat and sat down. Bosch noticed Langwiser reaching over and gripping Kretzler's forearm in a congratulatory gesture. It, too, was part of the well-practiced play.

The judge told the jurors that in light of the brevity of the prosecution's address the trial would proceed to the defense statement without a break. But the break came soon enough anyway when Fowkkes stood and moved to the lectern and proceeded to spend even less time than Kretzler addressing the jury.

'You know, ladies and gentlemen, all this talk about shoot the messenger, don't shoot the messenger, well let me tell you something about that. Those fine words you got from Mr. Kretzler there at the end, well let me tell you every prosecutor in this building says those at the start of every trial in this place. I mean they must have 'em printed up on cards they carry in their wallets, it seems to me.'

Kretzler stood and objected to what he called such 'wild exaggeration' and Houghton admonished Fowkkes but then advised the prosecutor that he might make better use of his objections. Fowkkes moved on quickly.

'If I was outta line, I'm sorry. I know it's a touchy thing with prosecutors and police. But all I'm saying, folks, is that where there's smoke there's usually fire. And in the course of this trial we are going to try to find our way through the smoke. We may or may not come upon a fire but one thing I do know for sure we will come upon is the conclusion that this man—'

He turned and pointed strongly at his client.

'—this man, David N. Storey, is without a shadow of a doubt not guilty of the crime he is charged with. Yes, he is a man of power and position but, remember, it is not a crime to be so. Yes, he knows a few celebrities but, last time I checked *People* magazine, this too was not yet a crime. Now I think you may find elements of Mr. Storey's personal life and appetites to be offensive to you. I know I do. But remember that these do not constitute crimes that he is charged with in these proceedings. The crime here is *murder.* Nothing less and nothing more. It is a crime of which David Storey is *NOT* guilty. And no matter what Mr. Kretzler and Ms. Langwiser and Detective Bosch and their witnesses tell you, there is absolutely no evidence of guilt in this case.'

After Fowkkes bowed to the jury and sat down, Judge Houghton announced the trial would break for an early lunch before testimony began in the afternoon.

Bosch watched the jury file out through the door next to the box. A few of them looked back over their shoulders at the courtroom. The juror who was last in line, a black woman of about fifty, looked directly back at Bosch. He lowered his eyes and then immediately wished he hadn't. When he looked back up she was gone.

16

McCaleb turned off the television when the trial broke for lunch. He didn't want to hear all the analysis of the talking heads. He thought the best point had been scored by the defense. Fowkkes had made a smooth move telling the jury that he, too, found his client's personal life and habits offensive. He was telling them that if he could stand it, so could they. He was reminding them that the case was about taking a life, not about how one lived a life.

He went back to preparing for his afternoon meeting with Jaye Winston. He'd gone back to the boat after breakfast and gathered up his files and books. Now, with a pair of scissors and some tape, he was putting together a presentation he hoped would not only impress Winston but convince her of something McCaleb was having a difficult time believing himself. In a way, putting together the presentation was a dress rehearsal for putting on a case. In that respect, McCaleb found the time he labored over what he would show and say to Winston very useful. It allowed him to see logic holes and prepare answers for the questions he knew Winston would ask.

While he considered exactly what he would say to Winston, she called on his cell phone.

'We might have a break on the owl. Maybe, maybe not.'

'What is it?'

'The distributor in Middleton, Ohio, thinks he knows where it came from. A place right here in Carson called Bird Barrier.'

'Why does he think that?'

'Because Kurt faxed photos of our bird, and the man he was dealing with in Ohio noticed that the bottom of the mold was open.'

'Okay. What's it mean?'

'Well, apparently these are shipped with the base enclosed so it can be filled with sand to make the bird stand up in wind and rain and whatever.'

'I understand.'

'Well, they have one subdistributor who orders the owls with the bottom of the base punched out. Bird Barrier. They take them with the open base because they fit the owls on top of some kind of gizmo that shrieks.'

'What do you mean, shrieks?'

'You know, like a real owl. I guess it helps really scare birds away. You know what Bird Barrier's slogan is? "Number one when it comes to birds going number two." Cute, huh? That's how they answer the phone there.'

McCaleb's mind was churning too quickly to register humor. He didn't laugh.

'This place is in Carson?'

'Right, not far from your marina. I've got to go to a meeting now but I was going to drop by before coming to see you. You want to meet there instead? Can you make it over in time?'

'That would be good. I'll be there.'

She gave him the address, which was about fifteen minutes from Cabrillo Marina, and they agreed to meet there at two. She said that the company's president, a man named Cameron Riddell, had agreed to see them.

'Are you bringing the owl with you?' McCaleb asked.

'Guess what, Terry? I've been a detective going on twelve years now. *And* I've had a brain even longer.'

'Sorry.'

'See you at two.'

After clicking off the phone, McCaleb took a leftover tamale out of the freezer, cooked it in the microwave and then wrapped it in foil and put it in his leather bag for eating while crossing the bay. He checked on his daughter, who was in the family room sleeping in the arms of their part-time nanny, Mrs. Perez. He touched the baby's cheek and left.

Bird Barrier was located in a commercial and upscale warehouse district that hugged the eastern side of the 405 Freeway just below the airfield where the Goodyear blimp was tethered. The blimp was in its place and McCaleb could see the leashes that held it straining against the afternoon wind coming in from the sea. When he pulled into the Bird Barrier lot he noticed an LTD with commercial hubs that he knew had to be Jaye Winston's car. He was right. She was sitting in a small waiting room when he came in through a glass door. On the floor next to her chair were a briefcase and a cardboard box sealed at the top with red tape marked EVIDENCE. She immediately got up and went to a reception window through which McCaleb could see a seated young man wearing a telephone headset.

'Can you tell Mr. Riddell we're both here?'

The young man, who was apparently on a call, nodded to her.

A few minutes later they were ushered into Cameron Riddell's office. McCaleb carried the box. Winston made the introductions, calling McCaleb her colleague. It was the truth but it also concealed his badgeless status.

Riddell was a pleasant-looking man in his mid-thirties who seemed anxious to help in the investigation. Winston put on a pair of latex gloves from her briefcase, then ran a key along the red tape on the box and opened it. She removed the owl and placed it on Riddell's desk.

'What can you tell us about this, Mr. Riddell?'

Riddell remained standing behind his desk and leaned across to look at the owl.

'I can't touch it?'

'Tell you what, why don't you put these on.'

Winston opened her briefcase and handed another pair of gloves from the cardboard dispenser to Riddell. McCaleb just watched, having decided that he would not jump in unless Winston asked him to or she made an obvious omission during the interview. Riddell struggled with the gloves, slowly pulling them on.

'Sorry,' Winston said. 'They're medium. You look like a large.'

Once he had the gloves on, Riddell picked the owl up with both hands and studied the underside of the base. He looked up into the hollow plastic mold and then held the bird directly in front of him, seemingly studying the painted eyes. He then placed it on the corner of the desk and went back around to his seat. He sat down and pressed a button on an intercom.

'Monique, it's Cameron. Can you go to the back and get one of the screeching owls off the line and bring it in to me? I need it now, too.'

'On my way.'

Riddell took off the gloves and flexed his fingers. He then looked at Winston, having sensed that she was the important one. He gestured to the owl.

'Yes, it's one of ours but it's been . . . I don't know what the word you would use would be. It's been changed, modified. We don't sell them like this.'

'How so?'

'Well, Monique's getting us one so you can see, but essentially this one has been repainted a little bit and the screeching mechanism has been removed. Also, we have a proprietary label we attach here at the base and that's gone.'

He pointed to the rear of the base.

'Let's start with the painting,' Winston said. 'What was done?'

Before Riddell answered, there was a single knock on the door and a woman came in carrying another owl which was wrapped in plastic. Riddell told her to put it down on the desk and remove the plastic. McCaleb noticed that she made a face when she saw the painted black eyes of the owl Winston had brought. Riddell thanked her and she left the office.

McCaleb studied the side-by-side owls. The evidence owl had been painted darker. The Bird Barrier owl had five colors on its feathers, including white and light blue, as well as plastic eyes with pupils rimmed in a reflective amber color. Also, the new owl was sitting atop a black plastic base.

'As you can see, the owl you brought has been repainted,' Riddell said. 'Especially the eyes. When you paint over them like that, you lose a lot of the effect. These are called foil-reflect eyes. The layer of foil in the plastic catches light and gives the eyes the appearance of movement.'

'So the birds think it is real.'

'Exactly. You lose that when you paint them like this.'

'We don't think the person that painted this was worried about birds. What else is different?'

Riddell shook his head.

'Just that the plumage has been darkened quite a bit. You can see that.'

'Yes. Now you said the mechanism has been removed. What mechanism?'

'We get these from Ohio and then we paint them and attach one of two mechanisms. What you see here is our standard model.'

Riddell picked the owl up and showed them the underside. The black plastic base swiveled as he turned it. It made a loud screeching sound.

'Hear the screech?'

'Yes, that's enough, Mr. Riddell.'

'Sorry. But you see, the owl sits on this base and reacts to the wind. As it turns, it emits the screech and sounds like a predator. Works well, as long as the wind is blowing. We also have a deluxe model with an electronic insert in the base. It contains a speaker that emits recorded sounds of predator birds like the hawk. No reliance on wind.'

'Can you get one without either one of the inserts?'

'Yes, you can purchase a replacement that fits over one of our proprietary bases. In case the owl is damaged or lost. With exposure, particularly in marine settings, the paint lasts two to three years and after that the owl might lose some of its effectiveness. You have to repaint or simply get a new owl. The reality is, the mold is the least expensive part of the ensemble.'

Winston looked over at McCaleb. He had nothing to add or ask in the line of questioning she was pursuing. He simply nodded at her and she turned back to Riddell.

'Okay, then, I think we want to see if there is a method of tracing this owl from this point to its eventual owner.'

Riddell looked at the owl for a long moment as if it might be able to answer the question itself.

'Well, that could be difficult. It's a commodity item. We sell several thousand a year. We ship to retail outlets as well as sell through mail-order catalogs and an internet website.'

He snapped his fingers.

'There is one thing that will cut it down some, though.'

'What's that?'

'They changed the mold last year. In China. They did some research and decided the horned owl was considered a higher threat to other birds than the round head. They changed to the horns.'

'I'm not quite following you, Mr. Riddell.'

He held up a finger as if to tell her to wait a moment. He then opened a desk drawer and dug through some paperwork. He came out with a catalog and quickly started turning pages. McCaleb saw that Bird Barrier's primary business was not plastic owls, but large-scale bird deterrent systems that encompassed netting and wire coils and spikes. Riddell found the page showing the plastic owls and turned the catalog so that Winston and McCaleb could view it.

'This is last year's catalog,' he said. 'You see the owl has the round head. The manufacturer changed last June, about seven months ago. Now we have these guys.'

He pointed to the two owls on the table.

'The feathering turns up into the two points, or ears, on the top of the head. The sales rep said these are called horns and that these types of owls are sometimes called devil owls.'

Winston glanced at McCaleb, who raised his eyebrows momentarily.

'So you're saying this owl we have was ordered or bought since June,' she said to Riddell.

'More like since August or maybe September. They changed in June but we probably didn't start receiving the new mold until late July. We also would have sold off our existing supplies of the round head first.'

Winston then questioned Riddell about sales records and determined that information from mail-order and website purchases was kept complete and current on the company's computer files. But point-of-purchase sales from shipments to major hardware and home and marine products retailers would obviously not be recorded. He turned to the computer on his desk and typed in a few commands. He then pointed to the screen, though McCaleb and Winston were not at angles where they could see it.

'All right, I asked for sales of those part numbers since August one,' he said.

'Part numbers?'

'Yes, for the standard and deluxe models and then the replacement molds. We show we self-shipped four hundred and fourteen total. We also shipped six hundred even to retailers.'

'And what you're telling us is that we can only trace, through you at least, the four hundred fourteen.'

'Correct.'

'You have the names of buyers and the addresses the owls were shipped to there?'

'Yes, we do.'

'And are you willing to share this information with us without need of a court order?'

Riddell frowned as if the question was absurd.

'You said you're working on a murder, right?'

'Right.'

'We don't require a court order. If we can help, we want to help.'

'That's very refreshing, Mr. Riddell.'

They sat in Winston's car and reviewed the computer printouts Riddell had given them. The evidence box containing the owl was between them on the seat. There were three printouts, divided by orders for the deluxe, standard or replacement owls. McCaleb asked to see the replacement list because his instincts told him the owl in Edward Gunn's apartment had been bought for the express purpose of playing a part in the murder scene and therefore no attachment mechanisms were needed. Additionally, the replacement owl was the least expensive.

'We better find something here,' Winston said as her eyes scanned the list of purchasers of the standard owl model. 'Because chasing down buyers through the Home Depots and other retailers is going to mean court orders and lawyers and – hey, the Getty's on here. They ordered four.'

McCaleb looked over at her and thought about that. Finally, he shrugged his shoulders and went back to his list. Winston moved on as well, continuing her listing of the difficulties they would face if they had to go to the retail outlets where the horned owl was sold. McCaleb tuned her out when he got to the third-to-last name on his list. He traced his finger from a name he recognized along a line on the printout detailing the address the owl was shipped to, method of payment, origin of purchase order and the name of the person receiving it if different from purchaser. His breath must have caught, because Winston picked up on his vibe.

'What?'

'I got something here.'

He held the printout across the seat to her and pointed to the line.

'This buyer. Jerome Van Aiken. He had one shipped the day before Christmas to Gunn's address and apartment number. The order was paid for by a money order.'

She took the printout from him and started reading the information.

'Shipped to the Sweetzer address but to a Lubbert Das care of Edward Gunn. Lubbert Das. Nobody named Lubbert Das came up in the investigation. I don't remember that name on the residents list of that building, either. I'll call Rohrshak to see if Gunn ever had a roommate with that name.'

'Don't bother. Lubbert Das never lived there.'

She looked up from the pages and over at him.

'You know who Lubbert Das is?'

'Sort of.'

Her brow creased deeply.

'Sort of? *Sort of?* What about Jerome Van Aiken?'

He nodded. Winston dropped the pages on the box between them. She looked at him with an expression that imparted both curiosity and annoyance.

'Well, Terry, I think it's about time you started telling me what you know.'

McCaleb nodded again and put his hand on the door handle.

'Why don't we go over to my boat? We can talk there.'

'Why don't we talk right here, right fucking now?'

McCaleb tried a small smile on her.

'Because it's what you'd call an audiovisual demonstration.'

He opened the door and got out, then looked back in at her.

'I'll see you over there, okay?'

She shook her head.

'You better have one hell of a profile worked out for me.'

Then he shook his head.

'I don't have a profile ready for you yet, Jaye.'

'Then what *do* you have?'

'A suspect.'

He closed the door then and he could hear her muffled curses as he walked to his car. As he crossed the parking lot a shadow fell over him and everything else. He looked up to see the Goodyear blimp cross overhead, totally eclipsing the sun.

17

They reconvened fifteen minutes later on *The Following Sea*. McCaleb got out some Cokes and told Winston to sit on the stuffed chair at the end of the coffee table in the salon. In the parking lot he had told her to bring the plastic owl with her to the boat. He now used two paper towels to remove it from its box and place it on the table in front of her. Winston watched him, her lips tight with annoyance. McCaleb told her he understood her anger at being manipulated on her own case but added that she would be back in control of things as soon as he presented his findings.

'All I can say, Terry, is that this better be fucking good.'

He remembered that he had once noted on the inside file flap on the first case he ever worked with her that she was prone to using profanity when under stress. He had also noted that she was smart and intuitive. He hoped now that those characteristics had not changed.

He stepped over to the counter where he had his presentation file waiting. He opened it and took the top sheet over to the coffee table. He pushed the Bird Barrier printout aside and put the sheet down at the base of the plastic owl.

'What do you think? This our bird?'

Winston leaned forward to study the color image he had put down. It was an enlarged detail from the Bosch painting *The Garden of Earthly Delights* showing the nude man embracing the dark owl with shining black eyes. He had cut it and other details from the Marijnissen book. He watched as Winston's eyes moved back and forth between the plastic owl and the detail from the painting.

'I'd say it's a match,' she finally said. 'Where'd you get this, the Getty? You should have told me about this yesterday, Terry. What the fuck is going on?'

McCaleb raised his hands in a calming gesture.

'I'll explain everything. Just let me show you this stuff the way I want to. Then I'll answer any question you ask.'

She waved a hand, indicating he could go on. He went over to the counter and got the second sheet and brought it over. He put it down in front of her.

'Same painter, different painting.'

She looked. It was a detail from *The Last Judgment* depicting the sinner bound in the reverse fetal position, waiting to be delivered to hell.

'Don't do this to me. Who painted these?'

'I'll tell you in a minute.'

He went back to the counter and the file.

'Is this guy still alive?' she called after him.

He walked the third sheet over and put it down on the table next to the other two.

'He's been dead about five hundred years.'

'Jesus.'

She picked up the third sheet and looked closely at it. It was the full copy of the *Seven Deadly Sins* tabletop.

'That's supposed to be God's eye seeing all the sins of the world,' McCaleb explained. 'You recognize the words in the center, running around the iris?'

'Beware, beware . . .' she whispered the translation. 'Oh, God, we've got a real nut here. Who is this?'

'One more. This one really falls into place now.'

He went back to the file for the fourth time and came back with another reproduction of a painting from the Bosch book. He handed it to her.

'It's called *The Stone Operation*. In medieval times it was believed by some that an operation to remove a stone from the brain was a cure for stupidity and deceit. Note the location of the incision.'

'I noted, I noted. Just like our guy. What's all of this around here?'

She traced the exterior of the circular painting with a finger. In the outer black margin were words that were once ornately painted in gold but which had deteriorated over time and were almost indecipherable.

'The translation is "Master, cut out the stone. My name is Lubbert Das." The critical literature on the painter who created this piece notes that in his time the name Lubbert was a derisive name applied to those who were perverted or stupid.'

Winston put the sheet down on top of the others and raised her hands, palms out.

'All right, Terry, enough. Who was the painter and who is this suspect you say you've come up with?'

McCaleb nodded. It was time.

'The painter's name was Jerome Van Aiken. He was Netherlandish, considered to be one of the greats of the Northern Renaissance. But his paintings were dark, full of monsters and phantasmic demons. Owls, too. Lots of owls. The literature suggests the owls found in his paintings symbolized everything from evil to doom to the fall of mankind.'

He sorted through the sheets on the coffee table and held up the detail of the man embracing the owl.

'This kind of says it all about him. Man's embracing of evil – the devil owl, to use Mr. Riddell's description – leads to the inevitable destiny of hell. Here's the whole painting.'

He went back to the file and brought to her the full copy of *The Garden of Earthly Delights*. He watched her eyes as she studied the images. He saw repulsion as well as fascination. He pointed out the four owls he had found in the painting, including the detail he had already shown her.

She suddenly pulled the sheet aside and looked at him.

'Wait a minute. I know I've seen this before. In a book or maybe an art class I took at CSUN. But I never heard of this Van Aiken, I don't think. He painted this?'

McCaleb nodded.

'*The Garden of Earthly Delights*. Van Aiken painted it but you've never heard of him because he wasn't known by his real name. He used the Latin version of Jerome and took the name of his hometown for a last name. He was known as Hieronymus Bosch.'

She just looked at him for a long moment as it all clicked together, the images he had shown her, the names on the printout, her knowledge of the Edward Gunn case.

'Bosch,' she said, almost as an expulsion of breath. 'Is Hieronymus ...?'

She didn't finish. McCaleb nodded.

'Yeah, that's Harry's real name.'

They were both pacing in the salon now, heads down but careful not to collide. Talking in sprints, a bad but fast-moving jazz in their blood.

'This is too far out there, McCaleb. Do you know what you are saying?'

'I know exactly what I'm saying. And don't think that I didn't think long and hard about it before I said it. I consider him to be a friend, Jaye. There was ... I don't know, at one time I thought we were a lot alike. But look at this stuff, look at the connections, the parallels. It fits. It all fits.'

He stopped and looked at her. She kept pacing.

'He's a cop! A homicide cop, for God's sake.'

'What, are you going to tell me it's beyond the realm because he's a cop? This is Los Angeles – the modern Garden of Earthly Delights. With all the same temptations and demons. You don't even have to go beyond the city limits for examples of cops crossing the line – dealing drugs, robbing banks, even murder.'

'I know, I know. It's just that ...'

She didn't finish.

'At minimum it fits well enough that you know we have to take a good hard look.'

She stopped and looked back at him.

'We? Forget it, Terry. I asked you to take a look at the book, not run down the leads. You're out after this.'

'Look, if I didn't run some of this down you'd have nothing. This owl would still be sitting on top of that guy Rohrshak's other building.'

'I'll give you that. And thank you very much. But you're a civilian. You're out.'

'I'm not walking away, Jaye. If I'm the one who puts Bosch under the glass, then I'm not walking away from it.'

Winston sat down heavily in the chair.

'All right, can we talk about that when and if we come to it? I'm still not sold on this.'

'Good. I'm not either.'

'Well, you sure made a nice show of giving me the pictures and building your case.'

'All I am saying is that Harry Bosch is connected to this. And that cuts two ways. One, he did it. Two, he's been set up. He's been a cop a long time.'

'Twenty-five, thirty years. The list of people he's put in the penitentiary has got to be a yard long. And the ones who have been in and out is probably half the list. It'll take a fucking year to run all of them down.'

McCaleb nodded.

'And don't think he didn't know that.'

She looked up sharply at him. He started pacing again, his head down. After too long a silence he glanced up and saw her staring at him.

'What?'

'You really like Bosch for this, don't you? You know something else.'

'No, I don't. I am trying to stay open. All avenues of possibility need to be pursued.'

'Bullshit, you're driving down one avenue.'

McCaleb didn't answer. He felt enough guilt about it without Winston having to apply more.

'Okay,' she said. 'Then why don't you spell it out for me? And don't worry, I'm not going to hold it against you when you end up wrong.'

He stopped and looked at her.

'Come on, spell it out for me.'

McCaleb shook his head.

'I'm not all the way there yet. All I know is that what we have here is way, way beyond the realm of coincidence. So there has to be an explanation.'

'So tell me the explanation involving Bosch. I know you. You've been thinking about it.'

'All right, but remember, it's all theory at this point.'

'I'll remember. Go.'

'First of all, you start with *Detective* Hieronymus Bosch believing – no, make that *knowing* – that this guy, Edward Gunn, walked on a homicide. Okay, then you have Gunn turn up strangled and looking like a figure out of a picture by the *painter* Hieronymus Bosch. You throw in one plastic owl and at least a half dozen other connection points between the two Boschs, let alone the name, and there it is.'

'What's there? Those connections don't mean it was Bosch who did it. You said it yourself, someone could have set this up for us to find and put on Bosch.'

'I don't know what it is. Gut instinct, I guess. There's something about Bosch – something off the page.'

He remembered how Vosskuhler had described the paintings.

'A darkness more than night.'

'What's that supposed to mean?'

McCaleb waved off the question. He reached over and picked up the detail of the owl embraced by the man. He held it up in front of her face.

'Look at the darkness there. In the eyes. There's something about Harry that is the same.'

'Now you're getting downright spooky, Terry. What are you saying, in a previous life Harry Bosch was a painting? I mean, listen to what you are saying here.'

He put the sheet back down and stepped away from her, shaking his head.

'I don't know *how* to say it,' he said. 'There's just something there. A connection of some kind between them that is more than the name.'

He made a motion of waving away the thought.

'All right, then let's move on,' Winston said. 'Why now, Terry? If it is Bosch, why now? And why Gunn? He walked away from him six years ago.'

'It's interesting that you say walked away from *him* and not justice.'

'I didn't mean anything by it. You just like to take—'

'Why now? Who knows? But there was that re-encounter the night before in the drunk tank and before that there was the time in October and it goes further back. Whenever this guy ended up in the can Bosch was there.'

'But on that last night Gunn was too drunk to talk.'

'Says who?'

She nodded. They only had Bosch's account of the drunk-tank encounter.

'All right, fine. But why Gunn? I mean, I don't want to put a qualitative judgment on a murderer or his victims but, come on, the guy stabbed a prostitute in a Hollywood hot sheet hotel. We all know that some count more than others and this one couldn't have counted for much. If you read the book, you saw – her own family didn't even care about her.'

'Then there's something missing, something else that we don't know. Because Harry cared. I don't think he's the kind who ever counts one case, one person more important than another, anyway. But there's something about Gunn we don't know yet. There has to be – six years ago it was enough for Harry to shove his lieutenant through a window and take a suspension for it. It was enough for him to visit Gunn every time he got hooked up and put in a cell.'

McCaleb nodded to himself.

'We need to find the trigger. The stressor. The thing that forced the action now as opposed to a year ago, two years ago, whenever.'

Winston abruptly stood up.

'Would you stop saying "we"? And, you know, there is something you are conveniently missing here. Why would this man, this veteran cop and homicide detective, kill this guy and leave all of these clues leading back to himself? It makes no sense – not with Harry Bosch. He'd be too smart for that.'

'Only from this side of it. These things may only seem obvious now that we have discovered them. And you are forgetting the act of murder itself is evidence of aberrant thinking, of a dissembling personality. If Harry Bosch has veered off the path and crashed into the ditch – into the abyss – then we can't assume anything about his thinking or planning of a murder. His leaving of these markers could be symptomatic.'

She waved off his explanation.

'That's the Quantico dance there. Too much mumbo jumbo.'

Winston picked the copy of *The Garden of Earthly Delights* off the table and studied it.

'I talked to Harry about this case two weeks ago,' she said. 'You talked to him yesterday. He wasn't exactly climbing the walls and foaming at the mouth. And look at this trial he's riding now. He's cool, calm and has his shit together. Know what some of the guys in the office call him, the ones who know him? The Marlboro Man.'

'Yeah, well, he stopped smoking. And maybe this Storey case was the stressor. A lot of pressure. It's gotta come out someplace.'

McCaleb could tell she wasn't listening. Her eyes had caught on something in the painting. She dropped the sheet and picked up the detail of the dark owl embraced by the nude man.

'Let me ask you something,' she said. 'If our guy sent the owl directly from that warehouse to our victim, then how the fuck did it get this nice custom paint job?'

McCaleb nodded.

'Good question. He must've painted it right there in the apartment. Maybe while watching Gunn try to stay alive.'

'There was no paint like this found in the apartment. And we checked the building's dumpster, too. I saw no paint.'

'He took it with him, got rid of it somewhere else.'

'Or maybe plans to use it again on the next one.'

She paused and thought for a long moment. McCaleb waited.

'So what do we do?' she finally asked.

'So it's "we" now?'

'For now. I changed my mind. I can't take this inside. Too dangerous. If it's wrong I could kiss everything good-bye.'

McCaleb nodded.

'Do you and your partner have other cases?'

'We've got three open files, including this one.'

'Well, put him on one of the others while you work this one – with me. We work on Bosch until we have something solid – one way or the other – that you can take in and make official.'

'And what do I do, call up Harry Bosch and tell him I need to talk to him because he's a suspect in a murder?'

'I'll take Bosch first. It will be less obvious if I make the first run. Let me get a feel for him and, who knows, maybe my current instincts will be wrong. Or maybe I'll find the trigger.'

'That's easier said than done. We move too close and he'll know. I don't want this blowing up in our faces – my face, in particular.'

'That's where I can be an advantage.'

'Yeah? How so?'

'I'm not a cop. I'll be able to get closer to him. I need to get inside his house, see how he lives. Meantime, you—'

'Wait a minute. You're not talking about breaking into his house. I can't be a party to that.'

'No, nothing illegal.'

'Then how are you going to get in?'

'Knock on the door.'

'Good luck. What were you going to say? Meantime, I do what?'

'You work the outside line, the obvious stuff. Trace down the money order for the owl. Find out more about Gunn and the murder six years ago. Find out about the incident between Harry and his old lieutenant – and find out about the lieutenant. Harry said the guy went out one night and ended up dead in a tunnel.'

'Damn, I remember that. That was related to Gunn?'

'I don't know. But Bosch made some kind of elliptical reference to it yesterday.'

'I can pull stuff on it and I can ask questions about the other stuff. But any one of these moves could get back to Bosch.'

McCaleb nodded. He thought it was a risk that had to be taken.

'You know anybody who knows him?' he said.

She shook her head in annoyance.

'Look, don't you remember? Cops are paranoid people. The minute I ask one question about Harry Bosch, people are going to know what we are doing.'

'Not necessarily. Use the Storey case. It's high profile. Maybe you've been watching the guy on TV and he doesn't look so good. "Is he all right? What's going on with him?" Like that. Make it like you're gossiping.'

She didn't look mollified. She stepped over to the sliding door and looked out across the marina. She leaned her forehead against the glass.

'I know his former partner,' she said. 'There's an informal group of women who get together once a month. We all work homicide from all the local departments. About a dozen of us. Harry's old partner Kiz Rider just got moved from Hollywood to Robbery–Homicide. The big time. But I think they were close. He was kind of a mentor. I might be able to hit on her. If I use a little finesse.'

McCaleb nodded and thought of something.

'Harry told me he was divorced. I don't know how long ago but you could ask Rider about him like, you know, you're interested and what's he like, that sort of thing. You ask like that and she might give you the real lowdown.'

Winston looked away from the slider and back at McCaleb.

'Yeah, that will make us good friends when she finds out it was all bullshit and I was setting up on her ex-partner – her mentor.'

'If she's a good cop she'll understand. You had to clear him or bag him and either way you wanted to do it as quietly as possible.'

Winston looked back out the door.

'I'm going to need deniability on this.'

'Meaning?'

'Meaning if we do this and you go in there and it all blows up, I need to be able to walk away.'

McCaleb nodded. He wished she hadn't said it but he could see her need to protect herself.

'I'm just telling you up front, Terry. If it all goes to hell it's going to look like you overstepped, that I asked you to take a look at the book and you went off on your own. I'm sorry but I have to protect myself here.'

'I understand, Jaye. I can live with it. I'll take my chances.'

18

Winston was silent for a long time while she stared out the salon's door. McCaleb sensed that she was building up to something and just waited.

'I'll tell you a story about Harry Bosch,' she finally said. 'The first time I ever met him was about four years ago. It was a joint case. Two kidnap-murders. The one in Hollywood was his, the one in West Hollywood was mine. Young women, girls really. Physical evidence tied the cases together. We were basically working them separately but would meet for lunch every Wednesday to compare notes.'

'Did you profile it?'

'Yeah. This was when Maggie Griffin was still out here at the bureau. She worked something up for us. The usual. Anyway, things heated up when a third one disappeared. A seventeen-year-old this time. The evidence from the first two indicated the doer was keeping them alive four or five days before he got tired of them and killed them. So we had a big clock on us. We got reinforcements and we were running down common denominators.'

McCaleb nodded. It sounded as though they were going by the book on tracking a serial.

'A long shot came up,' she said. 'All three of the victims used the same dry cleaner on Santa Monica near La Ciénega. The latest – the girl – had a summer job at Universal and took her uniforms in for dry cleaning. Anyway, before we even went in there to the management we went into the employee parking lot and took down tags to run, just in case we got something before we had to go in and announce ourselves. And we got a hit. The manager himself. He'd gotten popped about ten years before on a public indecency. We pulled the jacket and it was a garden-variety flasher case. He pulled up in a car next to a bus stop and opened the door so the woman on the bench could get a look at his johnson. Turned out she was an undercover – they knew a wagger was working the neighborhood and put out decoys. Anyway, he got probation and counseling. He lied about it on his application at the job and over the years worked his way up to manager of the shop.'

'Higher job, higher stress, higher level of offense.'

'That's what we thought. But we didn't have any evidence. So Bosch had an idea. He said all of us – me, him and our partners – would go see this guy, his name was Hagen, at his home. He said an FBI agent once told him to always brace a suspect at home if you get the chance because sometimes you get more from the surroundings than you get from their mouths.'

McCaleb suppressed a smile. It had been a lesson Bosch learned on the Cielo Azul case.

'So we followed Hagen home. He lived over in Los Feliz in a big old rundown house off Franklin. This was the fourth day of the third woman's disappearance, so we knew we were running out of time. We knocked on his door and the plan was to act like we didn't know about his record and that we were just there to enlist his help in checking out employees in the shop. You know, to see how he reacted or if he made a slip.'

'Right.'

'Well, we were in there in this guy's living room and I was doing most of the talking because Bosch wanted to see how the guy took it. You know, a woman in control. And we weren't there but five minutes when Bosch suddenly stood up and said, "It's him. She's here somewhere." And when he said that, Hagen up and bolted for the door. He didn't get far.'

'Was it a bluff or part of the plan?'

'Neither. Bosch just knew. On this little table next to the couch was one of those baby monitor things, you know? Bosch saw that and he just knew. It was the wrong end. It was the transmitter part. It meant the receiver was somewhere else. If you have a kid it's the other way around. You listen in the living room for noise from the baby room. But this was backwards. The profile from Griffin said this guy was a controller, that he likely used verbal coercion on his victim. Bosch saw that transmitter and something just clicked; this guy had her somewhere and got off on talking to her.'

'He was right?'

'Dead on. We found her in the garage in an unplugged freezer with three air holes drilled in it. It was like a coffin. The receiver part of the monitor was in there with her. She later told us that Hagen talked to her incessantly whenever he was in the house. He sang to her, too. Top forties. He'd change the words and sing about raping and killing her.'

McCaleb nodded. He wished he had been there on the case, for he knew what Bosch had felt, that sudden moment of coalescing, when the atoms smash together. When you just knew. A moment as thrilling as it was dreadful. The moment every homicide detective privately lives for.

'The reason I tell this story is because of what Bosch did and said after. Once we had Hagen in the back seat of one of the cars and started searching the house, Bosch stayed in the living room with that baby monitor. He turned it on and he spoke to her. He never stopped until we found her. He said, "Jennifer, we're here. It's all right, Jennifer, we're coming. You're safe and we're coming for you. Nobody's going to hurt you." He never stopped talking to her, soothing her like that.'

She stopped for a long moment and McCaleb saw her eyes were on the memory.

'After we found her we all felt so good. It was the best high I've ever had on this job. I went to Bosch and said, "You must have kids. You spoke to her like she was one of your own." And he just shook his head and said no. He said, "I just know what it's like to be alone and in the dark." Then he sort of walked away.'

She looked from the door back at McCaleb.

'Your talking about darkness reminded me of that.'

He nodded.

'What do we do if we come to a point that we know flat out that it was him?' she asked, her face turned back to the glass.

McCaleb answered quickly so that he wouldn't have to think about the question.

'I don't know,' he said.

After Winston had put the plastic owl back in the evidence box, gathered all of the pages he had shown her and left, McCaleb stood at the sliding door and watched her make her way up the ramp to the gate. He checked his watch and saw there was a lot of time before he needed to get ready for the night. He decided he would watch some of the trial on *Court TV*.

He looked back out the door and saw Winston putting the evidence box into the trunk of her car. Behind him somebody cleared his throat. McCaleb abruptly turned and there was Buddy Lockridge in the stairwell looking up at him from the lower deck. He had a pile of clothes clasped in his arms.

'Buddy, what the hell are you doing?'

'Man, that's one weird case you're working on.'

'I said *what* the hell are you doing?'

'I was going to do laundry and I came over here 'cause half my stuff was down in the cabin. Then you two showed up and when you started talking I knew I couldn't come up.'

He held the pile of clothes in his arms up as proof of his story.

'So I just sat down there on the bed and waited.'

'And listened to everything we said.'

'It's a crazy case, man. What are you going to do? I've seen that Bosch guy on *Court TV*. He kind of looks like he's wound a little too tight.'

'I know what I'm not going to do. I'm not going to talk about this with you.'

He pointed to the glass door.

'Leave, Buddy, and don't tell a word of this to anybody. You understand me?'

'Sure, I understand. I was just—'

'Leaving.'

'Sorry, man.'

'So am I.'

McCaleb opened the slider and Lockridge walked out like a dog with his tail between his legs. McCaleb had to hold himself back from kicking him in the rear. Instead he angrily slid the door closed and it banged loudly in its frame. He stood there looking out through the glass until he saw Lockridge make it all the way up the ramp and over to the facilities building where there was a coin laundry.

His eavesdropping had compromised the investigation. McCaleb knew he should page Winston immediately and tell her, see how she wanted to handle it. But he let it go. The truth was, he didn't want to make any move that might take him out of the investigation.

19

After putting his hand on the Bible and promising the whole truth, Harry Bosch took a seat in the witness chair and glanced up at the camera mounted on the wall above the jury box. The eye of the world was upon him, he knew. The trial was being broadcast live on *Court TV* and locally on Channel 9. He tried to give no appearance of nervousness. But the fact was that more than the jurors would be studying him and judging his performance and personality. It was the first time in many years of testifying in criminal trials that he did not feel totally at ease. Being on the side of the truth was not a comfort when he knew the truth had to run a treacherous obstacle course set before it by a wealthy, connected defendant and his wealthy, connected attorney.

He put the blue binder – the murder book – down on the front ledge of the witness box and pulled the microphone toward him, creating a high-pitched squeal that hurt every set of ears in the courtroom.

'Detective Bosch, please don't touch the microphone,' Judge Houghton intoned.

'Sorry, Your Honor.'

A deputy sheriff who acted as the judge's bailiff came over to the witness box, turned the microphone off and adjusted its location. When Bosch nodded at its new position, the bailiff turned it back on. The judge's clerk then asked Bosch to state his full, formal name and spell it for the record.

'Very well,' the judge said after Bosch finished. 'Ms. Langwiser?'

Deputy District Attorney Janis Langwiser got up from the prosecution table and went to the attorney's lectern. She carried a yellow legal tablet with her questions on it. She was second seat at the prosecution table but had worked with the investigators since the start of the case. It had been decided that she would handle Bosch's testimony.

Langwiser was a young up-and-coming lawyer in the DA's office. In the span of a few short years she had risen from a position of filing cases for more experienced lawyers in the office to handle to taking them all the way to court herself. Bosch had worked with her before on a politically sensitive and treacherous case known as the Angels Flight murders. The experience resulted in his recommendation of her as second chair to Kretzler. Since working with her again, Bosch had found his earlier impressions were well founded. She had complete command and recall of the facts of the case. While most other lawyers would have to sift through evidence reports to locate a piece of information, she would have the information and its location in the reports memorized. But her skill was not confined to the minutiae of the case. She never took her eye off the big picture – the fact that all their efforts were focused on putting David Storey away for good.

'Good afternoon, Detective Bosch,' she began. 'Could you please tell the jury a bit about your career as a police officer.'

Bosch cleared his throat.

'Yes. I've been with the Los Angeles Police Department twenty-eight years. I have spent more than half of that time investigating homicides. I am a detective three assigned to the homicide squad of the Hollywood Division.'

'What does "detective three" mean?'

'It means detective third grade. It is the highest detective rank, equivalent to sergeant, but there are no detective sergeants in the LAPD. From detective three the next rank up would be detective lieutenant.'

'How many homicides would you say you have investigated in your career?'

'I don't keep track. I would say at least a few hundred in fifteen years.'

'A few *hundred.*'

Langwiser looked over at the jury when she stressed the last word.

'Give or take a few.'

'And as a detective three you are currently a supervisor on the homicide squad?'

'I have some supervisory duties. I am also the lead officer on a three-person team that handles homicide investigations.'

'As such you were in charge of the team that was called to the scene of a homicide on October thirteenth of last year, correct?'

'That is correct.'

Bosch glanced over at the defense table. David Storey had his head down and was using his felt-tip pen to draw on the sketch pad. He'd been doing it since jury selection began. Bosch's eyes traveled to the defendant's attorney and locked on those of J. Reason Fowkkes. Bosch held the stare until Langwiser asked her next question.

'This was the murder of Donatella Speers?'

Bosch looked back over at Langwiser.

'Correct. That was the name she used.'

'It was not her real name?'

'It was her stage name, I guess you would call it. She was an actress. She changed her name. Her real name was Jody Krementz.'

The judge interrupted and asked Bosch to spell the names for the court reporter, then Langwiser continued.

'Tell us the circumstances of the call out. Walk us through it, Detective

Bosch. Where were you, what were you doing, how did this become your case?'

Bosch cleared his throat and had reached to the microphone to pull it closer when he remembered what happened the last time. He left the microphone where it was and leaned forward to it.

'My two partners and I were eating lunch at a restaurant called Musso and Frank's on Hollywood Boulevard. It was Friday and we usually eat there if we have the time. At eleven forty-eight my pager went off. I recognized the number as belonging to my supervisor, Lieutenant Grace Billets. While I was calling her, the pagers of my partners, Jerry Edgar and Kizmin Rider, also went off. At that point we knew we had probably drawn a case. I got ahold of Lieutenant Billets and she directed my team to one-thousand-one Nichols Canyon Road, where patrol officers had earlier responded along with paramedics to an emergency call at that location. They reported a young woman was found dead in her bed under suspicious circumstances.'

'You then went to the address?'

'No. I had driven all three of us to Musso's. So I drove back to the Hollywood station, which is a few blocks away, and dropped off my partners so they could get their own vehicles. Then all three of us proceeded separately to the address. You never know where you might have to go from a crime scene. It's good procedure for each detective to have his or her own car.'

'At this time did you know who the victim was or what the suspicious circumstances of her death were?'

'No, I did not.'

'What did you find when you got there?'

'It was a small two-bedroom house overlooking the canyon. Two patrol cars were on the scene. The paramedics had already left once it was determined the victim was dead. Inside the house were two patrol officers and a patrol sergeant. In the living room there was a woman seated on the couch. She was crying. She was introduced to me as Jane Gilley. She shared the house with Ms. Krementz.'

Bosch stopped there and waited for a question. Langwiser was bent over the prosecution table whispering to her co-prosecutor, Roger Kretzler.

'Ms. Langwiser, does that conclude your questioning of Detective Bosch?' Judge Houghton asked.

Langwiser jerked upright, not having noticed that Bosch had stopped.

'No, Your Honor.'

She moved back to the lectern.

'Go on, Detective Bosch, tell us what happened after you entered the house.'

'I spoke to Sergeant Kim and he informed me that there was a young woman who was deceased in her bed in the bedroom to the right rear of the house. He introduced the woman on the couch and he said that his people had backed out of the bedroom without disturbing anything once the paramedics determined that the victim was dead. I then went down the short hallway to the bedroom and entered.'

'What did you find in there?'

'I saw the victim in the bed. She was a white female of slim build and blond hair. Her identification would later be confirmed as Jody Krementz, age twenty-three.'

Langwiser asked permission to show a set of photographs to Bosch. Houghton allowed it and Bosch identified the police evidence photos as being that of the victim in situ – as the body had been seen at first by police. The body was face up. The bedclothes were pulled to the side to reveal the body to be nude with the legs spread about two feet apart at the knees. The large breasts held their full shape despite the body being in a horizontal position, an indication of breast implants. The left arm was extended over the stomach. The palm of the left hand covered the pubic region. Two fingers of the left hand penetrated the vagina.

The victim's eyes were closed and her head rested on a pillow but at a sharp angle to her neck. Wrapped tightly around her neck was a yellow scarf with one end looped up and over the top crossbar of the bed's headboard. The end of the scarf came off the crossbar and extended to the victim's right hand on the pillow above her head. The end of the silk scarf was wrapped several times around the hand.

The photographs were in color. A purplish-red bruise could be seen on the victim's neck where the scarf had tightened against the skin. There was a rouge-like discoloration in and around the eye sockets. There was also a bluish discoloration running down the complete left side of the body, including the left arm and leg.

After Bosch identified the photographs as being of Jody Krementz in situ, Langwiser asked that they be shown to the jury. J. Reason Fowkkes objected, stating that the photos would be highly inflammatory and prejudicial for jurors to see. The judge overruled the objection but told Langwiser to choose just one photo which would be representative of the lot. Langwiser chose the photo taken closest to the victim and it was handed to a man who sat in the first seat of the jury. While the photo was slowly passed from juror to juror and then to the alternates, Bosch watched their faces tighten with shock and horror. He pushed back on his seat and drank from a paper cup of water. After he drained it he caught the eye of the sheriff's deputy and signaled for a refill. He then pulled himself back close to the microphone.

After the photo made its way through the jury, it was delivered to the clerk. It would be returned to the jurors, along with all other exhibits presented during the trial, during deliberation of a verdict.

Bosch watched Langwiser return to the lectern to continue the questioning. He knew she was nervous. They'd had lunch together in the basement cafeteria of the other court building and she had voiced her concerns. Though she was second seat to Kretzler, it was a big trial with potential career enhancing or destroying aspects for both of them.

She checked her legal pad before going on.

'Detective Bosch, did there come a time after you had inspected the body that you declared the death to be subject to a homicide investigation?'

'Right away – before my partners even got there.'

'Why is that? Did it not appear to be an accidental death?'

'No, it—'

'Ms. Langwiser,' Judge Houghton interrupted. 'One question at a time, please.'

'Sorry, Your Honor. Detective, did it not appear to you that the woman may have accidentally killed herself?'

'No, it did not. It appeared to me that someone attempted to make it look that way.'

Langwiser looked down at her pad for a long moment before going on. Bosch was pretty sure the pause was planned, now that the photograph and his testimony had secured the full attention of the jury.

'Detective, are you familiar with the term autoerotic asphyxia?'

'Yes, I am.'

'Could you please explain it to the jury?'

Fowkkes stood up and objected.

'Y'Honor, Detective Bosch may be a lot of things but there has been no proffer made to the court that he is an expert in human sexuality.'

There was a murmur of quiet laughter in the courtroom. Bosch saw a couple of the jurors suppress smiles. Houghton hit his gavel once and looked at Langwiser.

'What about that, Ms. Langwiser?'

'Your Honor, I can make a proffer.'

'Proceed.'

'Detective Bosch, you said you have worked hundreds of homicides. Have you investigated deaths that turned out not to be caused by homicide?'

'Yes, probably hundreds of those as well. Accidental deaths, suicides, even deaths by natural causes. It is routine for a homicide detective to be called out to a death scene by patrol officers to help in making a determination as to whether a death should be investigated as a homicide. This is what happened in this case. The patrol officers and their sergeant weren't sure what they had. They called it in as suspicious and my team got the call out.'

'Have you ever been called out or investigated a death that was ruled, either by you or the medical examiner's office, an accidental death by autoerotic asphyxia?'

'Yes.'

Fowkkes stood up again.

'Same objection, Y'Honor. This is leading to an area where Detective Bosch is not an expert.'

'Your Honor,' Langwiser said. 'It has clearly been established that Detective Bosch is an expert in the investigation of death – that would include all kinds. He has seen this before. He can testify to it.'

There was a note of exasperation in her voice. Bosch thought it was intended for the jury, not Houghton. It was a subliminal way of communicating to the twelve that she wanted to get at the truth, while others wanted to block the way.

'I tend to agree, Mr. Fowkkes,' Houghton said after a slight pause. 'Objections to this line of questioning are overruled. Proceed, Ms. Langwiser.'

'Thank you, Your Honor. So then, Detective Bosch, you are familiar with cases of autoerotic asphyxia?'

'Yes, I have worked on three or four. I have also studied the literature on the subject. It is referenced in books on homicide investigation techniques. I have also read summaries of in-depth studies conducted by the FBI and others.'

'Was this before this case occurred?'

'Yes, before.'

'What is autoerotic asphyxia? How does it occur?'

'Ms. Langwiser,' the judge began.

'Sorry, Your Honor. Restating. What is autoerotic asphyxia, Detective Bosch?'

Bosch took a drink of water, using the time to draw his thoughts together. They had gone over these questions during lunch.

'It is an accidental death. It occurs when the victim attempts to increase sexual sensations during masturbation by cutting off or disrupting the flow of arterial blood to the brain. This is usually done with a form of ligature around the neck. The tightening of the ligature results in hypoxia – the diminishing of oxygenation of the brain. It is believed by people who . . . uh, practice this that hypoxia – the light-headedness that ensues – heightens masturbatory sensations. However, it can lead to accidental death if the victim goes too far, to the point where he damages the carotid arteries and/ or passes out with the ligature still tightly in place and asphyxiates.'

'You said "he," Detective. But in this case the victim is a woman.'

'This case does not involve autoerotic asphyxia. The cases I have seen and investigated involving this form of death all involved male victims.'

'Are you saying that in this case the death was made to look like autoerotic asphyxia?'

'Yes, that was my immediate conclusion. It remains so today.'

Langwiser nodded and paused. Bosch sipped some water. As he brought the cup up to his mouth he glanced at the jury. Everyone in the box seemed to be paying close attention.

'Walk us through it, Detective. What led you to that conclusion?'

'Can I refer to my reports?'

'Please.'

Bosch opened the binder in front of him. The first four pages were the OIR – the original incident report. He turned to the fourth page, which included the lead officer's summary. The report had actually been typed out by Kiz Rider, though Bosch was the LO on the case. He quickly scanned the summary to refresh his mind, then looked up at the jury.

'Several things contradicted the death being an accident caused by autoerotic asphyxia. First off, I was immediately concerned because statistically it is rare that this occurs with female victims. It is not one hundred percent males but it is close. This knowledge made me pay very close attention to the body and the crime scene.'

'Would it be fair to say you were immediately skeptical of the crime scene?'

'Yes, that would be fair.'

'Okay, go on. What else concerned you?'

'The ligature. In almost all cases involving this that I have been aware of firsthand or through the literature on the subject, the victim uses some sort of padding around the neck to prevent bruising or breaking of the skin. Most often a piece of heavy clothing like a sweater or a towel is wrapped around the neck. The ligature is then wrapped around this padding. It prevents the ligature from making a contusion line running around the neck. In this case there was no padding.'

'And what did that mean to you?'

'Well, it didn't make sense if you looked at it from the victim's viewpoint. I mean, if you were to assume that she had engaged in this activity, then the scene didn't make sense. It would mean that she didn't use any kind of padding because she didn't mind having the bruises on her neck. This to me was a contradiction between what we had there at the scene and common sense. Add in that she was an actress – which I knew right away because she had a stack of head shots on the bureau – and the contradiction was even greater. She relied on her physical presence and attributes while seeking acting work. That she would knowingly engage in an activity, sexual or otherwise, that would leave visible bruises on her neck – I just didn't buy it. That and other things led me to conclude the scene was a setup.'

Bosch looked over at the defense table. Storey still had his head down and was working on the sketch pad as though he were sitting on a bench in a park somewhere. Bosch noticed Fowkkes was writing on a legal tablet. Harry wondered if he had said something in his last answer that could somehow be turned against him. He knew Fowkkes was an expert in taking phrases of testimony and giving them new meaning when taken out of context.

'What other things added to this conclusion?' Langwiser asked him.

Bosch looked at the OIR summary page again.

'The biggest single thing was the indication from postmortem lividity that the body had been moved.'

'In layman's terms, Detective, what does postmortem lividity mean?'

'When the heart ceases to pump blood through the body, the blood then settles in the lower half of the body, depending on the position of the body. Over time it creates a bruising effect on the skin. If the body is moved, the bruising remains in the original position because the blood has coagulated. Over time the bruising becomes more apparent.'

'What happened in this case?'

'In this case there was clear indication that the blood had settled in the left side of the body, meaning the victim's body had been lying on the left side at or shortly after the time of death.'

'However, that was not the way the body was found, correct?'

'That is correct. The body was found in the supine position – lying on the back.'

'What did you conclude from this?'

'That the body had been moved after death. That the woman had been positioned on her back as part of the setup to make her death look like an autoerotic asphyxiation.'

'What did you think was the cause of death?'

'At that point I wasn't sure. I just didn't think it was as presented. The bruising on the neck beneath the ligature led me to believe we were looking at a strangulation – just not at her own hands.'

'At what point did your partners arrive on the scene?'

'While I was making the initial observations of the body and crime scene.'

'Did they come to the same conclusions as you?'

Fowkkes objected, saying the question called for an answer that would be hearsay. The judge sustained the objection. Bosch knew it was a minor point. If Langwiser wanted the conclusions of Edgar and Rider on the record, she could just call them to testify.

'Did you attend the autopsy of Jody Krementz's body?'

'Yes, I did.' He flipped through the binder until he found the autopsy protocol. 'On October seventeenth. It was conducted by Dr. Teresa Corazón, chief of the medical examiner's office.'

'Was a cause of death determined by Dr. Corazón during autopsy?'

'Yes, the cause of death was asphyxiation. She was strangled.'

'By ligature?'

'Yes.'

'Now doesn't this contradict your theory that the death was not caused by autoerotic asphyxiation?'

'No, it confirmed it. The pose of autoerotic asphyxiation was used to cover the strangulation murder of the victim. The interior damage to both carotid arteries, to the muscular tissue of the neck and the hyoid bone, which was crushed, led Dr. Corazón to confirm that death was at the hand of another. The damage was too great to be knowingly self-inflicted.'

Bosch realized he was holding a hand to his neck as he described the injuries. He dropped it back down to his lap.

'Did the medical examiner find any independent evidence of homicide?'

He nodded.

'Yes, examination of the victim's mouth determined that there was a deep laceration caused by biting on the tongue. Such injury is common in cases of strangulation.'

Langwiser flipped a page over on her tablet.

'Okay, Detective Bosch, let's go back to the crime scene. Did you or your partners interview Jane Gilley?'

'Yes, I did. Along with Detective Rider.'

'From that interview were you able to ascertain where the victim had been in the twenty-four hours prior to the discovery of her death?'

'Yes, we first determined that she had met the defendant several days earlier at a coffee shop. He invited her to attend a premiere of a movie as his date on the night of October twelfth at the Chinese Theater in Hollywood. He picked her up between seven and seven-thirty that night. Ms. Gilley watched from a window in the house and identified the defendant.'

'Did Ms. Gilley know when Ms. Krementz returned that night?'

'No. Ms. Gilley left the house shortly after Ms. Krementz went on her date and spent the night elsewhere. Consequently, she did not know when her roommate returned home. It was when Ms. Gilley returned to the house at eleven A.M. on October thirteenth that she discovered Ms. Krementz's body.'

'What was the name of the movie which was premiered the night before?'

'It was called *Dead Point*.'

'And who directed it?'

'David Storey.'

Langwiser waited through a long pause before looking at her watch and then up at the judge.

'Your Honor,' she said, 'I am going to move into a new line of questioning now with Detective Bosch. If appropriate, this might be the best time to break for the day.'

Houghton pulled back the baggy black sleeve of his robe and looked at his watch. Bosch looked at his. It was a quarter to four.

'Okay, Ms. Langwiser, we'll adjourn until nine o'clock tomorrow morning.'

Houghton told Bosch he could step down from the witness stand. He then admonished the jurors not to read newspaper accounts or watch TV reports on the trial. Everyone stood as the jurors filed out. Bosch, who was now standing next to Langwiser at the prosecution table, glanced over at the defense side. David Storey was looking at him. His face betrayed no emotion at all. But Bosch thought he saw something in his pale blue eyes. He wasn't sure but he thought it was mirth.

Bosch was the first to look away.

20

After the courtroom emptied, Bosch conferred with Langwiser and Kretzler about their missing witness.

'Anything yet?' Kretzler asked. 'Depending on how long John Reason keeps you up there, we're going to need her tomorrow afternoon or the next morning.'

'Nothing yet,' Bosch said. 'But I've got something in the works. In fact, I better get going.'

'I don't like this,' Kretzler said. 'This could blow up. If she's not coming in, there's a reason. I've never been a hundred percent on her story.'

'Storey could have gotten to her,' Bosch offered.

'We need her,' Langwiser said. 'It shows pattern. You have to find her.'

'I'm on it.'

He got up from the table to leave.

'Good luck, Harry,' Langwiser said. 'And, by the way, so far I think you're doing very well up there.'

Bosch nodded.

'The calm before the storm.'

On his way down the hall to the elevators Bosch was approached by one of the reporters. He didn't know his name but he recognized him from the press seats in the courtroom.

'Detective Bosch?'

Bosch kept walking.

'Look, I've told everybody, I'm not commenting until the trial is over. I'm sorry. You'll have to get—'

'No, that's okay. I just wanted to see if you hooked up with Terry McCaleb.'

Bosch stopped and looked at the reporter.

'What do you mean?'

'Yesterday. He was looking for you here.'

'Oh, yeah, I saw him. You know Terry?'

'Yeah, I wrote a book a few years ago about the bureau. I met him then. Before he got the transplant.'

Bosch nodded and was about to move on when the reporter put out his hand.

'Jack McEvoy.'

Bosch reluctantly shook his hand. He recognized the name. Five years earlier the bureau had tracked a serial cop killer to L.A., where it was believed he was about to strike his next victim – a Hollywood homicide detective named Ed Thomas. The bureau had used information from McEvoy, a reporter for the *Rocky Mountain News* in Denver, to track the so-called Poet and Thomas's life was never threatened. He was retired from the force now and running a bookshop down in Orange County.

'Hey, I remember you,' Bosch said. 'Ed Thomas is a friend of mine.'

Both men appraised each other.

'You're covering this thing?' Bosch asked, an obvious question.

'Yeah. For the *New Times* and *Vanity Fair*. I'm thinking about a book, too. So when it's all over, maybe we can talk.'

'Yeah, maybe.'

'Unless you're doing something with Terry on it.'

'With Terry? No, that was something else yesterday. No book.'

'Okay, then keep me in mind.'

McEvoy dug into his pocket for his wallet and then removed a business card.

'I mostly work out of my home in Laurel Canyon. Feel free to give me a call if you want.'

Bosch held the card up.

'Okay. I gotta go. See you around, I guess.'

'Yeah.'

Bosch walked over and pushed the button for an elevator. He looked at the card again while he waited and thought about Ed Thomas. He then put the card into the pocket of his suit jacket.

Before the elevator came he looked down the hallway and saw McEvoy was still in the hallway, now talking to Rudy Tafero, the defense's investigator. Tafero was a big man and he was leaning forward, close to McEvoy, as if it was some sort of conspiratorial rendezvous. McEvoy was writing in a notebook.

The elevator opened and Bosch stepped on. He watched them until the doors closed.

Bosch took Laurel Canyon Boulevard over the hill and dropped down into Hollywood ahead of the evening traffic. At Sunset he took a right and pulled to the curb a few blocks into West Hollywood. He fed the meter and went into the small, drab white office building across Sunset from a strip bar. The two-story courtyard building catered to small production companies. They were small offices with small overheads. The companies lived from movie to movie. In between there was no need for opulent offices and space.

Bosch checked his watch and saw that he was right on time. It was quarter to five and the audition was set for five. He took the stairs up to the second floor and went through a door with a sign saying NUFF SAID PRODUCTIONS. It was a three-room suite, one of the biggest in the building. Bosch had been there before and knew the layout: a waiting room with a secretary's desk, the office of Bosch's friend, Albert 'Nuff' Said, and then a conference room. A woman behind the secretary's desk looked up at Bosch as he stepped in.

'I'm here to see Mr. Said. My name's Harry Bosch.'

She nodded and picked up the phone and punched a number. Bosch could hear it beep in the other room and recognized Said's voice answering.

'It's Harry Bosch,' the secretary said.

Bosch heard Said order her to send him in. He headed that way before she was off the phone.

'Go on in,' she said to his back.

Bosch stepped into an office that was furnished simply with a desk, two chairs, a black leather couch and a television/video console. The walls were crowded with framed one-sheet posters advertising Said's movies and other mementos, such as the back panels of the producers' chairs with the names of the movies printed on them. Bosch had known Said at least fifteen years, ever since the older man had hired him as a technical adviser on a movie thinly based on one of Bosch's cases. They had kept in touch sporadically over the ensuing decade, Said usually calling Bosch when he had a technical question about a police procedure he was using in a movie. Most of Said's productions were never seen on the silver screen. They were television and cable movies.

Albert Said stood up behind the desk and Bosch extended his hand.

'Hey, Nuff, howzit going?'

'Going fine, my friend.'

He pointed to the television.

'I watched your fine performance on *Court TV* today. Bravo.'

He politely clapped his hands. Bosch waved the demonstration off and looked at his watch again.

'Thanks. So are we all set here?'

'I believe so. Marjorie will have her wait for me in the conference room. You can take it from there.'

'I appreciate this, Nuff. Let me know what I can do to square it.'

'You can be in my next movie. You have a real presence, my friend. I watched the whole thing today. I taped it if you would like to see for yourself.'

'No, I don't think so. I don't think we'll have the time anyway. What have you got going these days?'

'Oh, you know, waiting for the light to turn green. I have a project I think is about to go with overseas financing. It is about this cop who gets sent to prison and the trauma of being stripped of his badge and his respect and everything gives him amnesia. And so there he is in prison and he can't remember which guys he put there and which ones he didn't. He's in a constant fight to survive. The one convict who befriends him turns out to be a serial killer he sent there in the first place. It's a thriller, Harry. What do you think? Steven Segal is reading the script.'

Said's bushy black eyebrows were arched into sharp points on his forehead. He was clearly excited by the premise of the movie.

'I don't know, Nuff,' Bosch said. 'I think it's been done before.'

'Everything's been done before. But what do you think?'

Bosch was saved by the bell. In the silence after Said's question they both could hear the secretary talking to someone in the next room. Then the speakerphone on Said's desk beeped and the secretary said, 'Ms. Crowe is here. She will be waiting in the conference room.'

Bosch nodded at Said.

'Thanks, Nuff,' he whispered. 'I'll take it from here.'

'Are you sure?'

'I'll let you know if I need any help.'

He turned to the office door but then went back to the desk and put out his hand.

'I may have to split kind of fast. So I'll say good-bye. Good luck with that project. Sounds like another winner.'

They shook hands.

'Yes, we shall see,' Said said.

Bosch left the office and crossed a small hallway and entered the conference room. There was a square, glass-topped table at center with a chair on each side. Annabelle Crowe sat in the chair on the side opposite the door. She was studying a black-and-white photograph of herself as Bosch entered. She looked up with a bright smile and perfect teeth. The smile held for a little longer than a second and then crashed off her face like a Malibu mudslide.

'What – what are you doing here?'

'Hello, Annabelle, how've you been?'

'This is an audition – you can't just—'

'You're right, this is an audition. I am auditioning you for the role of witness in a murder trial.'

The woman stood up. Her head shot and a résumé slipped off the table to the floor.

'You can't just – what is going on here?'

'You know what is going on. You moved and left no forwarding. Your parents wouldn't help. Your agent wouldn't help me. The only way I could get to you was to set up an audition. Now sit down and we're going to talk about where you've been and why you're ducking the trial.'

'So there is no part?'

Bosch almost laughed. She still didn't get it.

'No, no part.'

'And they're not remaking *Chinatown?*'

This time he did laugh but quickly covered.

'One of these days they'll get around to it. But you're too young for the part and I'm no Jake Gittes. Sit down, please.'

Bosch started to pull out the chair opposite hers. But she refused to sit down. She looked very put out. She was a beautiful young woman with a face that often got her what she wanted. But not this time.

'I said sit down,' Bosch said sternly. 'You have to understand something here, Miss Crowe. You broke the law when you did not respond to a court-issued subpoena to appear today. That means if I want, I can just place you under arrest and we can talk about this in lockup. Or the alternative is that we sit down here because they're letting us use the nice room and talk about this in a civilized manner. Your choice, Annabelle.'

She dropped back into her chair. Her mouth was a thin, tight line. The lipstick she had carefully painted on for a casting session was already starting to crack and wear. Bosch studied her for a long moment before beginning.

'Who got to you, Annabelle?'

She looked at him sharply.

'Look,' she said, 'I was scared, okay? I still am. David Storey is a powerful man. He has some scary people behind him.'

Bosch leaned across the table.

'Are you saying you were threatened by him? By them?'

'No, I am not saying that. They didn't need to threaten me. I know the picture.'

Bosch leaned back away from her and quietly studied her. Her eyes moved everywhere around the room but to him. The traffic noise from out on Sunset filtered through the room's one closed window. Somewhere in the building a toilet was flushed. Finally, she looked at Bosch.

'What? What do you want?'

'I want you to testify. I want you to make a stand against this guy. For what he tried to do to you. For Jody Krementz. And Alicia Lopez.'

'Who is Alicia Lopez?'

'Another one we found. She wasn't lucky like you.'

Bosch could read the turmoil on her face. She clearly viewed testifying as some sort of danger.

'If I testify I'll never work again. And maybe worse.'

'Who told you that?'

She didn't answer.

'Come on, who? Did that come from them, your agent, who?'

She hesitated and then shook her head as if she couldn't believe she was talking to him.

'I was working out at Crunch and I was on a Stairmaster and this guy got on the machine next to me. He was reading the newspaper. It was folded to the story he was reading. And I was minding my own business when suddenly he just started talking. He never looked at me. He just talked while he was looking down at the newspaper. He said the story he was reading was about the David Storey trial and how he'd hate to be a witness who went against him. He said that person would never work in this town again.'

She stopped but Bosch waited. He studied her. Her anguish in recounting the story seemed genuine. She was on the verge of tears.

'And I . . . I got so panicked with him right there next to me I just got off the machine and ran into the locker room. I stayed in there for an hour and even then I was scared that he might still be out there waiting for me. Watching me.'

She started crying. Bosch got up and left the room and looked into the bathroom in the hallway. There was a box of tissues. He took it back with him to the conference room and handed it to Annabelle Crowe. He sat back down.

'Where is Crunch?'

'Just down the street from here. Sunset and Crescent Heights.'

Bosch nodded. He knew where it was now. The same shopping and entertainment complex where Jody Krementz had met David Storey in a coffee shop. He wondered if there was a connection. Maybe Storey belonged to Crunch. Maybe he got a workout pal to threaten Annabelle Crowe.

'Did you get a look at the guy?'

'Yes, but it doesn't matter. I don't know who he was. I never saw him before or since.'

Bosch thought about Rudy Tafero.

'Do you know who the defense team's investigator is? A guy named Rudy Tafero? He's tall, black hair and a nice tan. Good-looking guy?'

'I don't know who that is but he's not the man who was there that day. This man was short and bald. He had glasses.'

The description didn't register with Bosch. He decided to let it go for the time being. He'd have to let Langwiser and Kretzler know about the threat. They might want to take it to Judge Houghton. They might want to have Bosch go to Crunch and start asking questions, see if he could confirm anything.

'So what are you going to do?' she asked. 'Are you going to make me testify?'

'It's not up to me. The prosecutors will decide after I tell them your story.'

'Do you believe it?'

Bosch hesitated and then nodded.

'You still have to show up. You're under subpoena. Be there between twelve and one tomorrow and they'll let you know what they want to do.'

Bosch knew that they would make her testify. They wouldn't care if the threat was real or not. They had the case to worry about. Annabelle Crowe would be sacrificed to get David Storey. A small fish to get a big fish, the name of the game.

Bosch made her empty her purse. He looked through her things and found an address and phone number written down. It was a temp apartment in Burbank. She admitted that she had put her belongings in storage and was living in the temp, waiting for the trial to be over.

'I'm going to give you a break, Annabelle, and not hold you in lockup overnight. But I found you this time and I can find you again. You don't show up tomorrow and I'll come looking for you. And you'll go right to lockup at Sybil Brand, you understand that?'

She nodded her head.

'You going to be there?'

She nodded again.

'I should've never come to you people.'

Bosch nodded. She was right.

'It's too late for that,' he said. 'You did the right thing. Now you have to live with it. That's the funny thing about the courts. You decide to be brave and stick your neck out and they don't let you back down from it.'

21

Art Pepper was on the stereo and Bosch was on the telephone with Janis Langwiser when there was a knock on his screen door. He stepped into the hallway from the kitchen and saw a figure looking in through the mesh. Annoyed by the intrusion of a solicitor, he walked to the door and was about to simply close it without a word when he recognized the visitor as Terry McCaleb. Still on the phone and listening to Langwiser fume about possible witness tampering, he flicked on the outside light, opened the screen door and signaled McCaleb in.

McCaleb made a signal that he would be quiet until Bosch was off the call. Bosch watched him walk through the living room and step out onto the rear deck to look down at the lights of the Cahuenga Pass. He tried to concentrate on what Langwiser was saying but he was curious as to why McCaleb would drive all the way up into the hills to see him.

'Harry, are you listening?'

'Yeah. What was that last part?'

'I said do you think Shootin' Houghton will delay the trial if we open up an investigation.'

Bosch didn't have to think long to answer that.

'No way. The show must go on.'

'Yeah, that's what I figure. I'm going to call Roger and see what he wants to do. Anyway, it's the least of our worries. As soon as you mention Alicia Lopez on the stand there's going to be a brutal fight.'

'I thought we already won that. Houghton ruled—'

'It doesn't mean Fowkkes won't try a new attack. We're not clear yet.'

There was a pause. There had not been much confidence in her voice.

'I guess I'll see you tomorrow, Harry.'

'All right, Janis, I'll see you.'

Bosch clicked the phone off and put it back in its cradle in the kitchen. When he stepped back out McCaleb was standing in the living room, looking at the shelves over the stereo, at a framed photograph of Bosch's wife in particular.

'Terry, what's up?'

'Hey, Harry, sorry to drop in unannounced like this. I didn't have your home number to call first.'

'How'd you find the place? You want a beer or something?'

Bosch pointed to his chest.

'Can you have a beer?'

'I can now. Just got clearance, in fact. I can drink again. In moderation. A beer sounds good.'

Bosch went into the kitchen. McCaleb continued talking from the living room.

'I've been here before. You don't remember?'

Bosch came out with two open bottles of Anchor Steam. He handed one to McCaleb.

'You need a glass? When were you here?'

McCaleb took the bottle.

'Cielo Azul.'

He took a long pull from the bottle, answering Bosch's question about the glass.

Cielo Azul, Bosch thought, and then he remembered. They had gotten drunk on the back porch once, both of them dulling the edges of a case that was too terrible to think deeply about with a sober mind. He remembered being embarrassed about it the next day, about how he had lost control and kept rhetorically asking in an alcohol-slowed voice, 'Where is God's hand, where is God's hand?'

'Oh, yeah,' Bosch said. 'One of my finer existential moments.'

'Yeah. Except the place is different now. The old one slide down the hill in the quake?'

'Just about. Red-tagged, the whole bit. Started over from the ground up.'

'Yeah, I didn't recognize it. I drove up here looking for the old place. But then I saw the Shamu and figured there couldn't be another cop in the neighborhood.'

Bosch thought about the black-and-white parked in the carport. He hadn't bothered to take it to the station to exchange for his personal car. It would save him time in the morning by allowing him to drive straight to court. The car was a slickback – a black-and-white without the emergency lights on top. Detectives from the divisions used them as part of a program designed to make it look as if there were more cops on the street than there really were.

McCaleb reached over and clicked Bosch's bottle with his own.

'To Cielo Azul,' he said.

'Yeah,' Bosch said.

He drank from the bottle. It was ice cold and good. His first beer since the start of the trial. He decided he would keep it to one, even if McCaleb pressed on.

'This your ex?' McCaleb asked, pointing to the photo on the shelves.

'My wife. Not my ex, yet – at least as far as I know. But I guess it's heading that way.'

Bosch stared at the photo of Eleanor Wish. It was the only picture of her he had.

'That's too bad, man.'

'Yeah. So what's up, Terry? I've got some stuff I have to go over for—'

'I know, the trial. I'm sorry to intrude, man. I know that's gotta be all-consuming. I just had a couple things on the Gunn case I wanted to clear up. But also I wanted to tell you something. I mean, show you, too.'

He pulled his wallet out of his back pocket, opened it and took out a photo. He handed it to Bosch. The photo had taken on the contour line of the wallet. It showed a dark-haired baby in the arms of a dark-haired woman.

'That's my daughter, Harry. And my wife.'

Bosch nodded and studied the photo. Both mother and child had dark hair and skin and were quite beautiful. He knew they were probably even more so to McCaleb.

'Beautiful,' he said. 'The baby looks brand new. So tiny.'

'She's about four months now. That picture's a month old, though. Anyway, I forgot to tell you yesterday at lunch. We named her Cielo Azul.'

Bosch's eyes came up from the photo to McCaleb's. They held for a moment and then he nodded.

'Nice.'

'Yeah, I told Graciela I wanted to do it and I told her why. She thought it was a good idea.'

Bosch handed the photo back.

'I hope someday the kid does, too.'

'Me, too. We call her CiCi most of the time. Anyway, remember that night up here, how you kept asking that question about the hand of God and how you couldn't find it in anything anymore? That happened to me, too. I lost it. This kind of job ... it's hard not to. Then ...'

He held up the photo.

'Here it is right here. I found it again. The hand of God. I see it in her eyes.'

Bosch looked at him for a long moment and then nodded.

'Good for you, Terry.'

'I mean, I'm not trying to come off like ... I mean I'm not trying to convert you or anything. I'm just saying I found that thing that was missing. And I don't know if you're still looking for it ... I just wanted to say, you know, that it is out there. Don't give up.'

Bosch glanced away from McCaleb and out the glass doors to the darkness.

'For some people I'm sure it is.'

He drained his bottle and went into the kitchen to break his promise to himself to have only one. He called back to McCaleb to see if he was ready for a second but his visitor passed. As he bent into the open refrigerator he paused and closed his eyes as the cool air caressed his face. He thought about what McCaleb had just told him.

'You don't think you are one of them?'

Bosch jerked up at the sound of McCaleb's voice. He was standing in the kitchen's doorway.

'What?'

'You said it was out there for some people. You don't think you are one of them?'

Bosch took a beer out of the refrigerator and slid it into the bottle opener mounted on the wall. He snapped the bottle open and drank deeply from it before answering.

'What is this, Terry, twenty questions? You thinking of becoming a priest or something?'

McCaleb smiled and shook his head.

'Sorry, Harry. A new father, you know? I guess I want to tell the world, that's all.'

'That's nice. You want to talk about Gunn now?'

'Sure.'

'Let's go out and look at the night.'

They walked out to the back deck and both looked at the view. The 101 was its usual ribbon of light, a glowing vein cutting through the mountains. The sky was clear, the smog having been washed out by rain the week before. Bosch could see the lights on the floor of the Valley seemingly extending into infinity. Closer to the house there was only darkness held in the brush on the hillside below. He could smell the eucalyptus from below; it was always strongest after the rain.

McCaleb was the first to speak.

'You've got a nice place here, Harry. A nice spot. You must hate having to ride down into the plague every morning.'

Bosch looked over at him.

'Not as long as I get a shot at the carriers every now and then. People like David Storey. I don't mind that.'

'And what about the ones who walk away? Like Gunn.'

'Nobody walks away, Terry. If I believed that they did, then I couldn't do this. Sure we might not get every one of them, but I believe in the circle. The big wheel. What goes around comes around. Eventually. I might not see the hand of God too often like you do but I believe in that.'

Bosch put his bottle down on the railing. It was empty and he wanted another but knew he had to put on the brakes. He'd need every brain cell he could muster in court the next day. He thought about a cigarette and knew there was a fresh pack in a kitchen cabinet. But he decided to hold off on that, too.

'Then I guess what happened with Gunn must be a confirmation of your faith in the big wheel theory.'

Bosch didn't say anything for a long time. He just stared out across the valley of light.

'Yeah,' he finally said. 'I guess it does.'

He broke his stare away and turned his back on the view. He leaned against the railing and looked at McCaleb again.

'So what about Gunn? I thought I told you everything there was to tell yesterday. You've got the file, right?'

McCaleb nodded.

'You probably did and I do have the file. But I was just wondering if anything else came up. You know, if maybe our conversation jump-started your thinking on it.'

Bosch sort of laughed and picked up the bottle before remembering it was empty.

'Terry, come on, man, I'm in the middle of a trial. I'm on the stand, I've been chasing down an AWOL wit. I mean I stopped thinking about your investigation the minute I got up from the table at Cupid's. What exactly do you want from me?'

'Nothing, Harry. I don't want anything from you that you don't have. I just thought it might be worth a shot, is all. I'm working on this thing and scratching around for anything. I thought maybe . . . don't worry about it.'

'You're a weird guy, McCaleb. I'm remembering that now. The way you used to stare at crime scene photos. You want another beer?'

'Yeah, why not?'

Bosch pushed off the railing and reached over for his bottle and then McCaleb's. It was still at least a third full. He put it back down.

'Well, finish that.'

He went into the house and got two more beers out of the refrigerator. This time McCaleb was standing in the living room when he came back from the kitchen. He handed Bosch his empty bottle and Bosch wondered for a moment if he had finished it or poured the beer over the side of the deck. He took the empty into the kitchen and when he came back McCaleb was standing at the stereo studying a CD case.

'This what's playing?' he asked. 'Art Pepper meets the Rhythm Section?'

Bosch stepped over.

'Yeah. Art Pepper and Miles's side men. Red Garland on piano, Paul Chambers on bass, Philly Joe Jones on drums. Recorded here in L.A., January 19, 1957. One day. The cork in the neck of Pepper's sax was supposedly cracked but it didn't matter. He had one shot with these guys. He made the most of it. One day, one shot, one classic. That's the way to do it.'

'These guys were in Miles Davis's band?'

'At the time.'

McCaleb nodded. Bosch leaned close to look at the CD cover in McCaleb's hands.

'Yeah, Art Pepper,' he said. 'When I was growing up I never knew who my father was. My mother, she used to have a lot of this guy's records. She hung out at some of the jazz clubs where he'd play. Handsome devil, Art was. For a hype. Just look at that picture. Too cool to fool. I made up this whole story about how he was my old man and he wasn't around 'cause he was always on the road and making records. Almost got to the point I believed it. Later on – I mean years later – I read a book about him. It said he was junk sick when they took that picture. He puked as soon as it was over and went back to bed.'

McCaleb studied the photograph on the CD. A handsome man leaning against a tree, his sax cradled in his right arm.

'Well, he could play,' McCaleb said.

'Yeah, he could,' Bosch agreed. 'Genius with a needle in his arm.'

Bosch stepped over and turned the volume up slightly. The song was 'Straight Life,' Pepper's signature composition.

'Do you believe that?' McCaleb asked.

'What, that he was a genius? Yeah, he was with the sax.'

'No, I mean do you think that every genius – musician, artist, even a detective – has a fatal flaw like that? The needle in the arm.'

'I think everybody's got a fatal flaw, whether they're a genius or not.'

Bosch turned it up louder. McCaleb put his beer down on top of one of the floor speakers. Bosch picked it up and handed it back. He used his palm to wipe the wet ring off the wood surface. McCaleb turned the music down.

'Come on, Harry, give me something.'

'What are you talking about?'

'I made the journey up here. Give me something on Gunn. I know you don't care about him – the wheel turned and he didn't walk away. But I don't like the way this one looked. This guy – whoever he is – is still out there. And he's going to do this again. I can tell.'

Bosch shrugged his shoulders like he still didn't care.

'All right, here's something. It's thin but it might be worth a try. When he was in the tank the night before he got put down and I checked in on him, I also talked with the Metro guys who brought him in on the duice. They said they asked him where he'd been drinking and he said he'd come out of a place called Nat's. It's on the Boulevard about a block from Musso's and on the south side.'

'Okay, I can find it,' McCaleb said, a what-about-it tone in his voice. 'What's the connection?'

'Well, see, Nat's was the same place he'd been drinking that night six years ago that I first made his acquaintance. It's where he picked up that woman, the one he killed.'

'So he was a regular.'

'Looks it.'

'Thanks, Harry. I'll check it out. How come you didn't tell this to Jaye Winston?'

Bosch shrugged his shoulders.

'I guess I didn't think about it and she didn't ask.'

McCaleb almost put his beer down on the speaker again but instead handed it to Bosch.

'I might go check down there tonight.'

'Don't forget.'

'Forget what?'

'You hook the guy who did it, you shake his hand for me.'

McCaleb didn't respond. He looked around the place as if he had just walked in.

'Can I use the bathroom?'

'Down the hall on the left.'

McCaleb headed that way while Bosch took the bottles into the kitchen and put them in the recycle bin with the others. He opened the refrigerator and saw he was down to one soldier left in the six-pack he'd bought on the way home from tricking Annabelle Crowe. He closed the refrigerator when McCaleb stepped into the room.

'That's a crazy fucking picture you got hanging in the hallway,' he said.

'What? Oh, yeah. I like that picture.'

'What's it supposed to mean?'

'I don't know. I guess it means the big wheel keeps turning. Nobody walks away.'

McCaleb nodded.

'I suppose.'

'You heading down there to Nat's?'

'Thinking about it. You want to go?'

Bosch considered it even though he knew it would be foolish. He had to review half of the murder book in preparation for his continuing testimony the next morning.

'Nah, I better do some work here. Get ready for tomorrow.'

'Okay. How'd it go today, anyway?'

'So far so good. But we're playing softball right now – direct. Tomorrow the ball goes to John Reason and he throws it back inside and fast.'

'I'll watch the news.'

McCaleb stepped over and stuck his hand out. Bosch shook it.

'Be careful out there.'

'You, too, Harry. Thanks for the beers.'

'No problem.'

He walked McCaleb to the door and then watched him get into a black Cherokee parked on the street. It started up immediately and pulled away, leaving Bosch standing in the lighted doorway.

Bosch locked up and turned off the living-room lights. He left the stereo on. It would automatically turn off at the end of Art Pepper's classic moment in time. It was early but Bosch was tired from the pressures of the day and the alcohol moving in his blood. He decided he would sleep now and wake up early to prepare for his testimony. He went into the kitchen and got the last bottle of beer out of the refrigerator.

On the way down the hall to his bedroom he stopped and looked at the framed picture McCaleb had referred to. It was a print of the Hieronymus Bosch painting called *The Garden of Earthly Delights*. He'd had it for a long time, since he was a kid. The surface of the print was warped and scratched. It was in bad shape. It had been Eleanor who moved it from the living room to the hallway. She didn't like it being in the place where they sat every night. Bosch never understood whether that was because of what was in the painting or because the print was old and deteriorated.

As he looked at the landscape of human debauchery and torment depicted in the painting, Bosch thought about maybe moving it back to its spot in the living room.

In Bosch's dream he was moving through dark water, unable to see his hands in front of his own face. There was a ringing sound and he pushed upward through the darkness.

He came awake. The light was on but all was silent. The stereo was off. He started to look at his watch when the phone rang again and he quickly grabbed it off the bedside table.

'Yeah.'

'Hey, Harry, it's Kiz.'

His old partner.

'Kiz, what's up?'

'You okay? You sound . . . out of it.'

'I'm fine. I was just . . . I was asleep.'

He looked at his watch. It was just after ten.

'Sorry, Harry, I thought you'd be burning the oil, getting ready for tomorrow.'

'I'm going to get up early and do it.'

'Well, you did good today. We had the box on in the squad. Everybody was pulling for you.'

'I'll bet. How is it going down there?'

'It's going. In a way I'm starting over. I've got to prove myself to them.'

'Don't worry about it. You'll be passing those guys like they're standing still. Just like you did with me.'

'Harry . . . you're the best. I learned more from you than you'll ever know.'

Bosch hesitated. He was genuinely touched by what she had said.

'That's nice of you to say, Kiz. You should call me more often.'

She laughed.

'Well, that's not why I'm calling. I told a friend I'd do this. It reminds me of high school but here goes. There's somebody that is interested in you. I said I'd check to see if you were back out in the field, if you know what I mean?'

Bosch didn't even have to think before answering.

'Nah, Kiz, I'm not. I . . . I'm not giving up on Eleanor yet. I'm still hoping she'll call or show up and maybe we can work it out. You know how it is.'

'I do. And that's cool, Harry. I just said I'd ask. But if you change your mind, she's a neat lady.'

'I know her?'

'Yeah, you know her. Jaye Winston, over at the sheriff's. We're in a women's group together. Dicks without Dicks. We got to talking about you tonight.'

Bosch didn't say anything. A strange constricting feeling filled his gut. He didn't believe in coincidences.

'Harry, you there?'

'Yeah, I'm here. I was just thinking about something.'

'Well, I'll let you go. And listen, Jaye asked me not to give you her name. You know, she just wanted to ask about you and put an anonymous feeler out. So next time you both run across each other on the job it wouldn't be embarrassing. So you didn't get it from me, right?'

'Right. She asked you questions about me?'

'A few. Nothing big. I hope you don't mind. I told her she made a good choice. I said if I wasn't, you know, the way I was, I'd be interested too.'

'Thanks, Kiz,' Bosch said but his mind was flying.

'Well, look, I'm gonna go. I'll see you. Knock 'em dead tomorrow, okay?'

'I'll try.'

She hung up and Bosch slowly put the phone back in its cradle. The tightening in his gut got more intense. He started thinking about McCaleb's visit and what he had asked and what Harry had said. Now Winston was asking questions about him.

He did not believe it was a coincidence. It was clear to Bosch that they had a bead on him. They were looking at him for the Edward Gunn killing. And he knew he had probably given McCaleb the right amount of psychological insight to believe he was on the right course.

Bosch drained the bottle of beer that was on the nightstand. The last swallow was room temperature and sour. He knew there were no more bottles in the refrigerator. He got up to get a cigarette instead.

22

Nat's was a railroad car-sized bar that was like a lot of Hollywood haunts – favored during daylight hours by hard-core drinkers, during early evening hours by casual hookers and their clientele, and late at night by the black leather and tattoo crowd. It was the kind of place where a person would stand out as a target if he tried to pay for drinks with a gold credit card.

McCaleb had stopped at Musso's for dinner – his body clock demanding nourishment before a complete shutdown occurred – and didn't get to Nat's until after ten. While eating his chicken pot pie he had wondered whether going to the bar to ask questions about Gunn was even worth the time. The tip had come from the suspect. Would the suspect knowingly point the investigator in the right direction? It seemed not, but McCaleb factored in Bosch's drinking and his being unaware of McCaleb's true mission during the visit to the house on the hill. The tip might very well be valid and he decided no part of the investigation should be overlooked.

As he walked in it took him a few seconds to adjust to the dim, reddish lighting. When the room became clear he saw it was half empty. It was the time between the early evening crowd and the late night group. Two women – one black, one white – sitting at one end of the bar that ran along the left side of the room sized him up and McCaleb could see *cop* register in their eyes at the same moment *hookers* registered in his. It secretly pleased him that he still had the look. He walked by them and further into the lounge. The booths lining the right side of the room were mostly full. No one in these bothered to give him a glance.

He stepped up to the bar between two empty stools and signaled one of the bartenders.

An old Bob Seger song, 'Night Moves,' was blaring from a jukebox in the back. The bartender leaned over the bar so she could get McCaleb's order. She was wearing a buttoned black vest with no shirt underneath. She had long straight black hair and a thin gold hoop pierced her left eyebrow.

'What can I get you?'

'Some information.'

McCaleb slid a driver's-license picture of Edward Gunn across the counter. It was a three-by-five blowup that had been in the files Winston gave him. The bartender looked at it for a moment and then back up at McCaleb.

'What about him? He's dead.'

'How do you know that?'

She shrugged her shoulders.

'I don't know. Word just got around, I guess. You a cop?'

McCaleb nodded, lowered his voice so the music would cover it and said, 'Something like that.'

The bartender leaned further over the bartop so she could hear him. This position opened the top of her vest, exposing most of her small but round breasts. There was a tattoo of a heart wrapped in barbed wire on the left side. It looked like a bruise on a pear, not very appetizing. McCaleb looked away.

'Edward Gunn,' he said. 'He was a regular, right?'

'He came in a lot.'

McCaleb nodded. Her acknowledgment confirmed Bosch's tip.

'You work New Year's Eve?'

She nodded.

'You know if he came in that night?'

She shook her head.

'I can't remember. A lot of people were in here New Year's Eve. We had a party. I don't know if he was here or not. It wouldn't surprise me, though. People came and went.'

McCaleb nodded toward the other bartender. A Latino who also wore a black vest with no shirt beneath.

'What about him? Think he'd remember?'

'No, 'cause he only started last week. I'm breaking him in.'

A thin smile played on her face. McCaleb ignored it. 'Twisting the Night Away' began playing. The Rod Stewart version.

'How well did you know Gunn?'

She let out a short burst of laughter.

'Honey, this is the kind of place where people don't exactly like to let on who they are or what they are. How well did I know him? I knew him, okay? Like I said, he came in. But I didn't even know his name until he was dead and people started talking about him. Somebody said Eddie Gunn got himself killed and I said, "Who the fuck is Eddie Gunn?" They had to describe him. The whiskey rocks who always had the paint in his hair. Then I knew who Eddie Gunn was.'

McCaleb nodded. He reached inside his coat pocket and brought out a folded piece of newspaper. He slid it across the bartop. She leaned down to look, showing another view of her breasts. McCaleb thought it was intentional.

'This is that cop, the one from the trial, right?'

McCaleb didn't answer the question. The newspaper had been folded to a photo of Harry Bosch that had run that morning in the *Los Angeles Times* as an advance on the testimony expected to begin in the Storey trial. It was a candid shot of Bosch standing outside the courtroom door. He probably didn't even know it had been taken.

'You seen him in here?'

'Yeah, he comes in. Why are you asking about him?'

McCaleb felt a charge go up the back of his neck.

'When does he come in?'

'I don't know, from time to time. I wouldn't call him a regular. But he'd come in. And he wouldn't stay long. A one-timer – one drink and out. He's ...'

She pointed a finger up and cocked her head to the side as she rifled through her interior files. She then slashed her finger down as if making a notch.

'Got it. Bottled beer. Asks for Anchor Steam every time because he always forgets we don't carry it – too expensive, we'd never sell it. He then settles for the old thirty-three.'

McCaleb was about to ask what that was when she answered his unspoken question.

'Rolling Rock.'

He nodded.

'Was he in here New Year's Eve?'

She shook her head.

'Same answer. I don't remember. Too many people, too many drinks, too many days since then.'

McCaleb nodded and pulled the newspaper back across the bar and put it in his pocket.

'He in some kind of trouble, that cop?'

McCaleb shook his head. One of the women at the end of the bar tapped the corner of her empty glass on the bartop and called to the bartender.

'Hey, Miranda, you got payin' customers over here.'

The bartender looked around for her partner. He was gone, apparently in the back room or the bathroom.

'Gotta go to work,' she said.

McCaleb watched her go to the end of the bar and make two fresh vodka rocks for the hookers. During a lull in the music, he overheard one of them tell her to stop talking to the cop so he would leave. As Miranda headed back toward McCaleb's position one of the hookers called after her.

'And stop giving him the freebie or he'll never leave.'

McCaleb acted like he didn't hear it. Miranda exhaled like she was tired when she got to him.

'I don't know where Javier went. I can't be standing here talking to you all night.'

'Let me ask you one last thing,' he said. 'You ever remember the cop being in here with Eddie Gunn at the same time – either together or apart?'

She thought a moment and leaned forward.

'Maybe, it could've happened. But I don't remember.'

McCaleb nodded. He was pretty sure that was the best he could get out of her. He wondered if he should leave some money on the bar. He'd never been good at that sort of thing when he was an agent. He never knew when it would be appropriate and when it would be insulting.

'Can I ask you something now?' Miranda asked.

'What?'

'You like what you see?'

He felt his face immediately begin to color with embarrassment.

'I mean, you were looking enough. I just thought I'd ask.'

She glanced over at the hookers and shared a smile. They were all enjoying McCaleb's embarrassment.

'They're real nice,' he said as he stepped away from the bar, leaving a twenty-dollar bill for her. 'I'm sure they keep people coming back. Probably kept Eddie Gunn comin' in.'

He headed toward the door and she called after him, her words hitting him in the back all the way to the door.

'Then maybe you oughta come back and try 'em out some time, *Officer!*'

As he went through the door he heard the hookers whoop and slap hands in a high five.

McCaleb sat in the Cherokee in front of Nat's and tried to shake off the embarrassment. He concentrated on the information he had gotten from the bartender. Gunn was a regular and might or might not have been in there on the last night of his life. Secondly, she was familiar with Bosch as a customer. He, too, might or might not have been in there on the last night of Gunn's life. The fact that this information had indirectly come from Bosch was puzzling. Again, he wondered why Bosch – if he was Gunn's killer – had given him a valid clue to follow. Was it arrogance, a belief that he would never be considered a suspect and therefore not be brought up during the questioning at the bar? Or could there be a deeper psychological motivation? McCaleb knew that many criminals make mistakes that ensure their apprehension because subconsciously they do not want to get away with their crimes. The big wheel theory, McCaleb thought. Maybe Bosch was subconsciously making sure the wheel turned for him as well.

He opened his cell phone and checked the signal. It was good. He called Jaye Winston's home number. He checked his watch while the phone was ringing and thought that it was not too late to call. After five rings she finally picked up.

'It's me. I've got some stuff.'

'So do I. But I'm still on the phone. Can I call you when I'm done?'

'Yeah, I'll be here.'

He clicked off and sat in the car waiting and thinking about things. He watched through the windshield as the white hooker from the bar stepped through the door with a man in a baseball cap in tow. They both lit cigarettes and headed down the sidewalk toward a motel called the Skylark.

His phone chirped. It was Winston.

'It's coming together, Terry. I'm a believer.'

'What did you get?'

'You first. You said you got some stuff.'

'No, you. What I got is minor. It sounds like you hooked something big.'

'Okay, listen to this. Harry Bosch's mother was a prostitute. In Hollywood. She got murdered when he was a little kid. And whoever did it got away with it. How is that for psychological underpinnings, Mr. Profiler?'

McCaleb didn't answer. The new information was stunning and provided many of the missing pieces in the working theory. He watched the hooker and her customer at the window of the motel office. The man passed cash through and received a key. They went in through a glass door.

'Gunn kills a prostitute and walks away,' Winston said when he didn't respond. 'Just like what happened with his mother.'

'How'd you find this out?' McCaleb finally asked.

'I made that call we talked about. To my friend, Kiz. I acted like I was interested in Bosch and asked her if she knew if he was, you know, over his divorce yet. She told me what she knew about him. The stuff about his mother apparently came out a few years ago in a civil trial when Bosch got sued for a wrongful death – the Dollmaker, you remember that one?'

'Yeah, the LAPD refused to call us in on that one. That was also a guy who killed prostitutes. Bosch killed him. He was unarmed.'

'There's a psychology going on here. A goddamn pattern.'

'What happened to Bosch after his mother was killed?'

'Kiz didn't really know. She called him an institutional man. It happened when he was ten or eleven. After that he grew up in youth halls and foster homes. He went into the service and then the department. The point is, this is the thing we were missing. The thing that turned a no-count case into something Bosch wouldn't let go.'

McCaleb nodded to himself.

'And there's more,' Winston said. 'I went through all the accumulated files – extraneous things I didn't put in the murder book. I looked at the autopsy on the woman Gunn killed six years ago. Her name was Frances Weldon, by the way. There was one thing in there that seems significant in light of what we now know about Bosch. Examination of the uterus and hips showed that at some point she'd had a child.'

McCaleb shook his head.

'Bosch wouldn't have known that. He pushed his lieutenant through a window and was on suspension by the time there was an autopsy.'

'True. But he could and probably did look at the case files after he came back. He would have known that Gunn did to some other kid what was done to him. You see, it is all fitting. Eight hours ago I thought you were grasping at straws. Now it looks to me like you're dead on.'

It didn't feel all that good to be dead on. But he understood Winston's excitement. When cases fell together the excitement could sometimes obscure the reality of the crime.

'What happened to her kid?' he asked.

'No idea. She probably gave the child up after the birth. That doesn't matter. What matters is what it meant to Bosch.'

She was right. But McCaleb didn't like the loose end.

'Going back to your call to Bosch's old partner. Is she going to call him and tell him you asked about him?'

'She already did.'

'This is tonight?'

'Yeah, this all just went down. That was that call, her getting back to me. He passed. He told her he was still holding out hope for his wife coming back.'

'Did she tell him it was you who was interested?'

'She wasn't supposed to.'

'But she probably did. This might mean he knows we're looking at him.'

'That's impossible. How?'

'I was just up there tonight. I was in his house. Then the same night he gets this call about you. A guy like Harry Bosch, he doesn't believe in coincidences, Jaye.'

'Well, when you were up there, how did you handle it?' Winston finally asked.

'Like we said. I wanted more info on Gunn but sidetracked into talking about Bosch. That's why I was calling you. I got some interesting stuff. Nothing that compares to what you got but stuff that also fits. But if he got this call about you right after I was there . . . I don't know.'

'Tell me about your stuff.'

'All little stuff. He's got the photo of the estranged wife prominently displayed in the living room. I was there less than an hour and the guy downed three beers. So there's the alcohol syndrome. Symptomatic of interior pressures. He also spoke of something he called "the big wheel." It's part of his belief system. He doesn't see the hand of God in things. He sees the big wheel. What goes around comes around. He said guys like Gunn don't really get away. Something always catches up to them. The wheel. I used some specific phrases to see if I could draw a reaction or disagreement. I called the world outside his door the plague. He didn't disagree. He said he could deal with the plague as long as he got his shots at the carriers. It's all very subtle, Jaye, but it's all there. He's got a Bosch print on the wall in the hallway. *The Garden of Earthly Delights*. It's got our owl in it.'

'So, he's named after the guy. If my name was Picasso I'd have a Picasso print on the wall.'

'I acted like I'd never seen it before and asked him what it meant. All he said was that it was the big wheel turning. That's what it meant to him.'

'Little pieces that fit.'

'There's still work to be done.'

'Well, are you still on it? Or are you going back?'

'For the time being I'm on it. I'll be staying over tonight. But I have a charter Saturday. I have to go back for that.'

She didn't say anything.

'You got anything else?' he finally asked.

'Yeah, I almost forgot.'

'What?'

'The owl from Bird Barrier. It was paid for with a money order from the Postal Service. I got the number from Cameron Riddell and ran a trace on it. It was bought December twenty-second at the post office on Wilcox in Hollywood. It's about four blocks from the police station where Bosch works.'

He shook his head.

'The laws of physics.'

'What do you mean?'

'For every action there is an equal and opposite reaction. When you look into the abyss the abyss looks into you. You know, all the clichés. They're clichés because they're true. You don't go into the darkness without it going into you and taking its piece. Bosch may have gone in too many times. He's lost his way.'

They were silent for a little while after that and then made plans to meet the following day. As he hung up he saw the hooker leaving the Skylark by herself and heading back up toward Nat's. She was wearing a denim jacket which she pulled tight around her against the cool night air. She adjusted her wig as she walked toward the bar where she would seek another customer.

Watching her and thinking about Bosch, McCaleb was reminded of all he had and how lucky in life he had been. He was reminded that luck could be a fleeting thing. It had to be earned and then guarded with everything you had. He knew he was not doing that now. He was leaving things unguarded while he went into the dark.

23

Trial resumed twenty-five minutes after the scheduled nine o'clock start because of the prosecution's unsuccessful bid to seek both sanctions against the defense for witness intimidation and a delay while the statements of Annabelle Crowe were fully investigated. Sitting behind his cherrywood desk in chambers, Judge Houghton encouraged the investigation but said the trial would not be delayed to accommodate it and no sanctions or other penalties would be issued unless evidence corroborating the witness's statements could be found. He warned the prosecutors and Bosch, who had taken part in the closed-door meeting by recounting his interview with Crowe, not to leak word of the witness's accusations to the media.

Five minutes later they were convened in the courtroom and the jurors were brought to their two rows of seats. Bosch returned to the witness stand and was reminded by the judge that he was still under oath. Janis Langwiser went back to the lectern with her legal pad.

'Now, Detective Bosch, we left off yesterday with your conclusion in regard to the death of Jody Krementz being determined to be a homicide. Is that correct?'

'Yes.'

'And that conclusion was based not only on your investigation but on the investigation and autopsy conducted by the coroner's office as well, correct?'

'Correct.'

'Could you please tell the jurors how the investigation proceeded once you had established the death as a homicide?'

Bosch turned in his seat so that he was looking directly at the jury box as he spoke. The movement was jarring. He had a pounding ache on the left side of his head that was so intense he wondered if people could actually see his temple throbbing.

'Well, my two partners – Jerry Edgar and Kizmin Rider – and I began to sit through – I mean, sift through the physical evidence we had accumulated. We also began conducting extensive interviews with those who knew the victim and were known to have been with her in the last twenty-four hours of her life.'

'You mentioned physical evidence. Please explain to the jury what physical evidence you had accumulated.'

'Actually, there was not a whole lot gathered. There were fingerprints throughout the house that we needed to run down. And there also was a quantity of fiber and hair evidence gathered from on and about the victim's body.'

J. Reason Fowkkes quickly objected before Bosch could continue his answer.

'Objection to the phrase "on or about" as being vague and misleading.'

'Your Honor,' Langwiser countered, 'I think if Mr. Fowkkes gave Detective Bosch a chance to finish the answer to the question there would be nothing vague or misleading. But interrupting a witness in mid-answer to say the answer is vague or misleading is not appropriate.'

'Overruled,' Judge Houghton said, before Fowkkes could get in a rejoinder. 'Let the witness complete his answer and then we'll see how vague it is. Go ahead, Detective Bosch.'

Bosch cleared his throat.

'I was going to say that several samples of pubic hair not—'

'What is "several," Your Honor,' Fowkkes said. 'My ongoing objection is to the lack of precision this witness is offering the jury.'

Bosch looked at Langwiser and saw how mad she was getting.

'Judge,' she said, 'could we please have direction from the court as to when objections can be raised? Defense counsel is seeking to constantly interrupt the witness because he knows we are moving into an area that is particularly devastating to his—'

'Ms. Langwiser, this isn't the time for closing arguments,' the judge said, cutting her off. 'Mr. Fowkkes, unless you are seeing a dire miscarriage of justice, I want objections stated either before a witness speaks or after he has completed at least a sentence.'

'Your Honor, the consequences *are* dire here. The state is trying to take away my client's life, simply because his moral views are—'

'Mr. Fowkkes!' the judge boomed. 'That goes for you, too, on the closing arguments. Let's continue the testimony, shall we?'

He turned to Bosch.

'Detective, continue – and try to be a little more precise in your answers.'

Bosch looked at Langwiser and saw her close her eyes momentarily. The judge's offhand direction to Bosch had been what Fowkkes was going for. A hint to the jurors that there might be vagueness, maybe even obfuscation in the prosecution's case. Fowkkes had successfully goaded the judge into appearing to agree with his objections.

Bosch glanced over at Fowkkes and saw him sitting with arms folded and a satisfied, if not smug, look on his face. Bosch looked back down at the murder book in front of him.

'Can I refer to my notes?' he asked.

He was told he could. He opened the binder and turned to the evidence reports. Looking at the medical examiner's evidence collection report, he began again.

'Prior to autopsy an evidence-collecting brush was passed through the victim's pubic hair. The comb collected eight samples of pubic hair that subsequent laboratory testing showed to have come from someone other than the victim.'

He looked up at Langwiser.

'Were those pubic hairs from eight different people?'

'No, the lab tests identified them as coming from the same unknown person.'

'And what did this indicate to you?'

'That the victim likely had sexual relations with someone between the time of her last bathing and her death.'

Langwiser looked down at her notes.

'Was there any other hair evidence collected on the victim or at the scene of the crime, Detective?'

Bosch turned a page in the murder book.

'Yes, a single strand of hair measuring two and one half inches long was found entangled on the clasp of a gold necklace the victim wore around her neck. The clasp was located at the back of the victim's neck. This, too, was identified during lab analysis as coming from someone other than the victim.'

'Going back for a moment to the pubic hair. Were there any other indications or evidence collected from the body or the crime scene indicating the victim had engaged in sexual relations in the time between bathing and her death?'

'No, there wasn't. No semen was collected from the vagina.'

'Is there a conflict between that and the finding of the pubic hair?'

'No conflict. It was simply an indication that a condom could have been used during the sex act.'

'Okay, moving on, Detective. Fingerprints. You mentioned fingerprints were found in the house. Please tell us about that area of the investigation.'

Bosch turned to the fingerprint report in the binder.

'There were a total of sixty-eight exemplars of fingerprints gathered inside the house where the victim was found. The victim and her roommate accounted for fifty-two of these. It was determined that the remaining sixteen were left by a total of seven people.'

'And who were these people?'

Bosch read the list of names from the binder. Through questioning from Langwiser he explained who each person was and how the detectives traced down when and why they had been in the house. They were friends of the roommates as well as family members, a former boyfriend and a prior date. The prosecution team knew that the defense would attempt to go to town on the prints, using them as red herrings to bait the jury away from the facts of the case. So the testimony moved slowly as Bosch tediously explained the location and origin of each fingerprint found and identified in the house. He ended with testimony about a full set of fingerprints found on the headboard of the bed in which the victim was found. He and Langwiser knew that these were the prints that Fowkkes would get the most yardage out of, so Langwiser attempted to minimize the potential damage by having it revealed during her examination of the witness.

'How far from the victim's body were these prints located?'

Bosch looked at the report in the binder.

'Two point three feet.'

'Exactly where on the headboard?'

'On the outside facing, between the headboard and the wall.'

'Was there a lot of space there?'

'About two inches.'

'How would someone get their fingerprints there?'

Fowkkes objected, saying it was outside Bosch's realm of expertise to determine how a set of fingerprints got anywhere, but the judge allowed the question.

'Only two ways I can think of,' Bosch answered. 'They got there when the bed was not pushed quite up to the wall. Or the person who left the prints had reached their fingers through the opening in the slats of the headboard and left them while holding onto that particular cross board.'

Langwiser introduced a photo taken by a fingerprint technician as an exhibit and it was shown to the jury.

'To accomplish the latter explanation you offered, the person would have to be lying in the bed, would they not?'

'It would seem that way.'

'Face down?'

'Yes.'

Fowkkes stood to object but the judge sustained it before the lawyer uttered a word.

'You are going too far afield with suppositions, Ms. Langwiser. Move on.'

'Yes, Your Honor.'

She referred to her pad for a moment.

'This print on the victim's bed, didn't that make you think the person who left it should be considered a prime suspect?'

'Not initially. It is impossible to tell how long a print has been at a specific location. Plus we had the additional factor that we knew the victim had not been killed in her bed, but rather taken to the bed after being killed elsewhere. It appeared to us that the location of the print was not a place that would have been touched by the killer when he put the body in the bed.'

'Who did these prints belong to?'

'A man named Allan Wiess, who had dated Ms. Krementz on three prior occasions, the most recent date being three weeks before her death.'

'Did you interview Allan Wiess?'

'Yes, I did. Along with Detective Edgar.'

'Did he acknowledge ever being in the victim's bed?'

'Yes, he did. He said he slept with her on that last occasion that he saw her, three weeks prior to her death.'

'Did he say he touched the bed board in the location you have shown us where the fingerprints were located?'

'He said he could have done it but he did not specifically remember doing it.'

'Did you investigate Allan Weiss's activities on the night of Jody Krementz's death?'

'Yes, we did. He had a solid alibi.'

'And what was that?'

'He told us he was in Hawaii at a real estate seminar. We checked airline and hotel records as well as with the seminar's producers. We confirmed he was there.'

Langwiser looked at Judge Houghton and said that it would be a good time to take the morning break. The judge said it was a little early but granted the request and ordered the jurors back in fifteen minutes.

Bosch knew she wanted the break now because she was about to move into questions about David Storey and wanted them clearly separated from all the other testimony. As he stepped off the witness stand and went back to the prosecution table, Langwiser was flipping through some files. She spoke to him without looking up.

'What's wrong, Harry?'

'What do you mean?'

'You're not crisp. Not like yesterday. Are you nervous about something?'

'No. Are you?'

'Yeah, the whole thing. We've got a lot riding on this.'

'I'll be crisper.'

'I'm serious, Harry.'

'So am I, Janis.'

He then walked away from the prosecution table and out through the courtroom.

He decided he would get a cup of coffee at the second-floor cafeteria. But first he stepped into the restroom next to the elevators and went to one of the sinks to splash cold water on his face. He bent fully over the sink, careful not to get water on his suit. He heard a toilet flush and when he straightened up and looked in the mirror he saw Rudy Tafero pass behind him and go to the sink furthest away. Bosch bent down again and brought more water up and held it. Its chill felt good against his eyes and eased his headache.

'What's it like, Rudy?' he asked without looking at the other man.

'What's what like, Harry?'

'You know, doing the devil's bidding. You get any sleep at night?'

Bosch walked over to the paper towel dispenser and tore off several sheets to dry his hands and face. Tafero came over and tore off a towel and began drying his hands.

'It's funny,' Tafero said. 'The only time in my life I had trouble sleeping was when I was a cop. I wonder why that was.'

He balled the towel in his hands and threw it into the wastebasket. He smiled at Bosch and then walked out. Bosch watched him go, still rubbing his hands on the towels.

24

Bosch could feel the coffee working in his blood. The second wind was coming. The headache was easing. He was ready. This would be how they planned it, how they had choreographed it. He leaned forward to the microphone and waited for the question.

'Detective Bosch,' Langwiser said from the lectern, 'did there come a time when the name David Storey came up in your investigation?'

'Yes, almost immediately. We received information from Jane Gilley, who was Jody Krementz's roommate, that on the last night of Jody's life she had a date with David Storey.'

'Did there come a time when you questioned Mr. Storey about that last night?'

'Yes. Briefly.'

'Why briefly, Detective Bosch? This *was* a homicide.'

'That was Mr. Storey's choosing. We attempted several times to interview him on that Friday that the body was discovered and the next day as well. He was difficult to locate. Finally, through his attorney, he agreed to be interviewed the next day, which was Sunday, on the condition that we come to him and conduct the interview in his office at Archway Studios. We reluctantly agreed to do it that way but did so in the spirit of cooperation and because we needed to talk to this man. At that point we were two days into the case and had not been able to talk to the last person known to have seen the victim alive. When we arrived at the office, Mr. Storey's personal attorney, Jason Fleer, was there. We began interviewing Mr. Storey but in less than five minutes his attorney terminated the interview.'

'Was this conversation tape-recorded?'

'Yes, it was.'

Langwiser made the motion to play the recording and it was approved by Judge Houghton over Fowkkes's objection. Fowkkes had asked the judge to simply allow jurors to read his already prepared transcripts of the short interview. But Langwiser objected to that, saying that she had not had time to check the transcripts for accuracy and that it was important for the jurors to hear David Storey's tone and demeanor. With the wisdom of Solomon the judge ruled that the tape would be heard and that the transcripts would be handed out anyway as an aid to the jurors. He encouraged Bosch and the prosecution team to read along as well so they could check the transcript for accuracy.

BOSCH: My name is Detective Hieronymus Bosch of the Los Angeles Police Department. I am accompanied by my partners, Detectives Jerry Edgar and Kizmin Rider. The date is October 15, 2000. We are interviewing David Storey in his offices at Archway Studios in regard to case number zero-zero-eight-nine-seven. Mr. Storey is accompanied by his attorney, Jason Fleer. Mr. Storey, Mr. Fleer? Any questions before we begin?

FLEER: No questions.

BOSCH: Oh, and, obviously, we are recording this statement. Mr. Storey, did you know a woman named Jody Krementz? Also known as Donatella Speers.

STOREY: You know the answer to that.

FLEER: David . . .

STOREY: Yes, I knew her. I was with her last Thursday night. It does not mean I killed her.

FLEER: David, please. Answer only the questions they ask you.

STOREY: Whatever.

BOSCH: Can I continue?

FLEER: By all means. Please.

STOREY: Yes, by all means. Please.

BOSCH: You mentioned that you were with her on Thursday evening. This was a date?

STOREY: Why ask things you already know the answer to? Yes, it was a date, if you want to call it that.

BOSCH: What do you want to call it?

STOREY: Doesn't matter.

(pause)

BOSCH: Could you give us a framework of time that you were with her?

STOREY: Picked her up at seven-thirty, dropped her off about midnight.

BOSCH: Did you enter her home when you came to pick her up?

STOREY: Matter of fact, I didn't. I was running very late and called on my cell phone to tell her to come outside because I didn't have time to come in. I think she wanted me to meet her roommate – another actress, no doubt – but I didn't have the time.

BOSCH: So when you pulled up she was waiting outside.

STOREY: That's what I said.

BOSCH: Seven-thirty until midnight. That is four and a half hours.

STOREY: You are good at math. I like that in a detective.

FLEER: David, let's try to get this done.

STOREY: I am.

BOSCH: Could you tell us what you did during the time period you were with Jody Krementz?

STOREY: We covered the three Fs. Film, food and a fuck.

BOSCH: Excuse me?

STOREY: We went to the premiere of my movie, then we went to the reception and had something to eat, then I took her to my place and we had sex. Consensual sex, Detective. Believe it or not, people do it on dates all the time. And not just Hollywood people. It happens across this great country of ours. It's what makes it great.

BOSCH: I understand. Did you take her home when you were finished?

STOREY: Always the gentleman, I did.

BOSCH: Did you enter her house at this time?

STOREY: No. I was in my fucking bathrobe. I just drove up, she got out and went inside. I then drove back home. Whatever happened after that I don't know. I am not involved in this in any way, shape or form. You people are—

FLEER: David, please.

STOREY: – completely full of shit if for one fucking moment you think—

FLEER: David, stop!

(pause)

Detective Bosch, I think we need to stop this.

BOSCH: We're in the middle of an interview here and—

FLEER: David, where are you going?

STOREY: Fuck these people. I'm going out for a smoke.

BOSCH: Mr. Storey has just left the office.

FLEER: I think at this point he is exercising his rights under the Fifth Amendment. This interview is over.

The tape went blank and Langwiser turned it off. Bosch looked at the jury. Several of them were looking at Storey. His arrogance had come through loud and clear on the tape. This was important because they would soon be asking the jury to believe that Storey had privately boasted to Bosch about the murder and how he would get away with it. Only an arrogant man would do that. The prosecution needed to prove Storey was not only a murderer, but an arrogant one at that.

'Okay, then,' Langwiser said. 'Did Mr. Storey return to continue the interview?'

'No, he did not,' Bosch answered. 'And we were asked to leave.'

'Did Mr. Storey's denial of any involvement in the murder of Jody Krementz end your interest in him?'

'No, it did not. We had an obligation to investigate the case fully and that included either ruling him in or ruling him out as a suspect.'

'Was his behavior during the short interview cause for suspicion?'

'You mean his arrogance? No, he—'

Fowkkes jumped up with an objection.

'Your Honor, one man's arrogance is another man's confidence in his innocence. There is no—'

'You are right, Mr. Fowkkes,' Houghton said.

He sustained the objection, struck Bosch's answer and turned to the jurors to tell them to ignore the remark.

'His behavior during the interview was not cause for suspicion,' Bosch began again. 'His being the last known person to be with the victim was cause for our immediate attention and focus. His lack of cooperation was suspicious but at this point we were keeping an open mind about everything. My partners and I have a combined total of more than twenty-five years' experience investigating homicides. We know that things are not always what they seem.'

'Where did the investigation go next?'

'We continued all avenues of investigation. One of those avenues was obviously Mr. Storey. Based on his statement that he and the victim had gone to his home on their date, my partners filed a search warrant application in Municipal Court and received approval to search David Storey's home.'

Langwiser brought the search warrant forward to the judge and it was received into evidence. She took it back with her to the lectern. Bosch then testified that the search of the home on Mulholland Drive was conducted at 6 A.M. two days after the initial interview with Storey.

'The search warrant authorized you to seize any evidence of Jody Krementz's murder, any evidence of her belongings and any evidence of her presence in that location, is that correct?'

'Correct.'

'Who conducted the search?'

'Myself, my partners and a two-man forensics team. We also had a photographer, for video and stills. A total of six.'

'How long did the search last?'

'Approximately seven hours.'

'Was the defendant present during the search?'

'For most of it. He had to leave at one point for a meeting with a movie actor he said he couldn't postpone. He was gone approximately two hours. During that time his personal attorney, Mr. Fleer, remained in the house and monitored the search. We were never left alone in the house, if that is what you are asking.'

Langwiser flipped through the pages of the search warrant, coming to the end of it.

'Now, Detective, when you seize any items during a court-approved search, you are required by law to keep an inventory on the search warrant receipt, correct?'

'Yes.'

'This receipt is then filed with the court, correct?'

'Yes.'

'Can you tell us then, why is this receipt blank?'

'We did not take any items from the house during the search.'

'You found nothing that indicated that Jody Krementz had been inside Mr. Storey's house, as he had told you she had been?'

'Nothing.'

'This search took place how many days after the evening Mr. Storey told you he had taken Ms. Krementz to his house and engaged in sexual relations with her?'

'Five days from the night of the murder, two days from our interview with Mr. Storey.'

'You found nothing in support of Mr. Storey's statement.'

'Nothing. The place was clean.'

Bosch knew she was trying to turn a negative into a positive, somehow trying to imply that the unsuccessful search was an indication of Storey's guilt.

'Would you call this an unsuccessful search?'

'No. Success doesn't enter into it. We were looking for evidence that would corroborate his statement as well as any evidence of possible foul play relating to Ms. Krementz. We found nothing in the house indicative of this. But sometimes it is not what you find, it's what you don't.'

'Can you explain that to the jury?'

'Well, it is true we didn't take any evidence from the house. But we found something missing that would later become important to us.'

'And what was that?'

'A book. A missing book.'

'How did you know it was missing if it wasn't there?'

'In the living room of the house there was a large built-in bookcase. Each shelf was full of books. On one shelf there was a space – a slot – where a book had been but was now gone. We could not find what book that might be. There were no books sitting out loose in the house. At the time it was just a small thing. Someone had obviously taken a book from the shelf and not replaced it. It was just kind of curious to us that we could not figure out where or what it was.'

Langwiser offered two still photographs of the bookcase taken during the search as exhibits. Houghton accepted them over a routine objection from Fowkkes. The photos showed the bookcase in its entirety and a close-up of the second shelf with the open space between a book called *The Fifth*

Horizon and a biography of the film director John Ford called *Print the Legend.*

'Now, Detective,' Langwiser said, 'you said that at the time you did not know if this missing book had any importance or bearing on the case, correct?'

'That is right.'

'Did you eventually determine what book had been taken from the shelf?'

'Yes, we did.'

Langwiser paused. Bosch knew what she was going to do. The dance had been choreographed. He thought of her as a good storyteller. She knew how to string it along, keep people hooked in, take them to the edge of the cliff and then pull them back.

'Well, let's take things in order,' she said. 'We'll come back to the book. Now did you have occasion to talk to Mr. Storey on the day of the search?'

'He mostly kept to himself and was on the phone most of the time. But we spoke when we first knocked on the door and announced the search. And then at the end of the day when I told him we were leaving and that we were not taking anything with us.'

'Did you wake him up when you came at six in the morning?'

'Yes, we did.'

'Was he alone in the house?'

'Yes.'

'Did he invite you in?'

'Not at first. He objected to the search. I told him—'

'Excuse me, Detective, we might make this easier if we show it. You said there was a videographer with you. Was he running the camera when you knocked at six in the morning?'

'Yes, he was.'

Langwiser then made the appropriate motions to introduce the search video. It was accepted under objection from the defense. A large television was rolled into the courtroom and placed at center in front of the jury box. Bosch was asked to identify the tape. The lights in the courtroom were dimmed and it was played.

The tape began with a focus on Bosch and the others outside the red front door of a house. He identified himself and the address and the case number. He spoke quietly. He then turned and knocked sharply on the door. He announced it was the police and knocked sharply again. They waited. Bosch knocked on the door every fifteen seconds until it was finally opened about two minutes after the first pounding. David Storey looked out through the opening, his hair disheveled, his eyes showing exhaustion.

'What?' he asked.

'We have a search warrant here, Mr. Storey,' Bosch said. 'It allows us to conduct a search of these premises.'

'You have to be fucking kidding.'

'No, we're not, sir. Could you step back and let us in? The sooner we're in the sooner we're out.'

'I'm calling my lawyer.'

Storey closed and locked the door. Bosch immediately stepped up and put his face close to the jamb. He called out loudly.

'Mr. Storey, you have ten minutes. If this door is not opened by six-fifteen then we're going to take it down. We have a court-ordered search warrant and we will execute it.'

He turned back to the camera and made the cut signal across his throat.

The video jumped to another focus on the door. The time readout in the bottom corner now showed it was 6:13 A.M. The door opened and Storey stepped back and signaled the search team in. His hair looked as though it had been combed with his hands. He was wearing black jeans and a black T-shirt. He was in bare feet.

'Do what you have to do and get out. My lawyer's coming and he's going to watch you people. You break one fucking thing in this house and I'm going to sue the shit out of you. This is a David Serrurier house. You so much as put a scratch on one of the walls and it'll be your jobs. All of you.'

'We'll be careful, Mr. Storey,' Bosch said as he walked in.

The cameraman was the last to enter the house. Storey looked into the lens as if seeing it for the first time.

'And get that shit off of me.'

He made a motion and the camera angle shot upward to the ceiling. It remained there while the voices of the videographer and Storey continued off camera.

'Hey! Don't touch the camera!'

'Then get it out of my face!'

'Okay. Fine. Just don't touch the camera.'

The screen went blank and the lights of the courtroom came back up. Langwiser continued the questioning.

'Detective Bosch, did you or members of the search team have further . . . conversation with Mr. Storey after that?'

'Not during the search. Once his lawyer got there Mr. Storey stayed in his office. When we searched his office he moved into the bedroom. When he was leaving for his appointment I questioned him briefly about that and he left. That was about it as far as it went during the search and while we were inside the house.'

'What about at the end of the day – seven hours later – when the search was completed, did you speak to the defendant again?'

'Yes, I spoke to him briefly at the front door. We were packed up and ready to leave. The lawyer had left. I was in my car with my partners. We were backing out when I realized I had forgotten about giving Mr. Storey a copy of the search warrant. It's required by law. So I went back to his door and knocked on it.'

'Did Mr. Storey answer the door himself?'

'Yes, he answered after about four hard knocks. I gave him the receipt and told him it was required.'

'Did he say anything to you?'

Fowkkes stood up and objected for the record but the issue had already been disposed of in pretrial motions and rulings. The judge noted the objection for the record and overruled it for the record. Langwiser asked the question again.

'Can I refer to my notes?'

'Please.'

Bosch turned to the notes he had taken in the car right after the conversation.

'First, he said, "You didn't find a goddamn thing, did you?" And I told him he was right, that we weren't taking anything with us. He then said, "Because there was nothing to take." I nodded and was turning to leave when he spoke again. He said, "Hey, Bosch." I turned back and he leaned toward me and said, "You'll never find what you are looking for." I said, "Oh really, what is it that I am looking for?" He didn't respond. He just looked at me and smiled.'

After a pause, Langwiser asked, 'Was that the end of it?'

'No. I sensed at that point that I might be able to bait him into saying more. I said to him, "You did it, didn't you?" He continued to smile and then he slowly nodded. And he said, "And I'll get away with it." He said, "I'm a —"'

'Bullshit! You're a fucking liar!'

It was Storey. He had stood up and was pointing at Bosch. Fowkkes had his hand on him and was trying to pull him back into his place. A deputy sheriff, who had been positioned at a desk to the rear of the defense table was up and moving toward Storey from behind.

'The defendant will sit DOWN!' the judge boomed from the bench at the same moment he brought the gavel down.

'He's fucking lying!'

'Deputy, sit him down!'

The deputy moved in, put both hands on Storey's shoulders from behind and roughly pulled him back down into his seat. The judge pointed another deputy toward the jury.

'Remove the jury.'

While the jurors were quickly hustled into the deliberation room, Storey continued to struggle with the deputy and Fowkkes. As soon as the jurors were gone he seemed to relax his efforts and then calmed. Bosch looked over at the reporters, trying to see if any of them had noted how Storey's demonstration ended as soon as the jurors were out of sight.

'Mr. Storey!' the judge yelled from a standing position. 'That behavior and language is not acceptable in this courtroom. Mr. Fowkkes, if you can't control your client, my people will. One more outburst and I will have him gagged and chained to that chair. Am I clear on this?'

'Absolutely, Your Honor. I apolo—'

'That is a zero tolerance rule. Any outburst from here on out and he'll be shackled. I don't care who he is or who his friends are.'

'Yes, Your Honor. We understand.'

'I am taking five minutes and then we'll start again.'

The judge abruptly left the bench, his feet resounding loudly as he quickly took the three steps down. He disappeared through a door to the rear hallway that led to his chambers.

Bosch looked over at Langwiser and her eyes betrayed her delight at what had just happened. To Bosch it was a trade-off. On one hand the jurors saw the defendant acting angry and out of control – possibly exhibiting the same rage that had led to murder. But on the other hand, he was registering his objection to what was happening to him in the courtroom. And that could register an empathic response from the jurors. Storey had to reach only one of them in order to walk.

Before the trial Langwiser had predicted that they would draw Storey into an outburst. Bosch had thought she was wrong. He thought Storey was too cool and calculating. Unless, of course, the outburst was a calculated move. Storey was a man who directed dramatic scenes and characters for a living. Bosch knew he should have seen that a time might come when he would be unwittingly used as a supporting actor in one of those scenes.

25

The judge returned to the bench two minutes after leaving and Bosch wondered if he had retreated to his chambers to put a holster on under the robes. As soon as he sat down Houghton looked at the defense table. Storey was sitting with his face somberly pointed down at the sketch pad in front of him.

'Are we ready?' the judge asked.

All parties murmured they were ready. The judge called for the jury and they were brought in, most of them looking directly at Storey as they entered.

'Okay, folks, we're going to try this again,' Judge Houghton said. 'The exclamations you heard a few minutes ago from the defendant are to be ignored. They are not evidence, they are not anything. If Mr. Storey wants to personally deny the charges or anything else said about him in testimony, he'll get that chance.'

Bosch watched Langwiser's eyes dance. The judge's comments were his way of slapping back at the defense. He was setting up the expectation that Storey would testify during the defense phase. If he didn't, then it could be a letdown for the jurors.

The judge turned it back over to Langwiser, who continued her questioning of Bosch.

'Before we were interrupted, you were testifying about your conversation with the defendant at the door to his house.'

'Yes.'

'You quoted the defendant as saying, "And I'll get away with it," is that correct?'

'Correct.'

'And you took this comment to be referring to the death of Jody Krementz, correct?'

'That's what we were talking about, yes.'

'Did he say anything else after that?'

'Yes.'

Bosch paused, wondering if Storey would make another outburst. He didn't.

'He said, "I am a god in this town, Detective Bosch. You don't fuck with the gods." '

Nearly ten seconds of silence went by before Langwiser was prompted by the judge to move on.

'What did you do after the defendant made this statement to you?'

'Well, I was kind of taken aback. I was surprised that he would say this to me.'

'You were not recording the conversation, is that correct?'

'That is correct. It was just a conversation at the door after I knocked.'

'So what happened next?'

'I went to the car and immediately wrote out these notes of the conversation so I would have it verbatim from when it was freshest in my mind. I told my partners what had just transpired and we decided to call the district attorney's office for advice as to whether this admission to me would give us probable cause to arrest Mr. Storey. Um, what happened was that none of us could get a signal on our cell phones because we were up there in the hills. We left the house and drove to the fire station on Mulholland just east of Laurel Canyon Boulevard. We asked to use a phone there and I made the call to the DA.'

'And who did you speak with?'

'You. I recounted the case, what had transpired during the search and what Mr. Storey said at the door. It was decided to continue the investigation at that point and not make the arrest.'

'Did you agree with that decision?'

'Not at the time. I wanted to arrest him.'

'Did Mr. Storey's admission change the investigation?'

'It pretty much closed the focus. The man had admitted the crime to me. We began looking only at him.'

'Did you ever consider that perhaps the admission was an empty boast, that at the same time you were in essence baiting the defendant, he was baiting you?'

'Yes, I considered it. But ultimately I believed he made the statements because they were true and because he believed he was in an invincible position at that point.'

There was a sharp ripping sound as Storey tore the top page off his sketch pad. He crumpled the paper and bounced it across the table. It hit a computer screen and bounced off the table to the floor.

'Thank you, Detective,' Langwiser said. 'Now, you said the decision was to continue the investigation. Can you tell the jury what that entailed?'

Bosch described how he and his partners had interviewed dozens of witnesses who had seen the defendant and the victim at the film premiere or at the reception that followed in a circus tent erected in a nearby parking lot. They also interviewed dozens more people who knew Storey or had worked with him. Bosch acknowledged that none of these interviews had produced information important to the investigation.

'You mentioned earlier that during the search of the defendant's home you became curious about a missing book, correct?'

'Yes.'

Fowkkes objected.

'There has been no evidence whatsoever about a missing book. There was a space on the shelf. It does not mean there was ever a book in that place.'

Langwiser promised she would tie it all up promptly and the judge overruled.

'Did there come a time when you determined what book had been in that space on the shelf in the defendant's home?'

'Yes, in the course of our gathering of background information on Mr. Storey, my partner, Kizmin Rider, who was aware of his work and professional reputation, remembered that she had read a story about him in a magazine called *Architectural Digest*. She was able to do an Internet search and determine that the issue she remembered was from February of last year. She then ordered a copy of the magazine from the publisher. What she had remembered was that there were photos in the article of Mr. Storey in his house. She remembered his bookshelves because she is an avid reader and was curious about what books this movie director would have on his shelves.'

Langwiser made a motion to introduce the magazine as her next exhibit. It was received by the judge and Langwiser gave it to Bosch on the witness stand.

'Is that the magazine your partner received?'

'Yes.'

'Could you turn to the story on the defendant and describe the photograph on the opening page of the story?'

Bosch flipped to a marker in the magazine.

'It is a photograph of David Storey sitting on the couch in the living room of his house. To his left are the bookshelves.'

'Can you read the titles of the books on the spines of the books?'

'Some of them. They are not all clear.'

'When you received this magazine from the publisher, what did you do with it?'

'We saw that not all of the books were clear. We contacted the publisher again and attempted to borrow the negative of this photo. We dealt with the editor in chief, who would not allow the negatives out of the office. He cited media law and free-press restraints.'

'So what happened next?'

'The editor said he would even fight a court order. An attorney from the city attorney's office was called in and began negotiating with the magazine's lawyer. The result was that I flew to New York City and was allowed access to the negative in the photo lab in the *Architectural Digest* offices.'

'For the record, what date were you there?'

'I took a redeye on October twenty-ninth. I was at the magazine's office the following morning. It was a Monday, October thirtieth.'

'And what did you do there?'

'I had the magazine's photo lab manager make blowups of the shot containing the bookshelves.'

Langwiser introduced two large blowup photographs on hard backing as her next exhibits. After they were approved over unsustained objection she put them on easels set in front of the jury. One showed the bookcase in full while the other was a blowup of one shelf. The image was grainy but the titles on the spines of the books could be read.

'Detective, did you compare these photos with those taken during the search of the defendant's house?'

'Yes, we did.'

Langwiser asked permission to set up a third and fourth easel and to put blowup photos taken during the search of the full bookcase and the shelf with the space for a missing book. The judge approved. She then asked Bosch to step down from the witness stand and use a pointer to explain what he found during his comparison study. It was obvious to anyone looking at the photos what he found but Langwiser was painstakingly going through the motions so that no juror could be confused.

Bosch put the pointer on the photo showing the open space in the shelved books. He then brought it over and put the tip on a book that was in the same spot.

'When we searched the house on October seventeenth there was no book here between *The Fifth Horizon* and *Print the Legend.* Here in this photo, taken ten months before, there is a book between *The Fifth Horizon* and *Print the Legend.*'

'And what is the title of that book?'

'*Victims of the Night.*'

'Okay, and did you look at photos you had from the search of the full bookcase in order to see if this book, *Victims of the Night,* had been shelved elsewhere?'

Bosch pointed to the October 17 blowup of the entire bookcase.

'We did. It's not there.'

'Did you find this book anywhere in the house?'

'No, we did not.'

'Thank you, Detective. You can return to the witness stand now.'

Langwiser introduced a copy of *Victims of the Night* as an exhibit and handed it to Bosch.

'Can you tell the jury what that is, Detective?'

'It is a copy of *Victims of the Night.*'

'Is that the book that was on the defendant's shelf when his photograph was taken for *Architectural Digest* in January of last year?'

'No, it's not. It's a copy of the same book. I bought it.'

'Where?'

'A place called Mystery Bookstore in Westwood.'

'Why did you buy it there?'

'I called around. It was the only place I could find that had it in stock.'

'Why was it so hard to find?'

'The man at Mystery Bookstore told me it was a small printing by a small publisher.'

'Did you read this book?'

'Parts of it. It is mostly photographs of unusual crime scenes and accident scenes, that sort of thing.'

'Is there anything in there that struck you as unusual or perhaps relating to the killing of Jody Krementz?'

'Yes, there is a photograph of a death scene on page seventy-three that immediately drew my attention.'

'Describe it, please.'

Bosch opened the book to a marker. He spoke as he looked at the full-page photograph on the right side of the book.

'It shows a woman in a bed. She's dead. A scarf is tied around her neck and looped over one of the bars of the headboard. She is nude from the waist down. Her left hand is between her legs and two of her fingers have penetrated the vagina.'

'Can you read the caption beneath the photo, please?'

'It says, "Autoerotic Death: This woman was found in her bed in New Orleans, a victim of autoerotic asphyxia. It is estimated that around the world more than five hundred people die from this accidental misadventure each year." '

Langwiser asked and received permission to place two more blowup photos on the easels as exhibits. She placed them right over two of the bookshelf photos. Side by side the photos were of Jody Krementz's body in her bed and of the page from *Victims of the Night.*

'Detective, did you make a comparison between the photo of the victim in this case, Jody Krementz, and the photo from the book?'

'Yes, I did. I found them to be very similar.'

'Did it appear to you that the body of Ms. Krementz could have been staged, using the photo from the book as a model or baseline?'

'Yes, it did.'

'Did you ever have occasion to ask the defendant what happened to his copy of the book *Victims of the Night?*'

'No, since the day of the search of his home, Mr. Storey and his attorneys have refused repeated requests for an interview.'

Langwiser nodded and looked at the judge.

'Your Honor, may I take these exhibits down and offer them to the court clerk?'

'Please do,' the judge responded.

Langwiser made a show of taking the photos of the two dead women down first by folding them in toward each other like two sides of a mirror closing. It was a little thing but Bosch saw the jurors watching.

'Okay, Detective Bosch,' Langwiser said when the easels were cleared. 'Did you make any inquiries or do any further investigation into autoerotic deaths?'

'Yes. I knew that if this case ever moved to a trial that the classification of the death as a homicide staged to look like this sort of accident might be challenged. I was also curious about what that caption in the book said. Frankly, I was surprised by the figure of five hundred deaths a year. I did some checking with the FBI and found that the figure was actually accurate, if not low.'

'And did that cause you to do any further research?'

'Yes, on a more local level.'

With Langwiser prompting, Bosch testified that he checked through records at the medical examiner's office for deaths due to autoerotic asphyxia. His search went back five years.

'And what did you find?'

'In those five years, sixteen deaths in Los Angeles County classified as accidental death by misadventure had been attributed specifically to autoerotic asphyxia.'

'And how many of these cases involved female victims?'

'Only one case involved a female.'

'Did you examine this case?'

Fowkkes was up with an objection and this time asked for a sidebar conference. The judge allowed it and the attorneys gathered at the side of the bench. Bosch could not hear the whispered conversation but knew that Fowkkes was most likely trying to stop the direction of the testimony. Langwiser and Kretzler had anticipated he would move once more to block any mention of Alicia Lopez in front of the jurors. It would likely be the pivotal decision in the trial – for both sides.

After five minutes of whispered argument, the judge sent the lawyers back to their places and told the jurors that the issue before the court would take longer than anticipated. He adjourned for another fifteen-minute break. Bosch returned to the prosecution table.

'Something new?' Bosch asked Langwiser.

'No, the same old argument. For some reason the judge wants to hear it again. Wish us luck.'

The lawyers and the judge retreated to chambers to argue the point. Bosch was left at the table. He used his cell phone to check messages at his home and office. There was one message at work. It was from Terry

McCaleb. He thanked Bosch for the tip from the night before. He said he got some good information at Nat's and that he'd be in touch. Bosch erased it and closed the phone, wondering what it was that McCaleb had picked up.

When the lawyers returned through the rear door of the courtroom, Bosch read the judge's decision in their faces. Fowkkes looked dour, with his eyes downcast. Kretzler and Langwiser came back smiling.

After the jurors were brought back and the trial resumed, Langwiser went directly in for the hit. She asked the court reporter to read back the last question before the objection.

'Did you examine this case?' the reporter read.

'Let's strike that,' Langwiser said. 'Let's not confuse the issue. Detective, the one female case of the sixteen you found in the medical examiner's records, what was the name of the deceased in that case?'

'Alicia Lopez.'

'Can you tell us a little bit about her?'

'She was twenty-four and lived in Culver City. She worked as an administrative assistant to the vice-president of production at Sony Pictures, also in Culver City. She was found dead in her bed on the twentieth of May, nineteen ninety-eight.'

'She lived alone?'

'Yes.'

'What were the circumstances of her death?'

'She was found in her bed by a coworker who became concerned when she had missed two days of work following the weekend without calling in. The coroner estimated she had been dead three to four days by the time she was found. Decomposition of the body was extensive.'

'Ms. Langwiser?' Judge Houghton interrupted. 'It was agreed that you would lay foundation connecting the cases quickly.'

'I'm right there, Your Honor. Thank you. Detective, did anything about this case alert you or draw your attention in any way?'

'Several things. I looked at photos taken at the death scene and though decomposition was extensive I was able to note that the victim in this case was in a posture closely paralleling that of the victim in the present case. I also noted that the ligature in the Lopez case was also used without a buffering, which was the same with the present case. I also knew from our backgrounding investigation of Mr. Storey that at the time of Ms. Lopez's death he was making a film for a company called Cold House Films, a company which was being financed in part by Sony Pictures.'

In the moment following his answer Bosch noticed that the courtroom had become unusually still and silent. No one was whispering in the gallery or clearing their throat. It was as if everyone – jurors, lawyers, spectators and media – all decided to hold their breath at once. Bosch glanced at the jurors and saw that almost all of them were looking at the defense table.

Bosch looked there as well and saw Storey, his face still aimed downward, silently seething. Langwiser finally broke the silence.

'Detective, did you make further inquiries about the Lopez case?'

'Yes, I spoke to the detective who handled it for the Culver City Police Department. I also made inquiries about Ms. Lopez's job at Sony.'

'And what did you learn about her that would have bearing on the present case?'

'I learned that at the time of her death she was acting as a liaison between the studio and the field production of the film David Storey was directing.'

'Do you recall the name of that film?'

'*The Fifth Horizon.*'

'Where was it being filmed?'

'In Los Angeles. Mostly in Venice.'

'And as a liaison would Ms. Lopez have had any direct contact with Mr. Storey?'

'Yes. She spoke with him by phone or in person every day of the shoot.'

Again the silence seemed to be roaring. Langwiser milked it for as long as she could and then started driving home the nails.

'Let me see if I have all of this straight, Detective. Your testimony is that in the past five years there has been only one death of a female in Los Angeles County attributed to autoerotic asphyxia and that the present case involving the death of Jody Krementz was staged to appear as an autoerotic asphyxia?'

'Objection,' Fowkkes interjected. 'Asked and answered.'

'Overruled,' Houghton said without argument from Langwiser. 'The witness may answer.'

'Yes,' Bosch said. 'Correct.'

'And that both of these women knew the defendant, David Storey?'

'Correct.'

'And that both of these deaths show similarities to a photograph of an autoerotic death contained in a book known at one time to be in the defendant's collection at home?'

'Correct.'

Bosch looked over at Storey as he said it, hoping he would look up so that they could lock eyes one more time.

'What did the Culver City Police Department have to say about this, Detective Bosch?'

'Based upon my inquiries they have reopened the case. But they are hampered.'

'Why is that?'

'The case is old. Because it was originally ruled an accidental death, not all the records were kept in archives. Because decomposition was advanced at the time of the body's discovery it is hard to make definitive observations and conclusions. And the body cannot be exhumed because it was cremated.'

'It was? By whom?'

Fowkkes stood and objected but the judge said the argument had already been heard and overruled. Langwiser prompted Bosch before Fowkkes had even sat back down.

'By whom, Detective Bosch?'

'By her family. But it was paid for ... the cremation, the service, everything was paid for by David Storey as a gift in Alicia Lopez's memory.'

Langwiser loudly flipped up a page on her legal tablet. She was on a roll and everybody knew it. It was what cops and prosecutors called being in the tube. It was a surfing reference. It meant they had ridden the case into the water tunnel where everything was going smoothly and perfectly and was surrounding them in glorious balance.

'Detective, subsequent to this part of the investigation, did there come a time when a woman named Annabelle Crowe came to see you?'

'Yes. A story had broken in the *Los Angeles Times* about the investigation and how David Storey was the focus. She read the story and came forward.'

'And who is she?'

'She's an actress. She lives in West Hollywood.'

'And what bearing did she have on this case?'

'She told me that she had dated David Storey at one time last year and he choked her while they were having sex.'

Fowkkes made another objection, this one without the force of his other protestations. But again he was overruled, as the testimony had been cleared by the judge in earlier motions.

'Where did Ms. Crowe say this incident took place?'

'In Mr. Storey's home on Mulholland Drive. I asked her to describe the place and she was able to do so accurately. She had been there.'

'Couldn't she have seen the issue of *Architectural Digest* that showed photos of the defendant's home?'

'She was able to describe in accurate detail areas of the master bedroom and bath that were not shown in the magazine.'

'What happened to her when the defendant choked her?'

'She told me she passed out. When she awoke Mr. Storey was not in the room. He was taking a shower. She grabbed her clothing and fled from the home.'

Langwiser underlined that with a long silence. She then flipped the pages of her pad down, glanced over at the defense table and then looked up at Judge Houghton.

'Your Honor, that is all I have for Detective Bosch at this time.'

26

McCaleb got to El Cochinito at quarter to twelve. He hadn't been inside the store-front restaurant in Silver Lake in five years but he remembered the place had only a dozen or so tables and they were usually taken quickly at lunchtime. And often those tables were taken by cops. Not because the name of the restaurant was a draw – the Little Pig – but because the food was of high quality and low cost. It had been McCaleb's experience that cops were highly skilled in finding such establishments among the many restaurants in any city. When he had traveled on assignment for the bureau, he would always ask the local street cops for recommendations on food. He had rarely been disappointed.

While he waited for Winston he carefully studied the menu and planned his meal. In the past year his palate had finally returned with a vengeance. For the first eighteen months of his life after surgery, his sense of taste had deserted him. He had not cared what he ate because it all tasted the same – bland. Even a heavy dousing of habañera sauce on everything from sandwiches to pasta only registered a minor blip on his tongue. But then, slowly, his taste started coming back and it became a second rebirth for him following the transplant itself. He now loved everything Graciela made. He even loved everything *he* made – and this despite his general ineptitude with anything other than the barbecue grill. He ate everything with a gusto he'd never had before, even before the transplant. A peanut butter and jelly sandwich in the middle of the night was something he privately savored as much as a trip overtown with Graciela to dine in style at Jozu on Melrose. Consequently, he had started filling out, gaining back the twenty-five pounds he'd lost while his own heart had withered and he'd waited for a new one. He was now back to his pre-illness weight of 180 and food intake, for the first time in four years, was something he had to watch. On his last cardio checkup, his doctor had taken notice and raised a warning. She told him that he had to slow down the intake of calories and fat.

But not at this lunch. He had been waiting a long time for a chance to come to this place. Years earlier he had spent a good bit of time in Florida on a serial case and the only good that had come out of it was his love of Cuban food. When he later transferred to the Los Angeles field office it was hard to find a Cuban restaurant that compared with the places where he had eaten in Ybor City outside of Tampa. Once on an L.A. case he'd come across a patrol cop who he learned was of Cuban descent. McCaleb asked him where he went to eat when he wanted real home cooking. The cop's answer was El Cochinito. And McCaleb quickly became a regular.

McCaleb decided that studying the menu was a waste of time because he had known all along what he wanted. Lechon asada with black beans and rice, fried bananas and yucca on the side and don't bother telling the doctor. He just wished Winston would hurry up and get there so he could place his order.

He put the menu aside and thought about Harry Bosch. McCaleb had spent most of the morning on the boat, watching the trial on television. He thought Bosch's performance on the witness stand had been outstanding. The revelation that Storey had been linked to another death was shocking to McCaleb and apparently to the media horde as well. During the breaks the talking heads in the studio were beside themselves with excitement over the prospect of this new fodder. They cut at one point to the hallway outside the courtroom where J. Reason Fowkkes was being peppered with questions about these new developments. Fowkkes, for probably the only time in his life, was not commenting. The talking heads were left to speculate about this new information and to comment on the methodical yet thoroughly gripping procession of the prosecution's case.

Still, watching the trial only caused uneasiness within McCaleb. He had a difficult time coming to terms with the idea that the man he had watched so capably describing the aspects and moves of a difficult investigation was also the man he was investigating, the man his gut instincts told him had committed the same kind of crime he was now involved in prosecuting.

At noon, their agreed-upon meeting time, McCaleb looked up from his thoughts to see Jaye Winston come through the restaurant's front door. She was followed by two men. One was black and one was white and that was the best way to differentiate between them because they wore almost identical gray suits and maroon ties. Before they even got to his table McCaleb knew they were bureau men.

Winston had a look of washed-out resignation on her face.

'Terry,' she said before sitting down, 'I want you to meet a couple guys.'

She indicated the black agent first.

'This is Don Twilley and this is Marcus Friedman. They're with the bureau.'

All three of them pulled out chairs and sat down. Friedman sat next to McCaleb, Twilley directly across from him. Nobody shook hands.

'I've never had Cuban food before,' Twilley said as he pulled a menu from the napkin stand. 'Is it good here?'

McCaleb looked at him.

'No. That's why I like to eat here.'

Twilley's eyes came up from the menu and he smiled.

'I know, stupid question.' He looked down at the menu and then back up at McCaleb. 'You know I know about you, Terry. You're a fucking legend in the FO. Not 'cause of the heart, 'cause of the cases. I'm glad to finally meet you.'

McCaleb looked over at Winston with a look that said what the hell is going on?

'Terry, Marc and Don are from the civil rights section.'

'Yeah? That's great. Did you guys come all the way from the field office to meet the legend and try Cuban food, or is there something else?'

'Uh . . .' Twilley began.

'Terry, the shit's hit the fan,' Winston said. 'A reporter called my captain this morning to ask if we were investigating Harry Bosch as a suspect in the Gunn case.'

McCaleb leaned back in his seat, shocked by the news. He was about to respond when the waiter came to the table.

'Give us a couple minutes,' Twilley said gruffly to the man, waving him off with a dismissive gesture, which annoyed McCaleb.

Winston continued.

'Terry, before we go further with this, I have to know something. Did you leak this?'

McCaleb shook his head in disgust.

'Are you kidding me? You're asking *me* that?'

'Look, all I know is that it didn't come from me. And I didn't tell anyone, not Captain Hitchens and not even my own partner, let alone a reporter.'

'Well, it wasn't me. Thanks for asking.'

He glanced at Twilley and then back at Winston. He hated having this dispute with Jaye in front of them.

'What are these guys doing here?' he asked. Then looking at Twilley again, he added, 'What do you want?'

'They're taking over the case, Terry,' Winston answered. 'And you're out.'

McCaleb looked back at Winston. His mouth opened a little before he realized how he looked and closed it.

'What are you talking about? I'm out? I'm the only one in. I've been working this as—'

'I know, Terry. But things are different now. After the reporter called Hitchens I had to tell him what was happening, what we'd been doing. He threw a fit and after he was done throwing a fit he decided the best way to handle this was to go to the bureau with it.'

'The civil rights section, Terry,' Twilley said. 'Investigating cops is our bread and butter. We'll be able to—'

'Fuck you, Twilley. Don't try that bureau rap with me. I used to be in the club, remember? I know how it goes. You guys will come in, piggyback my trail and then waltz Bosch past the cameras on the way to the lockup.'

'Is that what this is about?' Friedman said. 'Getting the credit?'

'You don't have to worry about that, Terry,' Twilley said. 'We can put you in front of the cameras if that's what you want.'

'It's *not* what I want. And don't call me Terry. You don't even fuckin' know me.'

He looked down at the table, shaking his head.

'Fuck, I've been waiting to come back to this place for a long time and now I don't even feel like eating.'

'Terry . . .' Winston said, not offering anything else.

'What, you're going to tell me this is right?'

'No. It's not right or wrong. It's just the way it is. The investigation is official now. You're not official. You knew this could happen from the start.'

He reluctantly nodded. He brought his elbows up onto the table and put his face into his hands.

'Who was the reporter?'

When Winston didn't answer he dropped his hands and looked pointedly at her.

'Who?'

'A guy named Jack McEvoy. He works for the *New Times*, an alternative weekly that likes to stir up shit.'

'I know what it is.'

'You know McEvoy?' Twilley asked.

McCaleb's cell phone began to chirp. It was in the pocket of his jacket draped over his chair. It got caught in the pocket as he tried to get it out. He anxiously struggled with it because he assumed it would be Graciela. Other than Winston and Buddy Lockridge, he'd only given the number to Brass Doran in Quantico and he had finished his business with her.

He finally answered after the fifth chirp.

'Hey, Agent McCaleb, it's Jack McEvoy from the *New Times*. You got a couple minutes to talk?'

McCaleb looked across the table at Twilley, wondering if he could hear the voice on the phone.

'Actually, I don't. I'm in the middle of something here. How'd you get this number?'

'Information on Catalina. I called the number and your wife answered. She gave me your cell. That a problem?'

'No, no problem. But I can't talk now.'

'When can we talk? It's important. Something's come up that I really want to talk—'

'Just call me later. In an hour.'

McCaleb closed the phone and put it down on the table. He looked at it, half expecting McEvoy to call back right away. Reporters were like that.

'Terry, everything all right?'

He looked up at Winston.

'Yeah, fine. My charter tomorrow. He wanted to know about the weather.'

He looked at Twilley.

'What was your question again?'

'Do you know Jack McEvoy? The reporter who called Captain Hitchens.'

McCaleb paused, looking at Winston and then back at Twilley.

'Yeah, I know him. You know I know him.'

'That's right, the Poet case. You had a piece of that.'

'A small piece.'

'When was the last time you talked to McEvoy?'

'Well, that would've been, let's see . . . that would have been a couple days ago.'

Winston visibly stiffened. McCaleb looked over at her.

'Relax, would you, Jaye? I ran into McEvoy at the Storey trial. I went up there to talk to Bosch. McEvoy's covering it for *New Times* and he said hello – I hadn't talked to him in five years. And I did *not* tell him what I was doing or what I was working on. In fact, at the time I saw him Bosch wasn't even a suspect.'

'Well, did he see you with Bosch?'

'I'm sure he did. Everybody did. There's as much media up there as there was for O. J. Did he specifically mention me to your captain?'

'If he did, Hitchens didn't tell me.'

'All right, then, if it wasn't you and it wasn't me, where else did the leak come from?'

'That's what we are asking you,' Twilley said. 'Before we come into this case we want to know the lay of the land and who's talking to who.'

McCaleb didn't reply. He was getting claustrophobic. Between the conversation and Twilley being in his face, and the people standing around in the small restaurant waiting for tables, he was beginning to feel like he couldn't breathe.

'What about this bar you went to last night?' Friedman asked.

McCaleb leaned back and looked over at him.

'What about it?'

'Jaye told us what you told her. You specifically asked about Bosch *and* Gunn there, right?'

'Yeah, right. And what? You think the bartender then jumped on the phone and called the *New Times* and asked for Jack McEvoy? All because I showed her a picture of Bosch? Give me a fucking break.'

'Hey, it's a media-conscious town. People are plugged in. People sell stories, info, data all the time.'

McCaleb shook his head, refusing to buy into the possibility that the bartender in the vest had enough intelligence to put together what he was doing and to then make a call to a reporter.

Suddenly, he realized who did have the intelligence and information to do it. Buddy Lockridge. And if it had been him, it might as well have been McCaleb who leaked the story. He felt sweat start to warm his scalp as he thought about Lockridge hiding down on the lower deck while he had made his case against Bosch to Winston.

'Did you have anything to drink while you were in the bar? I hear you take a mess of pills every day. Mixing that with alcohol . . . you know, loose lips sink ships.'

Twilley had asked the question but McCaleb looked sharply at Winston. He was stung with a sense of betrayal by the whole scene and at how quickly things had shifted. But before he could say anything he saw the apology in her eyes and he knew she wished things had been handled differently. He finally looked back at Twilley.

'You think maybe I mixed a few too many drinks and pills, Twilley? That it? You think I started shooting my mouth off in the bar?'

'I don't think that. I'm just asking, okay? No reason to get defensive here. I'm just trying to figure out how this reporter knows what he thinks he knows.'

'Well, figure it out without me.'

McCaleb pushed back his chair to get up.

'Try the lechon asada,' he said. 'It's the best in the city.'

As he began to get up, Twilley reached across the table and grabbed his forearm.

'Come on, Terry, let's talk about this,' Twilley said.

'Terry, please,' Winston said.

McCaleb pulled his arm loose from Twilley's grip and stood up. He looked over at Winston.

'Good luck with these guys, Jaye. You'll probably need it.'

Then he looked down at Friedman and then Twilley.

'And fuck you guys very much.'

He made his way through the crowd of people waiting and out the front door. Nobody followed him.

He sat in the Cherokee parked on Sunset and watched the restaurant while letting the anger slowly leach out of his body. On one level McCaleb knew the moves Winston and her captain were making were the right moves. But on another he didn't like being moved out of his own case. A case was like a car. You could be driving it or riding in the front or back. Or you could be left on the side of the road as the car went by. McCaleb had just gone from having his hands on the wheel to thumbing it from the side of the road. And it hurt.

He began to think about Buddy Lockridge and how he would handle him. If he determined that it had been Buddy who had talked to McEvoy after eavesdropping on McCaleb's briefing of Winston on the boat, then he would cleanly sever all ties to him. Partner or not, he wouldn't be able to work with Buddy again.

He realized that Buddy had the number to his cell phone and could have been the one who gave it to McEvoy. He got the phone out and called his home. Graciela answered, Fridays being one of her half days at the school.

'Graciela, did you give my cell number to anybody lately?'

'Yes, a reporter who said he knew you and needed to speak with you right away. A Jack something. Why, is something wrong?'

'No, nothing's wrong. I was just checking.'

'Are you sure?'

McCaleb got a call-waiting beep. He looked at his watch. It was ten to one. McEvoy wasn't supposed to call back until after one.

'Yes, I'm sure,' he told Graciela. 'Look, I've got another call. I'll be home by dark tonight. I'll see you then.'

He switched to the other call. It was McEvoy, who explained that he was at the courthouse and had to get back into the trial at one or he'd lose his precious seat. He couldn't wait the full hour to call back.

'Can you talk now?' he asked.

'What do you want?'

'I need to talk to you.'

'You keep saying that. About what?'

'Harry Bosch. I'm working on a story about—'

'I don't know anything about the Storey case. Only what's on TV.'

'It's not that. It's about the Edward Gunn case.'

McCaleb didn't answer. He knew this was not good. Dancing with a reporter over something like this could only lead to trouble. McEvoy spoke into the silence.

'Is that what you wanted to see Harry Bosch about the other day when I saw you here? Are you working on the Gunn case?'

'Listen to me. I can honestly tell you that I am not working on the Edward Gunn case. Okay?'

Good, McCaleb thought. So far he hadn't lied.

'*Were* you working on the case? For the sheriff's department?'

'Can I ask you something? Who told you this? Who said I was working this case?'

'I can't answer that. I have to protect my sources. If you want to give me information I will protect your identity as well. But if I give up a source, I'm fucked in this business.'

'Well, I'll tell you what, Jack. I'm not talking to you unless you are talking to me, know what I mean? It's a two-way street. You want to tell me who is saying this shit about me and I'll talk to you. Otherwise, we've got nothing to say to each other.'

He waited. McEvoy said nothing.

'I thought so. Take it easy, Jack.'

He closed the phone. Whether McEvoy had mentioned his name or not to Captain Hitchens, it was clear that McEvoy was tapped in to a credible pipeline of information. And again McCaleb narrowed it down to one person besides himself and Jaye Winston.

'Goddamnit!' he said out loud in the car.

A few minutes after one he watched Jaye Winston come out of El Cochinito. McCaleb was hoping for the chance to corner her and talk to her alone, maybe tell her about Lockridge. But Twilley and Friedman followed her out and all three got into the same car. A bureau car.

McCaleb watched them pull out into traffic and drive off in the direction of downtown. He got out of the Cherokee and went back into the restaurant. He was starved. There were no tables available so he made an order to go. He'd eat in the Cherokee.

The old woman who took his order looked up at him with sad brown eyes. She said it had been a busy week and the kitchen had just run out of lechon asada.

27

John Reason surprised the spectators, the jurors and probably most of the media when he reserved his cross-examination of Bosch until the defense's case began, but it had been anticipated by the prosecution team. If the defense strategy was to shoot the messenger, that messenger was Bosch and the best place from which to take the shot was during the presentation of the defense's side. That way, Fowkkes's attack on Bosch could be part of an orchestrated attack on the entire case against David Storey.

Following a lunch break during which Bosch and the prosecutors were relentlessly pursued by the media with questions about Bosch's testimony, the prosecution began to move quickly with the momentum gained in the morning's session. Kretzler and Langwiser took turns examining a series of witnesses with short stays on the stand.

The first of these was Teresa Corazón, chief of the medical examiner's office. Under Kretzler's questioning, she testified to her findings during the autopsy and put Jody Krementz's time of death at some point between midnight and 2 A.M. on Friday, October 13. She also gave corroborating testimony on the rarity of autoerotic deaths involving female victims.

Once more Fowkkes reserved the right to question the witness during the defense phase of the trial. Corazón was dismissed after less than a half hour on the stand.

Now that his own testimony was completed – as far as the prosecution's case went – it was not vital for Bosch to be in the courtroom for every moment of the trial. While Langwiser called the next witness – a lab tech who would identify the hair samples gathered from the victim's body as belonging to Storey – Bosch walked Corazón to her car. They had been lovers many years before in what current culture would term a casual relationship. But while there may not have been any love involved, there had been nothing casual about it to Bosch. In his view it had been two people who looked at death every day pushing it away with the ultimate life-affirming act.

Corazón had broken it off after she was named to the top slot in the coroner's office. Their relationship since that point had been strictly professional, though Corazón's new position reduced her time in the autopsy suites and Bosch did not see her often. The Jody Krementz case was different. Corazón had instinctively known it might become a case that drew the bead of the media horde and had taken the autopsy herself. It had paid off. Her testimony would be seen across the nation and probably around the globe. She was attractive, smart, skilled and thorough. That half hour on the stand would be like a half-hour commercial for lucrative jobs as an independent examiner or commentator. Bosch knew one thing about her from his time with her: Teresa Corazón always had her eye on the next step.

She was parked in the garage next to the state parole office on the back side of the justice complex. They spoke of banalities – the weather, Harry's attempts to stop smoking – until Corazón brought the case up.

'It seems to be going well.'

'So far.'

'It'd be nice if we won one of these big ones for a change.'

'It would.'

'I watched you testify this morning. In my office I had the TV on. You did very well, Harry.'

He knew her tone. She was leading to something.

'But?'

'But you look tired. And you know they're going to come after you. This kind of case, if they destroy the cop they destroy the case.'

'O. J. one-oh-one.'

'Right. So are you ready for them?'

'I think so.'

'Good. Just rest up.'

'Easier said than done.'

As they approached the garage Bosch looked over at the parole office and saw a gathering of the staff out front for some kind of presentation. The group was standing below a banner hanging from the roof line that said WELCOME BACK THELMA. A man in a suit was presenting a plaque to a heavyset black woman who was leaning on a cane.

'Oh . . . that's that parole agent,' Corazón said. 'The one who got shot last year. By that hit man from Vegas?'

'Right, right,' Bosch said, remembering the story. 'She came back.'

He noticed that there were no television cameras recording the presentation. A woman got shot in the line of duty and then fought her way back to the job. It apparently wasn't worth wasting videotape over.

'Welcome back,' he said.

Corazón's car was on the second floor. It was a two-seat, shining black Mercedes.

'I see the outside work must be going pretty well,' Bosch said.

Corazón nodded.

'In my last contract I got four weeks' professional leave. I'm making the most of it. Trials, TV, that sort of thing. I did a case on that autopsy show on HBO, too. It airs next month.'

'Teresa, you're going to be world famous before we know it.'

She smiled and stepped close to him and straightened his tie.

'I know what you think about it, Harry. That's okay.'

'Doesn't matter what I think about it. Are you happy?'

She nodded.

'Very.'

'Then I'm happy for you. I better get back in there. I'll see you, Teresa.'

She suddenly rose on her toes and kissed him on the cheek. It had been a long time since he had gotten one of those.

'I hope you make it through, Harry.'

'Yeah, me too.'

Bosch stepped out of the elevator into the hallway and headed toward the Department N courtroom. He saw a line of people cordoned off by the courtroom door: people waiting for a spectator seat to possibly open. A few reporters were milling about the open door of the pressroom but everybody else was at stations, watching the trial.

'Detective Bosch?'

Bosch turned. Standing in a pay-phone alcove was Jack McEvoy, the reporter he had met the day before. He stopped.

'I saw you walk out and I hoped I'd catch you.'

'I have to get back in there.'

'I know. I just wanted to tell you that it is very important that I talk to you about something. The sooner the better.'

'What are you talking about? What's so important?'

'Well, it's about you.'

McEvoy stepped out of the alcove so that he was closer to Bosch and did not have to speak as loud.

'What about me?'

'Do you know you are under investigation by the sheriff's department?'

Bosch looked up the hall toward the courtroom door and then back at McEvoy. The reporter was slowly bringing a pad of paper and pen up in his hands. He was ready to take notes.

'Wait a minute.' Bosch put his hand on the notebook. 'What are you talking about? What investigation?'

'Edward Gunn, you remember him? He's dead and you're their suspect.'

Bosch just stared at him, his mouth coming slightly open.

'I wondered if you wanted to comment on this. You know, defend yourself. I'll be writing a story for next week's edition and wanted you to have the chance to tell your—'

'No, no comment. I have to get back.'

Bosch turned and walked a few paces toward the courtroom door but then stopped. He walked back to McEvoy, who was writing in the notebook.

'What are you writing? I didn't say anything.'

'I know. That's what I'm writing.'

McEvoy looked up from the notebook to him.

'You said next week,' Bosch said. 'When does it come out?'

'*New Times* is published every Thursday morning.'

'So until when do I have, if I decide to talk to you?'

'About Wednesday lunch. But that will be pressing it. I won't be able to do much then but drop in some quotes. The time to talk is now.'

'Who told you this? Who's your source?'

McEvoy shook his head.

'I can't discuss sources with you. What I want to talk about is this allegation. Did you kill Edward Gunn? Are you some kind of avenging angel? That's what they think.'

Bosch studied the reporter for a long moment before finally speaking.

'Don't quote me on this, but fuck you. You know what I mean? I don't know if this is a bullshit bluff or not, but let me give you some advice. You better make damn sure you've got it right before you put anything in that paper of yours. A good investigator always knows the motivation of his sources – it's called having a bullshit meter. Yours better be working real well.'

He turned and walked quickly to the courtroom door.

Langwiser had just finished with the hair specialist when Bosch came back into the courtroom. Once again Fowkkes stood up and reserved the right to recall the witness during the defense case.

While the witness came through the gate behind the attorneys' lectern, Bosch slipped past him and went to his seat at the prosecution table. He didn't look at or say anything to Langwiser or Kretzler. He folded his arms and looked down at the notepad he had left on the table. He realized he had adopted the same position and posture he had seen David Storey take at the defense table. The posture of a guilty man. Bosch quickly dropped his arms to his lap and looked up at the seal of the State of California which hung on the wall above the judge's bench.

Langwiser got up and called the next witness, a fingerprint technician. His testimony was quick and more corroboration of Bosch's testimony. It went unchallenged by Fowkkes. The technician was followed to the stand by the patrol officer who answered the first call from Krementz's roommate and then by his sergeant, who was the next to arrive.

Bosch barely listened to the testimony. There was nothing new in it and his mind was racing in another direction. He was thinking about McEvoy and the story he was working on. He knew he should inform Langwiser and

Kretzler but wanted time to think about things. He decided to hold off until after the weekend.

The victim's roommate, Jane Gilley, was the first witness to appear who was not part of the law enforcement community. She was tearful and sincere in her testimony, confirming details of the investigation already revealed by Bosch but also adding more personal bits of information. She testified about how excited Jody Krementz had been at the prospect of dating a major Hollywood player and how both of them had spent the day before her date getting manicures, pedicures and hair stylings.

'She paid for me,' Gilley testified. 'That was so sweet.'

Her testimony put a very human face on what so far had been an almost antiseptic analysis by law enforcement professionals of a murder.

When Gilley's examination by Langwiser was concluded, Fowkkes finally broke with his pattern and announced he had a few questions for the witness. He stepped to the lectern without any notes. He clasped his hands behind his back and leaned slightly forward to the microphone.

'Now, Ms. Gilley, your roommate was an attractive young woman, wasn't she?'

'Yes, she was beautiful.'

'And was she popular? In other words, did she date a lot of fellows?'

Gilley nodded hesitantly.

'She went out.'

'A lot, a little, how often?'

'It would be hard to say. I wasn't her social secretary and I have my own boyfriend.'

'I see. Then let's take, say, the ten weeks prior to her death. How many of those ten weeks would you say went by without Jody going out on a date?'

Langwiser stood up and objected.

'Your Honor, this is ridiculous. It has nothing to do with the night of October twelfth going into the morning of the thirteenth.'

'Oh, but Your Honor, I think it does,' Fowkkes responded. 'And I think Ms. Langwiser knows it does. If you allow me a little bit of string here, I will be able to quickly tie it up.'

Houghton overruled the objection and told Fowkkes to ask the question again.

'In the ten weeks prior to her death, how many weeks went by without Jody Krementz having a date with a man?'

'I don't know. Maybe one. Maybe none.'

'Maybe none,' Fowkkes repeated. 'And, Ms. Gilley, how many of those weeks would you say your roommate had at least two dates?'

Langwiser objected again but was overruled again.

'I don't know the answer,' Gilley said. 'A lot of them.'

'A lot of them,' Fowkkes repeated.

Langwiser rose and asked the judge to direct Fowkkes not to repeat the witness's answer unless it was in the form of a question. The judge complied and Fowkkes went on as if he had not been corrected at all.

'Were these dates all with the same fellow?'

'No. Different guys mostly. A few repeats.'

'So she liked to play the field, is that correct?'

'I guess so.'

'Is that a yes or no, Ms. Gilley?'

'It's a yes.'

'Thank you. In the ten weeks prior to her death, weeks in which you said she most often had at least two dates, how many different men did she see?'

Gilley shook her head in exasperation.

'I have no idea. I didn't count them. Besides, what does this have to do—'

'Thank you, Ms. Gilley. I would appreciate it if you would just answer the questions I pose to you.'

He waited. She said nothing.

'Now, did Jody ever encounter difficulties when she stopped dating a man? When she moved on to the next?'

'I don't know what you mean.'

'I mean were all the men happy not to have a return engagement?'

'Sometimes they'd get mad if she didn't want to go out again. Nothing serious.'

'No threats of violence? She wasn't afraid of anyone?'

'Not that she told me about.'

'Did she tell you about every man she dated?'

'No.'

'Now, on these dates, did she often bring the men back to the home you two shared?'

'Sometimes.'

'Did they stay over?'

'Sometimes, I don't know.'

'You often weren't there, is that correct?'

'Yes, I often stayed at my boyfriend's.'

'Why is that?'

She gave a short laugh.

'Because I love him.'

'Well, did you ever stay together overnight at your home?'

'I don't remember him ever staying over.'

'Why is that?'

'I guess because he lives alone. It was more private.'

'Isn't it true, Ms. Gilley, that you stayed overnight several times a week at your boyfriend's home?'

'Sometimes. So what?'

'And that this was because you were unhappy with your roommate's constant procession of overnight guests.'

Langwiser stood up.

'Your Honor, that's not even a question. I object to its form and content. Jody Krementz's lifestyle is not on trial here. David Storey is on trial for her murder and it's not fair for the defense to be allowed to go after someone who—'

'Okay, Ms. Langwiser, that's enough,' Judge Houghton said. He looked over at Fowkkes. 'Mr. Fowkkes, that's about all the string I'm going to allow you to run with in that direction. Ms. Langwiser makes her point. I want you to move on with this witness.'

Fowkkes nodded. Bosch studied him. He was a perfect actor. In his demeanor he was able to convey the frustration of a man being pulled back from a hidden truth. He wondered if the jury would see it as an act.

'Very well, Your Honor,' Fowkkes said, putting the frustration into the inflection of his voice. 'I have no further questions for this witness at this time.'

The judge adjourned for the afternoon break of fifteen minutes. Bosch ushered Gilley through the reporters, down the elevator and out to her car. He told her she had done very well and handled Fowkkes's cross-examination perfectly. He then joined Kretzler and Langwiser in the second-floor DA's office where the prosecution team had a temporary office during the trial. There was a small coffeemaker in the room and it was half-filled with coffee brewed during the morning break. There wasn't enough time for a fresh brew so they all drank the stale coffee while Kretzler and Langwiser considered the progress of the day.

'I think the she's-a-whore defense is going to backfire on them big time,' Langwiser said. 'They have to have more than that.'

'He's just trying to show there were a lot of men,' Kretzler said. 'And it could have been any of them. The shotgun defense. You shoot a lot of pellets and one's bound to hit the target.'

'It's still not going to work.'

'I'll tell you one thing, with John Reason reserving on all of these wits, we're moving really quickly. He keeps this up, we're going to finish our case Tuesday or Wednesday.'

'Good. I can't wait to see what they've got.'

'I can,' Bosch interjected.

Langwiser looked at him.

'Oh, Harry. You've weathered these storms before.'

'Yeah, but I've got a bad feeling about this one.'

'Don't worry about it,' Kretzler said. 'We're going to kick their ass across the courtroom. We're in the tube, man, and we ain't coming out.'

They put their three Styrofoam cups together in a toast.

Bosch's current partner, Jerry Edgar, and former partner, Kizmin Rider, testified during the afternoon session. Both were asked by the prosecutors to recall the moments after the search of David Storey's home when Bosch got into the car and reported to them that Storey had just bragged of committing the crime. Their testimony was solidly in tandem with Bosch's own testimony and would act to buttress the case against defense assaults on Bosch's character. Bosch also knew that the prosecutors hoped to gain additional credence with the jury because both Edgar and Rider were black. Five members of the jury and the two alternates were black. In a time when the veracity of any white police officer in Los Angeles would fall under suspicion by black jurors, having Edgar and Rider join a line of solidarity with Bosch was a plus.

Rider testified first and Fowkkes passed on cross-examination. Edgar's testimony mirrored hers but he was asked additional questions because he had delivered the second search warrant issued in the case. This one was a court order seeking hair and blood samples from David Storey. It had been approved and signed by a judge while Bosch was in New York following the *Architectural Digest* lead and Rider was on a Hawaiian vacation planned before the murder. With a patrol officer in tow, Edgar had once again appeared at Storey's house at 6 A.M. with the warrant. He testified that Storey kept them waiting outside while he contacted his lawyer, who by now was the criminal defense attorney J. Reason Fowkkes.

Once Fowkkes was apprised of the situation he told Storey to cooperate and the suspect was taken to Parker Center in downtown where samples of his pubic hair, scalp hair and blood were collected by a lab nurse.

'Did you at any point during this traveling time and collection process question the defendant about the crime?' Kretzler asked.

'No, I did not,' Edgar responded. 'Before we left his residence he gave me his phone and I spoke to Mr. Fowkkes. He told me his client did not wish to be questioned or harassed, as he put it, in any way. So we basically drove in silence – at least on my part. And we didn't talk at Parker Center either. When we were finished, Mr. Fowkkes was there and he drove Mr. Storey home.'

'Did Mr. Storey make any unsolicited comments to you during the time he was with you?'

'Just one.'

'And where was that?'

'In the car while we were driving to Parker Center.'

'And what did he say?'

'He was looking out the window and just said, "You people are fucked if you think I'm going down for this." '

'And was this piece of conversation tape-recorded?'

'Yes, it was.'

'Why is that?'

'Because of his earlier admission to Detective Bosch, we thought there was a chance he might go ahead and make another statement like that. On the day I served the hair and blood warrant, I used a car borrowed from the narcotics unit. It's a car they use for making street buys. It is wired for sound.'

'Did you bring the tape from that day with you, Detective?'

'Yes.'

Kretzler introduced the tape as evidence. Fowkkes objected, saying that Edgar had already testified as to what was said and the audio wasn't necessary. Again the judge overruled and the tape was played. Kretzler started the tape well before the statement made by Storey so that the jurors would hear the hum of the car engine and traffic noise and know that Edgar did not violate the defendant's rights by questioning him in order to elicit the statement.

When the tape came to Storey's comment, the tone of arrogance and even hate for his investigators came through loud and clear.

Wanting that tone to be what carried the jurors into the weekend, Kretzler ended his questioning of Edgar.

Fowkkes, perhaps understanding the ploy, said he would have a brief cross-examination. He proceeded to ask Edgar a series of innocuous questions that added little to the record in favor of the defense or disfavor of the prosecution. At precisely 4:30 P.M. he ended the cross-examination and Judge Houghton promptly recessed for the weekend.

As the courtroom emptied into the hallway, Bosch looked around for McEvoy but didn't see him. Edgar and Rider, who had hung around after her testimony, came up to him.

'Harry, how 'bout we go get a drink?' Rider said.

'How 'bout we go get drunk?' Bosch replied.

28

They waited until ten-thirty Saturday morning for their charter clients to arrive but no one showed. McCaleb was sitting silently on the gunwale in the stern doing a slow burn over everything. The missing charter, his dismissal from the case, the most recent phone call from Jaye Winston, everything. Before he left the house Winston had called to apologize for how things had gone the day before. He feigned indifference and told her to forget about it. And he still didn't tell her about Buddy Lockridge overhearing them on the boat two days earlier. When Jaye said Twilley and Friedman had decided it would be best if he returned the copies of all the documents relating to the case, he told her to tell them they could come get them if they wanted them. He said he had a charter and had to go. They abruptly said good-byes and hung up.

Raymond was bent over the stern, fishing with a little spinner reel McCaleb had gotten him after they moved to the island. He was looking through the clear water at the moving shapes of the orange garibaldi fish twenty feet below. Buddy Lockridge was sitting in the fighting chair reading the Metro section of the *Los Angeles Times*. He seemed as relaxed as a summer wave. McCaleb had not yet confronted him with his suspicions that he was the leak. He had been waiting for the right moment.

'Hey, Terror, you see this story?' Lockridge said. 'About Bosch giving his testimony yesterday in Van Nuys court?'

'Nope.'

'Man, what they're hinting at here is that this director's a serial killer. Sounds like one of your old cases. And here the guy on the witness stand putting the finger on him is a—'

'Buddy, I told you, don't talk about that. Or did you forget what I said?'

'Okay, sorry. I was just saying, if this ain't irony I don't know what is, that's all.'

'Fine. Leave it at that.'

McCaleb checked his watch again. The clients should have been there at ten. He straightened up and went to the salon door.

'I'll make some calls,' he said. 'I don't want to be waiting around all day for these people.'

At the little chart table in the boat's salon he opened a drawer and took out the clipboard where they attached the charter reservations. There were only two pages on it. The current day's charter and a reservation for the following Saturday. The winter months were slow. He looked at the information on the top sheet. He was unfamiliar with it because Buddy had taken the reservation. The charter was for four men from Long Beach. They were supposed to come over Friday night and stay at the Zane Grey. A four-hour charter – ten to two on Saturday – and then they'd take a late ferry back to overtown. Buddy had taken the organizer's home number and the name of the hotel as well as a deposit of half the charter fee.

He looked at the list of hotels and phone numbers taped to the chart table and called the Zane Grey first. He quickly learned that no one with the charter organizer's name – the only one of the four names McCaleb had – was staying at the hotel. He then called the man's home number and got his wife. She said her husband wasn't home.

'Well, we're kind of waiting for him on a boat over here on Catalina. Do you know if he and his friends are on their way?'

There was a long silence.

'Ma'am, you there?'

'Uh, yes, yes. It's just that, they're not going fishing today. They told me they canceled that trip. They're out golfing right now. I can give you my husband's cell phone if you would like. You could talk—'

'That's not necessary, ma'am. Have a nice day.'

McCaleb closed his phone. He knew exactly what had happened. Neither he nor Buddy had checked the answering service that handled calls to the phone number they had placed on their charter ads in various phone books and fishing publications. He called the number now, punched in the code and, sure enough, there had been a message waiting since Wednesday. The party canceled the charter. They'd reschedule later.

'Yeah, sure,' McCaleb said.

He erased the message and closed the phone. He felt like throwing it through the glass slider at Buddy's head but he tried to calm himself. He walked into the little galley and got a quart carton of orange juice out of the cooler. He took it out with him to the stern.

'No charter today,' he said before taking a long drink from the carton.

'Why not?' Raymond asked, his disappointment obvious.

McCaleb wiped his mouth on the sleeve of his long-sleeve T-shirt. 'They canceled.'

Lockridge looked up from the newspaper and McCaleb hit him with a laser stare.

'Well, we keep the deposit, right?' Buddy asked. 'I took a two-hundred-dollar deposit on Visa.'

'No, we don't keep the deposit because they canceled on Wednesday.

We've both been too *busy* I guess to check the charter line like we're supposed to.'

'Ah, fuck! That's my fault.'

'Buddy, not in front of the boy. How many times do I have to tell you that?'

'Sorry. Sorry.'

McCaleb continued to stare at him. He had not wanted to talk about the leak to McEvoy until after the charter because he needed Buddy's help running a four-man fishing party. Now it didn't matter. Now was the time.

'Raymond,' he said while still staring at Lockridge. 'Do you still want to earn your money?'

'Yeah.'

'You mean "yes," don't you?'

'Yeah. I mean, yes. Yes.'

'Okay, then reel in, hook your line and start taking these rods in and put them in the rack. Can you do that?'

'Sure.'

The boy quickly reeled in his line, took off his bait and threw it into the water. He attached the hook to one of the rod's eyelets and then leaned it in the corner of the stern so he could take it home with him. He liked to practice his casting technique on the rear deck of the house, dropping a rubber practice weight onto the roofs and backyards below.

Raymond started taking the deep-sea rods out of the holders where Buddy had placed them in preparation for the charter. Two by two he took them into the salon and put them in the overhead racks. He had to stand on the couch to do it but it was an old couch in dire need of a new slipcover and McCaleb didn't care about it.

'Something wrong, Terror?' Buddy tried. 'It's just a charter, man. We knew it was going to be slow this month.'

'It's not the charter, Bud.'

'Then what? The case?'

McCaleb took a smaller gulp of juice and put the carton down on the gunwale.

'You mean the case I'm not on anymore?'

'I guess. I don't know. You're not on it anymore? When did that—'

'No, Buddy, I'm not on it. And there's something I want to talk to you about.'

He waited for Raymond to move another set of rods into the salon.

'You ever read the *New Times*, Buddy?'

'You mean that free weekly?'

'Yeah, that free weekly. The *New Times*, Buddy. Comes out every Thursday. There's always a stack in the laundry building at the marina. In fact, why am I asking this? I know you read the *New Times*.'

Lockridge's eyes suddenly fell to the deck. He looked crestfallen with guilt. He brought one hand up and rubbed his face. He kept it over his eyes when he spoke.

'Terry, I'm sorry. I never thought it would get back to you. What happened?'

'What's the matter, Uncle Buddy?'

It was Raymond in the door of the salon.

'Raymond, would you go inside and close that door for a few minutes?' McCaleb said. 'You can put on the TV. I need to talk to Buddy by myself.'

The boy hesitated, staring the whole time at Buddy covering his face.

'Raymond, please. And take this back to the cooler.'

The boy finally stepped out and took the orange juice carton. He went back in and slid the door closed. McCaleb looked back at Lockridge.

'How could you not think it would get back to me?'

'I don't know. I just thought nobody would know.'

'Well, you were wrong. And it has caused me a lot of trouble. But most of all it's a fucking betrayal, Buddy. I just can't believe you would do something like this.'

McCaleb glanced at the glass door to make sure the boy wasn't in earshot. There was no sign of Raymond. He must've gone down to one of the staterooms. McCaleb realized his breathing was way up. He was so angry he was hyperventilating. He had to end this and calm down.

'Does Graciela have to know about it?' Buddy asked in a pleading voice.

'I don't know. It doesn't matter what she knows. What matters is that we had this relationship and then you do something like this behind my back.'

Lockridge still hid his eyes behind his hand.

'I just didn't think it would mean that much to you, even if you found out. It was no big deal. I'm—'

'Don't try to mitigate it or tell me what kind of deal it is, okay? Don't even talk to me in that pleading, whiny voice. Just shut up.'

McCaleb walked to the stern, pressing his thighs against the padded combing. His back to Lockridge, he looked up the hillside above the commercial part of the little town. He could see his house. Graciela was on the deck holding the baby. She waved and then held Cielo's hand up in a baby wave. McCaleb waved back.

'What do you want me to do?' Buddy said from behind him. His voice was more controlled now. 'What do you want me to say? I won't do it again? Fine, I won't do it again.'

McCaleb didn't turn around. He continued looking up at his wife and his daughter.

'It doesn't matter what you won't do again. The damage is done. I have to think about this. We're partners as well as friends. Or we were, at least. All I want now is for you to just go. I'm going inside with Raymond. Take the skiff and go back to the pier. Take a ferry back tonight. I just don't want you around here, Buddy. Not now.'

'How will you guys get back to the pier?'

It was a desperate question with an obvious answer.

'I'll call the water taxi.'

'We've got a charter next Saturday. It's five people and—'

'I'll worry about Saturday when I come to it. I can cancel it if I have to or turn it over to Jim Hall's charter.'

'Terry, are you sure about this? All I did was—'

'I'm sure. Go on, Buddy. I don't want to talk anymore.'

McCaleb turned from the view and walked past Lockridge and to the salon door. He opened it and stepped in, then slid the door closed behind him. He didn't look back at Buddy. He went to the chart table and got an envelope out of the drawer. He slipped a five-dollar bill from his pocket into it, sealed it and wrote Raymond's name on it.

'Hey, Raymond, where are you?' he called out.

For dinner they had grilled cheese sandwiches and chili. The chili was from the Busy Bee. McCaleb had picked it up on his way up from the boat with Raymond.

McCaleb sat across the table from his wife with Raymond to his left and the baby to his right in a jumper seat perched on the table. They were eating inside as an evening fog had enshrouded the island in a chilly grip. McCaleb remained morosely quiet through the meal, as he had been through much of the day. When they had come back early, Graciela decided to keep her distance. She took Raymond for a hike in the Wrigley Botanical Garden in Avalon Canyon. McCaleb was left with the baby, who fussed most of the day. He didn't mind, though. It took his mind off things.

Finally, at dinner, there was no avoiding each other. McCaleb had made the sandwiches so he was the last to sit down. He had barely begun eating when Graciela asked him what his trouble was.

'Nothing,' he said. 'I'm fine.'

'Raymond said you and Buddy had an argument.'

'Maybe Raymond should mind his own business.'

He looked at the boy as he said this and Raymond looked down at his food.

'That's not fair, Terry,' Graciela said.

She was right. McCaleb knew it. He reached over and tousled the boy's hair. It was so soft. He liked doing it. He hoped the gesture conveyed his apology.

'I'm off the case because Buddy leaked it to a reporter.'

'What?'

'We came up – I came up – with a suspect. A cop. Buddy overheard me telling Jaye Winston about my findings. He turned around and told a reporter. The reporter turned around and started making calls. Jaye and her captain think I was the leak.'

'That doesn't make sense. Why would Buddy do that?'

'I don't know. He didn't say. Actually, he did say. He said he didn't think I'd care or that it mattered. Words to that effect. That was today on the boat.'

He gestured toward Raymond, meaning this was the tense conversation he had caught part of and told Graciela about.

'Well, did you call Jaye and tell her it was him?'

'No, it doesn't matter. It came through me. I was dumb enough to let him on the boat. Can we talk about something else? I'm tired of thinking and talking about this.'

'Fine, Terry, what else do you want to talk about?'

He was silent. She was silent. After a long moment he started to laugh.

'I can't think of anything right now.'

Graciela finished eating a bite of her sandwich. McCaleb looked over at Cielo, who was looking at a blue-and-white ball that was suspended over her on a wire attached to the side of her bouncer seat. She was trying to reach for it with her tiny hands but couldn't quite make it. McCaleb could see her getting frustrated and he understood the feeling.

'Raymond, tell your father what you saw today in the gardens,' Graciela said.

She had recently begun referring to McCaleb as Raymond's father. They had adopted him but McCaleb didn't want to put any pressure on the boy to think of or refer to him as his father. Raymond usually called him Terry.

'We saw a Channel Islands fox,' he said now. 'It was hunting in the canyon.'

'I thought foxes hunted at night and slept during the day.'

'Well, somebody woke him up then because we saw him. He was big.'

Graciela nodded, confirming the sighting.

'Pretty cool,' McCaleb said. 'Too bad you didn't get a picture.'

They ate in silence for a few minutes. Graciela used her napkin to clean spittle off the baby's chin.

'Anyway,' McCaleb said, 'I'm sure you're happy that I'm off it and things will be normal around here again.'

Graciela looked at him.

'I want you to be safe. I want the whole family to be together and safe. That's what makes me happy, Terry.'

He nodded and finished his sandwich. She continued.

'I want you to be happy but if that means working these cases, then that is a conflict with your personal well-being as far as your health is concerned and the well-being of this family.'

'Well, you don't have to worry about it anymore. I don't think anybody will come calling on me again after this.'

He got up to clear the table. But before picking up plates he leaned over his daughter's chair and bent the wire so that the blue-and-white ball would be within her reach.

'It's not supposed to be like that,' Graciela said.

McCaleb looked at her.

'Yes, it is.'

29

McCaleb stayed up into the early morning hours with the baby. He and Graciela alternated nights on duty so that at least one of them got a decent night of sleep. Cielo seemed to have an almost hourly feed clock. Each time she awoke he would feed her and walk her through the dark house. He would gently pat her back until he heard her burp and then he would put her down again. In an hour the process would begin again.

After each cycle McCaleb would walk through the house and check the doors. It was a nervous habit, his routine. The house, by virtue of being up on the hillside, was fogged in tight. Looking through the rear windows, he couldn't even see the lights of the pier down below. He wondered if the fog stretched across the bay to the mainland. Harry Bosch's house was up high. He wondered if he was standing at his window looking into the misty nothingness as well.

In the morning Graciela took the baby and McCaleb, exhausted from the night and everything else, slept until eleven. When he came to he found the house to be quiet. In his T-shirt and boxer shorts he wandered down the hall and found the kitchen and family room empty. Graciela had left a note on the kitchen table saying she had taken the children to St. Catherine's for the ten o'clock service and then to the market afterward. The note said they'd be back by noon.

McCaleb went to the refrigerator and got out the gallon jug of orange juice. He poured a full glass and then took his keys off the counter and went back into the hallway to the locking cabinet. He opened it up and got out a plastic Ziploc bag containing a morning dose of the drug therapy that kept him alive. The first of every month he and Graciela carefully put together the doses and put them in plastic bags marked with dates and whether they were the A.M. or P.M. dosage. It made it easier than having to open dozens of pill bottles twice a day.

He took the bag back to the kitchen and began taking the pills two and three at a time with gulps of juice. As he followed this routine he looked through the kitchen window and down to the harbor below. The fog had moved out. It was still misty but clear enough for him to see *The Following Sea* and a skiff tied at its fantail.

He went to one of the kitchen drawers and pulled out the set of binoculars Graciela liked to use when she was watching him on the boat heading in or out of the harbor with a charter party. He went out onto the deck and to the railing. He focused the binoculars. There was no one in the cockpit or up on the bridge of the boat. His view could not penetrate the reflective film on the sliding door of the salon. He moved his focus to the skiff. It was weathered green with a one-and-a-half-horse outboard. He recognized it as being one of the rentals from the concession on the pier.

McCaleb went back inside and left the binoculars on the counter while he swiped the remaining pills into his hand. He took them and the orange juice back to the bedroom. He quickly ingested the pills while he got dressed. He knew Buddy Lockridge would not have rented a boat to get to *The Following Sea*. Buddy knew which Zodiac was McCaleb's and would simply have borrowed that.

Somebody else was on his boat.

It took him twenty minutes to walk down to the pier because Graciela had the golf cart. He went to the boat rental booth first to ask who had rented the boat but the window was closed and there was a sign with a clock face that said the operator would not be back until twelve-thirty. McCaleb checked his watch. It was ten after twelve. He couldn't wait. He went down the ramp to the skiff dock and stepped onto his Zodiac and started the engine.

As McCaleb moved down the fairway toward *The Following Sea* he studied the side windows of the salon but still could not see any movement or indication that someone was on the boat. He cut the engine on the Zodiac when he was twenty-five yards away and the inflatable skiff glided the rest of the way silently. He unzipped the pocket of his windbreaker and removed the Glock 17, his service weapon from his time with the bureau.

The Zodiac bumped lightly into the fantail next to the rental skiff. McCaleb first looked into the skiff but saw nothing other than a life vest and a flotation cushion, nothing that indicated who had rented the boat. He stepped onto the fantail and while crouched behind the stern wrapped the Zodiac's line around one of the rear cleats. He looked over the transom and saw only himself in the sliding door. He knew he would have to approach the door not knowing if there would be someone on the other side watching him come in.

He crouched down again and looked around. He wondered if he should retreat and come back with the harbor patrol boat. After a moment he decided against it. He glanced up the hill at his house and then raised himself and swung his body over the transom. With the gun carried low and hidden behind his hip he walked to the door and looked down at the lock. There was no damage or indication it had been tampered with. He pulled the handle and the door slid open. McCaleb was sure he had locked it the day before when leaving with Raymond.

He stepped inside. The salon was empty, no sign of intruder or burglary. He slid the door closed behind him and listened. The boat was silent. There was the sound of water lapping against the outside surfaces and that was it. His eyes moved toward the steps leading to the lower-deck staterooms and the head. He moved that way, raising the gun in front of him now.

On the second of the four steps down McCaleb hit a cracked board that sighed with his weight. He froze and listened for a response. There was only silence and the relentless sound of water against the sides of the boat. At the bottom of the stairs was a short hallway with three doors. Directly ahead was the forward stateroom, which had been converted into an office and file storage room. To the right was the master stateroom. To the left was the head.

The door to the master stateroom was closed and McCaleb could not remember if it had been that way when he had left the boat twenty-four hours earlier. The door to the head was wide open and hooked on the inside wall so it wouldn't swing and slam when the boat was moving. The office door was partially open and swaying slightly with the movement of the boat. There was a light on inside the room and McCaleb could tell it was the light over the desk, which was built into the lower berth of a set of bunk beds to the left of the door. McCaleb decided he would check the head first, followed by the office and then the master last. As he approached the head he realized that he smelled cigarette smoke.

The head was empty and too small to be used as a hiding place anyway. As he turned toward the office door and raised his weapon, a voice called out from within.

'Come on in, Terry.'

He recognized the voice. He cautiously stepped forward and used his free hand to push open the door. He kept the gun raised.

The door swung open and there was Harry Bosch sitting at the desk, his body in a relaxed posture, leaning back and looking toward the door. Both his hands were in sight. Both were empty except for the unlit cigarette between two fingers of his right hand. McCaleb slowly moved into the small room, still holding the gun up and aimed at Bosch.

'You going to shoot me? You want to be my accuser *and* my executioner?'

'This is breaking and entering.'

'Then I guess that makes us even.'

'What are you talking about?'

'That little dance at my place the other night, what do you call that? "Harry, I gotta couple more questions about the case." Only you never asked any real questions, did you? Instead, you take a look at my wife's picture and ask about that, and you ask about the picture in the hallway and you drink my beer and, oh, yeah, you tell me all about finding God in your baby daughter's blue eyes. So what do you call all of that, Terry?'

Bosch casually turned the chair and glanced over his shoulder at the desk. McCaleb looked past him and saw his own laptop computer was open and turned on. On the screen he could see that Bosch had called up the file containing the notes for the profile he was going to compose until everything changed the day before. He wished he had protected it with a password.

'It feels like breaking and entering to me,' Bosch said, his eyes on the screen. 'Maybe worse.'

In Bosch's new posture the leather bomber jacket he was wearing fell open and McCaleb could see the pistol holstered on his hip. He continued to hold his own weapon up and ready.

Bosch looked back at him.

'I didn't get a chance to look at all of this yet. Looks like a lot of notes and analysis. Probably all first-rate stuff, knowing you. But somehow, someway, you got it wrong, McCaleb. I'm not the guy.'

McCaleb slowly slid back into the lower berth of the opposite set of bunks. He held the gun with a little less precision now. He sensed there was no immediate danger from Bosch. If he had wanted to, he could have ambushed him as he'd come in.

'You shouldn't be here, Harry. You shouldn't be talking to me.'

'I know, anything I say can and will be used against me in a court of law. But who am I going to talk to? You put the bead on me. I want it off.'

'Well, you're too late. I'm off the case. And you don't want to know who's on it.'

Bosch just stared at him and waited.

'The bureau's civil rights division. You think Internal Affairs has been a pain in your ass? These people live and breathe for one thing, taking scalps. And an LAPD scalp is worth more than Boardwalk and Park Place put together.'

'How'd that happen, the reporter?'

McCaleb nodded.

'I guess that means he talked to you, too.'

Bosch nodded.

'Tried to. Yesterday.'

Bosch looked around himself, noticed the cigarette in his hand and put it in his mouth.

'You mind if I smoke?'

'You already have been.'

Bosch pulled a lighter out of his jacket pocket and lit the cigarette. He pulled the trash can out from beneath the desk and next to his seat to be used as an ashtray.

'Can't seem to quit these.'

'Addictive personality. A good and bad attribute in a detective.'

'Yeah, whatever.'

He took a hit off the cigarette.

'We've known each other for what is it, ten, twelve years?'

'More or less.'

'We worked cases and you don't work a case with somebody without taking some kind of measure. Know what I mean?'

McCaleb didn't answer. Bosch flicked the cigarette on the side of the trash can.

'And you know what bothers me, even more than the accusation itself? It's that it came from you. It's how and why you could think this. You know, what was the measure you took of me that allowed you to make this jump?'

McCaleb gestured with both hands as if to say the answer was obvious.

'People change. If there was anything I learned about people from my job, it's that any one of us is capable of anything, given the right circumstances, the right pressures, the right motives, the right moment.'

'That's all psycho-bullshit. It doesn't . . .'

Bosch's sentence trailed off and he didn't finish. He looked back at the computer and the papers spread across the desk. He pointed the cigarette at the laptop's screen.

'You talk about darkness . . . a darkness more than night.'

'What about it?'

'When I was overseas . . .' He dragged deeply on the cigarette and exhaled, tilting his head back and shooting the smoke toward the ceiling. '. . .I was put into the tunnels and let me tell you, you want darkness? That was darkness. Down in there. Sometimes you couldn't see your fucking hand three inches in front of your face. It was so dark it hurt your eyes from straining to see just anything. Anything at all.'

He took another long hit from the cigarette. McCaleb studied Bosch's eyes. They were staring blankly at the memory. Then suddenly he was back. He reached down and ground the half-finished cigarette into the inside edge of the can and dropped it in.

'This is my way of trying to quit. I smoke these shitty menthol things and never more than a half at a time. I'm down to about a pack a week.'

'It's not going to work.'

'I know.'

He looked up at McCaleb and smiled crookedly in a sort of apologetic way. Quickly his eyes changed and he moved back to his story.

'And then sometimes it wasn't that dark down there. In the tunnels. Somehow there was just enough light to make your way. And the thing is, I never knew where it came from. It was like it was trapped down there with the rest of us. My buddies and me, we called it lost light. It was lost but we found it.'

McCaleb waited but that was all Bosch said.

'What are you telling me, Harry?'

'That you missed something. I don't know what it is but you missed something.'

He held McCaleb with his dark eyes. He reached back to the desk and picked up the stack of copied documents from Jaye Winston. He tossed them across the small room onto McCaleb's lap. McCaleb made no move to catch them and they spilled to the floor in a jumble.

'Look again. You missed something and what you did see added up to me. Go back in and find the missing piece. It will change the addition.'

'I told you, man, I'm off it.'

'I'm putting you back on it.'

It was said with a tone of permanence, as if there was no choice for McCaleb.

'You've got till Wednesday. That writer's deadline. You have to stop his story with the truth. You don't, and you know what J. Reason Fowkkes will do with it.'

They sat in silence for a long moment looking at each other. McCaleb had met and talked with dozens of killers in his time as a profiler. Few of them readily admitted their crimes. So in that Bosch was no different. But the intensity with which he stared unblinkingly at him was something McCaleb had never seen before in any man, guilty or innocent.

'Storey's killed two women, and those are just the two we know about. He's the monster you spent your life chasing, McCaleb. And now ... and now you're giving him the key that unlocks the door to the cage. He gets out, he'll do it again. You know his kind. You know he will.'

McCaleb could not compete with Bosch's eyes. He looked down at the gun in his hands.

'What made you think I would listen, that I would do this?' he asked.

'Like I said, you take somebody's measure. I got yours, McCaleb. You'll do this. Or the monster you set free will haunt you the rest of your life. If God is really in your daughter's eyes, how will you be able to look at her again?'

McCaleb unconsciously nodded and immediately wondered what he was doing.

'I remember you once told me something,' Bosch said. 'You said if God is in the details, so is the Devil. Meaning, the person you are looking for is usually right there in front of us, hiding in the details all the time. I always remember that. It still helps me.'

McCaleb nodded again. He looked down at the documents on the floor.

'Listen, Harry, you should know. I was convinced about this when I took it to Jaye. I'm not sure I can be turned the other way. If you want help, I'm probably the wrong one to go to.'

Bosch shook his head and smiled.

'That's exactly why you're the right one. If you can be convinced, the world can be convinced.'

'Yeah, where were you on New Year's Eve? Why don't we start with that.'

Bosch shrugged his shoulders.

'Home.'

'Alone?'

Bosch shrugged his shoulders again and didn't answer. He stood up to go. He put his hands in the pockets of his jacket. He went through the narrow door first and up the steps to the salon. McCaleb followed, now holding the gun at his side.

Bosch slid the door open with his shoulder. As he stepped out onto the cockpit he looked up at the cathedral of the hillside, then he looked at McCaleb.

'So all that talk at my place about finding God's hand, was that bullshit? Interview technique or something? A statement designed to get a response that could fit into a profile?'

McCaleb shook his head.

'No, no bullshit.'

'Good. I was hoping it wasn't.'

Bosch climbed over the transom to the fantail. He untied his rental boat and got in and sat down on the rear bench. Before starting the engine he looked once more at McCaleb and pointed to the back of the boat.

'*The Following Sea*. What's that mean?'

'My father named the boat. It was his originally. The following sea is the wave that comes up behind you, that hits you before you see it coming. I guess he named the boat as sort of a warning. You know, always watch your back.'

Bosch nodded.

'Overseas we used to tell each other, "Watch six."'

Now McCaleb nodded.

'Same thing.'

They were silent a moment. Bosch put his hand on the boat motor's pull handle but didn't start the engine.

'You know the history of this place, Terry? I'm talking about back before the missionaries came.'

'No, do you?'

'A little. I used to read a lot of history books. When I was a kid. Whatever they had in the library. I liked local history. L.A. mostly, and California. I just liked reading it. We took a field trip here from the youth hall once. So I read up on it.'

McCaleb nodded.

'The Indians that lived out here – the Gabrielinos – were sun worshippers,' Bosch said. 'The missionaries came and changed all of that – in fact, they were the ones who called them Gabrielinos. They called themselves something else but I don't remember what it was. But before all that happened they'd been here and they worshipped the sun. It was so important to life on the island I guess they figured it had to be a god.'

McCaleb watched Bosch's dark eyes scan across the harbor.

'And the mainland Indians thought of the ones out here as these fierce wizards who could control weather and waves through worship and sacrifices to their god. I mean, they had to be fierce and strong to be able to cross the bay so they could trade their pottery and sealskins on the mainland.'

McCaleb studied Bosch, trying to get a bead on the message he was sure the detective was trying to convey.

'What are you saying, Harry?'

Bosch shrugged his shoulders.

'I don't know. I guess I'm saying that people find God where they need Him to be. In the sun, in a new baby's eyes ... in a new heart.'

He looked at McCaleb, his eyes as dark and as unreadable as the painted owl's.

'And some people,' McCaleb began, 'find their salvation in truth, in justice, in that which is righteous.'

Now Bosch nodded and offered his crooked smile again.

'That sounds good.'

He turned and started the engine with one pull. He then mock saluted McCaleb and pulled away, angling the rental boat back toward the pier. Not knowing the etiquette of the harbor, he cut across the fairway and between unused mooring buoys. He didn't look back. McCaleb watched him all the way. A man all alone on the water in an old wooden boat. And in that thought came a question. Was he thinking about Bosch or himself?

30

On the ferry ride back Bosch bought a Coke at the concession stand and hoped it would settle his stomach and prevent seasickness. He asked one of the stewards where the steadiest ride on the boat was and he was directed to one of the middle seats on the inside. He sat down and drank some of the Coke, then pulled the folded pages he had printed in McCaleb's office out of his jacket pocket.

He had printed two files before he had seen McCaleb approaching in the Zodiac. One was titled SCENE PROFILE and the other was called SUBJECT PROFILE. He had folded them into his jacket and disconnected the portable printer from the laptop before McCaleb entered the boat. He'd only had time to glance at them on the computer and now began a thorough reading.

He took the scene profile first. It was only one page. It was incomplete and appeared to be simply a listing of McCaleb's rough notes and impressions from the crime scene video.

Still, it gave an insight into how McCaleb worked. It showed how his observations of a scene turned into observations about a suspect.

SCENE
1. Ligature
2. Nude
3. Head wound
4. Tape/gag – 'Cave'?
5. Bucket?
6. Owl – watching over?

highly organized
detail oriented
statement – the SCENE is his statement
he was there – he watched (the owl?)
exposure = victim humiliation
   = victim hatred, contempt
bucket – remorse?
killer – PRIOR KNOWLEDGE of victim

personal knowledge – previous interaction
personal hatred
KILLER INSIDE THE WIRE
what is the statement?

Bosch reread the page and then thought about it. Though he did not have full knowledge of the crime scene from which McCaleb's notes were drawn, he was impressed by the leaps in logic McCaleb had made. He had carefully gone down the ladder to the point where he concluded that Gunn's killer was someone he knew, that it was someone who would be found inside the perimeter wire that circled Gunn's existence. It was an important distinction to make in any case. Investigative priorities were usually set upon the determination of whether the suspect being sought had intersected with the victim only at the point of the killing or before. McCaleb's read on the nuances of the scene were that the killer was someone known to Gunn, that there was a prelude to this final and fatal crossing of killer and victim.

The second page continued the listing of shorthand notes that Bosch assumed McCaleb planned to turn into a fleshed-out profile. As he read he realized that some of the word groupings were phrases McCaleb had taken from him.

SUSPECT
Bosch:
institutional – youth hall, Vietnam, LAPD
outsider – alienation
obsessive-compulsive
eyes – lost, loss
mission man – avenging angel
the big wheel always turning –
    nobody walks away
what goes around comes around

alcohol
divorce – wife? why?
alienation/obsession
mother
cases
justice system – 'bullshit'
carriers of the plague
guilt?

Harry = Hieronymus
owl = evil

evil = Gunn
death of evil = release stressors

paintings – demons – devils – evil
darkness and light – the edge
punishment
mother – justice – Gunn
God's hand – police – Bosch
punishment = God's work

A <u>darkness</u> more than night – Bosch

Bosch wasn't sure how to interpret the notes. His eyes were drawn to the last line and he repeatedly read it, unsure what it was that McCaleb was saying about him.

After a while he carefully folded the page closed and sat still for a long moment. It felt somehow surrealistic to be sitting there on the boat, having just tried to interpret someone else's notes and reasons as to why he should be considered a murder suspect. He felt himself getting queasy and realized he might be getting seasick. He gulped down the rest of the Coke and got up, putting the pages back into his jacket pocket.

Bosch headed toward the front of the boat and pushed through the heavy door to the bow. The cool air blasted him immediately. He could see the dim outline of the mainland in the distance. He kept his eyes on the horizon and breathed in deeply. In a few minutes he started feeling better.

31

McCaleb sat on the old couch in the salon thinking about his encounter with Bosch for a long time. It was the first time in all of his experiences as an investigator that a murder suspect had come to him to enlist his aid. He had to decide if it had been the act of a desperate or a sincere man. Or, possibly, something else. What if McCaleb had not noticed the rental skiff and come to the boat. Would Bosch have waited for him?

He went down to the front stateroom and looked at the documents spread on the floor. He wondered if Bosch had intentionally tossed them so that they would fall to the floor and become mixed up. Had he taken something?

He went to the desk and studied his laptop. It was not attached to the printer but he knew that didn't mean anything. He closed the file that was on the screen and opened the print manager window. He clicked the jobs file and saw that two files had been printed that day – the scene and suspect profiles. Bosch had taken them.

McCaleb imagined Bosch riding on the *Express* ferry back across, sitting by himself and reading what McCaleb had written about him. It made him feel uncomfortable. He didn't think any suspect he had ever profiled had read the report McCaleb had put together on him.

He shook it off and decided to occupy his mind with something else. He slid off the chair to his knees and began picking up the murder book reports, putting them into a neat pile first before worrying about putting them back in order.

Once he had the mess cleaned up he sat down at the desk, the reports in a squared-off pile in front of him. McCaleb took a blank page of typing paper out of a drawer and wrote on it with the thick black marker he used for labeling cardboard boxes containing his files.

YOU MISSED SOMETHING

He took a piece of tape off a dispenser on the desk and taped the page to the wall behind the desk. He looked at it for a long time. Everything Bosch had said to him came down to that one line. He now had to decide if it was true, if it was possible. Or if it was the last manipulation of a desperate man.

He heard his cell phone begin to chirp. It was in the pocket of his jacket, which he had left on the couch in the salon. He hustled up the stairs and grabbed the jacket. When he reached into the pocket his hand closed around his gun. He then tried the other pocket and got the phone. It was Graciela.

'We're home,' she said. 'I thought you'd be here. I thought maybe we could all go down to lunch at El Encanto.'

'Um ...'

McCaleb didn't want to leave the office or his thoughts about Bosch. But the last week had strained things with Graciela. He needed to talk to her about that, about how he saw things changing.

'Tell you what,' he finally said. 'I'm just finishing some stuff here. Why don't you take the kids down and I'll meet you there.'

He looked at his watch. It was quarter of one.

'Is one-thirty too late?'

'Fine,' she said abruptly. 'What stuff?'

'Oh, just ... I'm sort of wrapping up this thing for Jaye.'

'I thought you told me you were off it.'

'I am but I have all the reports and I wanted to write up my final ... you know, just wrap it up.'

'Don't be late, Terry.'

She said it with a tone that implied that he would miss more than his lunch if he was.

'I won't. I'll see you there.'

He closed the phone and went back down to the office. He looked at his watch again. He had about a half hour before he'd have to get on the skiff and go back to the pier. The El Encanto was about a five-minute walk from there. It was one of the few restaurants that remained open on the island during the winter months.

He sat down and started putting the stack of investigative documents in order. It was not a difficult task. Each page had a date stamp on the upper right-hand corner. But McCaleb stopped almost as soon as he started. He looked up at the message he had taped on the wall. He decided that if he was going to look for something he had not noticed before, that he had missed, he should come at the information from another angle. He decided not to put the documents in their correct order. Instead, he would read them in the random order they were now in. Doing it this way he would avoid thinking about the flow of the investigation and how one step followed the other. He would simply have each report to consider as a single piece of the puzzle. It was a simple mind trick but he had used it before on cases with the bureau. Sometimes it shook something new out, something he had previously missed.

He checked his watch again and began with the first document on the pile. It was the autopsy protocol.

32

McCaleb walked briskly to the front steps of the El Encanto. He saw his golf cart parked at the curb. Mostly, the carts on the island looked the same, but he could identify his because of the baby seat with the pink-and-white cushioning. His family was still here.

He went up the steps and the hostess, recognizing him as a local, pointed to the table where his family was seated. He hurried over and pulled out a chair next to Graciela. They were close to being finished. He noticed that the waitress had already left the check on the table.

'Sorry I'm late.'

He took a chip out of the basket at the center of the table and dragged it through the salsa and guacamole bowls before shoving it into his mouth. Graciela looked at her watch and then pierced him with her deep brown eyes. He weathered it and got ready for the next one which he knew was surely coming.

'I can't stay.'

She loudly put her fork down on her plate. She was finished.

'Terry . . .'

'I know, I know. But something's come up. I have to go across tonight.'

'What could've possibly come up? You're off the case. It's Sunday. People are watching football, not running around trying to solve murders that they're not even asked to.'

She pointed to a television mounted in the upper corner of the room. Three talking heads with thick necks sat at a counter with a football field behind them. McCaleb knew that the day's games would determine the Super Bowl contenders. He couldn't care less, though he did suddenly remember he had promised Raymond that they would watch at least one of the games together.

'I have been asked, Graciela.'

'What are you talking about? You said they asked you *off* the case.'

He told her about discovering Bosch on the boat that morning and what he had asked McCaleb to do.

'And this is the guy you told Jaye probably did it?'

McCaleb nodded.

'How'd he know where you lived?'

'He didn't. He knew about the boat, not where we live. You don't have to worry about that.'

'I think I do. Terry, you are going too far with this and you are going completely blind to the dangers to yourself and your family. I think—'

'Really? I think—'

He stopped and reached into his pocket and pulled out two quarters. He turned to Raymond.

'Raymond, are you finished eating?'

'Yeah.'

'You mean yes?'

'Yes.'

'Okay, take these. Go play the video machine over there by the bar.'

The boy took the quarters.

'You're excused.'

Raymond hesitantly hopped down and then trotted into the next room where there were tabletop video games that they had played before. He chose a game McCaleb knew was Pac-Man and sat down. He was not out of McCaleb's sight.

McCaleb looked back at Graciela, who had her purse up on her lap and was taking money out and putting it down on the check.

'Graciela, forget about that. Look at me.'

She finished with the money and pushed her wallet back into the purse. She looked at him.

'We have to go. CiCi has to take her nap.'

The baby was in her bouncing chair on the table, one hand grasping the blue-and-white ball on the wire.

'She's fine. She can sleep right there. Just listen to me for a minute.'

He waited and she put a conceding look on her face.

'All right. Say what you have to say and then I have to leave.'

McCaleb turned and leaned close to Graciela so that his words would be heard only by her. He noticed the edge of one of her ears poking through her hair.

'We are heading toward a big problem here, aren't we?'

Graciela nodded and immediately the tears came down her cheeks. It was as if his saying the words out loud had knocked down the thin defensive mechanism she had constructed inside to protect herself and her marriage. McCaleb pulled the unused napkin out from beneath his silverware setting and handed it to her. He then put his hand on the back of her neck and pulled her toward him and kissed her on the cheek. Over the top of her head he saw Raymond watching them with a scared look on his face.

'We've talked about this, Graci,' he began. 'You have it in your head that we can't have our home and our family and everything else if this is what I do. The problem is in that word "if." That is the mistake here. Because there is no "if" here. It's not "if this is what I do." It *is* what I do. And I've gone too long thinking otherwise, trying to convince myself of something else.'

More tears came and she held the napkin to her face. She cried silently but McCaleb was sure people in the restaurant had noticed and were watching them instead of the television above them. He checked on Raymond and saw the boy was back to playing the video game.

'I know,' Graciela managed to say.

He was surprised by her acknowledgment. He took it as a good sign.

'So then what do we do? I'm not talking about just now and this case. I mean, for now and forever. What do we do? Graci, I am tired of trying to be what I'm not and of ignoring the thing inside that I know is what I am truly all about. It took this case to finally make me realize it and admit it to myself.'

She didn't say anything. He wasn't expecting her to.

'You know I love you and the kids. That's not the issue. I think I can have both and you think I can't. You've adopted this one-or-the-other attitude and I don't think it's right. Or fair.'

He knew his words were hurting her. He was drawing a line. One of them had to capitulate. He was saying it wasn't going to be him.

'Look, let's think about this. This isn't a good place to talk. What I am going to do is finish my work on this thing and then we'll sit down and talk about our future. Is that okay?'

She slowly nodded but didn't look at him.

'You do what you have to do,' she said in a tone McCaleb knew would make him feel guilty forever. 'I just hope you'll be careful.'

He pulled himself over and kissed her again.

'I've got too much here with you not to be.'

He got up and came around the table to the baby. He kissed her on top of the head and then unhitched the chair's safety belt and lifted her out.

'I'll take her down to the cart,' he said. 'Why don't you get Raymond?'

He carried the baby down to the cart and secured her in the safety seat. He put her bouncing chair in the rear storage compartment. Graciela came down with Raymond a few minutes later. Her eyes were swollen from the crying. McCaleb put his hand on Raymond's shoulder and walked him to the front passenger seat.

'Raymond, you're going to have to watch the second game without me. I have some work I have to do.'

'I can go with you. I can help you.'

'No, it's not a charter.'

'I know, but I can still help you.'

McCaleb knew Graciela was looking at him and he felt the guilt like the sun on his back.

'Thanks but maybe next time, Raymond. Put on your seat belt.'

Once the boy was safely in, McCaleb stepped back from the cart. He looked at Graciela, who was no longer looking at him.

'Okay,' he said. 'I'll be back as soon as I can. And I'll have the phone with me if you want to call.'

Graciela didn't acknowledge him. She pulled the cart away from the curb and headed up Marilla Avenue. He watched them until they were out of sight.

33

On the walk back to the pier his cell phone chirped. It was Jaye Winston returning his call. She was talking very quietly and said she was calling from her mother's house. McCaleb had difficulty hearing so he sat down on one of the benches along the casino walk. He leaned forward with his elbows on his knees, one hand holding the phone tightly to one ear, his other hand clasped over the other.

'We missed something,' he said. 'I missed something.'

'Terry, what are you talking about?'

'In the murder book. In Gunn's arrest record. He was—'

'Terry, what are you doing? You're off the case.'

'Says who, the FBI? I don't work for them anymore, Jaye.'

'Then says me. I don't want you getting any further—'

'I don't work for you, either, Jaye. Remember?'

There was a long silence on the phone.

'Terry, I don't know what you are doing but it's got to stop. You have no authority, no standing in this case anymore. If those guys Twilley and Friedman find out you're still snooping around on this, they can arrest you for interference. And you know they're just the type that will.'

'You want standing, I have standing.'

'What? I withdrew my authorization to you yesterday. You can't use me on this.'

McCaleb hesitated and then decided to tell her.

'I have standing. I guess you could say I'm working for the accused.'

Now Winston's silence was even longer. Finally she spoke, her words delivered very slowly.

'Are you telling me that you went to Bosch with this?'

'No. He came to me. He showed up on my boat this morning. I was right about the other night. The coincidence; me showing up at his place, then the call from his partner about you. He put it together. The reporter from the *New Times* called him, too. He knew what was going on without me having to tell him a thing. The point is, Jaye, none of that matters. What matters is that I think I jumped on Bosch too soon. I missed something and now I'm not so sure. There's a chance all of this could be a setup.'

'He's convinced you.'

'No, I convinced myself.'

There were voices in the background and Winston told McCaleb to hold on. He then heard voices muffled by a hand over the phone. It sounded like arguing. McCaleb stood up and continued walking toward the pier. Winston came back on in a few seconds.

'Sorry,' she said. 'This is not a good time. I'm in the middle of something right now.'

'Can we meet tomorrow morning?'

'What are you talking about?' Winston said, her voice almost shrill. 'You just told me you are working for the target of an investigation. I'm not going to meet with you. How the fuck would that look? Hold on—'

He heard her muffled voice apologizing for her language to someone. She then came back on the line.

'I really have to go.'

'Look, I don't care how it would look. I'm interested in the truth and I thought you would be, too. You don't want to meet me, fine, don't meet me. I've gotta go myself.'

'Terry, wait.'

He listened. She said nothing. He sensed that she was distracted by something there.

'What, Jaye?'

'What is this thing you said we missed?'

'It was in the arrest package from Gunn's last duice. I guess after Bosch told you he had spoken to him in lockup you pulled all the records. I just scanned through it the first time I looked at the book.'

'I pulled the records,' she said in a defensive tone. 'He spent the night of December thirtieth in the Hollywood tank. That's where Bosch saw him.'

'And he bonded out in the morning. Seven-thirty.'

'Yeah. Okay? I don't get it.'

'Look who bailed him out.'

'Terry, I'm at my parents'. I don't have—'

'Right, sorry. He was bailed out by Rudy Tafero.'

Silence. McCaleb was at the pier. He walked out toward the gangway that led down to the skiff dock and leaned on the railing. He cupped his free hand over his ear again.

'Okay, he was bailed out by Rudy Tafero,' Winston said. 'I assume he is a licensed bail bondsman. What does that mean?'

'You haven't been watching your TV. You're right, Tafero is a licensed bail bondsman – at least he put a license number on the bail sheet. But he's also a PI and security consultant. And – ready for this – he works for David Storey.'

Winston didn't say anything but McCaleb could hear her breathing into the phone.

'Terry, I think you better slow down. You are reading too much into this.'

'No coincidences, Jaye.'

'What coincidence? The man's a bail bondsman. It's what he does. He gets people out of jail. I'll bet you a box of doughnuts his office is right across the street from Hollywood station with all the others. He probably bails every third drunk and fourth prostitute out of the tank there.'

'You don't believe it's that simple and you know it.'

'Don't tell me what I believe.'

'This was when he was in the middle of preparing for Storey's trial. Why would Tafero come over and write a duice ticket himself?'

'Because maybe he's a one-man show and maybe, like I said, all he had to do was cross the street.'

'I don't buy it. And there's something else. On his booking slip it says Gunn got his one phone call at three A.M. December thirty-first. The number's on the slip – he called his sister in Long Beach.'

'Okay, what about it? We knew that.'

'I called her today and asked if she'd called a bondsman for him. She said no. She said she was tired of getting calls in the middle of the night and literally bailing him out all the time. She told him he was on his own this time.'

'So he went with Tafero. What about it?'

'How'd he get him? He already used his call.'

Winston had no answer for that. They were both silent for a while. McCaleb looked out across the harbor. The yellow taxi boat was moving slowly down one of the fairways, empty except for the man at the wheel. Men alone in their boats, McCaleb thought.

'What are you going to do?' Winston finally asked. 'Where are you going with this?'

'I'm coming back across tonight. Can you meet me in the morning?'

'Where? When?'

The tone of her voice revealed that she was put out by the prospect of a meeting.

'Seven-thirty, out front at the Hollywood station.'

There was a pause and then Winston said, 'Wait a minute, wait a minute. I can't do this. If Hitchens gets wind of it, that will be the end. He'll ship me out to Palmdale. I'll spend the rest of my career pulling bones out of the desert sand.'

McCaleb was ready for that protest.

'You said the bureau guys want the murder book back, right? You meet me, I'll have it with me. What's Hitchens going to say about that?'

There was silence as Winston considered this.

'Okay, that'll work. I'll be there.'

34

When Bosch got home that evening he found the message light on his phone machine was blinking. He pushed the button and listened to two messages, one from each of the prosecutors on the Storey case. He decided to call Langwiser back first. As he punched her number into the phone, he wondered what urgency had caused both members of the prosecution team to call him. He thought maybe they had been contacted by the FBI agents McCaleb had mentioned. Or possibly by the reporter.

'What's up?' he asked when Langwiser answered. 'With both of you guys calling me I know it must be big and bad.'

'Harry? How are you?'

'Hanging in. What do you two have cooking?'

'It's funny you should mention that. Roger's on his way over and I'm going to cook tonight. We're going to go over Annabelle Crowe's grand jury testimony one more time. You want to come by?'

He knew she lived up in Agua Dulce, an hour's drive north.

'Uh, you know what, I've been driving all day. Down to Long Beach and back. You think you really need me there?'

'Totally optional. Just didn't want you to feel left out. But that's not why we were calling.'

'What was the reason?'

He was in the kitchen, sliding a six-pack of Anchor Steam onto a shelf in the refrigerator. He pulled one bottle out of its sleeve and closed the door.

'Roger and I have been conferencing all weekend about this. We also talked to Alice Short about it.'

Alice Short was a chief deputy who was in charge of major trials. Their boss. It sounded as though they had been contacted about the Gunn case.

'What's the "it" you're talking about?' Bosch asked.

He slid the bottle into the opener and yanked down, popping the cap.

'Well, we think the case has really gone by the numbers. Really fallen together. In fact, it's bulletproof, Harry, and we think we should pull the trigger tomorrow.'

Bosch was quiet a moment while he tried to decipher all the weaponry coding.

'You're saying you're going to rest tomorrow?'

'We think so. We'll probably talk about it again tonight but we have Alice's blessing and Roger really thinks it's the right move. What we'd do is put on a bunch of cleanup wits in the morning and then bring Annabelle Crowe out after lunch. We'd end with her – a human story. She'll be our closer.'

Bosch was speechless. It might be the right move from a prosecutorial point of view. But that would put J. Reason Fowkkes in control of things as early as Tuesday.

'Harry, what do you think?'

He took a long pull on the bottle. The beer wasn't that cold. It had been in the car for a while.

'I think you only get one shot,' he said, continuing the weaponry imagery. 'You two better think long and hard about it tonight while you're making the pasta. You don't get a second chance to put on a case.'

'We know, Harry. And how'd you know I was making pasta?'

He could hear the smile in her voice.

'Lucky guess.'

'Well, don't worry, we'll think long and hard. We have been.'

She paused, allowing him a chance to respond but he was silent.

'In case we go this way, what's the status on Crowe?'

'She's waiting in the wings. Good to go.'

'Can you reach her tonight?'

'No problem. I'll tell her to be there by noon tomorrow.'

'Thanks, Harry. See you in the morning.'

They hung up. Bosch thought about things. He wondered if he should call McCaleb and tell him what was happening. He decided to wait. He walked out into the living room and turned on the stereo. The Art Pepper CD was still in the play slot. The music soon filled the room.

35

McCaleb was leaning against the Cherokee parked in front of the LAPD's Hollywood station when Winston pulled up in a BMW Z3 and parked. When she got out she saw McCaleb studying her car.

'I was running late. I didn't have time to pick up a company car.'

'I like your wheels. You know what they say about L.A., you are what you drive.'

'Don't start profiling me, Terry. It's too fucking early. Where's the book and the tape?'

He noted her profanity but kept his thoughts on that to himself. He pushed off the car and went around to the passenger side. He opened the door and took out the murder book and the crime scene tape. He handed them to her and she took them back to her car. McCaleb closed and locked the Cherokee, looking down through the window to the floor of the backseat where he had covered the Kinko's box with the morning newspaper. Before coming to the rendezvous he had gone to the twenty-four-hour shop on Sunset and photocopied the entire murder book. The tape was a problem; he didn't know where to get it dubbed on short notice. So he'd simply bought a videocassette at the Rite-Aid near the marina and slipped the blank tape into the case Winston had given him. It was his guess that she wouldn't check to make sure he had returned the correct tape.

When she came back from her car he pointed with his chin across the street.

'I guess I owe you a box of doughnuts.'

She looked. Across Wilcox from the station was a shabby two-story building with a handful of storefront bail bond operations with phone numbers advertised in each window in cheap neon, maybe to help prospective clients memorize them from the backseat of passing patrol cars. The middle business had a painted sign above the window: Valentino Bonds.

'Which one?' Winston asked.

'Valentino. As in Rudy Valentino Tafero. That's what they used to call him when he worked this side of the street.'

McCaleb appraised the small business again and shook his head.

'I still don't see how a neon bondsman and David Storey ever hooked up.'

'Hollywood is just street trash with money. So what are we doing here? I don't have a lot of time.'

'You bring your badge?'

She gave him a don't-fuck-with-me look and he explained what he wanted to do. They went up the steps and into the station. At the front desk Winston flashed her badge and asked for the A.M. watch sergeant. A man with Zucker on his name plate and sergeant's stripes on the sleeve of his uniform came out from the small office. Winston showed her badge again, introduced herself and then introduced McCaleb as her associate. Zucker knitted his healthy set of eyebrows together but didn't ask what associate meant.

'We're working a homicide case from New Year's Eve. The victim spent the night before in your tank. We—'

'Edward Gunn.'

'Right. You knew him?'

'He'd been in a few times. And of course I heard he won't be coming back.'

'We need to talk to whoever runs the tank on A.M. watch.'

'Well, that would be me, I guess. We don't have a specific duty. It's sort of catch as catch can around here. What do you want to know?'

McCaleb took a set of photocopies from the murder book out of his jacket pocket and spread them on the counter. He noticed Winston's look but ignored it.

'We're interested in how he made bail,' he said.

Zucker turned the pages around so he could read them. He put his finger on Rudy Tafero's signature.

'Says it right here. Rudy Tafero. He's got a place across the street. He came over and bailed him out.'

'Did someone call him?'

'Yeah, the guy did. Gunn.'

McCaleb tapped his finger on the copy of the booking slip.

'It says here that when he got his call he called this number. It's his sister.'

'Then she must've called Rudy for him.'

'So nobody gets two calls.'

'Nope, 'round here we're usually so busy they're lucky if they get the one.'

McCaleb nodded. He folded the photocopies and was about to put them back in his pocket when Winston took them from his hand.

'I'll hang on to those,' she said.

She slipped the folded copies into a back pocket of her black jeans.

'Sergeant Zucker,' she said. 'You wouldn't be the kind of nice guy who would call Tafero, being that he's former LAPD, and tip him that he had a potential fish over here in the tank, would you?'

Zucker stared at her for a moment, his face a stone.

'It's very important, Sergeant. If you don't tell us, it could come back on you.'

The stone cracked into a humorless smile.

'No, I'm not that kind of nice guy,' Zucker said. 'And I don't have any nice guys like that on A.M. watch. And speaking of which, I just got off shift which means I don't have to be talking to you anymore. Have a nice day.'

He started to step away from the counter.

'One last thing,' Winston said quickly.

Zucker turned back to her.

'Were you the one who called Harry Bosch and told him Gunn was in the tank?'

Zucker nodded.

'I had a standing request from him. Any and every time Gunn was brought in here, Bosch wanted to know about it. He'd come in and talk to the guy, try to get him to say something about that old case. Bosch wouldn't give up on it.'

'It says Gunn wasn't booked until two-thirty,' McCaleb said. 'You called Bosch in the middle of the night?'

'That was part of the deal. Bosch didn't care what time it was. And actually, the procedure was that I would page him and then he'd call in.'

'And that's what happened that last night?'

'Yeah, I paged and Bosch called in. I told him we had Gunn again and he came down to try to talk to him. I tried to tell him to wait until morning 'cause the guy was on his ass drunk – Gunn, I mean – but Harry came down anyway. Why are you asking so much about Harry Bosch?'

Winston didn't answer so McCaleb jumped in.

'We're not. We're asking about Gunn.'

'Well, that's all I know. Can I go home now? It's been a long one.'

'Aren't they all,' Winston said. 'Thank you, Sergeant.'

They stepped away from the counter and walked out to the front steps.

'What do you think?' Winston asked.

'He sounded legit to me. But you know what, let's watch the employee lot for a few minutes.'

'Why?'

'Humor me. Let's see what the sergeant drives home.'

'You're wasting my time, Terry.'

They got into McCaleb's Cherokee anyway and drove around the block until they came to the entrance–exit of the Hollywood station employee parking lot. McCaleb drove fifty yards past it and parked in front of a fire hydrant. He adjusted the side-view mirror so he could see any car that left the lot. They sat and waited in silence for a couple of minutes until Winston spoke.

'So if we are what we drive, what's this make you?'

McCaleb smiled.

'Never thought about it. A Cherokee . . . I guess that makes me the last of a breed or something.'

He glanced at her then looked back at the mirror.

'Yeah, and what about this coating of dust on everything, what does that—'

'Here we go. Think it's him.'

McCaleb watched a car leave the exit and turn left in their direction.

'Coming this way.'

Neither of them moved. The car drove up and stopped right next to them. McCaleb looked over casually and his eyes met Zucker's. The cop lowered his passenger-side window. McCaleb had no choice. He lowered his.

'You're parked in front of a plug there, Detective. Don't get a ticket.'

McCaleb nodded. Zucker saluted with two fingers and drove off. McCaleb noted that he was driving a Crown Victoria with commercial bumpers and wheels. It was a secondhand patrol car, the kind you pick up at auction for four hundred bucks and slap on an $89.95 paint job.

'Don't we look like a couple of assholes,' Winston said.

'Yeah.'

'So what's your theory about *that* car?'

'He's either an honest man or he drives the beater to work because he doesn't want people to see the Porsche.'

He paused.

'Or the Z3.'

He turned to her and smiled.

'Funny, Terry. Now what? Eventually, I have to get some real work done today. And I'm supposed to meet with your bureau buddies this morning as well.'

'Stick with me – and they aren't my buddies.'

He started the Cherokee and pulled away from the curb.

'You really think this car's dirty?' he asked.

36

The post office on Wilcox was a large World War II-era building with twenty-five-foot-high ceilings and murals depicting bucolic scenes of brotherhood and good deeds covering the upper walls. As they walked in, McCaleb's eyes scanned the murals but not for their artistic or philosophic merit. He counted three small cameras mounted above the public areas of the office. He pointed them out to Winston. They had a chance.

They waited in line and when it was their turn Winston flashed her badge and asked for the on-site security officer. They were directed to a door next to a row of vending machines and they waited nearly five minutes before it was opened and a small black man with gray hair looked out.

'Mr. Lucas?' Winston asked.

'That's right,' he said with a smile.

Winston showed the badge once more and introduced McCaleb simply by name. McCaleb had told her on the way over from Hollywood station that calling him an associate wasn't working.

'We're working a homicide investigation, Mr. Lucas, and an important piece of evidence is a money order that was purchased here and probably mailed here on December twenty-second.'

'The twenty-second? That's right in the Christmas rush.'

'That's right, sir.'

Winston looked at McCaleb.

'We noticed your cameras out there on the walls, Mr. Lucas,' she said. 'We'd be interested in knowing if you have a videotape from the twenty-second.'

'Videotape,' Lucas said, as if the word was foreign to him.

'You are the security officer here, right?' Winston said impatiently.

'Yes, I'm the security man. I run the cameras.'

'Can you take us back and show us your surveillance system, Mr. Lucas?' McCaleb said in a gentler tone.

'Yup, sure can. Just as soon as you get authorization I'll take you on back.'

'And how and where do we get authorization?' Winston asked.

'From L.A. Regional. Downtown.'

'Is there a specific person we talk to? We're on a homicide investigation, Mr. Lucas. Time is of the essence.'

'That would be Mr. Preechnar – he's a postal inspector – you would talk to. Yes.'

'Do you mind if we come back to your office and we call Mr. Preechnar together?' McCaleb asked. 'It would save us a lot of time and then Mr. Preechnar could just talk directly to you.'

Lucas thought about this for a moment and decided it was a good idea. He nodded.

'Let's see what we can do.'

Lucas opened the door and led them through a warren of huge mail baskets to a cubbyhole office with two desks squeezed together. On one of the desks was a video monitor with its screen cut into four camera views of the public area of the post office. McCaleb realized he had missed one of the cameras when he had searched the walls earlier.

Lucas ran his finger down a list of phone numbers taped to the top of the desk and made the call. Once he got ahold of his supervisor he explained the situation and then turned the phone over to Winston. She went through their explanation again and then turned the phone back over to Lucas. She nodded to McCaleb. They got the approval.

'Okay, then,' Lucas said after hanging up. 'Let's see what we've got here.'

He reached to his hip and pulled up a ring of keys on a retractable wire attached to his belt. He went to the other side of the office and unlocked a closet door which he opened to reveal a rack of video recorders and four upper shelves of videotapes marked with the numbers one through thirty-one on each shelf. On the floor were two cartons containing fresh videotapes.

McCaleb saw all of this and suddenly realized it was January 22, exactly one month from the day the money order was purchased.

'Mr. Lucas, stop the machines,' he said.

'Can't do that. The machines always gotta roll. If we're open for business, then the tapes are rolling.'

'You don't understand. December twenty-second is the day we want. We're taping over the day we want to look at.'

'Hold your horses, Detective McCallan. I have to explain the setup.'

McCaleb didn't bother correcting him on the name. There wasn't time. 'Then hurry, please.'

McCaleb looked at his watch. It was eight forty-eight. The post office had been open for forty-eight minutes. That was forty-eight minutes of the December 22 tape erased with forty-eight minutes of the current day's taping.

Lucas started explaining the taping procedure. One VCR for each of the four cameras. One tape in each machine at the start of each day. The cameras were set at thirty frames a minute, allowing one tape to cover the entire day. The tape for an individual day was held for a month and used again if not reserved because of an investigation by the postal inspectors service.

'We get a lot of scam artists and whatnot. You know how it is in Hollywood. We end up with a lot of tapes on reserve. The inspectors come in and get 'em. Or we send 'em on down in dispatch.'

'We understand, Mr. Lucas,' said Winston, an urgent tone in her voice as she apparently came to the same realization as McCaleb. 'Can you please turn off the machines or replace the tapes in them. We are taping over what could be valuable evidence.'

'Right away,' Lucas said.

But he proceeded to reach into the carton of new tapes and take out four cassettes. He then peeled labels off a dispenser roll and put them on the tapes. He took a pen from behind his ear and wrote the date and some sort of coding on the labels. Then, finally, he started popping tapes out of the VCRs and replacing them with the new cassettes.

'Now, how do you want to do this? These tapes are post office property. They are not leaving the premises. I can set you up over here at the desk. I've got a portable TV with built-in VCR if you want to use it.'

'Are you sure we just can't borrow them for the day?' Winston said. 'I could have them back by—'

'Not without a court order. That's what Mr. Preechnar told me. That's what I'm going to do.'

'Then I guess we don't have a choice,' Winston said, looking at McCaleb and shaking her head in frustration.

While Lucas went to get the TV, McCaleb and Winston decided that McCaleb would stay and watch the videotape while Winston went to her office for an 11 A.M. meeting with the bureau men, Twilley and Friedman. She said she would not be mentioning McCaleb's new investigation or the possibility that his earlier focus on Bosch might have been in error. She would return the copied murder book and crime scene tape.

'I know you don't believe in coincidences but that's all you have at the moment, Terry. You come up with something on the tape and I'll bring it to the captain and we'll blow Twilley and Friedman out of the water. But until you have it . . . I'm still in the doghouse and need something more than a coincidence to look anywhere other than at Bosch.'

'What about the call to Tafero?'

'What call?'

'Somehow he knew Gunn was in the tank and he came and bailed him out – so they could kill him that night and pin it on Bosch.'

'I don't know about the call – if it wasn't Zucker, it was probably somebody else in the station he's got a sweetheart deal with. And the rest of what you just said is pure speculation without a single fact backing it up.'

'I think it's—'

'Stop, Terry. I don't want to hear it until you have something backing it up. I'm going to work.'

As if on cue, Lucas came back pushing a cart with a small television on top of it.

'I'll set you up with this,' he said.

'Mr. Lucas, I need to go to an appointment,' Winston said. 'My colleague is going to look at the tapes. Thank you for your cooperation.'

'Happy to be of service, ma'am.'

Winston looked at McCaleb.

'Call me.'

'You want me to drive you back to your car?'

'It's just a few blocks. I'll walk it.'

He nodded.

'Happy hunting,' she said.

McCaleb nodded. She had said that to him once before on a case that had not turned out so happily for him.

37

Langwiser and Kretzler told Bosch they were going ahead with the plan to rest their case by the close of the day.

'We got him,' Kretzler said, smiling and enjoying the adrenaline ride that came with making the decision to pull the trigger. 'By the time we're done he'll be tied down nine ways till Sunday. We've got Hendricks and Crowe today. We've got everything we need.'

'Except motive,' Bosch said.

'Motive is not going to be important with a crime that is obviously the work of a psychopath,' Langwiser said. 'Those jurors aren't going to go back into their little room at the end of this and say, "Yeah, but what was his motive?" They're going to say this guy is a sick fuck and—'

Her voice dropped to a whisper when the judge entered the courtroom through the door behind the bench.

'– we're going to put him away.'

The judge called for the jury and after a few minutes the prosecutors were putting on their last witnesses of the trial.

The first three witnesses were film business people who had attended the premiere party on the night of Jody Krementz's death. Each testified to having seen David Storey at the film premiere and the following party with a woman they identified from exhibit photos as Jody Krementz. The fourth witness, a screenwriter named Brent Wiggan, testified that he left the premiere party a few minutes before midnight and that he waited at the valet stand for his car along with David Storey and a woman he also identified as Jody Krementz.

'Why are you so sure it was just a few minutes before midnight, Mr. Wiggan?' Kretzler asked. 'It was, after all, a party. Were you watching the clock?'

'One question at a time, Mr. Kretzler,' the judge barked.

'Sorry, Your Honor. Why are you so sure it was a few minutes before midnight, Mr. Wiggan?'

'Because I *was* watching the clock, actually,' Wiggan said. 'My watch, that is. I do my writing at night. I am most productive from midnight until six.

So I was watching the clock, knowing I had to get back to my house at close to midnight or I would fall behind in my work.'

'Would that also mean you were not drinking alcoholic beverages at the premiere party?'

'That is correct. I wasn't drinking because I didn't want to become tired or have my creativity dampened. People don't usually drink before they go to work at a bank or as a plane pilot – well, I guess most of them don't.'

He paused until the titters of laughter subsided. The judge looked annoyed but didn't say anything. Wiggan looked like he was enjoying his moment of attention. Bosch started feeling uneasy.

'I don't drink before I go on the job,' Wiggan finally continued. 'Writing is a craft but it is also a job and I treat it as such.'

'So are you crystal clear in your memory and identification of who David Storey was with at a few minutes before midnight?'

'Absolutely.'

'And David Storey, you personally already knew him, correct?'

'Yes, that's true. For several years.'

'Have you ever worked for David Storey on a film project?'

'No, I haven't. But not for lack of trying.'

Wiggan smiled ruefully. This part of the testimony, right down to the self-deprecating comment, had been carefully planned by Kretzler earlier. He needed to limit the potential for damage to Wiggan's testimony by walking him through the weak spots on direct.

'What do you mean by that, Mr. Wiggan?'

'Oh, I would say that in the last five years or so I have pitched film projects to David directly or to people in his production company maybe six or seven times. He never bought any of them.'

He hiked his shoulders in a sheepish gesture.

'Would you say this created a sense of animosity between you two?'

'No, not at all – at least not on my part. That's the way the Hollywood game is played. You keep pitching and pitching and hopefully somebody eventually bites. It helps to have a thick skin, though.'

He smiled and nodded to the jury. He was giving Bosch a full set of the creeps. He wished Kretzler would end it before they lost the jury.

'Thank you, that's all, Mr. Wiggan,' Kretzler said, apparently getting the same vibes as Bosch.

Wiggan's face seemed to fall as he realized his moment was ending.

But then Fowkkes, who had passed on cross-examining the first three witnesses of the day, stood up and went to the lectern.

'Good morning, Mr. Wiggan.'

'Good morning.'

Wiggan raised his eyebrows in a what-do-we-have-here look.

'Just a few questions. Could you list for the jury the titles of films that you have written that have been produced?'

'Well . . . so far, nothing's been made. I've got some options and I think in a few—'

'I understand. Would you be surprised to know that in the last four years you have pitched Mr. Storey or submitted film treatments to him on a total of twenty-nine occasions, all of which were rejected?'

Wiggan's face flushed with embarrassment.

'Well, I . . . I guess that could be true. I . . . don't really know. I don't keep a record of my rejections, as Mr. Storey apparently does.'

He delivered the last line in a snippish manner and Bosch almost winced. There was nothing worse than a witness on the stand who is caught in a lie and then gets defensive about it. Bosch glanced at the jury. Several of them were not looking at the witness, a sign that they were as uncomfortable as Bosch.

Fowkkes moved in for the kill.

'You were rejected by the defendant on twenty-nine occasions and yet you say to the jury that you bear him no malice, is that correct, sir?'

'That's just business as usual in Hollywood. Ask anyone.'

'Well, Mr. Wiggan, I am asking you. Are you telling this jury that you bear this man no ill will when he is the same man who has constantly and repeatedly said to you your work is not good enough?'

Wiggan almost mumbled his answer into the microphone.

'Yes, that is true.'

'Well, you're a better man than me, Mr. Wiggan,' Fowkkes said. 'Thank you, Your Honor. Nothing further at this time.'

Bosch could feel a good bit of the air go out of the prosecution's balloon. With four questions and less than two minutes Fowkkes had put Wiggan's entire credibility into question. And what was so absolutely perfect about the defense attorney's skillful surgery was that there was little Kretzler could do on redirect to resuscitate Wiggan. The prosecutor at least knew better than to try to perhaps dig the hole deeper. He dismissed the witness and the judge called for the mid-morning break of fifteen minutes.

After the jury was out and people started working their way out of the courtroom, Kretzler leaned across Langwiser to whisper to Bosch.

'We should've known that this guy was going to blow up,' he said angrily.

Bosch just looked around to make sure no reporters were within earshot. He leaned toward Kretzler.

'You're probably right,' he said. 'But six weeks ago you were the one who said he would do the vetting on Wiggan. He was your responsibility, not mine. I'm going to get coffee.'

Bosch got up and left the two prosecutors sitting there.

After the break the prosecutors decided they needed to come back strong immediately after the disastrous cross-examination of Wiggan. They dropped plans to have another witness testify about seeing Storey and the victim together at the premiere party and Langwiser called a home security technician named Jamal Hendricks to the stand.

Bosch walked Hendricks in from the hallway. He was a black man wearing blue pants and a light blue uniform top, his first name embroidered over one pocket and the Lighthouse Security emblem over the other. He was planning to go to work following his testimony.

As they went through the first set of doors to the courtroom Bosch asked Hendricks in a whisper if he was nervous.

'Nah, man, piece of cake,' Hendricks replied.

On the stand Langwiser took Hendricks through his pedigree as a service technician for the home security company. She then moved specifically to his work on the security system at David Storey's house. Hendricks said that eight months earlier he had installed a deluxe Millennium 21 system in the house on Mulholland.

'Can you tell us what some of the features are on the deluxe Millennium Twenty-one system?'

'Well, it's top of the line. It's got everything. Remote sensing and operation, voice recognition command software, automatic sensor polling, an innkeeper program ... you name it and Mr. Storey got it.'

'What is an innkeeper program?'

'Essentially, it's operation recording software. It lets you know what doors or windows have been opened and when, when the system has been turned on and off, what personal codes were used and whatnot. It keeps track of the whole system. It's primarily used in commercial-industrial applications but Mr. Storey wanted a commercial system and it came included.'

'So he didn't specifically ask for the innkeeper program?'

'I don't know about that. I didn't sell him the system. I only installed it.'

'But he could have had this program and not known about it.'

'Anything's possible, I guess.'

'Now did there come a time when Detective Bosch called Lighthouse Security and asked for a technician to meet him at Mr. Storey's home?'

'Yeah, he made the call and it was given to me because I had installed the system. I met him there at the house. This was after Mr. Storey had been arrested and was in lockup. Mr. Storey's lawyer was there, too.'

'When was that exactly?'

'That was November eleventh.'

'What did Detective Bosch ask you to do?'

'Well, first he showed me a search warrant. It allowed him to collect information from the system's chip.'

'And did you help him with that?'

'Yeah. I downloaded the innkeeper data file and printed it out for him.'

Langwiser first introduced the search warrant – the third executed during the investigation – as an exhibit, then she introduced the printout Hendricks had just testified about.

'Now Detective Bosch was interested in the innkeeper records for the evening of October twelfth going into the morning of October thirteenth, is that correct, Mr. Hendricks?'

'Right.'

'Can you look at the printout and read the entries for that time period?'

Hendricks studied the printout for several seconds before speaking.

'Well, it says the interior door leading to the garage was opened and the alarm system was engaged by Mr. Storey's voiceprint at seven-oh-nine the night of the twelfth. Then nothing happened until the next day, the thirteenth. At twelve-twelve A.M. the alarm system was disengaged by Mr. Storey's voiceprint and the interior garage door was opened again. He then put the alarm back on – once he was in the house.'

Hendricks studied the printout before continuing.

'The system remained at status until three-nineteen, when the alarm was shut off. The interior garage door was then opened and the alarm system was engaged once more by Mr. Storey's voiceprint. Then, forty-two minutes later, at four-oh-one A.M., the alarm was disengaged by Mr. Storey's voiceprint, the garage door was opened and the alarm system was engaged again. There was no other activity until eleven A.M., when the alarm was disengaged by the voice print of Betilda Lockett.'

'Do you know who Betilda Lockett is?'

'Yes, when I installed the system I set up her voice acceptance program. She's Mr. Storey's executive assistant.'

Langwiser asked permission to set up an easel with a board displaying the times and activities Hendricks had just testified to. It was approved over objection and Bosch helped Langwiser set up the display. The poster board had two columns on it showing the record of the house alarm's engagement and the usage of the door between the house and the garage.

ALARM	INTERIOR GARAGE DOOR
10/12 7:09 P.M. – engaged by D. Storey	opened/closed
10/13 12:12 A.M. – disengaged by D. Storey	opened/closed
10/13 12:12 A.M. – engaged by D. Storey	
10/13 3:19 A.M. – disengaged by D. Storey	opened/closed
10/13 3:19 A.M. – engaged by D. Storey	
10/13 4:01 A.M. – disengaged by D. Storey	opened/closed
10/13 4:01 P.M. – engaged by D. Storey	

Langwiser continued her questioning of Hendricks.

'Does this illustration accurately reflect your testimony about the alarm system in David Storey's home on the evening of October twelfth going into October thirteenth?'

The technician looked at the poster carefully and then nodded.

'Is that a yes?'

'It's a yes.'

'Thank you. Now, because these activities were instigated with the system's recognition and approval of David Storey's voiceprint, are you telling the jury that this is the record of David Storey's comings and goings during the time period in question?'

Fowkkes objected, saying the question assumed facts not in evidence. Houghton agreed and told Langwiser to rephrase or ask another question. Her point made with the jury, she moved on.

'Mr. Hendricks, if I had a tape-recording of David Storey's voice, could I play it into the Millennium Twenty-one's station microphone and receive clearance to engage or disengage the alarm?'

'No. There are two fail-safe mechanisms. You must use a password recognized by the computer and you must say the date. So you need voice, password, correct date or the system won't accept the command.'

'What was David Storey's password?'

'I don't know. It's private. The system is set so that he can change his password as often as he likes.'

Langwiser looked at the poster on the easel. She went up and took a pointer off the easel's ledge and used it to underline the entries for 3:19 and 4:01 in the morning.

'Can you tell from these entries whether someone with Mr. Storey's voice left the house at three-nineteen and returned at four-oh-one, or if it was the other way around; someone came in at three-nineteen and then left at four-oh-one?'

'Yes, I can.'

'How is that?'

'The system also records which transmitter stations are used to engage and disengage the system. In this house the stations are set on either side of three doors – you know, outside and inside the door. The three are the front door, the door to the garage and one of the doors to the rear deck. The transmitters are on the outside and the inside of each door. Whatever one is used gets recorded in the innkeeper program.'

'Can you look at the printout from Mr. Storey's system that you looked at earlier and tell us what transmitters were used during the three-nineteen and four-oh-one entries?'

Hendricks studied his paperwork before answering.

'Uh, yes. At three-nineteen the exterior transmitter was used. That means somebody was in the garage when they turned the alarm on in the house. Then at four-oh-one the same exterior transmitter was used to turn the alarm off. The door was then opened and closed, then the alarm was turned back on from the inside.'

'So someone came home at four-oh-one, is that what you are saying?'

'Yes. Right.'

'And the system computer registered this someone as David Storey, correct?'

'It identified his voice, yes.'

'And this person would have to have used Mr. Storey's password and given the correct date as well?'

'Yes, that's right.'

Langwiser said she had no further questions. Fowkkes told the judge he had a quick cross-examination. He bounded to the lectern and looked at Hendricks.

'Mr. Hendricks, how long have you worked for Lighthouse?'

'Three years next month.'

'So you were employed by Lighthouse on January first a year ago, the so-called Y-two-K changeover?'

'Yes,' Hendricks said hesitantly.

'Can you tell us what happened to many of Lighthouse's clients on that day?'

'Uh, we had a few problems.'

'A *few* problems, Mr. Hendricks?'

'We had system failures.'

'What system in particular?'

'The Millennium Twos had a program malfunction. But it was minor. We were able to—'

'How many clients with Millennium Twos were affected in the Los Angeles area?'

'All of them. But we found the bug and—'

'That's all, sir. Thank you.'

'We got it fixed.'

'Mr. Hendricks,' the judge barked. 'That's enough. The jury will disregard the last statement.'

He looked at Langwiser.

'Redirect, Ms. Langwiser?'

Langwiser said she had a few quick questions. Bosch had known about the Y2K problems and reported them to the prosecutors. Their hope had been that the defense would not learn of them or raise them.

'Mr. Hendricks, did Lighthouse fix the bug that infected the systems after Y-two-K?'

'Yes, we did. It was fixed right away.'

'Would it in any way have affected data gathered from the defendant's system a full ten months after Y-two-K?'

'Not at all. The problem was resolved. The system was repaired.'

Langwiser said that was all she had for the witness and sat down. Fowkkes then rose for re-cross.

'The bug that was fixed, Mr. Hendricks, that was the bug they knew about, correct?'

Hendricks gave a confused look.

'Yeah, that was the one that caused the problem.'

'So what you're saying is that you only know about these "bugs" when they cause a problem.'

'Uh, usually.'

'So there could be a program bug in Mr. Storey's security system and you wouldn't know about it until it creates a problem, correct?'

Hendricks shrugged his shoulders.

'Anything's possible.'

Fowkkes sat down and the judge asked Langwiser if she had anything else. The prosecutor hesitated a moment but then said she had nothing further. Hendricks was dismissed by Houghton, who then suggested an early break for lunch.

'Our next witness will be very brief, Your Honor. I'd like to get him in before the break. We plan to concentrate on one witness during the afternoon session.'

'Very well, go on.'

'We recall Detective Bosch.'

Bosch got up and went to the witness stand, carrying the murder book. This time he did not touch the microphone. He settled in and was reminded by the judge that he was still under oath.

'Detective Bosch,' Langwiser began. 'At some point during your investigation of the murder of Jody Krementz were you directed to drive from the defendant's home to the victim's home and then back again?'

'Yes, I was. By you.'

'And did you follow that direction?'

'Yes.'

'When?'

'On November sixteenth at three-nineteen A.M.'

'Did you time your drive?'

'Yes, I did. Both ways.'

'And can you tell us those times? You can refer to your notes, if you wish.'

Bosch opened the binder to a previously marked page. He took a moment to study the notations even though he knew them by heart.

'From Mr. Storey's house to Jody Krementz's house it took eleven minutes and twenty-two seconds, driving within posted speed limits. Coming back it took eleven minutes and forty-eight seconds. The round trip was twenty-three minutes, ten seconds.'

'Thank you, Detective.'

That was it. Fowkkes passed again on cross-examination, reserving the right to call Bosch back to the stand during the defense phase. Judge Houghton recessed the trial for lunch and the crowded courtroom slowly drained into the outside hallway.

Bosch was pushing and moving through the crowd of lawyers, spectators and reporters in the hallway and looking for Annabelle Crowe when a hand strongly grabbed his upper arm from behind. He swung around and looked into the face of a black man he didn't recognize. Another man, this one white, came up to them. The two men had on almost identical gray suits. Bosch knew they were bureau men before the first man said his first word.

'Detective Bosch, I'm Special Agent Twilley with the FBI. This is Special Agent Friedman. Can we talk to you somewhere privately?'

38

It took three hours to go carefully through the videotape. At the end of it McCaleb had nothing to show for his time except a parking ticket. Tafero had appeared nowhere in the video of the post office on the day the money order was purchased. Neither had Harry Bosch, for that matter. The missing forty-eight minutes of video, which had been taped over before McCaleb and Winston got there, now haunted him. If they had gone to the post office first and Hollywood station second, they might have had the killer on tape. Those forty-eight minutes might be the difference in the case, the difference in being able to clear Bosch or convict him.

McCaleb was thinking about what-if scenarios when he got to the Cherokee and found the parking ticket under the wiper. He cursed and pulled it off and looked at it. He had been so absorbed in watching the tape he had forgotten he had parked in a fifteen-minute zone in front of the post office. The ticket would cost him forty dollars and that stung. With few fishing charters in the winter months, his family had been living mostly off Graciela's small paycheck and his monthly pension from the bureau. There wasn't a lot of leeway with expenses for the two kids. This, coupled with Saturday's canceled charter, would hurt.

He slipped the ticket back into place on the windshield and started walking down the sidewalk. He decided he wanted to go into Valentino Bonds, even if he knew Rudy Tafero would likely be up in Van Nuys in court. It was in keeping with his practice of viewing the target subject in comfortable surroundings. The target might not be there this time, but the surroundings where he felt safe would.

As he walked he took out his cell phone and called Jaye Winston but got her machine. He hung up without leaving a message and paged her. Four blocks later, when he was almost to Valentino Bonds, she called back.

'I got nothing,' he reported.

'Nothing?'

'No Tafero and no Bosch.'

'Damn.'

'It had to have been on that missing forty-eight minutes.'

'We should have—'

'Gone to the post office first. I know. My fault. The one thing I did get was a parking ticket.'

'Sorry, Terry.'

'Which at least gives me an idea. It was right before Christmas and crowded. If he was in a fifteen-minute zone he might have gone over while waiting in line. The parking enforcement goons in this city are like Nazis. They wait in the shadows. There's always a chance there was a ticket. It should be checked.'

'Son of Sam?'

'Right.'

She was referring to the New York City serial killer who was tripped up in the 1970s by a parking ticket.

'I'll take a shot at it. See what I can do. What are you going to do?'

'I'm about to check out Valentino Bonds.'

'Is he there?'

'He's probably up in court. I'm going to go up there next, see if I can talk to Bosch about all of this.'

'Better be careful. Your colleagues from the bureau said they were going up to see him at lunch. They might still be around when you get there.'

'What, they're expecting Bosch to be so impressed by their suits that he confesses or something?'

'I don't know. Something like that. They were going to brace him. Get some stuff on the record and then go find the contradictions. You know, routine word trap.'

'Harry Bosch is not routine. They're wasting their time.'

'I know. I told 'em. But you can't tell an FBI agent anything, you know that.'

He smiled.

'Hey, if this goes the other way and we take down Tafero, I want the sheriff to pay for this ticket.'

'Hey, you're not working for me. You're working for Bosch, remember? He pays parking tickets. The sheriff only pays for pancakes.'

'All right. I'm gonna go.'

'Call me.'

He slid the phone into the pocket of his windbreaker and opened the glass door of Valentino Bonds.

It was a small white room with a waiting couch and a counter. It reminded McCaleb of a motel office. There was a calendar on the wall depicting a beach scene from Puerta Vallarta. Behind the counter a man sat with his head down, filling in a crossword puzzle. Behind him was a closed door to what was probably a rear office. McCaleb put a smile on his face and started walking with purpose around the counter before the man there even looked up.

'Rudy? Hey, Rudy, come on outta there!'

The man looked up as McCaleb passed him and opened the door. He stepped into an office that was more than twice the size of the front room.

'Rudy?'

The man from the counter came in right behind him.

'Hey, man, what are you doing?'

McCaleb turned, scanning the room.

'Looking for Rudy. Where is he?'

'He's not here. Now, if you would step—'

'He told me he'd be here, that he didn't have to be in court until later.'

Scanning the office, he saw the rear wall was covered with framed photos. He took a step closer. Most of them were shots of Tafero with celebrities he had either bailed out or worked with as a security consultant. Some of the photos were clearly from his days working across the street at the cop shop.

'Excuse me, just who are you?'

McCaleb looked at the man as if insulted. He looked like he might be Tafero's younger brother. The same dark hair and eyes with rough good looks.

'I'm a friend. Terry. We used to work together when he was across the street.'

McCaleb pointed to a group photo that was on the wall. It showed several men in suits and a few women standing in front of the brick facade of the Hollywood Division station. The detective squad. McCaleb saw both Harry Bosch and Rudy Tafero in the back row. Bosch's face was turned slightly away from the camera. There was a cigarette in his mouth and smoke rising from it partially obscured his face.

The man turned and started looking at the photo.

McCaleb's eyes took another swing around the office. The room was nicely appointed with a desk to the left and a sitting area to the right with two short couches and an oriental rug. He stepped closer to the desk to look at a file sitting at center on the blotter but the file, though an inch thick with documents, had nothing written on the tab.

'What the fuck, you're not on here.'

'Yes, I am,' McCaleb said without turning from the desk. 'I was smoking. You can't see my face.'

There was a file tray to the right of the blotter that was stacked with folders. McCaleb leaned his head at an angle to check the tabs. He saw an assortment of names, some of them recognizable as entertainers or actors but none of them correlating to his investigation.

'Bullshit, man, that ain't you. That's Harry Bosch.'

'Really? You know Harry?'

The man didn't answer. McCaleb turned around. The man was looking at him with angry, suspicious eyes. For the first time McCaleb saw that he held an old billyclub down at his side.

'Let me see.'

He walked over and looked at the framed photo.

'You know, you're right, that's Harry. I must've been in the one they took the year before. I was working undercover when they took this one and couldn't be in the picture.'

McCaleb nonchalantly took a step toward the door. Inside he was bracing to get hit with the bat.

'Just tell him I was here, okay? Tell him Terry stopped by.'

He made it to the door but one last framed photo caught his eye. It showed Tafero and another man side by side, jointly holding a polished wood plaque in their hands. The picture was old, Tafero looked almost ten years younger. His eyes were brighter and his smile seemed genuine. The plaque itself was hanging on the wall next to the photo. McCaleb leaned closer and read the brass plate attached at the bottom.

RUDY TAFERO

HOLLYWOOD BOOSTERS DETECTIVE OF THE MONTH

FEBRUARY 1995

He glanced back at the photo again and then moved through the door to the front room.

'Terry what?' the man said as he passed.

McCaleb walked to the front door before turning back to him.

'Just tell him it was Terry, the undercover guy.'

He left the office and walked back up the street without looking back.

McCaleb sat in his car in front of the post office. He felt uneasy, the way he always did when he knew the answer was within reach but he just couldn't quite see it. His gut told him he was on the right track. Tafero, the PI who hid his upscale Hollywood practice behind a bail bonds shack, was the key. McCaleb just couldn't find the door.

He realized he was very hungry. He started the car and thought about a place to eat. He was a few blocks from Musso's but had eaten there too recently. He wondered if they served food at Nat's but figured if they did that it would be dangerous to the stomach. Instead, he drove over to the In 'n Out on Sunset and ordered at the drive-through.

While he was eating his hamburger over the to-go box in the Cherokee, his phone chirped. He put the burger down in the box, wiped his hands on a napkin and opened the phone.

'You're a genius.'

It was Jaye Winston.

'What?'

'Tafero got a ticket on his Mercedes. A black four-thirty CLK. He was in the fifteen-minute zone right in front of the post office. The ticket was written at eight-nineteen A.M. on the twenty-second. He hasn't paid it yet. He has till five today and then it's overdue.'

McCaleb was silent as he considered this. He felt nerve synapses firing like dominoes running up his backbone. The ticket was a hell of a break. It proved absolutely nothing but it told him that he was following the correct path. And sometimes knowing you were on the right path was better than having the proof.

His thoughts jumped to his visit to Tafero's office and the photographs he had seen.

'Hey, Jaye, did you get a chance to look up anything on the case with Bosch's old lieutenant?'

'I didn't have to go looking. Twilley and Friedman already had a file on it with them today. Lieutenant Harvey Pounds. Somebody beat him to death about four weeks after he had that altercation with Bosch over Gunn. Because of the bad blood Bosch was a likely suspect. But he apparently was cleared – by the LAPD at least. The case is open but inactive. The bureau kind of watched from afar and has kept an open file, too. Twilley told me today that there are some people in the LAPD who think Bosch was cleared on it a little too quickly.'

'Oh, and I bet Twilley loves that.'

'He does. He already has Bosch down for it. He thinks Gunn is only the tip of the iceberg with Harry.'

McCaleb shook his head but immediately moved on. He couldn't dwell on other peoples' foibles and motivations. There was a lot to think about and plan for with the investigation at hand.

'By the way, do you have a copy of the parking ticket?' he asked.

'Not yet. It was all phone work. But it's being faxed. The thing is, you and I know what it means but it's a long way off from being proof of anything.'

'I know. But it will make a good prop when the time comes.'

'When the time comes for what?'

'To make our play. We'll use Tafero to get to Storey. You know that's where this is heading.'

'We? You've got it all planned out, don't you, Terry?'

'Not quite but I'm working on it.'

He didn't want to have an argument with her about his role in the investigation.

'Listen, my lunch is getting cold here,' he said.

'Well, excuse me. Go ahead and eat.'

'Call me later. I'm going up to see Bosch later on. Anything from Twilley and Friedman on that?'

'I think they're still up there with him.'

'All right. Check you later.'

He closed the phone, got out of the car and carried the food box to a trash can. He then jumped back in and started the engine. On the way back to the post office on Wilcox he opened all the windows to air the smell of greasy food out of the car.

39

Annabelle Crowe walked to the witness stand, drawing all eyes in the courtroom. She was stunningly attractive but there was an almost awkward quality about her movements. This mixture made her seem old and young at the same time and even more attractive. Langwiser would do the questioning. She waited until Crowe was seated before disturbing the room's vibe and getting up to go to the lectern.

Bosch had barely noticed the entrance of the final witness for the prosecution. He sat at the prosecution table with his eyes down, deep in thought about his visit from the two FBI agents. He had sized them up quickly. They smelled blood in the water and knew if they bagged Bosch on the Gunn case that there would be no end to the media ride they would get from it. He expected them to make their move at any moment.

Langwiser quickly moved through a series of general questions with Crowe, establishing that she was a neophyte actress with a few plays and commercials on her resume as well as one line in a feature film that had yet to be released. Her story seemed to confirm the difficulties of making it in Hollywood – a knock-down beauty who was only one in a town full of them. She still lived on stipends sent from her parents in Albuquerque.

Langwiser moved on to more salient testimony, keying in on the night of April 14 of the previous year when Annabelle Crowe went out on a date with David Storey. After quickly drawing brief descriptions of the dinner and drinks the couple enjoyed at Dan Tana's in West Hollywood, Langwiser moved to the latter half of the evening, when Annabelle accompanied Storey to his home on Mulholland Drive.

Crow testified that she and Storey shared a whole pitcher of margaritas on the back deck of his house before they went to his bedroom.

'And did you go willingly, Ms. Crowe?'

'Yes, I did.'

'You engaged in sexual relations with the defendant?'

'Yes, I did.'

'And this was consensual sexual intercourse?'

'Yes, it was.'

'Did anything happen that was unusual once you began having sexual relations with the defendant?'

'Yes, he started to choke me.'

'He started to choke you. How did that occur?'

'Well, I guess I closed my eyes at one point and it felt like he was changing positions or moving. He was on top of me and I felt his hand slide behind my neck and he sort of lifted my head off the pillow. Then I felt him slide something down . . .'

She stopped and put her hand to her mouth as she appeared to fight to maintain her composure.

'Take your time, Ms. Crowe.'

The witness looked as though she was genuinely trying to hold back tears. She finally dropped her hand and picked up her cup of water. She sipped from it and then looked up at Langwiser, a new resolve in her eyes.

'I felt him slide something down over my head and around my neck. I opened my eyes and he was tightening a necktie around my neck.'

She stopped and took another sip of water.

'Can you describe this necktie?'

'It had a pattern. It was blue diamonds on a field of purple. I remember it exactly.'

'What happened when the defendant pulled the tie tightly around your neck?'

'It was choking me!' Crowe replied shrilly, as if the question was stupid and the answer was obvious. 'He was choking me. And he kept . . . moving in me . . . and I tried to fight him but he was too strong for me.'

'Did he say anything at this time?'

'He just kept saying, "I have to do this, I have to do this," and he was breathing really hard and he kept on having sex with me. His teeth were clenched tight when he said it. I . . .'

She stopped again and this time single tears slid down both her cheeks, one slightly behind the other. Langwiser went to the prosecution table and took a box of tissues from her spot. She held them up and said, 'Your Honor, may I?'

The judge allowed her to approach the witness with the tissues. Langwiser made the delivery and then went back to the lectern. The courtroom was silent save for the crying sounds of the witness. Langwiser broke the moment.

'Ms. Crowe, do you need a minute?'

'No, I'm fine. Thank you.'

'Did you pass out when the defendant choked you?'

'Yes.'

'What do you remember next?'

'I woke up in his bed.'

'Was he there?'

'No, but I could hear the shower running. In the bathroom next to the bedroom.'

'What did you do?'

'I got up to get dressed. I wanted to leave before he came out of the shower.'

'Were your clothes where you had left them?'

'No. I found them in a bag – like a grocery bag – by the bedroom door. I put on my underwear.'

'Did you have a purse with you that night?'

'Yes. That was in the bag, too. But it was opened. I looked inside and he had taken the keys out. I—'

Fowkkes objected, saying the answer assumed facts not in evidence and the judge sustained it.

'Did you see the defendant take your keys out of your purse?' Langwiser asked.

'Well, no. But they had been inside my purse. I didn't take them out.'

'Okay, then someone – someone you didn't see because you were unconscious on the bed – took your keys out, is that correct?'

'Yes.'

'Okay, where did you find your keys after you realized they were not in your purse?'

'They were on his bureau next to his own keys.'

'Did you finish getting dressed and leave?'

'Actually, I was so scared I just grabbed my clothes and my keys and my purse and I ran out of there. I finished getting dressed when I got outside. I then ran down the street.'

'How did you get home?'

'I got tired of running and so I walked on Mulholland for a long time until I came to a fire station with a pay phone out front. I used it to call a cab, then I went home.'

'Did you call the police when you got home?'

'Um, I didn't.'

'Why not, Ms. Crowe?'

'Well, two things. When I got home David was leaving a message on my machine and I picked up. He apologized and said he got carried away. He told me he thought that the choking was going to increase my satisfaction while we had sex.'

'Did you believe him?'

'I don't know. I was confused.'

'Did you ask him why he had put your clothes in a bag?'

'Yes. He said he thought he was going to have to take me to the hospital if I didn't wake up by the time he was out of the shower.'

'Did you ask him why he thought he should take a shower before taking an unconscious woman in his bed to the hospital?'

'I didn't ask that.'

'Did you ask him why he didn't call for paramedics?'

'No, I didn't think of that.'

'What was the other reason you did not call the police?'

The witness looked down at her hands, which were grasping each other in her lap.

'Well, I was embarrassed. After he called I wasn't sure anymore what had happened. You know, whether he had tried to kill me or was ... trying to satisfy me more. I don't know. You always hear about Hollywood people and weird sex. I thought maybe I was ... I don't know, just being uncool and square about it.'

She kept her eyes down and two more tears went down the slopes of her cheeks. Bosch saw a drop hit the collar of her chiffon blouse and leave a wet mark. Langwiser continued in a very soft tone.

'When did you contact the police about what happened that night with you and the defendant?'

Annabelle Crowe responded in a softer tone.

'When I read about him being arrested for killing Jody Krementz the same way.'

'You talked to Detective Bosch then?'

She nodded.

'Yes. And I knew that if I'd ... I'd called the police that night that maybe she'd still ...'

She didn't finish. She grabbed tissues out of the box and started a full force cry. Langwiser told the judge she was finished with her examination. Fowkkes said there would be a cross-examination but suggested that it should follow a break during which time the defendant could compose herself. Judge Houghton said that was a good idea and called a fifteen-minute break.

Bosch stayed in the courtroom watching over Annabelle Crowe as she went through the box of tissues. When she was done her face was no longer as beautiful. It was distorted and red, her eye sockets swollen. Bosch thought she had been convincing but he knew she hadn't faced Fowkkes yet. How she fared during the cross would determine whether the jury believed anything she had said on direct.

When Langwiser came back in she told Bosch there was someone at the outer door of the courtroom who wanted to speak to him.

'Who is it?'

'I didn't ask. I just overheard him talking to the deputies as I went in. They wouldn't let him in.'

'Was he in a suit? A black guy?'

'No, street clothes. A windbreaker.'

'Keep an eye on Annabelle. And you better find another box of tissues.'

He got up and went to the courtroom doors, working his way past all of the people coming back in at the end of the break. At one point he came face-to-face with Rudy Tafero. Bosch moved to his right to go around him but Tafero moved to his left. They danced back and forth a couple of times and Tafero smiled broadly. Bosch finally stopped and didn't move until Tafero pushed by him.

In the hall he looked around but didn't see anyone he recognized. Then Terry McCaleb walked out of the men's room and they nodded to each other. Bosch walked over to the railing in front of one of the floor-to-ceiling windows that looked out on the plaza below. McCaleb walked up.

'I've got about two minutes, then I've got to get back in there.'

'I just want to know if we can talk after court today. Things are happening and I need some time with you.'

'I know things are happening. Two agents showed up here today.'

'What did you tell them?'

'To fuck off. It made them mad.'

'Federal agents don't take that sort of language that well, you should know that, Bosch.'

'Yeah, well, I'm a slow learner.'

'What about after?'

'I'll be around. Unless Fowkkes creams this wit. Then I don't know, my team might have to retreat somewhere to lick our wounds.'

'All right, then I'll hang out, watch it on TV.'

'Later.'

Bosch went back into the courtroom, wondering what McCaleb had come up with so quickly. The jury was back and the judge was giving Fowkkes the go-ahead. The defense attorney waited politely as Bosch moved by him to get to the prosecution table. Then he began.

'Now Ms. Crowe, is acting your full-time occupation?'

'Yes.'

'Have you been acting here today?'

Langwiser immediately objected, angrily accusing Fowkkes of harassing the witness. Bosch thought her reaction was a bit extreme but knew she was sending a message to Fowkkes that she was going to defend her witness tooth and nail. The judge overruled the objection, saying Fowkkes was within bounds in cross-examining a witness hostile to his client.

'No, I am not acting,' Crowe answered forcefully.

Fowkkes nodded.

'You testified that you have been in Hollywood three years.'

'Yes.'

'I counted five paying jobs you spoke of. Anything else?'

'Not yet.'

Fowkkes nodded.

'Good to be hopeful. It's very difficult to break in, isn't it?'

'Yes, very difficult, very discouraging.'

'But you are on TV right now, aren't you?'

She hesitated a moment, the realization that she had walked into a trap showing on her face.

'And so are you,' she said.

Bosch almost smiled. It was the best answer she could have given.

'Let's talk about this . . . event that allegedly took place between you and Mr. Storey,' Fowkkes said. 'This event is, in fact, something you concocted from newspaper stories following David Storey's arrest, correct?'

'No, not correct. He tried to kill me.'

'So you say.'

Langwiser stood up to object but before she did the judge admonished Fowkkes to keep such editorial comments to himself. The defense lawyer moved on.

'Now, after Mr. Storey supposedly choked you to the point of unconsciousness, did you develop bruises on your neck?'

'Yes, I had a bruise for almost a week. I had to stay inside. I couldn't go to auditions or anything.'

'And you took photographs of the bruise to document its existence, correct?'

'No, I didn't.'

'But you showed the bruise to your agent and friends, did you not?'

'No.'

'And why is that?'

'Because I didn't think it would ever come to this, where I would have to try to prove what he did. I just wanted it to go away and I didn't want anyone to know.'

'So we only have your word for the bruise, is that correct?'

'Yes.'

'Just as we only have your word for the entire alleged incident, correct?'

'He tried to kill me.'

'And you testified that when you got home that evening David Storey happened at that very moment to be leaving a message on your phone machine, correct?'

'Absolutely.'

'And you picked that call up – a call from the man you say tried to kill you. Do I have that right?'

Fowkkes gestured as if grabbing a telephone. He held his hand up until she answered.

'Yes.'

'And you saved that message on that tape to document his words and what had happened to you, correct?'

'No, I taped over it. By mistake.'

'By mistake. You mean you left it in the machine and eventually taped over it?'

'Yes. I didn't want to but I forgot and it got taped over.'

'You mean you forgot that someone tried to kill you and taped over it?'

'No, I didn't forget that he tried to kill me. I'll never forget that.'

'So as far as this tape goes, we only have your word for it, correct?'

'That's right.'

There was a measure of defiance in her voice. But in a way it seemed pitiful to Bosch. It was like yelling, 'Fuck you' into a jet engine. He sensed that she was about to be thrown into that jet engine and torn apart.

'Now, you testified that you are supported in part by your parents and that you have earned some monies as an actress. Is there any other source of income you haven't told us about?'

'Well ... not really. My grandmother sends me money. But not too often.'

'Anything else?'

'Not that I can think of.'

'Do you take money from men on occasion, Ms. Crowe?'

There was an objection from Langwiser and the judge called the lawyers to a sidebar. Bosch watched Annabelle Crowe the whole time the lawyers whispered. He studied her face. There was still a brushstroke of defiance but it was being crowded by fear. She knew something was coming. Bosch decided that Fowkkes had something legitimate that he was going after. It was something that was going to hurt her and thereby hurt the case.

When the sidebar broke up Kretzler and Langwiser returned to their seats at the prosecution table. Kretzler leaned over to Bosch.

'We're fucked,' he whispered. 'He's got four men that will testify they paid her for sex. Why didn't we know about this?'

Bosch didn't answer. She had been assigned to him for vetting. He had questioned her at length about her personal life and had run her prints for an arrest record. Her answers and the computer run were clean. If she'd never been popped for prostitution and she denied any criminal activities to Bosch, there wasn't much else he could have done.

Back at the lectern, Fowkkes rephrased the question.

'Ms. Crowe, have you ever taken money from men in exchange for sex?'

'No, absolutely not. That is a lie.'

'Do you know a man named Andre Snow?'

'Yes, I do.'

'If he were to testify under oath that he paid you for sexual relations, would he be lying?'

'Yes, he would.'

Fowkkes named three other men and they went through the same loop of Crowe acknowledging that she knew them but denying she had ever sold them sex.

'Then have you ever taken money from these men, but not for sex?' Fowkkes asked in a false tone of exasperation.

'Yes, on occasion. But it had nothing to do with whether we had sex or not.'

'Then what did it have to do with?'

'Them wanting to help me. I considered them friends.'

'Did you ever have sex with them?'

Annabelle Crowe looked down at her hands and shook her head.

'Are you saying no, Ms. Crowe?'

'I am saying that I didn't have sex with them every time they gave me money. They didn't give me money every time we had sex. One thing had nothing to do with the other. You are trying to make it look like something it's not.'

'I'm just asking questions, Ms. Crowe. As it is my job to do. As it is your job to tell this jury the truth.'

After a long pause Fowkkes said he had no further questions.

Bosch realized that he had been gripping the arms of his chair so tightly that his knuckles were white and had gone numb. He rubbed his hands together and tried to relax but he couldn't. He knew that Fowkkes was a master, a cut-and-run artist. He was brief and to the point and as devastating as a stiletto. Bosch realized that his discomfort was not only for Annabelle Crowe's helpless position and public humiliation, but for his own position. He knew the stiletto would be pointed at him next.

40

They settled into a booth at Nat's after getting bottles of Rolling Rock from the bartender with the tattoo of the barbed-wire-wrapped heart. While she pulled the bottles from the cold case and opened them, the woman hadn't said anything about McCaleb having come in the other night asking questions about the man he had now returned with. It was early and the place was empty except for groups of hard-cores at the bar and crowded into the booth all the way to the rear. Bruce Springsteen was on the jukebox singing, 'There's a darkness on the edge of town.'

McCaleb studied Bosch. He thought he looked pre-occupied by something, probably the trial. The last witness had been a wash at best. Good on direct, bad on cross. The kind of witness you don't use – if you have the choice.

'Looked like you guys got sandbagged there with your wit.'

Bosch nodded.

'My fault. I should've seen it coming. I looked at her and thought she was so beautiful she couldn't possibly ... I just believed her.'

'I know what you mean.'

'Last time I trust a face.'

'You guys still look like you're in good shape. What else you got coming?'

Bosch smirked.

'That's it. They were going to rest today but decided to wait until the morning so Fowkkes wouldn't have the night to get ready. But we've fired all the bullets in the gun. Starting tomorrow we see what they've got.'

McCaleb watched Bosch take down almost half the bottle in one long pull. He decided he'd better get to the real questions while Bosch was still sharp.

'So tell me about Rudy Tafero.'

Bosch shrugged his shoulders in a gesture of ambivalence.

'What about him?'

'I don't know. How well do you know him? How well *did* you know him?'

'Well, I knew him when he was on *our* team. He worked Hollywood detectives about five years while I was there. Then he pulled the pin, got his twenty-year pension and moved across the street. Started working on getting people we put in the bucket out of the bucket.'

'When you were both on the same team, both in Hollywood, were you close?'

'I don't know what close means. We weren't friends, we weren't drinking buddies, he worked burglaries and I worked homicides. What are you asking so much about him for? What's he got to do with—'

He stopped and looked at McCaleb, the wheels obviously turning inside. Rod Stewart was now singing 'Twisting the Night Away.'

'Are you fucking kidding me?' Bosch finally asked. 'You're looking at—'

'Let me just ask some questions,' McCaleb interjected. 'Then you can ask yours.'

Bosch drained his bottle and held it up until the bartender noticed.

'No table service, guys,' she called over. 'Sorry.'

'Fuck that,' Bosch said.

He slid out of the booth and went to the bar. He came back with four more Rocks, though McCaleb had barely begun to drink his first one.

'Ask away,' Bosch said.

'Why weren't you two close?'

Bosch put both elbows on the table and held a fresh bottle with both hands. He looked out of the booth and then at McCaleb.

'Five, ten years ago there were two groups in the bureau. And to a large extent it was this way in the department, too. It was like the saints and the sinners – two distinct groups.'

'The born agains and the born againsts?'

'Something like that.'

McCaleb remembered. It had become well known in local law enforcement circles a decade earlier that a group within the LAPD known as the 'born agains' had members in key positions and was holding sway over promotions and choice assignments. The group's numbers – several hundred officers of all ranks – were members of a church in the San Fernando Valley where the department's deputy chief in charge of operations was a lay preacher. Ambitious officers joined the church in droves, in hopes of impressing the deputy chief and enhancing their career prospects. How much spirituality was involved was in question. But when the deputy chief delivered his sermon every Sunday at the eleven o'clock service, the church would be packed to standing room only with off-duty cops casting their eyes fervently on the pulpit. McCaleb had once heard a story about a car alarm going off in the parking lot during an eleven o'clock service. The hapless hype rummaging through the vehicle's glove compartment soon found himself surrounded by a hundred guns pointed by off-duty cops.

'I take it you were on the sinners' team, Harry.'

Bosch smiled and nodded.

'Of course.'

'And Tafero was on the saints'.'

'Yeah. And so was our lieutenant at the time. A paper pusher named Harvey Pounds. He and Tafero had their little church thing going and so they were tight. I think anybody who was tight with Pounds, whether because of church or not, wasn't somebody I was going to gravitate toward, if you know what I mean. And they weren't going to gravitate toward me.'

McCaleb nodded. He knew more than he was letting on.

'Pounds was the guy who messed up the Gunn case,' he said. 'The one you pushed through the window.'

'He's the one.'

Bosch dropped his head and shook it in self-disgust.

'Was Tafero there that day?'

'Tafero? I don't know, probably.'

'Well, wasn't there an IAD investigation with witness reports?'

'Yeah, but I didn't look at it. I mean, I pushed the guy through a window in front of the squad. I wasn't going to deny it.'

'And later – what, a month or so? – Pounds ends up dead in the tunnel up in the hills.'

'Griffith Park, yeah.'

'And it's still open . . .'

Bosch nodded.

'Technically.'

'You said that before. What does that mean?'

'It means it's open but nobody's working it. The LAPD has a special classification for cases like it, cases they don't want to touch. It's what is called closed by circumstances other than arrest.'

'And you know those circumstances?'

Bosch finished his second bottle, slid it to the side and pulled a fresh bottle in front of him.

'You're not drinking,' he said.

'You're doing enough for both of us. Do you know those circumstances?'

Bosch leaned forward.

'Listen, I'm going to tell you something very few people know about, okay?'

McCaleb nodded. He knew better than to ask a question now. He would just let Bosch tell it.

'Because of that window thing I went on suspension. When I got tired of walking around my house staring at the walls, I started investigating an old case. A cold case. A murder case. I went freelancing on it and I ended up following a blind trail to some very powerful people. But at the time I had no badge, no real standing. So a few times, when I made some calls, I used Pounds's name. You know, I was trying to hide what I was doing.'

'If the department found out you were working a case while on suspension things would've gotten worse for you.'

'Exactly. So I used his name when I made what I thought were some routine, innocuous calls. But then one night somebody called Pounds up and told him that they had something for him, some urgent information. He went to the meet. By himself. Then they found him later in that tunnel. He'd been beaten pretty bad. Like they had tortured him. Only he couldn't answer their questions because he was the wrong guy. I was the one who had used his name. I was the one they wanted.'

Bosch dropped his chin to his chest and was silent for a long moment.

'I got him killed,' he said without looking up. 'The guy was a pure-bred asshole but my actions got him killed.'

Bosch suddenly jerked his head up and drank from his bottle. McCaleb saw his eyes were dark and shiny. They looked weary.

'Is that what you wanted to know, Terry? Does that help you?'

McCaleb nodded.

'How much of this would Tafero have known?'

'Nothing.'

'Could he have thought you were the one who called Pounds out that night?'

'Maybe. There were people who did and probably still do. But what does it mean? What's it got to do with Gunn?'

McCaleb took his first long drink of beer. It was cold and he felt the chill in his chest. He put the bottle down and decided it was time to give something back to Bosch.

'I need to know about Tafero because I need to know about reasons, motives. I have no proof of anything – yet – but I think Tafero killed Gunn. He did it for Storey. He set you in the frame.'

'Jesus . . .'

'Nice perfect frame. The crime scene is connected to the painter Hieronymus Bosch, the painter is connected to you as his namesake and then you are connected to Gunn. And you know when Storey probably got the idea for it?'

Bosch shook his head. He looked too stunned to talk.

'The day you tried to interview him in his office. You played the tape in court last week. You identified yourself on it by your full first name.'

'I always do. I . . .'

'He then connects with Tafero and Tafero has the perfect victim to put in the frame. Gunn – a man he knew walked away from you and a murder charge six years ago.'

Bosch lifted his bottle a couple of inches off the table and brought it back down hard.

'I think the plan was twofold. If they got lucky the connection would be made quickly and you'd be fighting a murder charge before Storey's trial even started. If that didn't happen, then Plan B. They would still have it to crush you with at trial. Destroy you, they destroy the case. Fowkkes already took out that woman today and potshotted a few of the other wits. What does the case rest on? You, Harry. They knew it would come down to you.'

Bosch turned his head slightly and his eyes seemed to go blank as he stared at the scarred table top while considering what McCaleb had said.

'I needed to know your background with Tafero. Because that's a question; why would *he* do this? Yes, there probably is money in it and a hook into Storey if he walks. But there had to be something more. And I think you just told me what it was. He's probably hated you for a long time.'

Bosch looked up from the table and directly at McCaleb.

'It's a payback.'

McCaleb nodded.

'For Pounds. And unless we get the proof of it, it might just work.'

Bosch was silent. He stared down at the table. He looked tired and washed out to McCaleb.

'Still want to shake his hand?' McCaleb asked.

Bosch raised his eyes.

'Sorry, Harry, that was a cheap shot.'

Bosch shook his head, shrugging it off.

'I deserve it. So tell me, what *do* you have?'

'Not a lot. But you were right. I missed something. Tafero bailed Gunn out on New Year's Eve. I think the plan was to kill him that night, set the scene and let things take their course. The Hieronymus Bosch connection would come to light – either through Jaye Winston or a bureau VICAP inquiry – and you'd become a natural target. But then Gunn went and got himself drunk in here.'

He raised his bottle and gestured to the bar.

'And then he got himself duiced while driving home. Tafero had to get him out so they could stay with the plan. So he could kill him. That bail slip is the one direct link we have.'

Bosch nodded. McCaleb could tell he was seeing the scheme.

'They leaked it to that reporter,' Bosch said. 'Once it hit the media they could jump on it and use it and act like it was news to them, like they were behind the curve when all along they were bending the goddamn curve.'

McCaleb nodded hesitantly. He didn't bring up Buddy Lockridge's admission because it threw a jam into the working theory.

'What?' Bosch asked.

'Nothing. I'm just thinking.'

'You've got nothing other than Tafero posting the bail?'

'A traffic ticket and that's it for now.'

In detail McCaleb described his morning's visits to Valentino Bonds and the post office and how his being forty-eight minutes late at the post office might be the difference in being able to clear Bosch and take down Tafero.

Bosch winced and picked up his bottle, but then put it down without drinking from it.

'The parking ticket puts him at the post office,' McCaleb offered.

'It's nothing. He's got an office five blocks away. He could claim it was the only parking place he could find. He could say he lent his car to somebody. It's nothing.'

McCaleb didn't want to concentrate on what they didn't have. He wanted to fill in pieces.

'Listen, the morning watch sergeant told us you had a standing request to be notified every time Gunn was brought in. Would Tafero have known about it? Either from before when he was still in the squad or some other way?'

'He could have. It wasn't a secret. I was working on Gunn. Someday I was going to break him.'

'By the way, what did Pounds look like?'

Bosch gave him a confused look.

'Short, wide and balding with a mustache?'

Bosch nodded and was about to ask a question when McCaleb answered it.

'His picture is on the wall in Tafero's office. Pounds giving him the detective-of-the-month plaque. I bet you never got one of those, Harry.'

'Not with Pounds making the pick.'

McCaleb looked up and saw that Jaye Winston had entered the bar. She was carrying a briefcase. He nodded to her and she started toward the booth, walking with her shoulders up as though she were carefully stepping through a landfill.

McCaleb moved over and she slid into the booth next to him.

'Nice place.'

'Harry,' McCaleb said, 'I believe you know Jaye Winston.'

Bosch and Winston looked at each other.

'First thing,' Winston said, 'I'm sorry about the thing with Kiz. I hope—'

'We do what we have to do,' Bosch said. 'You want a drink? They don't come to the table here.'

'I'd be shocked if they did. Maker's Mark, rocks, if they have it.'

'Terry, you cool?'

'Cool.'

Bosch slid out to get the drink. Winston turned to look at McCaleb.

'How is it going?'

'Little pieces, here and there.'

'How's he taking it?'

'Not bad, I guess, for a guy who's been put into a pretty big box. How'd you do?'

She smiled in a way that McCaleb could tell meant she had come up with something.

'I got you the photo and a couple other ... interesting ... pieces.'

Bosch put Winston's drink down in front of her and slid back into the booth.

'She laughed when I said Maker's Mark,' he said. 'That's the house swill there.'

'Wonderful. Thank you.'

Winston moved her glass to the side and brought her briefcase up onto the table. She opened it, removed a file and then closed the briefcase and put it back on the floor next to the booth. McCaleb watched Bosch watching her. There was an expectant look on his face.

Winston opened the file and slid a five-by-eight photo of Rudy Tafero over to McCaleb.

'That's from his bonding license. It's eleven months old.'

She then referred to a page of typed notes.

'I went to county lockup and pulled everything on Storey. He was held there until they transferred him to Van Nuys jail for the trial. During his stay in county he had nineteen visits from Tafero. The first twelve visits coming during the first three weeks he was in there. During that same period, Fowkkes only visited him four times. A lawyer in Fowkkes's office visited an additional four times and Storey's executive assistant, a woman named Betilda Lockett, visited six times. That's it. He was meeting with his investigator more often than his lawyers.'

'That's when they planned it,' McCaleb said.

She nodded and then smiled in that same way again.

'What?' McCaleb asked.

'Just saving the best for last.'

She brought her briefcase back up and opened it.

'The jail keeps records of all property and possessions of inmates – things that were brought in with them, things approved and passed to them by visitors. There is a notation in Storey's records that his assistant, Betilda Lockett, was allowed to give him a book during the second of her six visits. According to the property report, it was called *The Art of Darkness*. I went to the downtown library and checked it out.'

From her briefcase she took a large, heavy book with a blue cloth cover. She started opening it on the table. There was a yellow Post-it sticking out as a marker.

'It's a study of artists who used darkness as a vital part of the visual medium, according to the introduction.'

She looked up and smiled as she got to the Post-it.

'It has a rather long chapter on Hieronymus Bosch. Complete with illustrations.'

McCaleb lifted his empty bottle and clicked against her glass, which she still hadn't touched. He then leaned in, along with Bosch, to look at the pages.

'Beautiful,' he said.

Winston turned the pages. The book's illustrations of Bosch's work included all of the paintings from which pieces of the crime scene could be traced: *The Stone Operation, The Seven Deadly Sins* with the eye of God, *The Last Judgment* and *The Garden of Earthly Delights*.

'He planned the thing right there from his cell,' McCaleb marveled.

'Looks like it,' Winston said.

They both looked at Bosch, who was nodding his head almost imperceptibly.

'Now your turn, Harry,' McCaleb said.

Bosch looked perplexed.

'My turn at what?'

'At making good luck.'

McCaleb slid the picture of Tafero across the table and nodded toward the bartender. Bosch slid out and took the photo to the bar.

'We're still just dancing around the edges,' Winston said as they both watched Bosch question the bartender about the photo. 'We've got little pieces but that's it.'

'I know,' McCaleb said. He couldn't hear what was being said at the bar. The music was too loud, Van Morrison singing, 'The wild night is coming.'

Bosch nodded to the bartender and came back to the booth.

'She recognizes him – drinks Kahlúa and cream of all things. She can't put him here with Gunn, though.'

McCaleb shrugged his shoulders in a no-big-deal gesture.

'It was worth the shot.'

'You know where this is going, don't you?' Bosch said, his eyes shifting from McCaleb's to Winston's and then back. 'You're going to have to make a play. It's going to be the only way. And it's gotta be a damn good play because my ass is on the line.'

McCaleb nodded.

'We know,' he said.

'When? I'm running out of time.'

McCaleb looked at Winston. It was her call.

'Soon,' she said. 'Maybe tomorrow. I haven't gone into the office with this yet. I have to finesse my captain on it because last he knew, Terry here was banished and I was working with the bureau on you. I also have to get a DA involved because when we make the move we'll have to move fast. If it all works out I say we take Tafero in tomorrow night and make the play to him.'

Bosch looked down at the table with a rueful smile. He slid an empty bottle back and forth between his hands.

'I met those guys today. The agents.'

'I heard. You didn't exactly assure them of your innocence. They came back all hot and bothered.'

Bosch looked up.

'So what do you need from me on this?'

'We need you to sit tight,' Winston said. 'We'll let you know about tomorrow night.'

Bosch nodded.

'There is one thing,' McCaleb said. 'The exhibits from the trial, do you have access to them?'

'During court, yeah. Otherwise they stay with the clerk. Why?'

'Because Storey obviously had existing knowledge of the painter Hieronymus Bosch. He had to have recognized your name during that interview and known what he could do with it. So I'm thinking that book his assistant brought him in jail had to be his own. He told her to bring it to him.'

Bosch nodded.

'The picture of the bookcase.'

McCaleb nodded.

'You got it.'

'I'll let you know.' Bosch looked around the place. 'Are we done here?'

'We're done,' Winston said. 'We'll be in touch.'

She slid out of the booth, followed by Bosch and McCaleb. They left two beers and a whiskey rocks untouched on the table. At the door, McCaleb glanced back and saw a couple of the hard-cores moving in on the treasure. From the jukebox John Fogerty was singing, 'There's a bad moon on the rise . . .'

41

The chill off the water worked its way into McCaleb's bones. He shoved his hands deep into the pockets of his windbreaker and turtled his neck as far down into the collar as he could as he carefully made his way down the ramp to the Cabrillo Marina docks.

Though his chin was down his eyes were alert and scanning the docks for unusual movement. Nothing caught his attention. He glanced at Buddy Lockridge's sailboat as he passed. Despite all the junk – surfboards, bikes, gas grill, an ocean kayak and other assorted equipment and debris – crowding the deck, he could see the cabin lights were on. He walked quietly on the wood planking. He decided that whether Buddy was awake or not it was too late and McCaleb was too tired and cold to deal with his supposed partner. Still, as he approached *The Following Sea,* he couldn't help but move his mind over the sharp-edged anomaly in his working theory on the case. Back at the bar Bosch had been correct when he deduced that someone from the Storey camp had to have leaked the story of the Gunn investigation to the *New Times.* McCaleb knew that the only way the current case theory hung together was if Tafero, or maybe Fowkkes or even Storey from jail, had been Jack McEvoy's source. The problem was that Buddy Lockridge had told McCaleb that he had leaked the investigation to the weekly tabloid.

Now the only way, at least as it appeared to McCaleb, that this could work would be if both Buddy and someone in Storey's defense group leaked the same information to the same media source. And this, of course, was a coincidence that even a believer in coincidence would have a difficult time accepting.

McCaleb tried to put it out of his mind for the moment. He got to the boat, looked around again, and stepped down into the cockpit. He unlocked the slider and went in, turning on the lights. He decided that in the morning he would go over and question Buddy more carefully about what he had done and who he had talked to.

He locked the door and put his keys and the videotape he'd been carrying down on the chart table. He immediately went to the galley and poured a large glass of orange juice. He then turned the upper deck lights off and took the juice with him down to the lower deck where he went into the head and quickly began his evening pill ritual. As he swallowed the pills and orange juice he looked at himself in the small mirror over the sink. He thought about what Bosch had looked like. The weariness clearly set deep in his eyes. McCaleb wondered if he would get the same look in a few years, after a few more cases.

When he was finished with his medicine routine he stripped off his clothes and took a quick shower, the water feeling ice cold because the water heater hadn't been on since he had crossed in the boat the day before.

Shivering, he went into the master cabin and put on a pair of boxer shorts and a sweatshirt. He was dead tired but once he got into the bed he decided he should write a few notes about his thoughts on how Jaye Winston should run the play with Tafero. He reached down to the nightstand's drawer, where he kept pens and scratch pads. When he opened it he found a folded newspaper crammed into the small drawer space. He pulled it out, unfolded it and found it was the previous week's issue of *New Times*. The pages had been folded backward so that the rear advertising section was at the front. McCaleb was looking at a page full of matchbook-sized ads under a heading that said OUTCALL MASSAGE.

McCaleb got up quickly and went to his windbreaker, which he had tossed onto a chair. He pulled the cell phone out of the pocket and went back to the bed with it. Though McCaleb had been carrying the phone with him in recent days, it usually stayed in its charger on the boat. It was paid for out of charter funds and was carried as a business expense. It was used by clients during charter trips and by Buddy Lockridge while confirming reservations and running credit card authorizations.

The phone had a small digital screen with a menu he scrolled through. He opened the call log program and began scrolling through the last hundred numbers the phone had been used to call. Most of the numbers he quickly identified and eliminated. But every time he did not recognize a number he compared it to the phone numbers at the bottom of the ads on the massage page. The fourth unrecognized number he compared to the ads was a match. The number was for a woman who advertised herself as an 'Exotic Japanese-Hawaiian Beauty' named Leilani. Her ad said she specialized in 'full-service relaxation' and was not associated with any massage agency.

McCaleb closed the phone and got off the bed again. He started pulling on a pair of sweatpants as he tried to recall exactly what had been said when he had accused Buddy Lockridge of leaking the case information to the *New Times*.

By the time he was dressed, McCaleb realized he had never specifically accused Buddy of leaking information to the newspaper. He had only mentioned the *New Times* and Buddy had immediately begun to apologize. McCaleb now understood that Buddy's apology and embarrassment could have been over his using *The Following Sea* the week before when it was in the marina as a rendezvous point with the full-service masseuse. It explained why he had asked if McCaleb was going to tell Graciela what he had done.

McCaleb looked at his watch. It was ten after eleven. He grabbed the newspaper and went topside. He didn't want to wait until the morning to confirm this. He guessed that Buddy had used *The Following Sea* to meet the woman because his own boat was so small and cramped and looked like a forbidding floating rat trap. There was no master cabin – just one open space that was as crowded with junk as the deck above. If Buddy had *The Following Sea* available to him, he would have used it.

In the salon he didn't bother turning on the lights. He leaned over the couch and looked out the window to the boat's left. Buddy's boat, the *Double Down,* was four slips away and he could see the cabin lights were still on. Buddy was still awake, unless he had passed out with the lights on.

McCaleb went to the slider and was about to unlock it when he realized it was already open a half inch. He realized someone was on the boat, probably having entered while he had been in the shower and unable to hear the lock pop or feel the added weight on the boat. He quickly slid the door all the way open in an effort to escape. He was just stepping through when he was grabbed from behind. An arm came over his right shoulder and across the front of his neck. It bent at the elbow and his neck was shoved into the V it formed. His attacker's other forearm closed the triangle behind his neck. The hold closed like a vise on both sides of his neck, compressing the carotid arteries that carried oxygenated blood to his brain. McCaleb had an almost clinical understanding of what was happening. He was caught in a textbook choke hold. He began to struggle. He brought his arms up and tried to dig his fingers under the forearm and biceps on either side of his neck but it was no use. He was already weakening.

He was dragged back away from the door and into the darkness of the salon. He reached his left hand back to the point where his attacker's right hand gripped his left forearm – the weak point of the triangle. But he had no leverage and was losing power quickly. He tried to yell. Maybe Buddy would hear. But his voice was gone and nothing came out.

He remembered another defensive measure. He raised his right foot up and drove it down, heel first, toward his attacker's foot, with the last strength he could muster. But he missed. His heel hit the floor ineffectively and his attacker took another step backward, violently pulling McCaleb off balance and unable to attempt the kick release again.

McCaleb was quickly losing consciousness. His vision of the marina lights through the salon door was being crowded by a closing blackness with a reddish outline. His last thoughts were that he was in the grip of a classic choke hold, the kind taught at police departments across the country until too many deaths resulted from its use.

Soon even that thought drifted away and he saw no lights. The darkness moved in and took him.

42

McCaleb came awake to tremendous muscular pain in his shoulders and upper legs. When he opened his eyes he realized he was lying chest down across the master cabin's bed. His head was lying flat on the mattress, his left cheek down, and he was staring at the headboard. It took him a moment before he remembered that he had been on his way to visit Buddy Lockridge when he was attacked from behind.

He became completely conscious and tried to relax his aching muscles but realized he could not move. His wrists were bound behind his back and his legs were bent backward at the knees and were being held in that position by someone's hand.

He lifted his head off the mattress and tried to turn. He couldn't get the angle. He dropped back to the mattress and turned his head to the left. He lifted up once again and turned to see Rudy Tafero, standing next to the bed, smiling at him. With one gloved hand he was holding McCaleb's feet, which were bound at the ankles and folded back toward his thighs.

Comprehension rushed over him. McCaleb realized he was naked and that he was bound and held in the same posture as he had seen the body of Edward Gunn. The reverse fetal pose from the painting by Hieronymus Bosch. The cold chill of terror exploded in his chest. He instinctively flexed his leg muscles. Tafero was ready for it. His feet barely moved. But he heard three clicks behind his head and became aware of the ligature around his neck.

'Easy,' Tafero said. 'Easy now. Not yet.'

McCaleb stopped his movement. Tafero continued to press his ankles down toward the back of his thighs.

'You've seen the setup before,' Tafero said matter of factly. 'This one's a little different. I strung together a bunch of snap-cuffs, like every L.A. cop carries around in the trunk of his car.'

McCaleb understood the message. The plastic strips first invented to bundle cables together but found to be useful by police agencies faced with occasional social unrest and the need to make mass arrests. A cop can carry one set of handcuffs but hundreds of snap cuffs. String them around the wrists, slide the end through the lock. Tiny grooves in the plastic strip click and lock as the tie gets tighter. The only way to remove it is to cut it off. McCaleb realized that the clicking sound he had just heard had been a snap cuff tightening around his neck.

'So you be careful now,' Tafero said. 'Hold real steady.'

McCaleb put his face down into the mattress. His mind was racing, looking for the way out. He thought if he could engage Tafero he might buy some time. But time for what?

'How'd you find me?' he spoke into the mattress.

'Easy enough. My little brother followed you from my shop and got your plate. You should look around more often, make sure you aren't being followed.'

'I'll remember that.'

He understood the plan. It would look as if Gunn's killer had gotten McCaleb when he had come too close. He turned his head again so he could see Tafero.

'It's not going to work, Tafero,' he said. 'People know. They're not going to buy that it was Bosch.'

Tafero smiled down at him.

'You mean Jaye Winston? Don't worry about her. I'm going to go pay her a visit when I'm done here with you. Eighty-eight-oh-one Willoughby, apartment six, West Hollywood. She was easy to find, too.'

He raised his free hand and waved the fingers as though he were playing the piano or typing.

'Let your fingers do the walking through the voters registration – I've got it on CD-ROM. She's a registered Democrat, if you can believe it. A homicide cop who votes Democrat. Wonders never cease.'

'There are others. The FBI's on this. You—'

'They're on Bosch. Not me. I saw them today at the courthouse.'

He reached down and ticked one of the snap cuffs strung from McCaleb's legs to his neck.

'And these, I'm sure, will help bring them directly to Detective Bosch.'

He smiled at the genius of his own plan. And McCaleb knew his thinking was sound. Twilley and Friedman would go after Bosch like a pair of dogs chasing either side of a car.

'Hold steady now.'

Tafero let go of his feet and moved out of his sight. McCaleb strained to keep his legs from unfolding. Almost immediately he felt the muscles in his legs start to burn. He knew he didn't have the strength to hold them for long.

'Please . . .'

Tafero returned to view. He was holding a plastic owl in both hands, a delighted smile on his face.

'Took this off one of the boats down the dock. A little weathered but it'll work out nice. Gonna get another one for Winston.'

He looked around the room as if looking for a place for the owl. He settled on a shelf above the built-in bureau. He placed the owl there, looked back at McCaleb once and then adjusted it so the plastic bird's gaze was upon him.

'Perfect,' he said.

McCaleb closed his eyes. He could feel his muscles vibrating with the strain. An image of his daughter appeared in his mind. She was in his arms, her eyes were watching him over the bottle and telling him not to worry or be afraid. It soothed him. He concentrated on her face and somehow thought he could even smell her hair. He felt tears going down his face and his legs started to give way. He heard the clicking of the cuffs and –

Tafero grabbed his legs and held them.

'Not yet.'

Something hard banged off McCaleb's head and thudded on the mattress next to him. He turned his face and opened his eyes and saw it was the videotape he had gone back to borrow from Lucas, the post office security officer. He looked at the post office emblem of the flying eagle on the sticker Lucas had put on the tape for him.

'I hope you don't mind but while you were sleeping off the choke hold I took a look at the tape on your VCR. I couldn't find anything on it. It's blank. Why is that?'

McCaleb felt a pang of hope. He realized that the only reason he wasn't already dead was because of the tape. Tafero had found it and it raised too many questions. It was a break. McCaleb tried to think of a way to turn it further to his advantage. The tape was supposed to be blank. They had planned to use it as a prop when they brought Tafero in and tried to play him. It would have been part of a bluff. They would hold it up and tell him they had him on tape sending the money order. But they wouldn't actually play it. Now McCaleb thought he might be able to still use it – but in reverse.

Tafero shoved down hard on his ankles, so hard they came close to touching McCaleb's buttocks. McCaleb groaned from the stress on his muscles. Tafero eased back.

'I asked you a question, motherfucker. Now you fucking answer it.'

'It's nothing. It's supposed to be blank.'

'Bullshit. The label says "December twenty-second." It says "Wilcox surveillance." Why is it blank?'

He increased the pressure on McCaleb's legs but not to the point of a few moments before.

'Okay, I'll tell you the truth. I'll tell you.'

McCaleb took a deep breath and tried to relax. In the moment his body was still, when the air was held in his lungs, he thought he detected a movement of the boat that was out of rhythm with the gentle rise-and-fall cycle of the marina's wake. Somebody had stepped onto the boat. He could only think of Buddy Lockridge. And if it was him then he was most likely walking into his own doom. McCaleb started to speak quickly and loudly, hoping his voice would warn Lockridge off.

'It's just a prop, that's all. We were going to bluff you, tell you we had you on tape buying the money order that bought the owl. The plan, the plan was to get you to turn on Storey. We know it was his plan from the jail. You just followed orders. They want Storey more than they want you. I was going to—'

'All right, shut up!'

McCaleb was quiet. He wondered if Tafero had felt the boat move unusually or if he had heard something. But then McCaleb watched as the tape was lifted off the bed. He realized he had Tafero thinking. After a long moment of silence Tafero finally spoke.

'I think you are full of shit, McCaleb. I think this tape is out of one of those multiplex surveillance systems they use. It won't read on a regular VCR.'

If it didn't seem that every muscle in his body was screaming in pain, McCaleb might have smiled. He had Tafero. He was helplessly hogtied on the bed but he was playing his captor. Tafero was second-guessing his own plan.

'Who else has copies?' Tafero asked.

McCaleb didn't answer. He started thinking that he had been wrong about the boat's movement. Too much time had gone by. There was no one else onboard.

Tafero rapped the tape hard on the back of McCaleb's head.

'I said who else has copies?'

There was a new note in the tone of his voice. One part confidence had been removed and replaced with one equal part fear that there was a flaw in his perfect plan.

'Fuck you,' McCaleb said. 'You do what you have to do with me. Either way, you'll be finding out who's got copies soon enough.'

Tafero pushed down on his legs and leaned over him. McCaleb could feel his breath close to his ear.

'Listen to me, you fucking—'

There was a sudden loud crash from behind McCaleb.

'Don't fucking move!' a voice called.

In the same instant Tafero stood up and let go of McCaleb's legs. The sudden release of pressure coupled with the jarring noise made McCaleb startle and involuntarily flex his muscles at once. He heard the zipping sound of snap cuffs clicking in several places of his bindings. In chain reaction, the cuff around his neck pulled tight and locked. He tried to raise his legs but it was too late, the cuff was set. It was biting into his neck. He had no air. He opened his mouth but not a sound came out.

43

Harry Bosch stood in the doorway of the boat's downstairs cabin and pointed his gun at Rudy Tafero. His eyes widened as he took in the whole room. Terry McCaleb was naked on the bed, his arms and legs bound behind him. Bosch saw that several snap cuffs had been linked together and used to bind his wrists and ankles while a leader ran from his ankles and under his wrists to a loop around his neck. He couldn't see McCaleb's face but saw the plastic was digging tightly into his neck and the skin was a dark rouge. He was strangling.

'Turn around,' he yelled at Tafero. 'Get back against the wall.'

'He needs help, Bosch. You—'

'I said get back against the fucking wall! Now!'

He raised the gun to Tafero's chest level to drive home the order. Tafero raised his hands and started turning to the wall.

'Okay, okay, I'm turning around.'

As soon as Tafero had turned Bosch moved quickly into the room and shoved the big man up against the wall. He glanced at McCaleb. He could see his face now. It was getting redder. His eyes were opened and bugged. His mouth was opened in a desperate but fruitless bid for air.

Bosch pushed the barrel of his gun into Tafero's back and reached his other hand around him to check for a weapon. He pulled a handgun out of Tafero's belt and then stepped back. He looked at McCaleb again and knew he didn't have any time. The problem was controlling Tafero and getting to McCaleb to cut him free. He suddenly knew what needed to be done. He stepped back and brought his hands together so that the guns were side by side. He raised them over his head and brought the butts of both guns down violently into the back of Tafero's head. The big man pitched forward, going face-first into the wood-paneled wall and then dropping to the floor motionless.

Bosch turned and dropped both guns onto the bed and quickly pulled out his keys.

'Hold on, hold on, hold on.'

His fingers scrabbling, he pulled the blade out of the penknife attached to the key chain. He reached to the plastic cuff embedded around McCaleb's neck but couldn't get his fingers underneath it. He shoved McCaleb onto his side and quickly worked his fingers under the cuff at the front of his neck. He slipped the blade in and sliced through the cuff, the point of the knife just nicking the skin beneath it.

A horrible sound came from McCaleb's throat as he gulped air into his lungs and tried to speak at the same time. The words were unintelligible, lost in the instinctive urgency for oxygen intake.

'Shut up and breathe!' Bosch yelled. 'Just breathe!'

There came an interior rattling sound with each breath McCaleb took. Bosch saw a vibrant red line running the circumference of his neck. He gently touched McCaleb's neck, wanting to feel for possible damage to the trachea or larynx or the arteries. McCaleb roughly turned his head on the mattress and tried to move away.

'Just ... cut me loose.'

The words made him cough violently into the mattress, his whole body shaking from the trauma.

Bosch used the knife to cut his hands free and then his ankles. He saw red ligature marks on both sets of limbs. He pulled all the snap cuffs away and threw them on the floor. He looked around and saw the sweatpants and shirt on the floor. He picked them up and threw them onto the bed. McCaleb was slowly turning back to face him, his face still red.

'You ... you ... saved ...'

'Don't talk.'

There was a groan from the floor and Bosch saw Tafero start moving as he began to regain consciousness. Bosch stepped over and stood straddling him. He took his handcuffs off his belt, bent down and then violently pulled Tafero's arms behind his back to cuff him. While he worked he talked to McCaleb.

'Hey, you want to take this guy out, tie him to the anchor and drop him over the side, it'd be fine by me. I wouldn't even blink about it.'

McCaleb didn't respond. He was pulling himself into a sitting position. Finished with the cuffing process, Bosch straightened up and looked down at Tafero, who had now opened his eyes.

'Stay still, shithead. And get used to those cuffs. You are under arrest for murder, attempted murder and general conspiracy to be an asshole. I think you know your rights but do yourself a favor and don't say a word until I get the card out and read it to you.'

The moment he was done speaking Bosch became aware of a creaking sound coming from the hallway. In that second he realized someone had used his words as cover to get close to the doorway.

Things seemed to drop into a slow-motion sense of clarity. Bosch instinctively brought his left hand up to his hip but realized his gun was not there. He had left it on the bed. He started to turn to the bed but saw

McCaleb sitting up, still naked, and already pointing one of the guns at the doorway.

Bosch's eyes followed the aim of the gun to the door. A man was swinging into the opening in a crouched position, two hands on a pistol. He was taking aim at Bosch. There was a shot and wood splintered from the doorjamb. The gunman flinched and squinted his eyes. He recovered and started to level the aim of his gun. There was another shot and another and then another. The noise was deafening in the confines of the wood-paneled room. Bosch watched one bullet hit the wall and two hit the gunman in the chest, throwing him backward into the hallway wall. He sank to the floor but was still visible from the bedroom.

'No!' Tafero shouted from the floor. 'Jesse, no!'

The wounded gunman was still moving but having difficulty with motor controls. With one hand he awkwardly raised the gun again and made a pathetic attempt to aim it once more at Bosch.

There was another shot and Bosch saw the gunman's cheek explode with blood. His head snapped back against the wall behind him and he became still.

'No!' Tafero cried out again.

And then there was silence.

Bosch looked at the bed. McCaleb still held the gun aimed at the door. A cloud of blue gunpowder smoke was rising into the center of the room. The air smelled acrid and burned.

Bosch picked his gun up off the bed and went out to the hallway. He squatted down next to the gunman but didn't need to touch him to know he was dead. During the shooting he had thought he recognized him as Tafero's younger brother who worked in the bail bonds office. Now most of his face was gone.

Bosch got up and went into the head to grab a tissue, which he then used to take the gun out of the dead man's grip. He carried it back into the master cabin and put it down on the nightstand. The gun McCaleb had used was now lying on the bed. McCaleb stood on the other side of the bed. He had the sweatpants on and was pulling the shirt over his head. Once his head came through he looked at Bosch.

Their eyes held for a long moment. They had saved each other. Bosch finally nodded.

Tafero worked his way up into a sitting position against the wall. Blood had run out of his nose and down around both sides of his mouth. It looked like a grotesque Fu Manchu mustache. Bosch guessed that his nose had been broken when he'd gone face-first into the wall. He sat slumped against the wall, his eyes staring in horror through the doorway to the body in the hallway.

Bosch used the tissue to pick the gun up off the bed and put it next to the other one on the nightstand. He then took a cell phone out of his pocket and punched in a number. While he waited for the call to connect he looked at Tafero.

'You got your little brother killed, Rudy,' he said. 'That's too bad.'

Tafero lowered his eyes and started crying.

Bosch's call was answered at central dispatch. He gave the address of the marina and said he was going to need a homicide team from the officer involved–shooting unit. He would need a coroner's crew and techs from Scientific Investigation Division to respond as well. He told the dispatcher to make all notifications by landline. He didn't want the media to get wind of the incident from a police scanner until the time was right.

He closed the phone and held it up for McCaleb to see.

'You want an ambulance? You should get checked out.'

'I'm fine.'

'Your neck looks like it could—'

'I said I'm fine.'

Bosch nodded.

'Suit yourself.'

He came around the bed and stood in front of Tafero.

'I'm going to get him out of here, put him in the car.'

He dragged Tafero to his feet and pushed him to the door. As he passed his brother's body in the hallway Tafero let out a loud animal-like wail, a kind of sound Bosch was surprised to hear coming from such a big man.

'Yeah, it's too bad,' Bosch said without a note of sympathy in his voice. 'The kid had a bright future helping you kill people and getting people out of jail.'

He shoved Tafero toward the steps up to the salon.

On the way up the gangway to the parking lot Bosch saw a man standing on the deck of a sailboat cluttered with rafts and surfboards and other junk. The man looked at Bosch and then Tafero and then back to Bosch. His eyes were wide and it was clear he recognized them, probably from the trial coverage on TV.

'Hey, I heard shots. Is Terry okay?'

'He's going to be fine.'

'Can I go talk to him?'

'Better not. The cops are coming. Let them handle it.'

'Hey, you're Bosch, aren't you? From the trial?'

'Yeah. I'm Bosch.'

The man said nothing else. Bosch kept moving with Tafero.

When Bosch came back onto the boat a few minutes later McCaleb was in the galley drinking a glass of orange juice. Behind him and down the steps the splayed legs of the dead man were visible.

'A neighbor of yours out there asked about you.'

McCaleb nodded.

'Buddy.'

That's all he said.

Bosch looked out the window and back up at the parking lot. He thought he could hear sirens in the distance but thought it might just be the wind playing sound games.

'They're going to be here any minute,' he said. 'How's the throat? I hope you can talk, 'cause we're going to have a lot of explaining to do.'

'It's fine. Why were you here, Harry?'

Bosch put his car keys down on the countertop. He didn't answer for a long moment.

'I just sort of guessed you might be drawing a bead, that's all.'

'How so?'

'You busting in on his brother at the office this morning. I figured that if he followed you, he might've gotten a plate or something they could trace to you here.'

McCaleb looked pointedly at him.

'And what, you were hanging out in the marina and saw Rudy but not the little brother?'

'No, I just drove down and cruised around a little. I saw Rudy's old Lincoln parked up there in the lot and figured something was going on. I never saw the little brother – he must've been hiding somewhere and watching.'

'I'm thinking he was on the docks looking for an owl he could take off a boat to use at Winston's. They were improvising tonight.'

Bosch nodded.

'Anyway, I was looking around and saw the door open on your boat and decided to check it out. I thought it was too cold a night and you were too careful a guy to sleep with the door open like that.'

McCaleb nodded.

Bosch now heard the unmistakable sound of approaching sirens and looked out the window and across the docks to the parking lot. He saw two patrol cars glide in and stop near his slickback where Tafero was locked in the back. They killed the sirens but left the blue lights flashing.

'I better go meet the boys in blue,' he said.

44

For most of the night they were separated and questioned and then questioned again. Then the interrogators switched rooms and they heard the same questions once more from different mouths. Five hours after the shooting on *The Following Sea* the doors were opened and McCaleb and Bosch stepped out into a hallway at Parker Center. Bosch came up to McCaleb then.

'You okay?'

'Tired.'

'Yeah.'

McCaleb watched him put a cigarette in his mouth but not light it.

'I'm heading out to the sheriff's,' Bosch said. 'I want to be there.'

McCaleb nodded.

'I'll see you there.'

They stood side by side behind the one-way glass, squeezed in next to the videographer. McCaleb was close enough to smell Bosch's menthol cigarette breath and the glove-box cologne he had seen him put on in his car while driving behind him out to Whittier. He could see the faint reflection of Bosch's face in the glass and he realized he was looking through it into what was happening in the next room.

On the other side of the glass was a conference table with Rudy Tafero seated next to a public defender named Arnold Prince. Tafero had white tape spread across his nose and cotton in both nostrils. He had six stitches in the crown of his head which could not be seen because of his full head of hair. Paramedics had treated him for a broken nose and the head laceration at Cabrillo Marina.

Across from Tafero sat Jaye Winston. To her right was Alice Short, from the DA's office. To her left were Deputy Chief Irvin Irving of the LAPD and Donald Twilley of the FBI. The early morning hours had been spent with all law enforcement agencies remotely involved in the investigation jockeying for the best position to take advantage of what all players knew to be a major case. It was now six-thirty in the morning and time to question the suspect.

It had been decided that Winston would handle the questioning – it being her case from the beginning – while the other three looked on and were available to her for advice. She began the interview by stating the date, time and identities of those in the room. She then read Tafero his constitutional rights and had him sign an acknowledgment form. His attorney said that Tafero would not be making a statement at the present time.

'That's fine,' Winston said, her eyes on Tafero. 'I don't need him to talk to me. I want to talk to him. I want to give him an idea of what he is facing here. I don't want there to be any regrets down the line over miscommunications or his passing up the one opportunity to cooperate that he'll be given.'

She looked down at the file in front of her and opened it. McCaleb recognized the top sheet as a DA's office complaint form.

'Mr. Tafero,' Winston began, 'I want you to know that this morning we are charging you with the first-degree murder of Edward Gunn on January first of this year, the attempted murder of Terrell McCaleb on this date, and the murder of Jesse Tafero, also on this date. I know you know the law but I am compelled to explain the last charge. Your brother's death occurred during the commission of a felony. Therefore, under California law you, as his co-conspirator, are held responsible for his death.'

She waited a beat, staring into Tafero's seemingly dead eyes. She went back to reading the complaint.

'Further, you should know that the district attorney's office has agreed to file a count of special circumstances in regard to the murder of Edward Gunn. To wit, murder for hire. The addition of special circumstances will make it a death penalty case. Alice?'

Short leaned forward. She was an attractive, petite woman in her late thirties with big, engaging eyes. She was the deputy chief in charge of major trials. It was a lot of power in such a small body – especially when contrasted with the size of the man across the table from her.

'Mr. Tafero, you were a policeman for twenty years,' she said. 'You more than most know the gravity of your actions. There is not a case I can think of that cries out more for the death penalty. We will ask a jury for it. And I have no doubt we will get it.'

Her rehearsed part of the play finished, Short leaned back in her chair and deferred to Winston. There was a long silence while Winston stared at Tafero and waited for him to look back at her. Eventually, his eyes came up and held on hers.

'Mr. Tafero, you've been around and you've even been in the opposite position in rooms just like this before. I don't think we could play a game on you if we had a year to work it out. So no game. Just the offer. A one-time offer that will be rescinded, permanently, when we walk out of this room. It comes down to this.'

The focus of Tafero's eyes had dropped to the table again. Winston leaned forward and looked up into them.

'Do you want to live or do you want to take your chances with the jury? It's as simple as that. And before you answer, there are a few things to consider. Number one, the jurors are going to see photographic evidence of what you did to Edward Gunn. Two, they are going to hear Terry McCaleb describe what it was like to be so helpless and to feel his own life being choked away by your design. You know, I don't usually bet on such things but I'd give it less than an hour. My bet is that it will be one of the quickest death verdicts ever returned in the state of California.'

Winston pulled back and closed the file in front of her. McCaleb found himself nodding. She was doing very well.

'We want your employer,' Winston said. 'We want physical evidence that will link him to the Gunn case. I have a feeling that someone like you would take precautions before carrying out such a scheme. Whatever it is, we want what you have.'

She looked at Short and the prosecutor nodded, her way of saying well done.

Almost half a minute went by. Finally, Tafero turned to his attorney and was about to whisper a question. Then he turned back to Winston.

'Fuck it, I'll ask myself. Without acknowledging a fucking thing here, what if you drop the special circumstances? What am I facing?'

Winston immediately burst out laughing and shook her head. McCaleb smiled.

'Are you kidding?' Winston asked. ' "What am I facing?" Man, you are going to be buried in concrete and steel. That's what you are facing. You are never, *ever* going to see the light of day again. Deal, no deal, that is a given and non-negotiable.'

Tafero's attorney cleared his throat.

'Ms. Winston, this is hardly a professional manner in which—'

'I don't give a shit about my manner. This man is a killer. He's no different from a hit man except, no, he's worse. He used to carry a badge and that makes it all the more despicable. So this is what we'll do for your client, Mr. Prince. We'll take guilty pleas to the murder of Edward Gunn and the attempted on Terry McCaleb. Life without on both counts. Non-negotiable. We'll no-bill the charge on his brother. Maybe it will help him live with it better if he doesn't carry the charge. I don't really care. What I care about is that he understands that his life as he knows it is over. He's gone. And he can either go to death row or super max, but he's going to one of them and not coming back.'

She looked at her watch.

'You've got about five minutes and then we're out of here. You don't want the deal, fine, we'll take both of them to trial. Storey might be a long shot but there's no question about Mr. Tafero here. Alice is going to have prosecutors knocking down her door, sending her flowers and chocolates. Every day's going to be Valentine's Day – or Valentino's day, as the case may be. This one's a ticket to prosecutor of the year.'

Prince brought a slim briefcase up onto the table and slid his legal pad into it. He hadn't written a word on it.

'Thank you for your time,' he said. 'I think what we'll do is proceed to a bail hearing and go from there with discovery and other matters.'

He pushed his chair back and stood up.

Tafero slowly raised his head and looked at Winston, his eyes badly bloodshot from the hemorrhaging of his nose.

'It was his idea to make it look like a painting,' he said. 'David Storey's idea.'

There was a moment of stunned silence and then the defense attorney sat down heavily and closed his eyes in pain.

'Mr. Tafero,' Prince said. 'I am strongly advising—'

'Shut up,' Tafero barked. 'You little pissant. You're not the one facing the needle.'

He looked back at Winston.

'I'll take the deal. As long as I don't get charged with my brother.'

Winston nodded.

Tafero turned to Short and pointed his finger and waited. She nodded.

'Deal,' she said.

'One thing,' Winston said quickly. 'We're not going into this with your word against his. What else have you got?'

Tafero looked at her and a thin, dead smile cracked across his face.

In the viewing room, Bosch stepped closer to the glass. McCaleb saw his reflection more clearly on the glass. His eyes stared unblinking.

'I've got pictures,' Tafero said.

Winston hooked her hair behind her ear and narrowed her eyes. She leaned across the table.

'Pictures? What do you mean, photographs? Photographs of what?'

Tafero shook his head.

'No. Pictures. He drew pictures for me while we were in the attorney visiting room in the jail. Drawings of what he wanted the scene to look like. So it would look like the painting.'

McCaleb gripped his hands into fists at his sides.

'Where are the drawings?' Winston said.

Tafero smiled again.

'Safe-deposit box. City National Bank, Sunset and Doheny. The key's on the ring that was in my pocket.'

Bosch brought his hands up and slapped them together.

'Bang!' he exclaimed, loud enough that Tafero turned and looked toward the glass.

'Please!' the videographer whispered. 'We're taping.'

Bosch went to the door of the little room and stepped out. McCaleb followed. Bosch turned and looked at him. He nodded.

'Storey goes down,' he said. 'The monster goes back into the darkness from which it came.'

They looked at each other silently for a moment and then Bosch broke it away.

'I gotta go,' he said.

'Where?'

'Get ready for court.'

He turned and started walking through the deserted bullpen of the sheriff's department homicide squad. McCaleb saw him bang a fist on a desk and then punch it into the air above him.

McCaleb went back into the viewing room and watched the interview continue. Tafero was telling the assemblage in the interview room that David Storey had demanded that the killing of Edward Gunn take place on the first morning of the new year.

McCaleb listened for a while and then thought of something. He stepped out of the observation room and into the bullpen. Detectives were now filtering in to start the day of work. He went to an empty desk and tore a page off a notepad on its top. He wrote, 'Ask about the Lincoln' on it. He folded it and took it to the door of the interview room.

He knocked and after a moment Alice Short opened the door. He handed her the folded note.

'Give this to Jaye before the interview is over,' he whispered.

She nodded and closed the door. McCaleb went back into the observation room to watch.

45

Freshly showered and shaved, Bosch stepped off the elevator and headed toward the doors to the Division N courtroom. He walked with purpose. He felt like a true prince of the city. He had taken only a few strides when he was accosted by McEvoy, who stepped out of an alcove like a coyote that had been waiting in a cave for his unsuspecting prey. But nothing could dent Bosch's demeanor. He smiled as the reporter fell into stride with him.

'Detective Bosch, have you thought any more about what we talked about? I've got to start writing my story today.'

Bosch didn't slow his pace. He knew that once he got into the courtroom he wouldn't have a lot of time.

'Rudy Tafero,' he said.

'Excuse me?'

'He was your source. Rudy Tafero. I figured it out this morning.'

'Detective, I told you that I can't reveal—'

'Yeah, I know. But, see, I'm the one who's revealing it. Anyway, it doesn't matter.'

'Why not?'

Bosch suddenly stopped. McEvoy walked a few steps past and then came back.

'Why not?' he asked again.

'Today's your lucky day, Jack. I've got two good tips for you.'

'Okay. What?'

McEvoy started pulling a notebook from his back pocket. Bosch put his hand on his arm to stop him.

'Don't take that out. The other reporters see that, they'll think I'm telling you something.'

He gestured up the hall to the open door of the media room where a handful of reporters were loitering and waiting for the day's court session to begin.

'Then they'll come over and I'll have to tell them.'

McEvoy left the notebook in place.

'Okay. What are the tips?'

'First of all, you're full of shit on that story. In fact, your source was arrested this morning for the murder of Edward Gunn as well as the attempted murder of Terry McCaleb.'

'What? He got—'

'Wait. Let me talk. I don't have a lot of time.'

He waited and McEvoy nodded.

'Yeah, Rudy got popped. He killed Gunn. The plan was to put it on me and spring it on the world during the defense case.'

'Are you saying that Storey was a part of—'

'Exactly. Which brings me to tip number two. And that is, if I were you, I would be in that courtroom today long before the judge comes in and starts things. You see those guys standing down there? They're going to miss it, Jack. You don't want to be like them.'

Bosch left him there. He nodded to the deputy on the courtroom door and was allowed in.

Two deputies were walking David Storey to his place at the defense table as Bosch came into the courtroom. Fowkkes was already there and Langwiser and Kretzler were seated at the prosecution table. Bosch looked at his watch as he came through the gate. He had about fifteen minutes before the judge would take the bench and call for the jury.

He went to the prosecution table but remained standing. He leaned down and put both palms on the table and looked at the two prosecutors.

'Harry, you ready?' Langwiser began. 'Today's the day.'

'Today's the day but not because of what you think. You two would take a plea on this wouldn't you? If he copped to Jody Krementz *and* Alicia Lopez, you wouldn't go for the needle, right?'

They both looked at him with blank stares of confusion.

'Come on, we don't have a lot of time before the judge comes out. What if I could go over there and in five minutes get you two murder ones? Alicia Lopez's family would love you for it. You told them you didn't have a case.'

'Harry, what are you talking about?' Langwiser said. 'We floated a plea. Twice. Fowkkes shot it down both times.'

'And we don't have the evidence on Lopez,' Kretzler added. 'You know that – the grand jury passed. Nobody, no—'

'Listen, you want the plea or not? I think I can go over there and get it. I arrested Rudy Tafero for murder this morning. It was a setup orchestrated by Storey to get to me. It backfired and Tafero is taking a deal. He's talking.'

'Jesus Christ!' Kretzler said.

He said it too loudly. Bosch turned and looked over at the defense table. Both Fowkkes and Storey were looking at them. Just past the defense table he saw McEvoy take a seat in the media gallery that was closest to the defense table. No other reporters had come in and sat down yet.

'Harry, what are you talking about?' Langwiser said. 'What murder?'

Bosch ignored the questions.

'Let me go over there,' Bosch said. 'I want to look in Storey's eyes when I tell him.'

Kretzler and Langwiser looked at each other. Langwiser shrugged her shoulders and waved her hands in exasperation.

'Worth a try. We were only holding death as an ace in the hole.'

'Okay then,' Bosch said. 'See if you can get the clerk to buy me some time with the judge.'

Bosch stepped around the defense table and stood in front of it so he could look equally at Fowkkes and Storey. Fowkkes was writing something on a legal pad. Bosch cleared his throat and after a few moments the defense attorney slowly looked up.

'Yes, Detective? Shouldn't you be at your table preparing for—'

'Where's Rudy Tafero?'

Bosch looked at Storey as he asked it.

Fowkkes looked behind him to the seat against the rail where Tafero normally sat during court sessions.

'I'm sure he's on his way,' he said. 'We have a few minutes.'

Bosch smiled.

'On his way? Yeah, he's on his way. Up to super max at Corcoran, maybe Pelican Cove if he's lucky. I really wouldn't want to be a former cop doing my time in Corcoran.'

Fowkkes seemed unimpressed.

'Detective, I don't know what you are talking about. I am trying to prepare a defense strategy here because I think the prosecution is going to fold its tent today. So, if you don't mind.'

Bosch looked at Storey when he responded.

'There is no strategy. There is no defense. Rudy Tafero was arrested this morning. He's been charged with murder and attempted murder. I'm sure your client can tell you all about it, Counselor. That is, if you didn't know already.'

Fowkkes stood up abruptly as though he were making an objection.

'Sir, it is highly irregular for you to come to the defense table and—'

'He cut a deal about two hours ago. He's laying it all out.'

Again Bosch ignored Fowkkes and looked at Storey.

'So here's the deal. You've got about five minutes to go over there to Langwiser and Kretzler and agree to plead to murder one on Krementz *and* Lopez.'

'This is preposterous. I am going to complain to the judge about this.'

Bosch now looked at Fowkkes.

'You do that. But it doesn't change things. Five minutes.'

Bosch stepped away but went to the clerk's desk in front of the judge's bench. The exhibits were lying stacked on a side table. Bosch looked through them until he found the poster he wanted. He slid it out and carried it with him back to the defense table. Fowkkes was still standing but bending down so Storey could whisper in his ear. Bosch dropped the poster, containing the blowup photo of the bookcase in Storey's house, on the table. He tapped his finger on two of the books on an upper shelf. The titles on the spines were clearly readable. One title was *The Art of Darkness* and the other book was merely titled *Bosch*.

'There's your prior knowledge right there.'

He left the exhibit on the defense table and started to walk back to the prosecution table. But after two steps he came back and put his palms down flat on the defense table. He looked directly at Storey. He spoke in a voice that he knew would be loud enough for McEvoy to hear in the media gallery.

'You know what your big mistake was, David?'

'No,' Storey said, a sneer in his voice. 'Why don't you tell me?'

Fowkkes immediately grabbed his client's arm in a silencing gesture.

'Drawing out the scene for Tafero,' Bosch said. 'What he did was, he went and put those pretty pictures you made right into his safe-deposit box at City National. He knew they might come in handy and they sure did. He used them this morning to buy *his* way out of a death sentence. What are you going to use?'

Bosch saw the falter in Storey's eyes, the tell. For just a moment his eyes blinked without really blinking. But in that moment Bosch knew it was over because Storey knew it was over.

Bosch straightened up and casually looked at his watch, then at Fowkkes.

'About three minutes now, Mr. Fowkkes. Your client's life is on the line.'

He returned to the defense table and sat down. Kretzler and Langwiser leaned toward him and urgently whispered questions but Bosch ignored them.

'Let's just see what happens.'

Over the next five minutes he never once looked over at the defense table. He could hear muffled words and whispers but couldn't make out any of it. The courtroom filled with spectators and members of the media.

Nothing came from the defense table.

At precisely 9 A.M. the door behind the bench opened and Judge Houghton bounded up the steps to his spot. He took his seat and glanced at both the prosecution and defense tables.

'Ladies and gentlemen, are we ready for the jury?'

'Yes, Your Honor,' Kretzler said.

Nothing came from the defense table. Houghton looked over, a curious smile on his face.

'Mr. Fowkkes? Can I bring in our jury?'

Now Bosch leaned back so he could look past Langwiser and Kretzler at the defense table. Fowkkes sat slouched in his chair, a posture he had never exhibited in the courtroom before. He had an elbow on the arm of the chair and his hand up. He was wagging a pen in his fingers and seemed to be lost in deep, depressing thought. His client sat rigid next to him, face forward.

'Mr. Fowkkes? I'm waiting for an answer.'

Fowkkes finally looked up at the judge. Very slowly he rose from the seat and went to the lectern.

'Your Honor, may we approach at sidebar for a moment?'

The judge looked both curious and annoyed. It had been the routine of the trial to submit all non-public conference requests by 8:30 A.M. so that they could be considered and argued in chambers without cutting into court time.

'This can't be handled in open court, Mr. Fowkkes?'

'No, Your Honor. Not at this time.'

'Very well. Come on up.'

Houghton signaled the lawyers forward with both hands as though he were giving signals to a truck backing up.

The attorneys approached the side of the bench and huddled with the judge. From his angle Bosch could see all of their faces and he didn't need to hear what was being whispered. Fowkkes looked ashen and after a few words Kretzler and Langwiser seemed to grow in stature. Langwiser even glanced over at Bosch and he could read the victory message in her eyes.

He turned and looked over at the defendant. He waited and David Storey slowly turned and their eyes locked one final time. Bosch didn't smile. He didn't blink. He didn't do anything but hold the stare. Eventually, it was Storey who looked away and down at his hands lying in his lap. Bosch felt a trilling sensation move over his scalp. He'd felt it before, times when he had glimpsed the normally hidden face of the monster.

The sidebar conference broke up and the two prosecutors came back quickly to the table, excitement clearly showing in their strides and on their faces. By contrast J. Reason Fowkkes moved slowly to the defense table.

'That's all, Fowkkes,' Bosch said under his breath.

Langwiser grabbed Bosch by the shoulder as she sat down.

'He's going to plead,' she whispered excitedly. 'Krementz *and* Lopez. When you went over there, did you say consecutive or concurrent sentencing?'

'I didn't say either.'

'Okay. We just agreed on concurrent but we're going into chambers to work it out. We need to formally charge Storey with Lopez first. You want to come in and make the arrest?'

'Whatever. If you want me to.'

Bosch knew it was just a legal formality. Storey was already in custody.

'You deserve it, Harry. We want you to be there.'

'Fine.'

The judge tapped his gavel once and drew the courtroom's attention. The reporters in the media gallery were all leaning forward in their seats. They knew something big was going on.

'We'll stand in recess until ten o'clock,' the judge announced. 'I'll see all parties in chambers now.'

He stood up and quickly went down the three stairs to the rear door before the deputy had time to call, 'All rise.'

46

McCaleb stayed away from *The Following Sea,* even after the last detective and forensic technician had finished with it. From early afternoon until dark the boat was staked out by reporters and television news crews. The coupling of the shooting aboard the boat plus the arrest of Tafero and abrupt guilty pleas from David Storey had turned the boat into the central image of a story that had developed quickly through the day. Every local channel plus the networks shot their stand-up reports from the marina, *The Following Sea* serving as the backdrop with its yellow police tape strung across the salon door.

McCaleb hid out for most of the afternoon in Buddy Lockridge's boat, staying below decks and donning one of Buddy's floppy fishing hats if he poked his head up through a hatch to see what was going on outside. The two were talking again. Soon after leaving the sheriff's department and getting to the marina ahead of the media, McCaleb had sought out Buddy and apologized for assuming that his charter partner had leaked the story. Buddy in turn apologized for using *The Following Sea* – and McCaleb's cabin – as a rendezvous point for encounters with erotic masseuses. McCaleb agreed to tell Graciela he had been wrong about Buddy being the leak. He also agreed not to tell her about the masseuses. Buddy had explained that he didn't want Graciela thinking less of him than she probably already did.

While they hid out in the boat, they watched Buddy's little twelve-inch TV and remained up-to-the-minute with the day's developments. Channel 9, which had been carrying the Storey trial live, remained most current, staying on live and continuously reporting from the Van Nuys courthouse and the sheriff's Star Center.

McCaleb was left stunned and in awe by the day's events. David Storey abruptly filed guilty pleas in Van Nuys to two murders as he was simultaneously charged in the downtown Los Angeles courthouse with being a conspirator in the Gunn case. The movie director had avoided the death penalty in the first cases but still would face it in the Gunn case if he did not make another plea arrangement with prosecutors.

A televised news conference at the Star Center had featured Jaye Winston prominently. She answered questions from reporters after the sheriff, flanked by LAPD and FBI brass, read a statement announcing the day's events from an investigative standpoint. McCaleb's name was mentioned numerous times in the discussion of the investigation and subsequent shooting aboard *The Following Sea*. Winston also mentioned it at the end of the news conference when she expressed her thanks to him, saying it was his volunteer work on the case that broke it open.

Bosch was also prominently mentioned but took no part in any press conferences. After Storey's guilty verdicts were entered in the Van Nuys court, Bosch and the lawyers involved in the case were mobbed outside the doors to the courtroom. But McCaleb had seen video on one channel of Bosch pushing his way through the reporters and cameras and refusing to comment as he moved to a fire escape and disappeared down the stairs.

The only reporter who got to McCaleb was Jack McEvoy, who still had his cell phone number. McCaleb talked to him briefly but declined to comment on what had happened in the master cabin of *The Following Sea* and how close he had come to death. His thoughts about that were too personal and he would never share them with any reporter.

McCaleb had also talked to Graciela, calling her and filling her in on the events before she saw them on the news. He told her he probably wouldn't get home until the next day because he was sure the media pack would be watching the boat until well after dark. She said she was glad it was over and that he'd be coming home. He sensed there was still a high level of stress in her voice and knew it was something he would have to address when he got back to the island.

Late in the day McCaleb was able to slip out of Buddy's boat unnoticed when the media pack was distracted by activity in the marina parking lot. The LAPD was towing off the old Lincoln Continental that the Tafero brothers had been using the night before when they had come to the marina to kill McCaleb. While the news crews filmed and watched the mundane task of a car being hooked up and towed away, McCaleb was able to get to his Cherokee without being spotted. He started the car and drove out of the lot ahead of the tow truck. Not a single reporter followed.

It was fully dark by the time he got to Bosch's house. The front door was open as it had been the time before, the screen door in place. McCaleb rapped on the wooden frame and peered through the mesh into the darkness of the house. There was a single light – a reading light – on in the living room. He could hear music and thought it was the same Art Pepper CD that had been playing during his last visit. But he didn't see Bosch.

McCaleb looked away from the door to check the street and when he looked back Bosch was standing at the screen and it startled him. Bosch unhooked a latch and opened the screen. He was wearing the same suit

McCaleb had seen him in on the news. He was holding a bottle of Anchor Steam down at his side.

'Terry. Come on in. I thought maybe you were a reporter. Bugs the hell out of me when they come to your house. Seems like there should be one place they can't go.'

'Yeah, I know what you mean. They're all over the boat. I had to get away.'

McCaleb passed by Bosch in the entrance hallway and stepped into the living room.

'So reporters aside, how's it going, Harry?'

'Never better. A good day for our side. How's your neck doing?'

'Sore as hell. But I'm alive.'

'Yeah, that's what's important. Want a beer?'

'Uh, that would be good.'

While Bosch got the beer McCaleb went out to the rear deck.

Bosch had the deck lights off, making the lights of the city more brilliant in the distance. McCaleb could hear the ever-present sound of the freeway at the bottom of the pass. Searchlights cut across the sky from three different locations on the valley floor. Bosch came out and handed him a beer.

'No glass, right?'

'No glass.'

They looked out into the night and drank their beers silently for a little while. McCaleb thought about how he should say what he wanted to say. He was still working on it.

'The last thing they were doing before I left was hooking up Tafero's car,' he said after some time.

Bosch nodded.

'What about the boat? They finished with it?'

'Yeah, they're done.'

'Is it a mess? They always leave things a mess.'

'Probably. I haven't been inside. I'll worry about it tomorrow.'

Bosch nodded. McCaleb took a long draw on his beer and put the bottle down on the railing. He had taken too much. It backed up in his throat and burned his sinuses.

'Okay?' Bosch asked.

'Yeah, fine.' He wiped his mouth with the back of his hand. 'Harry, I came up to tell you I'm not going to be your friend anymore.'

Bosch started to laugh but then stopped.

'What?'

McCaleb looked at him. Bosch's eyes were still piercing in the darkness. They had caught a speck of reflected light from somewhere and McCaleb could see the two pinpoints holding on him.

'You should've hung around a little longer this morning while Jaye interviewed Tafero.'

'I didn't have the time.'

'She asked him about the Lincoln and he said it was his undercover car. He said he used it on jobs when he didn't want there to be any chance of a trace. It has stolen plates on it. And the registration is phony.'

'Makes sense, a guy like that, having a car for the wet work.'

'You don't get it, do you?'

Bosch had finished his beer. He was leaning with his elbows on the railing. He was peeling the label off the bottle and dropping the little pieces into the darkness below.

'No, I don't get it, Terry. Why don't you tell me what you're talking about?'

McCaleb picked up his beer but then put it back down without drinking any more.

'His real car, the one he used every day, is a Mercedes 430 CLK. That was the one he caught the ticket with. For parking at the post office when he sent the money order.'

'Okay, the guy had two cars. His secret car and his show car. What does it mean?'

'It means you knew something you shouldn't have known.'

'What are you talking about? Knew what?'

'Last night I asked you why you came onto my boat. You said you saw Tafero's Lincoln and knew there was something wrong. How did you know that Lincoln was his?'

Bosch was silent for a long moment. He looked out into the night and nodded.

'I saved your life,' he said.

'I saved yours.'

'So we're even. Leave it at that, Terry.'

McCaleb shook his head. It felt like there was a fist in his stomach pushing up into his chest, trying to get to his new heart.

'I think you knew that Lincoln and knew it meant trouble for me because you had watched Tafero before. Maybe on a night he was using the Lincoln. Maybe on a night he was watching Gunn and setting up the hit. Maybe on the night he made the hit. You saved my life because you knew something, Harry.'

McCaleb was quiet for a moment, giving Bosch an opportunity to say something in his defense.

'That's a lot of maybes, Terry.'

'Yeah. A lot of maybes and one guess. My guess is that somehow you knew or you figured out back when Tafero hooked up with Storey that they would have to come after you in court. So you watched Tafero and you saw him draw the bead on Gunn. You knew what was going to happen and you let it happen.'

McCaleb took another long drink of beer and put the bottle back down on the railing.

'A dangerous game, Harry. They almost pulled it off. But I guess if I hadn't come along you would've figured out some way of pointing it back at them.'

Bosch continued to stare out into the darkness and say nothing.

'The one thing I hope is that you weren't the one who tipped Tafero that Gunn was in the tank that night. Tell me you didn't make that call, Harry. Tell me you didn't help get him out so they could kill him like that.'

Again Bosch said nothing. McCaleb nodded.

'You want to shake somebody's hand, Harry, shake your own.'

Bosch dropped his gaze and looked down into the darkness below the deck. McCaleb watched him closely and saw him slowly shake his head.

'We do what we have to do,' Bosch said quietly. 'Sometimes you have choices. Sometimes there is no choice, only necessity. You see things happening and you know they're wrong but somehow they're also right.'

He was silent for a long moment and McCaleb waited.

'I didn't make that call,' Bosch said.

He turned and looked at McCaleb. Again McCaleb could see the shining points of light in the blackness of his eyes.

'Three people – three monsters – are gone.'

'But not that way. We don't do it that way.'

Bosch nodded.

'What about your play, Terry? Pushing past the little brother into the office. Like you didn't think that would start some shit. You pushed the action with that little move and you know it.'

McCaleb felt his face growing hot under Bosch's stare. He didn't answer. He didn't know what to say.

'You had your own plan, Terry. So what's the difference?'

'The difference? If you don't see it, then you have completely fallen. You are lost.'

'Yeah, well, maybe I'm lost and maybe I've been found. I'll have to think about it. Meantime, why don't you just go home now. Go back to your little island and your little girl. Hide behind what you think you see in her eyes. Pretend the world is not what you know it to be.'

McCaleb nodded. He'd said what he wanted to say. He stepped away from the railing, leaving his beer, and walked toward the door to the house. But Bosch hit him with more words as he entered the house.

'You think naming her after a girl nobody cared about or loved can make up for that lost girl? Well, you're wrong, man. Just go home and keep dreaming.'

McCaleb hesitated in the doorway and looked back.

'Good-bye, Harry.'

'Yeah, good-bye.'

McCaleb walked through the house. When he passed the reading chair where the light was on he saw the printout of his profile of Bosch sitting on the arm of the chair. He kept going. When he got to the front door he pulled it closed behind him.

47

Bosch stood with his arms folded on the deck railing and his head down. He thought about McCaleb's words, both spoken and printed. They were pieces of hot shrapnel ripping through him. He felt a deep tearing of his interior lining. It felt as though something within had seized him and was pulling him into a black hole, that he was imploding into nothingness.

'What did I do?' he whispered. 'What did I do?'

He straightened up and saw the bottle on the railing, its label gone. He grabbed it and threw it as far as he could out into the darkness. He watched its trajectory, able to follow its flight because of moonlight reflecting off the brown glass. The bottle exploded in the brush on the rocky hillside below.

He saw McCaleb's half-finished beer and grabbed it. He pulled his arm back, wanting to throw this one all the way to the freeway. Then he stopped. He put the bottle back on the railing and went inside.

He grabbed the printed profile off the arm of the chair and started ripping the two pages apart. He went to the kitchen, turned the water on and put the pieces into the sink. He flicked on the garbage disposal and pushed the pieces of paper into the drain. He waited until he could tell by the sound that the paper had been chewed into nothing and was gone. He turned off the disposal and just watched the water running into the drain.

Slowly, his eyes came up and he looked through the kitchen window and out through the Cahuenga Pass. The lights of Hollywood glimmered in the cut, a mirror reflection of the stars of all galaxies everywhere. He thought about all that was bad out there. A city with more things wrong than right. A place where the earth could open up beneath you and suck you into the blackness. A city of lost light. His city. It was all of that and, still, always still, a place to begin again. His city. The city of the second chance.

Bosch nodded and bent down. He closed his eyes, put his hands under the water and brought them up to his face. The water was cold and bracing, as he thought any baptism, the start of any second chance, should be.

48

He could still smell burned gunpowder. McCaleb stood in the master cabin and looked around. There were rubber gloves and other debris scattered on the floor. Black fingerprint dust was everywhere, on everything. The door to the room was gone and so was the doorjamb, cut right out of the wall. In the hallway an entire wall panel had been removed as well. McCaleb walked over and looked down at the floor where the little brother had died from the bullets he had fired. The blood had dried brown and would permanently stain the alternating light and dark wood strips in the floor. It would always be there to remind him.

Staring at the blood, he replayed the shots he had fired at the man, the images in his mind moving much slower than real time. He thought about what Bosch had said to him, out on the deck. About letting the little brother follow him. He considered his own culpability. Could his guilt be any less than Bosch's? They had both set things in motion. For every action there is an equal and opposite reaction. You don't go into the darkness without the darkness going into you.

'We do what we have to do,' he said out loud.

He went up into the salon and looked out the door at the parking lot. The reporters were still up there with their vans. He had sneaked in. Parked at the far end of the marina and then borrowed a skiff from somebody's boat to get to *The Following Sea*. He had climbed aboard and slipped in without anyone seeing him.

He noticed that the vans had their microwave towers cranked up and each crew was getting ready for the eleven o'clock report, the camera angles set so that *The Following Sea* would once more be in all the shots. McCaleb smiled and opened his phone. He hit a number on speed dial and Buddy Lockridge answered.

'Buddy, it's me. Listen, I'm on the boat and I gotta go home. I want you to do me a favor.'

'You gotta go tonight? Are you sure?'

'Yeah, this is what I want you to do. When you hear me turn the Pentas over, you come over and untie me. Do it fast. I'll do the rest.'

'You want me to go with you?'

'No, I'll be fine. Catch an *Express* over on Friday. We've got the charter on Saturday morning.'

'All right, Terror. I heard on the radio it's pretty flat out there tonight and no fog, but be careful.'

McCaleb closed the phone and went to the salon door. Most of the reporters and their crews were preoccupied and not looking at the boat because they had already assured themselves it was empty. He slid open the door and stepped out, shut the door and then quickly climbed the ladder to the bridge. He unzipped the plastic curtain that enclosed the bridge and slipped in. Making sure both throttles were in neutral, he engaged the choke and slid his key into the ignition.

He turned the key and the starters began to whine loudly. Looking back through the plastic curtain he saw the reporters had all turned to the boat. The engines finally turned over and he worked the throttles, revving the engines into a quick-start warm-up. He glanced back again and saw Buddy coming down the dock to the boat's stern. A couple of the reporters were hurrying down the gangway to the dock behind him.

Buddy quickly uncleated the two stern lines and threw them into the cockpit. He then moved down the side pier to get the bow line. McCaleb lost sight of him but then heard his call.

'Clear!'

McCaleb took the throttles out of neutral and moved the boat out of the slip. As he made the turn into the fairway he looked back and saw Buddy standing on the side pier and the reporters behind him on the dock.

Once he was away from the cameras he unzipped the curtains and took them down. The cool air swept into the bridge and braced him. He sighted the flashing red lights of the channel markers and put the boat on course. He looked ahead, past the markers, into the darkness but saw nothing. He turned on the Raytheon and saw that which he could not see ahead. The island was there on the radar screen.

Ten minutes later, after he had cleared the harbor break line, McCaleb pulled the phone out of his jacket and speed-dialed home. He knew it was too late to call and that he was risking waking the children. Graciela answered in a whispered urgency.

'Sorry, it's just me.'

'Terry, are you all right?'

'I am now. I'm coming home.'

'You're crossing in the dark?'

McCaleb thought a moment about the question.

'I'll be all right. I can see in the dark.'

Graciela didn't say anything. She had an ability to know when he was saying one thing and talking about something else.

'Put the deck light on,' he said. 'I'll look for it when I get close.'

He closed the phone and pushed the throttles up. The bow started to rise and then leveled off. He passed the last channel marker twenty yards to his left. He was right on course. A three-quarter moon was high in the sky ahead and laying down a shimmering path of liquid silver for him to follow home. He held on tightly to the wheel and thought about the moment when he had truly thought he was going to die. He remembered the image of his daughter that had come to him and had comforted him. Tears started to roll down his cheeks. Soon the wind off the water dried them on his face.

Acknowledgments

The author gratefully acknowledges the help of many people during the writing of this book. They include John Houghton, Jerry Hooten, Cameron Riddell, Dawson Carr, Terrill Lankford, Linda Connelly, Mary Lavelle and Susan Connelly.

For words of support of inspiration just when they were needed, thanks go to Sarah Crichton, Philip Spitzer, Scott Eyman, Ed Thomas, Steve Stilwell, Josh Meyer, John Sacret Young and Kathy Lingg.

The author is indebted to Jane Davis for her excellent management of *www.michaelconnelly.com*. Gerald Petievich and Robert Crais are owed many thanks for excellent career advice foolishly ingnored – to this point, at least – by the author.

This book, like those before it, would not exist in publishable form without the excellent efforts of its editor, Michael Pietsch, and copy editor, Betty Power, and the entire team at Little, Brown and Company.

And all this work would be for naught if not for the efforts of the many booksellers who put the stories into readers' hands. Thank you.

Lastly, special thanks to Raymond Chandler for inspiring the title of the book. Describing in 1950 the time and place from which he drew his early crime stories, Chandler wrote, 'The streets were dark with something more than night.'

Sometimes they still are.

Michael Connelly
Los Angeles

City of
Bones

This is for John Houghton,
for the help, the friendship and the stories

1

The old lady had changed her mind about dying but by then it was too late. She had dug her fingers into the paint and plaster of the nearby wall until most of her fingernails had broken off. Then she had gone for the neck, scrabbling to push the bloodied fingertips up and under the cord. She broke four toes kicking at the walls. She had tried so hard, shown such a desperate will to live, that it made Harry Bosch wonder what had happened before. Where was that determination and will and why had it deserted her until after she had put the extension cord noose around her neck and kicked over the chair? Why had it hidden from her?

These were not official questions that would be raised in his death report. But they were the things Bosch couldn't avoid thinking about as he sat in his car outside the Splendid Age Retirement Home on Sunset Boulevard east of the Hollywood Freeway. It was 4:20 P.M. on the first day of the year. Bosch had drawn holiday call-out duty.

The day more than half over and that duty consisted of two suicide runs – one a gunshot, the other the hanging. Both victims were women. In both cases there was evidence of depression and desperation. Isolation. New Year's Day was always a big day for suicides. While most people greeted the day with a sense of hope and renewal, there were those who saw it as a good day to die, some – like the old lady – not realizing their mistake until it was too late.

Bosch looked up through the windshield and watched as the latest victim's body, on a wheeled stretcher and covered in a green blanket, was loaded into the coroner's blue van. He saw there was one other occupied stretcher in the van and knew it was from the first suicide – a thirty-four-year-old actress who had shot herself while parked at a Hollywood overlook on Mulholland Drive. Bosch and the body crew had followed one case to the other.

Bosch's cell phone chirped and he welcomed the intrusion into his thoughts on small deaths. It was Mankiewicz, the watch sergeant at the Hollywood Division of the Los Angeles Police Department.

'You finished with that yet?'

'I'm about to clear.'

'Anything?'

'A changed-my-mind suicide. You got something else?'

'Yeah. And I didn't think I should go out on the radio with it. Must be a slow day for the media – getting more what's-happening calls from reporters than I am getting service calls from citizens. They all want to do something on the first one, the actress on Mulholland. You know, a death-of-a-Hollywood-dream story. And they'd probably jump all over this latest call, too.'

'Yeah, what is it?'

'A citizen up in Laurel Canyon. On Wonderland. He just called up and said his dog came back from a run in the woods with a bone in its mouth. The guy says it's human – an arm bone from a kid.'

Bosch almost groaned. There were four or five call outs like this a year. Hysteria always followed by simple explanation: animal bones. Through the windshield he saluted the two body movers from the coroner's office as they headed to the front doors of the van.

'I know what you're thinking, Harry. Not another bone run. You've done it a hundred times and it's always the same thing. Coyote, deer, whatever. But listen, this guy with the dog, he's an MD. And he says there's no doubt. It's a humerus. That's the upper arm bone. He says it's a child, Harry. And then, get this. He said . . .'

There was silence while Mankiewicz apparently looked for his notes. Bosch watched the coroner's blue van pull off into traffic. When Mankiewicz came back he was obviously reading.

'The bone's got a fracture clearly visible just above the medial epicondyle, whatever that is.'

Bosch's jaw tightened. He felt a slight tickle of electric current go down the back of his neck.

'That's off my notes, I don't know if I am saying it right. The point is, this doctor says it was just a kid, Harry. So could you humor us and go check out this humerus?'

Bosch didn't respond.

'Sorry, had to get that in.'

'Yeah, that was funny, Mank. What's the address?'

Mankiewicz gave it to him and told him he had already dispatched a patrol team.

'You were right to keep it off the air. Let's try to keep it that way.'

Mankiewicz said he would. Bosch closed his phone and started the car. He glanced over at the entrance to the retirement home before pulling away from the curb. There was nothing about it that looked splendid to him. The woman who had hung herself in the closet of her tiny bedroom had no next of kin, according to the operators of the home. In death, she would be treated the way she had been in life, left alone and forgotten.

Bosch pulled away from the curb and headed toward Laurel Canyon.

2

Bosch listened to the Lakers game on the car radio while he made his way into the canyon and then up Lookout Mountain to Wonderland Avenue. He wasn't a religious follower of professional basketball but wanted to get a sense of the situation in case he needed his partner, Jerry Edgar. Bosch was working alone because Edgar had lucked into a pair of choice seats to the game. Bosch had agreed to handle the call outs and to not bother Edgar unless a homicide or something Bosch couldn't handle alone came up. Bosch was alone also because the third member of his team, Kizmin Rider, had been promoted nearly a year earlier to Robbery-Homicide Division and still had not been replaced.

It was early third quarter, and the game with the Trail Blazers was tied. While Bosch wasn't a hardcore fan he knew enough from Edgar's constant talking about the game and begging to be left free of call-out duty that it was an important matchup with one of the Los Angeles team's top rivals. He decided not to page Edgar until he had gotten to the scene and assessed the situation. He turned the radio off when he started losing the AM station in the canyon.

The drive up was steep. Laurel Canyon was a cut in the Santa Monica Mountains. The tributary roads ranged up toward the crest of the mountains. Wonderland Avenue dead-ended in a remote spot where the half-million-dollar homes were surrounded by heavily wooded and steep terrain. Bosch instinctively knew that searching for bones in the area would be a logistical nightmare. He pulled to a stop behind a patrol car already at the address Mankiewicz had provided and checked his watch. It was 4:38, and he wrote it down on a fresh page of his legal pad. He figured he had less than an hour of daylight left.

A patrol officer he didn't recognize answered his knock. Her nameplate said Brasher. She led him back through the house to a home office where her partner, a cop whom Bosch recognized and knew was named Edgewood, was talking to a white-haired man who sat behind a cluttered desk. There was a shoe box with the top off on the desk.

Bosch stepped forward and introduced himself. The white-haired man said he was Dr. Paul Guyot, a general practitioner. Leaning forward Bosch could see that the shoe box contained the bone that had drawn them all together. It was dark brown and looked like a gnarled piece of driftwood.

He could also see a dog lying on the floor next to the doctor's desk chair. It was a large dog with a yellow coat.

'So this is it,' Bosch said, looking back down into the box.

'Yes, Detective, that's your bone,' Guyot said. 'And as you can see . . .'

He reached to a shelf behind the desk and pulled down a heavy copy of *Gray's Anatomy*. He opened it to a previously marked spot. Bosch noticed he was wearing latex gloves.

The page showed an illustration of a bone, anterior and posterior views. In the corner of the page was a small sketch of a skeleton with the humerus bone of both arms highlighted.

'The humerus,' Guyot said, tapping the page. 'And then we have the recovered specimen.'

He reached into the shoe box and gently lifted the bone. Holding it above the book's illustration he went through a point-by-point comparison.

'Medial epicondyle, trochlea, greater and lesser tubercle,' he said. 'It's all there. And I was just telling these two officers, I know my bones even without the book. This bone is human, Detective. There's no doubt.'

Bosch looked at Guyot's face. There was a slight quiver, perhaps the first showing of the tremors of Parkinson's.

'Are you retired, Doctor?'

'Yes, but it doesn't mean I don't know a bone when I see—'

'I'm not challenging you, Dr. Guyot.' Bosch tried to smile. 'You say it is human, I believe it. Okay? I'm just trying to get the lay of the land here. You can put that back into the box now if you want.'

Guyot replaced the bone in the shoe box.

'What's your dog's name?'

'Calamity.'

Bosch looked down at the dog. It appeared to be sleeping.

'When she was a pup she was a lot of trouble.'

Bosch nodded.

'So, if you don't mind telling it again, tell me what happened today.'

Guyot reached down and ruffled the dog's collar. The dog looked up at him for a moment and then put its head back down and closed its eyes.

'I took Calamity out for her afternoon walk. Usually when I get up to the circle I take her off the leash and let her run up into the woods. She likes it.'

'What kind of dog is she?' Bosch asked.

'Yellow Lab,' Brasher answered quickly from behind him.

Bosch turned and looked at her. She realized she had made a mistake by intruding and nodded and stepped back toward the door of the room where her partner was.

'You guys can clear if you have other calls,' Bosch said. 'I can take it from here.'

Edgewood nodded and signaled his partner out.

'Thank you, Doctor,' he said as he went.

'Don't mention it.'

Bosch thought of something.

'Hey, guys?'

Edgewood and Brasher turned back.

'Let's keep this off the air, okay?'

'You got it,' said Brasher, her eyes holding on Bosch's until he looked away.

After the officers left, Bosch looked back at the doctor and noticed that the facial tremor was slightly more pronounced now.

'They didn't believe me at first either,' he said.

'It's just that we get a lot of calls like this. But I believe you, Doctor, so why don't you continue with the story?'

Guyot nodded.

'Well, I was up on the circle and I took off the leash. She went up into the woods like she likes to do. She's well trained. When I whistle she comes back. Trouble is, I can't whistle very loud anymore. So if she goes where she can't hear me, then I have to wait, you see.'

'What happened today when she found the bone?'

'I whistled and she didn't come back.'

'So she was pretty far up there.'

'Yes, exactly. I waited. I whistled a few more times, and then finally she came down out of the woods next to Mr. Ulrich's house. She had the bone. In her mouth. At first I thought it was a stick, you see, and that she wanted to play fetch with it. But as she came to me I recognized the shape. I took it from her – had a fight over that – and then I called you people after I examined it here and was sure.'

You people, Bosch thought. It was always said like that, as if the police were another species. The blue species which carried armor that the horrors of the world could not pierce.

'When you called you told the sergeant that the bone had a fracture.'

'Absolutely.'

Guyot picked up the bone again, handling it gently. He turned it and ran his finger along a vertical striation along the bone's surface.

'That's a break line, Detective. It's a healed fracture.'

'Okay.'

Bosch pointed to the box, and the doctor returned the bone.

'Doctor, do you mind putting your dog on a leash and taking a walk up to the circle with me?'

'Not at all. I just need to change my shoes.'

'I need to change, too. How about if I meet you out front?'

'Right away.'

'I'm going to take this now.'

Bosch put the top back on the shoe box and then carried it with two hands, making sure not to turn the box or jostle its contents in any way.

Outside, Bosch noticed the patrol car was still in front of the house. The two officers sat inside it, apparently writing out reports. He went to his car and placed the shoe box on the front passenger seat.

Since he had been on call out he had not dressed in a suit. He had on a sport coat with blue jeans and a white oxford shirt. He stripped off his coat, folded it inside out and put it on the backseat. He noticed that the trigger from the weapon he kept holstered on his hip had worn a hole in the lining and the jacket wasn't even a year old. Soon it would work its way into the pocket and then all the way through. More often than not he wore out his coats from the inside.

He took his shirt off next, revealing a white T-shirt beneath. He then opened the trunk to get out the pair of work boots from his crime scene equipment box. As he leaned against the rear bumper and changed his shoes he saw Brasher get out of the patrol car and come back toward him.

'So it looks legit, huh?'

'Think so. Somebody at the ME's office will have to confirm, though.'

'You going to go up and look?'

'I'm going to try to. Not much light left, though. Probably be back out here tomorrow.'

'By the way, I'm Julia Brasher. I'm new in the division.'

'Harry Bosch.'

'I know. I've heard of you.'

'I deny everything.'

She smiled at the line and put her hand out but Bosch was right in the middle of tying one of the boots. He stopped and shook her hand.

'Sorry,' she said. 'My timing is off today.'

'Don't worry about it.'

He finished tying the boot and stood up off the bumper.

'When I blurted out the answer in there, about the dog, I immediately realized you were trying to establish a rapport with the doctor. That was wrong. I'm sorry.'

Bosch studied her for a moment. She was mid-thirties with dark hair in a tight braid that left a short tail going over the back of her collar. Her eyes were dark brown. He guessed she liked the outdoors. Her skin had an even tan.

'Like I said, don't worry about it.'

'You're alone?'

Bosch hesitated.

'My partner's working on something else while I check this out.'

He saw the doctor coming out the front door of the house with the dog on a leash. He decided not to get out his crime scene jumpsuit and put it on. He glanced over at Julia Brasher, who was now watching the approaching dog.

'You guys don't have calls?'

'No, it's slow.'

Bosch looked down at the MagLite in his equipment box. He looked at her and then reached into the trunk and grabbed an oil rag, which he threw over the flashlight. He took out a roll of yellow crime scene tape and the Polaroid camera, then closed the trunk and turned to Brasher.

'Then do you mind if I borrow your Mag? I, uh, forgot mine.'

'No problem.'

She slid the flashlight out of the ring on her equipment belt and handed it to him.

The doctor and his dog came up then.

'Ready.'

'Okay, Doctor, I want you to take us up to the spot where you let the dog go and we'll see where she goes.'

'I'm not sure you'll be able to stay with her.'

'I'll worry about that, Doctor.'

'This way then.'

They walked up the incline toward the small turnaround circle where Wonderland reached a dead end. Brasher made a hand signal to her partner in the car and walked along with them.

'You know, we had a little excitement up this way a few years ago,' Guyot said. 'A man was followed home from the Hollywood Bowl and then killed in a robbery.'

'I remember,' Bosch said.

He knew the investigation was still open but didn't mention it. It wasn't his case.

Dr Guyot walked with a strong step that belied his age and apparent condition. He let the dog set the pace and soon moved several paces ahead of Bosch and Brasher.

'So where were you before?' Bosch asked Brasher.

'What do you mean?'

'You said you were new in Hollywood Division. What about before?'

'Oh. The academy.'

He was surprised. He looked over at her, thinking he might need to reassess his age estimate.

She nodded and said, 'I know, I'm old.'

Bosch got embarrassed.

'No, I wasn't saying that. I just thought that you had been somewhere else. You don't seem like a rookie.'

'I didn't go in until I was thirty-four.'

'Really? Wow.'

'Yeah. Got the bug a little late.'

'What were you doing before?'

'Oh, a bunch of different things. Travel mostly. Took me a while to figure out what I wanted to do. And you want to know what I want to do the most?'

Bosch looked at her.

'What?'

'What you do. Homicide.'

He didn't know what to say, whether to encourage her or dissuade her.

'Well, good luck,' he said.

'I mean, don't you just find it to be the most fulfilling job ever? Look at what you do, you take the most evil people out of the mix.'

'The mix?'

'Society.'

'Yeah, I guess so. When we get lucky.'

They caught up to Dr. Guyot, who had stopped with the dog at the turnaround circle.

'This the place?'

'Yes. I let her go here. She went up through there.'

He pointed to an empty and overgrown lot that started level with the street but then quickly rose into a steep incline toward the crest of the hills. There was a large concrete drainage culvert, which explained why the lot had never been built on. It was city property, used to funnel storm water runoff away from the homes on the street. Many of the streets in the canyon were former creek and river beds. When it rained they would return to their original purpose if not for the drainage system.

'Are you going up there?' the doctor asked.

'I'm going to try.'

'I'll go with you,' Brasher said.

Bosch looked at her and then turned at the sound of a car. It was the patrol car. It pulled up and Edgewood put down the window.

'We got a hot shot, partner. Double D.'

He nodded toward the empty passenger seat. Brasher frowned and looked at Bosch.

'I hate domestic disputes.'

Bosch smiled. He hated them too, especially when they turned into homicides.

'Sorry about that.'

'Well, maybe next time.'

She started around the front of the car.

'Here,' Bosch said, holding out the MagLite.

'I've got an extra in the car,' she said. 'You can just get that back to me.'

'You sure?'

He was tempted to ask for a phone number but didn't.

'I'm sure. Good luck.'

'You too. Be careful.'

She smiled at him and then hurried around the front of the car. She got in and the car pulled away. Bosch turned his attention back to Guyot and the dog.

'An attractive woman,' Guyot said.

Bosch ignored it, wondering if the doctor had made the comment based on seeing Bosch's reaction to Brasher. He hoped he hadn't been that obvious.

'Okay, Doctor,' he said, 'let the dog go and I'll try to keep up.'

Guyot unhooked the leash while patting the dog's chest.

'Go get the bone, girl. Get a bone! Go!'

The dog took off into the lot and was gone from sight before Bosch had taken a step. He almost laughed.

'Well, I guess you were right about that, Doc.'

He turned to make sure the patrol car was gone and Brasher hadn't seen the dog take off.

'You want me to whistle?'

'Nah. I'll just go in and take a look around, see if I can catch up to her.'

He turned the flashlight on.

3

The woods were dark long before the sun disappeared. The overhead canopy created by a tall stand of Monterey pines blocked out most of the light before it got to the ground. Bosch used the flashlight and made his way up the hillside in the direction in which he had heard the dog moving through the brush. It was slow moving and hard work. The ground contained a foot-thick layer of pine needles that gave way often beneath Bosch's boots as he tried for purchase on the incline. Soon his hands were sticky with sap from grabbing branches to keep himself upright.

It took him nearly ten minutes to go thirty yards up the hillside. Then the ground started to level off and the light got better as the tall trees thinned. Bosch looked around for the dog but didn't see her. He called down to the street, though he could no longer see it or Dr. Guyot.

'Dr. Guyot? Can you hear me?'

'Yes, I hear you.'

'Whistle for your dog.'

He then heard a three-part whistle. It was distinct but very low, having the same trouble getting through the trees and underbrush as the sunlight had. Bosch tried to repeat it and after a few tries thought he had it right. But the dog didn't come.

Bosch pressed on, staying on the level ground because he believed that if someone was going to bury or abandon a body, then it would be done on even ground as opposed to the steep slope. Following a path of least resistance, he moved into a stand of acacia trees. And here he immediately came upon a spot where the earth had recently been disturbed. It had been overturned, as if a tool or an animal had been randomly rooting in the soil. He used his foot to push some of the dirt and twigs aside and then realized they weren't twigs.

He dropped to his knees and used the light to study the short brown bones scattered over a square foot of dirt. He believed he was looking at the disjointed fingers of a hand. A small hand. A child's hand.

Bosch stood up. He realized that his interest in Julia Brasher had distracted him. He had brought no means with him for collecting the bones. Picking them up and carrying them down the hill would violate every tenet of evidence collection.

The Polaroid camera hung on a shoelace around his neck. He raised it now and took a close-up shot of the bones. He then stepped back and took a wider shot of the spot beneath the acacia trees.

In the distance he heard Dr. Guyot's weak whistle. Bosch went to work with the yellow plastic crime scene tape. He tied a short length of it around the trunk of one of the acacia trees and then strung a boundary around the trees. Thinking about how he would work the case the following morning, he stepped out of the cover of the acacia trees and looked for something to use as an aerial marker. He found a nearby growth of sagebrush. He wrapped the crime scene tape around and over the top of the bush several times.

When he was finished it was almost dark. He took another cursory look around the area but knew that a flashlight search was useless and the ground would need to be exhaustively covered in the morning. Using a small penknife attached to his key chain, he began cutting four-foot lengths of the crime scene tape off the roll.

Making his way back down the hill, he tied the strips off at intervals on tree branches and bushes. He heard voices as he got closer to the street and used them to maintain his direction. At one point on the incline the soft ground suddenly gave way and he fell, tumbling hard into the base of a pine tree. The tree impacted his midsection, tearing his shirt and badly scratching his side.

Bosch didn't move for several seconds. He thought he might have cracked his ribs on the right side. His breathing was difficult and painful. He groaned loudly and slowly pulled himself up on the tree trunk so that he could continue to follow the voices.

He soon came back down into the street where Dr. Guyot was waiting with his dog and another man. The two men looked shocked when they saw the blood on Bosch's shirt.

'Oh my, what happened?' Guyot cried out.

'Nothing. I fell.'

'Your shirt is...there's blood!'

'Comes with the job.'

'Let me look at your chest.'

The doctor moved in to look but Bosch held his hands up.

'I'm okay. Who is this?'

The other man answered.

'I'm Victor Ulrich. I live there.'

He pointed to the house next to the lot. Bosch nodded.

'I just came out to see what was going on.'

'Well, nothing is going on at the moment. But there is a crime scene up there. Or there will be. We probably won't be back to work it until tomorrow morning. But I need both you men to keep clear of it and not to tell anybody about this. All right?'

Both of the neighbors nodded.

'And Doctor, don't let your dog off the leash for a few days. I need to go back down to my car to make a phone call. Mr. Ulrich, I am sure we will want to talk to you tomorrow. Will you be around?'

'Sure. Anytime. I work at home.'

'Doing what?'

'Writing.'

'Okay. We'll see you tomorrow.'

Bosch headed back down the street with Guyot and the dog.

'You really need me to take a look at your injury,' Guyot insisted.

'It'll be fine.'

Bosch glanced to his left and thought he saw a curtain quickly close behind a window of the house they were passing.

'The way you are holding yourself when you walk – you've damaged a rib,' Guyot said. 'Maybe you've broken it. Maybe more than one.'

Bosch thought of the small, thin bones he had just seen beneath the acacia trees.

'There's nothing you can do for a rib, broken or not,' he said.

'I can tape it. You'll breathe a hell of a lot easier. I can also take care of that wound.'

Bosch relented.

'Okay, Doc, you get out your black bag. I'm going to get my other shirt.'

Inside Guyot's house a few minutes later, the doctor cleaned the deep scratch on the side of Bosch's chest and taped his ribs. It did feel better, but it still hurt. Guyot said he could no longer write a prescription but suggested Bosch not take anything more powerful than aspirin anyway.

Bosch remembered that he had a prescription bottle with some Vicodin tablets left over from when he'd had a wisdom tooth removed a few months earlier. They would smooth out the pain if he wanted to go that way.

'I'll be fine,' Bosch said. 'Thanks for fixing me up.'

'Don't mention it.'

Bosch pulled on his good shirt and watched Guyot as he closed up his first-aid kit. He wondered how long it had been since the doctor had used his skills on a patient.

'How long have you been retired?' he asked.

'Twelve years next month.'

'You miss it?'

Guyot turned from the first-aid kit and looked at him. The tremor was gone.

'Every day. I don't miss the actual work – you know, the cases. But it was a job that made a difference. I miss that.'

Bosch thought about how Julia Brasher had described homicide work earlier. He nodded that he understood what Guyot was saying.

'You said there was a crime scene up there?' the doctor asked.

'Yes. I found more bones. I've got to make a call, see what we're going to do. Can I borrow your phone? I don't think my cell will work around here.'

'No, they never do in the canyon. Use the phone on the desk there and I'll give you some privacy.'

He headed out, carrying the first-aid kit with him. Bosch went behind the desk and sat down. The dog was on the ground next to the chair. The animal looked up and seemed startled when she saw Bosch in the master's spot.

'Calamity,' he said. 'I think you lived up to your name today, girl.'

Bosch reached down and rubbed the scruff of the dog's neck. The dog growled and he quickly took his hand away, wondering if it was the dog's training or something about himself that had caused the hostile response.

He picked up the phone and called the home of his supervisor, Lt. Grace Billets. He explained what had happened on Wonderland Avenue and his findings up on the hill.

'Harry, how old do these bones look?' Billets asked.

Bosch looked at the Polaroid he had taken of the small bones he had found in the dirt. It was a bad photo, the flash overexposing it because he was too close.

'I don't know, they look old to me. I'd say we're talking years here.'

'Okay, so whatever's there at the scene isn't fresh.'

'Maybe freshly uncovered, but no, it's been there.'

'That's what I'm saying. So I think we should stick a pin in it and gear up for tomorrow. Whatever is up there on that hill, it's not going anywhere tonight.'

'Yeah,' Bosch said. 'I'm thinking the same thing.'

She was silent a moment before speaking.

'These kind of cases, Harry . . .'

'What?'

'They drain the budget, they drain manpower . . . and they're the hardest to close, *if* you can close them.'

'Okay, I'll climb back up there and cover the bones up. I'll tell the doctor to keep his dog on a leash.'

'Come on, Harry, you know what I mean.' She exhaled loudly. 'First day of the year and we're going to start in the hole.'

Bosch was silent, letting her work through her administrative frustrations. It didn't take long. It was one of the things he liked about her.

'Okay, anything else happen today?'

'Not too much. A couple suicides, that's it so far.'

'Okay, when are you going to start tomorrow?'

'I'd like to get out there early. I'll make some calls and see what I can get going. And get the bone the dog found confirmed before we start anything.'

'Okay, let me know.'

Bosch agreed and hung up the phone. He next called Teresa Corazon, the county medical examiner, at home. Though their relationship outside of work had ended years before and she had moved at least two times since, she had always kept the same number and Bosch knew it by heart. It came in handy now. He explained what he had going and that he needed an official confirmation of the bone as human before he set other things in motion. He also told her that if it was confirmed he would need an archeological team to work the crime scene as soon as possible.

Corazon put him on hold for almost five minutes.

'Okay,' she said when she came back on the line. 'I couldn't get Kathy Kohl. She's not home.'

Bosch knew that Kohl was the staff archeologist. Her real expertise and reason for her inclusion as a full-time employee was retrieving bones from the body dump sites up in the desert of the north county, which was a weekly occurrence. But Bosch knew she would be called in to handle the search for bones off Wonderland Avenue.

'So what do you want me to do? I want to get this confirmed tonight.'

'Just hold your horses, Harry. You are always so impatient. You're like a dog with a bone, no pun intended.'

'It's a kid, Teresa. Can we be serious?'

'Just come here. I'll look at this bone.'

'And what about tomorrow?'

'I'll get things in motion. I left a message for Kathy and as soon as we hang up here I'll call the office and have her paged. She'll head up the dig as soon as the sun is up and we can get in there. Once the bones are recovered, there is a forensic anthropologist at UCLA we have on retainer and I can bring him in if he's in town. And I'll be there myself. Are you satisfied?'

This last part gave Bosch pause.

'Teresa,' he finally said, 'I want to try to keep this as low profile as I can for as long as I can.'

'And what are you implying?'

'That I'm not sure that *the* medical examiner for Los Angeles County needs to be there. And that I haven't seen you at a crime scene without a cameraman in tow for a long time.'

'Harry, he is a private videographer, okay? The film he takes is for future use by me and controlled solely by me. It doesn't end up on the six o'clock news.'

'Whatever. I just think we need to avoid any complications on this one. It's a child case. You know how they get.'

'Just get over here with that bone. I'm leaving in an hour.'

She abruptly hung up.

Bosch wished he had been a little more politic with Corazon but was glad he'd made his point. Corazon was a personality, regularly appearing on Court TV and network shows as a forensic expert. She had also taken to having a cameraman follow her so that her cases could be turned into documentaries for broadcast on any of the cop and legal shows on the vast cable and satellite spectrum. He could not and would not let her goals as a celebrity coroner interfere with his goals as an investigator of what might be the homicide of a child.

He decided he'd make the calls to the department's Special Services and K-9 units after he got confirmation on the bone. He got up and left the room, looking for Guyot.

The doctor was in the kitchen, sitting at a small table and writing in a spiral-bound notebook. He looked up at Bosch.

'Just writing a few notes on your treatment. I've kept notes on every patient I've ever treated.'

Bosch just nodded, even though he thought it was odd for Guyot to be writing about him.

'I'm going to go, Doctor. We'll be back tomorrow. In force, I'd expect. We might want to use your dog again. Will you be here?'

'I'll be here and be glad to help. How are the ribs?'

'They hurt.'

'Only when you breathe, right? That'll last about a week.'

'Thanks for taking care of me. You don't need that shoe box back, do you?'

'No, I wouldn't want that back now.'

Bosch turned to head toward the front door but then turned back to Guyot.

'Doctor, do you live alone here?'

'I do now. My wife died two years ago. A month before our fiftieth anniversary.'

'I'm sorry.'

Guyot nodded and said, 'My daughter has her own family up in Seattle. I see them on special occasions.'

Bosch felt like asking why only on special occasions but didn't. He thanked the man again and left.

Driving out of the canyon and toward Teresa Corazon's place in Hancock Park, he kept his hand on the shoe box so that it would not be jostled or slide off the seat. He felt a deep sense of dread rising from within. He knew it was because fate had certainly not smiled on him this day. He had caught the worst kind of case there was to catch. A child case.

Child cases haunted you. They hollowed you out and scarred you. There was no bulletproof vest thick enough to stop you from being pierced. Child cases left you knowing the world was full of lost light.

4

Teresa Corazon lived in a Mediterranean-style mansion with a stone turnaround circle complete with koi pond in front. Eight years earlier, when Bosch had shared a brief relationship with her, she had lived in a one-bedroom condominium. The riches of television and celebrity had paid for the house and the lifestyle that came with it. She was not even remotely like the woman who used to show up at his house unannounced at midnight with a cheap bottle of red wine from Trader Joe's and a video of her favorite movie to watch. The woman who was unabashedly ambitious but not yet skilled at using her position to enrich herself.

Bosch knew he now served as a reminder of what she had been and what she had lost in order to gain all that she had. It was no wonder their interactions were now few and far between but as tense as a visit to the dentist when they were unavoidable.

He parked on the circle and got out with the shoe box and the Polaroids. He looked into the pond as he came around the car and could see the dark shapes of the fish moving below the surface. He smiled, thinking about the movie *Chinatown* and how often they had watched it the year they were together. He remembered how much she enjoyed the portrayal of the coroner. He wore a black butcher's apron and ate a sandwich while examining a body. Bosch doubted she had the same sense of humor about things anymore.

The light hanging over the heavy wood door to the house went on, and Corazon opened it before he got there. She was wearing black slacks and a cream-colored blouse. She was probably on her way to a New Year's party. She looked past him at the slickback he had been driving.

'Let's make this quick before that car drips oil on my stones.'

'Hello to you, too, Teresa.'

'That's it?'

She pointed at the shoe box.

'This is it.'

He handed her the Polaroids and started taking the lid off the box. It was clear she was not asking him in for a glass of New Year's champagne.

'You want to do this right here?'

'I don't have a lot of time. I thought you'd be here sooner. What moron took these?'

'That would be me.'

'I can't tell anything from these. Do you have a glove?'

Bosch pulled a latex glove out of his coat pocket and handed it to her. He took the photos back and put them in an inside pocket of his jacket. She expertly snapped the glove on and reached into the open box. She held the bone up and turned it in the light. He was silent. He could smell her perfume. It was strong as usual, a holdover from her days when she spent most of her time in autopsy suites.

After a five-second examination she put the bone back down in the box.

'Human.'

'You sure?'

She looked up at him with a glare as she snapped off the glove.

'It's the humerus. The upper arm. I'd say a child of about ten. You may no longer respect my skills, Harry, but I do still have them.'

She dropped the glove into the box on top of the bone. Bosch could roll with all the verbal sparring from her, but it bothered him that she did that with the glove, dropping it on the child's bone like that.

He reached into the box and took the glove out. He remembered something and held the glove back out to her.

'The man whose dog found this said there was a fracture on the bone. A healed fracture. Do you want to take a look and see if you—'

'No. I'm late for an engagement. What you need to know right now is if it is human. You now have that confirmation. Further examination will come later under proper settings at the medical examiner's office. Now, I really have to go. I'll be there tomorrow morning.'

Bosch held her eyes for a long moment.

'Sure, Teresa, have a good time tonight.'

She broke off the stare and folded her arms across her chest. He carefully put the top back on the shoe box, nodded to her and headed back to his car. He heard the heavy door close behind him.

Thinking of the movie again as he passed the koi pond, he spoke the film's final line quietly to himself.

'Forget it, Jake, it's Chinatown.'

He got in the car and drove home, his hand holding the shoe box secure on the seat next to him.

5

By nine o'clock the next morning the end of Wonderland Avenue was a law enforcement encampment. And at its center was Harry Bosch. He directed teams from patrol, K-9, the Scientific Investigation Division, the medical examiner's office and the Special Services unit. A department helicopter circled above and a dozen police academy cadets milled about, waiting for orders.

Earlier, the aerial unit had locked in on the sagebrush Bosch had wrapped in yellow crime scene tape and used it as a base point to determine that Wonderland offered the closest access to the spot where Bosch had found the bones. The Special Services unit then swung into action. Following the trail of crime scene tape up the hillside, the six-man team hammered and strung together a series of wooden ramps and steps with rope guidelines that led up the hillside to the bones. Accessing and exiting the site would now be much easier than it had been for Bosch the evening before.

It was impossible to keep such a nest of police activity quiet. Also by 9 A.M. the neighborhood had become a media encampment. The media trucks were stacked behind the roadblocks set a half block from the turnaround circle. The reporters were gathering into press conference-sized groups. And no fewer than five news helicopters were circling at an altitude above the department's chopper. It all created a background cacophony that had already resulted in numerous complaints from residents on the street to police administrators at Parker Center downtown.

Bosch was getting ready to lead the first group up to the crime scene. He first conferred with Jerry Edgar, who had been apprised of the case the night before.

'All right, we're going to take the ME and SID up first,' he said, pronouncing the acronyms as Emmy and Sid. 'Then we'll take the cadets and the dogs up. I want you to oversee that part of it.'

'No problem. You see your pal the ME's got her damn cameraman with her?'

'Nothing we can do about it at the moment. Let's just hope she gets bored and goes back downtown, where she belongs.'

'You know, for all we know, these could be old Indian bones or something.'

Bosch shook his head.

'I don't think so. Too shallow.'

Bosch walked over to the first group: Teresa Corazon, her videographer and her four-person dig team, which consisted of archeologist Kathy Kohl and three investigators who would do the spadework. The dig team members were dressed in white jumpsuits. Corazon was in an outfit similar to what she was wearing the night before, including shoes with two-inch heels. Also in the group were two criminalists from SID.

Bosch signaled the group into a tighter circle so he could speak privately to them and not be overheard by all the others milling about.

'Okay, we're going to go up and start the documentation and recovery. Once we have all of you in place we'll bring up the dogs and the cadets to search the adjacent areas and possibly expand the crime scene. You guys—'

He stopped to reach his hand up to Corazon's cameraman.

'Turn that off. You can film her but not me.'

The man lowered his camera, and Bosch gave Corazon a look and then continued.

'You all know what you are doing so I don't need to brief you. The one thing I do want to say is that it is tough going getting up there. Even with the ramps and the stairs. So be careful. Hold on to the ropes, watch your footing. We don't want anybody hurt. If you have heavy equipment, break it up and make two or three trips. If you still need help I'll have the cadets bring it up. Don't worry about time. Worry about safety. All right, everybody cool?'

He got simultaneous nods from everybody. Bosch signaled Corazon away from the others and into a private conversation.

'You're not dressed right,' he said.

'Look, don't you start telling—'

'You want me to take my shirt off so you can see my ribs? The side of my chest looks like blueberry pie because I fell up there last night. Those shoes you've got on aren't going to work. It might look good for the camera but not—'

'I'm fine. I'll take my chances. Anything else?'

Bosch shook his head.

'I warned you,' he said. 'Let's go.'

He headed toward the ramp, and the others followed. Special Services had constructed a wooden gateway to be used as a checkpoint. A patrol officer stood there with a clipboard. He took each person's name and affiliation before they were allowed through.

Bosch led the way. The climbing was easier than the day before but his chest burned with pain as he pulled himself along on the rope guides and negotiated the ramps and steps. He said nothing and tried not to show it.

When he got to the acacia trees he signaled the others to hold back while he went under the crime scene tape to check first. He found the area of overturned earth and the small, brown bones he had seen the night before. They appeared undisturbed.

'Okay, come on in here and have a look.'

The group members came under the tape and stood over the bones in a semicircle. The camera started rolling and Corazon now took charge.

'All right, the first thing we're going to do is back out and take photos. Then we're going to set up a grid and Dr. Kohl will supervise the excavation and recovery. If you find anything, photograph it nine ways from Sunday before you collect it.'

She turned to one of the investigators.

'Finch, I want you to handle the sketches. Standard grid. Document everything. Don't assume we will be able to rely on photos.'

Finch nodded. Corazon turned to Bosch.

'Detective, I think we've got it. The less people in here the better.'

Bosch nodded and handed her a two-way radio.

'I'll be around. If you need me use the rover. Cell phones don't work up here. But be careful what you say.'

He pointed up at the sky, where the media helicopters were circling.

'Speaking of which,' Kohl said, 'I think we're going to string a tarp up off these trees so we can have some privacy as well as cut down on the sun glare. Is that okay with you?'

'It's your crime scene now,' Bosch said. 'Run with it.'

He headed back down the ramp with Edgar behind him.

'Harry, this could take days,' Edgar said.

'And maybe then some.'

'Well, they're not going to give us days. You know that, right?'

'Right.'

'I mean, these cases . . . we'll be lucky if we even come up with an ID.'

'Right.'

Bosch kept moving. When he got down to the street he saw that Lt. Billets was on the scene with her supervisor, Capt. LeValley.

'Jerry, why don't you go get the cadets ready?' Bosch said. 'Give them the crime scene one-oh-one speech. I'll be over in a minute.'

Bosch joined Billets and LeValley and updated them on what was happening, detailing the morning's activities right down to the neighborhood complaints about noise from the hammers, saws and helicopters.

'We've got to give something to the media,' LeValley said. 'Media Relations wants to know if you want them to handle it from downtown or you want to take it here.'

'I don't want to take it. What does Media Relations know about it?'

'Almost nothing. So you have to call them and they'll work up the press release.'

'Captain, I'm kind of busy here. Can I—'

'Make the time, Detective. Keep them off our backs.'

When Bosch looked away from the captain to the reporters gathered a half block away at the roadblock, he noticed Julia Brasher showing her badge to a patrol officer and being allowed through. She was in street clothes.

'All right. I'll make the call.'

He started down the street to Dr. Guyot's home. He was headed toward Brasher, who smiled at him as she approached.

'I've got your Mag. It's in my car down here. I have to go down to Dr. Guyot's house anyway.'

'Oh, don't worry about it. That's not why I'm here.'

She changed direction and continued with Bosch. He looked at her attire: faded blue jeans and a T-shirt from a 5K charity run.

'You're not on the clock, are you?'

'No, I work the three-to-eleven. I just thought you might need a volunteer. I heard about the academy call out.'

'You want to go up there and look for bones, huh?'

'I want to learn.'

Bosch nodded. They walked up the path to Guyot's door. It opened before they got there and the doctor invited them in. Bosch asked if he could use the phone in his office again and Guyot showed him the way even though he didn't have to. Bosch sat down behind the desk.

'How are the ribs?' the doctor asked.

'Fine.'

Brasher raised her eyebrows and Bosch picked up on it.

'Had a little accident when I was up there last night.'

'What happened?'

'Oh, I was just sort of minding my own business when a tree trunk suddenly attacked me for no reason.'

She grimaced and somehow managed to smile at the same time.

Bosch dialed Media Relations from memory and told an officer about the case in very general terms. At one point he put his hand over the phone and asked Guyot if he wanted his name put in the press release. The doctor declined. A few minutes later Bosch was finished and hung up. He looked at Guyot.

'Once we clear the scene in a few days the reporters will probably stick around. They'll be looking for the dog that found the bone, is my guess. So if you want to stay out of it, keep Calamity off the street or they'll put two and two together.'

'Good advice,' Guyot said.

'And you might want to call your neighbor, Mr. Ulrich, and tell him not to mention it to any reporters, either.'

On the way out of the house Bosch asked Brasher if she wanted her flashlight and she said she didn't want to bother carrying it while she was helping search the hillside.

'Get it to me whenever,' she said.

Bosch liked the answer. It meant he would get at least one more chance to see her.

Back at the circle Bosch found Edgar lecturing the academy cadets.

'The golden rule of the crime scene, people, is don't touch anything until it has been studied, photographed and charted.'

Bosch walked into the circle.

'Okay, we ready?'

'They're ready,' Edgar said. He nodded toward two of the cadets, who were holding metal detectors. 'I borrowed those from SID.'

Bosch nodded and gave the cadets and Brasher the same safety speech he had given the forensic crew. They then headed up to the crime scene, Bosch introducing Brasher to Edgar and then letting his partner lead the way through the checkpoint. He took up the rear, walking behind Brasher.

'We'll see if you want to be a homicide detective by the end of the day,' he said.

'Anything's got to be better than chasing the radio and washing puke out of the back of your car at the end of every shift.'

'I remember those days.'

Bosch and Edgar spread the twelve cadets and Brasher out in the areas adjacent to the stand of acacia trees and had them begin conducting side-by-side searches. Bosch then went down and brought up the two K-9 teams to supplement the search.

Once things were under way he left Edgar with the cadets and went back to the acacias to see what progress had been made. He found Kohl sitting on an equipment crate and supervising the placement of wooden stakes into the ground so that strings could be used to set the excavation grid.

Bosch had worked one prior case with Kohl and knew she was very thorough and good at what she did. She was in her late thirties with a tennis player's build and tan. Bosch had once run across her at a city park, where she was playing tennis with a twin sister. They had drawn a crowd. It looked like somebody hitting the ball off a mirrored wall.

Kohl's straight blonde hair fell forward and hid her eyes as she looked down at the oversized clipboard on her lap. She was making notations on a piece of paper with a grid already printed on it. Bosch looked over her shoulder at the chart. Kohl was labeling the individual blocks with letters of the alphabet as the corresponding stakes were placed in the ground. At the top of the page she had written 'City of Bones.'

Bosch reached down and tapped the chart where she had written the caption.

'Why do you call it that?'

She shrugged her shoulders.

'Because we're setting out the streets and the blocks of what will become a city to us,' she said, running her fingers over some of the lines on the chart in illustration. 'At least while we're working here it will feel like it. Our little city.'

Bosch nodded.

'In every murder is the tale of a city,' he said.

Kohl looked up at him.

'Who said that?'

'I don't know. Somebody did.'

He turned his attention to Corazon, who was squatting over the small bones on the surface of the soil, studying them while the lens of the video camera studied her. He was thinking of something to say about it when his rover was keyed and he took it off his belt.

'Bosch here.'

'Edgar. Better come on back over here, Harry. We already have something.'

'Right.'

Edgar was standing in an almost level spot in the brush about forty yards from the acacia trees. A half dozen of the cadets and Brasher had formed a circle and were looking down at something in the two-foot-high brush. The police chopper was circling in a tighter circle above.

Bosch got to the circle and looked down. It was a child's skull partially submerged in the soil, its hollow eyes staring up at him.

'Nobody touched it,' Edgar said. 'Brasher here found it.'

Bosch glanced at her and the humor she seemed to carry in her eyes and mouth were gone. He looked back at the skull and pulled the radio off his belt.

'Dr. Corazon?' he said into it.

It was a long moment before her voice came back.

'Yes, I'm here. What is it?'

'We are going to have to widen the crime scene.'

6

With Bosch acting as the general overseeing the small army that worked the expanded crime scene, the day progressed well. The bones came out of the ground and the hillside brush easily, as if they had been impatiently waiting a very long time. By noon, three blocks in the grid were being actively excavated by Kathy Kohl's team, and dozens of bones emerged from the dark soil. Like their archeological counterparts who unearthed the artifacts of the ancients, the dig team used small tools and brushes to bring these bones gently to light. They also used metal detectors and vapor probes. The process was painstaking yet it was moving at an even faster pace than Bosch had hoped for.

The finding of the skull had set this pace and brought a sense of urgency to the entire operation. It was removed from its location first, and the field examination conducted on camera by Teresa Corazon found fracture lines and surgical scarring. The record of surgery assured them they were dealing with relatively contemporary bones. The fractures in and of themselves were not definitive in the indication of homicide, but when added to the evidence that the body had been buried they gave a clear sense that the tale of a murder was unfolding.

By two o'clock, when the hillside crews broke for lunch, almost half of the skeleton had already been recovered from the grid. A small scattering of other bones had been found in the nearby brush by the cadets. Additionally, Kohl's crew had unearthed fragments of deteriorated clothing and a canvas backpack of a size most likely used by a child.

The bones came down the hillside in square wooden boxes with rope handles attached on the sides. By lunch, a forensic anthropologist was examining three boxes of bones in the medical examiner's office. The clothing, most of it rotten and unrecognizable, and the backpack, which had been left unopened, were transported to LAPD's Scientific Investigation Division lab for the same scrutiny.

A metal detector scan of the search grid produced a single coin – a quarter minted in 1975 – found at the same depth as the bones and approximately two inches from the left wing of the pelvis. It was assumed that the quarter had been in the left front pocket of pants that had rotted away along with the body's tissue. To Bosch, the coin gave one of the key parameters of time of death: If the assumption that the coin had been buried with the body was correct, the death could not have happened before 1975.

Patrol had arranged for two construction site lunch wagons to come to the circle to feed the small army working the crime scene. Lunch was late and people were hungry. One truck served hot lunches while the other served sandwiches. Bosch waited at the end of the line for the sandwich truck with Julia Brasher. The line was moving slowly but he didn't mind. They mostly talked about the investigation on the hillside and gossiped about department brass. It was get-to-know-you conversation. Bosch was attracted to her, and the more he heard her talk about her experiences as a rookie and a female in the department, the more he was intrigued by her. She had a mixture of excitement and awe and cynicism about the job that Bosch remembered clearly from his own early days on the job.

When he was about six people from the order window of the lunch truck, Bosch heard someone in the truck asking one of the cadets questions about the investigation.

'Are they bones from a bunch of different people?'

'I don't know, man. We just look for them, that's all.'

Bosch studied the man who had asked the question.

'Were they all cut up?'

'Hard to tell.'

Bosch broke from his spot with Brasher and walked to the back of the truck. He looked through the open door at the back and saw three men wearing aprons working in the truck. Or appearing to work. They did not notice Bosch watching. Two of the men were making sandwiches and filling orders. The man in the middle, the one who had asked the cadet questions, was moving his arms on the prep counter below the order window. He wasn't making anything, but from outside the truck it would appear he was creating a sandwich. As Bosch watched, he saw the man to the right slice a sandwich in half, put it on a paper plate and slide it to the man in the middle. The middle man then held it out through the window to the cadet who ordered it.

Bosch noticed that while the two real sandwich makers wore jeans and T-shirts beneath their aprons, the man in the middle had on cuffed slacks and a shirt with a button-down collar. Protruding from the back pocket of his pants was a notebook. The long, thin kind that Bosch knew reporters used.

Bosch stuck his head in the door and looked around. On a shelf next to the doorway he saw a sport jacket rolled into a ball. He grabbed it and stepped back away from the door. He went through the pockets of the jacket and found an LAPD-issued press pass on a neck chain. It had a picture of the middle sandwich maker on it. His name was Victor Frizbe and he worked at the *New Times*.

Holding the jacket to the side of the door, Bosch rapped on the outside of the truck, and when all three men turned to look he signaled Frizbe over. The reporter pointed to his chest with a *Who, me?* look and Bosch nodded. Frizbe came to the door and bent down.

'Yes?'

Bosch reached up and grabbed him by the top bib on the apron and jerked him out of the truck. Frizbe landed on his feet but had to run several steps to stop from falling. As he turned around to protest, Bosch hit him in the chest with the balled-up jacket.

Two patrol officers – they always ate first – were dumping paper plates into a nearby trash can. Bosch signaled them over.

'Take him back to the perimeter. If you see him crossing it again, arrest him.'

Each officer took Frizbe by an arm and started marching him down the street to the barricades. Frizbe started protesting, his face growing as red as a Coke can, but the patrol officers ignored everything about him but his arms and marched him toward his humiliation in front of the other reporters. Bosch watched for a moment and then took the press card out of his back pocket and dropped it in the trash can.

He rejoined Brasher in line. Now they were just two cadets away from being served.

'What was that all about?' Brasher asked.

'Health-code violation. Didn't wash his hands.'

She started laughing.

'I'm serious. The law's the law as far as I'm concerned.'

'God, I hope I get my sandwich before you see a roach or something and close the whole thing down.'

'Don't worry, I think I just got rid of the roach.'

Ten minutes later, after Bosch lectured the truck owner about smuggling the media into the crime scene, they took their sandwiches and drinks to one of the picnic tables Special Services had set up on the circle. It was a table that had been reserved for the investigative team, but Bosch didn't mind allowing Brasher to sit there. Edgar was there along with Kohl and one of the diggers from her crew. Bosch introduced Brasher to those who didn't know her and mentioned she had taken the initial call on the case and helped him the night before.

'So where's the boss?' Bosch asked Kohl.

'Oh, she already ate. I think she went off to tape an interview with herself or something.'

Bosch smiled and nodded.

'I think I'm going to get seconds,' Edgar said as he climbed over the bench and left with his plate.

Bosch bit into his BLT and savored its taste. He was starved. He wasn't planning to do anything but eat and rest during the break but Kohl asked if it was all right if she gave him some of her initial conclusions on the excavation.

Bosch had his mouth full. After he swallowed he asked her to wait until his partner came back. They talked in generalities about the condition of the bones and how Kohl believed that the shallow nature of the grave had allowed animals to disinter the remains and scatter the bones – possibly for years.

'We're not going to get them all,' she said. 'We won't come close. We're going to quickly reach a point where the expense and the effort won't be worth the return.'

Edgar returned with another plate of fried chicken. Bosch nodded to Kohl, who looked down at a notepad she had on the table to her left. She checked some of her notations and started talking.

'The things I want you to be mindful of are the grave depth and location terrain. I think these are key things. They're going to have to play somehow into who this child was and what happened to him.'

'Him?' Bosch asked.

'The hip spacing and the waistband of the underwear.'

She explained that included in the rotten and decomposed clothing was the rubber waistband, which was all that was left of the underwear that had been on the body when it was buried. Decomposition fluids from the body had led to the deterioration of the clothing. But the rubber waistband was largely intact and appeared to have come from a style of underwear made for males.

'Okay,' Bosch said. 'You were saying about grave depth?'

'Yes, well, we think that the hip assembly and lower spinal column were in undisturbed position when we uncovered them. Going on that, we're talking about a grave that wasn't more than six inches to a foot deep. A grave this shallow reflects speed, panic, a host of things indicative of poor planning. But—' she held up a finger '—by the same token, the location – very remote, very difficult – reflects the opposite. It shows careful planning. So you have some kind of contradiction going on here. The location appears to have been chosen because it was damn hard to get to, yet the burial appears to have been fast and furious. This person was literally just covered with loose topsoil and pine needles. I know pointing all of this out isn't necessarily going to help you catch the bad guy but I want you to see what I'm seeing here. This contradiction.'

Bosch nodded.

'It's all good to know. We'll keep it in mind.'

'Okay, good. The other contradiction – the smaller one – is the backpack. Burying it with the body was a mistake. The body decomposes at a much faster rate than the canvas. So if you get identifiers off the bag or its contents, it becomes a mistake made by the bad guy. Again poor planning in the midst of good planning. You're smart detectives, I'm sure you'll figure all this out.'

She smiled at Bosch and then studied her pad again, lifting the top page to look beneath it.

'I think that's it. Everything else we talked about up at the site. I think things are going very well up there. By the end of the day we'll have the main grave done. Tomorrow we'll do some sampling in the other grids. But this should probably wrap by tomorrow. Like I said, we're not going to get everything but we should get enough to do what we need to do.'

Bosch suddenly thought of Victor Frizbe's question to the cadet at the lunch wagon and realized that the reporter might have been thinking ahead of Bosch.

'Sampling? You think there's more than one body buried up there?'

Kohl shook her head.

'I have no indication of that at all. But we should make sure. We'll do some sampling, sink some gas probes. It's routine. The likelihood – especially in light of the shallow grave – is that this is a singular case, but we should be sure about it. As sure as we can be.'

Bosch nodded. He was glad he had eaten most of his sandwich because he was suddenly not hungry. The prospect of mounting an investigation with multiple victims was daunting. He looked at the others at the table.

'That doesn't leave this table. I already caught one reporter sniffing around for a serial killer, we don't want media hysteria here. Even if you tell them what we're doing is routine and just to make sure, it will be the top of the story. All right?'

Everyone nodded, including Brasher. Bosch was about to say something when there was a loud banging from the row of portable toilets on the Special Services trailer on the other side of the circle. Someone was inside one of the phone booth-sized bathrooms pounding on its thin aluminum skin. After a moment Bosch could hear a woman's voice behind the sharp banging. He recognized it and jumped up from the table.

Bosch ran across the circle and up the steps to the truck's platform. He quickly determined which toilet the banging was coming from and went to the door. The exterior hasp – used for securing the toilet for transport – had been closed over the loop and a chicken bone had been used to secure it.

'Hold on, hold on,' Bosch yelled.

He tried to pull the bone out but it was too greasy and slipped from his grip. The pounding and screaming continued. Bosch looked around for a tool of some kind but didn't see anything. Finally, he took his pistol out of his holster, checked the safety and used the butt of the weapon to hammer the bone through the hasp, careful all the time to aim the barrel of the gun at a downward angle.

When the bone finally popped out he put the gun away and flipped the hasp open. The door burst outward and Teresa Corazon charged out, almost knocking him over. He grabbed her to maintain his balance but she roughly pushed him away.

'You did that!'

'What? No, I didn't! I was over there the whole—'

'I want to know who did it!'

Bosch lowered his voice. He knew everyone in the encampment was probably looking at them. The media down the street as well.

'Look, Teresa, calm down. It was a joke, okay? Whoever did it did it as a joke. I know you don't like confined spaces but they didn't know that. Somebody just wanted to ease the tension around here a little bit, and you just happened to be—'

'It's because they're jealous, that's why.'

'What?'

'Of who I am, what I've done.'

Bosch was nonplussed by that.

'Whatever.'

She headed for the stairs, then abruptly turned around and came back to him.

'I'm leaving, you happy now?'

Bosch shook his head.

'Happy? That has nothing to do with anything here. I'm trying to conduct an investigation, and if you want to know the truth, not having the distraction of you and your cameraman around might be a help.'

'Then you've got it. And you know that phone number you called me on the other night?'

Bosch nodded. 'Yeah, what about—'

'Burn it.'

She walked down the steps, angrily hooked a finger at her cameraman and headed toward her official car. Bosch watched her go.

When he got back to the picnic table, only Brasher and Edgar remained. His partner had reduced his second order of fried chicken to bones. He sat with a satisfied smirk on his face.

Bosch dropped the bone he had knocked out of the hasp onto Edgar's plate.

'That went over real well,' he said.

He gave Edgar a look that told him he knew he had been the one who did it. But Edgar revealed nothing.

'The bigger the ego the harder they fall,' Edgar said. 'I wonder if her cameraman got any of that action on tape.'

'You know, it would have been good to keep her as an ally,' Bosch said. 'To just put up with her so that she was on our side when we needed her.'

Edgar picked up his plate and struggled to slide his large body out of the picnic table.

'I'll see you up on the hill,' he said.

Bosch looked at Brasher. She raised her eyebrows.

'You mean he was the one who did it?'

Bosch didn't answer.

7

The work in the city of bones lasted only two days. As Kohl had predicted, the majority of the pieces of the skeleton had been located and removed from the spot beneath the acacia trees by the end of the first day. Other bones had been found nearby in the brush in a scatter pattern indicative of disinterment over time by foraging animals. On Friday the searchers and diggers returned, but a daylong search of the hillside by fresh cadets and further excavation of the main squares of the grid found no more bones. Vapor probes and sample digs in all the remaining squares of the grid turned up no bones or other indications that other bodies had been buried beneath the acacia trees.

Kohl estimated that sixty percent of the skeleton had been collected. On her recommendation and with Teresa Corazon's approval the excavation and search were suspended pending further developments at dusk on Friday.

Bosch had not objected to this. He knew they were facing limited returns for a large amount of effort and he deferred to the experts. He was also anxious to proceed with the investigation and identification of the bones – elements which were largely stalled as he and Edgar had worked exclusively on Wonderland Avenue during the two days, supervising the collection of evidence, canvassing the neighborhood and putting together the initial reports on the case. It was all necessary work but Bosch wanted to move on.

On Saturday morning he and Edgar met in the lobby of the medical examiner's office and told the receptionist they had an appointment with Dr. William Golliher, the forensic anthropologist on retainer from UCLA.

'He's waiting for you in suite A,' the receptionist said after making a call to confirm. 'You know which way that is?'

Bosch nodded and they were buzzed through the gate. They took an elevator down to the basement level and were immediately greeted by the smell of the autopsy floor when they stepped out. It was a mixture of chemicals and decay that was unique in the world. Edgar immediately took a paper breathing mask out of a wall dispenser and put it on. Bosch didn't bother.

'You really ought to, Harry,' Edgar said as they walked down the hall. 'Do you know that all smells are particulate?'

Bosch looked at him.

'Thanks for that, Jerry.'

They had to stop in the hallway as a gurney was pushed out of an autopsy suite. There was a body on it, wrapped in plastic.

'Harry, you ever notice that they wrap 'em up the same way they do the burritos at Taco Bell?'

Bosch nodded at the man pushing the gurney.

'That's why I don't eat burritos.'

'Really?'

Bosch moved on down the hall without answering.

Suite A was an autopsy room reserved for Teresa Corazon for the infrequent times she actually left her administrative duties as chief medical examiner and performed an autopsy. Because the case had initially garnered her hands-on attention she had apparently authorized Golliher to use her suite. Corazon had not returned to the crime scene on Wonderland Avenue after the portable toilet incident.

They pushed through the double doors of the suite and were met by a man in blue jeans and a Hawaiian shirt.

'Please call me Bill,' Golliher said. 'I guess it's been a long two days.'

'Say that again,' Edgar said.

Golliher nodded in a friendly manner. He was about fifty with dark hair and eyes and an easy manner. He gestured toward the autopsy table that was in the center of the room. The bones that had been collected from beneath the acacia trees were now spread across the stainless steel surface.

'Well, let me tell you what's been going on in here,' Golliher said. 'As the team in the field has been collecting the evidence, I've been here examining the pieces, doing the radiograph work and generally trying to put the puzzle of all of this together.'

Bosch stepped over to the stainless steel table. The bones were laid out in place so as to form a partial skeleton. The most obvious pieces missing were the bones of the left arm and leg and the lower jaw. It was presumed that these were the pieces that had long ago been taken and scattered distantly by animals that had rooted in the shallow grave.

Each of the bones was marked, the larger pieces with stickers and the smaller ones with string tags. Bosch knew that notations on these markers were codes by which the location of each bone had been charted on the grid Kohl had drawn on the first day of the excavation.

'Bones can tell us much about how a person lived and died,' Golliher said somberly. 'In cases of child abuse, the bones do not lie. The bones become our final evidence.'

Bosch looked back at him and realized his eyes were not dark. They actually were blue but they were deeply set and seemed haunted in some way. He was staring past Bosch at the bones on the table. After a moment he broke from this reverie and looked at Bosch.

'Let me start by saying that we are learning quite a bit from the recovered artifacts,' the anthropologist said. 'But I have to tell you guys, I've consulted on a lot of cases but this one blows me away. I was looking at these bones and taking notes and I looked down and my notebook was smeared. I was crying, man. I was crying and I didn't even know it at first.'

He looked back at the outstretched bones with a look of tenderness and pity. Bosch knew that the anthropologist saw the person who was once there.

'This one is bad, guys. Real bad.'

'Then give us what you've got so we can go out there and do our job,' Bosch said in a voice that sounded like a reverent whisper.

Golliher nodded and reached back to a nearby counter for a spiral notebook.

'Okay,' Golliher said. 'Let's start with the basics. Some of this you may already know but I'm just going to go over all of my findings, if you don't mind.'

'We don't mind,' Bosch said.

'Good. Then here it is. What you have here are the remains of a young male Caucasoid. Comparisons to the indices of Maresh growth standards put the age at approximately ten years old. However, as we will soon discuss, this child was the victim of severe and prolonged physical abuse. Histologically, victims of chronic abuse often suffer from what is called growth disruption. This abuse-related stunting serves to skew age estimation. What you often get is a skeleton that looks younger than it is. So what I am saying is that this boy looks ten but is probably twelve or thirteen.'

Bosch looked over at Edgar. He was standing with his arms folded tightly across his chest, as if bracing for what he knew was ahead. Bosch took a notebook out of his jacket pocket and started writing notes in shorthand.

'Time of death,' Golliher said. 'This is tough. Radiological testing is far from exact in this regard. We have the coin which gives us the early marker of nineteen seventy-five. That helps us. What I am estimating is that this kid has been in the ground anywhere from twenty to twenty-five years. I'm comfortable with that and there is some surgical evidence we can talk about in a few minutes that adds support to that estimation.'

'So we've got a ten- to thirteen-year-old kid killed twenty to twenty-five years ago,' Edgar summarized, a note of frustration in his voice.

'I know I am giving you a wide set of parameters, Detective,' Golliher said. 'But at the moment it's the best the science can do for you.'

'Not your fault, Doc.'

Bosch wrote it all down. Despite the wide spread of the estimation, it was still vitally important to set a time frame for the investigation. Golliher's estimation put the time of death into the late seventies to early eighties.

Bosch momentarily thought of Laurel Canyon in that time frame. It had been a rustic, funky enclave, part bohemian and part upscale, with cocaine dealers and users, porno purveyors and burned out rock-and-roll hedonists on almost every street. Could the murder of a child have been part of that mix?

'Cause of death,' Golliher said. 'Tell you what, let's get to cause of death last. I want to start with the extremities and the torso, give you guys an idea of what this boy endured in his short lifetime.'

His eyes locked on Bosch's for a moment before returning to the bones. Bosch breathed in deeply, producing a sharp pain from his damaged ribs. He knew his fear from the moment he had looked down at the small bones on the hillside was now going to be realized. He instinctively knew all along that it would come to this. That a story of horror would emerge from the overturned soil.

He started scribbling on the pad, running the ballpoint deep into the paper, as Golliher continued.

'First of all, we only have maybe sixty percent of the bones here,' he said. 'But even still, we have incontrovertible evidence of tremendous skeletal trauma and chronic abuse. I don't know what your level of anthropological expertise is but I'm going to assume much of this will be new to you. I'm going to give you the basics. Bones heal themselves, gentlemen. And it is through the study of bone regeneration that we can establish a history of abuse. On these bones there are multiple lesions in different stages of healing. There are fractures old and new. We only have two of the four extremities but both of these show multiple instances of trauma. In short, this boy spent pretty much most of his life either healing or being hurt.'

Bosch looked down at the pad and pen clutched tightly in his hands. His hands were turning white.

'You will be getting a written report from me by Monday, but for now, if you want a number, I will tell you that I found forty-four distinct locations indicating separate trauma in various stages of healing. And these were just his bones, Detectives. It doesn't cover the damage that could have been inflicted on vital organs and the tissue. But it is without a doubt that this boy lived probably day in and day out with a lot of pain.'

Bosch wrote the number down on the pad. It seemed like a meaningless gesture.

'Primarily, the injuries I have catalogued can be noted on the artifacts by subperiosteal lesions,' Golliher said. 'These lesions are thin layers of new bone that grow beneath the surface in the area of trauma or bleeding.'

'Subperi – how do you spell that?' Bosch asked.

'What does it matter? It will be in the report.'

Bosch nodded.

'Take a look at this,' Golliher said.

Golliher went to the X-ray box on the wall and flipped on the light. There was already film on the box. It showed an X-ray of a long thin bone. He ran his finger along the stem of the bone, pointing out a slight demarcation of color.

'This is the one femur that was collected,' he said. 'The upper thigh. This line here, where the color changes, is one of the lesions. This means that this area – the boy's upper leg – had suffered a pretty strong blow in the weeks before his death. A crushing blow. It did not break the bone but it damaged it. This kind of injury would no doubt have caused surface bruising and I think affected the boy's walk. What I am telling you is that it could not have gone unnoticed.'

Bosch moved forward to study the X-ray. Edgar stayed back. When he was finished Golliher removed the X-ray and put up three more, covering the entire light box.

'We also have periosteal shearing on both of the limbs present. This is the stripping of the bone's surface, primarily seen in child abuse cases when the limb is struck violently by the adult hand or other instrument. Recovery patterns on these bones show that this particular type of trauma occurred repeatedly and over years to this child.'

Golliher paused to look at his notes, then he glanced at the bones on the table. He picked up the upper arm bone and held it up while he referred to his notes and spoke. Bosch noticed he wore no gloves.

'The humerus,' Golliher said. 'The right humerus shows two separate and healed fractures. The breaks are longitudinal. This tells us the fractures are the result of the twisting of the arm with great force. It happened to him once and then it happened again.'

He put the bone down and picked up one of the lower arm bones.

'The ulna shows a healed latitudinal fracture. The break caused a slight deviation in the attitude of the bone. This was because the bone was allowed to heal in place after the injury.'

'You mean it wasn't set?' Edgar asked. 'He wasn't taken to a doctor or an emergency room?'

'Exactly. This kind of injury, though commonly accidental and treated every day in every emergency room, can also be a defensive injury. You hold your arm up to ward off an attack and take the blow across the forearm. The fracture occurs. Because of the lack of indication of medical attention paid to this injury, my supposition is that this was not an accidental injury and was part of the abuse pattern.'

Golliher gently returned the bone to its spot and then leaned over the examination table to look down at the rib cage. Many of the rib bones had been detached and were lying separated on the table.

'The ribs,' Golliher said. 'Nearly two dozen fractures in various stages of healing. A healed fracture on rib twelve I believe may date to when the boy was only two or three. Rib nine shows a callus indicative of trauma only a few weeks old at the time of death. The fractures are primarily consolidated near the angles. In infants this is indicative of violent shaking. In older children this is usually indicative of blows to the back.'

Bosch thought of the pain he was in, of how he had been unable to sleep well because of the injury to his ribs. He thought of a young boy living with that kind of pain year in and year out.

'I gotta go wash my face,' he suddenly said. 'You can continue.'

He walked to the door, shoving his notebook and pen into Edgar's hands. In the hallway he turned right. He knew the layout of the autopsy floor and knew there were rest rooms around the next turn of the corridor.

He entered the rest room and went right to an open stall. He felt nauseous and waited but nothing happened. After a long moment it passed.

Bosch came out of the stall just as the door opened from the hallway and Teresa Corazon's cameraman walked in. They looked warily at each other for a moment.

'Get out of here,' Bosch said. 'Come back later.'

The man silently turned and walked out.

Bosch walked to the sink and looked at himself in the mirror. His face was red. He bent down and used his hands to cup cold water against his face and eyes. He thought about baptisms and second chances. Of renewal. He raised his face until he was looking at himself again.

I'm going to get this guy.

He almost said it out loud.

When Bosch returned to suite A all eyes were on him. Edgar gave him his notebook and pen back and Golliher asked if he was all right.

'Yeah, fine,' he said.

'If it is any help to you,' Golliher said, 'I have consulted on cases all over the world. Chile, Kosovo, even the World Trade Center. And this case . . .'

He shook his head.

'It's hard to comprehend,' he added. 'It's one of those where you have to think that maybe the boy was better off leaving this world. That is, if you believe in a God and a better place than this.'

Bosch walked over to a counter and pulled a paper towel out of a dispenser. He started wiping his face again.

'And what if you don't?'

Golliher walked over to him.

'Well, you see, this is why you must believe,' he said. 'If this boy did not go from this world to a higher plane, to something better, then . . . then I think we're all lost.'

'Did that work for you when you were picking through the bones at the World Trade Center?'

Bosch immediately regretted saying something so harsh. But Golliher seemed unfazed. He spoke before Bosch could apologize.

'Yes, it did,' he said. 'My faith was not shaken by the horror or the unfairness of so much death. In many ways it became stronger. It brought me through it.'

Bosch nodded and threw the towel into a trash can with a foot-pedal device for opening it. It closed with an echoing slam when he took his foot off the pedal.

'What about cause of death?' he said, getting back to the case.

'We can jump ahead, Detective,' Golliher said. 'All injuries, discussed and not discussed here, will be outlined in my report.'

He went back to the table and picked up the skull. He brought it over to Bosch, holding it in one hand close to his chest.

'In the skull we have the bad – and possibly the good,' Golliher said. 'The skull exhibits three distinct cranial fractures showing mixed stages of healing. Here is the first.'

He pointed to an area at the lower rear of the skull.

'This fracture is small and healed. You can see here that the lesions are completely consolidated. Then, next we have this more traumatic injury on the right parietal extending to the frontal. This injury required surgery, most likely for a subdural hematoma.'

He outlined the injury area with a finger, circling the forward top of the skull. He then pointed to five small and smooth holes which were linked by a circular pattern on the skull.

'This is a trephine pattern. A trephine is a medical saw used to open the skull for surgery or to relieve pressure from brain swelling. In this case it was probably swelling due to the hematoma. Now the fracture itself and the surgical scar show the beginning of bridging across the lesions. New bone. I would say this injury and subsequent surgery occurred approximately six months prior to the boy's death.'

'It's not the injury causing death?' Bosch asked.

'No. This is.'

Golliher turned the skull one more time and showed them another fracture. This one in the lower left rear of the skull.

'Tight spider web fracture with no bridging, no consolidation. This injury occurred at the time of death. The tightness of the fracture indicates a blow with tremendous force from a very hard object. A baseball bat, perhaps. Something like that.'

Bosch nodded and stared down at the skull. Golliher had turned it so that its hollow eyes were focused on Bosch.

'There are other injuries to the head, but not of a fatal nature. The nose bones and the zygomatic process show new bone formation following trauma.'

Golliher returned to the autopsy table and gently placed the skull down.

'I don't think I need to summarize for you, Detectives, but in short, somebody beat the shit out of this boy on a regular basis. Eventually, they went too far. It will all be in the report to you.'

He turned from the autopsy table and looked at them.

'There is a glimmer of light in all of this, you know. Something that might help you.'

'The surgery,' Bosch said.

'Exactly. Opening a skull is a very serious operation. There will be records somewhere. There had to be follow-up. The roundel is held back in place with metal clips after surgery. There were none found with the skull. I would assume they were removed in a second procedure. Again, there will be records. The surgical scar also helps us date the bones. The trephine holes are too large by today's standards. By the mid-eighties the tools were more advanced than this. Sleeker. The perforations were smaller. I hope this all helps you.'

Bosch nodded and said, 'What about the teeth? Anything there?'

'We are missing the lower mandible,' Golliher said. 'On the upper teeth present there is no indication of any dental work despite indication of ante-mortem decay. This in itself is a clue. I think it puts this boy in the lower levels of social classification. He didn't go to the dentist.'

Edgar had pulled his mask down around his neck. His expression was pained.

'When this kid was in the hospital with the hematoma, why wouldn't he tell the doctors what was happening to him? What about his teachers, his friends?'

'You know the answers to that as well as me, Detective,' Golliher said. 'Children are reliant on their parents. They are scared of them and they love them, don't want to lose them. Sometimes there is no explanation for why they don't cry out for help.'

'What about all these fractures and such? Why didn't the doctors see it and do something?'

'That's the irony of what I do. I see the history and tragedy so clearly. But with a living patient it might not be apparent. If the parents came in with a plausible explanation for the boy's injury, what reason would a doctor have to X-ray an arm or a leg or a chest? None. And so the nightmare goes unnoticed.'

Unsatisfied, Edgar shook his head and walked to the far corner of the room.

'Anything else, Doctor?' Bosch asked.

Golliher checked his notes and then folded his arms.

'That's it on a scientific level – you'll get the report. On a purely personal level, I hope you find the person who did this. They will deserve whatever they get, and then some.'

Bosch nodded.

'We'll get him,' Edgar said. 'Don't you worry about that.'

They walked out of the building and got into Bosch's car. Bosch just sat there for a moment before starting the engine. Finally, he hit the steering wheel hard with the heel of his palm, sending a shock down the injured side of his chest.

'You know it doesn't make me believe in God like him,' Edgar said. 'Makes me believe in aliens, little green men from outer space.'

Bosch looked over at him. Edgar was leaning his head against the side window, looking down at the floor of the car.

'How so?'

'Because a human couldn't have done this to his own kid. A spaceship must've come down and abducted the kid and done all that stuff to him. Only explanation.'

'Yeah, I wish that was on the checklist, Jerry. Then we could all just go home.'

Bosch put the car into drive.

'I need a drink.'

He started driving out of the lot.

'Not me, man,' Edgar said. 'I just want to go see my kid and hug him until this gets better.'

They didn't speak again until they got over to Parker Center.

8

Bosch and Edgar rode the elevator to the fifth floor and went into the SID lab, where they had a meeting set up with Antoine Jesper, the lead criminalist assigned to the bones case. Jesper met them at the security fence and took them back. He was a young black man with gray eyes and smooth skin. He wore a white lab coat that swayed and flapped with his long strides and always moving arms.

'This way, guys,' he said. 'I don't have a lot but what I got is yours.'

He took them through the main lab, where only a handful of other criminalists were working, and into the drying room, a large climate-controlled space where clothing and other material evidence from cases were spread on stainless steel drying tables and examined. It was the only place that could rival the autopsy floor of the medical examiner's office in the stench of decay.

Jesper led them to two tables where Bosch saw the open backpack and several pieces of clothing blackened with soil and fungus. There was also a plastic sandwich bag filled with an unrecognizable lump of black decay.

'Water and mud got into the backpack,' Jesper said. 'Leached in over time, I guess.'

Jesper took a pen out of the pocket of his lab coat and extended it into a pointer. He used it to help illustrate his commentary.

'We've got your basic backpack containing three sets of clothes and what was probably a sandwich or some kind of food item. More specifically, three T-shirts, three underwear, three sets of socks. And the food item. There was also an envelope, or what was left of an envelope. You don't see that here because documents has it. But don't get your hopes up, guys. It was in worse shape than that sandwich – *if* it was a sandwich.'

Bosch nodded. He made a list of the contents in his notebook.

'Any identifiers?' he asked.

Jesper shook his head.

'No personal identifiers on the clothing or in the bag,' he said. 'But two things to note. First, this shirt here has a brand-name identifier. 'Solid Surf.' Says it across the chest. You can't see it now but I picked it up with the black light. Might help, might not. If you are not familiar with the term 'Solid Surf,' I can tell you that it is a skateboarding reference.'

'Got it,' Bosch said.

'Next is the outside flap of the bag.'

He used his pointer to flip over the flap.

'Cleaned this up a little bit and came up with this.'

Bosch leaned over the table to look. The bag was made of blue canvas. On the flap was a clear demarcation of color forming a large letter B at the center.

'It looks like there was some kind of adhesive applicate at one time on the bag,' Jesper said. 'It's gone now and I don't really know if that occurred before or after this thing was put in the ground. My guess is before. It looks like it was peeled off.'

Bosch stepped back from the table and wrote a few lines in his notebook. He then looked at Jesper.

'Okay, Antoine, good stuff. Anything else?'

'Not on this stuff.'

'Then let's go to documents.'

Jesper led the way again through the central lab and then into a sub-lab where he had to enter a combination into a door lock to enter.

The documents lab contained two rows of desks that were all empty. Each desk had a horizontal light box and a magnifying glass mounted on a pivot. Jesper went to the middle desk in the second row. The nameplate on the desk said Bernadette Fornier. Bosch knew her. They had worked a case previously in which a suicide note had been forged. He knew she did good work.

Jesper picked up a plastic evidence pouch that was sitting in the middle of the desk. He unzipped it and removed two plastic viewing sleeves. One contained an unfolded envelope that was brown and smeared with black fungus. The other contained a deteriorated rectangular piece of paper that was broken into three parts along the folds and was also grossly discolored by decay and fungus.

'This is what happens when stuff gets wet, man,' Jesper said. 'It took Bernie all day just to unfold the envelope and separate the letter. As you can see, it came apart at the folds. And as far as whether we'll ever be able to tell what was in the letter, it doesn't look good.'

Bosch turned on the light box and put the plastic sleeves down on it. He swung the magnifier over and studied the envelope and the letter it had once contained. There was nothing remotely readable on either document. One thing he noted was that it looked like there was no stamp on the envelope.

'Damn,' he said.

He flipped the sleeves over and kept looking. Edgar came over next to him as if to confirm the obvious.

'Woulda been nice,' he said.

'What will she do now?' Bosch asked Jesper.

'Well, she'll probably try some dyes, some different lights. Try to get something that reacts with the ink, brings it up. But she wasn't too optimistic yesterday. So like I said, I wouldn't be getting my hopes up about it.'

Bosch nodded and turned off the light.

9

Near the back entrance to the Hollywood Division station was a bench with large sand-filled ashtrays on either side. It was called the Code 7, after the radio call for out-of-service or on break. At 11:15 P.M. on Saturday night Bosch was the only occupant on the Code 7 bench. He wasn't smoking, though he wished he was. He was waiting. The bench was dimly lit by the lights over the station's back door and had a view of the parking lot jointly shared by the station and the firehouse on the back end of the city complex.

Bosch watched as the patrol units came in from the three-to-eleven shift and the officers went into the station to change out of uniforms, shower and call it a night, if they could. He looked down at the MagLite he held in his hands and rubbed his thumb over the end cap and felt the scratchings where Julia Brasher had etched her badge number.

He hefted the light and then flipped it in his hand, feeling its weight. He flashed on what Golliher had said about the weapon that had killed the boy. He could add flashlight to the list.

Bosch watched a patrol car come into the lot and park by the motor pool garage. A cop he recognized as Julia Brasher's partner, Edgewood, emerged from the passenger side and headed into the station carrying the car's shotgun. Bosch waited and watched, suddenly unsure of his plan and wondering if he could abandon it and get into the station without being seen.

Before he decided on a move Brasher got out of the driver's side and headed toward the station door. She walked with her head down, the posture of someone tired and beat from a long day. Bosch knew the feeling. He also thought something might be wrong. It was a subtle thing, but the way Edgewood had gone in and left her behind told Bosch something was off. Since Brasher was a rookie, Edgewood was her training officer, even though he was at least five years younger than her. Maybe it was just an awkward situation because of age and gender. Or maybe it was something else.

Brasher didn't notice Bosch on the bench. She was almost to the station door before he spoke.

'Hey, you forgot to wash the puke out of the back seat.'

She looked back while continuing to walk until she saw it was him. She stopped then and walked over to the bench.

'I brought you something,' Bosch said.

He held out the flashlight. She smiled tiredly as she took it.

'Thank you, Harry. You didn't have to wait here to—'

'I wanted to.'

There was an awkward silence for a moment.

'Were you working the case tonight?' she asked.

'More or less. Started the paperwork. And we sort of got the autopsy earlier today. If you could call it an autopsy.'

'I can tell by your face it was bad.'

Bosch nodded. He felt strange. He was still sitting and she was still standing.

'I can tell by the way you look that you had a tough one, too.'

'Aren't they all?'

Before Bosch could say anything two cops, fresh from showers and in street clothes, came out of the station and headed toward their personal cars.

'Cheer up, Julia,' one of them said. 'We'll see you over there.'

'Okay, Kiko,' she said back.

She turned and looked back down at Bosch. She smiled.

'Some people from the shift are getting together over at Boardner's,' she said. 'You want to come?'

'Um . . .'

'That's okay. I just thought maybe you could use a drink or something.'

'I could. I need one. Actually, that's why I was waiting here for you. I just don't know if I want to get into a group thing at a bar.'

'Well, what were you thinking, then?'

Bosch checked his watch. It was now eleven-thirty.

'Depending on how long you take in the locker room, we could probably catch the last martini call at Musso's.'

She smiled broadly now.

'I love that place. Give me fifteen minutes.'

She headed toward the station door without waiting for a reply from him.

'I'll be here,' he called after her.

10

Musso and Frank's was an institution that had been serving martinis to the denizens of Hollywood – both famous and infamous – for a century. The front room was all red leather booths and quiet conversation with ancient waiters in red half-coats moving slowly about. The back room contained the long bar, where most nights it was standing room only while patrons vied for the attention of bartenders who could have been the fathers of the waiters. As Bosch and Brasher came into the bar two patrons slipped off their stools to leave. Bosch and Brasher quickly moved in, beating two black-clad studio types to the choice spots. A bartender who recognized Bosch came over and they both ordered vodka martinis, slightly dirty.

Bosch was already feeling at ease with her. They had spent lunch together at the crime scene picnic tables the last two days and she had never been far from his sight during the hillside searches. They had ridden over to Musso's together in his car and it seemed like a third or fourth date already. They small-talked about the division and the details Bosch was willing to part with about his case. By the time the bartender put down their martini glasses along with the sidecar carafes, he was ready to forget about bones and blood and baseball bats for a while.

They clinked glasses and Brasher said, 'To life.'

'Yeah,' Bosch said. 'Getting through another day.'

'Just barely.'

Bosch knew that now was the time to talk to her about what was troubling her. If she didn't want to talk, he wouldn't press it.

'That guy you called Kiko in the back lot, why'd he tell you to cheer up?'

She slumped a little and didn't answer at first.

'If you don't want to talk about—'

'No, it's not that. It's more like I don't want to *think* about it.'

'I know the feeling. Forget I asked.'

'No, it's okay. My partner's going to write me up and since I'm on probation, it could cost me.'

'Write you up for what?'

'Crossing the tube.'

It was a tactical expression, meaning to walk in front of the barrel of a shotgun or other weapon held by a fellow officer.

'What happened? I mean, if you want to talk about it.'

She shrugged and they both took long drinks from their glasses.

'Oh, it was a domestic – I hate domestics – and the guy locked himself in the bedroom with a gun. We didn't know if he was going to use it on himself, his wife or us. We waited for backup and then we were going to go in.'

She took another drink. Bosch watched her. Her inner turmoil showed clearly in her eyes.

'Edgewood had shotgun. Kiko had the kick. Fennel, Kiko's partner, and I had the door. So we did the deed. Kiko's big. He opened the door with one kick. Fennel and I went in. The guy was passed out on the bed. Seemed like no problem but Edgewood had a big problem with me. He said I crossed the tube.'

'Did you?'

'I don't think so. But if I did, then so did Fennel, and he didn't say jack to him.'

'You're the rookie. You're the one on probation.'

'Yeah, and I'm getting tired of it, that's for sure. I mean, how did you make it through, Harry? Right now you've got a job that makes a difference. What I do, just chasing the radio all day and night, going from dirtbag to dirtbag, it's like spitting on a house fire. We're not making any headway out there and on top of that I've got this uptight male asshole telling me every two minutes how I fucked up.'

Bosch knew what she was feeling. Every cop in a uniform went through it. You wade through the cesspool every day and soon it seems that that is all there is. An abyss. It was why he could never go back to working patrol. Patrol was a Band-Aid on a bullet hole.

'Did you think it would be different? When you were in the academy, I mean.'

'I don't know what I thought. I just don't know if I can make it through to a point where I think I'm making any difference.'

'I think you can. The first couple years are tough. But you dig in and you start seeing the long view. You pick your battles and you pick your path. You'll do all right.'

He didn't feel confident giving her the rah-rah speech. He had gone through long stretches of indecision about himself and his choices. Telling her to stick it out made him feel a little false.

'Let's talk about something else,' she said.

'Fine with me,' he said.

He took a long drink from his glass, trying to think of how to turn the conversation in another direction. He put his glass down, turned and smiled at her.

'So there you were, hiking in the Andes and you said to yourself, 'Gee, I wanna be a cop.''

She laughed, seemingly shaking off the blues of her earlier comments.

'Not quite like that. And I've never been in the Andes.'

'Well, what about the rich, full life you lived before putting on the badge? You said you were a world traveler.'

'Never made it to South America.'

'Is that where the Andes are? All this time I thought they were in Florida.'

She laughed again and Bosch felt good about successfully changing the subject. He liked looking at her teeth when she laughed. They were just a little bit crooked and in a way that made them perfect.

'So seriously, what did you do?'

She turned in the stool so they were shoulder to shoulder, looking at each other in the mirror behind all the colored bottles lined along the back wall of the bar.

'Oh, I was a lawyer for a while – not a defense lawyer, so don't get excited. Civil law. Then I realized that was bullshit and quit and just started traveling. I worked along the way. I made pottery in Venice, Italy. I was a horse guide in the Swiss Alps for a while. I was cook on a day-trip tourist boat in Hawaii. I did other things and I just saw a lot of the world – except for the Andes. Then I came home.'

'To L.A.?'

'Born and raised. You?'

'Same. Queen of Angels.'

'Cedars.'

She held out her glass and they clinked.

'To the few, the proud, the brave,' she said.

Bosch finished off his glass and poured in the contents of his sidecar. He was way ahead of Brasher but didn't care. He was feeling relaxed. It was good to forget about things for a while. It was good to be with somebody not directly related to the case.

'Born at Cedars, huh?' he asked. 'Where'd you grow up?'

'Don't laugh. Bel Air.'

'Bel Air? I guess somebody's daddy isn't too happy about her joining the cops.'

'Especially since his was the law firm she walked out of one day and wasn't heard from for two years.'

Bosch smiled and raised his glass. She clicked hers off it.

'Brave girl.'

After they put their glasses down, she said, 'Let's stop all the questions.'

'Okay,' Bosch said. 'And do what?'

'Just take me home, Harry. To your place.'

He paused for a moment, looking at her shiny blue eyes. Things were moving lightning fast, greased on the smooth runners of alcohol. But that was often the way it was between cops, between people who felt they were part of a closed society, who lived by their instincts and went to work each day knowing that how they made their living could kill them.

'Yeah,' he finally said, 'I was just thinking the same thing.'

He leaned over and kissed her on the mouth.

11

Julia Brasher stood in the living room of Bosch's house and looked at the CDs stored in the racks next to the stereo.

'I love jazz.'

Bosch was in the kitchen. He smiled when he heard her say it. He finished pouring the two martinis out of a shaker and came out to the living room and handed her a glass.

'Who do you like?'

'Ummm, lately Bill Evans.'

Bosch nodded, went to the rack and came up with *Kind of Blue*. He loaded it into the stereo.

'Bill and Miles,' he said. 'Not to mention Coltrane and a few other guys. Nothing better.'

As the music began he picked up his martini and she came over and tapped it with her glass. Rather than drink, they kissed each other. She started laughing halfway through the kiss.

'What?' he said.

'Nothing. I'm just feeling reckless. And happy.'

'Yeah, me too.'

'I think it was you giving me the flashlight.'

Bosch was puzzled.

'What do you mean?'

'You know, it's so phallic.'

The look on Bosch's face made her laugh again and she spilled some of her drink on the floor.

Later, when she was lying face down on his bed, Bosch was tracing the outline of the flaming sun tattooed on the small of her back and thinking about how comfortable and yet strange she felt to him. He knew almost nothing about her. Like the tattoo, there seemed to be a surprise from every angle of view he had on her.

'What are you thinking about?' she asked.

'Nothing. Just wondering about the guy who got to put this on your back. I wish it had been me, I guess.'

'How come?'

'Because there will always be a piece of him with you.'

She turned on her side, revealing her breasts and her smile. Her hair was out of its braid and down around her shoulders. He liked that, too. She reached up and pulled him down into a long kiss. Then she said, 'That's the nicest thing that's been said to me in a long time.'

He put his head down on her pillow. He could smell the sweet scent of perfume and sex and sweat.

'You don't have any pictures on your walls,' she said. 'Photos, I mean.'

He shrugged his shoulders.

She turned over so her back was to him. He reached under her arm and cupped one of her breasts and pulled her back into him.

'Can you stay till the morning?' he asked.

'Well . . . my husband will probably wonder where I am, but I guess I could call him.'

Bosch froze. Then she started laughing.

'Don't scare me like that.'

'Well, you never even asked me if I was involved with anyone.'

'You didn't ask me.'

'You were obvious. The lone detective type.' And then in a deep male voice: 'Just the facts, ma'am. No time for dames. Murder is my business. I have a job to do and I am—'

He ran his thumb down her side, over the indentations of her ribs. She cut off her words with laughter.

'You lent me your flashlight,' he said. 'I didn't think an 'involved' woman would have done that.'

'And I've got news for you, tough guy. I saw the Mag in your trunk. In the box before you covered it up. You weren't fooling anybody.'

Bosch rolled back on the other pillow, embarrassed. He could feel his face getting red. He brought his hands up to hide it.

'Oh, God . . . Mr. Obvious.'

She rolled over to him and peeled back his hands. She kissed him on the chin.

'I thought it was nice. Kinda made my day and gave me something to maybe look forward to.'

She turned his hands back and looked at the scarring across the knuckles. They were old marks and not very noticeable anymore.

'Hey, what is this?'

'Just scars.'

'I know that. From what?'

'I had tattoos. I took them off. It was a long time ago.'

'How come?'

'They made me take them off when I went into the army.'

She started to laugh.

'Why, what did it say, Fuck the army or something?'

'No, nothing like that.'

'Then what? Come on, I want to know.'

'It said H-O-L-D on one hand and F-A-S-T on the other.'

'Hold fast? What does 'hold fast' mean?'

'Well, it's kind of a long story . . .'

'I have time. My husband doesn't mind.'

She smiled.

'Come on, I want to know.'

'It's not a big deal. When I was a kid, one of the times I ran away I ended up down in San Pedro. Down around the fishing docks. And a lot of those guys down there, the fishermen, the tuna guys, I saw they had this on their hands. Hold fast. And I asked one of them about it and he told me it was like their motto, their philosophy. It's like when they were out there in those boats, way out there for weeks, and the waves got huge and it got scary, you just had to grab on and hold fast.'

Bosch made two fists and held them up.

'Hold fast to life . . . to everything that you have.'

'So you had it done. How old were you?'

'I don't know, sixteen, thereabouts.'

He nodded and then he smiled.

'What I didn't know was that those tuna guys got it from some navy guys. So a year later I go waltzing into the army with 'Hold Fast' on my hands and the first thing my sergeant told me was to get rid of it. He wasn't going to have any squid tattoo on one of his guys' hands.'

She grabbed his hands and looked closely at the knuckles.

'This doesn't look like laser work.'

Bosch shook his head.

'They didn't have lasers back then.'

'So what did you do?'

'My sergeant, his name was Rosser, took me out of the barracks and over to the back of the administration building. There was a brick wall. He made me punch it. Until every one of my knuckles was cut up. Then after they were scabbed up in about a week he made me do it again.'

'Jesus fucking Christ, that's barbaric.'

'No, that's the army.'

He smiled at the memory. It wasn't as bad as it sounded. He looked down at his hands. The music stopped and he got up and walked through the house naked to change it. When he came back to the bedroom, she recognized the music.

'Clifford Brown?'

He nodded and came toward the bed. He didn't think he had ever known a woman who could identify jazz music like that.

'Stand there.'

'What?'

'Let me look at you. Tell me about those other scars.'

The room was dimly lit by a light from the bathroom but Bosch became conscious of his nakedness. He was in good shape but he was more than fifteen years older than her. He wondered if she had ever been with a man so old.

'Harry, you look great. You totally turn me on, okay? What about the other scars?'

He touched the thick rope of skin above his left hip.

'This? This was a knife.'

'Where'd that happen?'

'A tunnel.'

'And your shoulder?'

'Bullet.'

'Where?'

He smiled.

'A tunnel.'

'Ouch, stay out of tunnels.'

'I try.'

He got into the bed and pulled the sheet up. She touched his shoulder, running her thumb over the thick skin of the scar.

'Right in the bone,' she said.

'Yeah, I got lucky. No permanent damage. It aches in the winter and when it rains, that's about it.'

'What did it feel like? Being shot, I mean.'

Bosch shrugged his shoulders.

'It hurt like hell and then everything sort of went numb.'

'How long were you down?'

'About three months.'

'You didn't get a disability out?'

'It was offered. I declined.'

'How come?'

'I don't know. I like the job, I guess. And I thought that if I stuck with it, someday I'd meet this beautiful young cop who'd be impressed by all my scars.'

She jammed him in the ribs and the pain made him grimace.

'Oh, poor baby,' she said in a mocking voice.

'That hurt.'

She touched the tattoo on his shoulder.

'What's that supposed to be, Mickey Mouse on acid?'

'Sort of. It's a tunnel rat.'

Her face lost all trace of humor.

'What's the matter?'

'You were in Vietnam,' she said, putting things together. 'I've been in those tunnels.'

'What do you mean?'

'When I was on the road. I spent six weeks in Vietnam. The tunnels, they're like a tourist thing now. You pay your money and you can go down into them. It must've been ... what you had to do must've been so frightening.'

'It was more scary afterward. Thinking about it.'

'They have them roped off so they can sort of control where you go. But nobody really watches you. So I went under the rope and went further in. It got so dark in there, Harry.'

Bosch studied her eyes.

'And did you see it?' he asked quietly. 'The lost light?'

She held his eyes for a moment and nodded.

'I saw it. My eyes adjusted and there was light. Almost like a whisper. But it was enough for me to find my way.'

'Lost light. We called it lost light. We never knew where it came from. But it was down there. Like smoke hanging in the dark. Some people said it wasn't light, that it was the ghosts of everybody who died in those things. From both sides.'

They spoke no more after that. They held each other and soon she was asleep.

Bosch realized he had not thought about the case for more than three hours. At first this made him feel guilty but then he let it go and soon he too was asleep. He dreamed he was moving through a tunnel. But he wasn't crawling. It was as if he were underwater and moving like an eel through the labyrinth. He came to a dead end and there was a boy sitting against the curve of the tunnel's wall. He had his knees up and his face down, buried in his folded arms.

'Come with me,' Bosch said.

The boy peeked his eyes over one arm and looked up at Bosch. A single bubble of air rose from his mouth. He then looked past Bosch as if something was coming up behind him. Bosch turned around but there was only the darkness of the tunnel behind him.

When he looked back at the boy, he was gone.

12

Late Sunday morning Bosch drove Brasher to the Hollywood station so she could get her car and he could resume work on the case. She was off duty Sundays and Mondays. They made plans to meet at her house in Venice that night for dinner. There were other officers in the parking lot when Bosch dropped her next to her car. Bosch knew that word would get around quickly that it appeared they had spent the night together.

'I'm sorry,' he said. 'I should have thought it out better last night.'

'I don't really care, Harry. I'll see you tonight.'

'Hey, look, you should care. Cops can be brutal.'

She made a face.

'Oh, police brutality, yeah, I've heard of it.'

'I'm serious. It's also against regs. On my part. I'm a D-three. Supervisor level.'

She looked at him a moment.

'Well, that's your call, then. I'll see you tonight. I hope.'

She got out and closed the door. Bosch drove on to his assigned parking slot and went into the detective bureau, trying not to think of the complications he might have just invited into his life.

It was deserted in the squad room, which was what he was hoping for. He wanted time alone with the case. There was still a lot of office work to do but he also wanted to step back and think about all the evidence and information that had been accumulated since the discovery of the bones.

The first thing to do was put together a list of what needed to be done. The murder book – the blue binder containing all written reports pertaining to the case – had to be completed. He had to draw up search warrants seeking medical records of brain surgeries at local hospitals. He had to run routine computer checks on all the residents living in the vicinity of the crime scene on Wonderland. He also had to read through all the call-in tips spawned by the media coverage of the bones on the hill and start gathering missing person and runaway reports that might match the victim.

He knew it was more than a day's work if he labored by himself but decided to keep with his decision to allow Edgar the day off. His partner, the father of a thirteen-year-old boy, had been greatly upset by Golliher's report the day before and Bosch wanted him to take a break. The days ahead would likely be long and just as emotionally upsetting.

Once Bosch had his list together he took his cup out of a drawer and went back to the watch office to get coffee. The smallest he had on him was a five-dollar bill but he put it in the coffee fund basket without taking any change. He figured he'd be drinking more than his share through the day.

'You know what they say?' someone said behind him as he was filling the cup.

Bosch turned. It was Mankiewicz, the watch sergeant.

'About what?'

'Fishing off the company dock.'

'I don't know. What do they say?'

'I don't know either. That's why I was asking you.'

Mankiewicz smiled and moved toward the machine to warm up his cup.

So already it was starting to get around, Bosch thought. Gossip and innuendo – especially anything with a sexual tone – moved through a police station like a fire racing up a hill in August.

'Well, let me know when you find out,' Bosch said as he started for the door of the watch office. 'Could be useful to know.'

'Will do. Oh, and one other thing, Harry.'

Bosch turned, ready for another shot from Mankiewicz.

'What?'

'Just stop fooling around and wrap up your case. I'm tired of my guys having to take all the calls.'

There was a facetious tone in his voice. In his humor and sarcasm was a legitimate complaint about his officers on the desk being tied up by the tip calls.

'Yeah, I know. Any good ones today?'

'Not that I could tell, but you'll get to slog through the reports and use your investigative wiles to decide that.'

'Wiles?'

'Yes, wiles. Like Wile E. Coyote. Oh, and CNN must've had a slow morning and picked up the story – good video, all you brave guys on the hill with your makeshift stairs and little boxes of bones. So now we're getting the long-distance calls. Topeka and Providence so far this morning. It's not going to end until you clear it, Harry. We're all counting on you back here.'

Again there was a smile – and a message – behind what he was saying.

'All right, I'll use all my wiles. I promise, Mank.'

'That's what we're counting on.'

Back at the table Bosch sipped his coffee and let the details of the case move through his mind. There were anomalies, contradictions. There were the conflicts between location choice and method of burial noticed by Kathy Kohl. But the conclusions made by Golliher added even more to the list of questions. Golliher saw it as a child abuse case. But the backpack full of clothes was an indication that the victim, the boy, was possibly a runaway.

Bosch had spoken to Edgar about it the day before when they returned to the station from the SID lab. His partner was not as sure of the conflict as Bosch but offered a theory that perhaps the boy was the victim of child abuse both at the hands of his parents and then an unrelated killer. He rightfully pointed out that many victims of abuse run away only to be drawn into another form of abusive relationship. Bosch knew the theory was legitimate but tried not to let himself go down that road because he knew it was even more depressing than the scenario Golliher had spun.

His direct line rang and Bosch answered, expecting it to be Edgar or Lt. Billets checking in. It was a reporter from the *L.A. Times* named Josh Meyer. Bosch barely knew him and was sure he'd never given him the direct line. He didn't let on that he was annoyed, however. Though tempted to tell the reporter that the police were running down leads extending as far as Topeka and Providence, he simply said there was no further update on the investigation since Friday's briefing from the Media Relations office.

After he hung up he finished his first cup of coffee and got down to work. The part of an investigation Bosch enjoyed the least was the computer work. Whenever possible he gave it to his partners to handle. So he decided to put the computer runs at the end of his list and started with a quick look through the accumulated tip sheets from the watch office.

There were about three dozen more sheets since he had last looked through the pile on Friday. None contained enough information to be helpful or worth pursuing at the moment. Each was from a parent or sibling or friend of someone who had disappeared. All of them permanently forlorn and seeking some kind of closure to the most pressing mystery of their lives.

He thought of something and rolled his chair over to one of the old IBM Selectrics. He inserted a sheet of paper and typed out four questions.

Do you know if your missing loved one underwent any kind of surgical procedure in the months before his disappearance?
If so, what hospital was he treated at?
What was the injury?
What was the name of his physician?

He rolled the page out and took it to the watch office. He gave it to Mankiewicz to be used as a template of questions to be asked of all callers about the bones.

'That wily enough for you?' Bosch asked.

'No, but it's a start.'

While he was there Bosch took a plastic cup and filled it with coffee and then came back to the bureau and dumped it into his cup. He made a note to ask Lt. Billets on Monday to procure some help in contacting all the callers of the last few days to ask the same medical questions. He then thought of Julia Brasher. He knew she was off on Mondays and would volunteer if needed. But he quickly dismissed it, knowing that by Monday the whole station would know about them and bringing her into the case would make matters worse.

He started the search warrants next. It was a matter of routine in homicide work to need medical records in the course of an investigation. Most often these records came from physicians and dentists. But hospitals were not unusual. Bosch kept a file with search warrant templates for hospitals as well as a listing of all twenty-nine hospitals in the Los Angeles area and the attorneys who handled legal filings at each location. Having all of this handy allowed him to draw up twenty-nine search warrants in a little over an hour. The warrants sought the records of all male patients under the age of sixteen who underwent brain surgery entailing the use of a trephine drill between 1975 and 1985.

After printing out the requests he put them in his briefcase. While normally it was proper on a weekend to fax a search warrant to a judge's home for approval and signature, it would certainly not be acceptable to fax twenty-nine requests to a judge on a Sunday afternoon. Besides, the hospital lawyers would not be available on a Sunday anyway. Bosch's plan was to take the warrants to a judge first thing Monday morning, then divide them with Edgar and hand-deliver them to the hospitals, thereby being able to push the urgency of the matter with the lawyers in person. Even if things went according to plan, Bosch didn't expect to start receiving returns of records from the hospitals until mid-week or later.

Bosch next typed out a daily case summary as well as a recap of the anthropological information from Golliher. He put these in the murder book and then typed up an evidence report detailing the preliminary SID findings on the backpack.

When he was finished Bosch leaned back and thought about the unreadable letter that had been found in the backpack. He did not anticipate that the documents section would have any success with it. It would forever be the mystery shrouded in the mystery of the case. He gulped the last of his second cup of coffee and opened the murder book to the page containing a copy of the crime scene sketch and chart. He studied the chart and noted that the backpack had been found right next to the spot Kohl had marked as the probable original location of the body.

Bosch wasn't sure what it all meant but instinctively he knew that the questions he now had about the case should be kept foremost in his mind as new evidence and details continued to be gathered. They would be the screen through which everything would be sifted.

He put the report into the murder book and then finished the updating of the paperwork by bringing the investigator's log – an hour-by-hour time chart with small entry blocks – up to date. He then put the murder book in his briefcase.

Bosch took his coffee cup to the sink in the rest room and washed it out. He then returned it to its drawer, picked up his briefcase and headed out the back door to his car.

13

The basement of Parker Center, the headquarters of the Los Angeles Police Department, serves as the record archives for every case the department has taken a report on in the modern era. Until the mid-nineties records were kept on paper for a period of eight years and then transferred to microfiche for permanent storage. The department now used computers for permanent storage and was also moving backward, putting older files into digital storage banks. But the process was slow and had not gone further back than the late eighties.

Bosch arrived at the counter in archives at one o'clock. He had two containers of coffee with him and two roast beef sandwiches from Philippe's in a paper bag. He looked at the clerk and smiled.

'Believe it or not I need to see the fiche on missing person reports, nineteen seventy-five to eighty-five.'

The clerk, an old guy with a basement pallor, whistled and said, 'Look out, Christine, here they come.'

Bosch smiled and nodded and didn't know what the man was talking about. There appeared to be no one else behind the counter.

'The good news is they break up,' the clerk said. 'I mean, I think it's good news. You looking for adult or juvy records?'

'Juveniles.'

'Then that cuts it up a bit.'

'Thanks.'

'Don't mention it.'

The clerk disappeared from the counter and Bosch waited. In four minutes the man came back with ten small envelopes containing microfiche sheets for the years Bosch requested. Altogether the stack was at least four inches thick.

Bosch went to a microfiche reader and copier, set out a sandwich and the two coffees and took the second sandwich back to the counter. The clerk refused the first offer but then took the sandwich when Bosch said it was from Philippe's.

Bosch went back to the machine and started fiche-ing, wading first into the year 1985. He was looking for missing person and runaway reports of young males in the age range of the victim. Once he got proficient with the machine he was able to move quickly through the reports. He would scan first for the 'closed' stamp that indicated the missing individual had returned home or been located. If there was no stamp his eyes would immediately go to the age and sex boxes on the form. If they fit the profile of his victim, he'd read the summary and then push the photocopy button on the machine to get a hard copy to take with him.

The microfiche also contained records of missing person reports forwarded to the LAPD by outside agencies seeking people believed to have gone to Los Angeles.

Despite his speed at the task, it took Bosch more than three hours to go through all the reports for the ten years he had requested. He had hard copies of more than three hundred reports in the tray to the side of the machine when he was finished. And he had no idea whether his effort had been worth the time or not.

Bosch rubbed his eyes and pinched the bridge of his nose. He had a headache from staring at the machine's screen and reading tale after tale of parental anguish and juvenile angst. He looked over and realized he hadn't eaten his sandwich.

He returned the stack of microfiche envelopes to the clerk and decided to do the computer work in Parker Center rather than drive back to Hollywood. From Parker Center he could jump on the 10 Freeway and shoot out to Venice for dinner at Julia Brasher's house. It would be easier.

The squad room of the Robbery-Homicide Division was empty except for the two on-call detectives who were sitting in front of a television watching a football game. One of them was Bosch's former partner, Kizmin Rider. The other Bosch didn't recognize. Rider stood up smiling when she saw it was Bosch.

'Harry, what are you doing here?' she asked.

'Working a case. I want to use a computer, that all right?'

'That bone thing?'

He nodded.

'I heard about it on the news. Harry, this is Rick Thornton, my partner.'

Bosch shook his hand and introduced himself.

'I hope she makes you look as good as she did me.'

Thornton just nodded and smiled and Rider looked embarrassed.

'Come on over to my desk,' she said. 'You can use my computer.'

She showed him the way and let him sit in her seat.

'We're just twiddling our thumbs here. Nothing happening. I don't even like football.'

'Don't complain about the slow days. Didn't anybody ever tell you that?'

'Yeah, my old partner. Only thing he ever said that made any sense.'

'I bet.'

'Anything I can do to help?'

'I'm just running the names – the usual.'

He opened his briefcase and took out the murder book. He opened it to a page where he had listed the names, addresses and birth dates of residents on Wonderland Avenue who had been interviewed during the neighborhood canvas. It was a matter of routine and due diligence to run the name of every person investigators came across in an investigation.

'You want a coffee or something?' Rider asked.

'Nah, I'm fine. Thanks, Kiz.'

He nodded in the direction of Thornton, who had his back to them and was on the other side of the room.

'How are things going?'

She shrugged her shoulders.

'Every now and then he lets me do some real detective work,' she said in a whisper.

'Well, you can always come back to Hollywood,' he whispered back with a smile.

He started typing in the commands for entering the National Crime Index Computer. Immediately, Rider made a sound of derision.

'Harry, you're still typing with two fingers?'

'It's all I know, Kiz. I've been doing it this way for almost thirty years. You expect me to suddenly know how to type with ten fingers? I'm still not fluent in Spanish and don't know how to dance, either. You've only been gone a year.'

'Just get up, dinosaur. Let me do it. You'll be here all night.'

Bosch raised his hands in surrender and stood up. She sat down and went to work. Behind her back Bosch secretly smiled.

'Just like old times,' he said.

'Don't remind me. I always get the shit work. And stop smiling.'

She hadn't looked up from her typing. Her fingers were a blur above the keyboard. Bosch watched in awe.

'Hey, it's not like I planned this. I didn't know you were going to be here.'

'Yeah, like Tom Sawyer didn't know he had to paint a fence.'

'What?'

'Never mind. Tell me about the boot.'

Bosch was stunned.

'What?'

'Is that all you can say? You heard me. The rookie you're, uh . . . seeing.'

'How the hell do you know about it already?'

'I'm a highly skilled gatherer of information. And I still have sources in Hollywood.'

Bosch stepped away from her cubicle and shook his head.

'Well, is she nice? That's all I wanted to know. I don't want to pry.'

Bosch came back.

'Yes, she's nice. I hardly know her. You seem to know more about her and me *than* me.'

'You havin' dinner with her tonight?'

'Yeah, I'm having dinner with her.'

'Hey, Harry?'

Rider's voice had lost any note of humor.

'What?'

'You got a pretty good hit here.'

Bosch leaned down and looked at the screen. After digesting the information he said, 'I don't think I'm going to make it to dinner tonight.'

14

Bosch pulled to a stop in front of the house and studied the darkened windows and porch.

'Figures,' Edgar said. 'The guy ain't even going to be home. Probably already in the wind.'

Edgar was annoyed with Bosch, who had called him in from home. The way he figured it, the bones had been in the ground twenty years, what was the harm of waiting until Monday morning to talk to this guy? But Bosch said he was going by himself if Edgar didn't come in.

Edgar came in.

'No, he's home,' Bosch said.

'How d'you know?'

'I just know.'

He looked at his watch and wrote the time and address down on a page in his small notebook. It occurred to him then that the house they were at was the one where he had seen the curtain pulled closed behind a window on the evening of the first call out.

'Let's go,' he said. 'You talked to him the first time, so you take the lead. I'll jump in when it feels right.'

They got out and walked up the driveway to the house. The man they were visiting was named Nicholas Trent. He lived alone in the house, which was across the street and two houses down from the hillside where the bones had been found. Trent was fifty-seven years old. He had told Edgar during his initial canvas of the neighborhood that he was a set decorator for a studio in Burbank. He was unmarried and had no children. He knew nothing about the bones on the hill and could offer no clues or suggestions that were helpful.

Edgar knocked hard on the front door and they waited.

'Mr. Trent, it's the police,' he said loudly. 'Detective Edgar. Answer your door, please.'

He had raised his fist to hit the door again when the porch light went on. The door was then opened and a white man with a shaved scalp stood in the darkness within. The light from the porch slashed across his face.

'Mr. Trent? It's Detective Edgar. This is my partner, Detective Bosch. We have a few follow-up questions for you. If you don't mind.'

Bosch nodded but didn't offer his hand. Trent said nothing and Edgar forced the issue by putting his hand against the door and pushing it open.

'All right if we come in?' he asked, already halfway across the threshold.

'No, it's not all right,' Trent said quickly.

Edgar stopped and put a puzzled look on his face.

'Sir, we just have a few more questions we'd like to ask.'

'Yeah, and that's bullshit!'

'Excuse me?'

'We all know what is going on here. I talked to my attorney already. Your act is just that, an act. A bad one.'

Bosch could see they were not going to get anywhere with the trick-or-treat strategy. He stepped up and pulled Edgar back by the arm. Once his partner had cleared the threshold he looked at Trent.

'Mr. Trent, if you knew we'd be back, then you knew we'd find out about your past. Why didn't you tell Detective Edgar about it before? It could have saved us some time. Instead, it gives us suspicion. You can understand that, I'm sure.'

'Because the past is the past. I didn't bring it up. I buried the past. Leave it that way.'

'Not when there are bones buried in it,' Edgar said in an accusatory tone.

Bosch looked back at Edgar and gave him a look that said use some finesse.

'See?' Trent said. 'This is why I am saying, "Go away." I have nothing to tell you people. Nothing. I don't know anything about it.'

'Mr. Trent, you molested a nine-year-old boy,' Bosch said.

'The year was nineteen sixty-six and I was punished for it. Severely. It's the past. I've been a perfect citizen ever since. I had nothing to do with those bones up there.'

Bosch waited a moment and then spoke in a calm and quieter tone.

'If that is the truth, then let us come in and ask our questions. The sooner we clear you, the sooner we move on to other possibilities. But you have to understand something here. The bones of a young boy were found about a hundred yards from the home of a man who molested a young boy in nineteen sixty-six. I don't care what kind of citizen he's been since then, we need to ask him some questions. And we *will* ask those questions. We have no choice. Whether we do it in your home right now or with your lawyer at the station with all of the news cameras waiting outside, that's going to be your choice.'

He paused. Trent looked at him with scared eyes.

'So you can understand our situation, Mr. Trent, and we can certainly understand yours. We are willing to move quickly and discreetly but we can't without your cooperation.'

Trent shook his head as though he knew that no matter what he did now, his life as he knew it was in jeopardy and probably permanently altered. He finally stepped back and signaled Bosch and Edgar in.

Trent was barefoot and wearing baggy black shorts that showed off thin ivory legs with no hair on them. He wore a flowing silk shirt over his thin upper body. He had the same build as a ladder, all hard angles. He led them to a living room cluttered with antiques. He sat down in the center of a couch. Bosch and Edgar took the two leather club chairs opposite. Bosch decided to keep the lead. He didn't like the way Edgar had handled the door.

'To be cautious and careful, I am going to read you your constitutional rights,' he said. 'Then I'll ask you to sign a waiver form. This protects you as well as us. I am also going to record our conversation so that nobody ends up putting words in anybody else's mouth. If you want a copy of the tape I will make it available.'

Trent shrugged and Bosch took it as reluctant agreement. When Bosch had the form signed he slipped it into his briefcase and took out a small recorder. Once he started it and identified those present as well as the time and date, he nodded to Edgar to assume the lead again. This was because Bosch thought that observations of Trent and his surroundings were going to be more important than his answers now.

'Mr. Trent, how long have you lived in this house?'

'Since nineteen eighty-four.'

He then laughed.

'What is funny about that?' Edgar asked.

'Nineteen eighty-four. Don't you get it? George Orwell? Big Brother?'

He gestured toward Bosch and Edgar as the front men of Big Brother. Edgar apparently didn't follow the statement and continued with the interview.

'Rent or own?'

'Own. Uh, at first I rented, then I bought the house in 'eighty-seven from the landlord.'

'Okay, and you are a set designer in the entertainment industry?'

'Set decorator. There is a difference.'

'What is the difference?'

'The designer plans and supervises the construction of the set. The decorator then goes in and puts in the details. The little character strokes. The characters' belongings or tools. Like that.'

'How long have you done this?'

'Twenty-six years.'

'Did you bury that boy up on the hillside?'

Trent stood up indignantly.

'Absolutely not. I've never even set foot on that hill. And you people are making a big mistake if you waste your time on me when the true killer of that poor soul is still out there somewhere.'

Bosch leaned forward in his chair.

'Sit down, Mr. Trent,' he said.

The fervent way in which Trent delivered the denial made Bosch instinctively think he was either innocent or one of the better actors he had come across on the job. Trent slowly sat down on the couch again.

'You're a smart guy,' Bosch said, deciding to jump in. 'You know exactly what we're doing here. We have to bag you or clear you. It's that simple. So why don't you help us out? Instead of dancing around with us, why don't you tell us how to clear you?'

Trent raised his hands wide.

'I don't know how! I don't know anything about the case! How can I help you when I don't know the first thing about it?'

'Well, right off the bat, you can let us take a look around here. If I can start to get comfortable with you, Mr. Trent, then maybe I can start seeing it from your side of things. But right now . . . like I said, I've got you with your record and I've got bones across the street.'

Bosch held up his two hands as if he was holding those two things in them.

'It doesn't look that good from where I'm looking at things.'

Trent stood up and threw one hand out in a gesture toward the interior of the house.

'Fine! Be my guest. Look around to your heart's content. You won't find a thing because I had nothing to do with it. Nothing!'

Bosch looked at Edgar and nodded, the signal being that he should keep Trent occupied while Bosch took a look around.

'Thank you, Mr. Trent,' Bosch said as he stood up.

As he headed into a hallway that led to the rear of the house, he heard Edgar asking if Trent had ever seen any unusual activity on the hillside where the bones had been found.

'I just remember kids used to play up—'

He stopped, apparently when he realized that any mention he made of kids would only further suspicion about him. Bosch glanced back to make sure the red light of the recorder was still on.

'Did you like watching the kids play up there in the woods, Mr. Trent?' Edgar asked.

Bosch stayed in the hallway, out of sight but listening to Trent's answer.

'No, I couldn't see them if they were up in the woods. On occasion I would be driving up or walking my dog – when he was alive – and I would see the kids climbing up there. The girl across the street. The Fosters next door. All the kids around here. It's a city-owned right-of-way – the only undeveloped land in the neighborhood. So they went up there to play.

Some of the neighbors thought the older ones went up there to smoke cigarettes, and the concern was they would set the whole hillside on fire.'

'How long ago are you talking about?'

'Like when I first moved here. I didn't get involved. The neighbors who had been here took care of it.'

Bosch moved down the hall. It was a small house, not much bigger than his own. The hallway ended at a conjunction of three doors. Bedrooms on the right and left and a linen closet in the middle. He checked the closet first, found nothing unusual, and then moved into the bedroom on the right. It was Trent's bedroom. It was neatly kept but the tops of the twin bureaus and bed tables were cluttered with knickknacks that Bosch assumed Trent used on the job in helping to turn sets into real places for the camera.

He looked in the closet. There were several shoe boxes on the upper shelf. Bosch started opening them and found they contained old, worn-out shoes. It was apparently Trent's habit of buying new shoes and putting his old ones in the box, then shelving them. Bosch guessed that these, too, became part of his work inventory. He opened one box and found a pair of work boots. He noticed that dirt had dried hard in some of the treads. He thought about the dark soil where the bones had been found. Samples of it had been collected.

He put the boots back and made a mental note of it for the search warrant. His current search was just a cursory look around. If they moved to the next step with Trent and he became a full-fledged suspect, then they would come back with a search warrant and literally tear the place apart looking for evidence tying him to the bones. The work boots might be a good place to start. He was already on tape saying he had never been up on that hillside. If the dirt in the treads matched the soil samples from the excavation, then they'd have Trent caught in a lie. Most of what sparring with suspects was about was the locking in of a story. It was then that the investigator looked for the lies.

There was nothing else in the closet that warranted Bosch's attention. Same with the bedroom or the attached bathroom. Bosch, of course, knew that if Trent was the killer, he'd had many years to cover his tracks. He would also have had the last three days – since Edgar first questioned him during the canvas – to double-check his trail and be ready.

The other bedroom was used as an office and a storage room for his work. On the walls hung framed one sheets advertising the films Bosch assumed Trent had worked on. Bosch had seen some of them on television but rarely went to theaters to see movies. He noticed that one of the frames held the one sheet for a film called *The Art of the Cape*. Years before, Bosch had investigated the murder of that film's producer. He had heard that after that, the one sheets from the movie had become collector items in underground Hollywood.

When he was finished looking around the rear of the house, Bosch went through a kitchen door into the garage. There were two bays, one containing Trent's minivan. The other was stacked with boxes with markings on them corresponding to rooms in a house. At first Bosch was shocked at the thought that Trent had still not completely unpacked after moving in nearly twenty years before. Then he realized the boxes were work related and used in the process of set decoration.

When he turned around he was looking at an entire wall hung with the heads of wild game, their black marble eyes staring at him. Bosch felt a nerve tickle run down his spine. All of his life he had hated seeing things like that. He wasn't sure why.

He spent another few minutes in the garage, mostly going through a box in the stack that was marked 'boy's room 9–12.' It contained toys, airplane models, a skateboard, and a football. He took the skateboard out for a few moments and studied it, all the while thinking about the shirt from the backpack with 'Solid Surf' printed on it. After a while he put the skateboard back in the box and closed it.

There was a side door to the garage that led to a path that went to the backyard. A pool took up most of the level ground before the yard rose into the steep, wooded hillside. It was too dark to see much and Bosch decided he would have to do the exterior look during daylight hours.

Twenty minutes after he left to begin the search Bosch returned to the living room empty-handed. Trent looked up at him expectantly.

'Satisfied?'

'I'm satisfied for now, Mr. Trent. I appreciate your—'

'You see? It never ends. "Satisfied for now." You people will never let it go, will you? I mean, if I was a drug dealer or a bank robber, my debt would be cleared and you people would leave me alone. But because I touched a boy almost forty years ago I am guilty for life.'

'I think you did more than touch him,' Edgar said. 'But we'll get the records. Don't worry.'

Trent put his face in his hands and mumbled something about it being a mistake to have cooperated. Bosch looked at Edgar, who nodded that he was finished and ready to go. Bosch stepped over and picked up his recorder. He slid it into the breast pocket of his jacket but didn't turn it off. He'd learned a valuable lesson on a case the year before – sometimes the most important and telling things are said after an interview is supposedly over.

'Mr. Trent, thank you for your cooperation. We're going to go. But we might need to talk to you tomorrow. Are you working tomorrow?'

'God, no, don't call me at work! I need this job and you'll ruin it. You'll ruin everything.'

He gave Bosch his pager number. Bosch wrote it down and headed toward the front door. He looked back at Edgar.

'Did you ask him about trips? He's not planning to go anywhere, is he?'

Edgar looked at Trent.

'Mr. Trent, you work on movies, you know how the dialogue goes. You call us if you plan to go out of town. If you don't and we have to find you . . . you're not going to like it very much.'

Trent spoke in a flat-line monotone, his eyes focused forward, somewhere far away.

'I'm not going anywhere at all. Now please leave. Just leave me alone.'

They walked out the door and Trent closed it hard behind them. At the bottom of the driveway was a large bougainvillea bush in full bloom. It blocked Bosch's view of the left side of the street until he got there.

A bright light suddenly flashed on and in Bosch's face. A reporter with a cameraman in tow moved in on the two detectives. Bosch was blinded for a few moments until his eyes started to adjust.

'Hi, Detectives. Judy Surtain, Channel Four news. Is there a break in the bones case?'

'No comment,' Edgar barked. 'No comment and turn that damn light off.'

Bosch finally saw her in the glare of the light. He recognized her from TV and from the gathering at the roadblock earlier in the week. He also recognized that a 'no comment' was not the way to leave this situation. He needed to defuse it and keep the media away from Trent.

'No,' he said. 'No breakthrough. We're just following routine procedures.'

Surtain shoved the microphone she was carrying toward Bosch's face.

'Why are you out here in the neighborhood again?'

'We're just finishing the routine canvas of the residents here. I hadn't had a chance to talk to the resident here before. We just finished up, that's all.'

He was talking with a bored tone in his voice. He hoped she was buying it.

'Sorry,' he added. 'No big story tonight.'

'Well, was this neighbor or any of the neighbors helpful to the investigation?'

'Well, everyone here has been very cooperative with us but as far as investigative leads go it has been difficult. Most of these people weren't even living in the neighborhood when the bones were buried. That makes it tough.'

Bosch gestured toward Trent's house.

'This gentleman, for example. We just found out that he didn't buy his home here until nineteen eighty-seven and we're pretty sure those bones were already up there by then.'

'So then it's back to the drawing board?'

'Sort of. And that's really all I can tell you. Good night.'

He pushed past her toward his car. A few moments later Surtain was on him at the car door. Without her cameraman.

'Detective, we need to get your name.'

Bosch opened his wallet and took out a business card. The one with the general station number printed on it. He gave it to her and said good night again.

'Look, if there is anything you can tell me, you know, off the record, I would protect you,' Surtain said. 'You know, off camera like this, whatever you want to do.'

'No, there is nothing,' Bosch said as he opened the door. 'Have a good night.'

Edgar cursed the moment the doors of the car were closed.

'How the hell did she know we were here?'

'Probably a neighbor,' Bosch said. 'She was out here the whole two days of the dig. She's a celebrity. She made nice with the residents. Made friends. Plus, we're sitting in a goddamn Shamu. Might as well have called a press conference.'

Bosch thought of the inanity of trying to do detective work in a car painted black and white. Under a program designed to make cops more visible on the street, the department had assigned detectives in the divisions to black-and-whites that didn't carry the emergency lights on top but were just as noticeable.

They watched as the reporter and her cameraman went to Trent's door.

'She's going to try to talk to him,' Edgar said.

Bosch quickly went into his briefcase and got out his cell phone. He was about to dial Trent's number and tell him not to answer when he realized he couldn't get a cell signal.

'Goddammit,' he said.

'Too late anyway,' Edgar said. 'Let's just hope he plays it smart.'

Bosch could see Trent at his front door, totally bathed in the white light from the camera. He said a few words and then made a waving gesture and closed the door.

'Good,' Edgar said.

Bosch started the car, turned it around and headed back through the canyon to the station.

'So what's next?' Edgar asked.

'We have to pull the records on his conviction, see what it was about.'

'I'll do that first thing.'

'No. First thing I want to deliver the search warrants to the hospitals. Whether Trent fits our picture or not, we need to ID the kid in order to connect him to Trent. Let's meet at Van Nuys Courthouse at eight. We get them signed and then split 'em up.'

Bosch had picked Van Nuys court because Edgar lived nearby and they could separate and go from there in the morning after the warrants had been approved by a judge.

'What about a warrant on Trent's place?' Edgar said. 'You see anything while you were looking around?'

'Not much. He's got a skateboard in a box in the garage. You know, with his work stuff. For putting on a set. I was thinking of our victim's shirt when I saw that. And there were some work boots with dirt in the treads. It might match the samples from the hill. But I'm not counting on a search coming through for us. The guy has had twenty years to make sure he's clear. *If* he's the guy.'

'You don't think so?'

Bosch shook his head.

'Timing's wrong. 'Eighty-four is on the late side. The far edge of our window.'

'I thought we were looking at 'seventy-five to 'eighty-five.'

'We are. In general. But you heard Golliher – twenty to twenty-five years ago. That's early eighties on the high side. I don't know about 'eighty-four being early eighties.'

'Well, maybe he moved to that house *because* of the body. He buried the kid there before and wanted to be close by so he moves into the neighborhood. I mean, Harry, these are sick fucks, these guys.'

Bosch nodded.

'There's that. But I just wasn't getting the vibe from the guy. I believed him.'

'Harry, your mojo's been wrong before.'

'Oh, yeah . . .'

'I think it's him. He's the guy. Hear how he said, "just because I touched a boy." Probably to him, sodomizing a nine-year-old is reaching out and touching somebody.'

Edgar was being reactionary but Bosch didn't call him on it. He was a father; Bosch wasn't.

'We'll get the records and we'll see. We also have to go to the Hall to check the reverses, see who was on that street back then.'

The reverses were phone books that listed residents by address instead of by name. A collection of the books for every year was kept in the Hall of Records. They would allow the detectives to determine who was living on the street during the 1975 to 1985 range they were looking at as the boy's time of death.

'That's going to be a lot of fun,' Edgar said.

'Oh, yeah,' Bosch said. 'I can't wait.'

They drove in silence the rest of the way. Bosch became depressed. He was disappointed with himself for how he had run the investigation so far. The bones were discovered Wednesday, and the full investigation took off on Thursday. He knew he should have run the names – a basic part of the investigation – sooner than Sunday. By delaying it he had given Trent the advantage. He'd had three days to expect and prepare for their questions.

He had even been briefed by an attorney. He could have even been practicing his responses and looks in a mirror. Bosch knew what his internal lie detector said. But he also knew that a good actor could beat it.

15

Bosch drank a beer on the back porch with the sliding door open so he could hear Clifford Brown on the stereo. Almost fifty years before, the trumpet player made a handful of recordings and then checked out in a car crash. Bosch thought about all the music that had been lost. He thought about young bones in the ground and what had been lost. And then he thought about himself and what he had lost. Somehow the jazz and the beer and the grayness he was feeling about the case had all mixed together in his mind. He felt on edge, like he was missing something that was right in front of him. For a detective it was just about the worst feeling in the world.

At 11 P.M. he came inside and turned the music down so he could watch the news on Channel 4. Judy Surtain's report was the third story after the first break. The anchor said, 'New developments in the Laurel Canyon bone case. We go to Judy Surtain at the scene.'

'Ah, shit,' Bosch said, not liking the sound of the introduction.

The program cut to a live shot of Surtain on Wonderland Avenue, standing on the street in front of a house Bosch recognized as Trent's.

'I'm here on Wonderland Avenue in Laurel Canyon, where four days ago a dog brought home a bone that authorities say was human. The dog's find led to the discovery of more bones belonging to a young boy who investigators believe was murdered and then buried more than twenty years ago.'

Bosch's phone started ringing. He picked it up off the arm of the TV chair and answered it.

'Hold on,' he said and then held the phone down by his side while he watched the news report.

Surtain said, 'Tonight the lead investigators on the case returned to the neighborhood to speak to one resident who lives less than one hundred yards from the place where the boy was buried. That resident is Nicholas Trent, a fifty-seven-year-old Hollywood set decorator.'

The program cut to tape of Bosch being questioned by Surtain that night. But it was used as visual filler while Surtain continued her report in a voice-over dub.

'Investigators declined to comment on their questioning of Trent, but Channel Four news has learned—'

Bosch sat down heavily on the chair and braced himself.

'—that Trent was once convicted of molesting a young boy.'

The sound was then brought up on the street interview just as Bosch said, 'That's really all I can tell you.'

The next jump was to video of Trent standing in his doorway and waving the camera off and closing the door.

'Trent declined comment on his status in the case. But neighbors in the normally quiet hillside neighborhood expressed shock upon learning of Trent's background.'

As the report shifted to a taped interview of a resident Bosch recognized as Victor Ulrich, Bosch hit the mute button on the TV remote and brought the phone up. It was Edgar.

'You watching this shit?' he asked.

'Oh, yeah.'

'We look like shit. We look like we told her. They used your quote out of context, Harry. We're going to be fucked by this.'

'Well, you didn't tell her, right?'

'Harry, you think I'd tell some—'

'No, I don't. I was confirming. You didn't tell her, right?'

'Right.'

'And neither did I. So, yeah, we're going to take some shit but we're clear on it.'

'Well, who else knew? I doubt Trent was the one who told her. About a million people now know he's a child molester.'

Bosch realized the only people who knew were Kiz, who had gotten the records flag while doing the computer work, and Julia Brasher, whom Bosch told while he was making his excuse for missing dinner. Suddenly a vision of Surtain standing at the roadblock on Wonderland came to him. Brasher had volunteered her help during both days of the hillside search and excavation. It was entirely possible that she had connected with Surtain in some way. Was she the reporter's source, the leak?

'There didn't have to be a leak,' Bosch said to Edgar. 'All she needed was Trent's name. She could have gotten any cop she knew to run it on the box for her. Or she could have looked it up on the sexual offenders CD. It's public record. Hold on.'

He had gotten a call-waiting beep on the phone. He switched over and learned it was Lt. Billets calling. He told her to hold while he got off the other line. He clicked over.

'Jerry, it's Bullets. I gotta call you back.'

'It's still me,' Billets said.

'Oh, sorry. Hold on.'

He tried again and this time made the switch back. He told Edgar he'd call him back if Billets said anything he needed to know right away.

'Otherwise, go with the plan,' he added. 'See you at Van Nuys at eight.'

He switched back over to Billets.

'Bullets?' she said. 'Is that what you guys call me?'

'What?'

'You said 'Bullets.' When you thought I was Edgar you called me 'Bullets.''

'You mean just now?'

'Yes, just now.'

'I don't know. I don't know what you're talking about. You mean when I was switching over to – '

'Never mind, it doesn't matter. I assume you saw Channel Four?'

'Yeah, I saw it. And all I can tell you is that it wasn't me and it wasn't Edgar. That woman got a tip that we were out there and we "no comment"-ed our way out of there. How she came up with his—'

'Harry, you didn't "no comment" your way out of there. They have you on tape, your mouth moving, and then I hear you say, "that's all I can say." If you say "that's all," that means you gave her something.'

Bosch shook his head, even though he was on the phone.

'I didn't give her shit. I just bullshitted my way by. I told her we were just finishing up the routine canvas of the neighborhood and I hadn't talked to Trent before.'

'Was that true?'

'Not really, but I wasn't going to say we were there because the guy's a child molester. Look, she didn't know about Trent when we were there. If she did, she would have asked me. She found out later, and how I don't know. That's what Jerry and I were just talking about.'

There was silence for a moment before Billets continued.

'Well, you better have your shit together on this tomorrow because I want a written explanation from you that I can send up the line. Before that report on Four was even over I got a call from Captain LeValley and she said she had already gotten a call from Deputy Chief Irving.'

'Yeah, yeah, typical. Right on down the food chain.'

'Look, you know that leaking the criminal record of a citizen is against departmental policy, whether that citizen is the target of an investigation or not. I just hope you have your story straight on this. I don't need to tell you that there are people in the department just waiting for you to make a mistake they can sink their teeth into.'

'Look, I'm not trying to downplay the leak. It was wrong and it was bad. But I'm trying to solve a murder here, Lieutenant, and now I've got a whole new obstacle to overcome. And that's what's typical. There is always something thrown in the way.'

'Then you should be more careful next time.'

'Careful of what? What did I do wrong? I'm following leads where they go.'

Bosch immediately regretted the explosion of frustration and anger. Of those people in the department waiting for his self-destruction, Billets certainly wasn't on the list. She was only the messenger here. In the same moment, he realized his anger was also self-directed because he knew Billets was right. He should have handled Surtain differently.

'Look, I'm sorry,' he said in a low, even tone. 'It's just the case. It's got its hooks, you know?'

'I think I do,' Billets answered just as quietly. 'And speaking of the case, what exactly is going on? This whole thing with Trent came out of left field for me. I thought you were going to keep me up to date.'

'It all came up today. Late. I was just going to fill you in in the morning. I didn't know Channel Four would be doing it for me. And doing it for LeValley and Irving as well.'

'Never mind them for now. Tell me about Trent.'

16

It was well after midnight by the time Bosch got to Venice. Parking on the little streets near the canals was nonexistent. He drove around looking for ten minutes and ended up parking in the lot by the library out on Venice Boulevard and then walking back in.

Not all of the dreamers drawn to Los Angeles came to make movies. Venice was the century-old dream of a man named Abbot Kinney. Before Hollywood and the film industry barely had a pulse, Kinney came to the marshlands along the Pacific. He envisioned a place built on a network of canals with arched bridges and a town center of Italian architecture. It would be a place emphasizing cultural and artistic learning. And he would call it Venice of America.

But like most of the dreamers who come to Los Angeles his vision was not uniformly shared or realized. Most financiers and investigators were cynical and passed on the opportunity to build Venice, putting their money into projects of less grand design. Venice of America was dubbed 'Kinney's Folly.'

But a century later many of the canals and the arched bridges reflected in their waters remained while the financiers and doomsayers and their projects were long swept away by time. Bosch liked the idea of Kinney's Folly outlasting them all.

Bosch had not been to the canals in many years, though for a short period in his life after returning from Vietnam he had lived there in a bungalow with three other men he knew from overseas. In the years since, many of the bungalows had been erased and modern two- and three-story homes costing a million dollars or more had replaced them.

Julia Brasher lived in a house at the corner of the Howland and Eastern canals. Bosch expected it to be one of the new structures. He guessed she probably used her law-firm money to buy it or even build it. But as he came to the address he saw that he was wrong. Her house was a small bungalow made of white clapboard with an open front porch overlooking the joining of the two canals.

Bosch saw lights on behind the windows of her house. It was late but not that late. If she worked the three-to-eleven shift, then it was unlikely she was used to going to bed before two.

He stepped up onto the porch but hesitated before knocking on the door. Until the doubts of the last hour had crept in, he had gotten only good feelings about Brasher and their fledgling relationship. He knew he now had to be careful. There could be nothing wrong and yet he could spoil everything if he misstepped here.

Finally, he raised his arm and knocked. Brasher answered right away.

'I was wondering if you were going to knock or stand out there all night.'

'You knew I was standing here?'

'The porch is old. It creaks. I heard it.'

'Well, I got here and then figured it was too late. I should have called first.'

'Just come in. Is anything wrong?'

Bosch came in and looked around. He didn't answer the question.

The living room had an unmistakable beach flavor to it, right down to the bamboo-and-rattan furniture and the surfboard leaning in one corner. The only deviation was her equipment belt and holster hanging on a wall rack near the door. It was a rookie mistake leaving it out like that, but Bosch assumed she was proud of her new career choice and wanted to remind friends outside the cop world of it.

'Sit down,' she said. 'I have some wine open. Would you like a glass?'

Bosch thought a moment about whether mixing wine with the beer he'd had an hour earlier would lead to a headache the next day when he knew he'd have to be focused.

'It's red.'

'Uh, I'll take just a little bit.'

'Got to be sharp tomorrow, huh?'

'I guess.'

She went into the kitchen while he sat down on the couch. He looked around the room and now saw a mounted fish with a long sharp point hanging over the white brick fireplace. The fish was a brilliant blue shading to black with a white and yellow underside. Mounted fish didn't bother him the way the heads of mounted game did but he still didn't like the eye of the fish always watching.

'You catch this thing?' he called out.

'Yeah. Off Cabo. Took me three and a half hours to bring it in.'

She then appeared with two glasses of wine.

'On fifty-pound test line,' she said. 'That was a workout.'

'What is it?'

'Black marlin.'

She toasted the fish with her glass and then toasted Bosch.

'Hold fast.'

Bosch looked at her.

'That's my new toast,' she said. 'Hold fast. It seems to cover everything.'

She sat down on the chair closest to Bosch. Behind her was the surfboard. It was white with a rainbow design in a border running along the edges. It was a short board.

'So you surf the wild waves, too.'

She glanced back at the board and then at Bosch and smiled.

'I try to. Picked it up in Hawaii.'

'You know John Burrows?'

She shook her head.

'Lot of surfers in Hawaii. What beach does he surf?'

'No, I mean here. He's a cop. He works Homicide out of Pacific Division. Lives on a walk street by the beach. Not too far from here. He surfs. On his board it says "To Protect and Surf." '

She laughed.

'That's cool. I like that. I'll have to get that put on my board.'

Bosch nodded.

'John Burrows, huh? I'll have to look him up.'

She said it with just a touch of teasing in her voice.

Bosch smiled and said, 'And maybe not.'

He liked the way she kidded him like that. It all felt good to Bosch, which made him feel all the more out of sorts because of his reason for being there. He looked at his wine glass.

'I've been fishing all day and didn't catch a thing,' he said. 'Microfiche mostly.'

'I saw you on the news tonight,' she said. 'Are you trying to put the squeeze on that guy, the child molester?'

Bosch sipped his wine to give himself time to think. She had opened the door. He now just had to step through very carefully.

'What do you mean?' he asked.

'Well, giving that reporter his criminal background. I figured you must be making some kind of play. You know, turning up the heat on him. To make him talk or something. It seems kind of risky.'

'Why?'

'Well, first of all, trusting a reporter is always risky. I know that from back when I was a lawyer and got burned. And second . . . and second, you never know how people are going to react when their secrets are no longer secrets.'

Bosch studied her for a moment and then shook his head.

'I didn't give it to her,' he said. 'Somebody else did.'

He studied her eyes for any kind of tell. There was nothing.

'There's going to be trouble over it,' he added.

She raised her eyebrows in surprise. Still no tell.

'Why? If you didn't give her the information, why would there . . .'

She stopped and now Bosch could see her put it together. He saw the disappointment fill her eyes.

'Oh, Harry . . .'

He tried to back out through the door.

'What? Don't worry about it. I'll be fine.'

'It wasn't me, Harry. Is that what you're here about? To see if I'm the leak or the source or whatever you'd call it?'

She abruptly put her wine glass down on the coffee table. Red wine lapped over the edge and onto the table. She didn't do anything about it. Bosch knew there was no use trying to avoid the collision. He had screwed up.

'Look, only four people knew . . .'

'And I was one of them. So you thought you'd come here undercover and find out if it was me.'

She waited for a response. Finally, all Bosch could do was nod.

'Well, it wasn't me. And I think you should go now.'

Bosch nodded and put down his glass. He stood up.

'Look, I'm sorry. I screwed it up. I thought the best way to not mess anything up, you know, between you and me, was to . . .'

He made a helpless gesture with his hands as he headed to the door.

'Was to do the undercover thing,' he continued. 'I just didn't want to mess it up, that's all. But I had to know. I think if you were me you would've felt the same way about it.'

He opened the door and looked back at her.

'I'm sorry, Julia. Thanks for the wine.'

He turned to go.

'Harry.'

He turned back. She came to him and reached up and grabbed the lapels of his jacket with both hands. She slowly pulled him forward and then pushed him backward, as if roughing up a suspect in slow motion. Her eyes dropped to his chest as her mind worked and she came to a decision.

She stopped shaking him but kept her grasp on his jacket.

'I can get over it,' she said. 'I think.'

She looked up to his eyes and pulled him forward. She kissed him hard on the mouth for a long time and then pushed him back. She let go.

'I hope. Call me tomorrow.'

Bosch nodded and stepped through the door. She closed it.

Bosch went down the porch to the sidewalk next to the canal. He looked at the reflection of the lights of all the houses on the water. An arched footbridge, lighted by the moon and nothing else, crossed the canal twenty yards away, its reflection perfect on the water. He turned and walked back up the steps to the porch. He hesitated at the door again and soon Brasher opened it.

'The porch creaks, remember?'

He nodded and she waited. He wasn't sure how to say what he wanted to say. Finally, he just began.

'One time when I was in one of those tunnels we were talking about last night I came up head-on with some guy. He was VC. Black pyjamas, greased face. We sort of looked at each other for a split second and I guess instincts took over. We both raised up and fired at the same time. Simultaneous. And then we fucking ran in opposite directions. Both of us scared shitless, screaming in the dark.'

He paused as he thought about the story, seeing it more than remembering it.

'Anyway, I thought he had to have hit me. It was almost point-blank, too close to miss. I thought my gun had backfired and jammed or something. The kick had felt wrong. When I got up top the first thing I did was check myself. No blood, no pain. I took all of my clothes off and checked myself. Nothing. He had missed. Point-blank and somehow the guy had missed.'

She stepped over the door's threshold and leaned against the front wall beneath the porch light. She didn't say anything and he pressed on.

'Anyway, then I checked my forty-five for a jam and I found out why he hadn't hit me. The guy's bullet was in the barrel of my gun. With mine. We had pointed at each other and his shot went right up the barrel of my gun. What were the chances of that? A million to one? A billion?'

As he spoke he held his empty hand out as a gun pointing at her. His hand was extended directly in front of his chest. The bullet that day in the tunnel had been meant for his heart.

'I guess I just want you to know that I know how lucky I was with you tonight.'

He nodded and then turned and went down the steps.

17

Death investigation is a pursuit with countless dead ends, obstacles and colossal chunks of wasted time and effort. Bosch knew this every day of his existence as a cop but was reminded of it once again when he got to the homicide table shortly before noon Monday and found his morning's time and effort had most likely been wasted while a brand-new obstacle awaited him.

The homicide squad had the area at the rear corner of the detective bureau. The squad consisted of three teams of three. Each team had a table consisting of the three detectives' desks pushed together, two facing each other, the third along one side. Sitting at Bosch's table, in the slot left vacant by Kiz Rider's departure, was a young woman in a business suit. She had dark hair and even darker eyes. They were eyes sharp enough to peel a walnut and they held on Bosch his whole way through the squad room.

'Can I help you?' he asked when he got to the table.

'Harry Bosch?'

'That's me.'

'Detective Carol Bradley, IAD. I need to take a statement from you.'

Bosch looked around. There were several people in the squad room trying to act busy while surreptitiously watching.

'Statement about what?'

'Deputy Chief Irving asked our division to determine if the criminal record of Nicholas Trent was improperly divulged to the media.'

Bosch still hadn't sat down. He put his hands on the top of his chair and stood behind it. He shook his head.

'I think it's pretty safe to assume it was improperly divulged.'

'Then I need to find out who did it.'

Bosch nodded.

'I'm trying to run an investigation here and all anybody cares about is—'

'Look, I know you think it's bullshit. And I may think it's bullshit. But I've got the order. So let's go into one of the rooms and put your story on tape. It won't take long. And then you can go back to your investigation.'

Bosch put his briefcase on the table and opened it. He took out his tape recorder. He had remembered it while driving around all morning delivering search warrants at the local hospitals.

'Speaking of tape, why don't you take this into one of the rooms and listen to it first? I had it on last night. It should end my involvement in this pretty quick.'

She hesitantly took the recorder, and Bosch pointed to the hallway that led to the three interview rooms.

'I'm still going to need to—'

'Fine. Listen to the tape, then we'll talk.'

'Your partner, too.'

'He should be in anytime now.'

Bradley went down the hall with the recorder. Bosch finally sat down and didn't bother to look at any of the other detectives.

It wasn't even noon but he felt exhausted. He had spent the morning waiting for a judge in Van Nuys to sign the search warrants for medical records and then driving across the city delivering them to the legal offices of nineteen different hospitals. Edgar had taken ten of the warrants and headed off on his own. With fewer to deliver, he was then going downtown to conduct record searches on Nicholas Trent's criminal background and to check the reverse directories and property records for Wonderland Avenue.

Bosch noticed that waiting for him was a stack of phone messages and the latest batch of call-in tips from the front desk. He took the phone messages first. Nine out of twelve of them were from reporters, all no doubt wanting to follow up on Channel 4's report on Trent the night before and then rebroadcast during the morning news program. The other three were from Trent's lawyer, Edward Morton. He had called three times between 8 and 9:30 A.M.

Bosch didn't know Morton but expected he was calling to complain about Trent's record being given to the media. He normally wasn't quick to return calls to lawyers but decided it would be best to get the confrontation over with and to assure Morton that the leak had not come from the investigators on the case. Even though he doubted that Morton would believe anything he said, he picked up the phone and called back. A secretary told him that Morton had gone to a court hearing but was due to check in at any moment. Bosch said he would be waiting for him to call again.

After hanging up Bosch dropped the pink slips with the reporters' numbers on them into the trash can next to his spot at the table. He started going through the call-in sheets and quickly noticed that the desk officers were now asking the questions he had typed out the morning before and given to Mankiewicz.

On the eleventh report in the pile he came across a direct hit. A woman named Sheila Delacroix had called at 8:41 A.M. that morning and said she had seen the Channel 4 report that morning. She said her younger brother

Arthur Delacroix disappeared in 1980 in Los Angeles. He was twelve years old at the time and was never heard from since.

In answer to the medical questions, she responded that her brother had been injured during a fall from a skateboard a few months before his disappearance. He suffered a brain injury that required hospitalization and neurosurgery. She did not remember the exact medical details but was sure the hospital was Queen of Angels. She could not recall the name of any of the doctors who treated her brother. Other than an address and call-back number for Sheila Delacroix, that was all the information on the report.

Bosch circled the word 'skateboard' on the sheet. He opened his briefcase and got out a business card Bill Golliher had given him. He called the first number and got a machine at the anthropologist's office at UCLA. He called the second and got Golliher while he was eating lunch in Westwood Village.

'Got a quick question. The injury that required surgery on the skull.'

'The hematoma.'

'Right. Could that have been caused by a fall from a skateboard?'

There was silence and Bosch let Golliher think. The clerk who took the calls to the general lines in the squad room came up to the homicide table and shot Bosch a peace sign. Bosch covered his receiver.

'Who is it?'

'Kiz Rider.'

'Tell her to hold.'

He uncovered the receiver.

'Doc, you there?'

'Yes, I'm just thinking. It might be possible, depending on what it was he hit. But a fall just to the ground, I would say it's not likely. You had a tight fracture pattern, which indicates a small area of surface-to-surface contact. Also, the location is high up on the cranium. It's not the back of the head, which you would normally associate with fall injuries.'

Bosch felt some of the wind going out of his sails. He had thought he might have an ID on the victim.

'Is this a particular person you are talking about?' Golliher asked.

'Yeah, we just got a tip.'

'Are there X-rays, surgical records?'

'I'm working on it.'

'Well, I'd like to see them to make a comparison.'

'As soon as I get them. What about the other injuries? Could they be from skateboarding?'

'Of course some of them could be from that,' Golliher said. 'But I would say not all. The ribs, the twist fractures – also, some of these injuries dated to very early childhood, Detective. There aren't many three-year-olds on skateboards, I would think.'

Bosch nodded and tried to think if there was anything else to ask.

'Detective, you do know that in abuse cases the reported cause of injury and the true cause are not often the same?'

'I understand. Whoever brought the kid into the emergency room wouldn't volunteer he hit him with a flashlight or whatever.'

'Right. There would be a story. The child would adhere to it.'

'Skateboard accident.'

'It's possible.'

'Okay, Doc, I gotta go. I'll get you the X-rays as soon as I get them. Thanks.'

He punched line two on the phone.

'Kiz?'

'Harry, hi, how're you doing?'

'Busy. What's up?'

'I feel awful, Harry. I think I fucked up.'

Bosch leaned back in his chair. He would have never guessed it was her.

'Channel Four?'

'Yeah. I, uh . . . yesterday after you left Parker and my partner stopped watching the football game, he asked what was up with you being in there. So I told him. I'm still trying to establish the relationship, Harry, you know? I told him I ran the names for you and there was a hit. One of the neighbors had a molestation record. That's all I told him, Harry. I swear.'

Bosch breathed out heavily. He actually felt better. His instinct about Rider had been right on. She was not the leak. She had simply trusted someone she should have been able to trust.

'Kiz, I got IAD sitting up here waiting to talk to me about this. How do you know Thornton gave it to Channel Four?'

'I saw the report on TV this morning when I was getting ready. I know Thornton knows that reporter. Surtain. Thornton and I worked a case a few months ago – an insurance murder on the Westside. It got some media play and he was feeding her stuff off the record. I saw them together. Then yesterday, after I told him about the hit, he said he had to go to the can. He picked the sports page up and went down the hall. But he didn't go to the can. We got a call out and I went down and banged on the door to tell him we were rolling. He didn't answer. I didn't really think anything about it until I saw the news today. I think he didn't go to the can because he went into another office or down to the lobby to use a phone to call her.'

'Well, it explains a lot.'

'I'm really sorry, Harry. That TV report didn't make you look good at all. I'm going to talk to IAD.'

'Just hold on to that, Kiz. For now. I'll let you know if I need you to talk to IAD. But what are *you* going to do?'

'Get a new partner. I can't work with this guy.'

'Be careful. You start jumping partners and pretty soon you'll be all alone.'

'I'd rather work alone than with some asshole I can't trust.'

'There's that.'

'What about you? The offer still stand?'

'What, I'm an asshole you can trust?'

'You know what I mean.'

'The offer stands. All you have to do is—'

'Hey, Harry, I gotta go. Here he comes.'

'Okay, bye.'

Bosch hung up and rubbed his mouth with his hand as he thought about what to do about Thornton. He could tell Kiz's story to Carol Bradley. But there was still too much room in it for error. He wouldn't feel comfortable going to IAD with it unless he was sure. The actual idea of going to IAD about anything repulsed him, but in this instance someone was harming Bosch's investigation.

And that was something he could not let pass.

After a few minutes he came up with a plan and checked his watch. It was ten minutes before noon. He called Kiz Rider back.

'It's Harry. Is he there?'

'Yeah, why?'

'Repeat after me, in a sort of excited voice. "You did, Harry? Great! Who was he?" '

'You did, Harry? That's great! Who was he?'

'Okay, now you're listening, listening, listening. Now say, "How did a ten-year-old get here from New Orleans?" '

'How did a ten-year-old get all the way here from New Orleans?'

'Perfect. Now hang up and don't say anything. If Thornton asks you, tell him we ID'd the kid through dental records. He was a ten-year-old runaway from New Orleans last seen in nineteen seventy-five. His parents are on a plane heading here now. And the chief is going to have a press conference about it all today at four.'

'Okay, Harry, good luck.'

'You, too.'

Bosch hung up and looked up. Edgar was standing across the table from him. He had heard the last part of the conversation and his eyebrows were up.

'No, it's all bullshit,' Bosch said. 'I'm setting up the leak. And that reporter.'

'The leak? Who is the leak?'

'Kiz's new partner. We think.'

Edgar slid into his chair and just nodded.

'But we do have a possible ID on the bones,' Bosch said.

He told Edgar about the call-in sheet on Arthur Delacroix and his subsequent conversations with Bill Golliher.

'Nineteen eighty? That's not going to work with Trent. I checked the reverses and property records. He wasn't on that street until 'eighty-four. Like he said last night.'

'Something tells me he isn't our guy.'

Bosch thought about the skateboard again. It wasn't enough to alter his gut feeling.

'Tell that to Channel Four.'

Bosch's phone rang. It was Rider.

'He just went to the can.'

'You tell him about the press conference?'

'I told him everything. He kept asking questions, the dipshit.'

'Well, if he tells her that everybody will have it at four, she'll go out with the exclusive on the noon news. I'm going to go watch.'

'Let me know.'

He hung up and checked his watch. He still had a few minutes. He looked at Edgar.

'By the way, IAD is in one of the rooms back there. We're under investigation.'

Edgar's jaw dropped. Like most cops, he resented Internal Affairs because even when you did a good and honest job, the IAD could still be on you for any number of things. It was like the Internal Revenue Service, the way just seeing a letter with the IRS return address in the corner was enough to pull your guts into a knot.

'Relax. It's about the Channel Four thing. We should be clear of it in a few minutes. Come with me.'

They went into Lt. Billets's office, where there was a small television on a stand. She was doing paperwork at her desk.

'You mind if we check out Channel Four's noon report?' Bosch asked.

'Be my guest. I'm sure Captain LeValley and Chief Irving are going to be watching as well.'

The news program opened with a report on a sixteen-car pileup in the morning fog on the Santa Monica Freeway. It wasn't that significant a story – no one was killed – but they had good video, so it led the program. But the 'dog bone' case had moved up to second billing. The anchor said they were going to Judy Surtain with another exclusive report.

The program cut to Surtain sitting at a desk in the Channel 4 newsroom.

'Channel Four has learned that the bones found in Laurel Canyon have been identified as those of a ten-year-old runaway from New Orleans.'

Bosch looked at Edgar and then at Billets, who was rising from her seat with an expression of surprise on her face. Bosch put out his hand as if to signal her to wait a moment.

'The parents of the boy, who reported him missing more than twenty-five years ago, are en route to Los Angeles to meet with police. The remains were identified through dental records. Later today, the chief of police is expected to hold a press conference where he will identify the boy and discuss the investigation. As reported by Channel Four last night, police are focusing on—'

Bosch turned the TV off.

'Harry, Jerry, what's going on?' Billets asked immediately.

'All of that was bogus. I was smoking out the leak.'

'Who?'

'Kiz's new partner. A guy named Rick Thornton.'

Bosch explained what Rider had explained to him earlier. He then outlined the scam he had just pulled.

'Where's the IAD detective?' Billets asked.

'One of the interview rooms. She's listening to a tape I had of me and the reporter last night.'

'A tape? Why didn't you tell me about it last night?'

'I forgot about it last night.'

'All right, I'll take it from here. You feel Kiz is clean on this?'

Bosch nodded.

'She has to trust her partner enough to tell him anything. He took that trust and gave it to Channel Four. I don't know what he's getting in return but it doesn't matter. He's fucking with my case.'

'All right, Harry, I said I would handle it. You go back to the case. Anything new I should know about?'

'We've got a possible ID – this one legit – that we'll be running down today.'

'What about Trent?'

'We're letting that sit until we find out if this is the kid. If it is, the timing is wrong. The kid disappeared in nineteen eighty. Trent didn't move into the neighborhood until four years later.'

'Great. Meantime, we've taken his buried secret and put it on TV. Last I heard from patrol, the media was camped in his driveway.'

Bosch nodded.

'Talk to Thornton about it,' he said.

'Oh, we will.'

She sat down behind her desk and picked up the phone. It was their cue to leave. On the way back to the table Bosch asked Edgar if he had pulled the file on Trent's conviction.

'Yeah, I got it. It was a weak case. Nowadays the DA probably wouldn't have even filed on it.'

They went to their respective spots at the table and Bosch saw that he had missed a callback from Trent's lawyer. He reached for the phone but then waited until Edgar finished his report.

'The guy worked as a teacher at an elementary school in Santa Monica. He was caught by another teacher in a stall in the bathroom holding an eight-year-old's penis while he urinated. He said he was teaching the kid how to aim it, that the kid kept pissing on the floor. What it came down to is the kid's story was all over the place but didn't back his. And the parents said the boy already knew how to aim by the time he was four. Trent was convicted and got a two plus one. He served fifteen months of it up at Wayside.'

Bosch thought about all of this. His hand was still on the phone.

'It's a long ass jump from that to beating a kid to death with a baseball bat.'

'Yeah, Harry, I'm beginning to like your mojo better all the time.'

'I wish I did.'

He picked up the phone and punched in the number for Trent's attorney, Edward Morton. He was transferred to the lawyer's cell phone. He was on his way to lunch.

'Hello?'

'Detective Bosch.'

'Bosch, yes, I want to know where he is.'

'Who?'

'Don't play this game, Detective. I've called every holding jail in the county. I want to be able to speak to my client. Right now.'

'I'm assuming you are speaking about Nicholas Trent. Have you tried his job?'

'Home and work, no answer. Pager, too. If you people have him, he's entitled to representation. And I am entitled to know. I'm telling you now, if you fuck with me on this, I will go right to a judge. And the media.'

'We don't have your man, counselor. I haven't seen him since last night.'

'Yes, he called me after you left. Then again after watching the news. You people fucked him over – you should be ashamed of yourself.'

Bosch's face burned with the rebuke but he didn't respond to it. If he didn't personally deserve it, then the department did. He'd take the bullet for now.

'Do you think he ran, Mr. Morton?'

'Why run if you are innocent?'

'I don't know. Ask O.J.'

A horrible thought suddenly shot into Bosch's gut. He stood up, the phone still pressed to his ear.

'Where are you now, Mr. Morton?'

'Sunset heading west. Near Book Soup.'

'Turn around and come back. Meet me at Trent's house.'

'I have a lunch. I'm not going—'

'Meet me at Trent's house. I'm leaving now.'

He put the phone in its cradle and told Edgar it was time to go. He'd explain on the way.

18

There was a small gathering of television reporters in the street in front of Nicholas Trent's house. Bosch parked behind the Channel 2 van and he and Edgar got out. Bosch didn't know what Edward Morton looked like but didn't see anyone in the group who looked like an attorney. After more than twenty-five years on the job, he had unerring instincts that allowed him to identify lawyers and reporters. Over the top of the car, Bosch spoke to Edgar before the reporters could hear them.

'If we have to go in, we'll do it around back – without the audience.'

'I gotya.'

They walked up to the driveway and were immediately accosted by the media crews, who turned on cameras and threw questions that went unanswered. Bosch noticed that Judy Surtain of Channel 4 was not among the reporters.

'Are you here to arrest Trent?'

'Can you tell us about the boy from New Orleans?'

'What about the press conference? Media Relations doesn't know anything about a press conference.'

'Is Trent a suspect or not?'

Once Bosch was through the crowd and on Trent's driveway, he suddenly turned back and faced the cameras. He hesitated a moment as if composing his thoughts. What he really was doing was giving them time to focus and get ready. He didn't want anyone to miss this.

'There is no press conference scheduled,' Bosch said. 'There has been no identification of the bones yet. The man who lives in this house was questioned last night as was every resident of this neighborhood. At no time was he called a suspect by the investigators on this case. Information leaked to the media by someone outside of the investigation and then broadcast without being checked first with the actual investigators has been completely wrong and damaging to the ongoing investigation. That's it. That's all I'm going to say. When there is some real and accurate information to report, we will give it to you through Media Relations.'

He turned back around and headed up the driveway to the house with

Edgar. The reporters threw more questions at them but Bosch gave no indication of even hearing them.

At the front door Edgar knocked sharply and called out to Trent, telling him it was the police. After a few moments he knocked again and made the same announcement. They waited again and nothing happened.

'The back?' Edgar asked.

'Yeah, or the garage has a door on the side.'

They walked across the driveway and started heading down the side of the house. The reporters yelled more questions. Bosch guessed they were so used to throwing questions that were not answered at people that it simply became natural for them to do it and natural for them to know they would not be answered. Like a dog barking in the backyard long after the master has left for work.

They passed the side door to the garage, and Bosch noted that he was correct in remembering that there was only a single key lock on the knob. They continued into the backyard. There was a kitchen door with a dead bolt and a key lock on the knob. There was also a sliding door, which would be easy to pop open. Edgar stepped over to it but looked down through the glass to the interior sliding track and saw that there was a wooden dowel in place that would prevent the door from being opened from the outside.

'This won't work, Harry,' he said.

Bosch had a small pouch containing a set of lock picks in his pocket. He didn't want to have to work the dead bolt on the kitchen door.

'Let's do the garage, unless . . .'

He walked over to the kitchen door and tried it. It was unlocked and he opened the door. In that moment he knew they would find Trent dead inside. Trent would be the helpful suicide. The one who leaves the door open so people don't have to break in.

'Shit.'

Edgar came over, pulling his gun from its holster.

'You're not going to need that,' Bosch said.

He stepped into the house and they moved through the kitchen.

'Mr. Trent?' Edgar yelled. 'Police! Police in the house! Are you here, Mr. Trent?'

'Take the front,' Bosch said.

They split up and Bosch went down the short hallway to the rear bedrooms. He found Trent in the walk-in shower of the master bath. He had taken two wire hangers and fashioned a noose which he had attached to the stem pipe of the shower. He had then leaned back against the tiled wall and dropped his weight and asphyxiated himself. He was still dressed in the clothes he had worn the night before. His bare feet were on the floor tiles. There were no indications at all that Trent had had second thoughts about killing himself. Being that it was not a suspension hanging, he could have stopped his death at any time. He didn't.

Bosch would have to leave it for the coroner's people but he judged by the darkening of the body's tongue, which was distended from the mouth, that Trent had been dead at least twelve hours. That would put his death in the vicinity of the very early morning, not long after Channel 4 had first announced his hidden past to the world and labeled him a suspect in the bones case.

'Harry?'

Bosch nearly jumped. He turned around and looked at Edgar.

'Don't do that to me, man. What?'

Edgar was staring at the body as he spoke.

'He left a three-page note out on the coffee table.'

Bosch stepped out of the shower and pushed past Edgar. He headed toward the living room, taking a pair of latex gloves from his pocket and blowing into them to expand the rubber before snapping them on.

'Did you read the whole thing?'

'Yeah, he says he didn't do the kid. He says he's killing himself because the police and reporters have destroyed him and he can't go on. Like that. There's some weird stuff, too.'

Bosch went into the living room. Edgar was a few steps behind him. Bosch saw three handwritten pages spread side by side on the coffee table. He sat down on the couch in front of them.

'This how they were?'

'Yup. I didn't touch them.'

Bosch started reading the pages. What he presumed were Trent's last words were a rambling denial of the murder of the boy on the hillside and a purging of anger over what had been done to him.

Now EVERYBODY will know! You people have ruined me, KILLED me. The blood is on you, not on me! I didn't do it, I didn't do it, no, no, NO! I never hurt anyone. Never, never, never. Not a soul on this earth. I love the children. LOVE!!!! No, it was you who hurt me. You. But it is I who can't live with the pain of what you have ruthlessly caused. I can't.

It was repetitive and almost as if someone had written down an extemporaneous diatribe rather than sat down with pen and paper and wrote out their thoughts. The middle of the second page was blocked off and inside the box were names under a heading of 'Those Found Responsible.' The list started with Judy Surtain, included the anchor on the Channel 4 nightly news, and listed Bosch, Edgar and three names Bosch didn't recognize. Calvin Stumbo, Max Rebner and Alicia Felzer.

'Stumbo was the cop and Rebner was the DA on the first case,' Edgar said. 'In the sixties.'

Bosch nodded.

'And Felzer?'

'Don't know that one.'

The pen with which the pages were apparently written was on the table next to the last page. Bosch didn't touch it because he planned to have it checked for Trent's fingerprints.

As he continued to read, Bosch noticed that each page was signed at the bottom with Trent's signature. At the end of the last page, Trent made an odd plea that Bosch didn't readily understand.

My one regret is for my children. Who will care for my children? They need food and clothes. I have some money. The money goes to them. Whatever I have. This is my last will and testament signed by me. Give the money to the children. Have Morton give the money and don't charge me anything. Do it for the children.

'His children?' Bosch asked.

'Yeah, I know,' Edgar said. 'Weird.'

'What are you doing here? Where is Nicholas?'

They looked at the doorway from the kitchen to the living room. A short man in a suit who Bosch guessed was a lawyer and had to be Morton stood there. Bosch stood up.

'He's dead. It looks like a suicide.'

'Where?'

'Master bath, but I wouldn't—'

Morton was already gone, heading to the bathroom. Bosch called after him.

'Don't touch anything.'

He nodded to Edgar to follow and make sure. Bosch sat back down and looked at the pages again. He wondered how long it took Trent to decide that killing himself was all that he had left and then to labor over the three-page note. It was the longest suicide note he had ever encountered.

Morton came back into the living room, Edgar just behind him. His face was ashen and his eyes held on the floor.

'I tried to tell you not to go back there,' Bosch said.

The lawyer's eyes came up and fixed on Bosch. They filled with anger, which seemed to restore some color to Morton's face.

'Are you people happy now? You completely destroyed him. Give a man's secret to the vultures, they put it on the air and this is what you get.'

He gestured with a hand in the direction of the bathroom.

'Mr. Morton, you've got your facts wrong, but essentially it looks like that's what happened. In fact, you'd probably be surprised by how much I agree with you.'

'Now that he's dead, that must be very easy for you to say. Is that a note? Did he leave a note?'

Bosch got up and gestured for him to take his spot on the couch in front of the three pages.

'Just don't touch the pages.'

Morton sat down, unfolded a pair of reading glasses and started studying the pages.

Bosch walked over to Edgar and said in a low voice, 'I'm going to use the phone in the kitchen to make the calls.'

Edgar nodded.

'Better get Media Relations on it. The shit is going to hit that fan.'

'Yeah.'

Bosch picked up the wall phone in the kitchen and saw it had a redial button. He pushed it and waited. He recognized the voice that answered as Morton's. It was an answering machine. Morton said he wasn't home and to leave a message.

Bosch called Lt. Billets's direct line. She answered right away and Bosch could tell she was eating.

'Well, I hate to break this to you while you're eating, but we're up here at Trent's place. It looks like he killed himself.'

There was silence for a long moment and then she asked Bosch if he was sure.

'I'm sure he's dead and I'm pretty sure he did it himself. Hung himself with a couple of wire hangers in the shower. There's a three-page note here. He denies anything to do with the bones. He blames his death on Channel Four and the police mostly – me and Edgar in particular. You're the first one I've called.'

'Well, we all know it wasn't you who—'

'That's okay, Lieutenant, I don't need the absolution. What do you want me to do here?'

'You handle the routine call outs. I'll call Chief Irving's office and tell him what has transpired. This is going to get hot.'

'Yes. What about Media Relations? There's already a gang of reporters out on the street.'

'I'll call them.'

'Did you do anything about Thornton yet?'

'Already in the pipeline. The woman from IAD, Bradley, is running with it. With this latest thing, I'd bet Thornton not only leaked his way out of a job, but they might want to go after him with a charge of some kind.'

Bosch nodded. Thornton deserved it. He still had no second thoughts about the scam he had devised.

'All right, well, we'll be here. For a while, at least.'

'Let me know if you find anything there that connects him to the bones.'

Bosch thought of the boots with the dirt in the treads and the skateboard.

'You got it,' he said.

Bosch clicked off the call and then immediately made calls to the coroner's office and SID.

In the living room Morton had finished reading the note.

'Mr. Morton, when was the last time you talked to Mr. Trent?' Bosch asked.

'Last night. He called me at home after the news on Channel Four. His boss had seen it and called him.'

Bosch nodded. That accounted for the last call.

'You know his boss's name?'

Morton pointed to the middle page on the table.

'Right here on the list. Alicia Felzer. She told him she was going to seek his termination. The studio makes movies for children. She couldn't have him on a set with a child. You see? The leaking of his record to the media destroyed this man. You recklessly took a man's existence and—'

'Let me ask the questions, Mr. Morton. You can save your outrage for when you go outside and talk to the reporters yourself, which I know you'll do. What about that last page? He mentions the children. His children. What does that mean?'

'I have no idea. He obviously was emotionally distraught when he wrote this. It may mean nothing.'

Bosch remained standing, studying the attorney.

'Why did he call you last night?'

'Why do you think? To tell me you had been here, that it was all over the news, that his boss had seen it and wanted to fire him.'

'Did he say whether he buried that boy up there on the hill?'

Morton put on the best indignant look he could muster.

'He certainly said that he did not have a thing to do with it. He believed he was being persecuted for a past mistake, a very distant mistake, and I'd say he was correct about that.'

Bosch nodded.

'Okay, Mr. Morton, you can leave now.'

'What are you talking about? I'm not going to—'

'This house is now a crime scene. We are investigating your client's death to confirm or deny it was by his own hand. You are no longer welcome here. Jerry?'

Edgar stepped over to the couch and waved Morton up.

'Come on. Time to go out there and get your face on TV. It'll be good for business, right?'

Morton stood up and left in a huff. Bosch walked over to the front windows and pulled the curtain back a few inches. When Morton came down the side of the house to the driveway, he immediately walked to the center of the knot of reporters and started talking angrily. Bosch couldn't hear what was said. He didn't need to.

When Edgar came back into the room, Bosch told him to call the watch office and get a patrol car up to Wonderland for crowd control. He had a feeling that the media mob, like a virus replicating itself, was going to start growing bigger and hungrier by the minute.

19

They found Nicholas Trent's children when they searched his home following the removal of his body. Filling the entire two drawers of a small desk in the living room, a desk Bosch had not searched the night before, were files, photographs and financial records, including several thick bank envelopes containing canceled checks. Trent had been sending small amounts of money on a monthly basis to a number of charitable organizations that fed and clothed children. From Appalachia to the Brazilian rain forest to Kosovo, Trent had been sending checks for years. Bosch found no check for an amount higher than twelve dollars. He found dozens and dozens of photographs of the children he was supposedly helping as well as small handwritten notes from them.

Bosch had seen any number of public-service ads for the charities on late-night television. He had always been suspicious. Not about whether a few dollars could keep a child from going hungry and unclothed, but about whether the few dollars would actually get to them. He wondered if the photos Trent kept in the drawers of his desk were the same stock shots sent to everybody who contributed. He wondered if the thank-you notes in childish printing were fake.

'Man,' Edgar said as he surveyed the contents of the desk. 'This guy, it's like I think he was paying a penance or something, sending all his cash to these outfits.'

'Yeah, a penance for what?'

'We may never know.'

Edgar went back to searching the second bedroom. Bosch studied some of the photos he had spread on the top of the desk. There were boys and girls, none looking older than ten, though this was hard to estimate because they all had the hollow and ancient eyes of children who have been through war and famine and indifference. He picked up one shot of a young white boy and turned it over. The information said the boy had been orphaned during the fighting in Kosovo. He had been injured in the mortar blast that killed his parents. His name was Milos Fidor and he was ten years old.

Bosch had been orphaned at age eleven. He looked into the boy's eyes and saw his own.

At 4 P.M. they locked Trent's home and took three boxes of seized materials to the car. A small group of reporters lingered outside during the whole afternoon, despite word from Media Relations that all information on the day's events would be distributed through Parker Center.

The reporters approached them with questions but Bosch quickly said that he was not allowed to comment on the investigation. They put the boxes in the trunk and drove off, heading downtown, where a meeting had been called by Deputy Chief Irvin Irving.

Bosch was uncomfortable with himself as he drove. He was ill at ease because Trent's suicide – and he had no doubts now that it was – had served to deflect the forward movement of the investigation of the boy's death. Bosch had spent half the day going through Trent's belongings when what he had wanted to be doing was nailing down the ID of the boy, running out the lead he had received in the call-in reports.

'What's the matter, Harry?' Edgar asked at one point on the drive.

'What?'

'I don't know. You're acting all morose. I know that's probably your natural disposition, but you usually don't show it so much.'

Edgar smiled but didn't get one in return from Bosch.

'I'm just thinking about things. This guy might be alive today if we had handled things differently.'

'Come on, Harry. You mean like if we didn't investigate him? There was no way. We did our job and things ran their course. Nothing we could do. If anybody's responsible it's Thornton, and he's gonna get his due. But if you ask me, the world's better off without somebody like Trent in it anyway. My conscience is clear, man. Crystal clear.'

'Good for you.'

Bosch thought about his decision to give Edgar the day off on Sunday. If he hadn't done that, Edgar might have been the one to make the computer runs on the names. Kiz Rider would've been out of the loop and the information would have never gotten to Thornton.

He sighed. Everything always seemed to work on a domino theory. If, then, if, then, if, then.

'What's your gut say on this guy?' he asked Edgar.

'You mean, like did he do the boy on the hill?'

Bosch nodded.

'I don't know,' Edgar said. 'Have to see what the lab says about the dirt and the sister says about the skateboard. If it is the sister and we get an ID.'

Bosch didn't say anything. But he always felt uncomfortable about relying on lab reports in determining which way to go with an investigation.

'What about you, Har?'

Bosch thought of the photos of all the children Trent thought he was caring for. His act of contrition. His chance at redemption.

'I'm thinking we're spinning our wheels,' he said. 'He isn't the guy.'

20

Deputy Chief Irvin Irving sat behind his desk in his spacious office on the sixth floor of Parker Center. Also seated in the room were Lt. Grace Billets, Bosch and Edgar and an officer from the Media Relations unit named Sergio Medina. Irving's adjutant, a female lieutenant named Simonton, stood in the open doorway of the office in case she was needed.

Irving had a glass-topped desk. There was nothing on it except for two pieces of paper with printing on them that Bosch could not read from his spot in front of Irving's desk and to the left.

'Now then,' Irving began. 'What do we know as fact about Mr. Trent? We know he was a pedophile with a criminal record of abusing a child. We know that he lived a stone's throw from the burial site of a murdered child. And we know that he committed suicide on the evening he was questioned by investigators in regard to the first two points just stated.'

Irving picked up one of the pages on his desk and studied it without sharing its contents with the room. Finally, he spoke.

'I have here a press release that states those same three facts and goes on to say, 'Mr. Trent is the subject of an ongoing investigation. Determination of whether he was responsible for the death of the victim found buried near his home is pending lab work and follow-up investigation.''

He looked at the page silently again and then finally put it down.

'Nice and succinct. But it will do little to quell the thirst of the media for this story. Or to help us avert another troubling situation for this department.'

Bosch cleared his throat. Irving seemed to ignore it at first but then spoke without looking at the detective.

'Yes, Detective Bosch?'

'Well, it sort of seems as though you're not satisfied with that. The problem is, what is on that press release is exactly where we stand. I'd love to tell you I think the guy did the kid on the hill. I'd love to tell you I *know* he did it. But we are a long way from that and, if anything, I think we're going to end up concluding the opposite.'

'Based on what?' Irving snapped.

It was becoming clear to Bosch what the purpose of the meeting was. He guessed that the second page on Irving's desk was the press release the deputy chief wanted to put out. It probably pinned everything on Trent and called his suicide the result of his knowing he would be found out. This would allow the department to handle Thornton, the leaker, quietly outside of the magnifying glass of the press. It would spare the department the humiliation of acknowledging that a leak of confidential information from one of its officers caused a possibly innocent man to kill himself. It would also allow them to close the case of the boy on the hill.

Bosch understood that everyone sitting in the room knew that closing a case of this nature was the longest of long shots. The case had drawn growing media attention, and Trent with his suicide had now presented them with a way out. Suspicions could be cast on the dead pedophile, and the department could call it a day and move on to the next case – hopefully one with a better chance of being solved.

Bosch could understand this but not accept it. He had seen the bones. He had heard Golliher run down the litany of injuries. In that autopsy suite Bosch had resolved to find the killer and close the case. The expediency of department politics and image management would be second to that.

He reached into his coat pocket and pulled out his notebook. He opened it to a page with a folded corner and looked at it as if he was studying a page full of notes. But there was only one notation on the page, written on Saturday in the autopsy suite.

44 separate indications of trauma

His eyes held on the number he had written until Irving spoke again.

'Detective Bosch? I asked, "Based on what?"'

Bosch looked up and closed the notebook.

'Based on the timing – we don't think Trent moved into that neighborhood until after that boy was in the ground – and on the analysis of the bones. This kid was physically abused over a long period of time – from when he was a small child. It doesn't add up to Trent.'

'Analysis of both the timing and the bones will not be conclusive,' Irving said. 'No matter what they tell us, there is still a possibility – no matter how slim – that Nicholas Trent was the perpetrator of this crime.'

'A very slim possibility.'

'What about the search of Trent's home today?'

'We took some old work boots with dried mud in the treads. It will be compared to soil samples taken where the bones were found. But they'll be just as inconclusive. Even if they match up, Trent could have picked up the dirt hiking behind his house. It's all part of the same sediment, geologically speaking.'

'What else?'

'Not much. We've got a skateboard.'

'A skateboard?'

Bosch explained about the call-in tip he had not had time to follow up on because of the suicide. As he told it, he could see Irving warming to the possibility that a skateboard in Trent's possession could be linked to the bones on the hill.

'I want that to be your priority,' he said. 'I want that nailed down and I want to know it the moment you do.'

Bosch only nodded.

'Yes, sir,' Billets threw in.

Irving went silent and studied the two pages on his desk. Finally, he picked up the one he had not read from – the page Bosch guessed was the loaded press release – and turned at his desk. He slid it into a shredder, which whined loudly as it destroyed the document. He then turned back to his desk and picked up the remaining document.

'Officer Medina, you may put this out to the press.'

He handed the document to Medina, who stood up to receive it. Irving checked his watch.

'Just in time for the six o'clock news,' he said.

'Sir?' Medina said.

'Yes?'

'Uh, there have been many inquiries about the erroneous reports on Channel Four. Should we—'

'Say it is against policy to comment on any internal investigation. You may also add that the department will not condone or accept the leaking of confidential information to the media. That is all, Officer Medina.'

Medina looked like he had another question to ask but knew better. He nodded and left the office.

Irving nodded to his adjutant and she closed the office door, remaining in the anteroom outside. The deputy chief then turned his head, looking from Billets to Edgar to Bosch.

'We have a delicate situation here,' he said. 'Are we clear on how we are proceeding?'

'Yes,' Billets and Edgar said in unison.

Bosch said nothing. Irving looked at him.

'Detective, do you have something to say?'

Bosch thought a moment before answering.

'I just want to say that I am going to find out who killed that boy and put him up in that hole. If it's Trent, fine. Good. But if it's not him, I'm going to keep going.'

Irving saw something on his desk. Something small like a hair or other near-microscopic particle. Something Bosch couldn't see. Irving picked it up with two fingers and dropped it into the trash can behind him. As he brushed his fingers together over the shredder, Bosch looked on and wondered if the demonstration was some sort of threat directed at him.

'Not every case is solved, Detective, not every case is solvable,' he said. 'At some point our duties may require us to move on to more pressing matters.'

'Are you giving me a deadline?'

'No, Detective. I am saying I understand you. And I just hope you understand me.'

'What's going to happen with Thornton?'

'It's under internal review. I can't discuss it with you at this time.'

Bosch shook his head in frustration.

'Watch yourself, Detective Bosch,' Irving said curtly. 'I've shown a lot of patience with you. On this case and others before it.'

'What Thornton did jammed up this case. He should—'

'If he is responsible he will be dealt with accordingly. But keep in mind he was not operating in a vacuum. He needed to get the information in order to leak it. The investigation is ongoing.'

Bosch stared at Irving. The message was clear. Kiz Rider could go down with Thornton if Bosch didn't fall into step with Irving's march.

'You read me, Detective?'

'I read you. Loud and clear.'

21

Before taking Edgar back to Hollywood Division and then heading out to
Venice, Bosch got the evidence box containing the skateboard out of the
trunk and took it back inside Parker Center to the SID lab. At the counter
he asked for Antoine Jesper. While he waited, he studied the skateboard. It
appeared to be made out of laminated plywood. It had a lacquered finish to
which several decals had been applied, most notably a skull and crossbones
located in the middle of the top surface of the board.

When Jesper came to the counter, Bosch presented him with the evidence
box.

'I want to know who made this, when it was made and where it was sold,'
he said. 'It's priority one. I got the sixth floor riding my back on this case.'

'No problem. I can tell you the make right now. It's a Boney board. They
don't make 'em anymore. He sold out and moved, I think, to Hawaii.'

'How do you know all of that?'

''Cause when I was a kid I was a boarder and this was what I wanted but
never had the dough for. Pretty ironic, huh?'

'What is?'

'A Boney board and the case. You know, bones.'

Bosch nodded.

'Whatever. I want whatever you can get me by tomorrow.'

'Um, I can try. I can't prom—'

'Tomorrow, Antoine. The sixth floor, remember? I'll be talking to you
tomorrow.'

Jesper nodded.

'Give me the morning, at least.'

'You got it. Anything happening with documents?'

Jesper shook his head.

'Nothing yet. She tried the dyes and nothing came up. I don't think you
should count on anything there, Harry.'

'All right, Antoine.'

Bosch left him there holding the box.

On the way back to Hollywood he let Edgar drive while he pulled the tip
sheet out of his briefcase and called Sheila Delacroix on his cell phone. She

answered promptly and Bosch introduced himself and said her call had been referred to him.

'Was it Arthur?' she asked urgently.

'We don't know, ma'am. That's why I'm calling.'

'Oh.'

'Will it be possible for me and my partner to come see you tomorrow morning to talk about Arthur and get some information? It will help us to be better able to determine if the remains are those of your brother.'

'I understand. Um, yes. You can come here, if that is convenient.'

'Where is there, ma'am?'

'Oh. My home. Off Wilshire in the Miracle Mile.'

Bosch looked at the address on the call-in sheet.

'On Orange Grove.'

'Yes, that's correct.'

'Is eight-thirty too early for you?'

'That would be fine, Officer. If I can help I would like to. It just bothers me to think that that man lived there all those years after doing something like this. Even if the victim wasn't my brother.'

Bosch decided it wasn't worth telling her that Trent was probably completely innocent in terms of the bone case. There were too many people in the world who believed everything they saw on television.

Instead, Bosch gave her his cell phone number and told her to call it if something came up and eight-thirty the next morning turned out to be a bad time for her.

'It won't be a bad time,' she said. 'I want to help. If it's Arthur, I want to know. Part of me wants it to be him so I know it is over. But the other part wants it to be somebody else. That way I can keep thinking he is out there someplace. Maybe with a family of his own now.'

'I understand,' Bosch said. 'We'll see you in the morning.'

22

It was a brutal drive to Venice and Bosch arrived more than a half hour late. His lateness was then compounded by his fruitless search for a parking space before he went back to the library lot in defeat. His delay was no bother to Julia Brasher, who was in the critical stage of putting things together in the kitchen. She instructed him to go to the stereo and put on some music, then pour himself a glass of wine from the bottle that was already open on the coffee table. She did not make a move to touch him or kiss him, but her manner was completely warm. He thought things seemed good, that maybe he had gotten past the gaffe of the night before.

He chose a CD of live recordings of the Bill Evans Trio at the Village Vanguard in New York. He had the CD at home and knew it would make for quiet dinner music. He poured himself a glass of red wine and casually walked around the living room, looking at the things she had on display.

The mantel of the white brick fireplace was crowded with small framed photos he hadn't gotten a chance to look at the night before. Some were propped on stands and displayed more prominently than others. Not all were of people. Some photos were of places he assumed she had visited in her travels. There was a ground shot of a live volcano billowing smoke and spewing molten debris in the air. There was an underwater shot of the gaping mouth and jagged teeth of a shark. The killer fish appeared to be launching itself right at the camera – and whoever was behind it. At the edge of the photo Bosch could see one of the iron bars of the cage the photographer – who he assumed was Brasher – had been protected by.

There was a photo of Brasher with two Aboriginal men on either side of her standing somewhere, Bosch assumed, in the Australian outback. And there were several other photos of her with what appeared to be fellow backpackers in other locations of exotic or rugged terrain that Bosch could not readily identify. In none of the photos in which Julia was a subject was she looking at the camera. Her eyes were always staring off in the distance or at one of the other individuals posed with her.

In the last position on the mantel, as if hidden behind the other photos, was a small gold-framed shot of a much younger Julia Brasher with a slightly older man. Bosch reached behind the photos and lifted it out so he could see it better. The couple was sitting at a restaurant or perhaps a wedding reception. Julia wore a beige gown with a low-cut neckline. The man wore a tuxedo.

'You know, this man is a god in Japan,' Julia called from the kitchen.

Bosch put the framed photo back in its place and walked to the kitchen. Her hair was down and he couldn't decide which way he liked it best.

'Bill Evans?'

'Yeah. It seems like they have whole channels of the radio dedicated to playing his music.'

'Don't tell me, you spent some time in Japan, too.'

'About two months. It's a fascinating place.'

It looked to Bosch like she was making a risotto with chicken and asparagus in it.

'Smells good.'

'Thank you. I hope it is.'

'So what do you think you were running from?'

She looked up at him from her work at the stove. A hand held a stirring spoon steady.

'What?'

'You know, all the travel. Leaving Daddy's law firm to go swim with sharks and dive into volcanoes. Was it the old man or the law firm the old man ran?'

'Some people would look at it as maybe I was running toward something.'

'The guy in the tuxedo?'

'Harry, take your gun off. Leave your badge at the door. I always do.'

'Sorry.'

She went back to work at the stove and Bosch came up behind her. He put his hands on her shoulders and pushed his thumbs into the indentations of her upper spine. She offered no resistance. Soon he felt her muscles begin to relax. He noticed her empty wine glass on the counter.

'I'll go get the wine.'

He came back with his glass and the bottle. He refilled her glass and she picked it up and clicked it off the side of his.

'Whether to something or away from something, here's to running,' she said. 'Just running.'

'What happened to "Hold fast"?'

'There's that, too.'

'Here's to forgiveness and reconciliation.'

They clicked glasses again. He came around behind her and started working her neck again.

'You know, I thought about your story all last night after you left,' she said.

'My story?'

'About the bullet and the tunnel.'

'And?'

She shrugged her shoulders.

'Nothing. It's just amazing, that's all.'

'You know, after that day, I wasn't afraid anymore when I was down in the darkness. I just knew that I was going to make it through. I can't explain why, I just knew. Which, of course, was stupid, because there are no guarantees of that – back then and there or anywhere else. It made me sort of reckless.'

He held his hands steady for a moment.

'It's not good to be too reckless,' he said. 'You cross the tube too often, you'll eventually get burned.'

'Hmm. Are you lecturing me, Harry? You want to be my training officer now?'

'No. I checked my gun and my badge at the door, remember?'

'Okay, then.'

She turned around, his hands still on her neck, and kissed him. Then she pulled back away.

'You know, the great thing about this risotto is that it can keep in the oven as long as we need it to.'

Bosch smiled.

Later on, after they had made love, Bosch got up from her bed and went out to the living room.

'Where are you going?' she called after him.

When he didn't answer she called out to him to turn the oven up. He came back into the room carrying the gold-framed photo. He got into the bed and turned on the light on the bed table. It was a low-wattage bulb beneath a heavy lamp shade. The room still was cast in shadow.

'Harry, what are you doing?' Julia said in a tone that warned he was treading close to her heart. 'Did you turn the oven up?'

'Yeah, three-fifty. Tell me about this guy.'

'Why?'

'I just want to know.'

'It's a private story.'

'I know. But you can tell me.'

She tried to take the photo away but he held it out of her reach.

'Is he the one? Did he break your heart and send you running?'

'Harry. I thought you took your badge off.'

'I did. And my clothes, everything.'

She smiled.

'Well, I'm not telling you anything.'

She was on her back, head propped on a pillow. Bosch put the picture on the bed table and then turned back and moved in next to her. Under the sheet he put his arm across her body and pulled her tightly to him.

'Look, you want to trade scars again? I got my heart broken twice by the same woman. And you know what? I kept her picture on a shelf in my living room for a long time. Then on New Year's Day I decided it had been a long enough time. I put her picture away. Then I got called out to work and I met you.'

She looked at him, her eyes moving slightly back and forth as she seemed to be searching his face for something, maybe the slightest hint of insincerity.

'Yes,' she finally said. 'He broke my heart. Okay?'

'No, not okay. Who is the creep?'

She started laughing.

'Harry, you're my knight in tarnished armor, aren't you?'

She pulled herself up into a sitting position, the sheet falling away from her breasts. She folded her arms across them.

'He was in the firm. I really fell for him – right down the old elevator shaft. And then . . . then he decided it was over. And he decided to betray me and to tell secret things to my father.'

'What things?'

She shook her head.

'Things I will never tell a man again.'

'Where was that picture taken?'

'Oh, at a firm function – probably the New Year's banquet, I don't remember. They have a lot of them.'

Bosch had become angled behind her. He leaned down and kissed her back, just above the tattoo.

'I couldn't be there anymore while he was there. So I quit. I said I wanted to travel. My father thought it was a midlife crisis because I had turned thirty. I just let him think it. But then I had to do what I said I wanted to do – travel. I went to Australia first. It was the farthest place I could think of.'

Bosch pulled himself up and stacked two pillows behind his back. He then pulled her back against his chest. He kissed the top of her head and kept his nose in her hair.

'I had a lot of money from the firm,' she said. 'I didn't have to worry. I just kept traveling, going wherever I wanted, working odd jobs when I felt like it. I didn't come home for almost four years. And when I did, that's when I joined the academy. I was walking along the boardwalk and saw the little Venice community service office. I went in and picked up a pamphlet. It all happened pretty fast after that.'

'Your history shows impulsive and possibly reckless decision-making processes. How did that get by the screeners?'

She gently elbowed him in the side, setting off a flare of pain from his ribs. He tensed.

'Oh, Harry, sorry. I forgot.'

'Yeah, sure.'

She laughed.

'I guess all you old guys know that the department's been pushing big time for what they term "mature" women cadets the last few years. To smooth off all the hard testosterone edges of the department.'

She rocked her hips back against Bosch's genitals to underline the point.

'And speaking of testosterone,' she said, 'you never told me how it went with old bullet head himself today.'

Bosch groaned but didn't answer.

'You know,' she said, 'Irving came to address our class one day on the moral responsibilities that come with carrying the badge. And everybody sitting there knew the guy probably makes more backroom deals up there on the sixth floor than there are days in the year. The guy's the classic fixer. You could practically cut the irony in the auditorium with a knife.'

Her use of the word 'irony' made Bosch flash on what Antoine Jesper had said about coupling the bones found on the hill with the bones on the skateboard. He felt his body tensing as thoughts of the case started encroaching on what had been an oasis of respite from the investigation.

She sensed his tightness.

'What is it?'

'Nothing.'

'You got all tense all of a sudden.'

'The case, I guess.'

She was quiet a moment.

'I think it's kind of amazing,' she then said. 'Those bones being up there all of these years and then coming up out of the ground. Like a ghost or something.'

'It's a city of bones. And all of them are waiting to come up.'

He paused.

'I don't want to talk about Irving or the bones or the case or anything else right now.'

'Then what do you want?'

He didn't answer. She turned to face him and started pushing him down off the pillows until he was flat on his back.

'How about a mature woman to smooth off all the hard edges again?'

It was impossible for Bosch not to smile.

23

Before dawn Bosch was on the road. He left Julia Brasher sleeping in her bed and started on his way to his home, after first stopping at Abbot's Habit for a coffee to go. Venice was like a ghost town, with the tendrils of the morning fog moving across the streets. But as he got closer to Hollywood the lights of cars on the streets multiplied and Bosch was reminded that the city of bones was a twenty-four-hour city.

At home he showered and put on fresh clothes. He then climbed back into his car and went down the hill to Hollywood Division. It was 7:30 when he got there. Surprisingly, a number of detectives were already in place, chasing paperwork and cases. Edgar wasn't among them. Bosch put his briefcase down and walked to the watch office to get coffee and to see if any citizen had brought in doughnuts. Almost every day a John Q who still kept the faith brought in doughnuts for the division. A little way of saying there were still those out there who knew or at least understood the difficulties of the job. Every day in every division cops put on the badge and tried to do their best in a place where the populace didn't understand them, didn't particularly like them and in many instances outright despised them. Bosch always thought it was amazing how far a box of doughnuts could go in undoing that.

He poured a cup and dropped a dollar in the basket. He took a sugar doughnut out of a box on the counter that had already been decimated by the patrol guys. No wonder. They were from Bob's Donuts in the farmers' market. He noticed Mankiewicz sitting at his desk, his dark eyebrows forming a deep V as he studied what looked like a deployment chart.

'Hey, Mank, I think we pulled a grade A lead off the call-in sheets. Thought you'd want to know.'

Mankiewicz answered without looking up.

'Good. Let me know when my guys can give it a rest. We're going to be short on the desk the next few days.'

Bosch knew this meant he was juggling personnel. When there weren't enough uniforms to put in cars – due to vacations, court appearances or sick-outs – the watch sergeant always pulled people off the desk and put them on wheels.

'You got it.'

Edgar still wasn't at the table when Bosch got back to the detective squad room. Bosch put his coffee and doughnut down next to one of the Selectrics and went to get a search warrant application out of a community file drawer. For the next fifteen minutes he typed out an addendum to the search warrant he had already delivered to the records custodian at Queen of Angels. It asked for all records from the care of Arthur Delacroix circa 1975 to 1985.

When he was finished he took it to the fax machine and sent it to the office of Judge John A. Houghton, who had signed all the hospital search warrants the day before. He added a note requesting that the judge review the addendum application as soon as possible because it might lead to the positive identification of the bones and therefore swing the investigation into focus.

Bosch returned to the table and from a drawer pulled out the stack of missing person reports he had gathered while fiche-ing in the archives. He started looking through them quickly, glancing only at the box reserved for the name of the missing individual. In ten minutes he was finished. There had been no report in the stack about Arthur Delacroix. He didn't know what this meant but he planned to ask the boy's sister about it.

It was now eight o'clock and Bosch was ready to leave to visit the sister. But still no Edgar. Bosch ate the remainder of his doughnut and decided to give his partner ten minutes to show before he would leave on his own. He had worked with Edgar for more than ten years and still was bothered by his partner's lack of punctuality. It was one thing to be late for dinner. It was another to be late for a case. He had always taken Edgar's tardiness as a lack of commitment to their mission as homicide investigators.

His direct line rang and Bosch answered it with an annoyed rasp, expecting it to be Edgar announcing he was running late. But it wasn't Edgar. It was Julia Brasher.

'So, you just leave a woman high and dry in bed, huh?'

Bosch smiled and his frustration with Edgar quickly drained away.

'I got a busy day here,' he said. 'I had to get going.'

'I know but you could've said good-bye.'

Bosch saw Edgar making his way through the squad room. He wanted to get going before Edgar started his coffee, doughnut and sports-page ritual.

'Well, I'm saying good-bye now, okay? I'm in the middle of something here and I gotta run.'

'Harry . . .'

'What?'

'I thought you were going to hang up on me or something.'

'I'm not, but I gotta go. Look, come by before you go up for roll call, okay? I'll probably be back by then.'

'All right. I'll see you.'

Bosch hung up and stood up just as Edgar got to the homicide table and dropped the folded sports page at his spot.

'You ready?'

'Yeah, I was just going to get—'

'Let's go. I don't want to keep the lady waiting. And she'll probably have coffee there.'

On the way out Bosch checked the incoming tray on the fax machine. His search warrant addendum had been signed and returned by Judge Houghton.

'We're in business,' Bosch said to Edgar, showing him the warrant as they walked to the car. 'See? You come in early, you get stuff done.'

'What's that supposed to mean? Is that a crack on me?'

'It means what it means, I guess.'

'I just want some coffee.'

24

Sheila Delacroix lived in a part of the city called the Miracle Mile. It was a neighborhood south of Wilshire that wasn't quite up to the standards of nearby Hancock Park but was lined with nicely kept homes and duplexes with modest stylistic adjustments to promote individuality.

Delacroix's home was the second floor of a duplex with pseudo-Beaux Arts styling. She invited the detectives into her home in a friendly manner, but when the first question Edgar asked was about coffee, she said it was against her religion. She offered tea, and Edgar reluctantly accepted. Bosch passed. He wondered which religion outlawed coffee.

They took seats in the living room while the woman made Edgar his tea in the kitchen. She called out to them, saying she only had an hour and then had to leave for work.

'What is it you do?' Bosch asked as she came out with a mug of hot tea, the tag from the tea bag looped over the side. She put it down on a coaster on a side table next to Edgar. She was a tall woman. She was slightly overweight with blonde hair cut short. Bosch thought she wore too much makeup.

'I'm a casting agent,' she said as she took a seat on the couch. 'Mostly independent films, some episodic television. I'm actually casting a cop show this week.'

Bosch watched Edgar sip some tea and make a face. He then held the mug so he could read the tea bag tag.

'It's a blend,' Delacroix said. 'Strawberry and Darjeeling. Do you like it?'

Edgar put the mug down on its coaster.

'It's fine.'

'Ms. Delacroix? If you're in the entertainment business, did you by any chance know Nicholas Trent?'

'Please, just call me Sheila. Now, that name, Nicholas Trent. It sounds familiar but I can't quite place it. Is he an actor or is he in casting?'

'Neither. He's the man who lived up on Wonderland. He was a set designer – I mean, decorator.'

'Oh, the one on TV, the man who killed himself. Oh, no wonder it was familiar.'

'So you didn't know him from the business, then?'

'No, not at all.'

'Okay, well I shouldn't have asked that. We're out of order here. Let's just start with your brother. Tell us about Arthur. Do you have a picture we can look at?'

'Yes,' she said, as she stood up and walked behind his chair. 'Here he is.'

She went to a waist-high cabinet Bosch hadn't noticed behind him. There were framed photos on it displayed in much the same way he had seen the photos on Julia Brasher's mantel. Delacroix chose one and turned around and handed it to Bosch.

The frame contained a photo of a boy and a girl sitting on a set of stairs Bosch recognized as the stairs they had climbed before knocking on her door. The boy was much smaller than the girl. Both were smiling at the camera and had the smiles of children who have been told to smile – a lot of teeth but not a legitimately turned-up mouth.

Bosch handed the photo to Edgar and looked at Delacroix, who had returned to the couch.

'Those stairs . . . was that taken here?'

'Yes, this is the home we grew up in.'

'When he disappeared, it was from here?'

'Yes.'

'Are any of his belongings still here in the house?'

Delacroix smiled sadly and shook her head.

'No, it's all gone. I gave his things to the charity rummage sale at church. That was a long time ago.'

'What church is that?'

'The Wilshire Church of Nature.'

Bosch just nodded.

'They're the ones who don't let you have coffee?' Edgar asked.

'Nothing with caffeine.'

Edgar put the framed photo down next to his tea.

'Do you have any other photos of him?' he asked.

'Of course, I have a box of old photos.'

'Can we look at those? You know, while we talk.'

Delacroix's eyebrows came together in confusion.

'Sheila,' Bosch said. 'We found some clothing with the remains. We would like to look at the photos to see if any of it matches. It will help the investigation.'

She nodded.

'I see. Well, then I'll be right back. I just need to go to the closet in the hallway.'

'Do you need help?'

'No, I can manage.'

After she was gone Edgar leaned over to Bosch and whispered, 'This Church of Nature tea tastes like piss water.'

Bosch whispered back, 'How would you know what piss water tastes like?'

The skin around Edgar's eyes drew tight with embarrassment as he realized he had walked into that one. Before he could muster a response Sheila Delacroix came back into the room carrying an old shoe box. She put it down on the coffee table and removed the lid. The box was filled with loose photographs.

'These aren't in any order or anything. But he should be in a lot of them.'

Bosch nodded to Edgar, who reached into the box for the first stack of photos.

'While my partner looks through these, why don't you tell me about your brother and when he disappeared?'

Sheila nodded and composed her thoughts before beginning.

'May fourth, nineteen eighty. He didn't come home from school. That's it. That's all. We thought he had run away. You said you found clothes with the remains. Well, my father looked in his drawers and said that Arthur had taken clothes. That was what made us think he had run away.'

Bosch wrote a few notes down in a notebook he had pulled from his coat pocket.

'You mentioned that he had been injured a few months before on a skateboard.'

'Yes, he hit his head and they had to operate.'

'When he disappeared, did he take his skateboard?'

She thought about this for a long moment.

'It was so long ago . . . all I know is that he loved that board. So I think he probably took it. But I just remember the clothes. My father found some of his clothes missing.'

'Did you report him missing?'

'I was sixteen years old at the time, so I didn't do anything. My father talked to the police though. I'm sure of it.'

'I couldn't find any record of Arthur being reported missing. Are you sure he reported him missing?'

'I drove with him to the police station.'

'Was it Wilshire Division?'

'I would assume but I don't really remember.'

'Sheila, where is your father? Is he still alive?'

'He's alive. He lives in the Valley. But he's not well these days.'

'Where in the Valley?'

'Van Nuys. In the Manchester Trailer Park.'

There was silence while Bosch wrote the information down. He had been to the Manchester Trailer Park before on investigations. It wasn't a pleasant place to live.

'He drinks . . .'

Bosch looked at her.

'Ever since Arthur . . .'

Bosch nodded that he understood. Edgar leaned forward and handed him a photograph. It was a yellowed 3 × 5. It showed a young boy, his arms raised in an effort to maintain balance, gliding on the sidewalk on a skateboard. The angle of the photograph showed little of the skateboard other than its profile. Bosch could not tell if it carried a bone design on it or not.

'Can't see much there,' he said as he started to hand the photo back.

'No, the clothes – the shirt.'

Bosch looked at the photo again. Edgar was right. The boy in the photo wore a gray T-shirt with SOLID SURF printed across the chest.

Bosch showed the photo to Sheila.

'This is your brother, right?'

She leaned forward to look at the photo.

'Yes, definitely.'

'That shirt he is wearing, do you remember if it is one of the pieces of clothing your father found missing?'

Delacroix shook her head.

'I can't remember. It's been – I just remember that he liked that shirt a lot.'

Bosch nodded and gave the photo back to Edgar. It wasn't the kind of solid confirmation they could get from X-rays and bone comparison but it was one more notch. Bosch was feeling more and more sure that they were about to identify the bones. He watched Edgar put the photo in a short stack of pictures he intended to borrow from Sheila's collection.

Bosch checked his watch and looked back at Sheila.

'What about your mother?'

Sheila immediately shook her head.

'Nope, she was long gone by the time all of this happened.'

'You mean she died?'

'I mean she took a bus the minute the going got tough. You see, Arthur was a difficult child. Right from the beginning. He needed a lot of attention and it fell to my mother. After a while she couldn't take it any longer. One night she went out to get some medicine at the drugstore and she never came back. We found little notes from her under our pillows.'

Bosch dropped his eyes to his notebook. It was hard to hear this story and keep looking at Sheila Delacroix.

'How old were you? How old was your brother?'

'I was six, so that would make Artie two.'

Bosch nodded.

'Did you keep the note from her?'

'No. There was no need. I didn't need a reminder of how she supposedly loved us but not enough to stay with us.'

'What about Arthur? Did he keep his?'

'Well, he was only two, so my father kept it for him. He gave it to him when he was older. He may have kept it, I don't know. Because he never really knew her, he was always very interested in what she was like. He asked me a lot of questions about her. There were no photos of her. My father had gotten rid of them all so he wouldn't have any reminders.'

'Do you know what happened to her? Or if she's still alive?'

'I haven't the faintest idea. And to tell you the truth, I don't care if she is alive or not.'

'What is her name?'

'Christine Dorsett Delacroix. Dorsett was her maiden name.'

'Do you know her birth date or Social Security number?'

Sheila shook her head.

'Do you have your own birth certificate handy here?'

'It's somewhere in my records. I could go look for it.'

She started to get up.

'No, wait, we can look for that at the end. I'd like to keep talking here.'

'Okay.'

'Um, after your mother was gone, did your father remarry?'

'No, he never did. He lives alone now.'

'Did he ever have a girlfriend, someone who might have stayed in the house?'

She looked at Bosch with eyes that seemed almost lifeless.

'No,' she said. 'Never.'

Bosch decided to move on to an area of discussion that would be less difficult for her.

'What school did your brother go to?'

'At the end he was going to The Brethren.'

Bosch didn't say anything. He wrote the name of the school down on his pad and then a large letter B beneath it. He circled the letter, thinking about the backpack. Sheila continued unbidden.

'It was a private school for troubled boys. My dad paid to send him there. It's off of Crescent Heights near Pico. It's still there.'

'Why did he go there? I mean, why was he considered troubled?'

'Because he got kicked out of his other schools for fighting mostly.'

'Fighting?' Edgar said.

'That's right.'

Edgar picked the top photograph off of his keeper file and studied it for a moment.

'This boy looks like he was as light as smoke. Was he the one starting these fights?'

'Most times. He had trouble getting along. All he wanted to do was be on

407

his skateboard. I think that by today's standards he would be diagnosed as having attention deficit disorder or something similar. He just wanted to be by himself all the time.'

'Did he get hurt in these fights?' Bosch asked.

'Sometimes. Black and blue mostly.'

'Broken bones?'

'Not that I remember. Just schoolyard fights.'

Bosch felt agitated. The information they were getting could point them in many different directions. He had hoped a clear-cut path might emerge from the interview.

'You said your father searched the drawers in your brother's room and found clothes missing.'

'That's right. Not a lot. Just a few things.'

'Any idea what was missing specifically?'

She shook her head.

'I can't remember.'

'What did he take the clothes in? Like a suitcase or something?'

'I think he took his schoolbag. Took out the books and put in some clothes.'

'Do you remember what that looked like?'

'No. Just a backpack. Everybody had to use the same thing at The Brethren. I still see kids walking on Pico with them, the backpacks with the *B* on the back.'

Bosch glanced at Edgar and then back at Delacroix.

'Let's go back to the skateboard. Are you sure he took it with him?'

She paused to think about this, then slowly nodded.

'Yes, I'm pretty sure he took it with him.'

Bosch decided to cut off the interview and concentrate on completing the identification. Once they confirmed the bones came from Arthur Delacroix, then they could come back to his sister.

He thought about Golliher's take on the injuries to the bones. Chronic abuse. Could it all have been injuries from schoolyard fights and skateboarding? He knew he needed to approach the issue of child abuse but did not feel the time was appropriate. He also didn't want to tip his hand to the daughter so that she could turn around and possibly tell the father. What Bosch wanted was to back out and come back in later when he felt he had a tighter grasp on the case and a solid investigative plan to go with.

'Okay, we're going to wrap things up here pretty quickly, Sheila. Just a few more questions. Did Arthur have some friends? Maybe a best friend, someone he might confide in?'

She shook her head.

'Not really. He mostly was by himself.'

Bosch nodded and was about to close his notebook when she continued.

'There was one boy he'd go boarding with. His name was Johnny Stokes.

He was from somewhere down near Pico. He was bigger and a little bit older than Arthur but they were in the same class at The Brethren. My father was pretty sure he smoked pot. So we didn't like Arthur being friends with him.'

'By "we," you mean your dad and you?'

'Yes, my father. He was upset about it.'

'Did either of you talk to Johnny Stokes after Arthur went missing?'

'Yes, that night when he didn't come home my father called Johnny Stokes, but he said he hadn't seen Artie. The next day when Dad went to the school to ask about him, he told me he talked to Johnny again about Artie.'

'And what did he say?'

'That he hadn't seen him.'

Bosch wrote down the friend's name in his notebook and underlined it.

'Any other friends you can think of?'

'No, not really.'

'What's your father's name?'

'Samuel. Are you going to talk to him?'

'Most likely.'

Her eyes dropped to the hands clasped in her lap.

'Is that a problem if we talk to him?'

'Not really. He's just not well. If those bones turn out to be Arthur ... I was thinking it would be better if he didn't ever know.'

'We'll keep that in mind when we talk to him. But we won't do it until we have a positive identification.'

'But if you talk to him, then he'll know.'

'It may be unavoidable, Sheila.'

Edgar handed Bosch another photo. It showed Arthur standing next to a tall blond man who looked faintly familiar to Bosch. He showed the photo to Sheila.

'Is this your father?'

'Yes, it's him.'

'He looks familiar. Was he ever—'

'He's an actor. Was, actually. He was on some television shows in the sixties and a few things after that, some movie parts.'

'Not enough to make a living?'

'No, he always had to work other jobs. So we could live.'

Bosch nodded and handed the photo back to Edgar but Sheila reached across the coffee table and intercepted it.

'I don't want that one to leave, please. I don't have many photos of my father.'

'Fine,' Bosch said. 'Could we go look for the birth certificate now?'

'I'll go look. You can stay here.'

She got up and left the room again, and Edgar took the opportunity to show Bosch some of the other photos he had taken to keep during the investigation.

'It's him, Harry,' he whispered. 'I got no doubt.'

He showed him a photo of Arthur Delacroix that had apparently been taken for school. His hair was combed neatly and he wore a blue blazer and tie. Bosch studied the boy's eyes. They reminded him of the photo of the boy from Kosovo he had found in Nicholas Trent's house. The boy with the thousand-yard stare.

'I found it.'

Sheila Delacroix came into the room carrying an envelope and unfolding a yellowed document. Bosch looked at it for a moment and then copied down the names, birth dates and Social Security numbers of her parents.

'Thanks,' he said. 'You and Arthur had the same parents, right?'

'Of course.'

'Okay, Sheila, thank you. We're going to go. We'll call you as soon as we know something for sure.'

He stood up and so did Edgar.

'All right if we borrow these photos?' Edgar asked. 'I will personally see that you get them back.'

'Okay, if you need them.'

They headed to the door and she opened it. While still on the threshold Bosch asked her one last question.

'Sheila, have you always lived here?'

She nodded.

'All my life. I've stayed here in case he comes back, you know? In case he doesn't know where to start and comes here.'

She smiled but not in any way that imparted humor. Bosch nodded and stepped outside behind Edgar.

25

Bosch walked up to the museum ticket window and told the woman sitting behind it his name and that he had an appointment with Dr. William Golliher in the anthropology lab. She picked up a phone and made a call. A few minutes later she rapped on the glass with her wedding band until it drew the attention of a nearby security guard. He came over and the woman instructed him to escort Bosch to the lab. He did not have to pay the admission.

The guard said nothing as they walked through the dimly lit museum, past the mammoth display and the wall of wolf skulls. Bosch had never been inside the museum, though he had gone to the La Brea Tar Pits often on field trips when he was a child. The museum was built after that, to house and display all of the finds that bubbled up out of the earth in the tar pits.

When Bosch had called Golliher's cell phone after receiving the medical records on Arthur Delacroix, the anthropologist said he was already working on another case and couldn't get downtown to the medical examiner's office until the next day. Bosch had said he couldn't wait. Golliher said he did have copies of the X-rays and photographs from the Wonderland case with him. If Bosch could come to him, he could make the comparisons and give an unofficial response.

Bosch took the compromise and headed to the tar pits while Edgar remained at Hollywood Division working the computer to see if he could locate Arthur and Sheila Delacroix's mother as well as run down Arthur's friend Johnny Stokes.

Now Bosch was curious as to what the new case was that Golliher was working. The tar pits were an ancient black hole where animals had gone to their death for centuries. In a grim chain reaction, animals caught in the miasma became prey for other animals, who in turn were mired and slowly pulled down. In some form of natural equilibrium the bones now came back up out of the blackness and were collected for study by modern man. All of this took place right next to one of the busiest streets in Los Angeles, a constant reminder of the crushing passage of time.

Bosch was led through two doors and into the crowded lab where the bones were identified, classified, dated and cleaned. There appeared to be boxes of bones everywhere on every flat surface. A half dozen people in white lab coats worked at stations, cleaning and examining the bones.

Golliher was the only one not in a lab coat. He had on another Hawaiian shirt, this one with parrots on it, and was working at a table in the far corner. As Bosch approached, he saw there were two wooden bone boxes on the worktable in front of him. In one of the boxes was a skull.

'Detective Bosch, how are you?'

'Doing okay. What's this?'

'This, as I'm sure you can tell, is a human skull. It and some other human bones were collected two days ago from asphalt that was actually excavated thirty years ago to make room for this museum. They've asked me to take a look before they make the announcement.'

'I don't understand. Is it ... old or ... from thirty years ago?'

'Oh, it's quite old. It was carbon-dated to nine thousand years ago, actually.'

Bosch nodded. The skull and the bones in the other box looked like mahogany.

'Take a look,' Golliher said and he lifted the skull out of the box.

He turned it so that the rear of the skull faced Bosch. He moved his finger in a circle around a star fracture near the top of the skull.

'Look familiar?'

'Blunt-force fracture?'

'Exactly. Much like your case. Just goes to show you.'

He gently replaced the skull in the wooden box.

'Show me what?'

'Things don't change that much. This woman – at least we think it was a woman – was murdered nine thousand years ago, her body probably thrown into the tar pit as a means of covering the crime. Human nature, it doesn't change.'

Bosch stared at the skull.

'She's not the first.'

Bosch looked up at Golliher.

'In nineteen fourteen the bones – a more complete skeleton, actually – of another woman were found in the tar. She had the same star fracture in the same spot on her skull. Her bones were carbon-dated as nine thousand years old. Same time frame as her.'

He nodded to the skull in the box.

'So, what are you saying, Doc, that there was a serial killer here nine thousand years ago?'

'It's impossible to know that, Detective Bosch. All we have are the bones.'

Bosch looked down at the skull again. He thought about what Julia Brasher had said about his job, about his taking evil out of the world. What she didn't know was a truth he had known for too long. That true evil could never be taken out of the world. At best he was wading into the dark waters of the abyss with two leaking buckets in his hands.

'But you have other things on your mind, don't you?' Golliher said, interrupting Bosch's thoughts. 'Do you have the hospital records?'

Bosch brought his briefcase up onto the worktable and opened it. He handed Golliher a file. Then, from his pocket he pulled the stack of photos he and Edgar had borrowed from Sheila Delacroix.

'I don't know if these help,' he said. 'But this is the kid.'

Golliher picked up the photos. He went through them quickly, stopping at the posed close-up of Arthur Delacroix in a jacket and tie. He went over to a chair where a backpack was slung over the armrest. He pulled out his own file and came back to the worktable. He opened the file and took out an 8 × 10 photo of the skull from Wonderland Avenue. For a long moment he held the photos of Arthur Delacroix and the skull side by side and studied them.

Finally, he said, 'The malar and superciliary ridge formation look similar.'

'I'm not an anthropologist, Doc.'

Golliher put the photos down on the table. He then explained by running his finger across the left eyebrow of the boy and then down around the outside of his eye.

'The brow ridge and the exterior orbit,' he said. 'It's wider than usual on the recovered specimen. Looking at this photo of the boy, we see his facial structure is in line with what we see here.'

Bosch nodded.

'Let's look at the X-rays,' Golliher said. 'There's a box back here.'

Golliher gathered the files and led Bosch to another worktable, where there was a light box built into the surface. He opened the hospital file, picked up the X-rays and began reading the patient history report.

Bosch had already read the document. The hospital reported that the boy was brought into the emergency room at 5:40 P.M. on February 11, 1980, by his father, who said he was found in a dazed and unresponsive state following a fall from a skateboard in which he struck his head. Neurosurgery was performed in order to relieve pressure inside the skull caused by swelling of the brain. The boy remained in the hospital under observation for ten days and was then released to his father. Two weeks later he was readmitted for follow-up surgery to remove the clips that had been used to hold his skull together following the neurosurgery.

There was no report anywhere in the file of the boy complaining about being mistreated by his father or anyone else. While recovering from the initial surgery he was routinely interviewed by an on-site social worker. Her report was less than half a page. It reported that the boy said he had hurt himself while skateboarding. There was no follow-up questioning or referral to juvenile authorities or the police.

Golliher shook his head while he finished his scan of the document.

'What is it?' Bosch asked.

'It's nothing. And that's the problem. No investigation. They took the boy at his word. His father was probably sitting right there in the room with him when he was interviewed. You know how hard it would have been for him to tell the truth? So they just patched him up and sent him right back to the person who was hurting him.'

'Hey, Doc, you're getting a little bit ahead of us. Let's get the ID, if it's there, and then we'll figure out who was hurting the kid.'

'Fine. It's your case. It's just that I've seen this a hundred times.'

Golliher dropped the reports and picked up the X-rays. Bosch watched him with a bemused smile on his face. It seemed that Golliher was annoyed because Bosch had not jumped to the same conclusions he had with the same speed he had.

Golliher put two X-rays down on the light box. He then went to his own file and brought out X-rays he had taken of the Wonderland skull. He flipped the box's light on and three X-rays glowed before them. Golliher pointed to the X-ray he had taken from his own file.

'This is a radiological X-ray I took to look inside the bone of the skull. But we can use it here for comparison purposes. Tomorrow when I get back to the medical examiner's office I will use the skull itself.'

Golliher leaned over the light box and reached for a small glass eyepiece that was stored on a nearby shelf. He held one end to his eye and pressed the other against one of the X-rays. After a few moments he moved to one of the hospital X-rays and pressed the eyepiece to the same location on the skull. He went back and forth numerous times, making comparison after comparison.

When he was finished, Golliher straightened up, leaned back against the next worktable and folded his arms.

'Queen of Angels was a government-subsidized hospital. Money was always tight. They should have taken more than two pictures of this kid's head. If they had, they might have seen some of his other injuries.'

'Okay. But they didn't.'

'Yeah, they didn't. But based on what they did do and what we've got here, I was able to make several comparison points on the roundel, the fracture pattern and along the squamous suture. There is no doubt in my mind.'

He gestured toward the X-rays still glowing on the light box.

'Meet Arthur Delacroix.'

Bosch nodded.

'Okay.'

Golliher stepped over to the light box and started collecting the X-rays.

'How sure are you?'

'Like I said, there's no doubt. I'll look at the skull tomorrow when I'm downtown, but I can tell you now, it's him. It's a match.'

'So, if we get somebody and go into court with it, there aren't going to be any surprises, right?'

Golliher looked at Bosch.

'No surprises. These findings can't be challenged. As you know, the challenge lies in the interpretation of the injuries. I look at this boy and see something horribly, horribly wrong. And I will testify to that. Gladly. But then you have these official records.'

He gestured dismissively to the open file of hospital records.

'They say skateboard. That's where the fight will be.'

Bosch nodded. Golliher put the two X-rays back into the file and closed it. Bosch put it back in his briefcase.

'Well, Doctor, thanks for taking the time to see me here. I think—'

'Detective Bosch?'

'Yes?'

'The other day you seemed very uncomfortable when I mentioned the necessity of faith in what we do. Basically, you changed the subject.'

'Not really a subject I feel comfortable talking about.'

'I would think that in your line of work it would be paramount to have a healthy spirituality.'

'I don't know. My partner likes blaming aliens from outer space for everything that's wrong. I guess that's healthy, too.'

'You're avoiding the question.'

Bosch grew annoyed and the feeling quickly slipped toward anger.

'What is the question, Doc? Why do you care so much about me and what I believe or don't believe?'

'Because it is important to me. I study bones. The framework of life. And I have come to believe that there is something more than blood and tissue and bone. There is something else that holds us together. I have something inside, that you'll never see on any X-ray, that holds me together and keeps me going. And so, when I meet someone who carries a void in the place where I carry my faith, I get scared for him.'

Bosch looked at him for a long moment.

'You're wrong about me. I have faith and I have a mission. Call it blue religion, call it whatever you like. It's the belief that this won't just go by. That those bones came out of the ground for a reason. That they came out of the ground for me to find, and for me to do something about. And that's what holds me together and keeps me going. And it won't show up on any X-ray either. Okay?'

He stared at Golliher, waiting for a reply. But the anthropologist said nothing.

'I gotta go, Doctor,' Bosch finally said. 'Thanks for your help. You've made things very clear for me.'

He left him there, surrounded by the dark bones the city had been built on.

26

Edgar was not at his spot at the homicide table when Bosch got back to the squad room.

'Harry?'

Bosch looked up and saw Lt. Billets standing in the doorway to her office. Through the glass window Bosch could see Edgar in there sitting in front of her desk. Bosch put his briefcase down and headed over.

'What's up?' he said as he entered the office.

'No, that's my question,' Billets said as she closed the door. 'Do we have an ID?'

She went around behind her desk and sat down as Bosch took the seat next to Edgar.

'Yes, we have an ID. Arthur Delacroix, disappeared May fourth, nineteen eighty.'

'The ME is sure of this?'

'Their bone guy says there is no doubt.'

'How close are we on time of death?'

'Pretty close. The bone guy said before we knew anything that the fatal impact to the skull came about three months after the kid had the earlier skull fracture and surgery. We got the records on that surgery today. February eleven, nineteen eighty at Queen of Angels. You add three months and we're almost right on the button – Arthur Delacroix disappeared May fourth, according to his sister. The point is, Arthur Delacroix was dead four years before Nicholas Trent moved into that neighborhood. I think that puts him in the clear.'

Billets reluctantly nodded.

'I've had Irving's office and Media Relations on my ass all day about this,' she said. 'They're not going to like it when I call them back with this.'

'That's too bad,' Bosch said. 'That's the way the case shakes out.'

'Okay, so Trent wasn't in the neighborhood in nineteen eighty. Do we have anything yet on where he was?'

Bosch blew out his breath and shook his head.

'You're not going to let this go, are you? We need to concentrate on the kid.'

'I'm not letting go because they're not. Irving called me himself this morning. He was very clear without having to say the words. If it turns out an innocent man killed himself because a cop leaked information to the media that held him up to public ridicule, then it's one more black eye for the department. Haven't we had enough humiliation in the last ten years?'

Bosch smiled without a hint of humor.

'You sound just like him, Lieutenant. That's really good.'

It was the wrong thing to say. He could see that it hurt her.

'Yeah, well, maybe I sound like him because I agree with him, for once. This department has had nothing but scandal after scandal. Like most of the decent cops around here, I for one am sick of it.'

'Good. So am I. But the solution is not to bend things to fit our needs. This is a homicide case.'

'I know that, Harry. I'm not saying bend anything. I'm saying we have to be sure.'

'We're sure. I'm sure.'

They were silent for a long moment, everyone's eyes avoiding the others'.

'What about Kiz?' Edgar finally asked.

Bosch sneered.

'Irving won't do a thing to Kiz,' he said. 'He knows it will make him look even worse if he touches her. Besides, she's probably the best cop they got down there on the third floor.'

'You're always so sure, Harry,' Billets said. 'It must be nice.'

'Well, I'm sure about this.'

He stood up.

'And I'd like to get back to it. We've got stuff happening.'

'I know all about it. Jerry was just telling me. But sit down and let's get back to this for one minute, okay?'

Bosch sat back down.

'I can't just talk to Irving the way I let you talk to me,' Billets said. 'This is what I am going to do. I am going to update him on the ID and everything else. I am going to say you are pursuing the case as is. I will then invite him to assign IAD to the background investigation of Trent. In other words, if he remains unconvinced by the circumstances of the ID, then he can have IAD or whoever he can find run the background on Trent to see where he was in nineteen eighty.'

Bosch just looked at her, giving no indication of approval or disapproval of her plan.

'Can we go now?'

'Yes, you can go.'

When they got back to the homicide table and sat down Edgar asked Bosch why he hadn't mentioned the theory that maybe Trent moved into the neighborhood because he knew the bones were up on the hillside.

'Because your "sick fuck" theory is too farfetched to go beyond this table for the time being. If that gets to Irving, next thing you know it's in a press release and is the official line. Now, did you get anything on the box or not?'

'Yeah, I got stuff.'

'What?'

'First of all, I confirmed Samuel Delacroix's address at the Manchester Trailer Park. So he's there when we want to go see him. In the last ten years he's had two DUIs. He drives on a restricted license at the moment. I also ran his Social and came up with a hit – he works for the city.'

Bosch's face showed his surprise.

'Doing what?'

'He works part-time at a driving range at the municipal golf course right next to the trailer park. I made a call to Parks and Recs – discreetly. Delacroix drives the cart that collects all the balls. You know, out on the range. The guy everybody tries to hit when he's out there. I guess he comes over from the trailer park and does it a couple times a day.'

'Okay.'

'Next, Christine Dorsett Delacroix, the name of the mother on Sheila's birth certificate. I ran her Social and got her now listed as a Christine Dorsett Waters. Address is in Palm Springs. Must've gone there to re-invent herself. New name, new life, whatever.'

Bosch nodded.

'You pull the divorce?'

'Got it. She filed on Samuel Delacroix in 'seventy-three. The boy would've been about five at the time. Cited mental and physical abuse. Details of what that abuse consisted of were not included. It never went to trial, so the details never came out.'

'He didn't contest it?'

'It looks like a deal was made. He got custody of the two kids and didn't contest. Nice and clean. The file's about twelve pages thick. I've seen some that are twelve inches. My own, for example.'

'If Arthur was five ... some of those injuries predate that, according to the anthropologist.'

Edgar shook his head.

'The extract says the marriage had ended three years prior and they were living separately. So it looks like she split when the boy was about two – like Sheila said. Harry, you usually don't refer to the vic by name.'

'Yeah, so?'

'Just pointing it out.'

'Thank you. Anything else in the file?'

'That's about it. I got copies if you want it.'

'Okay, what about the skateboard friend?'

'Got him, too. Still alive, still local. But there's a problem. I ran all the usual data banks and came up with three John Stokes in L.A. that fall into the right age range. Two are in the Valley, both clean. The third's a player.

Multiple arrests for petty theft, auto theft, burglary and possession going back to a full juvy jacket. Five years ago he finally ran out of second chances and got sent to Corcoran to iron out a nickel. Did two and a half to parole.'

'You talk to his agent? Is Stokes still on the line?'

'Talked to his agent, yes. No, Stokes isn't on the hook. He cleared parole two months ago. The agent doesn't know where he is.'

'Damn.'

'Yeah, but I got him to pull a look at the client bio. It has Stokes growing up mostly in Mid-Wilshire. In and out of foster homes. In and out of trouble. He's gotta be our guy.'

'The agent think he's still in L.A.?'

'Yeah, he thinks so. We just gotta find him. I already had patrol go by his last known – he moved out of there as soon as he cleared parole.'

'So he's in the wind. Beautiful.'

Edgar nodded.

'We have to put him on the box,' Bosch said. 'Start with—'

'Did it,' Edgar said. 'I also typed up a roll-call notice and gave it to Mankiewicz a while ago. He promised to get it read at all calls. I'm having a batch of visor photos made, too.'

'Good.'

Bosch was impressed. Getting photos of Stokes to clip to the sun visors of every patrol car was the sort of extra step Edgar usually didn't bother to make.

'We'll get him, Harry. I'm not sure what good he'll do us, but we'll get him.'

'He could be a key witness. If Arthur – I mean, the vic – ever told him his father was beating him, then we've got something.'

Bosch looked at his watch. It was almost two. He wanted to keep things moving, keep the investigation focused and urgent. For him the most difficult time was waiting. Whether it was for lab results or other cops to make moves, it was always when he became most agitated.

'What do you have going tonight?' he asked Edgar.

'Tonight? Nothing much.'

'You got your kid tonight?'

'No, Thursdays. Why?'

'I'm thinking about going out to the Springs.'

'Now?'

'Yeah, talk to the ex-wife.'

He saw Edgar check his watch. He knew that even if they left that moment, they still wouldn't get back until late.

'It's all right. I can go by myself. Just give me the address.'

'Nah, I'm going with you.'

'You sure? You don't have to. I just don't like waitin' around for something to happen, you know?'

'Yeah, Harry, I know.'

Edgar stood up and took his jacket off the back of his chair.

'Then I'll go tell Bullets,' Bosch said.

27

They were more than halfway across the desert to Palm Springs before either one of them spoke.

'Harry,' Edgar said, 'you're not talking.'

'I know,' Bosch said.

The one thing they had always had as partners was the ability to share long silences. Whenever Edgar felt the need to break the silence, Bosch knew there was something on his mind he wanted to talk about.

'What is it, J. Edgar?'

'Nothing.'

'The case?'

'No, man, nothing. I'm cool.'

'All right, then.'

They were passing a windmill farm. The air was dead. None of the blades were turning.

'Did your parents stay together?' Bosch asked.

'Yeah, all the way,' Edgar said, then he laughed. 'I think they wished sometimes they didn't but, yeah, they stuck it out. That's how it goes, I guess. The strong survive.'

Bosch nodded. They were both divorced but rarely talked about their failed marriages.

'Harry, I heard about you and the boot. It's getting around.'

Bosch nodded. This is what Edgar had wanted to bring up. Rookies in the department were often called 'boots.' The origin of the term was obscure. One school of thought was that it referred to boot camp, another that it was a sarcastic reference to rookies being the new boots of the fascist empire.

'All I'm saying, man, is be careful with that. You got rank on her, okay?'

'Yeah, I know. I'll figure something out.'

'From what I hear and have seen, she's worth the risk. But you still gotta be careful.'

Bosch didn't say anything. After a few minutes they passed a road sign that said Palm Springs was coming up in nine miles. It was nearing dusk.

Bosch was hoping to knock on the door where Christine Waters lived before it got dark.

'Harry, you going to take the lead on this, when we get there?'

'Yeah, I'll take it. You can be the indignant one.'

'That will be easy.'

Once they crossed the city boundary into Palm Springs they picked up a map at a gas station and made their way through the town until they found Frank Sinatra Boulevard and took it up toward the mountains. Bosch pulled the car up to the gate house of a place called Mountaingate Estates. Their map showed the street Christine Waters lived on was within Mountaingate.

A uniformed rent-a-cop stepped out of the gate house, eying the slickback they were in and smiling.

'You guys are a little ways off the beat,' he said.

Bosch nodded and tried to give a pleasant smile. But it only made him look like he had something sour in his mouth.

'Something like that,' he said.

'What's up?'

'We're going to talk to Christine Waters, three-twelve Deep Waters Drive.'

'Mrs. Waters know you're coming?'

'Not unless she's a psychic or you tell her.'

'That's my job. Hold on a second.'

He returned to the gate house and Bosch saw him pick up a phone.

'Looks like Christine Delacroix seriously traded up,' Edgar said.

He was looking through the windshield at some of the homes that were visible from their position. They were all huge with manicured lawns big enough to play touch football on.

The guard came out, put both hands on the window sill of the car and leaned down to look in at Bosch.

'She wants to know what it's about.'

'Tell her we'll discuss it with her at her house. Privately. Tell her we have a court order.'

The guard shrugged his shoulders in a have-it-your-way gesture and went back inside. Bosch watched him speaking on the phone for a few more moments. After he hung up, the gate started to open slowly. The guard stood in the open doorway and waved them in. But not without the last word.

'You know that tough-guy stuff probably works real well for you in L.A. Out here in the desert it's just—'

Bosch didn't hear the rest. He drove through the gate while putting the window up.

They found Deep Waters Drive at the far extreme of the development. The homes here looked to be a couple million dollars more opulent than those built near the entrance to Mountaingate.

'Who would name a street in the desert Deep Waters Drive?' Edgar mused.

'Maybe somebody named Waters.'

It dawned on Edgar then.

'Damn. You think? Then she really has traded up.'

The address Edgar came up with for Christine Waters corresponded with a mansion of contemporary Spanish design that sat at the end of a cul-de-sac at the terminus of Mountaingate Estates. It was most definitely the development's premier lot. The house was positioned on a promontory that afforded it a view of all the other homes in the development as well as a sweeping view of the golf course that surrounded it.

The property had its own gated drive but the gate was open. Bosch wondered if it always stood open or had been opened for them.

'This is going to be interesting,' Edgar said as they pulled into a parking circle made of interlocking paving stones.

'Just remember,' Bosch said, 'people can change their addresses but they can't change who they are.'

'Right. Homicide one-oh-one.'

They got out and walked under the portico that led to the double-wide front door. It was opened before they got to it by a woman in a black-and-white maid's uniform. In a thick Spanish accent the woman told them that Mrs. Waters was waiting in the living room.

The living room was the size and had the feel of a small cathedral, with a twenty-five-foot ceiling with exposed roof beams. High on the wall facing the east were three large stained-glass windows, a triptych depicting a sunrise, a garden and a moonrise. The opposite wall had six side-by-side sliding doors with a view of a golf course putting green. The room had two distinct groupings of furniture, as if to accommodate two separate gatherings at the same time.

Sitting in the middle of a cream-colored couch in the first grouping was a woman with blonde hair and a tight face. Her pale blue eyes followed the men as they entered and took in the size of the room.

'Mrs. Waters?' Bosch said. 'I am Detective Bosch and this is Detective Edgar. We're from the Los Angeles Police Department.'

He held out his hand and she took it but didn't shake it. She just held it for a moment and then moved on to Edgar's outstretched hand. Bosch knew from the birth certificate that she was fifty-six years old. But she looked close to a decade younger, her smooth tan face a testament to the wonders of modern medical science.

'Please have a seat,' she said. 'I can't tell you how embarrassed I am to have that car sitting in front of my house. I guess discretion is not the better part of valor when it comes to the LAPD.'

Bosch smiled.

'Well, Mrs. Waters, we're kind of embarrassed about it, too, but that's what the bosses tell us to drive. So that's what we drive.'

'What is this about? The guard at the gate said you have a court order. May I see it?'

Bosch sat down on a couch directly opposite her and across a black coffee table with gold designs inlaid on it.

'Uh, he must have misunderstood me,' he said. 'I told him we could get a court order, if you refused to see us.'

'I'm sure he did,' she replied, the tone of her voice letting them know she didn't believe Bosch at all. 'What do you want to see me about?'

'We need to ask you about your husband.'

'My husband has been dead for five years. Besides that, he rarely went to Los Angeles. What could he possibly—'

'Your first husband, Mrs. Waters. Samuel Delacroix. We need to talk to you about your children as well.'

Bosch saw a wariness immediately enter her eyes.

'I . . . I haven't seen or spoken to them in years. Almost thirty years.'

'You mean since you went out for medicine for the boy and forgot to come back home?' Edgar asked.

The woman looked at him as though he had slapped her. Bosch had hoped Edgar was going to use a little more finesse when he acted indignant with her.

'Who told you that?'

'Mrs. Waters,' Bosch said. 'I want to ask questions first and then we can get to yours.'

'I don't understand this. How did you find me? What are you doing? Why are you here?'

Her voice rose with emotion from question to question. A life she had put aside thirty years before was suddenly intruding into the carefully ordered life she now had.

'We are homicide investigators, ma'am. We are working on a case that may involve your husband. We—'

'He's *not* my husband. I divorced him twenty-five years ago, at least. This is crazy, you coming here to ask about a man I don't even know anymore, that I didn't even know was still alive. I think you should leave. I want you to leave.'

She stood up and extended her hand in the direction they had come in.

Bosch glanced at Edgar and then back at the woman. Her anger had turned the tan on her sculptured face uneven. There were blotches beginning to form, the tell of plastic surgery.

'Mrs. Waters, sit down,' Bosch said sternly. 'Please try to relax.'

'Relax? Do you know who I am? My husband built this place. The houses, the golf course, everything. You can't just come in here like this. I could pick up the phone and have the chief of police on the line in two—'

'Your son is dead, lady,' Edgar snapped. 'The one you left behind thirty years ago. So sit down and let us ask you our questions.'

She dropped back onto the couch as if her feet had been kicked out from beneath her. Her mouth opened and then closed. Her eyes were no longer on them, they were on some distant memory.

'Arthur . . .'

'That's right,' Edgar said. 'Arthur. Glad you at least remember it.'

They watched her in silence for a few moments. All the years and all the distance wasn't enough. She was hurt by the news. Hurt bad. Bosch had seen it before. The past had a way of coming back up out of the ground. Always right below your feet.

Bosch took his notebook out of his pocket and opened it to a blank page. He wrote 'Cool it' on it and handed the notebook to Edgar.

'Jerry, why don't you take some notes? I think Mrs. Waters wants to cooperate with us.'

His speaking drew Christine Waters out of her blue reverie. She looked at Bosch.

'What happened? Was it Sam?'

'We don't know. That's why we're here. Arthur has been dead a long time. His remains were found just last week.'

She slowly brought one of her hands to her mouth in a fist. She lightly started bumping it against her lips.

'How long?'

'He had been buried for twenty years. It was a call from your daughter that helped us identify him.'

'Sheila.'

It was as if she had not spoken the name in so long she had to try it out to see if it still worked.

'Mrs. Waters, Arthur disappeared in nineteen eighty. Did you know about that?'

She shook her head.

'I was gone. I left almost ten years before that.'

'And you had no contact with your family at all?'

'I thought . . .'

She didn't finish. Bosch waited.

'Mrs. Waters?'

'I couldn't take them with me. I was young and couldn't handle . . . the responsibility. I ran away. I admit that. I ran away. I thought that it would be best for them to not hear from me, to not even know about me.'

Bosch nodded in a way he hoped conveyed that he understood and agreed with her thinking at the time. It didn't matter that he did not. It didn't matter that his own mother had faced the same hardship of having a child too soon and under difficult circumstances but had clung to and protected him with a fierceness that inspired his life.

'You wrote them letters before you left? Your children, I mean.'

'How did you know that?'

'Sheila told us. What did you say in the letter to Arthur?'

'I just . . . I just told him I loved him and I'd always think about him, but I couldn't be with him. I can't really remember everything I said. Is it important?'

Bosch shrugged his shoulders.

'I don't know. Your son had a letter with him. It might have been the one from you. It's deteriorated. We probably won't ever know. In the divorce petition you filed a few years after leaving home, you cited physical abuse as a cause of action. I need you to tell us about that. What was the physical abuse?'

She shook her head again, this time in a dismissive way, as if the question was annoying or stupid.

'What do you think? Sam liked to bat me around. He'd get drunk and it was like walking on eggshells. Anything could set him off, the baby crying, Sheila talking too loud. And I was always the target.'

'He would hit you?'

'Yes, he would hit me. He'd become a monster. It was one of the reasons I had to leave.'

'But you left the kids with the monster,' Edgar said.

This time she didn't react as if struck. She fixed her pale eyes on Edgar with a deathly look that made Edgar turn his indignant eyes away. She spoke very calmly to him.

'Who are you to judge anyone? I had to survive and I could not take them with me. If I had tried none of us would have survived.'

'I'm sure they understood that,' Edgar said.

The woman stood up again.

'I don't think I am going to talk to you anymore. I'm sure you can find your way out.'

She headed toward the arched doorway at the far end of the room.

'Mrs. Waters,' Bosch said. 'If you don't talk to us now, we will go get that court order.'

'Fine,' she said without looking back. 'Do it. I'll have one of my attorneys handle it.'

'And it will become public record at the courthouse in town.'

It was a gamble but Bosch thought it might stop her. He guessed that her life in Palm Springs was built squarely atop her secrets. And that she wouldn't want anybody going down into the basement. The social gossips might, like Edgar, have a hard time viewing her actions and motives the way she did. Deep inside, she had a hard time herself, even after so many years.

She stopped under the archway, composed herself and came back to the couch. Looking at Bosch, she said, 'I will only talk to you. I want him to leave.'

Bosch shook his head.

'He's my partner. It's our case. He stays, Mrs. Waters.'

'I will still answer questions from you only.'

'Fine. Please sit down.'

She did so, this time sitting on the side of the couch farthest from Edgar and closest to Bosch.

'I know you want to help us find your son's killer. We'll try to be as fast as we can here.'

She nodded once.

'Just tell us about your ex-husband.'

'The whole sordid story?' she asked rhetorically. 'I'll give you the short version. I met him in an acting class. I was eighteen. He was seven years older, had already done some film work and to top it off was very, very handsome. You could say I quickly fell under his spell. And I was pregnant before I was nineteen.'

Bosch checked Edgar to see if he was writing any of this down. Edgar caught the look and started writing.

'We got married and Sheila was born. I didn't pursue a career. I have to admit I wasn't that dedicated. Acting just seemed like something to do at the time. I had the looks but soon I found out every girl in Hollywood had the looks. I was happy to stay at home.'

'How did your husband do at it?'

'At first, very well. He got a recurring role on *First Infantry*. Did you ever watch it?'

Bosch nodded. It was a World War II television drama that ran in the mid to late sixties, until public sentiment over the Vietnam War and war in general led to declining ratings and it was cancelled. The show followed an army platoon as it moved behind German lines each week. Bosch had liked the show as a kid and always tried to watch it, whether he was in a foster home or the youth hall.

'Sam was one of the Germans. His blond hair and Aryan looks. He was on it the last two years. Right up until I got pregnant with Arthur.'

She let some silence punctuate that.

'Then the show got cancelled because of that stupid war in Vietnam. It got cancelled and Sam had trouble finding work. He was typecast as this German. He really started drinking then. And hitting me. He'd spend his days going to casting calls and getting nothing. He'd then spend his nights drinking and being angry at me.'

'Why you?'

'Because I was the one who had gotten pregnant. First with Sheila and then with Arthur. Neither was planned and it all added up to too much pressure on him. He took it out on whoever was close.'

'He assaulted you.'

'Assaulted? It sounds so clinical. But yes, he assaulted me. Many times.'

'Did you ever see him strike the children?'

It was the key question they had come to ask. Everything else was window dressing.

'Not specifically,' she said. 'When I was carrying Arthur he hit me once. In the stomach. It broke my water. I went into labor about six weeks before my due date. Arthur didn't even weigh five pounds when he was born.'

Bosch waited. She was talking in a way that hinted she would say more as long as he gave her the space. He looked out through the sliding door behind her at the golf course. There was a deep sand trap guarding a putting green. A man in a red shirt and plaid pants was in the trap, flailing with a club at an unseen ball. Sprays of sand were flying up out of the trap onto the green. But no ball.

In the distance three other golfers were getting out of two carts parked on the other side of the green. The lip of the sand trap shielded them from view of the man in the red shirt. As Bosch watched, the man checked up and down the fairway for witnesses, then reached down and grabbed his ball. He threw it up onto the green, giving it the nice arc of a perfectly hit shot. He then climbed out of the trap, holding his club with both hands still locked in their grip, a posture that suggested he had just hit the ball.

Finally, Christine Waters began to talk again and Bosch looked back at her.

'Arthur only weighed five pounds when he was born. He was small right up through that first year and very sickly. We never talked about it but I think we both knew that what Sam had done had hurt that boy. He just wasn't right.'

'Aside from that incident when he struck you, you never saw him strike Arthur or Sheila?'

'He might have spanked Sheila. I don't really remember. He never hit the children. I mean, he had me there to hit.'

Bosch nodded, the unspoken conclusion being that once she was gone, who knows who became the target? Bosch thought of the bones laid out on the autopsy table and all the injuries Dr. Golliher had catalogued.

'Is my hus— is Sam under arrest?'

Bosch looked at her.

'No. We're in the fact-finding stage here. The indication from your son's remains is that there is a history of chronic physical abuse. We're just trying to figure things out.'

'And Sheila? Was she . . . ?'

'We haven't specifically asked her. We will. Mrs. Waters, when you were struck by your husband, was it always with his hand?'

'Sometimes he would hit me with things. A shoe once, I remember. He held me on the floor and hit me with it. And once he threw his briefcase at me. It hit me in the side.'

She shook her head.

'What?'

'Nothing. Just that briefcase. He carried it with him to all his auditions. Like he was so important and had so much going on. And all he ever had in it were a few head shots and a flask.'

Bitterness burned in her voice, even after so many years.

'Did you ever go to a hospital or an emergency room? Is there any physical record of the abuse?'

She shook her head.

'He never hurt me enough that I had to go. Except when I had Arthur, and then I lied. I said I fell and my water broke. You see, Detective, it wasn't something I wanted the world to know about.'

Bosch nodded.

'When you left, was that planned? Or did you just go?'

She didn't answer for a long moment as she watched the memory first on her inside screen.

'I wrote the letters to my children long before I left. I carried them in my purse and waited for the right time. On the night I left, I put them under their pillows and left with my purse and only the clothes I was wearing. And my car that my father had given us when we got married. That was it. I'd had enough. I told him we needed medicine for Arthur. He had been drinking. He told me to go out and get it.'

'And you never went back.'

'Never. About a year later, before I came out to the Springs, I drove by the house at night. Saw the lights on. I didn't stop.'

Bosch nodded. He couldn't think of anything else to ask. While the woman's memory of that early time in her life was good, what she was remembering wasn't going to help make a case against her ex-husband for a murder committed ten years after she had last seen him. Maybe Bosch had known that all along – that she wouldn't be a vital part of the case. Maybe he had just wanted to take the measure of a woman who had abandoned her children, leaving them with a man she believed was a monster.

'What does she look like?'

Bosch was momentarily taken aback by her question.

'My daughter.'

'Um, she's blonde like you. A little taller, heavier. No children, not married.'

'When will Arthur be buried?'

'I don't know. You would have to call the medical examiner's office. Or you could probably check with Sheila to see if . . .'

He stopped. He couldn't get involved in mending the thirty-year gaps in people's lives.

'I think we're finished here, Mrs. Waters. We appreciate your cooperation.'

'Definitely,' Edgar said, the sarcasm in his tone making its mark.

'You came all this way to ask so few questions.'

'I think that's because you have so few answers,' Edgar said.

They walked to the door and she followed a few paces behind. Outside, under the portico, Bosch looked back at the woman standing in the open doorway. They held each other's eyes for a moment. He tried to think of something to say. But he had nothing for her. She closed the door.

28

They pulled into the station lot shortly before eleven. It had been a sixteen-hour day that had netted very little in terms of evidence that could carry a case toward prosecution. Still, Bosch was satisfied. They had the identification and that was the center of the wheel. All things would come from that.

Edgar said good night and went straight to his car without going inside the station. Bosch wanted to check with the watch sergeant to see if anything had come up with Johnny Stokes. He also wanted to check for messages and knew that if he hung around until eleven he might see Julia Brasher when she got off shift. He wanted to talk to her.

The station was quiet. The midnight shift cops were up in roll call. The incoming and outgoing watch sergeants would be up there as well. Bosch went down the hallway to the detective bureau. The lights were out, which was in violation of an order from the Office of the Chief of Police. The chief had mandated that the lights in Parker Center and every division station should never be off. His goal was to let the public know that the fight against crime never slept. The result was that the lights glowed brightly every night in empty police offices across the city.

Bosch flicked on the row of lights over the homicide table and went to his spot. There were a number of pink phone message slips and he looked through these, but all were from reporters or related to other cases he had pending. He tossed the reporters' messages in the trash can and put the others in his top drawer to follow up on the next day.

There were two department dispatch envelopes waiting on the desk for him. The first contained Golliher's report and Bosch put it aside for reading later. He picked up the second envelope and saw it was from SID. He realized he had forgotten to call Antoine Jesper about the skateboard.

He was about to open the envelope when he noticed it had been dropped on top of a folded piece of paper on his calendar blotter. He unfolded it and read the short message. He knew it was from Julia, though she had not signed it.

Where are you, tough guy?

He had forgotten that he had told her to come by the squad room before she started her shift. He smiled at the note but felt bad about forgetting. He also thought once more about Edgar's admonishment to be careful with the relationship.

He refolded the page and put it in his drawer. He wondered how Julia would react to what he wanted to talk about. He was dead tired from the long hours but didn't want to wait until the next day.

The dispatch envelope from SID contained a one-page evidence analysis report from Jesper. Bosch read the report quickly. Jesper had confirmed that the board was made by Boneyard Boards Inc., a Huntington Beach manufacturer. The model was called a 'Boney Board.' The particular model at hand was made from February 1978 until June 1986, when design variations created a slight change in the board's nose.

Before Bosch could get excited by the implications of a match between the board and the time frame of the case, he read the last paragraph of the report, which put any match in doubt.

The trucks (wheel assemblies) are of a design first implemented by Boneyard in May 1984. The graphite wheels also indicate a later manufacture. Graphite wheels did not become commonplace in the industry until the mid-80s. However, because trucks and wheels are interchangeable and often are traded out or replaced by boarders, it is impossible to determine the exact date of manufacture of the skateboard in evidence. Best estimate pending additional evidence is manufacture between February 1978 and June 1986.

Bosch slid the report back into the dispatch envelope and dropped it on the desk. The report was inconclusive but to Bosch the factors Jesper had outlined leaned toward the skateboard not having been Arthur Delacroix's. In his mind the report tilted toward clearing rather than implicating Nicholas Trent in the boy's death. In the morning he would type up a report with his conclusions and give it to Lt. Billets to send up the chain to Deputy Chief Irving's office.

As if to punctuate the end of this line of investigation, the sound of the back door to the station banging open echoed down the hallway. Several loud male voices followed, all heading out into the night. Roll call was over and fresh troops were taking the field, their voices full of us-versus-them bravado.

The police chief's wishes notwithstanding, Bosch flicked off the light and headed back down the hallway to the watch office. There were two sergeants in the small office. Lenkov was going off duty, while Renshaw was just starting her shift. They both registered surprise at Bosch's appearance so late at night but then didn't ask him what he was doing in the station.

'So,' Bosch said, 'anything on my guy, Johnny Stokes?'

'Nothing yet,' Lenkov said. 'But we're looking. We're putting it out at all roll calls and we've got the pictures in the cars now. So . . .'

'You'll let me know.'

'We'll let you know.'

Renshaw nodded her agreement.

Bosch thought about asking if Julia Brasher had come in to end her shift yet but thought better of it. He thanked them and stepped back into the hallway. The conversation had felt odd, like they couldn't wait for him to get out of there. He sensed it was because of the word getting around about him and Julia. Maybe they knew she was coming off of shift and wanted to avoid seeing them together. As supervisors they would then be witnesses to what was an infraction of department policy. As minor and rarely enforced as the rule was, things would be better all the way around if they didn't see the infraction and then have to look the other way.

Bosch walked out the back door and into the parking lot. He had no idea whether Julia was in the station locker room, still out on patrol or had come and gone already. Mid-shifts were fluid. You didn't come in until the watch sergeant sent your replacement out.

He found her car in the parking lot and knew he hadn't missed her. He walked back toward the station to sit down on the Code 7 bench. But when he got to it, Julia was already sitting there. Her hair was slightly wet from the locker room shower. She wore faded blue jeans and a long-sleeved pullover with a high neck.

'I heard you were in the house,' she said. 'I checked and saw the light out and thought maybe I'd missed you.'

'Just don't tell the chief about the lights.'

She smiled and Bosch sat down next to her. He wanted to touch her but didn't.

'Or us,' he said.

She nodded.

'Yeah. A lot of people know, don't they?'

'Yeah. I wanted to talk to you about that. Can you get a drink?'

'Sure.'

'Let's walk over to the Cat and Fiddle. I'm tired of driving today.'

Rather than walk through the station together and out the front door, they took the long way through the parking lot and around the station. They walked two blocks up to Sunset and then another two down to the pub. Along the way Bosch apologized for missing her in the squad room before her shift and explained he had driven to Palm Springs. She was very quiet as they walked, mostly just nodding her head at his explanations. They didn't talk about the issue at hand until they reached the pub and slid into one of the booths by the fireplace.

They both ordered pints of Guinness and then Julia folded her arms on the table and fixed Bosch with a hard stare.

'Okay, Harry, I've got my drink coming. You can give it to me. But I have to warn you, if you are going to say you want to just be friends, well, I already have enough friends.'

Bosch couldn't help but break into a broad smile. He loved her boldness, her directness. He started shaking his head.

'Nah, I don't want to be your friend, Julia. Not at all.'

He reached across the table and squeezed her forearm. Instinctively, he glanced around the pub to make sure no one from the cop shop had wandered over for an after-shift drink. He didn't recognize anyone and looked back at Julia.

'What I want is to be with you. Just like we've been.'

'Good. So do I.'

'But we have to be careful. You haven't been around the department long enough. I have and I know how things get around, and so it's my fault. We should've never left your car in the station lot that first night.'

'Oh, fuck 'em if they can't take a joke.'

'No, it's—'

He waited while the barmaid put their beers down on little paper coasters with the Guinness seal on them.

'It's not like that, Julia,' he said when they were alone again. 'If we're going to keep going, we need to be more careful. We have to go underground. No more meeting at the bench, no more notes, no more anything like that. We can't even go here anymore because cops come here. We have to be totally underground. We meet outside the division, we talk outside the division.'

'You make it sound like we're a couple of spies or something.'

Bosch picked up his glass, clicked it off hers and drank deeply from it. It tasted so good after such a long day. He immediately had to stifle a yawn, which Julia caught and repeated.

'Spies? That's not too far off. You forget, I've been in this department more than twenty-five years. You're just a boot, a baby. I've got more enemies inside the wire than you've got arrests under your belt. Some of these people would take any opportunity to put me down if they could. It sounds like I'm just worrying about myself here, but the thing is if they need to go after a rookie to get to me, they'll do it in a heartbeat. I mean that. A heartbeat.'

She turtled her head down and looked both ways.

'Okay, Harry – I mean, Secret Agent double-oh-forty-five.'

Bosch smiled and shook his head.

'Yeah, yeah, you think it's all a joke. Wait until you get your first IAD jacket. Then you'll see the light.'

'Come on, I don't think it's a joke. I'm just having fun.'

They both drank from their beers, and Bosch leaned back and tried to relax. The heat from the fireplace felt good. The walk over had been brisk. He looked at Julia and she was smiling like she knew a secret about him.

'What?'

'Nothing. You just get so worked up.'

'I'm trying to protect you, that's all. I'm plus-twenty-five, so it doesn't matter as much to me.'

'What does that mean? I've heard people say that – 'plus-twenty-five' – like they're untouchable or something.'

Bosch shook his head.

'Nobody's untouchable. But after you hit twenty-five years in, you top out on the pension scale. So it doesn't matter if you quit at twenty-five years or thirty-five years, you get the same pension. So "plus-twenty-five" means you have some fuck-you room. You don't like what they're doing to you, you can always pull the pin and say have a nice day. Because you're not in it for the check and the bennies anymore.'

The waitress came back to the table and put down a basket of popcorn. Julia let some time go by and then leaned across the table, her chin almost over the mouth of her pint.

'Then what are you in it for?'

Bosch shrugged his shoulders and looked down at his glass.

'The job, I guess. . . . Nothing big, nothing heroic. Just the chance to maybe make things right every now and then in a fucked-up world.'

He used his thumb to draw patterns on the frosted glass. He continued speaking without taking his eyes off the glass.

'This case, for example . . .'

'What about it?'

'If we can just figure it out and put it together . . . we can maybe make up a little bit for what happened to that kid. I don't know, I think it might mean something, something really small, to the world.'

He thought about the skull Golliher had held up to him that morning. A murder victim buried in tar for 9,000 years. A city of bones, and all of them waiting to come up out of the ground. For what? Maybe nobody cares anymore.

'I don't know,' he said. 'Maybe it doesn't mean anything in the long run. Suicide terrorists hit New York and three thousand people are dead before they've finished their first cup of coffee. What does one little set of bones buried in the past matter?'

She smiled sweetly and shook her head.

'Don't go existential on me, Harry. The important thing is that it means something to you. And if it means something to you, then it is important to do what you can. No matter what happens in the world, there will always be the need for heroes. I hope someday I get a chance to be one.'

'Maybe.'

He nodded and kept his eyes from hers. He played some more with his glass.

'Do you remember that commercial that used to be on TV, where there's this old lady who's on the ground or something and she says, "I've fallen and I can't get up," and everybody used to make fun of it?'

'I remember. They sell T-shirts that say that on Venice Beach.'

'Yeah, well . . . sometimes I feel like that. I mean, plus twenty-five. You can't go the distance without screwing up from time to time. You fall down, Julia, and sometimes you feel like you can't get up.'

He nodded to himself.

'But then you get lucky and a case comes along and you say to yourself, this is the one. You just feel it. This is the one I can get back up with.'

'It's called redemption, Harry. What's that song say, "Everybody wants a shot at it"?'

'Something like that. Yeah.'

'And maybe this case is your shot?'

'Yeah, I think it is. I hope so.'

'Then here's to redemption.'

She picked up her glass for a toast.

'Hold fast,' he said.

She banged it off of his. Some of her beer sloshed into his almost empty glass.

'Sorry. I need to practice that.'

'It's okay. I needed a refill.'

He raised his glass and drained it. He put it back down and wiped his mouth with the back of his hand.

'So are you coming home with me tonight?' he asked.

She shook her head.

'No, not with you.'

He frowned and started to wonder if his directness had offended her.

'I'm *following* you home tonight,' she said. 'Remember? Can't leave the car at the division. Everything's got to be top secret, hush-hush, eyes only from now on.'

He smiled. The beer and her smile were like magic on him.

'You got me there.'

'I hope in more ways than one.'

29

Bosch came in late to the meeting in Lt. Billets's office. Edgar was already there, a rarity, as well as Medina from Media Relations. Billets pointed him to a seat with a pencil she was holding, then picked up her phone and punched in a number.

'This is Lieutenant Billets,' she said when her call was answered. 'You can tell Chief Irving that we are all here now and ready to begin.'

Bosch looked at Edgar and raised his eyebrows. The deputy chief was still keeping his hand directly in the case.

Billets hung up and said, 'He's going to call back and I'll put him on the speaker.'

'To listen or to tell?' Bosch asked.

'Who knows?'

'While we're waiting,' Medina said, 'I've started getting a few calls about a BOLO you guys put out. A man named John Stokes? How do you want me to handle that? Is he a new suspect?'

Bosch was annoyed. He knew the Be on the Lookout flier distributed at roll calls would eventually leak to the media. He didn't anticipate it happening so quickly.

'No, he's not a suspect at all,' he said to Medina. 'And if the reporters screw that up like they did Trent, we'll never find him. He's just somebody we want to talk to. He was an acquaintance of the victim. Many years ago.'

'Then you have the victim's ID?'

Before Bosch could answer, the phone buzzed. Billets answered and put Deputy Chief Irving on the speaker.

'Chief, we have Detectives Bosch and Edgar here, along with Officer Medina from Media Relations.'

'Very good,' Irving's voice boomed from the phone's speaker. 'Where are we at?'

Billets started tapping a button on the phone to turn down the volume.

'Uh, Harry, why don't you take that?' she said.

Bosch reached into his inside coat pocket and took out his notebook. He took his time about it. He liked the idea of Irving sitting behind his spotless glass desk in his office at Parker Center, waiting for voices over the phone.

He opened the notebook to a page full of jottings he had made that morning while eating breakfast with Julia.

'Detective, are you there?' Irving said.

'Uh, yes, sir, I'm right here. I was just going through some notes here. Um, the main thing is we have made a positive identification of the victim. His name is Arthur Delacroix. He disappeared from his home in the Miracle Mile area on May fourth, nineteen eighty. He was twelve years old.'

He stopped there, anticipating questions. He noticed that Medina was writing the name down.

'I'm not sure we want to put that out yet,' Bosch said.

'Why is that?' Irving asked. 'Are you saying the identification is not positive?'

'No, we're positive on it, Chief. It's just that if we put the name out, we might be telegraphing which way we're moving here.'

'Which is?'

'Well, we are very confident that Nicholas Trent was clear on this. So we are looking elsewhere. The autopsy – the injuries to the bones – indicate chronic child abuse, dating to early childhood. The mother was out of the picture, so we are looking at the father now. We haven't approached him yet. We're gathering string. If we were to announce that we have an ID and the father saw it, we would be putting him on notice before we need to.'

'If he buried the kid there, then he already is on notice.'

'To a degree. But he knows if we can't come up with a legit ID we'll never link it to him. The lack of an ID is what keeps him safe. And it gives us time to look at him.'

'Understood,' Irving said.

They sat in silence for a few moments, Bosch expecting Irving to say something else. But he didn't. Bosch looked at Billets and spread his hands in a what-gives gesture. She shrugged her shoulders.

'So then . . .,' Bosch began, 'we're not putting it out, right?'

Silence. Then:

'I think that is the prudent course to follow,' Irving said.

Medina tore the page he had written on out of his notebook, crumpled it and tossed it into a trash can in the corner.

'Is there anything we *can* put out?' he asked.

'Yes,' Bosch said quickly. 'We can clear Trent.'

'Negative,' Irving said just as quickly. 'We do that at the end. When and if you make a case, then we will clean up the rest.'

Bosch looked at Edgar and then at Billets.

'Chief,' he said. 'If we do it that way, we could be hurting our case.'

'How so?'

'It's an old case. The older the case, the longer the shot. We can't take chances. If we don't go out there and tell them Trent is clear, we'll be giving the guy we eventually take down a defense. He'll be able to point at Trent and say he was a child molester, he did it.'

'But he will be able to do that, whether we clear Trent now or later.'

Bosch nodded.

'True. But I am looking at it from the standpoint of testifying at trial. I want to be able to say we checked Trent out and quickly dismissed him. I don't want some lawyer asking me why, if we so quickly dismissed him, we waited a week or two weeks to announce it. Chief, it will look like we were hiding something. It's going to be subtle but it will have an impact. People on juries look for any reason not to trust cops in general and the LAPD in par—'

'Okay, Detective, you have made your point. My decision still stands. There will be no announcement on Trent. Not at this time, not until we have a solid suspect we can come forward with.'

Bosch shook his head and slumped a bit in his seat.

'What else?' Irving said. 'I have a briefing with the chief in two minutes.'

Bosch looked at Billets and shook his head again. He had nothing else he wanted to share. Billets spoke up.

'Chief, at this time I think that's pretty much where we stand.'

'When do you plan to approach the father, Detectives?'

Bosch poked his chin at Edgar.

'Uh, Chief, Detective Edgar here. We are still looking for a witness that could be important to talk to before approaching the father. That would be a boyhood friend of the victim. We're thinking he might have knowledge of the abuse the boy suffered. We're planning to give it the day. We believe he's here in Hollywood and we have a lot of eyes out there on the—'

'Yes, that is fine, Detective. We will reconvene this conversation tomorrow morning.'

'Yes, Chief,' Billets said. 'At nine-thirty again?'

There was no answer. Irving was already gone.

30

Bosch and Edgar spent the rest of the morning updating reports and the murder book and calling hospitals all over the city to cancel the records searches they had requested by warrant on Monday morning. But by noon Bosch had had enough of the office work and said he had to get out of the station.

'Where you want to go?' Edgar asked.

'I'm tired of waiting around,' Bosch said. 'Let's go take a look at him.'

They used Edgar's personal car because it was unmarked and there were no undercover units left in the motor pool. They took the 101 up into the Valley and then the 405 north before exiting in Van Nuys. The Manchester Trailer Park was on Sepulveda near Victory. They drove by it once before coming back and driving in.

There was no gate house, just a yellow-striped speed bump. The park road circled the property, and Sam Delacroix's trailer was at the rear of the tract, where it bumped up against a twenty-foot-high sound-retention wall next to the freeway. The wall was designed to knock down the nonstop roar of the freeway. All it did was redirect and change its tone, but it was still there.

The trailer was a single-wide with rust stains dripping down the aluminum skin from most of the steel rivet seams. There was an awning with a picnic table and a charcoal grill beneath it. A clothesline ran from one of the awning's support poles to a corner of the next trailer in line. Near the back of the narrow yard an aluminum storage shed about the size of an outhouse was pushed up against the sound wall.

The windows and door of the trailer were closed. There was no vehicle in the lone parking spot. Edgar kept the car going by at an even five miles an hour.

'Looks like nobody's home.'

'Let's try the driving range,' Bosch said. 'If he's over there, maybe you can hit a bucket of balls or something.'

'Always like to practice.'

The range had few customers when they got there but it looked like it had been a busy morning. Golf balls littered the entire range, which was three hundred yards deep, extending to the same sound wall that backed the trailer park. At the far end of the property, netting was erected on high utility poles to protect the freeway drivers from long balls. A small tractor with ball harvesters attached at the rear was slowly traversing the far end of the range, its driver secured in a safety cage.

Bosch watched for a few moments alone until Edgar came up with a half bucket of balls and his golf bag, which had been in the trunk of his car.

'I guess that's him,' Edgar said.

'Yeah.'

Bosch went over to a bench and sat down to watch his partner hit some balls from a little square of rubber grass. Edgar had taken off his tie and jacket. He didn't look that much out of place. Hitting balls a few green squares down from him were two men wearing suit pants and button-down shirts, obviously using their lunch break from the office to fine-tune their game.

Edgar propped his bag on a wooden stand and chose one of the irons. He put on a glove, which he had taken from the bag, took a few warm-up swings and then started striking balls. The first few were grounders that made him curse. Then he started getting some air underneath them and he seemed pleased with himself.

Bosch was amused. He had never played golf a single time in his life and couldn't understand the draw it had for many men – in fact, most of the detectives in the squad room played religiously, and there was a whole network of police tournaments around the state. He enjoyed watching Edgar get worked up even though hitting range balls didn't count.

'Take a shot at him,' he instructed after he thought Edgar was fully warmed up and ready.

'Harry,' Edgar said. 'I know you don't play but I got news for you. In golf you hit the ball at the pin – the flag. No moving targets in golf.'

'Then how come the ex-presidents are always hitting people?'

'Because they're allowed to.'

'Come on, you said everybody tries to hit the guy in the tractor. Take a shot.'

'Everybody but the serious golfers.'

But he angled his body so that Bosch could tell he was going to take a shot at the tractor as it came to the end of a crossing and was making the U-turn to go back the other way. Judging by the yardage markers, the tractor was a hundred forty yards out.

Edgar swung but the ball was another grounder.

'Dammit! See, Harry? This could hurt my game.'

Bosch started laughing.

'What are you laughing at?'

'It's just a game, man. Take another shot.'

'Forget it. It's childish.'

'Take the shot.'

Edgar didn't say anything. He angled his body again, taking aim at the tractor, which was now in the middle of the range. He swung and hit the ball, sending it screaming down the middle but a good twenty feet over the tractor.

'Nice shot,' Bosch said. 'Unless you were aiming for the tractor.'

Edgar gave him a look but didn't say anything. For the next five minutes he hit ball after ball at the range tractor but never came closer to it than ten yards. Bosch never said anything but Edgar's frustrations increased until he turned and angrily said, 'You want to try?'

Bosch feigned confusion.

'Oh, you're still trying to hit him? I didn't realize.'

'Come on, let's go.'

'You still have half your balls there.'

'I don't care. This will set my game back a month.'

'That's all?'

Edgar angrily shoved the club he had been using into his bag and gave Bosch his dead-eye look. It was all Bosch could do not to burst into laughter.

'Come on, Jerry, I want to get a look at the guy. Can't you hit a few more? It looks like he's gotta be done soon.'

Edgar looked out at the range. The tractor was now near the fifty-yard markers. Assuming he had started back at the sound wall, he would be finished soon. There weren't enough new balls out there – just Edgar's and the two business guys' – to warrant going back over the entire range.

Edgar silently relented. He took out one of his woods and went back to the green square of fake grass. He hit a beautiful shot that almost carried to the sound wall.

'Tiger Woods, kiss my ass,' he said.

The next shot he put into the real grass ten feet from the tee.

'Shit.'

'When you play for real, do you hit off that fake grass?'

'No, Harry, you don't. This is practice.'

'Oh, so in practice you don't re-create the actual playing situation.'

'Something like that.'

The tractor pulled off the range and up to a shed behind the concession stand where Edgar had paid for his bucket of balls. The cage door opened and a man in his early sixties got out. He started pulling wire-mesh baskets full of balls out of the harvester and carrying them into the shed. Bosch told Edgar to keep hitting balls so that they wouldn't be obvious. Bosch nonchalantly walked toward the concession stand and bought another half bucket of balls. This put him no more than twenty feet from the man who had been driving the tractor.

It was Samuel Delacroix. Bosch recognized him from a driver's license photo Edgar had pulled and shown him. The man who once played a blond, blue-eyed Aryan soldier and had put a spell on an eighteen-year-old girl was now about as distinguished as a ham sandwich. He was still blond but it obviously came from a bottle and he was bald to the crown of his head. He had day-old whiskers that shone white in the sun. His nose was swollen by time and alcohol and pinched by a pair of ill-fitting glasses. He carried a beer paunch that would've been a ticket to a discharge in anybody's army.

'Two-fifty.'

Bosch looked at the woman behind the cash register.

'For the balls.'

'Right.'

He paid her and picked up the bucket by the handle. He took a last glance at Delacroix, who suddenly looked over at Bosch at the same time. Their eyes locked for a moment and Bosch casually looked away. He headed back toward Edgar. That was when his cell phone started to chirp.

He quickly handed the bucket to Edgar and pulled the phone out of his back pocket. It was Mankiewicz, the day-shift watch sergeant.

'Hey, Bosch, what are you doing?'

'Just hitting some balls.'

'Figures. You guys fuck off while we do all the work.'

'You found my guy?'

'We think so.'

'Where?'

'He's working at the Washateria. You know, picking up some tips, loose change.'

The Washateria was a car wash on La Brea. It employed day laborers to vacuum and wipe down cars. They worked mostly for tips and what they could steal out of the cars without getting caught.

'Who spotted him?'

'Couple guys from vice. They're eighty percent sure. They want to know if you want them to make the move or do you want to be on scene.'

'Tell them to sit tight and that we're on the way. And you know what, Mank? We think this guy's a rabbit. You got a unit we can use as an extra backup in case he runs?'

'Um . . .'

There was silence and Bosch guessed that Mankiewicz was checking his deployment chart.

'Well, you're in luck. I got a couple three-elevens starting early. They should be out of roll call in fifteen. That work for you?'

'Perfect. Tell them to meet us in the parking lot of the Checkers at La Brea and Sunset. Have the vice guys meet us there, too.'

Bosch signaled to Edgar that they were going to roll.

'Uh, one thing,' Mankiewicz said.

'What's that?'

'On the backup, one of them's Brasher. Is that going to be a problem?'

Bosch was silent a moment. He wanted to tell Mankiewicz to put somebody else on it but knew it was not his place to. If he tried to influence deployment or anything else based on his relationship with Brasher, then he could leave himself open to criticism and the possibility of an IAD investigation.

'No, no problem.'

'Look, I wouldn't do it but she's green. She's made a few mistakes and needs this kind of experience.'

'I said no problem.'

31

They planned the takedown of Johnny Stokes on the hood of Edgar's car. The vice guys, Eyman and Leiby, drew the layout of the Washateria on a legal pad and circled the spot where they had spotted Stokes working under the waxing canopy. The car wash was surrounded on three sides by concrete walls and other structures. The area fronting La Brea was almost fifty yards, with a five-foot retention wall running the border except for entry and exit lanes at each corner of the property. If Stokes decided to run, he could go to the retention wall and climb it, but it was more likely that he would go for one of the open lanes.

The plan was simple. Eyman and Leiby would cover the car wash entrance, and Brasher and her partner, Edgewood, would cover the exit. Bosch and Edgar would drive Edgar's car in as customers and make the move on Stokes. They switched their radios to a tactical unit and worked out a code; red meant Stokes had rabbitted, and green meant he had been taken peaceably.

'Remember something,' Bosch said. 'Almost every wiper, rubber, soaper and vacuum guy on that lot is probably running from something – even if it's just *la migra*. So even if we take Stokes without a problem, the others may rumble. Cops showing up at a car wash is like yelling fire in a theater. Everybody scatters till they see who's the one who's it.'

Everybody nodded and Bosch looked pointedly at Brasher, the rookie. In keeping with the plan agreed to the night before, they made no showing of knowing each other as anything other than fellow cops. But now he wanted to make sure she understood just how fluid a takedown like this could become.

'You got that, boot?' he said.

She smiled.

'Yeah, I got it.'

'All right, then let's concentrate. Let's go.'

He thought he saw the smile stay on Brasher's face as she and Edgewood walked to their patrol car.

He and Edgar walked to Edgar's Lexus. Bosch stopped when he got to it and realized that it looked like it had just been washed and waxed.

'Shit.'

'What can I say, Harry? I take care of my car.'

Bosch looked around. Behind the fast-food restaurant was an open Dumpster in a concrete alcove that had recently been washed down. There was a puddle of black water pooling on the pavement.

'Drive through that puddle a couple times,' he said. 'Get it on your car.'

'Harry, I'm not going to get that shit on my car.'

'Come on, your car has to look like it needs to be washed or it might be a tell. You said yourself, the guy's a rabbit. Let's not give him a reason.'

'But we're not actually going to get the car washed. I splash that shit on there, it stays there.'

'Tell you what, Jerry. If we get this guy, I'll have Eyman and Leiby drive him in while you get your car washed. I'll even pay for it.'

'Shit.'

'Come on, just drive through the puddle. We're wasting time.'

After messing up Edgar's car they made the drive to the car wash in silence. As they came up on it, Bosch could see the vice car parked at the curb a few car lengths from the car wash entrance. Further down the block past the car wash, the patrol unit was stopped in a lane of parked cars. Bosch went to his rover.

'Okay, everybody set?'

He got two return clicks on the mike from the vice guys. Brasher responded by voice.

'All ready.'

'Okay. We're going in.'

Edgar pulled into the car wash and drove into the service lane, where customers delivered their cars to the vacuum station and ordered the kind of wash or wax they wanted. Bosch's eyes immediately started moving among the workers, all of whom were dressed in identical orange jumpsuits and baseball caps. It slowed the identification process but Bosch soon saw the blue wax canopy and picked out Johnny Stokes.

'He's there,' he said to Edgar. 'On the black Beemer.'

Bosch knew that once they stepped out of the car most of the cons on the lot would be able to identify them as cops. In the same way Bosch could spot a con ninety-eight percent of the time, they in turn could spot a cop. He would have to move swiftly in on Stokes.

He looked over at Edgar.

'Ready?'

'Let's do it.'

They cracked the doors at the same time. Bosch got out and turned toward Stokes, who was twenty-five yards away with his back turned. He was crouched down and spraying something on the wheels of a black BMW. Bosch heard Edgar tell someone to skip the vacuum and that he'd be right back.

Bosch and Edgar had covered half the distance to their target when they were made by other workers on the lot. From somewhere behind him, Bosch heard a voice call out, 'Five-oh, five-oh, five-oh.'

Immediately alerted, Stokes stood up and started turning. Bosch started running.

He was fifteen feet from Stokes when the ex-con realized he was the target. His obvious escape was to his left and then out through the car wash entrance but the BMW was blocking him. He made a move to his right but then seemed to stop when he realized it was a dead end.

'No, no!' Bosch called out. 'We just want to talk, we just want to talk.'

Stokes visibly slumped. Bosch moved directly toward him while Edgar moved out to the right in case the ex-con decided to make a break.

Bosch slowed and opened his hands wide as he got close. One hand held his rover.

'LAPD. We just want to ask you a few questions, nothing else.'

'Man, about what?'

'About—'

Stokes suddenly raised his arm and sprayed Bosch in the face with the tire cleaner. He then bolted to his right, seemingly toward the dead end, where the high rear wall of the car wash joined the side wall of a three-story apartment building.

Bosch instinctively brought his hands up to his eyes. He heard Edgar yell at Stokes and then the scuffling sound of his shoes on concrete as he gave chase. Bosch couldn't open his eyes. He put his mouth to the radio and yelled, 'Red! Red! Red! He's heading toward the back corner.'

He then dropped the radio to the concrete, using his shoe to break its fall. He used the sleeves of his jacket to wipe at his burning eyes. He finally could open them for brief moments at a time. He spotted a hose coiled on a faucet near the rear of the BMW. He made his way to it, turned it on and doused his face and eyes, not caring how wet his clothes got. His eyes felt like they had been dropped in boiling water.

After a few moments the water eased the burning sensation and he dropped the hose without turning it off and went back to get the radio. His vision was blurred at the edges but he could see well enough to get moving. As he bent down for the radio he heard laughter from some of the other men in orange jumpsuits.

Bosch ignored it. He switched the rover to the Hollywood patrol channel and spoke into it.

'Hollywood units, officers in pursuit of assault suspect, La Brea and Santa Monica. Suspect white male, thirty-five YOA, dark hair, orange jumpsuit. Suspect in the vicinity of Hollywood Washateria.'

He couldn't remember the exact address of the car wash but wasn't worried. Every cop on patrol would know it. He switched the rover to the department's main communication channel and requested that a paramedic unit respond as well to treat an injured officer. He had no idea what had been sprayed into his eyes. They were beginning to feel better but he didn't want to take a chance on long-term injury.

Lastly, he switched back to the tactical channel and asked for the others' locations. Only Edgar came back up on the radio.

'There was a hole in the back corner. He went through to the alley. He's in one of these apartment complexes on the north side of the car wash.'

'Where are the others?'

Edgar's return was broken up. He was moving into a radio void.

'They're back ... spread out. I think ... garage. You ... ight, Harry?'

'I'll make it. Backup's on the way.'

He didn't know if Edgar had heard that. He put the rover in his pocket and hustled to the back corner of the car wash lot, where he found the hole Stokes had slipped through. Behind a two-high pallet of fifty-five-gallon drums of liquid soap, the concrete wall was broken in. It appeared that at one time a car in the alley on the other side had struck the wall, creating the hole. Intentionally done or not, it was probably a well-known escape hatch for every wanted man who worked at the car wash.

Bosch crouched down and slipped through, momentarily catching his jacket on a rusty piece of rebar protruding from the broken wall. On the other side he got up in an alley that ran behind rows of apartment buildings on either side for the length of the block.

The patrol car was stopped at an angle forty yards down the alley. It was empty, both doors open. Bosch could hear the sound of the main communications channel playing over the dash radio. Further down, at the end of the block, the vice car was parked across the alley.

He quickly moved down the alley toward the patrol car, looking and listening for anything. When he got to the car he pulled the rover out again and tried to raise someone on tactical. He got no response.

He saw the patrol car was parked in front of a ramp that dipped down into an underground garage beneath the largest of the apartment complexes on the alley. Remembering auto theft was in Edgar's recitation of Stokes's criminal record, Bosch suddenly knew that Stokes would go for the garage. His only way out was to get a car.

He trotted down the garage ramp into the dark.

The garage was huge and appeared to follow the imprint of the building above. There were three parking lanes and a ramp leading to an even lower level. Bosch saw no one. The only sound he heard was a dripping from the overhead pipes. He moved swiftly down the middle lane, drawing his weapon for the first time. Stokes had already fashioned a weapon out of a spray bottle. There was no telling what he might find in the garage to also use as a weapon.

As he moved, Bosch checked the few vehicles in the garage – everyone was at work, he guessed – for signs of break-in. He saw nothing. He was raising the rover to his mouth when he heard the sound of running footsteps echo up the ramp from the lower level of the garage. He quickly moved to the ramp and descended, careful to keep the rubber soles of his shoes as quiet as he could.

The lower garage was even darker, with less natural light finding its way down. As the incline leveled, his eyes adjusted. He saw no one, but the ramp structure blocked his view of half of the space. As he began his way around the ramp he suddenly heard a high and taut voice coming from the far end. It was Brasher's.

'Right there! Right there! Don't move!'

Bosch followed the sound, moving in tight to the side of the ramp and holding his weapon up. His training told him to call out, to alert the other officer to his presence. But he knew that if Brasher was alone with Stokes his calling might distract her and give Stokes another chance to break or make a move on her.

As he cut beneath the underside of the ramp, Bosch saw them at the far wall, no more than fifty feet away. Brasher had Stokes up against the wall, legs and arms spread. She held him there with one hand pressed against his back. Her flashlight was on the ground next to her right foot, its beam lighting the wall on which Stokes leaned.

It was perfect. Bosch felt relief flood his body and almost immediately he understood it was relief that she had not been hurt. He came out of the semi-crouch he was in and started toward them, lowering his weapon.

He was directly behind them. After he had taken only a few steps he saw Brasher take her hand off Stokes and step back from him, glancing to either side as she did it. This immediately registered with Bosch as the wrong thing to do. It was completely out of training. It would allow Stokes to make another run if he wanted to.

Things seemed to slow down then. Bosch started to yell to her but the garage suddenly filled with the flash and shattering blast of a gunshot. Brasher went down, Stokes remained up. The blast echo reverberated through the concrete structure, obscuring its origin.

All Bosch could think was, where is the gun?

He raised his weapon while lowering his body into a combat crouch. He started to turn his head to look for the gun. But he saw Stokes start turning from the wall. He then saw Brasher's arm rising up from the ground, her gun pointed at Stokes's turning body.

Bosch aimed his Glock at Stokes.

'Freeze!' he yelled. 'Freeze! Freeze! Freeze!'

In a second he was on them.

'Don't shoot, man,' Stokes yelled. 'Don't shoot!'

Bosch kept his eyes unwavering on Stokes. They still burned and needed relief but he knew even one blink now could be a fatal mistake.

'Down! Get on the ground. Now!'

Stokes dropped onto his stomach and spread his arms at ninety-degree angles to his body. Bosch stepped over him and with a move performed a thousand times before quickly cuffed his wrists behind his back.

He then holstered his weapon and turned to Brasher. Her eyes were wide and moving in a back-and-forth pattern. Blood had spattered onto her neck and had already soaked the front of her uniform shirt. He knelt over her and ripped open her shirt. Still, there was so much blood it took him a moment to find the wound. The bullet had entered her left shoulder, just an inch or so from the Velcro shoulder strap of her Kevlar vest.

The blood was flowing freely from the wound, and Bosch could see Brasher's face was losing color quickly. Her lips were moving but not making any sound. He looked around for something and saw a car wash rag poking out of Stokes's back pocket. He yanked it out and pressed it down on the wound. Brasher moaned in pain.

'Julia, this is going to hurt but I have to stop the bleeding.'

With one hand he stripped off his tie and pushed it under her shoulder and then over the top. He tied a knot that was just tight enough to keep the rag compress in place.

'Okay, hang on, Julia.'

He grabbed his rover off the ground and quickly switched the frequency knob to the main channel.

'CDC, officer down, lower-level garage at the La Brea Park apartments, La Brea and Santa Monica. We need paramedics right NOW! Suspect in custody. Confirm CDC.'

He waited for what seemed to be an interminable time before a CDC dispatcher came on the air to say he was breaking up and needed to repeat his call. Bosch clicked the call button and yelled, 'Where's my paramedics? Officer DOWN!'

He switched to tactical.

'Edgar, Edgewood, we're in the lower level of the garage. Brasher is down. I've got Stokes controlled. Repeat, Brasher is down.'

He dropped the radio and yelled Edgar's name as loud as he could. He took off his jacket and balled it together.

'Man, I didn't do it,' Stokes yelled. 'I don't know what—'

'Shut up! Shut the fuck up!'

Bosch put his jacket under Brasher's head. Her teeth were clenched in pain, her chin jutting upward. Her lips were almost white.

'Paramedics are coming, Julia. I called 'em before this even went down. I must be psychic or something. You just gotta hold on, Julia. Hold on.'

She opened her mouth, though it looked like a terrible struggle. But before she could say anything Stokes yelled out again in a voice now tinged with fear bordering on hysteria.

'I did not do that, man. Don't let them kill me, man. I didn't DO it!'

Bosch leaned over, putting his weight on Stokes's back. He bent down and spoke in a loud voice directly into his ear.

'Shut the fuck up or I'll kill you myself!'

He turned his attention back to Brasher. Her eyes were still open. Tears were going down her cheeks.

'Julia, just a few more minutes. You've got to hang on.'

He pulled the gun out of her right hand and put it on the ground, far away from Stokes. He then held her hand in both of his.

'What happened? What the hell happened?'

She opened and then closed her mouth again. Bosch could hear running feet on the ramp. He heard Edgar call his name.

'Over here!'

In a moment both Edgar and Edgewood were there.

'Julia!' Edgewood cried out. 'Oh, shit!'

Without a moment's hesitation Edgewood stepped forward and delivered a vicious kick to Stokes's side.

'You motherfucker!'

He readied himself to do it again when Bosch yelled.

'No! Get back! Get away from him!'

Edgar grabbed Edgewood and pulled him away from Stokes, who had let out a hurt animal cry at the impact of the kick and was now murmuring and moaning in fear.

'Take Edgewood up and get the paramedics down here,' Bosch said to Edgar. 'The rovers aren't for shit down here.'

Both of them seemed frozen.

'Go! Now!'

As if on cue, the sound of sirens could be heard in the distance.

'You want to help her? Go get them!'

Edgar turned Edgewood around and they both ran back toward the ramp.

Bosch turned back to Brasher. Her face was now the color of death. She was going into shock. Bosch didn't understand. It was a shoulder wound. He suddenly wondered if he had heard two shots. Had the blast and echo obscured a second shot? He checked her body again but found nothing. He didn't want to turn her to check her back for fear of causing more damage. But there was no blood coming from beneath her.

'Come on, hang in there, Julia. You can do it. You hear that? The paramedics are just about here. Just hang in there.'

She opened her mouth again, jutted her chin and started to speak.

'He . . . he grabbed . . . he went for . . .'

She clenched her teeth and rocked her head back and forth on his coat. She tried to talk again.

'It wasn't . . . I'm not . . .'

Bosch leaned his face close to hers and lowered his voice to an urgent whisper.

'Shhhh, shhhh. Don't talk. Just stay alive. Concentrate, Julia. Hold fast. Stay alive. Please, stay alive.'

He could feel the garage rumble with noise and vibration. In a moment red lights were bouncing off the walls and then a paramedic truck was pulling up next to them. A patrol cruiser was behind it and other uniformed officers, as well as Eyman and Leiby, were running down the ramp and flooding the garage.

'Oh God, oh please,' Stokes mumbled. 'Don't let it happen . . .'

The first paramedic reached them and the first thing he did was put a hand on Bosch's shoulder and gently push him back. Bosch went willingly, realizing he was only complicating things now. As he moved backward away from Brasher, her right hand suddenly grasped his forearm and pulled him back toward her. Her voice was now as thin as paper.

'Harry, don't let them—'

The paramedic put a breathing mask over her face and her words were lost.

'Officer, please get back,' the paramedic said firmly.

As Bosch crawled backward on hands and knees he reached over and gripped Brasher's ankle for a moment and squeezed it.

'Julia, you'll be all right.'

'Julia?' said the second paramedic as he crouched next to her with a large equipment case.

'Julia.'

'Okay, Julia,' the paramedic said. 'I'm Eddie and that there's Charlie. We're going to fix you up here. Like your buddy just said, you're going to be all right. But you gotta be tough for us. You gotta want it, Julia. You gotta fight.'

She said something that was garbled through the mask. Just one word but Bosch thought he recognized it. Numb.

The paramedics started stabilizing procedures, the one called Eddie talking to her all the while. Bosch got up and moved over to Stokes. He pulled him up into a standing position and pushed him away from the rescue scene.

'My ribs are broken,' Stokes complained. 'I need the paramedics.'

'Trust me, Stokes, there's nothing they can do about it. So just shut the fuck up.'

Two uniforms came up to them. Bosch recognized them from the other night when they had told Julia they would meet her at Boardner's. Her friends.

'We'll take him to the station for you.'

Bosch pushed Stokes past them without hesitation.

'No, I got him.'

'You need to stay here for OIS, Detective Bosch.'

They were right. The Officer Involved Shooting team would soon descend on the scene and Bosch would be questioned as a primary witness. But he wasn't putting Stokes into any hands he did not explicitly trust.

He walked Stokes up the ramp toward the light.

'Listen, Stokes, you want to live?'

The younger man didn't answer. He was walking with his upper body hunched forward because of the injury to his ribs. Bosch tapped him lightly in the spot Edgewood had kicked him. Stokes groaned loudly.

'Are you listening?' Bosch asked. 'Do you want to stay alive?'

'Yes! I want to stay alive.'

'Then you listen to me. I'm going to put you in a room and you don't talk to anybody but me. You understand that?'

'I understand. Just don't let them hurt me. I didn't do anything. I don't know what happened, man. She said get against the wall and I did what I was told. I swear to God all I did was—'

'Shut up!' Bosch ordered.

More cops were coming down the ramp and he just wanted to get Stokes out of there.

When they got to daylight, Bosch saw Edgar standing on the sidewalk talking on his cell phone and using his other hand to signal a transport ambulance into the parking garage. Bosch pushed Stokes toward him. As they approached, Edgar closed the phone.

'I just talked to the lieutenant. She's on the way.'

'Great. Where's your car?'

'Still at the car wash.'

'Go get it. We're taking Stokes to the division.'

'Harry, we can't just leave the scene of a—'

'You saw what Edgewood did. We need to get this shitbag to a place of safety. Go get your car. If we get any shit for it, I'll take it.'

'You got it.'

Edgar started running in the direction of the car wash.

Bosch saw a utility pole near the corner of the apartment building. He walked Stokes to it and recuffed him with his arms around it.

'Wait here,' he said.

He then stepped away and ran a hand through his hair.

'What the hell happened back there?'

He didn't realize he had spoken out loud until Stokes started answering the question, stammering about him not doing anything wrong.

'Shut up,' Bosch said. 'I wasn't talking to you.'

32

Bosch and Edgar walked Stokes through the squad room and down the short hallway leading to the interview rooms. They took him into room 3 and cuffed him to the steel ring bolted to the middle of the table.

'We'll be back,' Bosch said.

'Hey, man, don't leave me in here,' Stokes began. 'They'll come in here, man.'

'Nobody's coming in but me,' Bosch said. 'Just sit tight.'

They left the room and locked it. Bosch went to the homicide table. The squad room was completely empty. When a cop went down in the division everybody responded. It was part of keeping the faith in the blue religion. If it was you who went down, you'd want everybody coming. So you responded in kind.

Bosch needed a smoke, he needed time to think and he needed some answers. His mind was crowded with thoughts about Julia and her condition. But he knew it was out of his hands and the best way to control his thoughts was to concentrate on something still in his hands.

He knew he had little time before the OIS detail would pick up the trail and come for him and Stokes. He picked up the phone and called the watch office. Mankiewicz answered. He was probably the last cop in the station.

'What's the latest?' Bosch asked. 'How is she?'

'I don't know. I hear it's bad. Where are you?'

'In the squad. I've got the guy here.'

'Harry, what are you doing? OIS is all over this. You should be at the scene. Both of you.'

'Let's just say I was fearful of a deteriorating situation. Listen, let me know the minute you hear something about Julia, okay?'

'You got it.'

Bosch was about to hang up when he remembered something.

'And Mank, listen. Your guy Edgewood tried to kick the shit out of the suspect. He was cuffed and on the ground at the time. He's probably got four or five broken ribs.'

Bosch waited. Mankiewicz didn't say anything.

'Your choice. I can go formal with it or I can let you take care of it your way.'

'I'll take care of it.'

'All right. Remember, let me know what you know.'

He hung up and looked at Edgar, who nodded his approval on the way Bosch was handling the Edgewood matter.

'What about Stokes?' Edgar said. 'Harry, what the fuck happened in that garage?'

'I'm not sure. Listen, I'm going to go in there and talk to him about Arthur Delacroix, see what I can get before OIS storms the place and takes him away. When they get here, see if you can stall them.'

'Yeah, and this Saturday I'm planning to kick Tiger Woods's ass on Riviera.'

'Yeah, I know.'

Bosch went into the rear hallway and was about to enter room 3 when he realized he had not gotten his recorder back from Detective Bradley of IAD. He wanted to record his interview with Stokes. He walked past the door to room 3 and stepped into the adjoining video room. He turned on the room 3 camera and auxiliary recorder and then went back to room 3.

Bosch sat across from Stokes. The life appeared drained from the younger man's eyes. Less than an hour before he had been waxing a BMW, picking up a few bucks. Now he was looking at a return to prison – if he was lucky. He knew cop blood in the water brought out the blue sharks. Many were the suspects who were shot trying to escape or inexplicably hung themselves in rooms just like this. Or so it was explained to the reporters.

'Do yourself a big favor,' Bosch said. 'Calm the fuck down and don't do anything stupid. Don't do anything with these people that gets you killed. You understand me?'

Stokes nodded.

Bosch saw the package of Marlboros in the breast pocket of Stokes's jumpsuit. He reached across the table, causing Stokes to flinch.

'Relax.'

He took the pack of cigarettes and fired one up with a match from a book slipped behind the cellophane. From the corner of the room he pulled a small trash can next to his chair and dropped in the match.

'If I wanted to hurt you I would've done it in the garage. Thanks for the smoke.'

Bosch savored the smoke. It had been at least two months since he'd had a cigarette.

'Can I have one?' Stokes asked.

'No, you don't deserve one. You don't deserve shit. But I'm going to make a little deal with you here.'

Stokes raised his eyes to Bosch's.

'You know that little kick in the ribs you got back there? I'll trade you.

You forget about it and take it like a man and I'll forget about you spraying me in the face with that shit.'

'My ribs are broke, man.'

'My eyes still burn, man. That was a commercial cleaning chemical. The DA will be able to get assault on a police officer out of that faster than you can say five to ten in Corcoran. You remember being in the Cork, don't you?'

Bosch let that sink in for a long moment.

'So do we have a deal?'

Stokes nodded but said, 'What difference is it going to make? They're going to say I shot her. I—'

'But I know you didn't.'

Bosch saw a glimmer of hope returning to Stokes's eyes.

'And I will tell them exactly what I saw.'

'Okay.'

Stokes's voice was barely a whisper.

'So let's start at the start. Why'd you run?'

Stokes shook his head.

'Because it's what I do, man. I run. I'm a convict and you're the Man. I run.'

Bosch realized that in all of the confusion and haste, nobody had searched Stokes. He told him to stand up, which could only be accomplished by Stokes leaning over the table because of his shackled wrists. Bosch moved around behind him and started checking his pockets.

'You got any needles?'

'No, man, no needles.'

'Good, I don't want to get stuck. I get stuck and all deals are off.'

As he searched he held the cigarette in his lips. The smoke stung his already burning eyes. Bosch took out a wallet, a set of keys and roll of cash totaling $27 in ones. Stokes's tips for the day. There was nothing else. If Stokes had been carrying drugs for sale or personal use, he had tossed them while trying to make his escape.

'They'll be out there with dogs,' Bosch said. 'If you tossed a stash, they'll find it and there won't be anything I can do about it.'

'I didn't toss anything. If they find something, they planted it.'

'Yeah. Just like O.J.'

Bosch sat back down.

'What was the first thing I said to you? I said, "I just want to talk." It was the truth. All of this . . .'

Bosch made a sweeping gesture with his hands.

'It could have all been avoided if you had just listened.'

'Cops never want to talk. They always want something more.'

Bosch nodded. He had never been surprised by how accurate the street knowledge of ex-convicts was.

'Tell me about Arthur Delacroix.'

Confusion tightened Stokes's eyes.

'What? Who?'

'Arthur Delacroix. Your skateboard buddy. From the Miracle Mile days. Remember?'

'Jesus, man, that was—'

'A long time ago. I know. That's why I'm asking.'

'What about him? He's long gone, man.'

'Tell me about him. Tell me about when he disappeared.'

Stokes looked down at his cuffed hands and slowly shook his head.

'That was a long time ago. I can't remember that.'

'Try. Why did he disappear?'

'I don't know. He just couldn't take no more of the shit and ran away.'

'Did he tell you he was running away?'

'No, man, he just left. One day he was just gone. And I never saw him again.'

'What shit?'

'What do you mean?'

'You said he couldn't take any more of the shit and ran away. That shit. What are you talking about?'

'Oh, you know, like all the shit in his life.'

'Did he have trouble at home?'

Stokes laughed. He mocked Bosch in an imitation.

"Did he have trouble at home?' Like, who didn't, man?'

'Was he abused – physically abused – at home? is what I mean.'

Again, laughter.

'Who wasn't? My old man, he'd rather take a shot at me than talk to me about anything. When I was twelve he hit me from across the room with a full can of beer. Just because I ate a taco he wanted. They took me away from him for that.'

'You know, that's a real shame, but we're talking about Arthur Delacroix here. Did he ever tell you his father hit him?'

'He didn't have to, man. I saw the bruises. The guy always had a black eye is what I remember.'

'That was from skateboarding. He fell a lot.'

Stokes shook his head.

'Fuck that, man. Artie was the best. That's all he did. He was too good to get hurt.'

Bosch's feet were flat on the floor. He could tell by the sudden vibrations through his soles that there were people in the squad room now. He reached over and pushed the button lock on the doorknob.

'You remember when he was in the hospital? He'd hurt his head. Did he tell you that it was from a skateboarding accident?'

Stokes knitted his brow and looked down. Bosch had jogged loose a direct memory. He could tell.

'I remember he had a shaved head and stitches like a fucking zipper. I can't remember what he—'

Someone tried the door from the outside and then there was a harsh banging on the door. A muffled voice came through.

'Detective Bosch, this is Lieutenant Gilmore, OIS. Open the door.'

Stokes suddenly reared back, panic filling his eyes.

'No! Don't let them—'

'Shut up!'

Bosch leaned across the table, grabbed Stokes by the collar and pulled him forward.

'Listen to me, this is important.'

There was another knock on the door.

'Are you saying that Arthur never told you his father hurt him?'

'Look, man, take care of me here and I'll say whatever the fuck you want me to say. Okay? His father was an asshole. You want me to say Artie told me his father beat him with the goddamn broomstick, I'll say it. You want it to be a baseball bat? Fine, I'll say—'

'I don't want you to say anything but the truth, goddammit. Did he ever tell you that or not?'

The door came open. They had gotten a key from the drawer at the front desk. Two men in suits came in. Gilmore, whom Bosch recognized, and another OIS detective Bosch didn't recognize.

'All right, this is over,' Gilmore announced. 'Bosch, what the fuck are you doing?'

'Did he?' Bosch said to Stokes.

The other OIS detective took keys from his pocket and started taking the cuffs off of Stokes's wrists.

'I didn't do anything,' Stokes started to protest. 'I didn't—'

'Did he ever tell you?' Bosch yelled.

'Get him out of here,' Gilmore barked to the other detective. 'Put him in another room.'

The detective physically lifted Stokes from his seat and half carried, half pushed him out of the room. Bosch's cuffs remained on the table. Bosch stared blankly at them, thinking of the answers Stokes had given him and feeling a terrible weight on his chest from the knowledge that the whole thing had been a dead end. Stokes added nothing to the case. Julia had been shot and it was for nothing.

He finally looked up at Gilmore, who closed the door and then turned to face Bosch.

'Now, like I said, what the fuck were you doing, Bosch?'

33

Gilmore twiddled a pencil in his fingers, drumming the eraser on the table. Bosch never trusted an investigator who took notes in pencil. But that's what the Officer Involved Shooting team was all about, making stories and facts fit the picture the department wanted to present to the public. It was a pencil squad. To get it right often meant using the pencil and eraser, never ink, never a tape recorder.

'So we're going to go over this again,' he said. 'Tell me once more, what did Officer Brasher do?'

Bosch looked past him. He had been moved to the suspect's chair in the interview room. He was facing the mirror – the one-way glass behind which he was sure there were at least a half dozen people, probably including Deputy Chief Irving. He wondered if anybody had noticed that the video had been running. If they had, it would have immediately been shut off.

'Somehow she shot herself.'

'And you saw this.'

'Not exactly. I saw it from the rear. Her back was to me.'

'Then how do you know she shot herself?'

'Because there was no one else there but her, me and Stokes. I didn't shoot her and Stokes didn't shoot her. She shot herself.'

'During the struggle with Stokes.'

Bosch shook his head.

'No, there was no struggle at the moment of the shooting. I don't know what happened before I got there, but at the moment of the shooting Stokes had both hands flat on the wall and his back to her when the gun went off. Officer Brasher had her hand on his back, holding him in place. I saw her step back from him and drop her hand. I didn't see the gun but I then heard the shot and saw the flash originate in front of her. And she went down.'

Gilmore drummed his pencil loudly on the table.

'That's probably messing up the recording,' Bosch said. 'Oh, that's right, you guys never put anything on tape.'

'Never mind that. Then what happened?'

'I started moving toward them at the wall. Stokes started to turn to see what had happened. From the ground Officer Brasher raised her right arm and took aim with her weapon at Stokes.'

'But she didn't fire, did she?'

'No. I yelled 'Freeze!' to Stokes and she did not fire and he did not move. I then moved to the scene and put Stokes on the ground. I handcuffed him. I then used the radio to call for help and tried to tend to Officer Brasher's wound as best I could.'

Gilmore was also chewing gum in a loud way that annoyed Bosch. He worked it for several chews before speaking.

'See, what I'm not getting here is why would she shoot herself?'

'You'll have to ask her that. I'm only telling you what I saw.'

'Yeah, but I'm asking you. You were there. What do you think?'

Bosch waited a long moment. Things had happened so fast. He had put off thinking about the garage by concentrating on Stokes. Now the images of what he had seen kept replaying in his mind. He finally shrugged.

'I don't know.'

'I'll tell you what, let's go your way with it for a minute. Let's assume she was re-holstering her weapon – which would have been against procedures, but let's assume it for the sake of argument. She's reholstering so she can cuff the guy. Her holster is on her right hip and the entry wound is on the left shoulder. How does that happen?'

Bosch thought about Brasher's questioning him a few nights earlier about the scar on his left shoulder. About being shot and what it had felt like. He felt the room closing in, getting tight on him. He started sweating.

'I don't know,' he said.

'You don't know very much, do you, Bosch?'

'I only know what I saw. I told you what I saw.'

Bosch wished they hadn't taken away Stokes's pack of cigarettes.

'What was your relationship with Officer Brasher?'

Bosch looked down at the table.

'What do you mean?'

'From what I hear you were fucking her. That's what I mean.'

'What's it have to do with anything?'

'I don't know. Maybe you tell me.'

Bosch didn't answer. He worked hard not to show the fury building inside.

'Well, first off, this relationship of yours was a violation of department policy,' Gilmore said. 'You know that, don't you?'

'She's in patrol. I'm in detective services.'

'You think that matters? That doesn't matter. You're a D-three. That's supervisor level. She's a grunt and a rookie no less. If this was the military you'd get a dishonorable just for starters. Maybe even some custody time.'

'But this is the LAPD. So what's it get me, a promotion?'

That was the first offensive move Bosch had made. It was a warning to

Gilmore to go another way. It was a veiled reference to several well-known and not so well-known dalliances between high-ranking officers and members of the rank and file. It was known that the police union, which represented the rank and file to the level of sergeant, was waiting with the goods ready to challenge any disciplinary action taken under the department's so-called sexual harassment policy.

'I don't need any smart remarks from you,' Gilmore said. 'I'm trying to conduct an investigation here.'

He followed this with an extended drum roll while he looked at the few notes he had written on his pad. What he was doing, Bosch knew, was conducting a reverse investigation. Start with a conclusion and then gather only the facts that support it.

'How are your eyes?' Gilmore finally asked without looking up.

'One of them still stings like a son of a bitch. They feel like poached eggs.'

'Now, you say that Stokes hit you in the face with a shot from his bottle of cleaner.'

'Correct.'

'And it momentarily blinded you.'

'Correct.'

Now Gilmore stood up and started pacing in the small space behind his chair.

'How long between the moment you were blinded and when you were down in that dark garage and supposedly saw her shoot herself?'

Bosch thought for a moment.

'Well, I used a hose to wash my eyes, then I followed the pursuit. I would say not more than five minutes. But not too much less.'

'So you went from blind man to eagle scout – able to see everything – inside of five minutes.'

'I wouldn't characterize it like that but you have the time right.'

'Well, at least I got something right. Thank you.'

'No problem, Lieutenant.'

'So you're saying you didn't see the struggle for control of Officer Brasher's gun before the shot occurred. Is that correct?'

He had his hands clasped behind his back, the pencil between two fingers like a cigarette. Bosch leaned across the table. He understood the game of semantics Gilmore was playing.

'Don't play with the words, Lieutenant. There was no struggle. I saw no struggle because there was no struggle. If there had been a struggle I would have seen it. Is that clear enough for you?'

Gilmore didn't respond. He kept pacing.

'Look,' Bosch said, 'why don't you just go do a GSR test on Stokes? His hands, his jumpsuit. You won't find anything. That should end this pretty quick.'

Gilmore came back to his chair and leaned down on it. He looked at Bosch and shook his head.

'You know, Detective, I would love to do that. Normally in a situation like this, first thing we'd do is look for gunshot residue. The problem is, you broke the box. You took it upon yourself to take Stokes out of the crime scene and bring him back here. The chain of evidence was broken, you understand that? He could've washed himself, changed his clothes, I don't know what else, because you took it upon yourself to take him from the crime scene.'

Bosch was ready for that.

'I felt there was a safety issue there. My partner will back me on that. So will Stokes. And he was never out of my custody and control until you came busting in here.'

'That doesn't change the fact that you thought your case was more important than us getting the facts about a shooting of an officer of this department, does it?'

Bosch had no answer for that. But he was now coming to a full understanding of what Gilmore was doing. It was important for him and the department to conclude and be able to announce that Brasher was shot during a struggle for control of her gun. It was heroic that way. And it was something the department public relations machine could take advantage of and run with. There was nothing like the shooting of a good cop – a female rookie, no less – in the line of duty to help remind the public of all that was good and noble about their police department and all that was dangerous about the police officer's duty.

The alternative, to announce that Brasher had shot herself accidentally – or even something worse – would be an embarrassment for the department. One more in a long line of public relations fiascos.

Standing in the way of the conclusion Gilmore – and therefore Irving and the department brass – wanted was Stokes, of course, and then Bosch. Stokes was no problem. A convicted felon facing prison time for shooting a cop, whatever he said would be self-serving and unimportant. But Bosch was an eyewitness with a badge. Gilmore had to change his account or failing that, taint it. The first soft spot to attack was Bosch's physical condition – considering what had been thrown in his eyes, could he actually have seen what he claimed to have seen? The second move was to go after Bosch the detective. In order to preserve Stokes as a witness in his murder case, would Bosch go so far as to lie about seeing Stokes shoot a cop?

To Bosch, it was so outlandish as to be bizarre. But over the years he had seen even worse things happen to cops who had stepped in front of the machinery that produced the image of the department that was delivered to the public.

'Wait a minute, you – ' Bosch said, able to hold himself from calling a superior officer an expletive. 'If you're trying to say I would lie about Stokes shooting Julia – uh, Officer Brasher – so he would stay in the clear for my case, then you – with all due respect – are out of your fucking mind.'

'Detective Bosch, I am exploring all possibilities here. It is my job to do so.'

'Well, you can explore them without me.'

Bosch stood up and went to the door.

'Where are you going?'

'I'm done with this.'

He glanced at the mirror and opened the door, then looked back at Gilmore.

'I got news for you, Lieutenant. Your theory is for shit. Stokes is nothing to my case. A zero. Julia getting shot, it was for nothing.'

'But you didn't know that until you got him in here, did you?'

Bosch looked at him and then slowly shook his head.

'Have a good day, Lieutenant.'

He turned to go through the door and almost stepped into Irving. The deputy chief stood ramrod straight in the hallway outside the room.

'Step back inside for a moment, Detective,' he said calmly. 'Please.'

Bosch backed into the room. Irving followed him in.

'Lieutenant, give us some space here,' the deputy chief said. 'And I want everyone out of the viewing room as well.'

He pointed at the mirror as he said this.

'Yes, sir,' Gilmore said and he left the room, closing the door behind him.

'Take your seat again,' Irving said.

Bosch moved back to the seat facing the mirror. Irving remained standing. After a moment he also started pacing, moving back and forth in front of the mirror, a double image for Bosch to track.

'We are going to call the shooting accidental,' Irving said, not looking at Bosch. 'Officer Brasher apprehended the suspect and while reholstering her weapon inadvertently fired the shot.'

'Is that what she said?' Bosch asked.

Irving looked momentarily confused, then shook his head.

'As far as I know, she only spoke to you and you said she didn't say anything specifically in regard to the shooting.'

Bosch nodded.

'So that's the end of it?'

'I don't see why it should go any further.'

Bosch thought of the photo of the shark on Julia's mantel. About what he knew about her in such a short time with her. Again the images of what he saw in the garage played back in slow motion. And things didn't add up.

'If we can't be honest with ourselves, how can we ever tell the truth to the people out there?'

Irving cleared his throat.

'I am not going to debate things with you, Detective. The decision has been made.'

'By you.'

'Yes, by me.'

'What about Stokes?'

'That will be up to the District Attorney's Office. He could be charged under the felony-murder law. His action of fleeing ultimately led to the shooting. It will get technical. If it is determined he was already in custody when the fatal shot occurred, then he might be able to – '

'Wait a minute, wait a minute,' Bosch said, coming out of his chair. 'Felony-*murder* law? Did you say *fatal* shot?'

Irving turned to face him.

'Lieutenant Gilmore did not tell you?'

Bosch dropped back into the chair and put his elbows on the table. He covered his face with his hands.

'The bullet hit a bone in her shoulder and apparently ricocheted inside her body. It cut through her chest. Pierced her heart. And she was dead on arrival.'

Bosch lowered his face so that his hands were now on top of his head. He felt himself get dizzy and he thought he might fall out of the chair. He tried to breathe deeply until it passed. After a few moments Irving spoke into the darkness of his mind.

'Detective, there are some officers in this department they call "shit magnets." I am sure you have heard the term. Personally, I find the phrase distasteful. But its meaning is that things always seem to happen to these particular officers. Bad things. Repeatedly. Always.'

Bosch waited in the dark for what he knew was coming.

'Unfortunately, Detective Bosch, you are one of those officers.'

Bosch unconsciously nodded. He was thinking about the moment that the paramedic put the breathing mask over Julia's mouth as she was speaking.

Don't let them—

What did she mean? Don't let them what? He was beginning to put things together and to know what she was going to say.

'Detective,' Irving said, his strong voice cutting through Bosch's thoughts. 'I have shown tremendous patience with you over the cases and over the years. But I have grown tired of it. So has this department. I want you to start thinking about retirement. Soon, Detective. Soon.'

Bosch kept his head down and didn't respond. After a moment he heard the door open and close.

34

In keeping with the wishes of Julia Brasher's family that she be buried in accordance with her faith, her funeral was late the next morning at Hollywood Memorial Park. Because she had been killed accidentally while in the line of duty, she was accorded the full police burial ceremony, complete with motorcycle procession, honor guard, twenty-one-gun salute and a generous showing of the department's brass at graveside. The department's aero squadron also flew over the cemetery, five helicopters flying in 'missing man' formation.

But because the funeral was not even twenty-four hours after her death it was not well attended. Line-of-duty deaths routinely bring at least token representations of officers from departments all over the state and the southwest. It was not to be with Julia Brasher. The quickness of the ceremony and the circumstances of her death added up to it being a relatively small affair – by police burial standards. A death in a gun battle would have crowded the small cemetery from stone to stone with the trappings of the blue religion. A cop killing herself while holstering her weapon did not engender much of the mythology and danger of police work. The funeral simply wasn't a draw.

Bosch watched from the outer edges of the funeral group. His head was throbbing from a night of drinking and trying to dull the guilt and pain he felt. Bones had come out of the ground and now two people were dead for reasons that made little sense to him. His eyes were badly bloodshot and swollen but he knew he could pass that off, if he had to, to being sprayed with the tire cleaner by Stokes the day before.

He saw Teresa Corazon, for once without her video-grapher, seated in the front row line of brass and dignitaries, what few of them there were in attendance. She wore sunglasses but Bosch could tell when she had noticed him. Her mouth seemed to settle into a hard, thin line. A perfect funeral smile.

Bosch was the first to look away.

It was a beautiful day for a funeral. Brisk overnight winds from the Pacific had temporarily cleared the smog out of the sky. Even the view of the Valley from Bosch's home had been clear that morning. Cirrus clouds scudded across the upper reaches of the sky along with contrails left by high-flying jets. The air in the cemetery smelled sweet from all the flowers arranged near the grave. From his standpoint, Bosch could see the crooked letters of the Hollywood sign, high up on Mount Lee, presiding over the service.

The chief of police did not deliver the eulogy as was his custom in line-of-duty deaths. Instead, the academy commander spoke, using the moment to talk about how danger in police work always comes from the unexpected corner and how Officer Brasher's death might save other cops by being a reminder never to let down the guard of caution. He never called her anything but Officer Brasher during his ten-minute speech, giving it an embarrassingly impersonal touch.

During the whole thing Bosch kept thinking about photos of sharks with open mouths and volcanoes disgorging their molten flows. He wondered if Julia had finally proven herself to the person she believed she needed to.

Amidst the blue uniforms surrounding the silver casket was a swath of gray. The lawyers. Her father and a large contingent from the firm. In the second row behind Brasher's father Bosch could see the man from the photo on the mantel of the Venice bungalow. For a while Bosch fantasized about going up to him and slapping him or bringing a knee up into his genitals. Doing it right in the middle of the service for all to see, then pointing to the casket and telling the man that he sent her on the path to this.

But he let it go. He knew that explanation and assignment of blame was too simple and wrong. Ultimately, he knew, people chose their own path. They can be pointed and pushed, but they always get the final choice. Everybody's got a cage that keeps out the sharks. Those who open the door and venture out do so at their own risk.

Seven members of Brasher's rookie class were chosen for the salute. They pointed rifles toward the blue sky and fired three rounds of blanks each, the ejected brass jackets arcing through the light and falling to the grass like tears. While the shots were still echoing off the stones, the helicopters made their pass overhead and then the funeral was over.

Bosch slowly made his way toward the grave, passing people heading away. A hand tugged his elbow from behind and he turned around. It was Brasher's partner, Edgewood.

'I, uh, just wanted to apologize about yesterday, about what I did,' he said. 'It won't happen again.'

Bosch waited for him to make eye contact and then just nodded. He had nothing to say to Edgewood.

'I guess you didn't mention it to OIS and I, uh, just want to say I appreciate it.'

Bosch just looked at him. Edgewood became uncomfortable, nodded once and walked away. When he was gone Bosch found himself looking at a woman who had been standing right behind the cop. A Latina with silver hair. It took Bosch a moment to recognize her.

'Dr. Hinojos.'

'Detective Bosch, how are you?'

It was the hair. Almost seven years earlier, when Bosch had been a regular visitor to Hinojos's office, her hair had been a deep brown without a hint of gray. She was still an attractive woman, gray or brown. But the change was startling.

'I'm doing okay. How're things in the psych shop?'

She smiled.

'They're fine.'

'I hear you run the whole show now.'

She nodded. Bosch felt himself getting nervous. When he had known her before, he had been on an involuntary stress leave. In twice-a-week sessions he had told her things he had never told anyone before or since. And once he was returned to duty he had never spoken to her again.

Until now.

'Did you know Julia Brasher?' he asked.

It wasn't unusual for a department shrink to attend a line-of-duty funeral; to offer on-the-spot counseling to those close to the deceased.

'No, not really. Not personally. As head of the department I reviewed her academy application and screening interview. I signed off on it.'

She waited a moment, studying Bosch for a reaction.

'I understand you were close to her. And that you were there. You were the witness.'

Bosch nodded. People leaving the funeral were passing on both sides of them. Hinojos took a step closer to him so that she would not be overheard.

'This is not the time or place but, Harry, I want to talk to you about her.'

'What's there to talk about?'

'I want to know what happened. And why.'

'It was an accident. Talk to Chief Irving.'

'I have and I'm not satisfied. I doubt you are, either.'

'Listen, Doctor, she's dead, okay? I'm not going to—'

'I signed off on her. My signature put that badge on her. If we missed something – if I missed something – I want to know. If there were signs, we should have seen them.'

Bosch nodded and looked down at the grass between them.

'Don't worry, there were signs I should've seen. But I didn't put it together either.'

She took another step closer. Now Bosch could look nowhere but directly at her.

'Then I am right. There is something more to this.'

He nodded.

'Nothing overt. It's just that she lived close to the edge. She took risks –

she crossed the tube. She was trying to prove something. I don't think she was even sure she wanted to be a cop.'

'Prove something to who?'

'I don't know. Maybe herself, maybe somebody else.'

'Harry, I knew you as a man of great instincts. What else?'

Bosch shrugged.

'It's just things she did or said. . . . I have a scar on my shoulder from a bullet wound. She asked me about it. The other night. She asked how I got shot and I told her how I had been lucky that it hit me where it did because it was all bone. Then . . . where she shot herself, it's the same spot. Only with her . . . it ricocheted. She didn't expect that.'

Hinojos nodded and waited.

'What I've been thinking I can't stand thinking, know what I mean?'

'Tell me, Harry.'

'I keep replaying it in my head. What I saw and what I know. She pointed her gun at him. And I think if I hadn't been there and yelled that maybe she would have shot him. Once he was down she would have wrapped his hands around the gun and fired a shot into the ceiling or maybe a car. Or maybe into him. It wouldn't matter as long as he ended up dead with paraffin on his hands and she could claim he went for her gun.'

'What are you suggesting, that she shot herself in order to kill him and make herself look like a hero?'

'I don't know. She talked about the world needing heroes. Especially now. She said she hoped to get a chance to be a hero one day. But I think there was something else in all of this. It was like she wanted the scar, the experience of it.'

'And she was willing to kill for it?'

'I don't know. I don't know if I'm even right about any of this. All I know is that she might have been a rookie but she had already reached the point where there was a line between us and them, where everybody without a badge is a scumbag. She saw it happening to herself. She might have been just looking for a way out . . .'

Bosch shook his head and looked off to the side. The cemetery was almost deserted now.

'I don't know. Saying it out loud makes it sound . . . I don't know. It's a crazy world.'

He took a step back from Hinojos.

'I guess you never really know anybody, do you?' he asked. 'You might think you do. You might be close enough to sleep with somebody but you'll never know what's really going on inside.'

'No, you won't. Everybody's got secrets.'

Bosch nodded and was about to step away.

'Wait, Harry.'

She lifted her purse and opened it. She started digging through it.

'I still want to talk about this,' she said as she came out with a business card and handed it to him. 'I want you to call me. Completely unofficial, confidential. For the good of the department.'

Bosch almost laughed.

'The department doesn't care about it. The department cares about the image, not the truth. And when the truth endangers the image, then fuck the truth.'

'Well, I care, Harry. And so do you.'

Bosch looked down at the card and nodded and put it in his pocket.

'Okay, I'll call you.'

'My cell phone's on there. I carry it with me all the time.'

Bosch nodded. She stepped forward and reached out. She grasped his arm and squeezed it.

'What about you, Harry? Are you okay?'

'Well, other than losing her and being told by Irving to start thinking about retiring, I'm doing okay.'

Hinojos frowned.

'Hang in there, Harry.'

Bosch nodded, thinking about how he had used the same words with Julia at the end.

Hinojos went off and Bosch continued his trek to the grave. He thought he was alone now. He grabbed a handful of dirt from the fill mound and walked over and looked down. A whole bouquet and several single flowers had been dropped on top of the casket. Bosch thought about holding Julia in his bed just two nights before. He wished he had seen what was coming. He wished he had been able to take the hints and put them into a clear picture of what she was doing and where she was going.

Slowly, he raised his hand out and let the dirt slide through his fingers.

'City of bones,' he whispered.

He watched the dirt fall into the grave like dreams disappearing.

'I assume you knew her.'

Bosch quickly turned. It was her father. Smiling sadly. They were the only two left in the cemetery. Bosch nodded.

'Just recently. I got to know her. I'm sorry for your loss.'

'Frederick Brasher.'

He put out his hand. Bosch started to take it but then held up.

'My hand's dirty.'

'Don't worry. So is mine.'

They shook hands.

'Harry Bosch.'

Brasher's hand stopped its shaking movement for a moment as the name registered.

'The detective,' he said. 'You were there yesterday.'

'Yes. I tried . . . I did what I could to help her. I . . .'

He stopped. He didn't know what to say.

'I'm sure you did. It must've been an awful thing to be there.'

Bosch nodded. A wave of guilt passed through him like an X-ray lighting his bones. He had left her there, thinking she would be all right. Somehow it hurt almost as bad as the fact she had died.

'What I don't understand is how it happened,' Brasher said. 'A mistake like that, how could it kill her? And then the District Attorney's Office today saying this man Stokes would not face any charge in the shooting. I'm a lawyer but I just don't understand. They are letting him go.'

Bosch studied the older man, saw the misery in his eyes.

'I'm sorry, sir. I wish I could tell you. I have the same questions as you.'

Brasher nodded and looked into the grave.

'I'm going now,' he said after a long moment. 'Thank you for coming, Detective Bosch.'

Bosch nodded. They shook hands again and Brasher started to walk away.

'Sir?' Bosch asked.

Brasher turned back.

'Do you know when someone from the family will be going to her house?'

'Actually, I was given her keys today. I was going to go now. Take a look at things. Try to get a sense of her, I guess. In recent years we hadn't . . .'

He didn't finish. Bosch stepped closer to him.

'There's something that she had. A picture in a frame. If it's not . . . if it's okay with you, I'd like to keep it.'

Brasher nodded.

'Why don't you come now? Meet me there. Show me this picture.'

Bosch looked at his watch. Lt. Billets had scheduled a one-thirty meeting to discuss the status of the case. He probably had just enough time to make it to Venice and back to the station. There would be no time for lunch but he couldn't see himself eating anything anyway.

'Okay, I will.'

They parted and headed toward their cars. On the way Bosch stopped on the grass where the salute had been fired. Combing the grass with his foot, he looked until he saw the glint of brass and bent down to pick up one of the ejected rifle shells. He held it on his palm and looked at it for a few moments, then closed his hand and dropped it into his coat pocket. He had picked up a shell from every cop funeral he had ever attended. He had a jar full of them.

He turned and walked out of the cemetery.

35

Jerry Edgar had a warrant knock that sounded like no other Bosch had ever heard. Like a gifted athlete who can focus the forces of his whole body into the swinging of a bat or the dunking of a basketball, Edgar could put his whole weight and six-foot-four frame into his knock. It was as though he could call down and concentrate all the power and fury of the righteous into the fist of his large left hand. He'd plant his feet firmly and stand sideways to the door. He'd raise his left arm, bend the elbow to less than thirty degrees and hit the door with the fleshy side of his fist. It was a backhand knock, but he was able to fire the pistons of this muscle assembly so quickly that it sounded like the staccato bark of a machine gun. What it sounded like was Judgment Day.

Samuel Delacroix's aluminum-skinned trailer seemed to shudder from end to end when Edgar hit its door with his fist at 3:30 on Thursday afternoon. Edgar waited a few seconds and then hit it again, this time announcing 'POLICE!' and then stepping back off the stoop, which was a stack of unconnected concrete blocks.

They waited. Neither had a weapon out but Bosch had his hand under his jacket and was gripping his gun in its holster. It was his standard procedure when delivering a warrant on a person not believed to be dangerous.

Bosch listened for movements from inside but the hiss from the nearby freeway was too loud. He checked the windows; none of the closed curtains were moving.

'You know,' Bosch whispered, 'I'm starting to think it comes as a relief when you yell it's just the cops after that knock. At least then they know it's not an earthquake.'

Edgar didn't respond. He probably knew it was just nervous banter from Bosch. It wasn't anxiety about the door knock – Bosch fully expected Delacroix to be easy. He was anxious because he knew the case was all coming down to the next few hours with Delacroix. They would search the trailer and then have to make a decision, largely communicated in partners' code, on whether to arrest Delacroix for his son's murder. Somewhere in that process they would need to find the evidence or elicit the confession that would change a case largely built on theory into one built on lawyer-resistant fact.

So in Bosch's mind they were quickly approaching the moment of truth, and that always made him nervous.

Earlier, in the case status meeting with Lt. Billets, it had been decided that it was time to talk to Sam Delacroix. He was the victim's father, he was the chief suspect. What little evidence they had still pointed to him. They spent the next hour typing up a search warrant for Delacroix's trailer and taking it to the downtown criminal courts building to a judge who was normally a soft touch.

But even this judge took some convincing. The problem was the case was old, the evidence directly linking the suspect was thin and the place Bosch and Edgar wanted to search was not where the homicide could have occurred and was not even occupied by the suspect at the time of the death.

What the detectives had in their favor was the emotional impact that came from the list in the warrant of all the injuries that the boy's bones indicated he had sustained over his short life. In the end, it was all those fractures that won the judge over and he signed the warrant.

They had gone to the driving range first but were informed that Delacroix was finished driving the tractor for the day.

'Give him another shot,' Bosch told Edgar outside the trailer.

'I think I can hear him coming.'

'I don't care. I want him rattled.'

Edgar stepped back up onto the stoop and hit the door again. The concrete blocks wobbled and he didn't plant his feet firmly. The resulting knock didn't carry the power and terror of the first two assaults on the door.

Edgar stepped back down.

'That wasn't the police,' Bosch whispered. 'That was a neighbor complaining about the dog or something.'

'Sorry, I—'

The door came open and Edgar shut up. Bosch went into high alert. Trailers were tricky. Unlike most structures, their doors opened outward so that the interior space didn't have to accommodate the swing. Bosch was positioned on the blind side, so that whoever answered was looking at Edgar but couldn't see Bosch. The problem was Bosch couldn't see whoever had opened the door either. If there was trouble Edgar's job was to yell a warning to Bosch and get himself clear. Without hesitation Bosch would empty his gun into the door of the trailer, the bullets tearing through the aluminum and whoever was on the other side like they were paper.

'What?' a man's voice said.

Edgar held up his badge. Bosch studied his partner for any warning sign of trouble.

'Mr. Delacroix, police.'

Seeing no sign of alarm, Bosch stepped forward and grabbed the knob and pulled the door all the way open. He kept his jacket flipped back and his hand on the grip of his gun.

The man he had seen on the golf range the day before was standing there. He wore an old pair of plaid shorts and a washed-out maroon T-shirt with permanent stains under the arms.

'We have a warrant allowing us to search these premises,' Bosch said. 'Can we come in?'

'You guys,' Delacroix said. 'You guys were at the range yesterday.'

'Sir,' Bosch said forcefully, 'I said that we have a search warrant for this trailer. Can we come in and conduct the search?'

Bosch took the folded warrant out of his pocket and held it up, but not within Delacroix's reach. That was the trick. To get the warrant they had to show all their cards to a judge. But they didn't want to show the same cards to Delacroix. Not just yet. So while Delacroix was entitled to read and study the warrant before granting the detectives entrance, Bosch was hoping to get inside the trailer without that happening. Delacroix would soon know the facts of the case, but Bosch wanted to control the delivery of information to him so that he could take readings and make judgments based on the suspect's reactions.

Bosch started putting the warrant back into his inside coat pocket.

'What's this about?' Delacroix asked in muted protest. 'Can I at least see that thing?'

'Are you Samuel Delacroix?' Bosch replied quickly.

'Yes.'

'This is your trailer, correct, sir?'

'It's my trailer. I lease the spot. I want to read the—'

'Mr. Delacroix,' Edgar said. 'We'd rather not stand out here in the view of your neighbors discussing this. I'm sure you don't want that either. Are you going to allow us to lawfully execute the search warrant or not?'

Delacroix looked from Bosch to Edgar and then back to Bosch. He nodded his head.

'I guess so.'

Bosch was first onto the stoop. He entered, squeezing by Delacroix on the threshold and picking up the odor of bourbon and bad breath and cat urine.

'Starting early, Mr. Delacroix?'

'Yeah, I've had a drink,' Delacroix said with a mixture of so-what and self-loathing in his voice. 'I'm done my work. I'm entitled.'

Edgar came in then, a much tighter squeeze past Delacroix, and he and Bosch scanned what they could see of the dimly lit trailer. To the right from the doorway was the living room. It was wood paneled and had a green Naugahyde couch and a coffee table with pieces of the wood veneer scraped off, exposing the particleboard beneath. There was a matching lamp table with no lamp on it and a television stand with a TV awkwardly stacked on top of a videocassette recorder. There were several videotapes stacked on top of the television. Across from the coffee table was an old recliner with its shoulders torn open – probably by a cat – and stuffing leaking out. Under the coffee table was a stack of newspapers, most of them gossip tabloids with blaring headlines.

To the left was a galley-style kitchen with sink, cabinets, stove, oven and refrigerator on one side and a four-person dining booth on the right. There was a bottle of Ancient Age bourbon on the table. On the floor under the table were a few crumbs of cat food on a plate and an old plastic margarine tub half full of water. There was no sign of the cat, other than the smell of its urine.

Beyond the kitchen was a narrow hallway leading back to one or two bedrooms and a bathroom.

'Let's leave the door open and open up a few windows,' Bosch said. 'Mr. Delacroix, why don't you sit down on the couch there?'

Delacroix moved toward the couch and said, 'Look, you don't have to search the place. I know why you're here.'

Bosch glanced at Edgar and then at Delacroix.

'Yeah?' Edgar said. 'Why are we here?'

Delacroix dropped himself heavily into the middle of the couch. The springs were shot. He sank into the midsection, and the ends of the cushion on either side of him rose into the air like the bows of twin *Titanics* going down.

'The gas,' Delacroix said. 'And I hardly used any of it. I don't go anywhere but back and forth from the range. I have a restricted license because of my DUI.'

'The gas?' Edgar asked. 'What are—'

'Mr. Delacroix, we're not here about you stealing gas,' Bosch said.

He picked up one of the videotapes off the stack on the television. There was tape on the spine with writing on it. *First Infantry, episode 46*. He put it back down and glanced at the writing on some of the other tapes. They were all episodes of the television show Delacroix had worked on as an actor more than thirty years before.

'That's not really our gig,' he added, without looking at Delacroix.

'Then what? What do you want?'

Now Bosch looked at him.

'We're here about your son.'

Delacroix stared at him for a long moment, his mouth slowly coming open and exposing his yellowed teeth.

'Arthur,' he finally said.

'Yeah. We found him.'

Delacroix's eyes dropped from Bosch's and seemed to leave the trailer as he studied a far-off memory. In his look was knowledge. Bosch saw it. His instincts told him that what they would tell Delacroix next he would already know. He glanced over at Edgar to see if he had seen it. Edgar gave a single short nod.

Bosch looked back at the man on the couch.

'You don't seem very excited for a father who hasn't seen his son in more than twenty years,' he said.

Delacroix looked at him.

'I guess that's because I know he's dead.'

Bosch studied him for a long moment, his breath holding in his lungs.

'Why would you say that? What would make you think that?'

'Because I know. I've known all along.'

'What have you known?'

'That he wasn't coming back.'

This wasn't going the way of any of the scenarios Bosch had imagined. It seemed to him that Delacroix had been waiting for them, expecting them, maybe for years. He decided that they might have to change the strategy and arrest Delacroix and advise him of his rights.

'Am I under arrest?' Delacroix asked, as if he had joined Bosch in his thoughts.

Bosch glanced at Edgar again, wondering if his partner had sensed how their plan was now slipping away from them.

'We thought we might want to talk first. You know, informally.'

'You might as well arrest me,' Delacroix said quietly.

'You think so? Does that mean you don't want to talk to us?'

Delacroix shook his head slowly and went into the long-distance stare again.

'No, I'll talk to you,' he said. 'I'll tell you all about it.'

'Tell us about what?'

'How it happened.'

'How what happened?'

'My son.'

'You know how it happened?'

'Sure I know. I did it.'

Bosch almost cursed out loud. Their suspect had literally just confessed before they had advised him of his rights, including the right to avoid giving self-incriminating statements.

'Mr. Delacroix, we're going to cut this off right here. I am going to advise you of your rights now.'

'I just want to—'

'No, please, sir, don't say anything else. Not yet. Let's get this rights thing taken care of and then we'll be more than happy to listen to anything you want to tell us.'

Delacroix waved a hand like it didn't matter to him, like nothing mattered.

'Jerry, where's your recorder? I never got mine back from IAD.'

'Uh, in the car. I don't know about the batteries, though.'

'Go check.'

Edgar left the trailer and Bosch waited in silence. Delacroix put his elbows on his knees and his face in his hands. Bosch studied his posture. It didn't happen often, but it wouldn't be the first time he had scored a confession during his first meeting with a suspect.

Edgar came back in with a tape recorder but shook his head.

'Batteries are dead. I thought you had yours.'

'Shit. Then take notes.'

Bosch took out his badge case and took out one of his business cards. He'd had them made with the Miranda rights advisory printed on the back, along with a signature line. He read the advisory statement and asked Delacroix if he understood his rights. Delacroix nodded his head.

'Is that a yes?'

'Yes, it's a yes.'

'Then sign on the line beneath what I just read to you.'

He gave Delacroix the card and a pen. Once it was signed, Bosch returned the card to his badge wallet. He stepped over and sat on the edge of the recliner chair.

'Now, Mr. Delacroix, do you want to repeat what you just said to us a few minutes ago?'

Delacroix shrugged like it was no big deal.

'I killed my son. Arthur. I killed him. I knew you people would show up someday. It took a long time.'

Bosch looked over at Edgar. He was writing in a notebook. They would have some record of Delacroix's admission. He looked back at the suspect and waited, hoping the silence would be an invitation for Delacroix to say more. But he didn't. Instead, the suspect buried his face in his hands again. His shoulders soon began shaking as he started to cry.

'God help me ... I did it.'

Bosch looked back at Edgar and raised his eyebrows. His partner gave a quick thumbs-up sign. They had more than enough to move to the next stage; the controlled and recorded setting of an interview room at the police station.

'Mr. Delacroix, do you have a cat?' Bosch asked. 'Where's your cat?'

Delacroix peeked his wet eyes through his fingers.

'He's around. Probably sleepin' in the bed. Why?'

'Well, we're going to call Animal Control and they'll come get him to take care of him. You're going to have to come with us. We're going to place you under arrest now. And we'll talk more at the police station.'

Delacroix dropped his hands and seemed upset.

'No. Animal Control won't take care of him. They'll gas him the minute they find out I won't be coming back.'

'Well, we can't just leave him here.'

'Mrs. Kresky will take care of him. She's next door. She can come in and feed him.'

Bosch shook his head. The whole thing was foundering because of a cat.

'We can't do that. We have to seal this place until we can search it.'

'What do you have to search it for?' Delacroix said, real anger in his voice now. 'I'm telling you what you need to know. I killed my son. It was an accident. I hit him too hard, I guess. I . . .'

Delacroix put his face back into his hands and tearfully mumbled, 'God . . . what did I do?'

Bosch checked Edgar; he was writing. Bosch stood up. He wanted to get Delacroix to the station and into one of the interview rooms. His anxiety was gone now, replaced by a sense of urgency. Attacks of conscience and guilt were ephemeral. He wanted to get Delacroix locked down on tape – video and audio – before he decided to talk to a lawyer and before he realized that he was talking himself into a 9×6 room for the rest of his life.

'Okay, we'll figure out the cat thing later,' he said. 'We'll leave enough food for now. Stand up, Mr. Delacroix, we're going to go.'

Delacroix stood up.

'Can I change into something nicer? This is just old stuff I was wearing around here.'

'No, don't worry about that,' Bosch said. 'We'll bring you clothes to wear later on.'

He didn't bother telling him that those clothes wouldn't be his. What would happen was that he'd be given a county jail-issued jumpsuit with a number across the back. His jumpsuit would be yellow, the color given to custodies on the high-power floor – the murderers.

'Are you going to handcuff me?' Delacroix asked.

'It's department policy,' Bosch said. 'We have to.'

He came around the coffee table and turned Delacroix so he could cuff his hands behind his back.

'I was an actor, you know. I once played a prisoner in an episode of *The Fugitive*. The first series, with David Janssen. It was just a small role. I sat on a bench next to Janssen. That's all I did. I was supposed to be on drugs, I think.'

Bosch didn't say anything. He gently pushed Delacroix toward the trailer's narrow door.

'I don't know why I just remembered that,' Delacroix said.

'It's all right,' Edgar said. 'People remember the strangest things at a time like this.'

'Just be careful on these steps,' Bosch said.

They led him out, Edgar in front and Bosch behind him.

'Is there a key?' Bosch asked.

'On the kitchen counter there,' Delacroix said.

Bosch went back inside and found the keys. He then started opening cabinets in the kitchenette until he found the box of cat food. He opened it and dumped it out onto the paper plate under the table. There was not very much food. Bosch knew he would have to do something about the animal later.

When Bosch came out of the trailer Edgar had already put Delacroix into the rear of the slickback. He saw a neighbor watching from the open front door of a nearby trailer. He turned and closed and locked Delacroix's door.

36

Bosch stuck his head into Lt. Billets's office. She was turned sideways at her desk and working on a computer at a side table. Her desk had been cleared. She was about to go home for the day.

'Yes?' she said without looking to see who it was.

'Looks like we got lucky,' Bosch said.

She turned from the computer and saw it was Bosch.

'Let me guess. Delacroix invites you in and just sits down and confesses.'

Bosch nodded.

'Just about.'

Her eyes grew wide in surprise.

'You are fucking kidding me.'

'He says he did it. We had to shut him up so we could get him back here on tape. It was like he had been waiting for us to show up.'

Billets asked a few more questions and Bosch ended up recapping the entire visit to the trailer, including the problem they had in not having a working tape recorder with which to take Delacroix's confession. Billets grew concerned and annoyed, equally with Bosch and Edgar for not being prepared and Bradley of IAD for not returning Bosch's tape recorder.

'All I can say is that this better not put hair on the cake, Harry,' she said, referring to the possibility of a legal challenge to any confession because Delacroix's initial words were not on tape. 'If we lose this one because of a screwup on our part . . .'

She didn't finish but didn't need to.

'Look, I think we'll be all right. Edgar got everything he said down verbatim. We stopped as soon as we got enough to hook him up and now we'll lock it all down with sound and video.'

Billets seemed barely placated.

'And what about Miranda? You're confident we will not have a Miranda situation,' she said, the last part not a question but an order.

'I don't see it. He started spouting off before we had a chance to advise him. Then he kept talking afterward. Sometimes it goes like that. You're ready to go with the battering ram and they just open the door for you.

479

Whoever he gets as a lawyer might have a heart attack and start screaming about it but nothing's going to come of it. We're clean, Lieutenant.'

Billets nodded, a sign that Bosch was convincing her.

'I wish they were all this easy,' she said. 'What about the DA's office?'

'I'm calling them next.'

'Okay, which room if I want to take a look?'

'Three.'

'Okay, Harry, go wrap him up.'

She turned back to her computer. Bosch threw a salute at her and was about to duck out of the doorway when he stopped. She sensed he had not left and turned back to him.

'What is it?'

Bosch shrugged his shoulders.

'I don't know. The whole way in I was thinking about what could have been avoided if we just went to him instead of dancing around him, gathering string.'

'Harry, I know what you're thinking and there's no way in the world you could have known that this guy – after twenty-some years – was just waiting for you to knock on his door. You handled it the right way and if you had it to do again you would still do it the same way. You circle the prey. What happened with Officer Brasher had nothing to do with how you ran this case.'

Bosch looked at her for a moment and then nodded. What she said would help ease his conscience.

Billets turned back to her computer.

'Like I said, go wrap him up.'

Bosch went back to the homicide table to call the District Attorney's Office to advise that an arrest had been made in a murder case and that a confession was being taken. He talked to a supervisor named O'Brien and told her that either he or his partner would be coming in to file charges by the end of the day. O'Brien, who was familiar with the case only through media reports, said she wanted to send a prosecutor to the station to oversee the handling of the confession and the forward movement of the case at this stage.

Bosch knew that with rush hour traffic out of downtown it would still be a minimum of forty-five minutes before the prosecutor got to the station. He told O'Brien the prosecutor was welcome but that he wasn't going to wait for anyone before taking the suspect's confession. O'Brien suggested he should.

'Look, this guy wants to talk,' Bosch said. 'In forty-five minutes or an hour it could be a different story. We can't wait. Tell your guy to knock on the door at room three when he gets here. We'll bring him into it as soon as we can.'

In a perfect world the prosecutor would be there for an interview but

Bosch knew from years working cases that a guilty conscience doesn't always stay guilty. When someone tells you they want to confess to a killing, you don't wait. You turn on the tape recorder and say, 'Tell me all about it.'

O'Brien reluctantly agreed, citing her own experiences, and they hung up. Bosch immediately picked the phone back up and called Internal Affairs and asked for Carol Bradley. He was transferred.

'This is Bosch, Hollywood Division, where's my damn tape recorder?'

There was silence in response.

'Bradley? Hello? Are you—'

'I'm here. I have your recorder here.'

'Why did you take it? I told you to listen to the tape. I didn't say take my machine, I don't need it anymore.'

'I wanted to review it and have the tape checked, to make sure it was continuous.'

'Then open it up and take the tape. Don't take the machine.'

'Detective, sometimes they need the original recorder to authenticate the tape.'

Bosch shook his head in frustration.

'Jesus, why are you doing this? You know who the leak is, why are you wasting time?'

Again there was a pause before she answered.

'I needed to cover all bases. Detective, I need to run my investigation the way I see fit.'

Now Bosch paused for a moment, wondering if he was missing something, if there was something else going on. He finally decided he couldn't worry about it. He had to keep his eyes on the prize. His case.

'Cover the bases, that's great,' he said. 'Well, I almost lost a confession today because I didn't have my machine. I would appreciate it if you would get it back to me.'

'I'm finished with it and am putting it in inter-office dispatch right now.'

'Thank you. Good-bye.'

He hung up, just as Edgar showed up at the table with three cups of coffee. It made Bosch think of something they should do.

'Who's got the watch down there?' he asked.

'Mankiewicz was in there,' Edgar said. 'So was Young.'

Bosch poured the coffee from the Styrofoam container into the mug he got out of his drawer. He then picked up the phone and dialed the watch office. Mankiewicz answered.

'You got anybody in the bat cave?'

'Bosch? I thought you might take some time off.'

'You thought wrong. What about the cave?'

'No, nobody till about eight today. What do you need?'

'I'm about to take a confession and don't want any lawyer to be able to open the box once I wrap it. My guy smells like Ancient Age but I think he's straight. I'd like to make a record of it, just the same.'

'This the bones case?'

'Yeah.'

'Bring him down and I'll do it. I'm certified.'

'Thanks, Mank.'

He hung up and looked at Edgar.

'Let's take him down to the cave and see what he blows. Just to be safe.'

'Good idea.'

They took their coffees into interview room 3, where they had earlier shackled Delacroix to the table's center ring. They released him from the cuffs and let him take a few gulps of his coffee before walking him down the back hallway to the station's small jail facility. The jail essentially consisted of two large holding cells for drunks and prostitutes. Arrestees of a higher order were usually transported to the main city or county jail. There was a small third cell that was known as the bat cave, as in blood alcohol testing.

They met Mankiewicz in the hallway and followed him to the cave, where he turned on the Breathalyzer and instructed Delacroix to blow into a clear plastic tube attached to the machine. Bosch noticed that Mankiewicz had a black mourning ribbon across his badge for Brasher.

In a few minutes they had the result. Delacroix blew a .003, not even close to the legal limit for driving. There was no standard set for giving a confession to murder.

As they took Delacroix out of the tank Bosch felt Mankiewicz tap his arm from behind. He turned to face him while Edgar headed back up the hallway with Delacroix.

Mankiewicz nodded.

'Harry, I just wanted to say I'm sorry. You know, about what happened out there.'

Bosch knew he was talking about Brasher. He nodded back.

'Yeah, thanks. It's a tough one.'

'I had to put her out there, you know. I knew she was green but—'

'Hey, Mank, you did the right thing. Don't second-guess anything.'

Mankiewicz nodded.

'I gotta go,' Bosch said.

While Edgar returned Delacroix to his spot in the interview room Bosch went into the viewing room, focused the video camera through the one-way glass and put in a new cassette he took from the supply cabinet. He then turned on the camera as well as the backup sound recorder. Everything was set. He went back into the interview room to finish wrapping the package.

37

Bosch identified the three occupants of the interview room and announced the date and time, even though both of these would be printed on the lower frame of the video being recorded of the session. He put a rights waiver form on the table and told Delacroix he wanted to advise him one more time of his rights. When he was finished he asked Delacroix to sign the form and then moved it to the side of the table. He took a gulp of coffee and started.

'Mr. Delacroix, earlier today you expressed to me a desire to talk about what happened to your son, Arthur, in nineteen eighty. Do you still wish to speak to us about that?'

'Yes.'

'Let's start with the basic questions and then we can go back and cover everything else. Did you cause the death of your son, Arthur Delacroix?'

'Yes, I did.'

He said it without hesitation or emotion.

'Did you kill him?'

'Yes, I did. I didn't mean to, but I did. Yes.'

'When did this occur?'

'It was in May, I think, of nineteen eighty. I think that's when it was. You people probably know more about it than me.'

'Please don't assume that. Please answer each question to the best of your ability and recollection.'

'I'll try.'

'Where was your son killed?'

'In the house where we lived at the time. In his room.'

'How was he killed? Did you strike him?'

'Uh, yes. I . . .'

Delacroix's businesslike approach to the interview suddenly eroded and his face seemed to close in on itself. He used the heels of his palms to wipe tears from the corners of his eyes.

'You struck him?'

'Yes.'

'Where?'

'All over, I guess.'

'Including the head?'

'Yes.'

'This was in his room, you said?'

'Yes, his room.'

'What did you hit him with?'

'What do you mean?'

'Did you use your fists or an object of some kind?'

'Yes, both. My hands and an object.'

'What was the object you struck your son with?'

'I really can't remember. I'll have to ... it was just something he had there. In his room. I have to think.'

'We can come back to it, Mr. Delacroix. Why on that day did you – first of all, when did it happen? What time of day?'

'It was in the morning. After Sheila – she's my daughter – had gone to school. That's really all I remember, Sheila was gone.'

'What about your wife, the boy's mother?'

'Oh, she was long gone. She's the reason I started—'

He stopped. Bosch assumed he was going to lay blame for his drinking on his wife, which would conveniently blame her for everything that came out of the drinking, including murder.

'When was the last time you talked to your wife?'

'Ex-wife. I haven't talked to her since the day she left. That was ...'

He didn't finish. He couldn't remember how long.

'What about your daughter? When did you talk to her last?'

Delacroix looked away from Bosch and down at his hands on the table.

'Long time,' he said.

'How long?'

'I don't remember. We don't talk. She helped me buy the trailer. That was five or six years ago.'

'You didn't talk to her this week?'

Delacroix looked up at him, a curious look on his face.

'This week? No. Why would—'

'Let me ask the questions. What about the news? Did you read any newspapers in the last couple weeks or watch the news on TV?'

Delacroix shook his head.

'I don't like what's on television now. I like to watch tapes.'

Bosch realized he had gotten off track. He decided to get back to the basic story. What was important for him to achieve here was a clear and simple confession to Arthur Delacroix's death. It needed to be solid and detailed enough to stand up. Without a doubt Bosch knew that at some point after Delacroix got a lawyer, the confession would be withdrawn. They always were. It would be challenged on all fronts – from the procedures followed to the suspect's state of mind – and Bosch's duty was not only to take the confession but to make sure it survived and could eventually be delivered to twelve jurors.

'Let's get back to your son, Arthur. Do you remember what the object was you struck him with on the day of his death?'

'I'm thinking it was this little bat he had. A miniature baseball bat that was like a souvenir from a Dodgers game.'

Bosch nodded. He knew what he was talking about. They sold bats at the souvenir stands that were like the old billy clubs cops carried until they went to metal batons. They could be lethal.

'Why did you hit him?'

Delacroix looked down at his hands. Bosch noticed his fingernails were gone. It looked painful.

'Um, I don't remember. I was probably drunk. I . . .'

Again the tears came in a burst and he hid his face in his tortured hands. Bosch waited until he dropped his hands and continued.

'He . . . he should have been in school. And he wasn't. I came in the room and there he was. I got mad. I paid good money – money I didn't have – for that school. I started to yell. I started to hit and then . . . then I just picked up the little bat and I hit him. I hit him too hard, I guess. I didn't mean to.'

Bosch waited again but Delacroix didn't go on.

'He was dead then?'

Delacroix nodded.

'That means yes?'

'Yes. Yes.'

There was a soft knock on the door. Bosch nodded to Edgar, who got up and went out. Bosch assumed it was the prosecutor but he wasn't going to interrupt things now to make introductions. He pressed on.

'What did you do next? After Arthur was dead.'

'I took him out the back and down the steps to the garage. Nobody saw me. I put him in the trunk of my car. I then went back to his room, I cleaned up and put some of his clothes in a bag.'

'What kind of bag?'

'It was his school bag. His backpack.'

'What clothes did you put into it?'

'I don't remember. Whatever I grabbed out of the drawer, you know?'

'All right. Can you describe this backpack?'

Delacroix shrugged his shoulders.

'I don't remember. It was just a normal backpack.'

'Okay, after you put clothes in it, what did you do?'

'I put it in the trunk. And I closed it.'

'What car was that?'

'That was my 'seventy-two Impala.'

'You still have it?'

'I wish; it'd be a classic. But I wrecked it. That was my first DUI.'

'What do you mean "wrecked"?'

'I totaled it. I wrapped it around a palm tree in Beverly Hills. It was taken to a junkyard somewhere.'

Bosch knew that tracing a thirty-year-old car would be difficult, but news that the vehicle had been totaled ended all hope of finding it and checking the trunk for physical evidence.

'Then let's go back to your story. You had the body in the trunk. When did you dispose of it?'

'That night. Late. When he didn't come home from school that day we started looking for him.'

'We?'

'Sheila and me. We drove around and we looked. We went to all the skateboard spots.'

'And all the time Arthur's body was in the trunk of the car you were in?'

'That's right. You see, I didn't want her to know what I had done. I was protecting her.'

'I understand. Did you make a missing person report with the police?' Delacroix shook his head.

'No. I went to the Wilshire station and talked to a cop. He was right there where you walk in. At the desk. He told me Arthur probably ran away and he'd be back. To give it a few days. So I didn't make out the report.'

Bosch was trying to cover as many markers as he could, going over story facts that could be verified and therefore used to buttress the confession when Delacroix and his lawyer withdrew it and denied it. The best way to do this was with hard evidence or scientific fact. But cross-matching stories was also important. Sheila Delacroix had already told Bosch and Edgar that she and her father had driven to the police station on the night Arthur didn't come home. Her father went in while she waited in the car. But Bosch found no record of a missing person report. It now seemed to fit. He had a marker that would help validate the confession.

'Mr. Delacroix, are you comfortable talking to me?'

'Yeah, sure.'

'You are not feeling coerced or threatened in any way?'

'No, I'm fine.'

'You are talking freely to me, right?'

'That's right.'

'Okay, when did you take your son's body from the trunk?'

'I did that later. After Sheila went to sleep I went back out to the car and I took it to where I could hide the body.'

'And where was that?'

'Up in the hills. Laurel Canyon.'

'Can you remember more specifically where?'

'Not too much. I went up Lookout Mountain past the school. Up in around there. It was dark and I . . . you know, I was drinking because I felt so bad about the accident, you know.'

'Accident?'

'Hitting Arthur too hard like I did.'

'Oh. So up past the school, do you remember what road you were on?'

'Wonderland.'

'Wonderland? Are you sure?'

'No, but that's what I think it was. I've spent all these years . . . I tried to forget as much about this as I could.'

'So you're saying you were intoxicated when you hid the body?'

'I was drunk. Don't you think I'd have to be?'

'It doesn't matter what I think.'

Bosch felt the first tremor of danger go through him. While Delacroix was offering a complete confession, Bosch had elicited information that might be damaging to the case as well. Delacroix being drunk could explain why the body had apparently been hurriedly dropped in the hillside woods and quickly covered with loose soil and pine needles. But Bosch recalled his own difficult climb up the hill and couldn't imagine an intoxicated man doing it while carrying or dragging the body of his own son along with him.

Not to mention the backpack. Would it have been carried along with the body or did Delacroix climb back up the hill a second time with the bag, somehow finding the same spot in the dark where he had left the body?

Bosch studied Delacroix, trying to figure out which way to go. He had to be very careful. It would be case suicide to bring out a response that a defense attorney could later exploit for days in court.

'All I remember,' Delacroix suddenly said unbidden, 'is that it took me a long time. I was gone almost all night. And I remember that I hugged him as tight as I could before I put him down in the hole. It was like I had a funeral for him.'

Delacroix nodded and searched Bosch's eyes as if looking for an acknowledgment that he had done the right thing. Bosch returned nothing with his look.

'Let's start with that,' he said. 'The hole you put him into, how deep was it?'

'It wasn't that deep, maybe a couple feet at the most.'

'How did you dig it? Did you have tools with you?'

'No, I didn't think about that. So I had to dig with my hands. I didn't get very far either.'

'What about the backpack?'

'Um, I put it there, too. In the hole. But I'm not sure.'

Bosch nodded.

'Okay. Do you remember anything else about this place? Was it steep or flat or muddy?'

Delacroix shook his head.

'I can't remember.'

'Were there houses there?'

'There was some right nearby, yeah, but nobody saw me, if that's what you mean.'

Bosch finally concluded that he was going too far down a path of legal peril. He had to stop and go back and clean up a few details.

'What about your son's skateboard?'

'What about it?'

'What did you do with it?'

Delacroix leaned forward to consider this.

'You know, I don't really remember.'

'Did you bury it with him?'

'I can't . . . I don't remember.'

Bosch waited a long moment to see if something would come out. Delacroix said nothing.

'Okay, Mr. Delacroix, we're going to take a break here while I go talk to my partner. I want you to think about what we were just talking about. About the place where you took your son. I need you to remember more about it. And about the skateboard, too.'

'Okay, I'll try.'

'I'll bring you back some more coffee.'

'That would be good.'

Bosch got up and took the empties from the room. He immediately went to the viewing room and opened the door. Edgar and another man were in there. The man, whom Bosch didn't know, was looking at Delacroix through the one-way glass. Edgar was reaching to the video to turn it off.

'Don't turn it off,' Bosch said quickly.

Edgar held back.

'Let it run. If he starts remembering more stuff I don't want anybody to try to say we gave it to him.'

Edgar nodded. The other man turned from the window and put out his hand. He looked like he was no more than thirty. He had dark hair that was slicked back and very white skin. He had a broad smile on his face.

'Hi, George Portugal, deputy district attorney.'

Bosch put the empty cups down on a table and shook his hand.

'Looks like you've got an interesting case here,' Portugal said.

'And getting more so all the time,' Bosch said.

'Well, from what I've seen in the last ten minutes, you don't have a worry in the world. This is a slam dunk.'

Bosch nodded but didn't return the smile. What he wanted to do was laugh at the inanity of Portugal's statement. He knew better than to trust the instincts of young prosecutors. He thought of all that had happened before they had gotten Delacroix into the room on the other side of the glass. And he knew there was no such thing as a slam dunk.

38

At 7 P.M. Bosch and Edgar drove Samuel Delacroix downtown to be booked at Parker Center on charges of murdering his son. With Portugal in the interview room taking part in the questioning, they had interrogated Delacroix for almost another hour, gleaning only a few new details about the killing. The father's memory of his son's death and his part in it had been eroded by twenty years of guilt and whiskey.

Portugal left the room still believing the case was a slam dunk. Bosch, on the other hand, was not so sure. He was never as welcoming of voluntary confessions as other detectives and prosecutors were. He believed true remorse was rare in the world. He treated the unanticipated confession with extreme caution, always looking for the play behind the words. To him, every case was like a house under construction. When a confession came into play, it became the concrete slab the house was built upon. If it was mixed wrong or poured wrong, the house might not withstand the jolt of the first earthquake. As he drove Delacroix toward Parker Center, Bosch couldn't help but think there were unseen cracks in this house's foundation. And that the earthquake was coming.

Bosch's thoughts were interrupted by his cell phone chirping. It was Lt. Billets.

'You guys slipped out of here before we had a chance to talk.'

'We're taking him down to booking.'

'You sound happy about it.'

'Well . . . I can't really talk.'

'You're in the car with him?'

'Yeah.'

'Is it serious or are you just playing mother hen?'

'I don't know yet.'

'I've got Irving and Media Relations calling me. I guess word is already out through the DA's press office that charges are coming. How do you want me to handle it?'

Bosch looked at his watch. He figured that after booking Delacroix they could get to Sheila Delacroix's house by eight. The trouble was that an announcement to the media might mean that reporters would get to her before that.

'Tell you what, we want to get to the daughter first. Can you get to the DA's office and see if they can hold it till nine? Same with Media Relations.'

'No problem. And look, after you dump the guy, call me when you can talk. At home. If there's a problem, I want to know about it.'

'You got it.'

He closed the phone and looked over at Edgar.

'First thing Portugal must've done was call his press office.'

'Figures. Probably his first big case. He's going to milk it for all he can.'

'Yeah.'

They drove in silence for a few minutes. Bosch thought about what he had insinuated to Billets. He couldn't quite place his reason for discomfort. The case was now moving from the realm of the police investigation to the realm of the court system. There was still a lot of investigative work to be done, but all cases changed once a suspect was charged and in custody and the prosecution began. Most times Bosch felt a sense of relief and fulfillment at the moment he was taking a killer to be booked. He felt as though he was a prince of the city, that he had made a difference in some way. But not this time and he wasn't sure why.

He finally tied off his feelings on his own missteps and the uncontrollable movements of the case. He decided he could not celebrate or feel much like a prince of the city when the case had cost so much. Yes, they had the admitted killer of a child in the car with them and they were taking him to jail. But Nicholas Trent and Julia Brasher were dead. The house he had built of the case would always have rooms containing their ghosts. They would always haunt him.

'Was that my daughter you were talking about? You're going to talk to her?'

Bosch looked up into the rearview mirror. Delacroix was hunched forward because his hands were cuffed behind his back. Bosch had to adjust the mirror and turn on the dome light to see his eyes.

'Yeah. We're going to give her the news.'

'Do you have to? Do you have to bring her into this?'

Bosch watched him in the mirror for a moment. Delacroix's eyes were shifting back and forth.

'We've got no choice,' Bosch said. 'It's her brother, her father.'

Bosch put the car onto the Los Angeles Street exit. They would be at the booking entrance at the back of Parker Center in five minutes.

'What are you going to tell her?'

'What you told us. That you killed Arthur. We want to tell her before the reporters get to her or she sees it on the news.'

He checked the mirror. He saw Delacroix nod his approval. Then the man's eyes came up and looked at Bosch's in the mirror.

'Will you tell her something for me?'

'Tell her what?'

Bosch reached inside his coat pocket for his recorder but then realized he didn't have it with him. He silently cursed Bradley and his own decision to cooperate with IAD.

Delacroix was quiet for a moment. He moved his head as he looked from side to side as if searching for the thing he wanted to say to his daughter. Then he looked back up at the mirror and spoke.

'Just tell her that I'm sorry for everything. Just like that. Sorry for everything. Tell her that.'

'You're sorry for everything. I got it. Anything else?'

'No, just that.'

Edgar shifted in his seat so he could look back at Delacroix.

'You're sorry, huh?' he said. 'Seems kind of late after twenty years, don't you think?'

Bosch turned right onto Los Angeles Street. He couldn't check the mirror for Delacroix's reaction.

'You don't know anything,' Delacroix angrily retorted. 'I've been crying for twenty years.'

'Yeah,' Edgar threw back. 'Crying in your whiskey. But not enough to do anything about it until we showed up. Not enough to crawl out of your bottle and turn yourself in and get your boy out of the dirt while there was still enough of him for a proper burial. All we have is bones, you know. Bones.'

Bosch now checked the mirror. Delacroix shook his head and leaned even further forward, until his head was against the back of the front seat.

'I couldn't,' he said. 'I didn't even—'

He stopped himself and Bosch watched the mirror as Delacroix's shoulders started to shake. He was crying.

'Didn't even what?' Bosch asked.

Delacroix didn't respond.

'Didn't even what?' Bosch asked louder.

Then he heard Delacroix vomit onto the floor of the back compartment.

'Ah, shit!' Edgar yelled. 'I knew this was going to happen.'

The car filled with the acrid smell of a drunk tank. Alcohol-based vomit. Bosch lowered his window all the way despite the brisk January air. Edgar did the same. Bosch turned the car into Parker Center.

'It's your turn, I think,' Bosch said. 'I got the last one. That wit we pulled out of Bar Marmount.'

'I know, I know,' Edgar said. 'Just what I wanna be doing before dinner.'

Bosch pulled into one of the spaces near the intake doors that were reserved for vehicles carrying prisoners. A booking officer standing by the door started heading toward the car.

Bosch recalled Julia Brasher's complaint about having to clean vomit out of the back of patrol cars. It was almost like she was jabbing him in the sore ribs again, making him smile despite the pain.

39

Sheila Delacroix answered the door of the home where she and her brother had lived but only one of them had grown up. She was wearing black leggings and a long T-shirt that went almost to her knees. Her face was scrubbed of makeup and Bosch noticed for the first time that she had a pretty face when it was not hidden by paint and powder. Her eyes grew wide when she recognized Bosch and Edgar.

'Detectives? I wasn't expecting you.'

She made no move to invite them in. Bosch spoke.

'Sheila, we have been able to identify the remains from Laurel Canyon as those of your brother, Arthur. We are sorry to have to tell you this. Can we come in for a few minutes?'

She nodded as she received the information and leaned for just a moment on the door frame. Bosch wondered if she would leave the place now that there was no chance of Arthur ever coming back.

She stepped aside and waved them in.

'Please,' she said, signaling them to sit down as they moved to the living room.

Everybody took the same seats as they had before. Bosch noticed the box of photos she had retrieved the other day was still on the coffee table. The photos were neatly stacked in rows in the box now. Sheila noticed his glance.

'I kind of put them in order. I had been meaning to get around to it for a long time.'

Bosch nodded. He waited until she took her seat before sitting down last and continuing. He and Edgar had worked out how the visit should go on the way over. Sheila Delacroix was going to be an important component of the case. They had her father's confession and the evidence of the bones. But what would pull it all together would be her story. They needed her to tell what it was like growing up in the Delacroix house.

'Uh, there's more, Sheila. We wanted to talk to you before you saw it on the news. Late today your father was charged with Arthur's murder.'

'Oh, my God.'

She leaned forward and brought her elbows down to her knees. She clasped her hands into fists and held them tight against her mouth. She closed her eyes and her hair fell forward, helping to hide her face.

'He's being held down at Parker Center pending his arraignment tomorrow and a bail hearing. I would say that from the looks of things – his lifestyle, I mean – I don't think he'll be able to make the kind of bail they're going to be talking about.'

She opened her eyes.

'There must be some kind of mistake. What about the man, the man across the street? He killed himself, he must be the one.'

'We don't think so, Sheila.'

'My father couldn't have done this.'

'Actually,' Edgar said softly, 'he confessed to it.'

She straightened herself, and Bosch saw the true surprise on her face. And this surprised him. He thought she would have always harbored the idea, the suspicion about her father.

'He told us that he hit him with a baseball bat because he skipped school,' Bosch said. 'Your father said he was drinking at the time and that he just lost it and he hit him too hard. An accident, according to him.'

Sheila stared back at him as she tried to process this information.

'He then put your brother's body in the trunk of the car. He told us that when you two drove around looking for him that night, he was in the trunk all along.'

She closed her eyes again.

'Then, later that night,' Edgar continued, 'while you were sleeping, he snuck out and drove up into the hills and dumped the body.'

Sheila started shaking her head like she was trying to fend off the words. 'No, no, he . . .'

'Did you ever see your father strike Arthur?' Bosch asked.

Sheila looked at him, seemingly coming out of her daze.

'No, never.'

'Are you sure about that?'

She shook her head.

'Nothing more than a swat on the behind when he was small and being a brat. That's all.'

Bosch looked over at Edgar and then back at the woman, who was leaning forward again, looking down at the floor by her feet.

'Sheila, I know we're talking about your father here. But we're also talking about your brother. He didn't get much of a chance at life, did he?'

He waited and after a long moment she shook her head without looking up.

'We have your father's confession and we have evidence. Arthur's bones tell us a story, Sheila. There are injuries. A lot of them. From his whole life.'

She nodded.

'What we need is another voice. Someone who can tell us what it was like for Arthur to grow up in this house.'

'To try to grow up,' Edgar added.

Sheila straightened herself and used her palms to smear tears across her cheeks.

'All I can tell you is that I never saw him hit my brother. Never once.'

She wiped more tears away. Her face was becoming shiny and distorted.

'This is unbelievable,' she said. 'All I did . . . all I wanted was to see if that was Arthur up there. And now . . . I should have never called you people. I should've . . .'

She didn't finish. She pinched the bridge of her nose in an effort to stop the tears.

'Sheila,' Edgar said. 'If your father didn't do it, why would he tell us he did?'

She sharply shook her head and seemed to grow agitated.

'Why would he tell us to tell you he said he was sorry?'

'I don't know. He's sick. He drinks. Maybe he wants the attention, I don't know. He was an actor, you know. '

Bosch pulled the box of photos across the coffee table and used his finger to go through one of the rows. He saw a photo of Arthur as maybe a five-year-old. He pulled it out and studied it. There was no hint in the picture that the boy was doomed, that the bones beneath the flesh were already damaged.

He slid the photo back into its place and looked up at the woman. Their eyes held.

'Sheila, will you help us?'

She looked away from him.

'I can't.'

40

Bosch pulled the car to a stop in front of the drainage culvert and quickly cut the engine. He didn't want to draw any attention from the residents on Wonderland Avenue. Being in a slickback exposed him. But he hoped it was late enough that all the curtains would be drawn across all the windows.

Bosch was alone in the car, his partner having gone home for the night. He reached down and pushed the trunk release button. He leaned to the side window and looked up into the darkness of the hillside. He could tell that the Special Services unit had already been out and removed the network of ramps and staircases that led to the crime scene. This was the way Bosch wanted it. He wanted it to be as close as possible to the way it was when Samuel Delacroix had dragged his son's body up the hillside in the dead of night.

The flashlight came on and momentarily startled Bosch. He hadn't realized he had his thumb on the button. He turned it off and looked out at the quiet houses on the circle. Bosch was following his instincts, returning to the place where it had all begun. He had a guy in lockup for a murder more than twenty years old but it didn't feel good to him. Something wasn't right and he was going to start here.

He reached up and switched the dome light off. He quietly opened the door and got out with the flashlight.

At the back of the car he looked around once more and raised the lid. Lying in the trunk was a test dummy he had borrowed from Jesper at the SID lab. Dummies were used on occasion in the restaging of crimes, particularly suspicious suicide jumps and hit-and-runs. The SID had an assortment ranging in size from infant to adult. The weight of each dummy could be manipulated by adding or removing one-pound sandbags from zippered pockets on the torso and limbs.

The dummy in Bosch's trunk had SID stenciled across the chest. It had no face. In the lab Bosch and Jesper had used sandbags to make it weigh seventy pounds, the estimated weight Golliher had given to Arthur Delacroix based on bone size and the photos of the boy. The dummy wore a store-bought backpack similar to the one recovered during the excavation.

It was stuffed with old rags from the trunk of the slickback in an approximation of the clothing found buried with the bones.

Bosch put the flashlight down and grabbed the dummy by its upper arms and pulled it out of the trunk. He hefted it up and over his left shoulder. He stepped back to get his balance and then reached back into the trunk for the flashlight. It was a cheap drugstore light, the kind Samuel Delacroix told them he had used the night he buried his son. Bosch turned it on, stepped over the curb and headed for the hillside.

Bosch started to climb but immediately realized he needed both his hands to grab tree limbs to help pull him up the incline. He shoved the flashlight into one of his front pockets and its beam largely illuminated the upper reaches of the trees and was useless to him.

He fell twice in the first five minutes and quickly exhausted himself before getting thirty feet up the steep slope. Without the flashlight illuminating his path he didn't see a small leafless branch he was passing and it raked across his cheek, cutting it open. Bosch cursed but kept going.

At fifty feet up Bosch took his first break, dropping the dummy next to the trunk of a Monterey pine and then sitting down on its chest. He pulled his T-shirt up out of his pants and used the cloth to help stanch the flow of blood on his cheek. The wound stung from the sweat that was dripping down his face.

'Okay, Sid, let's go,' he said when he had caught his breath.

For the next twenty feet he pulled the dummy up the slope. The progress was slower but it was easier than carrying the full weight and it was also the way Delacroix told them he remembered doing it.

After one more break Bosch made it the last thirty feet to the level spot and dragged the dummy into the clearing beneath the acacia trees. He dropped to his knees and sat back on his heels.

'Bullshit,' he said while gulping breath. 'This is bullshit.'

He couldn't see Delacroix doing it. He was maybe ten years older than Delacroix had been when he had supposedly accomplished the same feat but Bosch was in good shape for a man his age. He was also sober, something Delacroix claimed he had not been.

Even though Bosch had been able to get the body to the burial spot, his gut instinct told him Delacroix had lied to them. He had not done it the way he claimed. He either didn't take the body up the hill or he'd had help. And there was a third possibility, that Arthur Delacroix had been alive and climbed up the hill by himself.

His breathing finally returned to normal. Bosch leaned his head back and looked up through the opening in the canopy of the trees. He could see the night sky and a partial piece of the moon behind a cloud. He realized he could smell burning wood from a fireplace in one of the houses on the circle below.

He pulled the flashlight from his pocket and reached down to a strap sewn onto the back of the dummy. Since taking the dummy down the hill was not part of the test, he intended to pull it by the carrying strap. He was about to get up when he heard movement in the ground cover about thirty feet to his left.

Bosch immediately extended the flashlight in the direction of the noise and caught a fleeting glimpse of a coyote moving in the brush. The animal quickly moved out of the light beam and disappeared. Bosch swept the light back and forth but couldn't find it. He got up and started dragging the dummy toward the slope.

The law of gravity made going down easier but just as treacherous. As he carefully and slowly chose his steps, Bosch wondered about the coyote. He wondered how long coyotes lived and if the one he had seen tonight could have watched another man twenty years before as he buried a body in the same spot.

Bosch made it down the hill without falling. When he carried the dummy out to the curb he saw Dr. Guyot and his dog standing next to the slickback. The dog was on a leash. Bosch quickly went to the trunk, dumped in the dummy and then slammed it closed. Guyot came around to the back of his car.

'Detective Bosch.'

He seemed to know better than to ask what Bosch was doing.

'Dr. Guyot. How are you?'

'Better than you, I'm afraid. You've hurt yourself again. That looks like a nasty laceration.'

Bosch touched his cheek. It still stung.

'It's all right. Just a scratch. You better keep Calamity on the leash. I just saw a coyote up there.'

'Yes, I never take her off the leash at night. The hills are full of roaming coyotes. We hear them at night. You better come with me to the house. I can butterfly that. If you don't do it right it will scar.'

A memory of Julia Brasher asking about his scars suddenly came into Bosch's mind. He looked at Guyot.

'Okay.'

They left the car on the circle and walked down to Guyot's house. In the back office Bosch sat on the desk while the doctor cleaned the cut on his cheek and then used two butterfly bandages to close it.

'I think you'll recover,' Guyot said as he closed his first-aid kit. 'I don't know if your shirt will, though.'

Bosch looked down at his T-shirt. It was stained with his blood at the bottom.

'Thanks for fixing me up, Doc. How long do I have to leave these things on?'

'Few days. If you can stand it.'

Bosch gently touched his cheek. It was swelling slightly but the wound was no longer stinging. Guyot turned from his first-aid kit and looked at him and Bosch knew he wanted to say something. He guessed he was going to ask about the dummy.

'What is it, Doctor?'

'The officer that was here that first night. The woman. She was the one who got killed?'

Bosch nodded.

'Yes, that was her.'

Guyot shook his head in genuine sadness. He slowly stepped around the desk and sank into the chair.

'It's funny sometimes how things go,' he said. 'Chain reaction. Mr. Trent across the street. That officer. All because a dog fetched a bone. A most natural thing to do.'

All Bosch could do was nod. He started tucking in his shirt to see if it would hide the part with blood stains.

Guyot looked down at his dog, who was lying in the spot next to the desk chair.

'I wish that I'd never taken her off that leash,' he said. 'I really do.'

Bosch slid off the desk and stood up. He looked down at his midsection. The blood stain could not be seen but it didn't matter because the shirt was stained with his sweat.

'I don't know about that, Dr. Guyot,' he said. 'I think if you start thinking that way, then you'll never be able to come out your door again.'

They looked at each other and exchanged nods. Bosch pointed to his cheek.

'Thanks for this,' he said. 'I can find my way out.'

He turned toward the door. Guyot stopped him.

'On television there was a commercial for the news. They said the police announced an arrest in the case. I was going to watch it at eleven.'

Bosch looked back at him from the doorway.

'Don't believe everything you see on TV.'

41

The phone rang just as Bosch had finished watching the first session of Samuel Delacroix's confession. He picked up the remote and muted the sound on his television and then answered the call. It was Lieutenant Billets.

'I thought you were going to call me.'

Bosch took a pull from the bottle of beer he was holding and put it down on the table next to his television chair.

'Sorry, I forgot.'

'Still feeling the same way about things?'

'More so.'

'Well, what is it, Harry? I don't think I've ever seen a detective more upset about a confession before.'

'It's a lot of things. Something's going on.'

'What do you mean?'

'I mean I'm beginning to think that maybe he didn't do it. That maybe he's setting something up and I don't know what.'

Billets was quiet a long moment, probably not sure how to respond.

'What does Jerry think?' she finally asked.

'I don't know what he thinks. He's happy to clear the case.'

'We all are, Harry. But not if he's not the guy. Do you have anything concrete? Anything to back up these doubts you are having?'

Bosch gently touched his cheek. The swelling had gone down but the wound itself was sore to the touch. He couldn't stop himself from touching it.

'I went up to the crime scene tonight. With a dummy from SID. Seventy pounds. I got it up there but it was a hell of a fight.'

'Okay, so you proved it could be done. Where's the problem?'

'I hauled a dummy up there. This guy was dragging his dead son's body. I was straight; Delacroix says he was looped. I had been up there before; he hadn't. I don't think he could've done it. At least not alone.'

'You think he had help? The daughter maybe?'

'Maybe he had help and maybe he was never there. I don't know. We talked to the daughter tonight and she won't come across on the father. Won't say a word. So you start to think, maybe it was the two of them. But then, no. If she was involved, why would she call us and give us the ID on the bones? Doesn't make sense.'

Billets didn't respond. Bosch looked at his watch and saw it was eleven o'clock. He wanted to watch the news. He used the remote to turn off the VCR and put the TV on Channel 4.

'You got the news on?' he asked Billets.

'Yes. Four.'

It was the lead story – father kills son and then buries the body, arrested twenty-some years later because of a dog. A perfect L.A. story. Bosch watched silently and so did Billets on her end. The report by Judy Surtain had no inaccuracies that Bosch picked up on. He was surprised.

'Not bad,' he said when it was over. 'They finally get it right.'

He muted the television again just as the anchor segued to the next story. He was silent for a moment as he watched the television. The story was about the human bones found at the La Brea Tar Pits. Golliher was shown at a press conference, standing in front of a cluster of microphones.

'Harry, come on,' Billets said. 'What else is bugging you? There's got to be more than just your feeling that he couldn't have done it. And as far as the daughter goes, it doesn't bug me that she made the call with the ID. She saw it on the news, right? The story about Trent. Maybe she thought she could just pin it on Trent. After twenty years of worrying, she had a way to put it on somebody else.'

Bosch shook his head, though he knew she could not see this. He just didn't think Sheila would call the tip line if she had been involved in her brother's death.

'I don't know,' he said. 'It doesn't really work for me.'

'Then what are you going to do?'

'I'm going through everything now. I'll start over.'

'When's the arraignment, tomorrow?'

'Yup.'

'You don't have enough time, Harry.'

'I know. But I'm doing it. I already picked up a contradiction I didn't see before.'

'What?'

'Delacroix said he killed Arthur in the morning after he discovered the boy hadn't gone to school. When we interviewed the daughter the first time, she said Arthur didn't come home from school. There's a difference there.'

Billets made a chortling sound in the phone.

'Harry, that's minor. It's been more than twenty years and he's a drunk. I assume you are going to check the school's records?'

'Tomorrow.'

'Then you get it ironed out then. But how would the sister know for sure whether he went to school or not? All she knows is that he wasn't home afterward. You're not convincing me of anything.'

'I know. I'm not trying to. I'm just telling you about the things I'm looking at.'

'Did you guys find anything when you searched his trailer?'

'We didn't search it yet. He started talking almost as soon as we got in there. We're going tomorrow after the arraignment.'

'What's the window on the warrant?'

'Forty-eight hours. We're all right.'

Talking about the trailer made Bosch suddenly remember Delacroix's cat. They had gotten so involved in the suspect's confession that Bosch had forgotten to make arrangements for the animal.

'Shit.'

'What?'

'Nothing. I forgot about the guy's cat. Delacroix has a cat. I said I'd get a neighbor to take care of it.'

'Should've called Animal Control.'

'He was on to us about that. Hey, you have cats, right?'

'Yeah, but I'm not taking in this guy's.'

'No, I don't mean that. I just want to know, like, how long do they last without food and some water?'

'You mean you didn't leave any food for the cat?'

'No, we did, but it's probably gone by now.'

'Well, if you fed it today it can probably last until tomorrow. But it won't be too happy about it. Maybe tear the place up a little bit.'

'Looked like it already had. Listen, I gotta go. I want to watch the rest of the tape and see how we sit.'

'All right, I'll let you go. But, Harry, don't kick a gift horse in the mouth. You know what I mean?'

'I think so.'

They hung up then and Bosch started the videotape of the confession again. But almost immediately he turned it back off. The cat was bugging him. He should have made arrangements for it to be taken care of. He decided to go back out.

42

As Bosch approached Delacroix's trailer he saw light behind every curtain of every window. There had been no lights on when they left with Delacroix twelve hours earlier. He drove on by and pulled into the open parking space of a lot several trailers away. He left the box of cat food in the car, walked back to Delacroix's trailer and watched it from the same position where he had stood when Edgar had hit the door with his warrant knock. Despite the late hour the freeway's hiss was ever present and hindered his ability to hear sounds or movement from within the trailer.

He slipped his gun out of its holster and went to the door. He carefully and quietly stepped up onto the cinder blocks and tried the doorknob. It turned. He leaned to the door and listened but still could hear nothing from within. He waited another moment, slowly and silently turned the knob and then pulled the door open while raising his weapon.

The living room was empty. Bosch stepped in and swept the trailer with his eyes. No one. He pulled the door closed without a sound.

He looked through the kitchen and down the hallway to the bedroom. The door was partially closed and he could not see anyone, but he heard banging sounds, like somebody closing drawers. He started moving through the kitchen. The smell of cat urine was horrible. He noticed the plate on the floor under the table was clean, the water bowl almost empty. He moved into the hallway and was six feet from the bedroom door when it opened and a head-down figure came toward him.

Sheila Delacroix screamed when she looked up and saw Bosch. Bosch raised his gun and then immediately lowered it when he recognized who it was. Sheila raised her hand to her chest, her eyes growing wide.

'What are you doing here?' she said.

Bosch holstered his weapon.

'I was going to ask you the same thing.'

'It's my father's place. I have a key.'

'And?'

She shook her head and shrugged.

'I was . . . I was worried about the cat. I was looking for the cat. What happened to your face?'

Bosch moved past her in the tight space and stepped into the bedroom. 'Had an accident.'

He looked around the room and saw no cat or anything else that drew his attention.

'I think he's under the bed.'

Bosch looked back at her.

'The cat. I couldn't get him out.'

Bosch came back to the door and touched her shoulder, directing her to the living room.

'Let's go sit down.'

In the living room she sat down in the recliner while Bosch remained standing.

'What were you looking for?'

'I told you, the cat.'

'I heard you opening and closing drawers. The cat like to hide in drawers?'

Sheila shook her head as if to say he was bothering over nothing.

'I was just curious about my father. While I was here I looked around, that's all.'

'And where's your car?'

'I parked it by the front office. I didn't know if there'd be any parking here, so I parked there and walked in.'

'And you were going to walk the cat back on a leash or something?'

'No, I was going to carry him. Why are you asking me all these questions?'

Bosch studied her. He could tell she was lying but he wasn't sure what he should or could do about it. He decided to throw her a fastball.

'Sheila, listen to me. If you were in any way involved with what happened to your brother, now's the time to tell me and to try to make a deal.'

'What are you talking about?'

'Did you help your father that night? Did you help him carry your brother up the hill and bury him?'

She brought her hands up to her face so quickly it was as if Bosch had thrown acid in her eyes. Through her hands she yelled, 'Oh my God, oh my God, I can't believe this is happening! What are you—'

She just as abruptly dropped her hands and stared at him with bewildered eyes.

'You think *I* had something to do with it? How could you think that?'

Bosch waited a moment for her to calm down before answering.

'I think you're not telling me the truth about what's going on here. So it makes me suspicious and it means I have to consider all possibilities.'

She abruptly stood up.

'Am I under arrest?'

Bosch shook his head.

'No, Sheila, you're not. But I would appreciate it if you'd tell me the—'

'Then I'm leaving.'

She stepped around the coffee table and headed for the door with a purposeful stride.

'What about the cat?' Bosch asked.

She didn't stop. She was through the door and into the night. Bosch heard her answer from outside.

'You take care of it.'

Bosch stepped to the door and watched her walking down the trailer park's access road, out toward the management building, where her car was parked.

'Yeah,' he said to himself.

He leaned against the door frame and breathed some of the untainted air from the outside. He thought about Sheila and what she might have been doing. After a while he checked his watch and looked back over his shoulder at the interior of the trailer. It was after midnight and he was tired. But he decided he was going to stay and look for whatever it was she had been looking for.

He felt something brush up against his leg and looked down to see a black cat rubbing up against him. He gently pushed it away with his leg. He didn't care much for cats.

The animal came back and insisted on rubbing its head against Bosch's leg again. Bosch stepped back into the trailer, causing the cat to make a cautionary retreat of a few feet.

'Wait here,' Bosch said. 'I've got some food in the car.'

43

Downtown arraignment court was always a zoo. When Bosch entered the courtroom at ten minutes before nine on Friday morning, he saw no judge yet on the bench but a flurry of lawyers conferring and moving about the front of the courtroom like ants on a kicked-over hill. It took a seasoned veteran to know and understand what was going on at any given time in arraignment court.

Bosch first scanned the rows of public seating for Sheila Delacroix but didn't see her. He next looked for his partner and Portugal, the prosecutor, but they weren't in the courtroom either. He did notice that two cameramen were setting up equipment next to the bailiff's desk. Their position would give them a clear view of the glass prisoner docket once court was in session.

Bosch moved forward and pushed through the gate. He took out his badge, palmed it and showed it to the bailiff, who had been studying a computer printout of the day's arraignment schedule.

'You got a Samuel Delacroix on there?' he asked.

'Arrested Wednesday or Thursday?'

'Thursday. Yesterday.'

The bailiff flipped the top sheet over and ran his finger down a list. He stopped at Delacroix's name.

'Got it.'

'When will he come up?'

'We've still got some Wednesdays to finish. When we get to Thursdays it will depend on who his lawyer is. Private or public?'

'It'll be a PD, I think.'

'They go in order. You're looking at an hour, at least. That's if the judge starts at nine. Last I heard he wasn't here yet.'

'Thanks.'

Bosch moved toward the prosecution table, having to weave around two groupings of defense lawyers telling war stories while waiting for the judge to take the bench. In the first position at the table was a woman Bosch didn't recognize. She would be the arraignments deputy assigned to the courtroom. She would routinely handle eighty percent of the arraignments, as most of the cases were minor in nature and had not yet been assigned to prosecutors. In front of her on the table was a stack of files – the morning's cases – half a foot high. Bosch showed her his badge, too.

'Do you know if George Portugal is coming down for the Delacroix arraignment? It's a Thursday.'

'Yes, he is,' she said, without looking up. 'I just talked to him.'

She now looked up and Bosch saw her eyes go to the cut on his cheek. He'd taken the butterfly bandages off before his shower that morning but the wound was still quite noticeable.

'It's not going to happen for an hour or so. Delacroix has a public defender. That looks like it hurts.'

'Only when I smile. Can I use your phone?'

'Until the judge comes out.'

Bosch picked up the phone and called the DA's Office, which was three floors above. He asked for Portugal and was transferred.

'Yeah, it's Bosch. All right if I come up? We've gotta talk.'

'I'm here until I'm called down to arraignments.'

'See you in five.'

On the way out Bosch told the bailiff that if a detective named Edgar checked in he should be sent up to the DA's Office. The bailiff said no problem.

The hallway outside the courtroom was teeming with lawyers and citizens, all with some business with the courts. Everybody seemed to be on a cell phone. The marble floor and high ceiling took all of the voices and multiplied them into a fierce cacophony of white noise. Bosch ducked into the little snack bar and had to wait more than five minutes in line just to buy a coffee. After he was out, he legged it up the fire exit stairs because he didn't want to lose another five minutes waiting for one of the horribly slow elevators.

When he stepped into Portugal's small office Edgar was already there.

'We were beginning to wonder where you were,' Portugal said.

'What the hell happened to you?' Edgar added after seeing Bosch's cheek.

'It's a long story. And I'm about to tell it.'

He took the other chair in front of Portugal's desk and put his coffee down on the floor next to him. He realized he should have brought cups for Portugal and Edgar, so he decided not to drink in front of them.

He opened his briefcase on his lap and took out a folded section of the *Los Angeles Times*. He closed the briefcase and put it on the floor.

'So what's going on?' Portugal said, clearly anxious about the reason Bosch had called the meeting.

Bosch started unfolding the newspaper.

'What's going on is we charged the wrong guy and we better fix it before he gets arraigned.'

'Whoa, shit. I knew you were going to say something like that,' Portugal said. 'I don't know if I want to hear this. You are messing up a good thing, Bosch.'

'I don't care what I'm doing. If the guy didn't do it, he didn't do it.'

'But he *told* us he did it. *Several* times.'

'Look,' Edgar said to Portugal. 'Let Harry say what he wants to say. We don't want to fuck this up.'

'It may be too late with Mr. Can't-Leave-A-Good-Thing-Alone here.'

'Harry, just go on. What's wrong?'

Bosch told them about taking the dummy up to Wonderland Avenue and re-creating Delacroix's supposed trek up the steep hillside.

'I made it – just barely,' he said, gently touching his cheek. 'But the point is, Del—'

'Yeah, you made it,' Portugal said. 'You made it, so Delacroix could have made it. What's the problem with that?'

'The problem is that I was sober when I did it and he says he wasn't. I also knew where I was going. I knew it leveled off up there. He didn't.'

'This is all minor bullshit.'

'No, what's bullshit is Delacroix's story. Nobody dragged that kid's body up there. He was alive when he was up there. Somebody killed him up there.'

Portugal shook his head in frustration.

'This is all wild conjecture, Detective Bosch. I'm not going to stop this whole process because—'

'It's conjecture. Not wild conjecture.'

Bosch looked over at Edgar but his partner didn't look back at him. He had a glum look on his face. Bosch looked back at Portugal.

'Look, I'm not done. There's more. After I got home last night I remembered Delacroix's cat. We left it in his trailer and told him we'd take care of it but we forgot. So I went back.'

Bosch could hear Edgar breathing heavily and he knew what the problem was. Edgar had been left out of the loop by his own partner. It was embarrassing for him to be getting this information at the same time as Portugal. In a perfect world Bosch would have told him what he had before going to the prosecutor. But there hadn't been time for that.

'All I was going to do was feed the cat. But when I got there somebody was already in the trailer. It was his daughter.'

'Sheila?' Edgar said. 'What was she doing there?'

The news was apparently surprising enough for Edgar to no longer care if Portugal knew he was out of the latest investigative moves.

'She was searching the place. She claimed she was there for the cat, too, but she was searching the place when I got there.'

'For what?' Edgar said.

'She wouldn't tell me. She claimed she wasn't looking for anything. But after she left I stayed. I found some things.'

Bosch held up the newspaper.

'This is Sunday's Metro section. It has a pretty big story on the case, mostly a generic feature about forensics on cases like this. But there's a lot of detail about our case from an unnamed source. Mostly about the crime scene.'

Bosch thought after reading the article the first time in Delacroix's trailer the night before that the source was probably Teresa Corazon, since she was quoted by name in the article in regard to generic information about bone cases. He was aware of the trading that went on between reporters and sources; direct attribution for some information, no attribution for other information. But the identity of the source wasn't important to the present discussion and he didn't bring it up.

'So there was an article,' Portugal asked. 'What does it mean?'

'Well, it reveals that the bones were in a shallow grave and that it appeared that the body was not buried with the use of any tools. It also says that a knapsack had been buried along with the body. A lot of other details. Also details left out, like no mention of the kid's skateboard.'

'Your point being?' Portugal asked with a bored tone in his voice.

'That if you were going to put together a false confession, a lot of what you'd need is right here.'

'Oh, come on, Detective. Delacroix gave us much more than the crime scene details. He gave us the killing itself, the driving around with the body, all of that.'

'All of that was easy. It can't be proved or disproved. There were no witnesses. We'll never find the car because it's been squashed to the size of a mailbox in some junkyard in the Valley. All we have is his story. And the only place where his story meets the physical evidence is the crime scene. And every marker he gave us he could have gotten from this.'

He tossed the newspaper onto Portugal's desk but the prosecutor didn't even look at it. He leaned his elbows on the desk and brought his hands flat against each other and spread his fingers wide. Bosch could see his muscles flexing under his shirtsleeves and realized he was doing some kind of an at-your-desk exercise. Portugal spoke while his hands pushed against each other.

'I work out the tension this way.'

He finally stopped, releasing his breath loudly and leaning back in his seat.

'Okay, he had the ability to concoct a confession if he wanted to do it. Why would he want to do it? We're talking about his own son. Why would he say he killed his own son if he didn't?'

'Because of these,' Bosch said.

He reached into his inside jacket pocket and took out an envelope that was folded in half. He leaned forward and gently put it down on top of the newspaper on Portugal's desk.

As Portugal picked up the envelope and started to open it, Bosch said, 'I think that was what Sheila was looking for in the trailer last night. I found it in the night table next to her father's bed. It was underneath the bottom drawer. A hiding place there. You had to take the drawer out to find it. She didn't do that.'

From the envelope Portugal took a stack of Polaroid photos. He started looking through them.

'Oh, God,' he said almost immediately. 'Is this her? The daughter? I don't want to look at these.'

He shuffled through the remaining photos quickly and put them down on the desk. Edgar got up and leaned over the desk. With one finger he spread the photos out on the desk so he could view them. His jaw drew tight but he didn't say anything.

The photos were old. The white borders were yellowed, the colors of the images almost washed out by time. Bosch used Polaroids on the job all the time. He knew by the degradation of the colors that the photos on the desk were far more than a decade old and some of them were older than others. There were fourteen photos in all. The constant in each was a naked girl. Based on physical changes to the girl's body and hair length, he had guessed that the photos spanned at least a five-year-period. The girl innocently smiled in some of the photos. In others there was sadness and maybe even anger evident in her eyes. It had been clear to Bosch from the moment he first looked at them that the girl in the photos was Sheila Delacroix.

Edgar sat back down heavily. Bosch could no longer tell if he was upset by being so far behind on the case or by the content of the photos.

'Yesterday this was a slam dunk,' Portugal said. 'Today it's a can of worms. I assume you are going to give me your theory on these, Detective Bosch?'

Bosch nodded.

'You start with a family,' he said.

As he spoke he leaned forward and collected the photos, squared the edges and put them back in the envelope. He didn't like them being on display. He held the envelope in his hand.

'For one reason or another, the mother's weak,' he said. 'Too young to marry, too young to have kids. The boy she has is too hard to handle. She sees where her life is going and she decides she doesn't want to go there. She ups and splits and that leaves Sheila . . . to pick up with the boy and to fend for herself with the father.'

Bosch glanced from Portugal to Edgar to see how he was playing so far. Both men seemed hooked by the story. Bosch held the envelope with the photos up.

'Obviously, a hellish life. And what could she do about it? She could blame her mother, her father, her brother. But who could she lash out against? Her mother was gone. Her father was big and overpowering. In control. That only left ... Arthur.'

He noticed a subtle shake of Edgar's head.

'What are you saying, that she killed him? That doesn't make sense. She's the one who called us and gave us the ID.'

'I know. But her father doesn't know she called us.'

Edgar frowned. Portugal leaned forward and started doing his hand exercise again.

'I don't think I am following you, Detective,' he said. 'How does this have anything to do with whether or not he killed the son?'

Bosch also leaned forward and became more animated. He held the envelope up again, as if it was the answer to everything.

'Don't you see? The bones. All the injuries. We had it wrong. It wasn't the father who hurt him. It was her. Sheila. She was abused and she turned right around and became the abuser. To Arthur.'

Portugal dropped his hands to the desk and shook his head.

'So you *are* saying that she killed the boy and then twenty years later called up and gave you a key clue in the investigation. Don't tell me, you're going to say she has amnesia about killing him, right?'

Bosch let the sarcasm go.

'No, I'm saying she didn't kill him. But her record of abuse led her father to suspect she did. All these years Arthur's been gone, the father thought she did it. And he knew why.'

Once more Bosch proffered the envelope of photos.

'And so he carried the guilt of knowing his actions with Sheila caused it all. Then the bones come up, he reads it in the paper and puts two and two together. We show up and he starts confessing before we're three feet in the door.'

Portugal raised his hands wide.

'Why?'

Bosch had been turning it over in his mind ever since he had found the photos.

'Redemption.'

'Oh, please.'

'I'm serious. The guy's getting old, broken down. When you have more to look back at than forward to, you start thinking about the things you've done. You try making up for things. He thinks his daughter killed his son because of his own actions. So now he's willing to take the fall for her. After all, what's he got to lose? He lives in a trailer next to the freeway and works at a driving range. This is a guy who once had a shot at fame and fortune. Now look at him. He could be looking at this as his last shot at making up for everything.'

'And he's wrong about her but doesn't know it.'

'That's right.'

Portugal kicked his chair back from his desk. It was on wheels and he let it bang into the wall behind his desk.

'I got a guy waiting down there I could put in Q with one hand tied to my balls and you come in here and want me to kick him loose.'

Bosch nodded.

'If I'm wrong, you could always charge him again. But if I'm right, he's going to try to plead guilty down there. No trial, no lawyer, nothing. He wants to plead and if the judge lets him, then we're done. Whoever really killed Arthur is safe.'

Bosch looked over at Edgar.

'What do you think?'

'I think you got your mojo working.'

Portugal smiled but not because he found any humor in the situation.

'Two against one. That's not fair.'

'There's two things we can do,' Bosch said. 'To help be sure. He's probably down there in the holding tank by now. We can go down there, tell him it was Sheila who gave us the ID and flat out ask him if he's covering for her.'

'And?'

'Ask him to take a polygraph.'

'They're worthless. We can't admit them in—'

'I'm not talking about court. I'm talking about bluffing him. If he's lying, he won't take it.'

Portugal pulled his chair back to his desk. He picked up the paper and glanced at the story for a moment. His eyes then appeared to take a roving inventory of the desktop while he thought and came to a decision.

'Okay,' he finally said. 'Go do it. I'm dropping the charge. For now.'

44

Bosch and Edgar walked out to the elevator alcove and stood silently after Edgar pushed the down button.

Bosch looked at his blurred image reflected in the stainless steel doors of the elevator. He looked over at Edgar's reflection and then directly at his partner.

'So,' he said. 'How pissed off are you?'

'Somewhere between very and not too.'

Bosch nodded.

'You really left me with my dick in my hand in there, Harry.'

'I know. I'm sorry. You want to just take the stairs?'

'Have patience, Harry. What happened to your cell phone last night? You break it or something?'

Bosch shook his head.

'No, I just wanted to – I wasn't sure of what I was thinking and so I wanted to check things out on my own first. Besides, I knew you had the kid on Thursday nights. Then running into Sheila at the trailer, that was out of left field.'

'What about when you started searching the place? You coulda called. My kid was back home asleep by then.'

'Yeah, I know. I should have, Jed.'

Edgar nodded and that was the end of it.

'You know this theory of yours puts us at ground zero now,' he said.

'Yeah, ground zero. We're gonna have to start over, look at everything again.'

'You going to work it this weekend?'

'Yeah, probably.'

'Then call me.'

'I will.'

Finally, Bosch's impatience got the better of him.

'Fuck it. I'm taking the stairs. I'll see you down there.'

He left the alcove and went to the emergency stairwell.

45

Through an assistant in Sheila Delacroix's office Bosch and Edgar learned that she was working out of a temporary production office on the Westside, where she was casting a television pilot called *The Closers*.

Bosch and Edgar parked in a reserved lot full of Jaguars and BMWs and went into a brick warehouse that had been divided into two levels of offices. There were paper signs taped on the wall that said CASTING and showed arrows pointing the way. They went down a long hallway and then up a rear staircase.

When they reached the second floor they came into another long hallway that was lined with men in dark suits that were rumpled and out of style. Some of the men wore raincoats and fedoras. Some were pacing and gesturing and talking quietly to themselves.

Bosch and Edgar followed the arrows and turned into a large room lined with chairs holding more men in bad suits. They all stared as the partners walked to a desk at the far end of the room where a young woman sat, studying the names on a clipboard. There were stacks of 8 × 10 photos on the desk and script pages. From beyond a closed door behind the woman, Bosch could hear the muffled sounds of tense voices.

They waited until the woman looked up from her clipboard.

'We need to see Sheila Delacroix,' Bosch said.

'And your names?'

'Detectives Bosch and Edgar.'

She started to smile and Bosch took out his badge and let her see it.

'You guys are good,' she said. 'Did you get the sides already?'

'Excuse me?'

'The sides. And where are your head shots?'

Bosch put it together.

'We're not actors. We're real cops. Would you please tell her we need to see her right away?'

The woman continued to smile.

'Is that real, that cut on your cheek?' she said. 'It looks real.'

Bosch looked at Edgar and nodded toward the door. Simultaneously they went around both sides of her desk and approached the door.

'Hey! She's taking a reading! You can't—'

Bosch opened the door and stepped into a small room where Sheila Delacroix was sitting behind a desk watching a man seated on a folding chair in the middle of the room. He was reading from a page of script. A young woman was in the corner behind a video camera on a tripod. In another corner two men sat on folding chairs watching the reading.

The man reading the script didn't stop when Bosch and Edgar entered.

'The proof's in your pudding, you mutt!' he said. 'You left your DNA all over the scene. Now get up and get against—'

'Okay, okay,' Delacroix said. 'Stop there, Frank.'

She looked up at Bosch and Edgar.

'*What* is this?'

The woman from the desk roughly pushed past Bosch into the room.

'I'm sorry, Sheila, these guys just bullied their way in like they're real cops or something.'

'We need to talk to you, Sheila,' Bosch said. 'Right now.'

'I'm in the middle of a reading. Can't you see that I—'

'We're in the middle of a murder investigation. Remember?'

She threw a pen down on the desk and pushed her hands up through her hair. She turned to the woman on the video camera, which was now focused on Bosch and Edgar.

'Okay, Jennifer, turn that off,' she said. 'Everybody, I need a few minutes. Frank, I am very sorry. You were doing great. Can you stay and wait a few minutes? I promise to take you first, as soon as I am done.'

Frank stood up and smiled brilliantly.

'No problem, Sheila. I'll be right outside.'

Everybody shuffled out of the room, leaving Bosch and Edgar alone with Sheila.

'Well,' she said after the door closed. 'With an entrance like that, you really should be actors.'

She tried smiling but it didn't work. Bosch came over to the desk. He remained standing. Edgar leaned his back against the door. They had decided on the way over that Bosch would handle her.

She said, 'The show I'm casting is about two detectives called 'the closers' because they have a perfect record of closing cases nobody else seems able to. I guess there's no such thing in real life, is there?'

'Nobody's perfect,' Bosch said. 'Not even close.'

'What is so important that you had to come bursting in here, embarrassing me like that?'

'Couple things. I thought you might want to know that I found what you were looking for last night and – '

'I told you, I wasn't—'

'—your father was released from custody about an hour ago.'

'What do you mean *released*? You said last night he wouldn't be able to make bail.'

'He wouldn't have been able to. But he's not charged with the crime anymore.'

'But he confessed. You said he—'

'Well, he de-confessed this morning. That was after we told him we were going to put him on a polygraph machine and mentioned that it was you who called us up and gave us the tip that led to the ID of your brother.'

She shook her head slightly.

'I don't understand.'

'I think you do, Sheila. Your father thought you killed Arthur. You were the one who hit him all the time, who hurt him, who put him in the hospital that time after hitting him with the bat. When he disappeared your father thought maybe you'd finally gone all the way and killed him, then hidden the body. He even went into Arthur's room and got rid of that little bat in case you had used that again.'

Sheila put her elbows on the desk and hid her face in her hands.

'So when we showed up he started confessing. He was willing to take the fall for you to make up for what he did to you. For this.'

Bosch reached into his pocket and took out the envelope containing the photos. He dropped it onto the desk between her elbows. She slowly lowered her hands and picked it up. She didn't open the envelope. She didn't have to.

'How's that for a reading, Sheila?'

'You people ... is this what you do? Invade people's lives like this? I mean, their secrets, everything?'

'We're the closers, Sheila. Sometimes we have to.'

Bosch saw a case of water bottles on the floor next to her desk. He reached down and opened a bottle for her. He looked at Edgar, who shook his head. Bosch got another bottle for himself, pulled the chair Frank had used close to her desk and sat down.

'Listen to me, Sheila. You were a victim. You were a kid. He was your father, he was strong and in control. There is no shame for you in being a victim.'

She didn't respond.

'Whatever baggage you carry with you, now is the time to lose it. To tell us what happened. Everything. I think there is more than what you told us before. We're back at square one and we need your help. This is your brother we're talking about.'

He opened the bottle and took a long draw of water. For the first time he noticed how warm it was in the room. Sheila spoke while he took his second drink from the bottle.

'I understand something now ...'

'What is that?'

She was staring down at her hands. When she spoke it was like she was speaking to herself. Or to nobody.

'After Arthur was gone, my father never touched me again. I never . . . I thought it was because I had become undesirable in some way. I was overweight, ugly. I think now maybe it was because . . . he was afraid of what he thought I had done or what I might be able to do.'

She put the envelope back down on the desk. Bosch leaned forward again.

'Sheila, is there anything else about that time, about that last day, that you didn't tell us before? Anything that can help us?'

She nodded very slightly and then bowed her head, hiding her face behind her raised fists.

'I knew he was running away,' she said slowly. 'And I didn't do anything to stop him.'

Bosch moved forward on the edge of the seat. He spoke gently to her.

'How so, Sheila?'

There was a long pause before she answered.

'When I came home from school that day. He was there. In his room.'

'So he did come home?'

'Yes. For a little bit. His door was open a crack and I looked in. He didn't see me. He was putting things into his book bag. Clothes, things like that. I knew what he was doing. He was packing and was going to run. I just . . . I went into my room and closed the door. I wanted him to go. I guess I hated him, I don't know. But I wanted him gone. To me he was the cause of everything. I just wanted him to be gone. I stayed in my room until I heard the front door close.'

She raised her face and looked at Bosch. Her eyes were wet but Bosch had often before seen that in a purging of guilt and truth came a strength. He saw it in her eyes now.

'I could have stopped him but I didn't. And that's what I've had to live with. Now that I know what happened to him . . .'

Her eyes went off past Bosch, somewhere over his shoulder, where she could see the wave of guilt coming toward her.

'Thank you, Sheila,' Bosch said softly. 'Is there anything else you know that could help us?'

She shook her head.

'We'll leave you alone now.'

He got up and moved the chair back to the spot in the middle of the room. He then came back to the desk and picked up the envelope containing the Polaroids. He headed toward the office door and Edgar opened it.

'What will happen to him?' she asked.

They turned around and looked back. Edgar closed the door. Bosch knew she was talking about her father.

'Nothing,' he said. 'What he did to you is long past any statute of limitation. He goes back to his trailer.'

She nodded without looking up at Bosch.

'Sheila, he may have been a destroyer at one time. But time has a way of changing things. It's a circle. It takes power away and gives it to those who once had none. Right now your father is the one who is destroyed. Believe me. He can't hurt you anymore. He's nothing.'

'What will you do with the photographs?'

Bosch looked down at the envelope in his hand and then back up at her. 'They have to go into the file. Nobody will see them.'

'I want to burn them.'

'Burn the memories.'

She nodded. Bosch was turning to go when he heard her laugh and he looked back at her. She was shaking her head.

'What?'

'Nothing. It's just that I've got to sit here and listen to people trying to talk and sound like you all day. And I know right now nobody will come close. Nobody will get it right.'

'That's show business,' Bosch said.

As they headed back down the hallway to the stairs Bosch and Edgar passed by all the actors again. In the stairwell the one named Frank was saying his lines out loud. He smiled at the true detectives as they passed.

'Hey, guys, you guys are for real, right? How do you think I was doing in there?'

Bosch didn't answer.

'You were great, Frank,' Edgar said. 'You're a closer, man. The proof is in the pudding.'

46

At two o'clock Friday afternoon Bosch and Edgar made their way through the squad room to the homicide table. They had driven from the Westside to Hollywood in virtual silence. It was the tenth day of the case. They were no closer to the killer of Arthur Delacroix than they had been during all the years that Arthur Delacroix's bones had lain silently on the hillside above Wonderland Avenue. All they had to show for their ten days was a dead cop and the suicide of an apparently reformed pedophile.

As usual there was a stack of pink phone messages left for Bosch at his place. There was also an inter-office dispatch envelope. He picked up the envelope first, guessing he knew what was in it.

'About time,' he said.

He opened the envelope and slid his mini-cassette recorder out of it. He pushed the play button to check the battery. He immediately heard his own voice. He lowered the volume and turned off the device. He slipped it into his jacket pocket and dropped the envelope into the trash can by his feet.

He shuffled through the phone messages. Almost all were from reporters. Live by the media, die by the media, he thought. He would leave it to the Media Relations Office to explain to the world how a man who confessed to and was charged with a murder one day was exonerated and released the next.

'You know,' Bosch said to Edgar, 'in Canada the cops don't have to tell the media jack about a case until it's over. It's like a media blackout on every case.'

'Plus, they've got that round bacon up there,' Edgar replied. 'What're we doing here, Harry?'

There was a message from the family counselor at the medical examiner's office telling Bosch that the remains of Arthur Delacroix had been released to his family for burial on Sunday. Bosch put it aside so he could call back to find out about the funeral arrangements and which member of the family had claimed the remains.

He went back to the messages and came upon a pink slip that immediately gave him pause. He leaned back in his chair and studied it, a tightness coming over his scalp and going down the back of his neck. The message came in at ten-thirty-five and was from a Lieutenant Bollenbach in the Office of Operations – the O-3 as it was more popularly known by the rank and file. The O-3 was where all personnel assignments and transfers were issued. A decade before when Bosch was moved to the Hollywood Division he had gotten the word after a forthwith from the O-3. Same thing with Kiz Rider going to RHD the year before.

Bosch thought about what Irving had said to him in the interview room three days earlier. He guessed that the O-3 was now about to begin an effort to achieve the deputy chief's wish for Bosch's retirement. He took the message as a sign he was being transferred out of Hollywood. His new assignment would likely involve some freeway therapy – a posting far from his home and requiring long drives each day to and from work. It was a frequently used management tool for convincing cops they might be better off turning in the badge and doing something else.

Bosch looked at Edgar. His partner was going through his own collection of phone messages, none of which appeared to have stopped him the way the one in Bosch's hand had. He decided not to return the call yet or to tell Edgar about it. He folded the message and put it in his pocket. He took a look around the squad room, at all the bustling activity of the detectives. He would miss it if the new assignment wasn't a posting with the same kind of ebb and flow of adrenaline. He didn't care about freeway therapy. He could take the best punch they could give and not care. What he did care about was the job, the mission. He knew that without it he was lost.

He went back to the messages. The last one in the stack, meaning it was the first one received, was from Antoine Jesper in SID. He had called at ten that morning.

'Shit,' Bosch said.

'What?' Edgar said.

'I'm going to have to go downtown. I still have the dummy I borrowed last night in my trunk. I think Jesper needs it back.'

He picked up the phone and was about to call SID when he heard his and Edgar's names called from the far end of the squad room. It was Lieutenant Billets. She signaled them to her office.

'Here we go,' Edgar said as he got up. 'Harry, you can have the honors. You tell her where we're at on this thing. More like where we aren't at.'

Bosch did. In five minutes he brought Billets completely up to date on the case and its latest reversal and lack of progress.

'So where do we go from here?' she asked when he was finished.

'We start over, look at everything we've got, see what we missed. We go to the kid's school, see what records they have, look at yearbooks, try to contact classmates. Things like that.'

Billets nodded. If she knew anything about the call from the O-3, she wasn't letting on.

'I think the most important thing is that spot up there on the hill,' Bosch added.

'How so?'

'I think the kid was alive when he got up there. That's where he was killed. We have to figure out what or who brought him up there. We're going to have to go back in time on that whole street. Profile the whole neighborhood. It's going to take time.'

She shook her head.

'Well, we don't have time to work it full-time,' she said. 'You guys just sat out of the rotation for ten days. This isn't RHD. That's the longest I've been able to hold a team out since I got here.'

'So we're back in?'

She nodded.

'And right now it's your up – the next case is yours.'

Bosch nodded. He had assumed that was coming. In the ten days they'd been working the case, the two other Hollywood homicide teams had both caught cases. It was now their turn. It was rare to get such a long ride on a divisional case anyway. It had been a luxury. Too bad they hadn't turned the case, he thought.

Bosch also knew that by putting them back on the rotation Billets was making a tacit acknowledgment that she wasn't expecting the case to clear. With each day that a case stayed open, the chances of clearing it dropped markedly. It was a given in homicide and it happened to everybody. There were no closers.

'Okay,' Billets said. 'Anything else anybody wants to talk about?'

She looked at Bosch with a raised eyebrow. He suddenly thought maybe she did know something about the call from the O-3. He hesitated, then shook his head along with Edgar.

'Okay, guys. Thanks.'

They went back to the table and Bosch called Jesper.

'The dummy's safe,' he said when the criminalist picked up the phone. 'I'll bring it down later today.'

'Cool, man. But that wasn't why I called. I just wanted to tell you I can make a little refinement on that report I sent you on the skateboard. That is, if it still matters.'

Bosch hesitated for a moment.

'Not really, but what do you want to refine, Antoine?'

Bosch opened the murder book in front of him and leafed through it until he found the SID report. He looked at it as Jesper spoke.

'Well, in there I said we could put manufacture of the board between February of 'seventy-eight and June of 'eighty-six, right?'

'Right. I'm looking at it.'

'Okay, well, I can now cut more than half of that time period. This particular board was made between 'seventy-eight and 'eighty. Two years. I don't know if that means anything to the case or not.'

Bosch scanned the report. Jesper's amendment to the report didn't really matter, since they had dropped Trent as a suspect and the skateboard had never been linked to Arthur Delacroix. But Bosch was curious about it, anyway.

'How'd you cut it down? Says here the same design was manufactured until 'eighty-six.'

'It was. But this particular board has a date on it. Nineteen eighty.'

Bosch was puzzled.

'Wait a minute. Where? I didn't see any—'

'I took the trucks off – you know, the wheels. I had some time here between things and I wanted to see if there were any manufacture markings on the hardware. You know, patent or trademark coding. There weren't. But then I saw that somebody had scratched the date in the wood. Like carved it in on the underside of the board and then it was covered up by the truck assembly.'

'You mean like when the board was made?'

'No, I don't think so. It's not a professional job. In fact it was hard to read. I had to put it under glass and angled light. I just think it was the original owner's way of marking his board in a secret way in case there was ever a dispute or something over ownership. Like if somebody stole it from him. Like I said in the report, Boney boards were the choice board for a while there. They were hard to get – might've been easier to steal one than find one in a store. So the kid who had this one took off the back truck – this would have been the original truck, not the current wheels – and carved in the date. Nineteen eighty A.D. '

Bosch looked over at Edgar. He was on the phone speaking with his hand cupped over the mouthpiece. A personal call.

'You said A.D.?'

'Yeah, you know, as in anno Domini or however you say it. It's Latin. Means the year of our Lord. I looked it up.'

'No, it means Arthur Delacroix.'

'What? Who's that?'

'That's the vic, Antoine. Arthur Delacroix. As in A.D.'

'Damn! I didn't have the vic's name here, Bosch. You filed all of this evidence while he was still a John Doe and never amended it, man. I didn't even know you had an ID.'

Bosch wasn't listening to him. A surge of adrenaline was moving through his body. He knew his pulse was quickening.

'Antoine, don't move. I'm coming down there.'

'I'll be here.'

47

The freeway was crowded with people getting an early start on the weekend. Bosch couldn't keep his speed as he headed downtown. He had a feeling of pulsing urgency. He knew it was because of Jesper's discovery and the message from the O-3.

He turned his wrist on the wheel so he could see his watch and check the date. He knew that transfers usually took place at the end of a pay period. There were two pay periods a month – beginning the first and the fifteenth. If the transfer they were going to put on him was immediate, he knew that gave him only three or four days to wrap up the case. He didn't want to be taken off it, to leave it in Edgar's or anybody else's hands. He wanted to finish it.

Bosch reached into his pocket and brought out the phone slip. He unfolded it, driving with the heels of his palms on the wheel. He studied it for a moment and then got out his phone. He punched in the number from the message and waited.

'Office of Operations, Lieutenant Bollenbach speaking.'

Bosch clicked the phone off. He felt his face grow hot. He wondered if Bollenbach had caller ID on his phone. He knew that delaying the call was ridiculous because what was done was done whether he called in to get the news or not.

He put the phone and the message aside and tried to concentrate on the case, particularly the latest information Antoine Jesper had provided about the skateboard found in Nicholas Trent's house. Bosch realized that after ten days the case was wholly out of his grasp. A man he had fought with others in the department to clear was now the only suspect – with apparent physical evidence tying him to the victim. The thought that immediately poked through all of this was that maybe Irving was right. It was time for Bosch to go.

His phone chirped and he immediately thought it was Bollenbach. He was not going to answer but then decided his fate was unavoidable. He flipped open the phone. It was Edgar.

'Harry, what are you doing?'

'I told you. I had to go to SID.'

He didn't want to tell him about Jesper's latest discovery until he had seen it for himself.

'I could've gone with you.'

'Would've been a waste of your time.'

'Yeah, well, listen, Harry, Bullets is looking for you and, uh, there's a rumor floatin' around up here that you caught a transfer.'

'Don't know anything about it.'

'Well, you're going to let me know if something's happening, aren't you? We've been together a long time.'

'You'll be the first, Jerry.'

When Bosch got to Parker Center he had one of the patrolmen stationed in the lobby help him lug the dummy up to SID, where he returned it to Jesper, who took it and carried it easily to its storage closet.

Jesper led Bosch into a lab where the skateboard was on an examination table. He turned on a light that was mounted on a stand next to the board, then turned off the overhead light. He swung a mounted magnifying glass over the skateboard and invited Bosch to look. The angled light created small shadows in the etchings of the wood, allowing the letters to be clearly seen.

1980 A.D.

Bosch could definitely see why Jesper had jumped to the conclusion he did about the letters, especially since he did not have the case victim's name.

'It looks like somebody sanded it down,' Jesper said while Bosch continued to look. 'I bet what happened was that the whole board was rehabbed at one point. New trucks and new lacquer.'

Bosch nodded.

'All right,' he said after straightening up from the magnifying glass. 'I'm going to need to take this with me, maybe show it to some people.'

'I'm done with it,' Jesper said. 'It's all yours.'

He turned the overhead light back on.

'Did you check under these other wheels?'

''Course. Nothing there, though. So I put the truck back on.'

'You got a box or something?'

'Oh, I thought you were going to ride it out of here, Harry.'

Bosch didn't smile.

'That's a joke.'

'Yeah, I know.'

Jesper left the room and came back with an empty cardboard file box that was long enough to contain the skateboard. He put the skateboard in it along with the detached set of wheels and the screws, which were in a small plastic bag. Bosch thanked him.

'Did I do good, Harry?'

Bosch hesitated and then said, 'Yeah, I think so, Antoine.'

Jesper pointed to Bosch's cheek.

'Shaving?'

'Something like that.'

The drive back to Hollywood was even slower on the freeway. Bosch finally bailed at the Alvarado exit and worked his way over to Sunset. He took it the rest of the way in, not making any better time and knowing it.

As he drove he kept thinking about the skateboard and Nicholas Trent, trying to fit explanations into the framework of time and evidence that they had. He couldn't do it. There was a piece missing from the equation. He knew that at some level and at some place it all made sense. He was confident he would get there, if he had enough time.

At four-thirty Bosch banged through the back door into the station house carrying the file box containing the skateboard. He was heading quickly down the hallway to the squad room, when Mankiewicz ducked his head into the hallway from the watch office.

'Hey, Harry?'

Bosch looked back at him but kept walking.

'What's up?'

'I heard the news. We're gonna miss you around here.'

The word traveled fast. Bosch held the box with his right arm and raised his left hand palm down and made a sweeping gesture across the flat surface of an imaginary ocean. It was a gesture usually reserved for drivers of patrol cars passing on the street. It said, Smooth sailing to you, brother. Bosch kept going.

Edgar had a large white board lying flat across his desk and covering most of Bosch's as well. He had drawn what looked like a thermometer on it. It was Wonderland Avenue, the turnaround circle at the end being the bulb at the bottom of the thermometer. From the street there were lines drawn signifying the various homes. Extending from these lines were names printed in green, blue and black marker. There was a red X that marked the spot where the bones had been found.

Bosch stood and stared at the street diagram without asking a question.

'We should've done this from the start,' Edgar said.

'How's it work?'

'The green names are residents in nineteen eighty who moved sometime after. The blue names are anybody who came after 'eighty but has already left. The black names are current residents. Anywhere you see just a black name – like Guyot right here – that means they've been there the whole time.'

Bosch nodded. There were only two names in black. Dr. Guyot and someone named Al Hutter, who was at the end of the street farthest from the crime scene.

'Good,' Bosch said, though he didn't know what use the chart would be now.

'What's in the box?' Edgar asked.

'The skateboard. Jesper found something.'

Bosch put the box down on his desk and took off the top. He told and showed Edgar the scratched date and initials.

'We've got to start looking at Trent again. Maybe look at that theory you had about him moving into the neighborhood *because* he had buried the kid up there.'

'Jesus, Harry, I was almost joking about that.'

'Yeah, well, it's no joke now. We have to go back, put together a whole profile on Trent going all the way back to nineteen eighty, at least.'

'And meantime we catch the next case here. That's real sweet.'

'I heard on the radio it's supposed to rain this weekend. If we're lucky it will keep everybody inside and quiet.'

'Harry, inside is where most of the killing is done.'

Bosch looked across the squad room and saw Lt. Billets standing in her office. She was waving him in. He had forgotten that Edgar said she was looking for him. He pointed a finger at Edgar and then back at himself, asking if she wanted to see them both. Billets shook her head and pointed back only at Bosch. He knew what it was about.

'I gotta go see Bullets.'

Edgar looked up at him. He knew what it was about, too.

'Good luck, partner.'

'Yeah, partner. If that's still the case.'

He crossed the squad room to the lieutenant's office. She was now seated behind her desk. She didn't look at him when she spoke.

'Harry, you've got a forthwith from the Oh-Three. Call Lieutenant Bollenbach before you do anything else. That's an order.'

Bosch nodded.

'Did you ask him where I'm going?'

'No, Harry, I'm too pissed off about it. I was afraid if I asked I'd get into it with him and it's got nothing to do with him. Bollenbach's just the messenger.'

Bosch smiled.

'You're pissed off?'

'That's right. I don't want to lose you. Especially because of some bullshit grudge somebody up top has against you.'

He nodded and shrugged.

'Thanks, Lieutenant. Why don't you call him on speakerphone? We'll get this over with.'

Now she looked up at him.

'You sure? I could go get a coffee so you can have the office to yourself if you want.'

'It's all right. Go ahead and make the call.'

She put the phone on speaker and called Bollenbach's office. He answered right away.

'Lieutenant, this is Lieutenant Billets. I have Detective Bosch in my office.'

'Very good, Lieutenant. Just let me find the order here.'

There was the sound of papers rustling, then Bollenbach cleared his throat.

'Detective High ... Heronyim ... is that—'

'Hieronymus,' Bosch said. 'Rhymes with anonymous.'

'Hieronymus then. Detective Hieronymus Bosch, you are ordered to report for duty at Robbery-Homicide Division at oh-eight-hundred January fifteen. That is all. Are these orders clear to you?'

Bosch was stunned. RHD was a promotion. He had been demoted from RHD to Hollywood more than ten years earlier. He looked at Billets, who also had a look of suspicious surprise on her face.

'Did you say RHD?'

'Yes, Detective, Robbery-Homicide Division. Are these orders clear?'

'What's my assignment?'

'I just told you. You report at—'

'No, I mean what do I do at RHD? What's my assignment there?'

'You'll have to get that from your new commanding officer on the morning of the fifteenth. That's all I have for you, Detective Bosch. You have your orders. Have a nice weekend.'

He clicked off and a dial tone came from the speaker.

Bosch looked at Billets.

'What do you think? Is this some kind of a joke?'

'If it is, it's a good one. Congratulations.'

'But three days ago Irving told me to quit. Then he turns around and sends me downtown?'

'Well, maybe it's because he wants to watch you more closely. They don't call Parker Center the glass house for nothing, Harry. You better be careful.'

Bosch nodded.

'On the other hand,' she said, 'we both know you should be down there. You should've never been taken out of there in the first place. Maybe it's just the circle closing. Whatever it is, we're going to miss you. I'll miss you, Harry. You do good work.'

Bosch nodded his thanks. He made a move toward leaving but then looked back up at her and smiled.

'You're not going to believe this, especially in light of what just happened, but we're looking at Trent again. The skateboard. SID found a link to the boy on it.'

Billets threw her head back and laughed loudly, loud enough to draw the attention of everyone in the squad room.

'Well,' she said, 'when Irving hears that, he's definitely going to change RHD to Southeast Division, for sure.'

Her reference was to the gang-infested district at the far end of the city. A posting that would be the pure-form example of freeway therapy.

'I wouldn't doubt it,' Bosch said.

Billets dropped the smile and got serious. She asked Bosch about the latest turn in the case and listened intently while he outlined the plan to put together what would basically be a full-life profile on the dead set decorator.

'I'll tell you what,' she said when he was finished. 'I'll take you guys off rotation. No sense in you pulling a new case if you're splitting for RHD. I'm also authorizing weekend OT. So work on Trent and hit it hard and let me know. You've got four days, Harry. Don't leave this one on the table when you go.'

Bosch nodded and left the office. On his way back to his space he knew all eyes in the squad room were on him. He gave nothing away. He sat down at his space and kept his eyes down.

'So?' Edgar eventually whispered. 'What did you get?'

'RHD.'

'RHD?'

He had practically yelled it. It would now be known to all in the squad room. Bosch felt his face getting red. He knew everybody else would be looking at him.

'Jesus Christ,' Edgar said. 'First Kiz and now you. What am I, fucking chopped liver?'

48

Kind of Blue played on the stereo. Bosch held a bottle of beer and leaned back in the recliner with his eyes closed. It had been a confusing day at the end of a confusing week. He now just wanted to let the music move through him and clear out his insides. He felt sure that what he was looking for he already had in his possession. It was a matter of ordering things and getting rid of the unimportant things that cluttered the view.

He and Edgar had worked until seven before deciding on an early night. Edgar couldn't concentrate. The news of Bosch's transfer had affected him more deeply than it did Bosch. Edgar perceived it as a slight against him because he wasn't chosen to go to RHD. Bosch tried to calm him by assuring him that it was a pit of snakes that Bosch would be entering, but it was no use. Bosch pulled the plug and told his partner to go home, have a drink and get a good night's sleep. They would work through the weekend gathering information on Trent.

Now it was Bosch who was having the drink and falling asleep in his chair. He sensed he was at a threshold of some sort. He was about to begin a new and clearly defined time in his life. A time of higher danger, higher stakes and higher rewards. It made him smile, now that he knew no one was watching him.

The phone rang and Bosch bolted upright. He clicked off the stereo and went into the kitchen. When he answered, a woman's voice told him to hold for Deputy Chief Irving. After a long moment Irving's voice came on the line.

'Detective Bosch?'

'Yes?'

'You received your transfer orders today?'

'Yes, I did.'

'Good. I wanted to let you know that I made the decision to bring you back to Robbery-Homicide Division.'

'Why is that, Chief?'

'Because I decided after our last conversation to hold out one last chance to you. This assignment is that chance. You will be in a position where I can watch your moves very closely.'

'What position is that?'

'You were not told?'

'I was just told to report to RHD next pay period. That was it.'

There was silence on the phone and Bosch thought now he would find the sand in the engine oil. He was going back to RHD, but as what? He tried to think, What was the worst assignment within the best assignment?

Irving finally spoke.

'You are getting your old job back. Homicide Special. An opening came up today when Detective Thornton turned in his badge.'

'Thornton.'

'That is correct.'

'I'll be working with Kiz Rider?'

'That will be up to Lieutenant Henriques. But Detective Rider is currently without a partner and you have an established working relationship with her.'

Bosch nodded. The kitchen was dark. He was elated but did not want to transmit his feelings over the phone to Irving.

As if knowing these thoughts, Irving said, 'Detective, you may feel as though you fell into the sewer but came out smelling like a rose. Do not think that. Do not make any assumptions. Do not make any mistakes. If you do, I will be there. Am I clear?'

'Crystal clear.'

Irving hung up without another word. Bosch stood there in the dark holding the phone to his ear until it started making a loud, annoying tone. He hung up and went back into the living room. He thought about calling Kiz and seeing what she knew but decided he would wait. When he sat back down on the recliner he felt something hard jab into his hip. He knew it wasn't his gun because he had already unclipped it. He reached into his pocket and came up with his mini-cassette recorder.

He turned it on and listened to his verbal exchange with Surtain, the TV reporter outside Trent's house on the night he killed himself. Filtering it through the history of what would happen, Bosch felt guilty and thought that maybe he should have done or said more in an effort to stop the reporter.

After he heard the car door slam on the tape he stopped it and hit the rewind button. He realized that he had not yet heard the whole interview with Trent because he had been out of earshot while searching some parts of the house. He decided he would listen to the interview now. It would be a starting point for the weekend's investigation.

As he listened, Bosch tried to analyze the words and sentences for new meanings, things that would reveal a killer. All the while he was warring with his own instincts. As he listened to Trent speak in almost desperate tones he still felt convinced the man was not the killer, that his protests of innocence had been true. And this of course contradicted what he now knew. The skateboard – found in Trent's house – had the dead boy's initials on it and the year he both got the skateboard and was killed. The skateboard now served as a tombstone of sorts. A marker for Bosch.

He finished the Trent interview, but nothing in it, including the parts he had not previously heard, sparked any ideas in him. He rewound the tape and decided to play it again. And it was early in the second go-through that he picked up on something that made his face suddenly grow hot, almost with a feeling of being feverish. He quickly reversed the tape and replayed the exchange between Edgar and Trent that had drawn his attention. He remembered standing in the hallway in Trent's house and listening to this part of the interview. But he had missed its significance until this moment.

'Did you like watching the kids play up there in the woods, Mr. Trent?'

'No, I couldn't see them if they were up in the woods. On occasion I would be driving up or walking my dog – when he was alive – and I would see the kids climbing up there. The girl across the street. The Fosters next door. All the kids around here. It's a city-owned right-of-way – the only undeveloped land in the neighborhood. So they went up there to play. Some of the neighbors thought the older ones went up there to smoke cigarettes, and the concern was they would set the whole hillside on fire.'

He turned off the tape and went back to the kitchen and the phone. Edgar answered after one ring. Bosch could tell he had not been asleep. It was only nine o'clock.

'You didn't bring anything home with you, did you?'

'Like what?'

'The reverse directory lists?'

'No, Harry, they're at the office. What's up?'

'I don't know. Do you remember when you were making that chart on the board today, was there anybody named Foster on Wonderland?'

'Foster. You mean last name of Foster?'

'Yeah, last name.'

He waited. Edgar said nothing.

'Jerry, you remember?'

'Harry, take it easy. I'm thinking.'

More silence.

'Um,' Edgar finally said. 'No Foster. None that I can remember.'

'How sure are you?'

'Well, Harry, come on. I don't have the board or the lists here. But I think I would've remembered that name. Why is it so important? What's going on?'

'I'll call you back.'

Bosch took the phone with him out to the dining room table where he had left his briefcase. He opened it and took out the murder book. He quickly turned to the page that listed the current residents of Wonderland Avenue with their addresses and phone numbers. There were no Fosters on the list. He picked up the phone and punched in a number. After four rings it was answered by a voice he recognized.

'Dr. Guyot, this is Detective Bosch. Am I calling too late?'

'Hello, Detective. No, it's not too late for me. I spent forty years getting phone calls at all hours of the night. Nine o'clock? Nine o'clock is for amateurs. How are your various injuries?'

'They're fine, Doctor. I'm in a bit of a hurry and I need to ask you a couple questions about the neighborhood.'

'Well, go right ahead.'

'Going way back, nineteen eighty or so, was there ever a family or a couple on the street named Foster?'

There was silence as Guyot thought over the question.

'No, I don't think so,' he finally said. 'I don't remember anybody named Foster.'

'Okay. Then can you tell me if there was anybody on the street that took in foster kids?'

This time Guyot answered without hesitation.

'Uh, yes, there was. That was the Blaylocks. Very nice people. They helped many children over the years, taking them in. I admired them greatly.'

Bosch wrote the name down on a blank piece of paper at the front of the murder book. He then flipped to the report on the neighborhood canvas and saw there was no one named Blaylock currently living on the block.

'Do you remember their first names?'

'Don and Audrey.'

'What about when they moved from the neighborhood? Do you remember when that was?'

'Oh, that would have been at least ten years ago. After the last child was grown, they didn't need that big house anymore. They sold it and moved.'

'Any idea where they moved to? Are they still local?'

Guyot said nothing. Bosch waited.

'I'm trying to remember,' Guyot said. 'I know I know this.'

'Take your time, Doctor,' Bosch said, even though it was the last thing he wanted Guyot to do.

'Oh, you know what, Detective?' Guyot said. 'Christmas. I saved all the cards I received in a box. So I know who to send cards to next year. My wife always did that. Let me put the phone down and get the box. Audrey still sends me a card every year.'

'Go get the box, Doctor. I'll wait.'

Bosch heard the phone being put down. He nodded to himself. He was going to get it. He tried to think about what this new information could mean but then decided to wait. He would gather the information and then sift through it after.

It took Guyot several minutes to come back to the phone. The whole time Bosch waited with his pen poised to write the address on the note page.

'Okay, Detective Bosch, I've got it here.'

Guyot gave him the address and Bosch almost sighed out loud. Don and Audrey Blaylock had not moved to Alaska or some other far reach of the world. They were still within a car drive. He thanked Guyot and hung up.

49

At 8 A.M. Saturday morning Bosch was sitting in his slickback watching a small wood-frame house a block off the main drag in the town of Lone Pine three hours north of Los Angeles in the foothills of the Sierra Nevadas. He was sipping cold coffee from a plastic cup and had another one just like it ready to take over when he was finished. His bones ached from the cold and a night spent driving and then trying to sleep in the car. He had made it to the little mountain town too late to find a motel open. He also knew from experience that coming to Lone Pine without a reservation on a weekend was not advisable anyway.

As dawn's light came up he saw the blue-gray mountain rising in the mist behind the town and reducing it to what it was; insignificant in the face of time and the natural pace of things. Bosch looked up at Mt. Whitney, the highest point in California, and knew it had been there long before any human eyes had ever seen it and would be there long after the last set was gone. Somehow it made it easier to know all that he knew.

Bosch was hungry and wanted to go over to one of the diners in town for steak and eggs. But he wouldn't leave his post. If you moved from L.A. to Lone Pine it wasn't just because you hated the crowds, the smog and the pace of the big city. It was because you also loved the mountain. And Bosch wasn't going to risk missing Don and Audrey Blaylock to a morning mountain hike while he was eating breakfast. He settled for turning the car on and running the heater for five minutes. He had been parceling out the heat and the gas that way all night.

Bosch watched the house and waited for a light to come on or someone to pick up the newspaper that had been dropped on the driveway from a passing pickup two hours earlier. It was a thin roll of newspaper. Bosch knew it wasn't the *L.A. Times.* People in Lone Pine didn't care about Los Angeles or its murders or its detectives.

At nine Bosch saw smoke start to curl out of the house's chimney. A few minutes later, a man of about sixty wearing a down vest came out and got the paper. After picking it up he looked a half block down the street to Bosch's car. He then went back inside.

Bosch knew his car stood out on the street. He hadn't been trying to hide himself. He was just waiting. He started the car and drove down to the Blaylocks' house and pulled into the driveway.

When Bosch got to the door the man he had seen earlier opened it before he had to knock.

'Mr. Blaylock?'

'Yeah, that's me.'

Bosch showed his badge and ID.

'I was wondering if I could talk to you and your wife for a few minutes. It's about a case I'm working.'

'You alone?'

'Yeah.'

'How long've you been out there?'

Bosch smiled.

'Since about four. Got here too late to get a room.'

'Come in. We have coffee on.'

'If it's hot, I'll take it.'

He led Bosch in and pointed him toward a seating arrangement of chairs and a couch near the fireplace.

'I'll get my wife and the coffee.'

Bosch stepped over to the chair nearest the fireplace. He was about to sit down when he noticed all the framed photographs on the wall behind the couch. He stepped over to study them. They were all of children and young adults. They were of all races. Two had obvious physical or mental handicaps. The foster children. He turned and took the seat closest to the fire and waited.

Soon Blaylock returned with a large mug of steaming coffee. A woman came into the room behind him. She looked a little bit older than her husband. She had eyes still creased by sleep but a kind face.

'This is my wife, Audrey,' Blaylock said. 'Do you take your coffee black? Every cop I ever knew took it black.'

The husband and wife sat next to each other on the couch.

'Black's fine. Did you know a lot of cops?'

'When I was in L.A. I did. I worked thirty years for the city fire department. Quit as a station commander after the 'ninety-two riots. That was enough for me. Came in right before Watts and left after 'ninety-two.'

'What is it you want to talk to us about?' Audrey asked, seemingly impatient with her husband's small talk.

Bosch nodded. He had his coffee and the introductions were over.

'I work homicide. Out of Hollywood Division. I'm on a—'

'I worked six years out of fifty-eights,' Blaylock said, referring to the fire station that was behind the Hollywood Division station house.

Bosch nodded again.

'Don, let the man tell us why he came all the way up here,' Audrey said.

'Sorry, go ahead.'

'I'm on a case. A homicide up in Laurel Canyon. Your old neighborhood, actually, and we're contacting people who lived on the street back in nineteen eighty.'

'Why then?'

'Because that is when the homicide took place.'

They looked at him with puzzled faces.

'Is this one of those cold cases?' Blaylock said. 'Because I don't remember anything like that happening in our neighborhood back then.'

'In a way it's a cold case. Only the body wasn't discovered until a couple weeks ago. It had been buried up in the woods. In the hills.'

Bosch studied their faces. No tells, just shock.

'Oh, my God,' Audrey said. 'You mean all that time we were living there, somebody was dead up there? Our kids used to play up there. Who was it who was killed?'

'It was a child. A boy twelve years old. His name was Arthur Delacroix. Does that name mean anything to either of you?'

The husband and wife first searched their own memory banks and then looked at each other and confirmed the results, each shaking their head.

'No, not that name,' Don Blaylock said.

'Where did he live?' Audrey Blaylock asked. 'Not in the neighborhood, I don't think.'

'No, he lived down in the Miracle Mile area.'

'It sounds awful,' Audrey said. 'How was he killed?'

'He was beaten to death. If you don't mind – I mean, I know you're curious about it, but I need to ask the questions starting out.'

'Oh, I'm sorry,' Audrey said. 'Please go on. What else can we tell you?'

'Well, we are trying to put together a profile of the street – Wonderland Avenue – at that time. You know, so we know who was who and who was where. It's really routine.'

Bosch smiled and knew right away it didn't come off as sincere.

'And it's been pretty tough so far. The neighborhood has sort of turned over a lot since then. In fact, Dr. Guyot and a man down the street named Hutter are the only residents still there since nineteen eighty.'

Audrey smiled warmly.

'Oh, Paul, he is such a nice man. We still get Christmas cards from him, even since his wife passed away.'

Bosch nodded.

'Of course, he was too expensive for us. We mostly took our kids to the clinics. But if there was ever an emergency on a weekend or when Paul was home, he never hesitated. Some doctors these days are afraid to do anything because they might get – I'm sorry, I'm going off like my husband, and that's not what you came here to hear.'

'It's all right, Mrs. Blaylock. Um, you mentioned your kids. I heard from some of the neighbors that you two had a foster home, is that right?'

'Oh, yes,' she said. 'Don and I took in children for twenty-five years.'

'That's a tremendous, uh, thing you did. I admire that. How many children was it?'

'It was hard to keep track of them. We had some for years, some for only weeks. A lot of it was at the whim of the juvenile courts. It used to break my heart when we were just getting started with a child, you know, making them feel comfortable and at home, and then the child would be ordered home or to the other parent or what have you. I always said that to do foster work you had to have a big heart with a big callus on it.'

She looked at her husband and nodded. He nodded back and reached over and took her hand. He looked back at Bosch.

'We counted it up once,' he said. 'We had a total of thirty-eight kids at one time or another. But realistically, we say we raised seventeen of them. These were kids that were with us long enough for it to have an impact. You know, anywhere from two years to – one child was with us fourteen years.'

He turned so he could see the wall over the couch and reached up and pointed to a picture of a boy in a wheelchair. He was slightly built and had thick glasses. His wrists were bent at sharp angles. His smile was crooked.

'That's Benny,' he said.

'Amazing,' Bosch said.

He took a notebook out of his pocket and flipped it open to a blank page. He took out a pen. Just then his cell phone started chirping.

'That's me,' he said. 'Don't worry about it.'

'Don't you want to answer it?' Blaylock asked.

'They can leave a message. I didn't even think there'd be clear service this close to the mountain.'

'Yeah, we even get TV.'

Bosch looked at him and realized he had somehow been insulting.

'Sorry, I didn't mean anything. I was wondering if you could tell me what children you had living in your home in nineteen eighty.'

There was a moment when everyone looked at one another and said nothing.

'Is one of our kids involved in this?' Audrey asked.

'I don't know, ma'am. I don't know who was living with you. Like I said, we're trying to put together a profile of that neighborhood. We need to know exactly who was living there. And then we'll go from there.'

'Well, I am sure the Division of Youth Services can help you.'

Bosch nodded.

'Actually, they changed the name. It's now called the Department of Children's Services. And they're not going to be able to help us until Monday at the earliest, Mrs. Blaylock. This is a homicide. We need this information now.'

Again there was a pause as they all looked at one another.

'Well,' Don Blaylock finally said, 'it's going to be kind of hard to remember exactly who was with us at any given time. There are some obvious ones. Like Benny and Jodi and Frances. But every year we'd have a few kids that, like Audrey said, would be dropped in and then taken out. They're the tough ones. Let's see, nineteen eighty . . .'

He stood up and turned so he could see the breadth of the wall of photos. He pointed to one, a young black boy of about eight.

'William there. He was nineteen eighty. He—'

'No, he wasn't,' Audrey said. 'He came to us in 'eighty-four. Don't you remember, the Olympics? You made him that torch out of foil.'

'Oh, yeah, 'eighty-four.'

Bosch leaned forward in his seat. The location near the fire was now getting too warm for him.

'Let's start with the three you mentioned. Benny and the two others. What were their full names?'

He was given their names, and when he asked how they could be contacted he was given phone numbers for two of them but not Benny.

'Benny passed away six years ago,' Audrey said. 'Multiple sclerosis.'

'I'm sorry.'

'He was very dear to us.'

Bosch nodded and waited for an appropriate silence to go by.

'Um, who else? Didn't you keep records of who came and for how long?'

'We did but we don't have them here,' Blaylock said. 'They're in storage in L.A.'

He suddenly snapped his fingers.

'You know, we have a list of the names of every child we tried to help or did help. It's just not by year. We could probably cut it down a little bit, but would that help you?'

Bosch noticed Audrey give her husband a momentary look of anger. Her husband didn't see it but Bosch did. He knew her instincts would be to protect her children from the threat, real or not, that Bosch represented.

'Yes, that would help a lot.'

Blaylock left the room and Bosch looked at Audrey.

'You don't want him to give me that list. Why is that, Mrs. Blaylock?'

'Because I don't think you are being honest with us. You are looking for something. Something that will fit your needs. You don't drive three hours in the middle of the night from Los Angeles for a "routine questioning," as you call it. You know these children come from tough backgrounds. They weren't all angels when they came to us. And I don't want any of them blamed for something just because of who they were or where they came from.'

Bosch waited to make sure she was done.

'Mrs. Blaylock, have you ever been to the McClaren Youth Hall?'

'Of course. Several of our children came from there.'

'I came from there, too. And an assortment of foster homes where I never lasted very long. So I know what these children were like because I was one myself, all right? And I know that some foster homes can be full of love and some can be just as bad as or worse than the place you were taken from. I know that some foster parents are committed to the children and some are committed to the subsistence checks from Children's Services.'

She was quiet a long moment before answering.

'It doesn't matter,' she said. 'You still are looking to finish your puzzle with any piece that fits.'

'You're wrong, Mrs. Blaylock. Wrong about that, wrong about me.'

Blaylock came back into the room with what looked like a green school folder. He placed it down on the square coffee table and opened it. Its pockets were stuffed with photos and letters. Audrey continued despite his return.

'My husband worked for the city like you do, so he won't want to hear me say this. But, Detective, I don't trust you or the reasons you say you are here. You are not being honest with us.'

'Audrey!' Blaylock yelped. 'The man is just trying to do his job.'

'And he'll say anything to do it. And he'll hurt any of our children to do it.'

'Audrey, please.'

He turned his attention back to Bosch and offered a sheet of paper. There was a list of handwritten names on it. Before Bosch could read them Blaylock took the page back and put it down on the table. He went to work on it with a pencil, putting check marks next to some of the names. He spoke as he worked.

'We made this list just so we could sort of keep track of everybody. You'd be surprised, you can love somebody to death but when it comes time to remember twenty, thirty birthdays you always forget somebody. The ones I'm checking off here are the kids that came in more recent than nineteen eighty. Audrey will double-check when I'm done.'

'No, I won't.'

The men ignored her. Bosch's eyes moved ahead of Blaylock's pencil and down the list. Before he was two-thirds to the bottom he reached down and put his finger on a name.

'Tell me about him.'

Blaylock looked up at Bosch and then over at his wife.

'Who is it?' she asked.

'Johnny Stokes,' Bosch said. 'You had him in your home in nineteen eighty, didn't you?'

Audrey stared at him for a moment.

'There, you see?' she said to her husband while looking only at Bosch. 'He already knew about Johnny when he came in here. I was right. He's not an honest man.'

50

By the time Don Blaylock went to the kitchen to brew a second pot of coffee Bosch had two pages of notes on Johnny Stokes. He had come to the Blaylock house through a DYS referral in January 1980 and was gone the following July, when he was arrested for stealing a car and going on a joyride through Hollywood. It was his second arrest for car theft. He was incarcerated at the Sylmar Juvenile Hall for six months. By the time his period of rehabilitation was completed he was returned by a judge to his parents. Though the Blaylocks heard from him on occasion and even saw him during his infrequent visits to the neighborhood, they had other children still in their care and soon drifted from contact with the boy.

When Blaylock went to make the coffee Bosch settled into what he thought would be an uncomfortable silence with Audrey. But then she spoke to him.

'Twelve of our children graduated from college,' she said. 'Two have military careers. One followed Don into the fire service. He works in the Valley.'

She nodded at Bosch and he nodded back.

'We've never considered ourselves to be one hundred percent successful with our children,' she continued. 'We did our best with each one. Sometimes the circumstances or the courts or the youth authorities prevented us from helping a child. John was one of those cases. He made a mistake and it was as if we were to blame. He was taken from us . . . before we could help him.'

All Bosch could do was nod.

'You seemed to know of him already,' she said. 'Have you already spoken to him?'

'Yes. Briefly.'

'Is he in jail now?'

'No, he's not.'

'What has his life been since . . . we knew him?'

Bosch spread his hands apart.

'He hasn't done well. Drugs, a lot of arrests, prison.'

She nodded sadly.

'Do you think he killed that boy in our neighborhood? While he was living with us?'

Bosch could tell by her face that if he were to answer truthfully he would knock down everything she had built out of what was good in what they had done. The whole wall of pictures, the graduation gowns and the good jobs would mean nothing next to this.

'I don't really know. But we do know he was a friend of the boy who was killed.'

She closed her eyes. Not tightly, just as if she were resting them. She said nothing else until Blaylock came back into the room. He went past Bosch and put another log on the fire.

'Coffee will be up in a minute.'

'Thank you,' Bosch said.

After Blaylock walked back to the couch, Bosch stood up.

'I have some things I would like you to look at, if you don't mind. They're in my car.'

He excused himself and went out to the slickback. He grabbed his briefcase from the front seat and then went to the trunk to get the file box containing the skateboard. He thought it might be worth a try showing it to the Blaylocks.

His phone chirped just as he closed the trunk and this time he answered it. It was Edgar.

'Harry, where are you?'

'Up in Lone Pine.'

'Lone Pine! What the fuck are you doing up there?'

'I don't have time to talk. Where are you?'

'At the table. Like we agreed. I thought you—'

'Listen, I'll call you back in an hour. Meantime, put out a new BOLO on Stokes.'

'What?'

Bosch checked the house to make sure the Blaylocks weren't listening or in sight.

'I said put out another BOLO on Stokes. We need him picked up.'

'Why?'

'Because he did it. He killed the kid.'

'What the fuck, Harry?'

'I'll call you in an hour. Put out the BOLO.'

He hung up and this time turned the phone off.

Inside the house Bosch put the file box down on the floor and then opened his briefcase on his lap. He found the envelope containing the family photos borrowed from Sheila Delacroix. He opened it and slid them out. He split the stack in two and gave one-half to each of the Blaylocks.

'Look at the boy in these pictures and tell me if you recognize him, if he ever came to your house. With Johnny or anybody else.'

He watched as the couple looked at the photos and then exchanged stacks. When they were finished they both shook their heads and handed the photos back.

'Don't recognize him,' Don Blaylock said.

'Okay,' Bosch said as he put the photos back into the envelope.

He closed his briefcase and put it on the floor. He then opened the file box and lifted out the skateboard.

'Has either of you—'

'That was John's,' Audrey said.

'Are you sure?'

'Yes, I recognize it. When he was . . . taken from us, he left it behind. I told him we had it. I called his house but he never came for it.'

'How do you know that this is the one that was his?'

'I just remember. I didn't like the skull and crossbones. I remember those.'

Bosch put the skateboard back in the box.

'What happened to it if he never came for it?'

'We sold it,' Audrey said. 'When Don retired after thirty years and we decided to move up here, we sold all of our junk. We had a gigantic garage sale.'

'More like a house sale,' her husband added. 'We got rid of everything.'

'Not everything. You wouldn't sell that stupid fire bell we have in the backyard. Anyway, that was when we sold the skateboard.'

'Do you remember who you sold it to?'

'Yes, the man who lived next door. Mr. Trent.'

'When was this?'

'Summer of 'ninety-two. Right after we sold the house. We were still in escrow, I remember.'

'Why do you remember selling the skateboard to Mr. Trent? 'Ninety-two was a long time ago.'

'I remember because he bought half of what we were selling. The junky half. He gathered it all up and offered us one price for everything. He needed it all for his work. He was a set designer.'

'Set decorator,' her husband corrected. 'There is a difference.'

'Anyway, he used everything he bought from us on movie sets. I always hoped I would see something in a movie that I'd know came from our house. But I never did.'

Bosch scribbled some notes in his pad. He had just about everything he needed from the Blaylocks. It was almost time to head south, back to the city to put the case together.

'How did you get the skateboard?' Audrey asked him.

Bosch looked up from his notepad.

'Uh, it was in Mr. Trent's possessions.'

'He's still on the street?' Don Blaylock asked. 'He was a great neighbor. Never a problem at all with him.'

'He was until recently,' Bosch said. 'He passed away, though.'

'Oh, my gosh,' Audrey proclaimed. 'What a shame. And he wasn't that old a man.'

'I just have a couple more questions,' Bosch said. 'Did John Stokes ever tell either of you how he came to have the skateboard?'

'He told me that he had won it during a contest with some other boys at school,' Audrey said.

'The Brethren School?'

'Yes, that's where he went. He was going when he first came to us and so we continued it.'

Bosch nodded and looked down at his notes. He had everything. He closed the notebook, put it in his coat pocket and stood up to go.

51

Bosch pulled the car into a space in front of the Lone Pine Diner. The booths by all the windows were filled and almost all of the people in them looked out at the LAPD car two hundred miles from home.

He was starved but knew he needed to talk to Edgar before delaying any further. He took out the cell phone and made the call. Edgar answered after half a ring.

'It's me. Did you put the BOLO out?'

'Yeah, it's out. But it's a little hard to do when you don't know what the fuck is going on, *partner*.'

He said the last word as if it was a synonym for asshole. It was their last case together and Bosch felt bad that they were going to end their time this way. He knew it was his fault. He had cut Edgar out of the case for reasons Bosch wasn't even sure about.

'Jerry, you're right,' he said. 'I fucked up. I just wanted to keep things moving and that meant driving through the night.'

'I would've gone with you.'

'I know,' Bosch lied. 'I just didn't think. I just drove. I'm coming back now.'

'Well, start at the beginning so I know what the fuck is going on in our own case. I feel like a moron here, putting out a BOLO and not even knowing why.'

'I told you, Stokes is the guy.'

'Yeah, you told me that and you didn't tell me anything else.'

Bosch spent the next ten minutes watching diners eat their food while he recounted his moves for Edgar and brought him up to date.

'Jesus Christ, and we had him right here,' Edgar said when Bosch was finished.

'Yeah, well, it's too late to worry about that. We have to get him back.'

'So you're saying that when the kid packed up and ran away, he went to Stokes. Then Stokes leads him up there into the woods and just kills him.'

'More or less.'

'Why?'

'That's what we have to ask him. I've got a theory, though.'

'What, the skateboard?'

'Yeah, he wanted the skateboard.'

'He'd kill a kid over a skateboard?'

'We've both seen it done for less and we don't know if he intended to kill him or not. It was a shallow grave, dug by hand. Nothing premeditated about that. Maybe he just pushed him and knocked him down. Maybe he hit him with a rock. Maybe there was something else going on between them we don't even know about.'

Edgar didn't say anything for a long moment and Bosch thought maybe they were finished and he could get some food.

'What did the foster parents think about your theory?'

Bosch sighed.

'I didn't really spin it for them. But put it this way, they weren't too surprised when I started asking questions about Stokes.'

'You know something, Harry, we've been spinning our wheels is what we've been doing.'

'What do you mean?'

'This whole case. It comes down to what? – a thirteen-year-old killing a twelve-year-old over a fucking toy. Stokes was a juvy when this went down. Ain't nobody going to prosecute him now.'

Bosch thought about this for a moment.

'They might. Depends on what we get out of him after we pick him up.'

'You just said yourself there was no sign of premed. They're not going to file it, partner. I'm telling you. We've been chasing our tail. We close the case but nobody goes away for it.'

Bosch knew Edgar was probably right. Under the law, it was rare that adults were prosecuted for crimes committed while they were juveniles as young as thirteen. Even if they pulled a full confession out of Stokes he would probably walk.

'I should have let her shoot him,' he whispered.

'What's that, Harry?'

'Nothing. I'm going to grab something to eat and get on the road. You going to be there?'

'Yeah, I'm here. I'll let you know if anything happens.'

'All right.'

He hung up and got out of the car, thinking about the likelihood of Stokes walking away from his crime. As he entered the warm diner and was hit with the smells of grease and breakfast, he suddenly realized he had lost his appetite.

52

Bosch was just coming down out of the squiggle of treacherous freeway called The Grapevine when his phone chirped. It was Edgar.

'Harry, I've been trying to call you. Where y'at?'

'I was in the mountains. I'm less than an hour out. What's going on?'

'They've got a fix on Stokes. He's squatting in the Usher.'

Bosch thought about this. The Usher was a 1930s hotel a block off Hollywood Boulevard. For decades it was a weekly flophouse and prostitution center until redevelopment on the boulevard pushed up against it and suddenly made it a valuable property again. It was sold, closed and readied to go through a major renovation and restoration that would allow it to rejoin the new Hollywood as an elegant grande dame. But the project had been delayed by city planners who held final approval. And in that delay was an opportunity for the denizens of the night.

While the Hotel Usher awaited rebirth, the rooms on its thirteen floors became the homes of squatters who snuck past the fences and plywood barriers to find shelter. In the previous two months Bosch had been inside the Usher twice while searching for suspects. There was no electricity. There was no water, but the squatters used the toilets anyway and the place smelled like an aboveground sewer. There were no doors on any of the rooms and no furniture. People used rolled-up carpets in the rooms as their beds. It was a nightmare to try to search safely. You moved down the hall and every doorway was open and a possible blind for a gunman. You kept your eyes on the openings and you might step on a needle.

Bosch flipped on the car's emergency lights and put his foot hard on the pedal.

'How do we know he's in there?' he asked.

'From last week when we were looking for him. Some guys in narcs were working something in there and got a line on him squatting all the way up on the thirteenth floor. You gotta be scared of something to go all the way to the top in a place with the elevators shut down.'

'Okay, what's the plan?'

'We're going to go in big. Four teams from patrol, me and the narcs. We start at the bottom and work our way up.'

'When do you go?'

'We're about to go into roll call now and talk it out, then we go. We can't wait for you, Harry. We have to take this guy before he gets out and about.'

Bosch wondered for a moment if Edgar's hurry was legitimate or simply an effort to get even with Bosch for his cutting him out of several of the investigative moves on the case.

'I know,' he finally said. 'You going to have a rover with you?'

'Yeah, we're using channel two.'

'Okay, I'll see you there. Put your vest on.'

He said the last not because he was concerned about Stokes being armed, but because he knew a heavily armed team of cops in the enclosed confinement of a dark hotel hallway had danger written all over it.

Bosch closed the phone and pushed the pedal down even harder. Soon he crossed the northern perimeter of the city and was in the San Fernando Valley. Saturday traffic was light. He switched freeways twice and was cruising through the Cahuenga Pass into Hollywood a half hour after hanging up with Edgar. As he exited onto Highland he could see the Hotel Usher rising a few blocks to the south. Its windows were uniformly dark, the curtains stripped out in preparation for the work ahead.

Bosch had no rover with him and had forgotten to ask Edgar where the command post for the search would be located. He didn't want to simply drive up to the hotel in his slickback and risk exposing the operation. He took out his phone and called the watch office. Mankiewicz answered.

'Mank, you ever take a day off?'

'Not in January. My kids celebrate Christmas and Chanukah. I need the OT. What's up?'

'Can you get me the CP location on the thing at the Usher?'

'Yeah, it's the parking lot at Hollywood Presbyterian.'

'Got it. Thanks.'

Two minutes later Bosch pulled into the church parking lot. There were five squad cars parked there along with a slickback and a narc car. The cars were parked up close to the church so that they were shielded from view of the windows of the Usher, which rose into the sky on the other side of the church.

Two officers sat in one of the patrol cars. Bosch parked and walked over to the driver side window. The car was running. Bosch knew it was the pickup car. When the others grabbed Stokes in the Usher, a radio call would go out for the pickup. They would drive over and pick up the prisoner.

'Where are they?'

'Twelfth floor,' said the driver. 'Nothing yet.'

'Let me borrow your rover.'

The cop handed his radio out the window to Bosch. Bosch called Edgar on channel two.

'Harry, you here?'

'Yeah, I'm coming up.'

'We're almost done.'

'I'm still coming up.'

He gave the radio back to the driver and started walking out of the parking lot. When he got to the construction fence that surrounded the Usher property he went to the north end, where he knew he would find the seam in the fence the squatters used to get in. It was partially hidden behind a construction sign announcing the arrival soon of historic luxury apartments. He pulled back the loose fence and ducked through.

There were two main staircases at either end of the building. Bosch assumed there would be a team of uniform officers posted at the bottom of each in case Stokes somehow slipped through the search and tried to escape. Bosch took out his badge and held it up and out as he opened the exterior stairwell door on the east side of the building.

As he stepped into the stairwell he was met by two officers who held their weapons out and at their sides. Bosch nodded and the cops nodded back. Bosch started up the stairs.

He tried to pace himself. Each floor had two runners of stairs and a landing for the turn. He had twenty-four to climb. The smell from the overflowing toilets was stifling and all he could think about was what Edgar had told him about all odors being particulate. Sometimes knowledge was an awful thing.

The hallway doors had been removed and with them the floor markings. Though someone had taken it upon himself to paint numbers on the walls of the lower landings, as Bosch got higher the markings disappeared and he lost count and became unsure what floor he was on.

At either the ninth or tenth floor he took a breather. He sat down on a reasonably clean step and waited for his breathing to become more regular. The air was cleaner this high up. Fewer squatters used the upper floors of the building because of the climb.

Bosch listened but he heard no human sounds. He knew the search teams had to be on the top floor by now. He was wondering if the tip on Stokes had been wrong, or if the suspect had slipped out.

Finally, he stood and started up again. A minute later he realized he had counted wrong – but in his favor. He stepped up onto the last landing and the open door of the penthouse – the thirteenth floor.

He blew out his breath and almost smiled at the prospect of not having to climb another set of stairs when he heard shouts coming from the hallway.

'There! Right there!'

'Stokes, no! Police! Free—'

Two quick and brutally loud gunshots sounded and echoed down the hall, obliterating the voices. Bosch drew his gun and quickly moved to the doorway. As he began to peek around the jamb he heard two more shots and pulled back.

The echo prevented him from identifying the origin of the shots. He leaned around the jamb again and looked into the hallway. It was dark with light slashing through it from the doorways of the rooms on the west side. He saw Edgar standing in a combat crouch behind two uniformed officers. Their backs were to Bosch and their weapons were pointed at one of the open doorways. They were fifty feet down the hall from Bosch.

'Clear!' a voice yelled. 'We're clear in here!'

The men in the hall raised their weapons up in unison and moved toward the open doorway.

'LAPD in the back!' Bosch yelled and then stepped into the hallway.

Edgar glanced back at him as he followed the two uniforms into the room.

Bosch walked quickly down the hallway and was about to enter the room when he had to step back to let a uniform officer out. He was talking on his rover.

'Central, we need paramedics to forty-one Highland, thirteenth floor. Suspect down, gunshot wounds.'

As Bosch entered the room he looked back. The cop on the rover was Edgewood. Their eyes locked for just a moment and then Edgewood disappeared into the shadows of the hallway. Bosch turned back to view the room.

Stokes was sitting in a closet that had no door. He was leaning back against the rear wall. His hands were in his lap, one holding a small gun, a .25 caliber pocket rocket. He wore black jeans and a sleeveless T-shirt that was covered with his own blood. He had entry wounds on his chest and right below his left eye. His eyes were open but he was clearly dead.

Edgar was squatted in front of the body. He didn't touch it. There was no use trying for a pulse and everybody knew it. The smell of burnt cordite invaded Bosch's nose and it was a welcome relief from the smell outside the room.

Bosch turned around to take in the whole room. There were too many people in the small space. There were three uniforms, Edgar, and a plainclothes Bosch assumed was a narc. Two of the uniforms were huddled together at the far wall, studying two bullet holes in the plaster. One raised a finger and was about to probe one of the holes.

'Don't touch that,' Bosch barked. 'Don't touch anything. I want everybody to back out of here and wait for OIS. Who fired a weapon?'

'Edge did it,' said the narc. 'The guy was waitin' for us in the closet and we—'

'Excuse me, what's your name?'

'Phillips.'

'Okay, Phillips, I don't want to hear your story. Save it for OIS. Go get Edgewood and go back downstairs and wait. When the paramedics get here tell them never mind. Save them a trip up the steps.'

The cops reluctantly shuffled out of the room, leaving only Bosch and Edgar. Edgar got up and walked over to the window. Bosch went to the corner farthest from the closet and looked back at the body. He then approached the body and squatted down in the same spot where Edgar had been.

He studied the gun in Stokes's hand. He assumed that when it was removed from the hand OIS investigators would find the serial number had been burned away by acid.

He thought about the shots he had heard while on the stairway landing. Two and two. It was hard to judge them by memory, especially considering his position at the time. But he thought the first two rounds had been louder and heavier than the second two. If that was so it would mean Stokes had fired his little popper after Edgewood had fired his service weapon. It would mean Stokes had gotten off two shots after he had been hit in the face and chest – wounds that appeared instantly fatal to Bosch.

'What do you think?'

Edgar had come up behind him.

'It doesn't matter what I think,' Bosch said. 'He's dead. It's an OIS case now.'

'What it is is a closed case, partner. I guess we didn't have to worry about whether the DA would file the case after all.'

Bosch nodded. He knew there would be wrap-up investigation and paperwork, but the case was finished. It would ultimately be classified as 'closed by other means,' meaning no trial and no conviction but carried in the solved column just the same.

'Guess not,' he said.

Edgar swatted him on the shoulder.

'Our last case together, Harry. We go out on top.'

'Yeah. Tell me something, did you mention the DA and about it being a juvy case during the briefing in the roll-call room this morning?'

After a long moment Edgar said, 'Yeah, I might've mentioned something about it.'

'Did you tell them we were spinning our wheels, the way you said it to me? That the DA probably wouldn't even file a case on Stokes?'

'Yeah, I might've said it like that. Why?'

Bosch didn't answer. He stood up and walked over to the room's window. He could see the Capitol Records building and farther past it the Hollywood sign up on the crest of the hill. Painted on the side of a building a few blocks away was an anti-smoking sign showing a cowboy with a drooping cigarette in his mouth accompanied by a warning about cigarettes causing impotence.

He turned back to Edgar.

'You going to hold the scene until OIS gets here?'

'Yeah, sure. They're going to be pissed off about having to hump the thirteen floors.'

Bosch headed toward the door.

'Where are you going, Harry?'

Bosch walked out of the room without answering. He used the stairwell at the farthest end of the hallway so that he wouldn't catch up to the others as he was going down.

53

The living members of what had once been a family stood as points of a hard-edged triangle with the grave in the middle. They stood on a sloping hillside in Forest Lawn, Samuel Delacroix on one side of the coffin while his ex-wife stood across from him. Sheila Delacroix's spot was at the end of the coffin opposite the preacher. The mother and daughter had black umbrellas open against the light drizzle that had been falling since dawn. The father had none. He stood there getting wet, and neither woman made a move to share her protection with him.

The sound of the rain and the freeway hissing nearby drowned out most of what the rented preacher had to say before it got to Bosch. He had no umbrella either and watched from a distance and the protection of an oak tree. He thought that it was somehow appropriate that the boy should be formally buried on a hill and in the rain.

He had called the medical examiner's office to find out which funeral home was handling the service and it had led him to Forest Lawn. He had also learned that it had been the boy's mother who had claimed the remains and planned the service. Bosch came to the funeral for the boy, and because he wanted to see the mother again.

Arthur Delacroix's coffin looked like it had been made for an adult. It was polished gray with brushed chrome handles. As coffins went it was beautiful, like a newly waxed car. The rain beaded on its surface and then slid down into the hole beneath. But it was still too big for those bones and somehow that bothered Bosch. It was like seeing a child in ill-fitting clothes, obvious hand-me-downs. It always seemed to say something about the child. That they were wanting. That they were second.

When the rain started coming down harder the preacher raised an umbrella from his side and held his prayer book with one hand. A few of his lines managed to drift over to Bosch intact. He was talking about the greater kingdom that had welcomed Arthur. It made Bosch think of Golliher and his unfaltering faith in that kingdom despite the atrocities he studied and documented every day. For Bosch, though, the jury was still out on all of that. He was still a dweller in the lesser kingdom.

Bosch noticed that none of the three family members looked at one another. After the coffin was lowered and the preacher made the final sign of the cross, Sheila turned and started walking down the slope to the parking road. She had never once acknowledged her parents.

Samuel immediately followed and when Sheila looked back and saw him coming after her she picked up speed. Finally, she just dropped the umbrella and started running. She made it to her car and drove away before her father could catch up.

Samuel watched his daughter's car cutting through the vast cemetery until it disappeared through the gate. He then went back and picked up the discarded umbrella. He took it to his own car and left as well.

Bosch looked back at the burial site. The preacher was gone. Bosch looked about and saw the top of a black umbrella disappearing over the crest of the hill. Bosch didn't know where the man was going, unless he had another funeral to officiate on the other side of the hill.

That left Christine Waters at the grave. Bosch watched her say a silent prayer and then walk toward the two remaining cars on the road below. He chose an angle of intersection and headed that way. As he got close she calmly looked at him.

'Detective Bosch, I am surprised to see you here.'

'Why is that?'

'Aren't detectives supposed to be aloof, not get emotionally involved? Showing up at a funeral shows emotional attachment, don't you think? Especially rainy-day funerals.'

He fell into stride next to her and she gave him half of the umbrella's protection.

'Why did you claim the remains?' he asked. 'Why did you do this?'

He gestured back toward the grave on the hill.

'Because I didn't think anybody else would.'

They got to the road. Bosch's car was parked in front of hers.

'Good-bye, Detective,' she said as she broke from him, walked between the cars and went to the driver's door of hers.

'I have something for you.'

She opened the car door and looked back at him.

'What?'

He opened his door and popped the trunk. He walked back between the cars. She closed her umbrella and threw it into her car and then came over.

'Somebody once told me that life was the pursuit of one thing. Redemption. The search for redemption.'

'For what?'

'For everything. Anything. We all want to be forgiven.'

He raised the trunk lid and took out a cardboard box. He held it out to her.

'Take care of these kids.'

She didn't take the box. Instead she lifted the lid and looked inside. There were stacks of envelopes held together by rubber bands. There were loose photos. On top was the photo of the boy from Kosovo who had the thousand-yard stare. She reached into the box.

'Where are they from?' she asked, as she lifted an envelope from one of the charities.

'It doesn't matter,' he said. 'Somebody has to take care of them.'

She nodded and carefully put the lid back on. She took the box from Bosch and walked it back to her car. She put it on the backseat and then went to the open front door. She looked at Bosch before getting in. She looked like she was about to say something but then she stopped. She got in the car and drove away. Bosch closed the trunk of his car and watched her go.

54

The edict of the chief of police was once again being ignored. Bosch turned on the squad room lights and went to his spot at the homicide table. He put down two empty cardboard boxes.

It was late Sunday, near midnight. He'd decided to come in and clear out his desk and files when no one else would be around to watch. He still had one more day in Hollywood Division but he didn't want to spend it packing boxes and exchanging insincere good-byes with anyone. His plan was to have a clean desk at the start of the day and a three-hour lunch at Musso & Frank's to end it. He'd say a few good-byes to those who mattered and then slip out the back door before anyone even knew he was gone. It was the only way to do it.

He started with his file cabinet, taking the murder books of the open cases that still kept him awake some nights. He wasn't giving up on them just yet. His plan was to work the cases during the downtimes in RHD. Or to work them at home alone.

With one box full he turned to his desk and started emptying the file drawers. When he pulled out the mason jar full of bullet shells, he paused. He had not yet put the shell collected at Julia Brasher's funeral into the jar. Instead he had put that one on a shelf in his home. Next to the picture of the shark he would always keep there as a reminder of the perils of leaving the safety cage. Her father had allowed him to take it.

He carefully put the jar into the corner of the second box and made sure it was held secure by the other contents. He then opened the middle drawer and started collecting all the pens and pads and other office supplies.

Old phone messages and business cards from people he had met on cases were scattered throughout the drawer. Bosch checked each one before deciding whether to keep it or drop it into the trash can. After he had a stack of keepers he put a rubber band around it and dropped it into the box.

When the drawer was almost clear, he pulled out a folded piece of paper and opened it. There was a message on it.

Where are you, tough guy?

Bosch studied it for a long time. Soon it made him think about all that had happened since he had pulled his car to a stop on Wonderland Avenue just thirteen days before. It made him think about what he was doing and where he was going. It made him think of Trent and Stokes and most of all Arthur Delacroix and Julia Brasher. It made him think about what Golliher had said while studying the bones of the murder victims from millenniums ago. And it made him know the answer to the question on the piece of paper.

'Nowhere,' he said out loud.

He folded the paper and put it in the box. He looked down at his hands, at the scars across the knuckles. He ran the fingers of one hand across the markings on the other. He thought about the interior scars left from punching all of the brick walls he couldn't see.

He had always known that he would be lost without his job and his badge and his mission. In that moment he came to realize that he could be just as lost with it all. In fact, he could be lost *because* of it. The very thing he thought he needed the most was the thing that drew the shroud of futility around him.

He made a decision.

He reached into his back pocket and took out his badge wallet. He slid the ID card out from behind the plastic window and then unclipped the badge. He ran his thumb along the indentations where it said *Detective*. It felt like the scars on his knuckles.

He put the badge and the ID card in the desk drawer. He then pulled his gun from its holster, looked at it for a long moment and put it in the drawer, too. He closed the drawer and locked it with a key.

He stood up and walked through the squad room to Billets's office. The door was unlocked. He put the key to his desk drawer and the key to his slickback down on her blotter. When he didn't show up in the morning he was sure she would get curious and check out his desk. She'd then understand that he wasn't coming back. Not to Hollywood Division and not to RHD. He was turning in his badge, going Code 7. He was done.

On the walk back through the squad room Bosch looked about and felt a wave of finality move through him. But he didn't hesitate. At his desk he put one box on top of the other and carried them out through the front hallway. He left the lights on behind him. After he passed the front desk he used his back to push open the heavy front door of the station. He called to the officer sitting behind the counter.

'Hey, do me a favor. Call a cab for me.'

'You got it. But with the weather it might be a while. You might want to wait in—'

The door closed, cutting off the cop's voice. Bosch walked out to the curb. It was a crisp, wet night. There was no sign of the moon beyond the cloud cover. He held the boxes against his chest and waited in the rain.

AUTHOR'S NOTE

In 1914 the bones of a female homicide victim were recovered from the La Brea Tar Pits in Los Angeles. The bones were nine thousand years old, making the woman the earliest known murder victim in the place now known as Los Angeles. The tar pits continue to churn the past and bring bones to the surface for study. However, the finding of a second homicide victim mentioned in this book is wholly fictional – as of this writing.

Chasing the
Dime

This is for Holly Wilkinson

1

The voice on the phone was a whisper. It had a forceful, almost desperate quality to it.

Henry Pierce told the caller he had the wrong number. But the voice became insistent.

'Where is Lilly?' the man asked.

'I don't know,' Pierce said. 'I don't know anything about her.'

'This is her number. It's on the site.'

'No, you have the wrong number. There is no one named Lilly here. And I don't know anything about any site. Okay?'

The caller hung up without responding. Then Pierce hung up, annoyed. He had plugged in the new phone only fifteen minutes earlier and already he had gotten two calls for someone named Lilly.

He put the phone down on the floor and looked around the almost empty apartment. All he had was the black leather couch he sat on, the six boxes of clothes in the bedroom and the new phone. And now the phone was going to be a problem.

Nicole had kept everything – the furniture, the books, the CDs and the house on Amalfi Drive. She didn't keep it, actually: he had given it all to her. The price of his guilt for letting things slip away. The new apartment was nice. It was high luxury and security, a premier address in Santa Monica. But he was going to miss the house on Amalfi. And the woman who was still living in it.

He looked down at the phone on the beige carpet, wondering if he should call Nicole and let her know he had moved from the hotel to the apartment and had the new number. But then he shook his head. He had already sent her the e-mail with all the new information. To call her would be breaking the rules she had set and he had promised to follow on their last night together.

The phone rang. He leaned down and checked the caller ID screen this time. The call was coming from the Casa Del Mar again. It was the same guy. Pierce thought about letting it ring through to the message service that came with the new phone number, but then he picked up the phone and clicked the talk button.

'Look, man, I don't know what the problem is. You have the wrong number. There is nobody here named—'

The caller hung up without saying a word.

Pierce reached over to his backpack and pulled out the yellow pad on which his assistant had written down the voice mail instructions. Monica Purl had set up the phone service for him, as he had been too busy in the lab all week preparing for the following week's presentation. And because that was what personal assistants were for.

He tried to read the notes in the dying light of the day. The sun had just slipped beneath the Pacific and he had no lamps yet for the new apartment's living room. Most new places had sunken lights in the ceiling. Not this one. The apartments were newly renovated, with new kitchens and windows, but the building was old. And slab ceilings without internal wiring could not be renovated in a cost-effective way. Pierce didn't think about that when he rented the place. The bottom line was he needed lamps.

He quickly read through instructions on using the phone's caller ID and caller directory features. He saw that Monica had set him up with something called the convenience package – caller ID, caller directory, call waiting, call forwarding, call everything. And she noted on the page that she had already sent the new number out to his A-level e-mail list. There were almost eighty people on this list. People who he would want to be able to reach him at any time, almost all of them business associates or business associates he also considered friends.

Pierce pressed the talk button again and called the number Monica had listed for setting up and accessing his voice mail program. He then followed the instructions provided by an electronic voice for creating a pass code number. He decided on 92102 – the day Nicole had told him that their three-year relationship was over.

He decided not to record a personal greeting. He would rather hide behind the disembodied electronic voice that announced the number and instructed the caller to leave a message. It was impersonal, but it was an impersonal world out there. He didn't have time to make everything personal.

When he was finished setting up the program a new electronic voice told him he had nine messages. Pierce was surprised by the number – his phone had not been put into service until that morning – but immediately hopeful that maybe one was from Nicole. Maybe several. He suddenly envisioned himself returning all the furniture Monica had ordered for him online. He saw himself carrying the cardboard boxes of his clothes back inside the house on Amalfi Drive.

But none of the messages were from Nicole. None of them were from Pierce's associates or associates/friends, either. Only one was for him – a 'welcome to the system' message delivered by the now familiar electronic voice.

The next eight messages were all for Lilly, no last name mentioned. The same woman he had already fielded three calls for. All the messages were from men. Most of them gave hotel names and numbers to call back. A few gave cell numbers or what they said was a private office line. A few mentioned getting her number off the net or the site, without being more specific.

Pierce erased each message after listening to it. He then turned the page on his notebook and wrote down the name Lilly. He underlined it while he thought about things. Lilly – whoever she was – had apparently stopped using the number. It had been dropped back into circulation by the phone company and then reassigned to him. Judging by the all-male caller list, the number of calls from hotels and the tone of trepidation and anticipation in the voices he had listened to, Pierce guessed that Lilly might be a prostitute. Or an escort, if there was a difference. He felt a little thrill of curiosity and intrigue go through him. Like he knew some secret he wasn't supposed to know. Like when he called up the security cameras on his screen at work and surreptitiously watched what was going on in the hallways and common areas of the office.

He wondered how long the phone number would have been out of use before it was reassigned to him. The number of calls to the line in one day indicated that the phone number was still out there – probably on the website mentioned in a few of the messages – and people still believed it was Lilly's valid number.

'Wrong number,' he said out loud, though he rarely spoke to himself when he wasn't looking at a computer screen or engaged in an experiment in the lab.

He flipped the page back and looked at the information Monica had written down for him. She had included the phone company's customer service number. He could and should call to get the number changed. He also knew it would be an annoying inconvenience to have to resend and receive e-mail notifications correcting the number.

Something else made him hesitate about changing the number. He was intrigued. He admitted it to himself. Who was Lilly? Where was she? Why did she give up the telephone number but leave it on the website? There was a flaw in the logic flow there, and maybe that was what gripped him. How did she maintain her business if the website delivered the wrong number to the client base? The answer was that she didn't. She couldn't. Something was wrong and Pierce wanted to know what and why.

It was Friday evening. He decided to let things stand until Monday. He would call about changing the number then.

Pierce got up from the couch and walked through the empty living room to the master bedroom, where the six cardboard boxes of his clothing were lined against one wall and a sleeping bag was unrolled alongside another. Before moving into the apartment and needing it, he hadn't used the sleeping bag in almost three years – since a trip to Yosemite with Nicole. Back when he had time to do things, before the chase began, before his life became about only one thing.

He went onto the balcony and stared out at the cold blue ocean. He was twelve floors up. The view stretched from Venice on the south side to the ridge of the mountains sliding into the sea off Malibu to the north. The sun was gone but there were violent slashes of orange and purple still in the sky. This high up, the sea breeze was cold and bracing. He put his hands in the pockets of his pants. The fingers of his left hand closed around a coin and he brought it out. A dime. Another reminder of what his life had become.

The neon lights on the Ferris wheel on the Santa Monica Pier were on and flashing a repetitive pattern. It made him remember a time two years earlier when the company had rented the pier's entire amusement park for a private party celebrating the approval of the company's first batch of patents on molecular memory architecture. No tickets, no lines, no getting off a ride if you were having fun. He and Nicole had stayed in one of the open yellow gondolas of the Ferris wheel for at least a half hour. It had been cold that night, too, and they huddled against each other. They'd watched the sun go down. Now he couldn't look at the pier or even a sunset without thinking about her.

In acknowledging this about himself, he realized he had rented an apartment with views of the very things that would remind him of Nicole. There was a subliminal pathology there that he didn't want to explore.

He put the dime on his thumbnail and flipped it into the air. He watched it disappear into the darkness. There was a park below, a strip of green between the building and the beach. He had already noticed that homeless people snuck in at night and slept in sleeping bags under the trees. Maybe one of them would find the fallen dime.

The phone rang. He went back into the living room and saw the tiny LED screen glowing in the darkness. He picked up the phone and read the screen. The call was coming from the Century Plaza Hotel. He thought about it for two more rings and then answered without saying hello.

'Are you calling for Lilly?' he asked.

A long moment of silence went by but Pierce knew someone was there. He could hear television sounds in the background.

'Hello? Is this call for Lilly?'

Finally a man's voice answered.

'Yes, is she there?'

'She's not here at the moment. Can I ask how you got this number?'

'From the site.'

'What site?'

The caller hung up. Pierce held the phone to his ear for a moment and then clicked it off. He walked across the room to return the phone to its cradle when it rang again. Pierce hit the talk button without looking at the caller ID display.

'You've got the wrong number,' he said.

'Wait, Einstein, is that you?'

Pierce smiled. It wasn't a wrong number. He recognized the voice of Cody Zeller, one of the A-list recipients of his new number. Zeller often called him Einstein, one of the college nicknames Pierce still endured. Zeller was a friend first and a business associate second. He was a computer security consultant who had designed numerous systems for Pierce over the years as his company grew and moved to larger and larger spaces.

'Sorry, Code,' Pierce said. 'I thought you were somebody else. This new number is getting a lot of calls for somebody else.'

'New number, new place, does this mean you're free, white and single again?'

'I guess so.'

'Man, what happened with Nicki?'

'I don't know. I don't want to talk about it.'

He knew talking about it with friends would add a permanency to the end of their relationship.

'I'll tell you what happened,' Zeller said. 'Too much time in the lab and not enough between the sheets. I warned you about that, man.'

Zeller laughed. He'd always had a way of looking at a situation or set of facts and cutting away the bullshit. And his laughter told Pierce he was not overly sympathetic to his plight. Zeller was unmarried and Pierce could never remember him in a long-term relationship. As far back as college he promised Pierce and their friends he would never practice monogamy in his lifetime. He also knew the woman in question. In his capacity as a security expert he also handled online backgrounding of employment applicants and investors for Pierce. In that role he worked closely at times with Nicole James, the company's intelligence officer. Make that former intelligence officer.

'Yeah, I know,' Pierce said, though he didn't want to talk about this with Zeller. 'I should've listened.'

'Well, maybe this means you'll be able to take your spoon out of retirement and meet me out at Zuma one of these mornings.'

Zeller lived in Malibu and surfed every morning. It had been nearly ten years since Pierce had been a regular on the waves with him. In fact, he had not even taken his board with him when he moved out of the house on Amalfi. It was up on the rafters in the garage.

'I don't know, Code. I've still got the project, you know. I don't think my time is going to change much just because she—'

'That's right, she was only your fiancée, not the project.'

'I don't mean it like that. I just don't think I'm—'

'What about tonight? I'll come down. We'll hit the town like the old days. Put on your black jeans, baby.'

Zeller laughed in encouragement. Pierce didn't. There had never been old days like that. Pierce had never been a player. He was blue jeans, not black jeans. He'd always preferred to spend the night in the lab looking into a scanning tunneling microscope than pursuing sex in a club with an engine fueled by alcohol.

'I think I'm going to pass, man. I've got a lot of stuff to do and I need to go back to the lab tonight.'

'Hank, man, you've got to give the molecules a rest. One night out. Come on, it will straighten you out, shake up your own molecules for once. You can tell me all about what happened with you and Nicki, and I'll pretend to feel sorry for you. I promise.'

Zeller was the only one on the planet who called him Hank, a name Pierce hated. But Pierce was smart enough to know that telling Zeller to stop was out of the question, because it would prompt his friend to use the name at all times.

'Call me next time, all right?'

Zeller reluctantly backed off and Pierce promised to keep the next weekend open for a night out. He made no promises about surfing. They hung up and Pierce put the phone in its cradle. He picked up his backpack and headed for the apartment door.

2

Pierce used his scramble card to enter the garage attached to Amedeo Technologies and parked his 540 in his assigned space. The entrance to the building came open as he approached, the approval coming from the night man at the dais behind the double glass doors.

'Thanks, Rudolpho,' Pierce said as he went by.

He used his electronic key to take the elevator to the third floor, where the administrative offices were located. He looked up at the camera in the corner and nodded, though he doubted Rudolpho was watching him. It was all being digitized and recorded for later. If ever needed.

In the third-floor hallway he worked the combo lock on his office door and went in.

'Lights,' he said as he went behind his desk.

The overhead lights came on. He turned on his computer and entered the passwords after it booted up. He plugged in the phone line so he could quickly check his e-mail messages before going to work. It was 8 p.m. He liked working at night, having the lab to himself.

For security reasons he never left the computer on or attached to a phone line when he wasn't working on it. For the same reason he carried no cell phone, pager or personal digital assistant. Though he had one, he rarely carried a laptop computer, either. Pierce was paranoid by nature – just a gene splice away from schizophrenia, according to Nicole – but also a cautious and practical researcher. He knew that every time he plugged an outside line into his computer or opened a cellular transmission, it was as dangerous as sticking a needle into his arm or having sex with a stranger. You never knew what you might be bringing into the pipeline. For some people, that was probably part of the thrill of sex. But it wasn't part of the thrill of chasing the dime.

He had several messages but only three that he decided to read this night. The first was from Nicole and he opened it immediately, again with a hope in his heart that made him uncomfortable because it verged on being maudlin.

But the message was not what he was looking for. It was short, to the point and so professional that it was devoid of any reference to their ill-fated romance. Just a former employee's last sign-off before moving on to bigger and better things – in career and romance.

Hewlett,

I'm out of here.

Everything's in the files. (by the way, the Bronson deal finally hit the media – SJMN got it first. nothing new but you might want to check it out.)

Thanks for everything and good luck.

Nic

Pierce stared at the message for a long time. He noted that it had been sent at 4:55 p.m., just a few hours earlier. There was no sense in replying, because her e-mail address would have been wiped from the system at 5 p.m. when she turned in her scramble card. She was gone and there seemed to be nothing so permanent as being wiped from the system.

She had called him Hewlett and he wondered about that for a long moment. In the past she had used the name as an endearment. A secret name only a lover would use. It was based on his initials – HP, as in Hewlett-Packard, the huge computer manufacturer that these days was one of the Goliaths to Pierce's David. She always said it with a sweet smile in her voice. Only she could get away with nicknaming him with a competitor's name. But her using it in this final message, what did it mean? Was she smiling sweetly when she wrote this? Smiling sadly? Was she faltering, changing her mind about them? Was there still a chance, a hope of reconciliation?

Pierce had never been able to judge the motives of Nicole James. He couldn't now. He put his hands back on the keyboard and saved the message, moving it to a file where he kept all her e-mails, going back the entire three years of their relationship. The history of their time together – good and bad, moving from co-workers to lovers – could be read in the messages. Almost a thousand messages from her. He knew keeping them was obsessive but it was a routine for him. He also had files for e-mail storage in regard to a number of his business relationships. The file for Nicole had started out that way, but then they moved from business associates to what he thought would be partners in life.

He scrolled through the e-mail list in the Nicole James file, reading the captions in the subject lines the way a man might look through photos of an old girlfriend. He outright smiled at a few of them. Nicole was always the master of the witty or sarcastic subject line. Later – by necessity, he knew –

she mastered the cutting line and then the hurtful line. One line caught his eye during the scroll – 'Where do you live?' – and he opened the message. It had been sent four months before and was as good a clue as any as to what would become of them. In his mind this message represented the start of the descent for them – the point of no return.

I was just wondering where you live because I haven't seen you at Amalfi in four nights.

Obviously this is not working, Henry. We need to talk but you are never home to talk. Do I have to come to that lab to talk about us? That would certainly be sad.

He remembered going home to talk to her after that one, resulting in their first breakup. He spent four days in a hotel, living out of a suitcase, lobbying her by phone, e-mail and flowers before being invited to return to Amalfi Drive. A genuine effort on his part followed. He came home every night by eight for at least a week, it seemed, before he started to slip and his lab shifts began lasting into the small hours again.

Pierce closed the message and then the file. Someday he planned to print out the whole scroll of messages and read it like a novel. He knew it would be the very common, very unoriginal story of how a man's obsession led him to lose the thing that was most important to him. If it were a novel, he would call it *Chasing the Dime*.

He went back to the current e-mail list and the next message he read was from his partner Charlie Condon. It was just an end-of-the-week reminder about the presentation scheduled for the next week, as if Pierce needed to be reminded. The subject line read 'RE: Proteus' and was a return on a message Pierce had sent Charlie a few days before.

It's all set with God. He's coming in Wednesday for a ten o'clock Thursday. The harpoon is sharpened and ready. Be there or be square.

CC

Pierce didn't bother replying. It was a given that he would be there. A lot was riding on it. No, everything was riding on it. The God referred to in the message was Maurice Goddard. He was a New Yorker, an ET investor Charlie was hoping would be their whale. He was coming in to look at the Proteus project before making his final decision. They were giving him a first look at Proteus, hoping it would be the closer on the deal. The following Monday they would file for patent protection on Proteus and begin seeking other investors if Goddard didn't come on board.

The last message he read was from Clyde Vernon, head of Amedeo security. Pierce figured he could guess what it said before he opened it, and he wasn't wrong.

Trying to reach you. We need to talk about Nicole James. Please call me ASAP.

Clyde Vernon

Pierce knew Vernon wanted to know how much Nicole knew and the circumstances of her abrupt departure. Vernon wanted to know what action he would need to take.

Pierce smirked at the security man's inclusion of his full name. He then decided not to waste time on the other e-mails and turned off the computer, careful to unplug the phone line as well. He left the office and went down the hallway, past the wall of fame, to Nicole's office. Her former office.

Pierce had the override combination for all doors on the third floor. He used it now to open the door and step into the office.

'Lights,' he said.

But the overhead lights did not respond. The office's audio receptor was still registered to Nicole's voice. That would likely be changed on Monday. Pierce went to the wall switch and turned on the lights.

The top of the desk was clear. She had said she'd be gone by Friday at five and she had made good on the promise, probably sending him that e-mail as her last official act at Amedeo Technologies.

Pierce walked around the desk and sat down in her chair. He could still pick up a scent of her perfume – a whisper of lilac. He opened the top drawer. It was empty except for a paper clip. She was gone. That was for sure. He checked the three other drawers and they were all empty except for a small box he found in the bottom drawer. He took it out and opened it. It was half full of business cards. He took one out and looked at it.

Nicole R. James
Director of Competitive Intelligence
Public Information Officer

Amedeo Technologies
Santa Monica, California

After a while he put the card back in the box, and the box back in the drawer. He got up and went to the row of file cabinets against the wall opposite the desk.

She'd insisted on hard copies of all intelligence files. There were four double-drawer cabinets. Pierce took out his keys and used one to unlock a drawer labeled BRONSON. He opened the drawer and took out the blue file – under Nicole's filing system the most current file on any competitor was blue. He opened the file and glanced through the printouts and a photocopy of a news clipping from the business section of the *San Jose Mercury News.* He'd seen everything before except for the clipping.

It was a short story about one of his chief competitors in the private sector getting an infusion of cash. It was dated two days earlier. He had heard about the deal in general already – through Nicole. Word traveled fast in the emerging-technologies world. A lot faster than through the news media. But the story was a confirmation of everything he'd already heard – and then some.

Bronson Tech Gets Boost from Japan

By Raul Puig

Santa Cruz–based Bronson Technologies has agreed to a partnership with Japan's Tagawa Corporation that will provide funding for the firm's molecular electronics project, the parties announced Wednesday.

Under terms of the agreement Tagawa will provide $16 million in research funds over the next four years. In return Tagawa will hold a 20 percent interest in Bronson.

Elliot Bronson, president of the six-year-old company, said the money will help put his company into the lead in the vaunted race to develop the first practical molecular computer. Bronson and a host of private companies, universities and governmental agencies are engaged in a race to develop molecular-based random access memory (RAM) and link it to integrated circuitry. Though practical application of molecular computing is still seen by some as at least a decade away, it is believed by its proponents that it will revolutionize the world of electronics. It is also seen as a potential threat to the multibillion-dollar silicon-based computer industry.

The potential value and application of molecular computing is seen as limitless and, therefore, the race to develop it is heated. Molecular computer chips will be infinitely more powerful and smaller than the silicon-based chips that currently support the electronics field.

'From diagnostic computers that can be dropped into the bloodstream to the creation of "smart streets" with microscopic computers contained in the asphalt, molecular computers will change this world,' Bronson said Tuesday. 'And this company is going to be there to help change it.'

Among Bronson's chief competitors in the private sector are Amedeo Technologies of Los Angeles and Midas Molecular in Raleigh, N.C. Also, Hewlett-Packard has partnered with scientists at the University of California, Los Angeles. And more than a dozen other universities and private firms are putting significant funding into research into nanotechnology and molecular RAM. The Defense Advanced Research Projects Agency is partially or wholly funding many of these programs.

A handful of companies have chosen to seek private backing instead of relying on the government or universities. Bronson explained that the decision makes the company more nimble, able to move quickly with projects and experimentation without having to seek government or university approval.

'The government and these big universities are like battleships,' Bronson said. 'Once they get moving in the right direction, then watch out. But it takes them a long while to make the turns and get pointed the right way. This field is too competitive and changes too rapidly for that. It's better to be a speed boat at the moment.'

Non-reliance on government or university funding also means less sharing of the wealth as patents in the area become more valuable in years to come.

Several significant advances in the development of molecular computing have occurred in the last five years, with Amedeo Tech seemingly leading the way.

Amedeo is the oldest company in the race. Henry Pierce, 34, the chemist who founded the company a year after leaving Stanford, has been granted numerous patents in the areas of molecular circuitry and the creation of molecular memory and logic gates – the basic component of computing.

Bronson said he hopes to now level the playing field with the funding from Tagawa.

'I think it will be a long and interesting race but we're going to be there at the finish line,' he said. 'With this deal, I guarantee it.'

The move to a significant source of financial support – a 'whale' in the parlance of the emerging-technologies investment arena – is becoming favored by the smaller companies. Bronson's move follows Midas Molecular, which secured $16 million in funding from a Canadian investor earlier this year.

'There is no two ways about it, you need the money to be competitive,' Bronson said. 'The basic tools of this science are expensive. To outfit a lab costs more than a million before you even get to the research.'

Amedeo's Pierce did not return calls but sources in the industry indicated his company is also seeking a significant investor.

'Everybody is out hunting whales,' said Daniel F. Daly, a partner in Daly & Mills, a Florida-based investment firm that has monitored the emergence of nanotechnology. 'Money from the hundred-thousand-dollar investor gets eaten up too quickly, so everybody's into one-stop shopping – finding the one investor who will see a project all the way through.'

Pierce closed the file, the newspaper clip inside it. Little in the story was new to him but he was intrigued by the first quote from Bronson mentioning molecular diagnostics. He wondered if Bronson was toeing the industry line, talking up the sexier side of the science, or whether he knew something about Proteus. Was he talking directly to Pierce? Using the newspaper and his newfound Japanese money to throw down the gauntlet?

If he was, then he had a shock coming soon. Pierce put the file back in its place in the drawer.

'You sold out too cheap, Elliot,' he said as he closed it.

As he left the office he turned off the lights by hand.

Outside in the hallway, Pierce momentarily scanned what they called the wall of fame. Framed articles on Amedeo and Pierce and the patents and the research covered the wall for twenty feet. During business hours, when employees were about in the offices, he never stopped to look at these. It was only in private moments that he glimpsed the wall of fame and felt a sense of pride. It was a scoreboard of sorts. Most of the articles came from science journals, and the language was impenetrable to the layman. But a few times the company and its work poked through into the general media. Pierce stopped before the piece that privately made him the most proud. It was a *Fortune* magazine cover nearly five years old. It showed a photograph of him – in his ponytail days – holding a plastic model of the simple molecular circuit he had just received a patent for. The caption to the right side of his smile asked, 'The Most Important Patent of the Next Millennium?'

Then in small type beneath it added, 'He thinks so. Twenty-nine-year-old wunderkind Henry Pierce holds the molecular switch that could be the key to a new era in computing and electronics.'

The moment was only five years old but it filled Pierce with a sense of nostalgia as he looked at the framed magazine cover. The embarrassing label of wunderkind notwithstanding, Pierce's life changed when that magazine hit the newsstands. The chase started in earnest after that. The investors came to him, rather than the other way around. The competitors came. Charlie Condon came. Even Jay Leno's people came calling about the longhaired surfer chemist and his molecules. The best moment of all that Pierce remembered was when he wrote the check that paid off the scanning electron microscope.

The pressure came then, too. The pressure to perform, to make the next stride. And then the next. Given the choice, he wouldn't go back. Not a chance. But Pierce liked to remember the moment for all that he didn't know then. There was nothing wrong with that.

3

The lab elevator descended so slowly that there was no physical indication it was even moving. The lights above the door were the only way to know for sure. It was designed that way, to eliminate as many vibrations as possible. Vibrations were the enemy. They skewed readings and measurements in the lab.

The door slowly opened on the basement level and Pierce stepped out. He used his scramble card to enter the first door of the mantrap and then, once inside the small passageway, punched in the October combination on the second door. He opened it and entered the lab.

The lab was actually a suite of several smaller labs clustered around the main room, or day room, as they called it. The suite was completely windowless. Its walls were lined on the inside with insulation containing copper shavings that knocked down electronic noise from the outside. On the surface of these walls the decorations were few, largely limited to a series of framed prints from the Dr. Seuss book *Horton Hears a Who!*

The secondary labs included the chemlab to the left. This was a 'clean room' where the chemical solutions of molecular switches were made and refrigerated. There was also an incubator for the Proteus project which they called the cell farm.

Opposite the chemlab was the wire lab, or the furnace room, as most of the lab rats called it, and next to it was the imaging lab, which housed the electron microscope. All the way to the rear of the day room was the laser lab. This room was sheathed in copper for added protection against intruding electronic noise.

The lab suite appeared empty, the computers off and the probe stations unmanned, but Pierce picked up the familiar smell of cooking carbon. He checked the sign-in log and saw that Grooms had signed in but had not yet signed out. He walked over to the wire lab and looked through the little glass door. He didn't see anyone. He opened the door and stepped in, immediately being hit with the heat and the smell. The vacuum oven was operating, a new batch of carbon wires being made. Pierce assumed Grooms had started the batch and then left the lab to take a break or get something to eat. It was understandable. The smell of cooking carbon was intolerable.

He left the wire lab and closed the door. He went to a computer next to one of the probe stations and typed in the passwords. He pulled up the data on the switch tests he knew Grooms had been planning to conduct after Pierce had gone home early to set up his phone. According to the computer log, Grooms had run two thousand tests on a new group of twenty switches. The chemically synthesized switches were basic on/off gates that one day could – or would – be used to build computer circuitry.

Pierce leaned back in the computer seat. He noticed a half full cup of coffee on the counter next to the monitor. He knew it was Larraby's because it was black. Everybody else in the lab used cream but the immunologist assigned to the Proteus project.

As Pierce thought about whether to continue with the gateway confirmation tests or to go into the imaging lab and pull up Larraby's latest work on Proteus, his eyes drifted up toward the wall behind the computers. Scotch-taped to the wall was a dime. Grooms had put it up a couple years earlier. A joke, yes, but a solid reminder of their goal. Sometimes it seemed to be mocking them. Roosevelt turning the side of his face, looking the other way, ignoring them.

It wasn't until that moment that Pierce realized he wasn't going to be able to work this night. He had spent so many nights working in the confines of the lab suite that it had cost him Nicole. That and other things. Now that she was gone, he was free to work without hesitation or guilt and he suddenly realized he couldn't do it. If he ever spoke to her again, he would tell her this. Maybe it would mean he was changing. Maybe it would mean something to her.

Behind him there was a sudden loud banging sound and Pierce jumped in his seat. Turning around and expecting to see Grooms returning, he saw Clyde Vernon come through the mantrap instead. Vernon was a wide and husky man with just a fringe of hair around the outer edges of his head. He had a naturally ruddy complexion that always gave him a look of consternation. In his mid-fifties, Vernon was by far the oldest person working at the company. After him Charlie Condon was probably the oldest at forty.

This time the look of consternation Vernon carried was real.

'Hey, Clyde, you scared me,' Pierce said.

'I didn't mean to.'

'We do a lot of sensitive readings in here. Banging the door open like that could ruin an experiment. Luckily, I was just reviewing experiments, not conducting any.'

'I'm sorry, Dr. Pierce.'

'Don't call me that, Clyde. Call me Henry. So let me guess, you put out a "be on the look out for" on me, and Rudolpho called it in when I came through. And that made you come all the way in from home. I hope you don't live too far away, Clyde.'

Vernon ignored Pierce's fine deductive work.

'We need to talk,' he said instead. 'Did you get my message?'

They were in the early stages of getting to know each other. Vernon might be the oldest person working at Amedeo, but he was also the newest. Pierce had already noticed that Vernon had difficulty calling him by name. He thought maybe it was an age thing. Pierce was the president of the company but at least twenty years younger than Vernon, who had come to the company a few months earlier after putting in twenty-five years with the FBI. Vernon probably thought it would be improper to address Pierce by his first name, and the gulf in age and real-life experience made it difficult to call him Mr. Pierce. Dr. Pierce seemed a bit easier for him, even though it was based on academic degrees not medical ones. His real plan seemed to be to never address him by any name if possible. To the point it was noticeable, especially in e-mail and telephone conversations.

'I just got your e-mail about fifteen minutes ago,' Pierce said. 'I was out of the office. I was probably going to call you when I got finished here. You want to talk about Nicole?'

'Yes. What happened?'

Pierce shrugged his shoulders in a helpless gesture.

'What happened is that she left. She quit her job and she, uh, quit me. I guess you could say she quit me first.'

'When did this happen?'

'Hard to tell, Clyde. It was happening for a while. Like slow motion. But it all sort of hit the fan a couple weeks ago. She agreed to stay until today. Today was her last day. I know when we brought you in here you warned me about fishing off the company dock. I think that's what you called it. I guess you were right.'

Vernon took a step closer to Pierce.

'Why wasn't I told about this?' he protested. 'I should've been told.'

Pierce could see the color moving higher on Vernon's cheeks. He was angry and trying to control it. It wasn't about Nicole so much as his need to solidify his position in the company. After all, he didn't leave the bureau after so many years to be kept in the dark by some punk scientist boss who probably smoked pot on the weekends.

'Look, I know you should have been told but because there were some personal issues involved I just . . . I didn't really want to talk about it. And to tell you the truth, I probably wasn't going to call you tonight, because I still don't want to talk about it.'

'Well, we need to talk about it. She was the intelligence officer of this company. She shouldn't have been allowed to just waltz out the door at the end of the day.'

'All the files are still there. I checked, even though I didn't need to. Nicki would never do anything like you are suggesting.'

'I am not suggesting any impropriety. I am just trying to be thorough and cautious about this. That's all. Did she take another job that you know of?'

'Not as of the last time we spoke. But she signed a no-compete contract when we hired her. We don't have to worry about that, Clyde.'

'So you think. What were the financial arrangements of the separation?'

'Why is that your business?'

'Because a person in need of finances is vulnerable. It's my business to know if a former or current employee with intimate knowledge of the project is vulnerable.'

Pierce was beginning to get annoyed with Vernon's rapid questioning and condescending demeanor, even though it was the same demeanor he treated the security man with on a daily basis.

'First of all, her knowledge of the project was limited. She gathered intelligence on the competitors, not on us. To do that, she had to have a sense of what we're doing in here. But I don't think she was in a position to know exactly what we're doing or where we are in any of the projects. Just like you don't, Clyde. It is safer that way.

'And second, I'll answer your next question before you ask it. No, I never told her on a personal level the details of what we are doing. It never came up. In fact, I don't even think she cared. She treated the job like a job, and that probably was the main problem with us. I didn't treat it as a job. I treated it like it was my life. Now, anything else, Clyde? I want to get some work done.'

He hoped camouflaging the one lie in verbiage and indignation would get it by Vernon.

'When did Charlie Condon know about this?' Vernon asked.

Condon was the company's chief financial officer, but more important, he was the man who had hired Vernon.

'We told him yesterday,' Pierce said. 'Together. I heard she'd made an appointment to talk to him last before she left today. If Charlie didn't tell you, there is nothing I can do about that. I guess he didn't see it as necessary, either.'

That was a shot, reminding Vernon that he had been left out of the loop by his own sponsor. But the former FBI man shook it off with a quick frown and moved on.

'You didn't answer before. Did she receive a severance?'

'Of course. Yes. Six months' pay, two years' medical and life insurance. She's also selling the house and keeping all proceeds. Satisfied? I hardly think she's vulnerable. She should clear more than a hundred grand on that house alone.'

Vernon seemed to calm a bit. Knowing that Charlie Condon had been in the loop eased things for him. Pierce knew Vernon viewed Charlie as being the practical business side of the company while Pierce was the more ephemeral talent side. And somehow Pierce's being on the talent side lowered Vernon's respect for him. Charlie was different. He was all business. If he had signed off on Nicole James's departure, then it was going to be okay.

But then again, if Vernon was satisfied, he wasn't going to say so to Pierce.

'I am sorry if you don't like the questions,' he said. 'But it's my job and my duty to maintain the security of this firm and its projects. There are many people and companies whose investment must be safeguarded.'

He was alluding to the reason he was there. Charlie Condon had hired him as a showpiece. Vernon was there to placate potential investors who needed to know that the company's projects were safe and secure and, therefore, that their investments would be safe and secure. Vernon's pedigree was impressive and more vitally important to the company than the actual security work he performed.

When Maurice Goddard had made his first trip out from New York to be shown around the place and receive the initial presentation, he had also been introduced to Vernon and had spent twenty minutes talking about plant security and personnel with him.

Pierce now looked at Clyde Vernon and felt like screaming at him, letting him know how close they were to running out of significant funding and how inconsequential he was in the scheme of things.

But he held his tongue.

'I understand your concerns perfectly, Clyde. But I don't think you have to worry about Nicole. Everything is cool.'

Vernon nodded and finally conceded, perhaps sensing the growing tension behind Pierce's eyes.

'I think you're probably right.'

'Thank you.'

'Now, you said you were selling the house.'

'I said she's selling it.'

'Yes. Have you moved yet? Do you have a number where you can be reached?'

Pierce hesitated. Vernon had not been on the A-list of people who had gotten his new number and address. Respect was a two-way street. While Pierce viewed Vernon as capable, he also knew what had gotten the man the job was his FBI pedigree. Of his twenty-five years in the bureau, Vernon had spent half in the L.A. field office on white collar crime and corporate espionage investigations.

But Pierce viewed Vernon largely as a poseur. He was always on the move, charging down hallways and banging through doors like a man on a mission. But the bottom line was that there wasn't a whole lot to the mission of providing project security to a firm that employed thirty-three people, only ten of which could get through the mantrap and inside the lab, where all the secrets were kept.

'I've got a new phone number but I don't remember it,' Pierce said. 'I'll get it to you as soon as I can.'

'What about the address?'

'It's over in the Sands on the beach. Apartment twelve oh one.'

Vernon took out a little notebook and wrote down the information. He looked just like a cop from an old movie, his big hands crowding the small notebook as he scribbled. *Why do they always have such small notebooks?* It was a question Cody Zeller had once posited after they'd seen a cop flick together.

'I'm going to get back to work now, Clyde. After all, all those investors are counting on us, right?'

Vernon looked up from his notebook, one eyebrow raised as he tried to gauge whether Pierce was being sarcastic.

'Right,' he said. 'Then I'll let you get back to it.'

But after the security man had retreated through the mantrap, Pierce again realized he could not get back to it. An inertia had set in. For the first time in three years he was unencumbered by interests outside the lab and free to do the work. But for the first time in three years he didn't want to.

He shut down the computer and got up. He followed in Vernon's wake through the mantrap.

4

When he got back to his office Pierce turned the lights on by hand. The voice-recognition switch was bullshit and he knew it. Something installed simply to impress the potential investors Charlie Condon walked through the place every few weeks. It was a gimmick. Just like all the cameras and Vernon. But Charlie said it was all necessary. It symbolized the cutting-edge nature of what they did. He said it helped investors envision the company's projects and importance. It made them feel good about writing a check.

But the result was that the offices sometimes seemed to Pierce to be as soulless as they were high-tech. He had started the company in a low-rent warehouse in Westchester, having to take readings on experiments in between takeoffs and landings at LAX. He had no employees. Now he had so many he needed an employee relations officer. He drove a fender-dented Volkswagen Beetle then – the old kind. And now he drove a BMW. There was no doubt, he and Amedeo had certainly come a long way. But with increasing frequency he would drift off to memories of that warehouse lab beneath the flight pattern of runway 17. His friend Cody Zeller, always looking for a movie reference, had once told him that 'runway 17' would be his 'Rosebud,' the last words whispered from his dying lips. Other similarities to *Citizen Kane* notwithstanding, Pierce thought there was a possibility Zeller might be right about that.

Pierce sat down at his desk and thought about calling Zeller and telling him he'd changed his mind about going out. He also thought about calling the house to see if Nicole wanted to talk. But he knew he couldn't do that. It was her move to make and he had to wait her out – even if it never happened.

He took the pad out of his backpack and called the number for accessing his home voice mail by remote location. He tapped in the password and was told electronically that he had one new message. He played it and heard the nervous voice of a man he didn't know.

'Uh, yes, hello, my name is Frank. I'm at the Peninsula. Room six twelve. So give me a call when you can. I got your number from the website and I wanted to see if you're available tonight. I know it's late but I thought I'd try. Anyway, it's Frank Behmer, room six twelve at the Peninsula. Hope to hear from you soon.'

Pierce erased the message but once more felt the weird magic of secretly being inside somebody's hidden world. He thought for a few moments and then called Information to get the number for the Peninsula in Beverly Hills. Frank Behmer had been so nervous while leaving the message that he hadn't included the callback number.

He called the hotel and asked for Behmer in room 612. The call was picked up after five rings.

'Hello?'

'Mr. Behmer?'

'Yes?'

'Hi. Did you call for Lilly?'

Behmer hesitated before answering.

'Who is this?'

Pierce didn't hesitate. He had been anticipating the question.

'My name is Hank. I handle Lilly's calls. She's kind of busy at the moment but I'm trying to reach her for you. To set it up for you.'

'Yes, I tried the cell number but she didn't call back.'

'The cell number?'

'The one on the site.'

'Oh, I see. You know, she is listed on several sites. Do you mind my asking which one you got her numbers from? We're trying to figure out which one is most effective, if you know what I mean.'

'I saw it on the L.A. Darlings site.'

'Oh, L.A. Darlings. Right. That's one of our better sites.'

'That's really her on there, right? In the picture?'

'Uh, yes, sir, that's really her.'

'Beautiful.'

'Yes. Okay, well, like I said, I'll get her to call you as soon as I get ahold of her. Shouldn't take too long. But if you don't hear from either me or Lilly within an hour, then it's not going to happen.'

'Really?'

Disappointment tumbled off his voice.

'She's very busy, Mr. Behmer. But I'll try my best. Good night.'

'Well, tell her I'm just in town on business for a few days and I'd treat her real nice, if you know what I mean.'

Now there was a slight note of pleading in his voice. It made Pierce feel guilty about the subterfuge. He felt that he suddenly knew too much about Behmer and his life.

'I know what you mean,' he said. 'Good-bye.'

'Good-bye.'

Pierce hung up. He tried to put his misgivings aside. He didn't know what he was doing or why, but something was pulling him down a pathway.

He rebooted his computer and jacked in the phone line. He then went online and tried a variation of web configurations until he hit on www.la-darlings.com and was connected to a site.

The first page was text. It was a warning/waiver form explaining that there was explicit adult fare waiting on the website. By clicking the ENTER button, the visitor was acknowledging that he or she was over eighteen years old and was not offended by nudity or adult content. Without reading all the fine print, Pierce clicked on the ENTER button and the screen changed to the site's home page. Running along the left border was a photo of a naked woman holding a towel in front of herself and a raised finger in front of her lips in a don't-tell-anyone pose. The site titling was in a large purple font.

L.A. Darlings
A free directory of adult entertainment and services

Beneath was a row of red tabs labeled with the available services, ranging from escorts categorized by race and hair color to massage and fetish experts of all genders and sexual orientation. There was even a tab for hiring actual porno stars for private sessions. Pierce knew there were countless sites like these all over the Internet. It was likely that every Internet provider in every city and town had at least one of these sites – the equivalent of an online bordello – sitting in its chips. He had never taken the time to explore one, though he knew that Charlie Condon had once used such a site to hire an escort for a potential investor. It was a decision he regretted and never repeated – the investor was drink-drugged and robbed by the escort before any sex act even took place. Needless to say, he did not invest in Amedeo Technologies.

Pierce clicked on the BLONDE ESCORTS tab for no reason other than it was a place to start looking for Lilly. The page opened in two halves. On the left side of the page was a scrolling panel of thumbnail photos of the blonde escorts with their first names appearing under each picture. When he clicked on one of the thumbnails, the escort's page would then open on the right – the photo enlarged for easier and better viewing.

Pierce scrolled down the panel, looking at the names. There were nearly forty different escorts, but none was named Lilly. He closed it out and went to the brunettes section next. Halfway through the thumbnails he came to an escort with the name Tiger Lilly under her picture. He clicked on the photo and her page appeared on the right. He checked the phone number – it wasn't the same as his.

He closed the page and went back to the thumbnails panel. Further down he came to another escort named simply Lilly. He clicked her page open and checked the number. It was a match. He had found the Lilly whose phone number he now had.

The photo on the ad was of a woman in her mid-twenties. She had dark shoulder-length hair and brown eyes, a deep tan. She was kneeling on a bed with brass railings and was naked beneath a black fishnet negligee. The curves of her breasts were clearly visible. The tan lines of her crotch were seen also. Her eyes looked directly into the camera. Her full lips formed what Pierce thought was meant to be an inviting pout.

If the photo had not been altered and if it was really Lilly, then she was beautiful. Just as Frank Behmer had said. Pure fantasy, an escort dream. Pierce understood why his phone had been ringing constantly since he had plugged it in. The wealth of competition on this website and all the others on the net didn't matter. A man scrolling through the photos – shopping for a woman, as it were – would be hard-pressed to go past this one without picking up the phone.

There was a blue ribbon posted below the photo. Pierce moved the cursor to it and a pop-up caption said 'photo verified by staff,' meaning the model in the photo was actually the woman who had placed the ad. In other words, you got what you saw if you arranged to meet the escort. Supposedly.

'Photo verifier,' Pierce said. 'That's not a bad job.'

His eyes moved to the ad copy below the photo and he scrolled down as he read it.

Special Desires

Hello, Gentlemen. My name is Lilly and I'm the most soothing, pleasing and down-to-earth escort on the whole Westside. I'm 23 yoa, 34-25-34 (all natural), 5-1 and 105 lbs. and don't smoke. I'm part Spanish and part Italian and all American! So if you're looking for the time of your life, then give me a call and come visit me at my safe and secure townhouse near the beach. I never rush and satisfaction is guaranteed! All special desires considered. And if you want to double your pleasure, visit my girlfriend Robin's page in the Blonde Escorts section. We work together as a team – on you or ourselves! I love my work and love to work. So call me!

Incall only. VIPs only.

Below the ad was the phone number now assigned to Pierce's apartment, as well as a cell phone number.

Pierce picked up the phone and called the cell number. He got her voice mail.

'Hi, it's Lilly. Leave your name and number and I'll call you right back. I don't return calls to pay phones. And if you're in a hotel, remember to leave your full name or they won't put my call through. Thanks. I hope to see you real soon. Bye-bye.'

Pierce had made the call before he was sure of what he wanted to say. The beep sounded and he started talking.

'Uh, yes, Lilly, my name is Henry. I sort of have a problem because I have your old phone number. What I mean is, the phone company gave it to me – it's in my apartment and . . . I don't know . . . I'd like to talk to you about it.'

He blurted out the number and hung up.

'Shit!'

He knew he had sounded like an idiot. He wasn't even sure why he was calling her. If she had given up the number, there was nothing she could do about it now to help him except get it off the website. And that thought raised the primary question: Why was the number still on her site?

He looked at her photo on the screen again. He studied it. Lilly was stunningly beautiful and he felt a heaviness at his center, the growing hunger of lust. Finally, a single thought pushed through: What am I doing?

It was a good and valid question. He knew what he needed to do was pull the plug on the computer, get a new number on Monday and then concentrate on the work and forget about all of this.

But he couldn't. He went back to the keyboard and closed Lilly's page and went back to the home page. He then opened the Blonde Escorts panel again and scrolled down until he found a thumbnail photo with the name Robin beneath it.

He opened the page. The woman named Robin was blonde as advertised. She lay naked on her back on a bed. Red rose petals were piled on her stomach and strategically used to partially cover her breasts and crotch. She had a red lipstick smile. There was a blue ribbon beneath the picture, indicating that the photo had been verified. He scanned down to the ad copy.

American Beauty

Hello, Gentlemen. My name is Robin and I'm the girl you have been dreaming about. I'm a true blonde and blue-eyed all-American girl. I'm 24 yoa, 38-30-36 and almost six feet tall. I don't smoke but I love champagne. I can come to you or you can come to me. It doesn't matter because I never rush you. Absolutely positive GFE. And if you want to double your pleasure, visit my girlfriend Lilly's page in the brunettes section. We work together as a team – on you or on ourselves! So give me a call. Satisfaction guaranteed!

VIPs only please.

There was a phone number and a pager number at the bottom of the ad. Without thinking too much about it, Pierce wrote them down in his notebook. He then moved back up to the photo. Robin was attractive but not in the aching sort of way that Lilly was. Robin had sharp lines to her mouth and eyes and a colder look. She was more in line with what Pierce had always thought he would find on one of these sites. Lilly wasn't.

Pierce reread the ad and was left wondering what 'absolutely positive GFE' meant. He had no clue. He then realized that the ad copy on both pages – Robin's and Lilly's – had likely been written by the same person. Repetitive phrases and structure indicated this. He also noticed as he looked at the photo that the same brass bed was in both photos. He pulled down his Internet directory and quickly switched back to Lilly's web page to confirm.

The bed was the same. He didn't know what this meant other than perhaps another confirmation that the two women worked together.

The main difference he picked up from the copy was that Lilly only entertained clients at her apartment. Robin worked it either way, going to a client or allowing him to come to her. Again, he didn't know if this meant anything in the world in which they lived and worked.

He leaned back in his chair, looking at the computer screen and wondering what to do next. He looked at his watch. It was almost eleven.

Abruptly he leaned forward and picked up the phone. Checking his notes, he called the number from Robin's page. He lost his nerve and was about to hang up after four rings when a woman answered in a sleepy, smoky voice.

'Uh, Robin?'

'Yes.'

'I'm sorry, did I wake you?'

'No, I'm awake. Who's this?'

'Um, my name's Hank. I, uh, saw your page on L.A. Darlings. Am I calling too late?'

'No, you're fine. What's Amedeo Techno?'

He realized she had caller ID. A shock of fear went through him. Fear of scandal, of people like Vernon knowing something secret about him.

'Actually, it's Amedeo Technologies. Your readout must not show the whole name.'

'Is that where you work?'

'Yes.'

'Are you Mr. Amedeo?'

Pierce smiled.

'No, there is no Mr. Amedeo. Not anymore.'

'Really? Too bad. What happened to him?'

'Amedeo was Amedeo Avogadro. He was a chemist who about two hundred years ago was the first to tell the difference between molecules and atoms. It was an important distinction but he wasn't taken seriously for about fifty years, until after he was dead. He was just a man ahead of his time. The company was named after him.'

'What do you do there? Play around with atoms and molecules?'

He heard her yawn.

'Sort of. I'm a chemist, too. We're building a computer out of molecules.'

He yawned.

'Really? Cool.'

Pierce smiled again. She sounded neither impressed nor interested.

'Anyway, the reason I'm calling is that I see that you work with Lilly. The brunette escort?'

'I did.'

'You mean not anymore?'

'No, not anymore.'

'What happened? I've been trying to call her and—'

'I'm not talking about Lilly with you. I don't even know you.'

Her voice had changed. It had taken on a sharper edge. Pierce instinctively knew he could lose her if he didn't play it right.

'Okay, sorry. I was just asking because I liked her.'

'You'd been with her?'

'Yeah. A couple times. She seemed like a nice girl and I was wondering where she went. That's all. She suggested the last time that maybe all three of us could get together next time. Do you think you could get a message to her?'

'No. She's long gone and whatever happened to her . . . just happened. That's all.'

'What do you mean? What exactly happened?'

'You know, mister, you're really creeping me out, asking all of these questions. And the thing is, I don't have to talk to you. So why don't you just spend the night with your own molecules.'

She hung up.

Pierce sat there with the phone still to his ear. He was tempted to call back but instinctively knew it would be fruitless attempting to get anything out of Robin. He had spoiled it with the way he had handled it.

He finally hung up and thought about what he had gathered. He looked at the photo of Lilly still on his computer screen. He thought about Robin's cryptic comment about something having happened to her.

'What happened to you?'

He moved the screen back to the home page and clicked on a tab marked ADVERTISE WITH US. It led to a page with instructions for placing ads on the site. It could be done through the net by submitting a credit card number, ad copy and a digital photograph. But in order to receive the blue ribbon signaling a verified photo on the ad, the advertiser had to submit all the materials in person so that she could be confirmed as the woman in the photograph. The site's brick-and-mortar location was on Sunset Boulevard in Hollywood. This was apparently what Lilly and Robin had done. The page listed the office's hours as Monday through Saturday, nine to five during the week and ten to three on Saturdays.

Pierce wrote the address and hours down on his notepad. He was about to disconnect from the site when he decided to call up Lilly's page once again. He printed out a color copy of her photo on the DeskJet. He then shut down the computer and disconnected the phone line. Again a voice inside told him he had gone as far with this as he could go. As he should go. It was time to change his phone number and forget about it.

But another voice – a louder voice from the past – told him something else.

'Lights,' he said.

The office dropped into darkness. Pierce didn't move. He liked the darkness. He always did his best thinking in the dark.

5

The stairway was dark and the boy was scared. He looked back to the street and saw the waiting car. His stepfather saw the hesitation and put his hand out the car window. He waved the boy forward, waved him in. The boy turned back and looked up into the darkness. He turned on the flashlight and started up.

He kept the light down on the steps, not wanting to announce he was coming up by lighting the room at the top. Halfway there one of the stairs creaked loudly under his foot. He stood frozen still. He could hear his own heartbeat banging in his chest. He thought about Isabelle and the fear she probably carried in her own chest every day and night after night. He drew his resolve from this and started up again.

Three steps from the top he cut the light off and waited for his eyes to adjust. In a few moments he thought he could see a dim light from the room up ahead of him. It was candlelight licking at the ceiling and walls. He pushed himself against the side wall and took the last three steps up.

The room was large and crowded. He could see the makeshift beds lined against the two long walls. Still figures, like heaps of rummage sale clothes, slept on each. At the end of the room a single candle burned and a girl, a few years older and dirtier, heated a bottle cap over the flame. The boy studied her face in the uneven light. He could see that it wasn't Isabelle.

He started moving down the center of the room, between the sleeping bags and the newspaper pallets. From side to side he looked, searching for the familiar face. It was dark but he could tell. He'd know her when he saw her.

He got to the end, by the girl with the bottle cap. And Isabelle wasn't there.

'Who are you looking for?' asked the girl.

She was drawing back the plunger on the hypodermic, sucking the brown-black liquid through a cigarette butt filter from the bottle cap. In the murky light the boy could see the needle scarring on her neck.

'Just somebody,' he said.

She looked away from her work and up to his face, surprised by his voice. She saw the young face in the camouflage of oversized and dirty clothes.

'You're a young one,' she said. 'You better get out of here before the houseman comes back.'

The boy knew what she meant. All the squats in Hollywood had somebody in charge. The houseman. He exacted a fee in money or drugs or flesh.

'He finds you, he'll bust your cherry ass and put you out on – '

She suddenly stopped and blew out the candle, leaving him in the dark. He turned back to the door and the stairs, and all his fears seized up in him like a fist closing on a flower. A silhouette of a man stood at the top of the steps. A big man. Wild hair. The houseman. The boy involuntarily took a step back and tripped over someone's leg. He fell, the flashlight clattering on the floor next to him and going out.

The man in the doorway moved and started coming at him.

'Hanky boy!' the man yelled. 'Come here, Hank!'

6

Pierce awoke at dawn, the sun rescuing him from the dream of running from a man whose face he could not see. He had no curtains in the apartment yet and the light streamed through the windows and burned through his eyelids. He crawled out of the sleeping bag, looked at the photo of Lilly he had left on the floor and went into the shower. When he was finished he had to dry off with two T-shirts he'd dug out of one of the clothing boxes. He'd forgotten to buy towels.

He walked over to Main Street to get coffee, a citrus smoothie and the newspaper. He read and drank slowly, almost feeling guilty about it. Most Saturdays he was in the lab by dawn.

When he was finished with the paper it was almost nine. He walked back to the Sands and got into his car, but he didn't go to the lab as usual.

Fifteen minutes before ten o'clock Pierce got to the Hollywood address he had written down for L.A. Darlings. The location was a multi-level office complex that looked as legitimate as a McDonald's. L.A. Darlings was located in Suite 310. On the glazed glass door the largest lettering read ENTREPRENEURIAL CONCEPTS UNLIMITED. Beneath this was a listing in smaller letters of ten different websites, including L.A. Darlings, that apparently fell under the Entrepreneurial Concepts umbrella. Pierce could tell by the titling of the site addresses that they were all sexually oriented and part of the Internet's dark universe of adult entertainment.

The door was locked but Pierce was a few minutes early. He decided to use the time by taking a walk and thinking about what he was going to say and how he was going to play this.

'Here, I'll open it.'

He turned as a woman approached the door with a key. She was about twenty-five and had crazy blonde hair that seemed to point in all directions. She wore cutoff jeans and sandals and a short shirt that exposed her pierced navel. She had looped over her shoulder a purse that looked big enough to hold a pack of cigarettes but not the matches. And she looked as though ten o'clock was definitely too early for her.

'You're early,' she said.

'I know,' Pierce said. 'I came from the Westside and I thought there'd be more traffic.'

He followed her in. There was a waiting area with a raised reception counter in front of a partition that guarded an entrance to a rear hallway. To the right and unguarded was a closed door with the word PRIVATE on it. Pierce watched as the woman walked behind the counter and threw her purse into a drawer.

'You'll have to wait a couple minutes until I get set up. I'm the only one here today.'

'Slow on Saturdays?'

'Most of the time.'

'Well, who is watching the machines if you're the only one here?'

'Oh, well, there's always somebody back there. I just meant I'm by myself up front today.'

She slid into a chair behind the counter. The silver ring protruding from her stomach caught Pierce's eye and reminded him of Nicole. She had worked at Amedeo for more than a year before he happened upon her in a coffee shop on Main Street on a Sunday afternoon. She had just come from a workout and was dressed in gray sweatpants and a sports bra, exposing a gold ring piercing her navel. It was like discovering a secret about someone of longtime acquaintance. She had always been a beautifully attractive woman in his eyes but everything changed after that moment in the coffee shop. Nicole became erotic to him and he went after her, wanting to check for hidden tattoos and to know all of her secrets.

Pierce wandered around the confines of the waiting room while the woman behind the counter did whatever it was she had to do to get set up. He heard a computer start booting up and some drawers opening and closing. He noticed on one wall an arrangement of logos of various websites operated through Entrepreneurial Concepts. He saw L.A. Darlings and several others. Most of them were pornography sites, where a $19.95-a-month subscription bought access to thousands of downloadable photos of your favorite sex acts and fetishes. It was all presented on the wall in complete, unashamed legitimacy. The PinkMink.com banner could have been the same as an advertisement for acne ointment.

Next to the wall of banners was the door marked Private. Pierce glanced back at the woman behind the counter and saw that she was preoccupied with something on her computer screen. He turned back and tried the doorknob. It was unlocked and he opened the door. It led to an unlit hallway with three sets of double doors spaced twenty feet apart on the left side.

'Um, excuse me,' the woman said from behind him. 'You can't go in there.'

Signs hanging on thin chains from the ceiling in front of the doors marked them as studio A, studio B and studio C.

Pierce backed out and closed the door. He returned to the counter. He saw that she was now wearing a pin with her name on it.

'I thought it was the rest rooms. What is that back there?'

'Those are the photo studios. We don't have public facilities here. They're down in the building's lobby.'

'I can wait.'

'What can I do for you?'

He leaned his elbows on the counter.

'I've sort of got a problem, Wendy. One of the advertisers with a page on L.A. Darlings dot com has my phone number. Calls that should be going to her are going to me instead. And I think if I were to show up at somebody's hotel room door, there'd be some disappointment involved.'

He smiled but she apparently didn't appreciate his attempt at humor.

'A misprint?' she said. 'I can fix that.'

'It's not exactly a misprint.'

He told his story of getting a new phone number, only to learn that it was the same line on the web page ad for the woman named Lilly.

She was sitting behind the counter. She looked up at him with suspicious eyes.

'If you just got the number, why don't you just get another?'

'Because I didn't realize I had this problem and I already had change-of-address cards with the number on it printed and mailed out. It would be very expensive and time-consuming to do that all over again with a new number. I'm sure if you told me how to contact this woman, she'd agree to alter her page. I mean, she's not getting any business off it if all her calls are going to me anyway, right?'

Wendy shook her head like his explanation and reasoning were beyond her.

'All right, let me see something.'

She turned to the computer and went to the L.A. Darlings site and into the Brunette Escorts list. She clicked on the picture of Lilly and then scrolled down to the phone number.

'You're saying this is your number, not hers, but it used to be hers.'

'Exactly.'

'Then if she changed her number, why wouldn't she change it with us, too?'

'I don't know. That's why I'm here. Would you have another way of contacting her?'

'Not that I can give you. Our client information is confidential.'

Pierce nodded. He had expected that.

'That's fine. But can you see if there is another contact number and then you could call her and tell her about this problem?'

'What about this cell number?'

'I tried it. It takes voice mail. I've left three messages for her explaining all of this but she hasn't called back. I don't think she's getting the messages.'

Wendy scrolled up and looked at the photo of Lilly.

'She's hot,' she said. 'I bet you're getting a lot of calls.'

'I've only had the phone a day and it's driving me nuts.'

Wendy pushed her chair back and stood up.

'I'm going to check something. I'll be right back.'

She went around the partition behind the counter and disappeared into the back hallway, the slapping sound of her sandals receding as she went. Pierce waited a moment and then leaned over the counter and scanned all surfaces. His guess was that Wendy was not the only one who worked at the counter. It was probably a job shared by two or three minimum-wage employees. Employees who might need help remembering passwords to the system.

He looked for Post-its on the computer and the back of the counter's facade but saw nothing. He reached down and lifted the blotter but there was nothing under it but a dollar bill. He dug his finger around in a dish of paper clips but found nothing. He reached further across the counter to see if there was a pencil drawer. There wasn't.

Just as he thought of something, he heard the sound of her sandals. She was coming back. He quickly reached into his pocket, found a dollar and then reached back over the counter. He lifted the blotter, put down the dollar and grabbed the one that was there. He put it in his pocket without looking at it. His hand was still there when she came around the partition, holding a thin file, and sat down.

'Well, I figured out one part of the problem,' she said.

'What's that?'

'This girl stopped paying her bill.'

'When was that?'

'In June she paid up through August. Then she didn't pay for September.'

'Then why's her page still on the site?'

'Because sometimes it takes a while to clean out the deadbeats. Especially when they look like this chick.'

She gestured to the computer screen with the file and then put it down on the counter.

'I wouldn't be surprised if Mr. Wentz wanted to keep her on there even though she didn't pay. Guys see girls like that on the site and they'll keep coming back.'

Pierce nodded.

'And the number of hits on the site is how they determine the rates for the ads, right?'

'You got it.'

Pierce looked at the screen. In a way, Lilly was still working. If not for herself, then for Entrepreneurial Concepts Unlimited. He looked back at Wendy.

'Is Mr. Wentz back there? I'd like to speak to him.'

'No, it's Saturday. You'd be lucky even to catch him here during the week, but I've never seen him on a Saturday.'

'Well, what can be done about this? My phone's ringing off the hook.'

'Well, I can take notes and then maybe on Monday somebody could—'

'Look, Wendy, I don't want to wait until Monday. I have a problem now. If Mr. Wentz isn't here, then go get the guy baby-sitting the servers. There has to be somebody who can go into the server and take her page down. It's a simple process.'

'There's one guy back there but I don't think he's authorized to do anything. Besides, he was sort of asleep when I looked in there.'

Pierce leaned over the counter and put a forceful tone into his voice.

'Lilly – I mean, Wendy, listen to me. I insist that you go back there and wake him up and bring him out here. You have to understand something here. You are in a legally precarious position. I have informed you that your website has my phone number on it. Because of this error I am repeatedly receiving phone calls of what I consider to be an offensive and embarrassing nature. So much so that I was here at your place of business this morning before you even opened. I want this fixed. If you put it off until Monday, then I am going to sue you, this company, Mr. Wentz and anybody else I can find associated with this place. Do you understand?'

'You can't sue me. I just work here.'

'Wendy, you can sue anybody you want to in this world.'

She stood up, an angry look in her eyes, and pirouetted around the partition without a word. Pierce didn't care if she was angry. What he cared about was that she had left the file on the counter.

As soon as the sound of her sandals was gone he bent over and flipped open the file. There was a copy of the photo of Lilly, along with a printout of her ad copy and an advertiser's information form. This was what Pierce wanted. He felt a surge of adrenaline zing through him as he read the sheet and tried to commit everything to memory.

Her name was Lilly Quinlan. Her contact number was the same cell phone number she had put on her web page. On the address line she had put a Santa Monica address and apartment number. Pierce quickly read it silently three times and then put everything back in the file just as he heard the sandals and another pair of shoes approaching from the other side of the partition.

7

The first thing Pierce did when he got back to the car was grab a pen from the ashtray and write Lilly Quinlan's address on an old valet parking stub. After that he pulled the dollar bill out of his pocket and examined it. It had been face down under the blotter. He now studied it and found the words *Arbadac Arba* written across George Washington's forehead on the front of the bill.

'Abra Cadabra,' he said, reading each word backwards.

He thought there was a good chance that the words were a user name and password for entering the Entrepreneurial Concepts computer system. While he was pleased with the moves he'd made in getting the words, he was unsure how useful they would be now that he had gotten Lilly Quinlan's name and address out of the hard-copy file.

He started the car and headed back toward Santa Monica. The address of Lilly's apartment was on Wilshire Boulevard near the Third Street Promenade. As he got close and started reading the numbers on the buildings, he realized that there were no apartment complexes in the vicinity of the address she had written on the advertiser's information sheet. When he finally pulled up in front of the business with the matching address on the door, he saw that it was a private mail drop, a business called All American Mail. The apartment number Lilly Quinlan had written on the info sheet was actually a box number. Pierce parked at the curb out front but wasn't sure what he could do. It appeared that he was at a dead end. He thought for a few minutes about a plan of action and then got out.

Pierce walked into the business and immediately went into the alcove where the mailboxes were. He was hoping the individual doors would have glass in them so he could look into Lilly Quinlan's and see if there was any mail. But the boxes all had aluminum doors with no glass. She had listed her address as apartment 333 on the info sheet. He located box 333 and just stared at it for a moment, as if it might give him some sort of answer. It didn't.

Pierce eventually left the alcove and went to the counter. A young man with a swath of pimples on each cheek and a name tag that said *Curt* asked how he could help him.

'This is sort of weird,' Pierce said. 'I need a mailbox but I want a specific number. It sort of goes with the name of my business. It's called Three Cubed Productions.'

The kid seemed confused.

'So what number do you want?'

'Three three three. I saw you have a box with that number. Is it available?'

It was the best Pierce could come up with while sitting in the car. Curt reached under the counter and came back up with a blue binder, which he opened to pages listing boxes by number and their availability. His finger drew down a column of numbers and stopped.

'Oh, this one.'

Pierce tried to read what was on the page but it was upside down and too far away.

'What?'

'Well, it's occupied at the moment but it might not be for long.'

'What's that mean?'

'It means there's a person in that box, but she didn't pay this month's rent. So she's in the grace period. If she shows up and pays, she keeps the box. If she doesn't show up by the end of the month, then she's out and you're in – if you can wait that long.'

Pierce put a concerned look on his face.

'That's kind of long. I wanted to get this set up. Do you know if there's a number or an address for this person? You know, to contact her and ask if she still wants the box.'

'I've sent out two late notices and put one in the box. We usually don't call.'

Pierce became excited but didn't show it. What Curt had said meant that there was another address for Lilly Quinlan. This excitement was immediately tempered by the fact that he had no idea how to get it from the young man who had it.

'Well, is there a number? If you could call this woman right now and find something out, I'd be willing to rent the box right now. And I'd pay for a year up front.'

'Well, I'll have to look it up. It will take me a minute.'

'Take your time. I'd rather get all of this done now than have to come back.'

Curt went to a desk that was against the wall behind the counter and sat down. He opened a file drawer and took out a thick hanging file. He was still too far away for Pierce to be able to read any of the documents he was going through. Curt ran his finger down one page and then held it on a spot. With his other hand he picked up the phone on the desk but was interrupted before making the call by a customer who had entered the shop.

'I need to send a fax to New York,' she said.

Curt got up and went to the counter. From underneath he pulled out a fax cover sheet and told the woman to fill it out. He returned to the desk. He put his finger back on the document and lifted the phone.

'Am I going to be charged for faxing this cover sheet?'

It was the other customer.

'No, ma'am. Only the documents you need to fax.'

He said it like he had said it only a million times before.

Finally, he punched in a number on the phone. Pierce tried to watch his finger and get the number but it was too fast. Curt waited a long time before finally speaking into the phone.

'This is a message for Lilly Quinlan. Could you please call us at All American Mail. Rent on your box is overdue and we'll be re-renting it if we do not hear from you. My name is Curt. Thank you very much.'

He gave the number and hung up, then came toward Pierce at the counter. The woman with the fax shook it at him.

'I'm in a big hurry,' she said.

'I'll be right with you, ma'am,' Curt said.

He looked at Pierce and shook his head.

'I got her machine. There's really nothing that I can do until either I hear from her or the end of the month comes and I don't. That's the policy.'

'I understand. Thanks for trying.'

Curt started running his finger down the columns in the binder again.

'You want to leave a number where I can reach you if I hear from her?'

'I'll just check with you tomorrow.'

Pierce took a business card off a plastic rack on the counter and headed toward the door. Curt called after him.

'What about twenty-seven?'

Pierce turned back.

'What?'

'Twenty-seven. Isn't that what three cubed is?'

Pierce slowly nodded. Curt was smarter than he looked.

'I've got that box open if you want it.'

'I'll think about it.'

He waved and returned to the door. Behind him he heard the woman telling Curt that he shouldn't make paying customers wait.

In the car Pierce put the business card in his shirt pocket and checked his watch. It was almost noon. He had to get back to his apartment to meet Monica Purl, his assistant. She'd agreed to wait at his apartment for the shipment of furniture he had ordered. The delivery window was noon until four and Pierce had decided Friday morning that he'd rather pay someone else to wait while he used the time in the lab preparing the next week's presentation for Goddard. Now he doubted he was going to go to the lab, but he would still use Monica to wait for the delivery. He also now had another plan for her as well.

When he got to the Sands he found her waiting in the lobby. The security officer on the door would not let her go up to the twelfth floor without approval of the resident she was going to visit.

'Sorry about that,' Pierce said. 'Were you waiting long?'

She was carrying a stack of magazines for reading while she waited for the delivery.

'Just a few minutes,' Monica said.

They went into the elevator alcove and had to wait. Monica Purl was a tall, thin blonde with the kind of skin that was so pale that just touching it might leave a mark. She was about twenty-five and had been with the company since she was twenty. She had been Pierce's personal assistant for only six months, getting the promotion from Charlie Condon for her five years of service. In that time Pierce had learned that the aura of fragility her build and coloring projected was false. Monica was organized and opinionated and got things done.

The elevator opened and they got on. Pierce hit the twelve button and they started to ascend, the elevator moving quickly.

'You sure you want to be in this place when the big one hits?' Monica asked.

'This building was engineered to take an eight point oh,' he replied. 'I checked before I rented. I trust the science.'

'Because you're a scientist?'

'I guess.'

'But do you trust the builders who carry out the science?'

It was a good point. He didn't have anything to say to that. The door slid open on twelve and they walked down the hall to his apartment.

'Where am I going to tell them to put everything?' Monica asked. 'Do you have like a design plan or a layout in mind?'

'Not really. Just tell them to put stuff where you think it will look good. I also need you to do a favor for me before I leave.'

He opened the door.

'What kind of favor?' Monica said suspiciously.

Pierce realized that she thought he might be making a move on her. Now that he and Nicole were no more. He had a theory that all attractive women thought that all men were out to make a move on them. He almost laughed but didn't.

'Just a phone call. I'll write it down.'

In the living room he picked up the phone. There was a broken dial tone and when he checked messages there was only one and it was for Lilly. But it was not from Curt at All American Mail. It was just another potential client checking on her availability. He erased the message and tried to figure it out, finally deciding that Lilly had put down her cell phone number on the mailbox application forms. Curt had called her cell phone.

It wouldn't change his plan.

He brought the phone to the couch and sat down and wrote the name

Lilly Quinlan on a fresh page of his notebook. He then pulled the business card out of his pocket.

'I want you to call this number and say you are Lilly Quinlan. Ask for Curt and tell him you got his message. Tell him his call was the first you'd heard about your payment being overdue and ask him why they didn't send you a notice in the mail. Okay?'

'Why – what is this for?'

'I can't explain it all to you but it's important.'

'I don't know if I want to impersonate somebody. It's not—'

'What you are doing is totally harmless. It's what hackers call social engineering. What Curt is going to tell you is that he did send you a notice. Then you say, 'Oh, really? What address did you send it to?' When he gives you the address write it down. That's what I need. The address. As soon as you get it you can get off the call. Just tell him you'll come by as soon as you can to pay, and hang up. I just need that address.'

She looked at him in a way she had never looked at him before during the six months she had worked directly for him.

'Come on, Monica, it's no big deal. It's not harming anyone. And it might actually be helping someone. In fact, I think it will.'

He put the notebook and pen on her lap.

'Are you ready? I'll dial the number.'

'Dr. Pierce, this doesn't seem—'

'Don't call me Dr. Pierce. You never call me Dr. Pierce.'

'Then Henry. I don't want to do this. Not without knowing what I am doing.'

'All right then, I'll tell you. You know the new phone number you got me?'

She nodded.

'Well, it belonged previously to a woman who has disappeared, or something has happened to her. I'm getting her calls and I'm trying to figure out what happened to her. You see? And this call I want you to make might get me an address where she lives. That's all I want. I want to go there and see if she's okay. Nothing else. Now, will you make the call?'

She shook her head as if warding off too much information. Her face looked as if Pierce had just told her he'd been taken aboard a spaceship and sodomized by an alien.

'This is crazy. How did you ever get caught up in this? Did you know this woman? How do you know she disappeared?'

'No, I don't know her. It was purely random. Because I got the wrong number. But now I know enough to know I have to find out what happened or make sure she's okay. Will you please do this for me, Monica?'

'Why don't you just change your number?'

'I will. First thing Monday I want you to change it.'

'And meantime, just call the police.'

'I don't have enough information yet to call the police. What would I tell them? They'll think I'm a nut.'

'And they might be right.'

'Look, will you do this or not?'

She nodded in resignation.

'If it will make you happy and it will keep my job.'

'Whoa. Wait a minute. I'm not threatening you about your job. If you don't want to do it, fine, I'll get somebody else. It's got nothing to do with your job. Are we clear on that?'

'Yes, clear. But don't worry, I'll do it. Let's just get it over with.'

He went over the call with her once more and then dialed the number of All American Mail and handed the phone to Monica. She asked for Curt and then pulled off the call as planned, with only a few moments of bad acting and confusion. Pierce watched as she wrote down an address on the notepad. He was ecstatic but didn't show it. When she hung up she handed him the pad and the phone.

Pierce checked the address – it was in Venice – then tore the page off the pad, folded it and put it in his pocket.

'Curt seemed like a nice guy,' Monica said. 'I feel bad about lying to him.'

'You could always go visit him and ask him out for a date. I've seen him. Believe me, one date with you would make him happy the rest of his life.'

'You've seen him? Were you the one he was talking about? He said a guy was in there and wanted my mailbox. I mean, Lilly Quinlan's mailbox.'

'Yeah, that was me. That's how I—'

The phone rang and he answered it. But the caller hung up. Pierce looked at the caller ID directory. The call had come from the Ritz-Carlton in the Marina.

'Look,' he said, 'you need to leave the phone plugged in so when the furniture comes, security can call up here for approval to let them up. But meantime, you're probably going to get a lot of calls for Lilly. Since you're a woman, they're going to think you're her. So you might want to say something right off like "This isn't Lilly, you've got the wrong number." Something like that. Otherwise—'

'Well, maybe I should pretend I'm her so I can get more information for you.'

'No, you don't want to do that.'

He opened his backpack and pulled out the printout of the photo from Lilly's web page.

'That's Lilly. I don't think you want to pretend you're her with these callers.'

'Oh my God!' Monica exclaimed as she looked at the photo. 'Is she like a prostitute or something?'

'I think so.'

'Then what are you doing trying to find this prostitute when you should be—'

She stopped abruptly. Pierce looked at her and waited for her to finish. She didn't.

'What?' he said. 'I should be what?'

'Nothing. It's not my business.'

'Did you talk with Nicki about her and me?'

'No. Look, it's nothing. I don't know what I was going to say. I just think it's strange that you're running around trying to find out if this prostitute is all right. It's weird.'

Pierce sat back down on the couch. He knew she was lying about Nicole. They had gotten close and used to go to lunch together all the times Pierce couldn't get out of the lab – which was almost every day. Why would it end now that Nicki was gone? They were probably still talking every day, exchanging stories about him.

He also knew that she was right about what he was doing. But he was too far down the road and around the bend. His life and career had been built on following his curiosity. In his last year at Stanford he sat in on a lecture about the next generation of microchips. The professor spoke of nanochips so small that the supercomputers of the day could and would be built to the size of a dime. Pierce became hooked and had been pursuing his curiosity – chasing the dime – ever since.

'I'm just going to go over to Venice,' he told Monica. 'I'm just going to check things out and leave it at that.'

'You promise?'

'Yes. You can call me at the lab after the furniture gets here and you're leaving.'

He stood up and slung his backpack over his shoulder.

'If you talk to Nicki, don't mention anything about this, okay?'

'Sure, Henry. I won't.'

He knew he couldn't count on that but it would have to do for the moment. He headed to the apartment door and left. As he went down the hall to the elevator he thought about what Monica had said and considered the difference between private investigation and private obsession. Somewhere there was a line between them. But he wasn't sure where it was.

8

There was something wrong about the address, something that didn't fit. But Pierce couldn't place it. He worried over it as he drove into Venice but it didn't open up to him. It was like something hidden behind a shower curtain. It was blurred but it was there.

The address Lilly Quinlan had given as a contact address to All American Mail was a bungalow on Altair Place, a block off the stretch of stylish antiques stores and restaurants on Abbot Kinney Boulevard. It was a small white house with gray trim that somehow made Pierce think of a seagull. There was a fat royal palm squatting in the front yard. Pierce parked across the street and for several minutes sat in his car, studying the house for signs of recent life.

The yard and ornamentation were neatly trimmed. But if it was a rental, that could have been taken care of by a landlord. There was no car in the driveway or in the open garage in back and no newspapers piling up near the curb. Nothing seemed outwardly amiss.

Pierce finally decided on the direct approach. He got out of the BMW, crossed the street and followed the walkway to the front door. There was a button for a doorbell. He pushed it and heard an innocuous chime sound from somewhere inside. He waited.

Nothing.

He pushed the bell again, then knocked on the door.

He waited.

And nothing.

He looked around. The Venetian blinds behind the front windows were closed. He turned and nonchalantly surveyed the homes across the street while he reached a hand behind his back and tried the doorknob. It was locked.

Not wanting the day's journey to end without his getting some piece of new information or revelation, he stepped away from the door and walked over to the driveway, which went down the left side of the house to a single stand-alone garage in the rear yard. A huge Monterey pine that dwarfed the house was buckling the driveway with its roots. They were headed for the house and Pierce guessed that in another five years there would be structural damage and the question would be whether to save the tree or the house.

The garage door was open. It was made of wood that had been bowed by time and its own weight. It looked like it was permanently fixed in the open position. The garage was empty except for a collection of paint cans lined against the rear wall.

To the right of the garage was a postage-stamp-sized yard that offered privacy because of a tall hedge that ran along the borders. Two lounge chairs sat in the grass. There was a birdbath with no water in it. Pierce looked at the lounge chairs and thought about the tan lines he had seen on Lilly's body in the web page photo.

After hesitating for a moment in the yard, Pierce went to the rear door and knocked again. The door had a window cut into its upper half. Without waiting to see if someone answered, he cupped his hands against the glass and looked in. It was the kitchen. It appeared neat and clean. There was nothing on the small table pushed against the wall to the left. A newspaper was neatly folded on one of the two chairs.

On the counter next to the toaster was a large bowl filled with dark shapes that Pierce realized were rotten pieces of fruit.

Now he had something. Something that didn't fit, something that showed something wasn't right. He knocked sharply on the door's window, even though he knew no one was inside who could answer. He turned and looked around the yard for something to maybe break the window with. He instinctively grabbed the knob and turned it while he was pivoting.

The door was unlocked.

Pierce wheeled back around. The knob still in his hand, he pushed and the door opened six inches. He waited for an alarm to sound but his intrusion was greeted with only silence. And almost immediately he could smell the sickly sweet stench of the rotten fruit. Or maybe, he thought, it was something else. He took his hand off the knob and pushed the door open wider, leaned in and yelled.

'Lilly? Lilly, it's me, Henry.'

He didn't know if he was doing it for the neighbors' sake or his own but he yelled her name two more times, expecting and getting no results. Before entering, he turned around and sat down on the stoop. He considered the decision, whether to go in or not. He thought about Monica's reaction earlier to what he was doing and what she had said: Just call the cops.

Now was the moment to do that. Something was wrong here and he certainly had something to call about. But the truth was he wasn't ready to give this away. Not yet. Whatever it was, it was his still and he wanted to pursue it. His motivations, he knew, were not only in regard to Lilly Quinlan. They reached further and were entwined with the past. He knew he was trying to trade the present for the past, to do now what he hadn't been able to do back then.

He got up off the back step and opened the door fully. He stepped into the kitchen and closed the door behind him.

There was the low sound of music coming from somewhere in the house. Pierce stood still and scanned the kitchen again and found nothing wrong except for the fruit in the bowl. He opened the refrigerator and saw a carton of orange juice and a plastic bottle of low fat milk. The milk had an August 18 use-by date. The juice's was August 16. It had been well over a month since the contents of each had expired.

Pierce went to the table and slid back the chair. On it was the *Los Angeles Times* edition from August 1.

There was a hallway running off the left side of the kitchen to the front of the house. As Pierce moved into the hall he saw the pile of mail building below the slot in the front door. But before he got to the front of the house he explored the three doorways that broke up the hallway. One was to a bathroom, where he found every horizontal surface crowded with perfumes and female beauty aids, all of it waiting under a fine layer of dust. He chose a small green bottle and opened it. He raised it to his nose and smelled the scent of lilac perfume. It was the same stuff Nicole used; he had recognized the bottle. After a moment he closed and returned the bottle to its place and then stepped back into the hallway.

The other two doors led to bedrooms. One appeared to be the master bedroom. Both closets in this room were open and jammed with clothing on wood hangers. The music was coming from an alarm clock radio located on a night table on the right side. He checked both tables for a phone and possibly an answering machine, but there was none.

The other bedroom appeared to be used as a workout location. There was no bed. There was a stair machine and a rowing machine on a grass mat, a small television in front of them. Pierce opened the only closet and found more clothing on hangers. He was about to close it when he realized something. These clothes were different. Almost two feet of hanger space was devoted to small things – negligees and leotards. He saw something familiar and reached in for the hanger. It was the black fishnet negligee she had posed in for the website photo.

This reminded him of something. He put the hanger back in its place and went back into the other bedroom. It was the wrong bed. Not the brass railings of the photo. In that moment he realized what was wrong, what had bothered him about the Venice address. Her ad copy. Lilly had said she met clients at a clean and safe townhouse on the Westside. This was no townhouse and that was the wrong bed. It meant there was still another address connected to Lilly Quinlan that he still had to find.

Pierce froze when he heard a noise from the front of the house. He realized as an amateur break-in artist he had made a mistake. He should have quickly scanned the whole house to make sure it was empty instead of starting at the back and moving slowly toward the front.

He waited but there was no other sound. It had been a singular banging sound followed by what sounded like something being rolled across the wood floor. He slowly moved toward the door of the bedroom and then looked down the hall. Just the pile of mail on the floor at the front door.

He stepped to the side of the hallway, where he felt the wood was probably less likely to creak, and made his way slowly to the front of the house. The hallway opened to a living room on the left and a dining room on the right. There was no one in either room. He saw nothing that would explain the sound he had heard.

The living room was kept neat. It was filled with Craftsman-style furniture that was in keeping with the house. What wasn't was the double rack of high-end electronics below the plasma television hanging on the wall. Lilly Quinlan had a home entertainment station that had probably run her twenty-five grand – a tweakhead's wet dream. It seemed out of character with everything else he had seen so far.

Pierce stepped over to the door and squatted by the pile of mail. He started looking through it. Most of it was junk mail addressed to 'current resident.' There were two envelopes from All American Mail – the late notices. There were credit card bills and bank statements. There was a large envelope from the University of Southern California. He looked specifically for letters – bills – from the phone company and found none. He thought this was odd but quickly assumed her phone bills might have been sent to the box at All American Mail. He put one of the bank statements and a Visa bill into the back pocket of his jeans without a second thought – the first being that he was compounding the crime of breaking and entering with a federal mail theft rap. He decided not to pursue thoughts on this and got up.

In the dining room he found a rolltop desk against the rear wall. He turned a chair from the table to the desk, opened it and sat down. He quickly went through the drawers and determined that this was her bill paying station. There were checkbooks, stamps and pens in the center drawer. The drawers going down either side of the desk were filled with envelopes from credit card companies and utilities and other bills. He found a stack of envelopes from Entrepreneurial Concepts Unlimited, though these had been addressed to the mail drop. On each envelope Lilly had written the date the bill was paid. Again noticeably missing was a stack of old phone bills. Even if she did not receive the bills by mail at this address, it did appear she paid her bills at this desk. But there were no receipts, no envelopes with the date of payment written on them.

Pierce didn't have time to dwell on it or to go through all the bills. He wasn't sure what he would find in them that might help him determine what had happened to Lilly Quinlan anyway. He went back to the center drawer and quickly went through the registers of the checkbooks. There had been no activity in either account since the end of July. Going back quickly through one of the books, he found record of payment to the telephone company ending in June. So she did pay the phone bill with the account he held in his hand and very likely at the desk where he sat. But he could find no other record of the billing in the drawers. He couldn't even find a phone.

Feeling hurried by the situation, he gave up on the contradiction and closed the drawer. He reached to the handle to pull the rolltop down when he saw a small book pushed far into one of the storage slots at the top of the desk. He reached in for it and found it to be a small personal phone book. He used his thumb to buzz through the pages and saw that it was filled with hand-written entries. Without another thought, he shoved the book into his back pocket along with the mail he had decided to take.

He rolled the top down, stood up and took a last survey of the two front rooms, looking for a phone and not finding one. Almost immediately he saw a shadow move behind the closed blinds of the living room window. Someone was going to the front door.

A blade of sheer panic sliced through Pierce. He didn't know whether to hide or run down the hallway and out the back door. Instead, he couldn't do anything. He stood there, unable to move his feet as he heard a footstep on the tiled stoop outside the front door.

A metallic clack made him jump. Then a small stack of mail was pushed through the slot in the door and fell to the floor on top of the other mail. Pierce closed his eyes.

'Jesus!' he whispered as he let out his breath and tried to relax.

The shadow crossed the living room blinds again, going the other way. And then it was gone.

Pierce stepped over and looked at the latest influx of mail. A few more bills but mostly junk mail. He used his foot to push the envelopes around to make sure and then he saw a small envelope addressed by hand. He bent down to pick it up. In the upper left corner of the envelope it said *V. Quinlan* but there was no return address to go with it. The postmark was partially smeared and he could only make out the letters *pa, Fla*. He turned the envelope over and checked the seal. He would have to tear the envelope to open it.

Something about opening this obviously personal piece of mail seemed more intrusive and criminal to him than anything else he had done so far. But his hesitation didn't last long. He used a fingernail to pry open the envelope and pulled out a small piece of folded paper. It was a letter dated four days earlier.

Lilly,

I am worried sick about you. If you get this, please just call me to let me know you are okay. Please, honey? Since you have stopped calling me I haven't been able to think right. I am very worried about you and that job of yours. Things around here were never really the best and I know I didn't do everything right. But I don't think that you shouldn't tell me if you are all right. Please call me if and when you get this.

Love,
Mom

He read it twice and then refolded the page and returned it to the envelope. More than anything else in the apartment, including the rotten fruit, the letter stabbed Pierce with a sense of doom. He didn't think the letter from V. Quinlan would ever be answered by a phone call or otherwise.

He closed the envelope as best as he could and quickly buried it in the pile of mail on the floor. The intrusion of the mail carrier had served to instill in him a sense of the risk he was running by being in the house. He'd had enough. He quickly turned and headed back down the hallway to the kitchen.

He went through the back door and closed it but left it unlocked. As nonchalantly as an amateur criminal can be, he walked around the corner of the house and down the driveway toward the street.

Halfway down the side of the house he heard a loud bang from up on the roof and then a large pinecone rolled off the eave and landed in front of him. As Pierce stepped over it he realized what had made the startling noise while he had been in the house. He nodded as he put it together. At least he had solved one mystery.

9

'Lights.'

Pierce swung around behind his desk and sat down. From his backpack he pulled out the things he had taken from Lilly Quinlan's house. He had a Visa bill and a bank statement and the phone book.

He started paging through the phone book first. There were several listings for men by first name or first name with a following initial only. These numbers ran the gamut of area codes. Many local but still more from area codes outside of Los Angeles. There were also several listings for local hotels and restaurants, as well as a Lexus dealer in Hollywood. He saw a listing for Robin and another listing for ECU, which he knew was Entrepreneurial Concepts Unlimited.

Under the heading 'Dallas' there were several numbers for hotels, restaurants and male first names listed. The same was true of a heading for Las Vegas.

He found a listing for Vivian Quinlan with an 813 area code phone number and an address in Tampa, Florida. That solved the mystery of the smeared postmark on the letter. Near the end of the book he found an entry for someone listed as Wainwright that included a phone number and an address in Venice that Pierce knew was not far from the home on Altair.

He flipped back to the Q listings and used his desk phone to call the number for Vivian Quinlan. A woman answered the phone in two rings. Her voice sounded like a broom sweeping a sidewalk.

'Hello?'

'Mrs. Quinlan?'

'Yes?'

'Uh, hi, I'm calling from Los Angeles. My name's Henry Pierce and—'

'Is this about Lilly?'

Her voice had an immediate, desperate tone to it.

'Yes. I'm trying to locate her and I was wondering if you could help me.'

'Oh, thank God! Are you police?'

'Uh, no, ma'am, I'm not.'

'I don't care. Someone finally cares.'

'Well, I'm just trying to find her, Mrs. Quinlan. Have you heard from her lately?'

'Not in more than seven weeks and that just isn't like her. She always checked in. I'm very worried.'

'Have you contacted the police?'

'Yes, I called and talked to the Missing Persons people. They weren't interested because she's an adult and because of what she does for a living.'

'What does she do for a living, Mrs. Quinlan?'

There was a hesitation.

'I thought you said you knew her.'

'I'm just an acquaintance.'

'She works as a gentleman's escort.'

'I see.'

'No sex or anything. She told me she goes to dinner with men in tuxedos mostly.'

Pierce let that go by as a mother's denial of the obvious. It was something he had seen before in his own family.

'What did the police say to you about her?'

'Just that she probably went off with one of these fellows and that I'd probably hear from her soon.'

'When was that?'

'A month ago. You see, Lilly calls me every Saturday afternoon. When two weeks went by with no phone calls I called the police. They didn't call me back. After the third week I called again and talked to Missing Persons. They didn't even take a report or anything, just told me to keep waiting. They don't care.'

For some reason a vision bled into his mind and distracted him. It was the night he had come home from Stanford. His mother was waiting for him in the kitchen, the lights off. Just waiting there in the dark to tell him the news about his sister, Isabelle.

When Lilly Quinlan's mother spoke, it was his own mother.

'I called in a private detective but he's been no help. He can't find her neither.'

The content of what she was saying finally brought him out of it.

'Mrs. Quinlan, is Lilly's father there? Can I talk to him?'

'No, he's long gone. She never knew him. He hasn't been here in about twelve years – ever since the day I caught him with her.'

'Is he in prison?'

'No, he's just gone.'

Pierce didn't know what to say.

'When did Lilly come out to L.A.?'

'About three years ago. She first went to a flight attendant school out in Dallas but never did that job. Then she moved to L.A. I wish she'd become a flight attendant. I told her that in the escort business even if you don't have sex with those men, people will still think that you did.'

Pierce nodded. He supposed that it was sound motherly advice. He pictured a heavyset woman with big hair and a cigarette in the corner of her mouth. Between that and her father, no wonder Lilly went about as far as she could get from Tampa. He was surprised it was only three years ago that she left.

'Where did you hire a private detective, there in Tampa or out here in L.A.?'

'Out there. Not much use to hire one here.'

'How did you hire one out here?'

'The policeman in Missing Persons sent me a list. I picked from there.'

'Did you come out here to look for her, Mrs. Quinlan?'

'I'm not in good health. Doctor says I've got emphysema and I've got my oxygen that I'm hooked up to. There wasn't much I could do comin' out there.'

Pierce reconstructed his vision of her. The cigarette was gone and the oxygen tube replaced it. The big hair remained. He thought about what else he could ask or what information he might be able to get from the woman.

'Lilly told me she was sending you money.'

It was a guess. It seemed to go with the whole mother-daughter relationship.

'Yes, and if you find her, tell her I'm getting real short about now. I'm real low. I had to give a lot of what I had to Mr. Glass.'

'Who is Mr. Glass?'

'He's the private detective I hired. But I don't hear from him anymore. Now that I can't pay him anymore.'

'Can you give me his full name and a number for him?'

'I have to look it up.'

She put down the phone and it was two minutes before she came back and gave him the number and address for the private investigator. His full name was Philip Glass. His office was in Culver City.

'Mrs. Quinlan, are there any other contacts you have for Lilly out here? Any friends or anything like that?'

'No, she never gave me any numbers or told me about any friends. Except she once mentioned this girl Robin who she worked with sometimes. Robin was from New Orleans and they had stuff in common, she told me.'

'Did she say what?'

'I think they both had the same kind of trouble with men in their family when they were young. That's what I expect she meant.'

'I understand.'

Pierce was trying to think like a detective. Vivian Quinlan seemed like an important piece of the puzzle, yet he could not think of anything else to ask her. She was three thousand miles away and was obviously kept literally and figuratively distant from her daughter's world. He looked down at the phone book on the desk in front of him and finally came up with something to ask.

'Does the name Wainwright mean anything to you, Mrs. Quinlan? Did Lilly or Mr. Glass ever mention that name?'

'Um, no. Mr. Glass didn't mention any names. Who is it?'

'I don't know. It's just someone she knew, I guess.'

That was it. He had nothing else.

'Okay, Mrs. Quinlan, I'm going to keep trying to find her and I'll tell her to call you when I do.'

'I'd appreciate that and make sure you tell her about the money, that I'm getting real low.'

'Right. I will.'

He hung up and thought for a few moments about what he knew. Probably too much about Lilly. It made him feel depressed and sad. He hoped one of her clients did take her away with a promise of riches and luxury. Maybe she was in Hawaii somewhere or in a rich man's penthouse in Paris.

But he doubted it.

'Guys in tuxedos,' he said out loud.

'What?'

He looked up. Charlie Condon was standing in the door. Pierce had left it open.

'Oh, nothing. Just talking to myself. What are you doing here?'

He realized that Lilly Quinlan's phone book and the mail were spread in front of him. He nonchalantly picked up the daily planner he kept on the desk, looked at it like he was checking a date and then put it down on top of the envelopes with her name on them.

'I called your new number and got Monica. She said you were supposed to be here while she waited for furniture to be delivered. But nobody answered in the lab or in your office, so I came by.'

He leaned against the door frame. Charlie was a handsome man with what seemed like a perpetual tan. He had worked as a model in New York for a few years before getting bored and going back to school for a master's in finance. They had been introduced by an investment banker who knew Condon was skilled at taking underfinanced emerging-technology firms and matching them with investors. Pierce had joined with him because he'd promised to do it with Amedeo Technologies without Pierce having to sacrifice his controlling interest to investors. In return, Charlie would hold 10 percent of the company, a stake that could ultimately be worth hundreds of millions – if they won the race and went public with a stock offering.

'I missed your calls,' Pierce said. 'I just got here, actually. Stopped to get something to eat first.'

Charlie nodded.

'I thought you'd be in the lab.'

Meaning, why aren't you in the lab? There is work to be done. We're in a race. We've got a presentation to a whale to make. You can't chase the dime from your office.

'Yeah, don't worry, I'll get there. I just have some mail to go through. You came all the way in to check on me?'

'Not really. But we only have until Thursday to get our shit together for Maurice. I wanted to make sure everything was all right.'

Pierce knew they were placing too much importance on Maurice Goddard. Even Charlie's e-mail reference to the investor as God was a subliminal indication of this. It was true that Thursday's dog and pony show would be the dog and pony show of all time, but Pierce had growing concern about Condon's reliance on this deal. They were seeking an investor willing to commit at least $6 million a year over three or four years, minimum. Goddard, according to the due diligence conducted by Nicole James and Cody Zeller, was worth $250 million, thanks to his getting in early on a few investments like Microsoft. It was clear that Goddard had the money. But if he didn't come across with a significant funding plan after Thursday's presentation, then there had to be another investor out there. It would be Condon's job to go out and find him.

'Don't worry,' Pierce said. 'We'll be ready. Is Jacob coming in for it?'

'He'll be here.'

Jacob Kaz was the company's patent attorney. They had fifty-eight patents already granted or applied for and Kaz was going to file nine more the Monday after the presentation to Goddard. Patents were the key to the race. Control the patents and you are in on the ground floor and will eventually control the market. The nine new patent applications were the first to come out of the Proteus project. They would send a shock wave through the nanoworld. Pierce almost smiled at the thought of it. And Condon seemed to read his thoughts.

'Did you look at the patents yet?' he asked.

Pierce reached down into the kneehole beneath his desk and knocked his fist on the top of the steel safe bolted there to the floor. The patent drafts were in there. Pierce had to sign off on them before they were filed but it was very dry reading, and he'd been distracted by other things even before Lilly Quinlan came up.

'Right here. I'm planning to get to them today or come back in tomorrow.'

It would be against company policy for Pierce to take the applications home to review.

Condon nodded his approval.

'Great. So, everything else okay? You doin' all right?'

'You mean with Nicki and everything?'

Charlie nodded.

'Yeah, I'm cool. I'm trying to keep my mind on other things.'

'Like the lab, I hope.'

Pierce leaned back in his chair, spread his hands and smiled. He wondered how much Monica had told him when he had called the apartment.

'I'm here.'

'Well, good.'

'By the way, Nicole left a new clip in the Bronson file on the Tagawa deal. It's hit the media.'

'Anything?'

'Nothing we didn't know already. Elliot said something about biologicals. Very general, but you never know. Maybe he's gotten wind of Proteus.'

As he said it Pierce looked past Condon at the framed one-sheet poster on his office wall next to the door. It was the poster from the 1966 movie *Fantastic Voyage*. It showed the white submarine *Proteus* descending through a multicolor sea of bodily fluids. It was an original poster. He had gotten it from Cody Zeller, who had obtained it through an online Hollywood memorabilia auction.

'Elliot just likes to talk,' Condon said. 'I don't know how he could know anything about Proteus. But after the patent is granted he'll know about it. And he'll be shitting bricks. And Tagawa will know they backed the wrong horse.'

'Yeah, I hope so.'

They had flirted with Tagawa earlier in the year. But the Japanese company wanted too large a piece of the company for the money, and negotiations broke down early. Though Proteus was mentioned in the early meetings, the Tagawa representatives were never fully briefed and never got near the lab. Now Pierce had to concern himself with exactly how much about the project was mentioned, because it stood to reason that the information was passed on to Tagawa's new partner, Elliot Bronson.

'Let me know if you need anything and I'll get it done,' Condon said.

It brought Pierce out of his thoughts.

'Thanks, Charlie. You going back home now?'

'Probably. Melissa and I are going to Jar tonight for dinner. You want to go? I could call and make it for three.'

'Nah, that's okay. But thanks. I've got the furniture coming in today and I'll probably work on getting my place set up.'

Charlie nodded and then hesitated for a moment before asking the next question.

'You going to change your phone number?'

'Yeah, I think I have to. First thing Monday. Monica told you, huh?'

'A little bit. She said you got some prostitute's old number and guys are calling all the time.'

'She's an escort, not a prostitute.'

'Oh, I didn't know there was a big difference.'

Pierce couldn't believe he had jumped to defend a woman he didn't even know. He felt his face getting red.

'There probably isn't. Anyway, when I see you Monday I'll probably give you a new number, okay? I want to get done here so I can get in the lab and do something today.'

'Okay, man, I'll see you Monday.'

Condon left then, and after Pierce was sure he was down the hall he got up and closed his door. He wondered how much more Monica had told him, whether she was spreading alarm about his activities. He thought about calling her but decided to wait until later, to talk about it with her in person.

He went back to Lilly's phone book, leafing through it once again. Almost to the end he came across a listing he hadn't noticed before. It simply said USC and had a number. Pierce thought about the envelope he had seen in her house. He picked up the phone and called the number. He got a recording for the admissions office of the University of Southern California. The office was closed on weekends.

Pierce hung up. He wondered if Lilly had been in the process of applying to USC when she disappeared. Maybe she had been trying to get out of the escort business. Maybe it was the reason she had disappeared.

He put the phone book aside and opened the Visa statement. It showed zero purchases on the card for the month of August and notice for an overdue payment on a $354.26 balance. The payment had been due by August 10.

The bank statement from Washington Savings & Loan was next. It was a combined statement showing balances in checking and savings accounts. Lilly Quinlan had not made a deposit in the month of August but had not been short of funds. She had $9,240 in checking and $54,542 in savings. It wasn't enough for four years at USC but it would have been a start if Lilly was changing her direction.

Pierce looked through the statement and the collection of posted checks the bank had returned to her. He noticed one to a Vivian Quinlan for $2,000 and assumed that was the monthly installment on maternal upkeep. Another check, this one for $4,000, was made out to James Wainwright and on the memo line Lilly had written, 'Rent.'

He tapped the check lightly against his chin as he thought about what this meant. It seemed to him that $4,000 was an excessively high monthly rent for the bungalow on Altair. He wondered if she had paid for more than one month with the check.

He put the check back in the stack and finished looking through the bank records. Nothing else hooked his interest and he put the checks and the statement back in the envelope.

The third-floor copy room was a short walk down the hall from Pierce's office. Along with a copier and a fax machine, the small room contained a power shredder. Pierce entered the room, opened up his backpack and fed the pieces of Lilly Quinlan's opened mail into the shredder, the whine of the machine seemingly loud enough to draw the attention of security. But no one came. He felt a sense of guilt drop over him. He didn't know anything about federal mail theft laws but was sure he had probably just compounded the first offense of stealing the mail by now destroying it.

When he was finished he stuck his head out into the hall and checked to make sure he was still alone on the floor. He then returned and opened one of the storage cabinets where stacks of packages containing copier paper were stored. From his backpack he removed Lilly Quinlan's phone book and then reached into the cabinet with it, dropping it behind one of the stacks of paper. He believed it could go as long as a month there without being discovered.

Once finished with hiding and destroying the evidence of his crime, Pierce took the lab elevator down to the basement and passed through the mantrap into the suite. He checked the sign-in log and saw that Grooms had been in that morning as well as Larraby and a few of the lower-tier lab rats. They had all come and gone. He picked up the pen and was about to sign in when he thought better of it and put the pen back down.

At the computer console Pierce entered the three passwords in correct order for a Saturday and logged in. He called up the testing protocols for the Proteus project. He started to read the summary of the most recent testing of cellular energy conversion rates, which had been conducted by Larraby that morning.

But then he stopped. Once again he could not do it. He could not concentrate on the work. He was consumed by other thoughts, and he knew from past experience – the Proteus project being an example – that he must run out the clock on the thing that consumed him if he was to ever return to the work.

He shut down the computer and left the lab. Back up in his office he took his notebook out of his backpack and called the number he had for the private investigator, Philip Glass. As he expected for a Saturday afternoon, he got a machine and left a message.

'Mr. Glass, my name is Henry Pierce. I would like to talk to you as soon as possible about Lilly Quinlan. I got your name and number from her mother. I hope to talk to you soon. You can call me back at any time.'

He left both his apartment number and the direct line to his office and hung up. He realized that Glass might recognize the apartment number as having once belonged to Lilly Quinlan.

He drummed his fingers on the edge of his desk. He tried to figure out the next step. He decided he was going up the coast to see Cody Zeller. But first he called his apartment number and Monica answered in a gruff voice.

'What?'

'It's me, Henry. My stuff get there yet?'

'They just got here. Finally. They're bringing in the bed first. Look, you can't blame me if you don't like where I tell them to put stuff.'

'Tell me something. Are you having them put the bed in the bedroom?'

'Of course.'

'Then I'm sure I'll like it just fine. What are you so short about?'

'It's just this goddamn phone. Every fifteen minutes some creep calls for Lilly. I'll tell you one thing: wherever she is, she must be rich.'

Pierce had a growing feeling that wherever she was, money didn't matter. But he didn't say that.

'The calls are still coming in? They told me they'd get her page off the website by three o'clock.'

'Well, I got a call about five minutes ago. Before I could say I wasn't Lilly the guy asked if I'd do a prostate massage, whatever that is. I hung up on him. It's totally gross.'

Pierce smiled. He didn't know what it was, either. But he tried to keep the humor out of his voice.

'I'm sorry. Hopefully they won't take long getting it all up there and you can leave as soon as they are finished.'

'Thank God.'

'I need to go to Malibu, or else I'd come back now.'

'Malibu? What's in Malibu?'

Pierce regretted mentioning it. He had forgotten about her earlier interest and disapproval of what he was doing.

'Don't worry, nothing to do with Lilly Quinlan,' he lied. 'I'm going to see Cody Zeller about something.'

He knew it was weak but it would have to do for now. They hung up and Pierce started putting his notebook back in his backpack.

'Lights,' he said.

10

The drive north on the Pacific Coast Highway was slow but nice. The highway skirted the ocean, and the sun hung low in the sky over Pierce's left shoulder. It was warm but he had the windows down and the sunroof open. He couldn't remember the last time he had taken a drive like this. Maybe it was the time he and Nicole had ducked out of Amedeo for a long lunch and driven up to Geoffrey's, the restaurant overlooking the Pacific and favored by Malibu's movie set.

When he got into the first stretch of the beach town and his view of the coast was stolen by the houses crowding the ocean's edge, he slowed down and watched for Zeller's house. He didn't have the address offhand and had to recognize the house, which he hadn't seen in more than a year. The houses on this stretch were jammed side to side and all looked the same. No lawns, built right to the curb, flat as shoe boxes.

He was saved by the sight of Zeller's black-on-black Jaguar XKR, which was parked out in front of his house's closed garage. Zeller had long ago illegally converted his garage into a workroom and had to pay garage rent to a neighbor to protect his $90,000 car. The car's being outside meant Zeller had either just gotten home or was about to head out. Pierce was just in time. He pulled a U-turn and parked behind the Jag, careful not to bump the car Zeller treated like a baby sister.

The front door of the house was opened before he reached it – either Zeller had seen him on one of the cameras mounted under the roof's eave or Pierce had tripped a motion sensor. Zeller was the only person Pierce knew who rivaled him in paranoia. It was probably what had bonded them at Stanford. He remembered that when they were freshmen Zeller had an often spoken theory that President Reagan had lapsed into a coma after the assassination attempt in the first year of his presidency and had been replaced by a double who was a puppet of the far right. The theory was good for laughs but he was serious about it.

'Dr. Strangelove, I presume,' Zeller said.

'Mein führer, I can walk,' Pierce replied.

It had been their standard greeting since Stanford when they saw the movie together at a Kubrick retrospective in San Francisco.

They gave each other a handshake invented by the loose group of friends they belonged to in college. They called themselves the Doomsters, after the Ross MacDonald novel. The handshake consisted of fingers hooked together like train car couplings and then three quick squeezes like gripping a rubber ball at a blood bank – the Doomsters had sold plasma on a regular basis while in college in order to buy beer, marijuana and computer software.

Pierce hadn't seen Zeller in a few months and his hair hadn't been cut since then. Sun-bleached and unkempt, it was loosely tied at the back of his neck. He wore a Zuma Jay T-shirt, baggies and leather sandals. His skin was the copper color of smoggy sunsets. Of all the Doomsters he always had the look the others had aspired to. Now it was wearing a little long in the tooth. At thirty-five he was beginning to look like an aging surfer who couldn't let it go, which made him all the more endearing to Pierce. In many ways Pierce felt like a sellout. He admired Zeller for the path he had cut through life.

'Check him out, Dr. Strange himself out in the Big Bad 'Bu. Man, you don't have your wets with you and I don't see any board, so to what do I owe this unexpected pleasure?'

He beckoned Pierce inside and they walked into a large loft-style home that was divided in half, with living quarters to the right and working quarters to the left. Beyond these distinct areas was a wall of floor-to-ceiling glass that opened to the deck and the ocean just beyond. The steady pounding of the ocean's waves was the heartbeat of the house. Zeller had once informed Pierce that it was impossible to sleep in the house without earplugs and a pillow over one's head.

'Just thought I'd take a ride out and check on things here.'

They moved across the beech flooring toward the view. In a house like this it was an automatic reflex. You gravitated to the view, to the blue-black water of the Pacific. Pierce saw a light misting out on the horizon but not a single boat. As they got close to the glass he could look down through the deck railing and see the swells rolling in. A small company of surfers in multicolor wets sat on their boards and waited for the right moment. Pierce felt an internal tug. It had been a long time since he'd been out there. He'd always found the waiting on the swells, the camaraderie of the group, to be more fulfilling than the actual ride in on the wave.

'Those are my boys out there,' Zeller said.

'They look like Malibu High teenagers.'

'They are. And so am I.'

Pierce nodded. Feel young, stay young – a common Malibu life ethic.

'I keep forgetting about how nice you got it out here, Code.'

'For a college dropout, I can't complain. Beats selling one's purity of essence for twenty-five bucks a bag.'

He was talking about plasma. Pierce turned away from the view. In the living area there were matching gray couches and a coffee table in front of a freestanding fireplace with an industrial, concrete finish. Behind this was the kitchen. To the left was the bedroom area.

'Beer, dude? I've got Pacifica and Saint Mike.'

'Yeah, sure. Either one.'

While Zeller went to the kitchen Pierce moved toward the work area. A large floor-to-ceiling rack of electronics acted to knock down the exterior light and partition off the area where Zeller made his living. There were two desks and another bank of shelves containing code books and software and system manuals. He stepped through the plastic curtain that used to be where the door to the garage was. He took a step down and was in a climate-controlled computer room. There were two complete computer bays on either side of the room, each equipped with multiple screens. Each system seemed to be at work. Slowly unspooling data trails moved across each screen. Digital inchworms crawling through whatever was Zeller's project at the moment. The walls of the room were covered in black foam padding to dampen exterior noise. The room was dimly lit by mini-spots. There was an unseen stereo playing an old Guns N' Roses disc that Pierce had not heard in more than ten years.

Affixed to the padding of the rear wall was a procession of stickers depicting company logos and trademark names. Most were household words, companies pervasive in daily life. There were many more stickers on the wall than the last time Pierce visited. He knew that Zeller put up a logo every time he conducted a successful intrusion into that company's computer services system. They were the notches on his belt.

Zeller earned $500 an hour as a white-hat hacker. He was the best of the best. He worked as an independent, usually hired by one of the Big Six accounting firms to conduct penetration tests on its clients. In a way it was a racket. The system that Zeller could not defeat was rare. And after each successful penetration his employer usually turned around and got a fat digital security contract from the client, with a nice bonus going to Zeller. He had once told Pierce that digital security was the fastest growth area in the corporate accounting industry. He was constantly fielding high-price offers to come on board full-time with one or another of the big firms, but he always demurred, saying he liked working for himself. Privately, he told Pierce that it was also because working for himself allowed him to eschew the random drug testing of the corporate world.

Zeller came into the clean room with two brown bottles of San Miguel. They double-clicked bottles before drinking. Another tradition. It tasted good to Pierce, smooth and cold. Bottle in hand, he pointed to a red and white square affixed to the wall. It was the most recognized corporate symbol in the world.

'That one's new, isn't it?'

'Yeah, I just got that one. Took the job out of Atlanta. You know how they got some secret formula for making the drink? They were – '

'Yeah, cocaine.'

'That's the urban myth. Anyway, they wanted to see how well the formula was protected. I went in from total scratch. Took me about seven hours and then I e-mailed the formula to the CEO. He didn't know we were doing a penetration test – it was handled by people below him. I was told he almost had a goddamn coronary. He had visions of the formula going out across the net, falling into the hands of the Pepsi and Dr. Pepper people, I guess.'

Pierce smiled.

'Cool. You working on something right now? It looks busy.'

He indicated the screens with his bottle.

'No, not really. I'm just doing a little trolling. Looking for somebody I know is out there hiding.'

'Who?'

Zeller looked at him and smiled.

'If I told you that, I'd have to kill you.'

It was business. Zeller was saying that part of what he sold was discretion. They were friends who went back to good times and one seriously bad time – at least for Pierce – in college. But business was business.

'I understand,' Pierce said. 'And I don't want to intrude, so let me get to it. Are you too busy to take on something else?'

'When would I need to start?'

'Uh, yesterday would be nice.'

'A quickie. I like quickies. And I like working for Amedeo Tech.'

'Not for the company. For me. But I'll pay you.'

'I like that better. What do you need?'

'I need to run some people and some businesses, see what comes up.'

Zeller nodded thoughtfully.

'Heavy people?'

'I don't really know but I'd use all precautions. It involves the adult entertainment field, you could say.'

Now Zeller smiled broadly, his burned skin crinkling around the eyes.

'Oh, baby, don't tell me you bumped your dick into something.'

'No, nothing like that.'

'Then what?'

'Let's sit down. And you'd better bring something to take notes with.'

In the living room Pierce gave him all the information he had on Lilly Quinlan without explanation about where it was coming from. He also asked Zeller to find what he could on Entrepreneurial Concepts Unlimited and Wentz, the man who operated it.

'You got a first name?'

'No. Just Wentz. Can't be too many in the field, I would guess.'

'Full scans?'

'Whatever you can get.'

'Stay inside the lines?'

Pierce hesitated. Zeller kept his eyes level on him. He was asking if Pierce wanted him to stay within the bounds of the law. Pierce knew from experience that there was much more out there to be found if Zeller crossed the lines and went into systems he was not authorized to enter. And he knew Zeller was an expert at crossing them. The Doomsters were formed when they were college sophomores. Computer hacking was just coming into vogue for their generation and the members of the group, largely under the direction of Zeller, did more than hold their own. They mostly committed pranks, their best being the time they hacked into the local telephone company's 411 information bank and changed the number for the Domino's Pizza closest to campus to the home number of the dean of the Computer Sciences Department.

But their best moment was also their worst. All six of the Doomsters were busted by the police and later suspended. On the criminal side everybody got probation with the charges to be expunged after six months without further trouble. Each boy also had to complete 160 hours of community service. On the school side they were all suspended for one semester. Pierce went back after serving both the suspension and the probation. Under the magnifying glass of police and school administrators, he switched from computer sciences to a chemistry curriculum and never looked back.

Zeller never looked back, either. He didn't go back to Stanford. He was scooped up by a computer security firm and given a nice salary. Like a gifted athlete who leaves school early for the pros, he could not go back to school once he sampled the joys of having money and doing what he loved for a living.

'Tell you what,' Pierce finally answered. 'Get whatever you can get. In fact, on Entrepreneurial Concepts, I think some variation of *abra cadabra* might help you get in. Try it backwards first.'

'Thanks for the head start. When do you need this?'

'Like I said, yesterday will be fine.'

'Right, a quickie. You sure you didn't stick your dick into something nasty?'

'Not that I know of.'

'Nicole know about this?'

'Nope, there's no reason. Nicole's gone, remember?'

'Right, right. This the reason why?'

'You don't give up, do you? No, it's got nothing to do with her.'

Pierce finished his beer. He didn't want to hang around, because he wanted Zeller to get to work on the assignment he was giving him. But Zeller seemed in no hurry to start.

'Want another beer, commander?'

'Nah, I'm gonna pass. I've gotta get back to my apartment. I have my assistant baby-sitting the furniture movers. Besides, you're going to get on this thing, aren't you?'

'Oh, yeah, man. Right away.'

He gestured toward his work area.

'Right now all my machines are booked. But I'll get on it tonight. I'll call you by tomorrow night.'

'All right, Code. Thanks.'

He got up. They pumped each other's hand. Blood brothers. Doomsters again.

11

By the time Pierce got to his apartment the movers were gone but Monica was still there. She'd had them arrange the furnishings in a way that was acceptable. It didn't really take advantage of the view from the floor-to-ceiling windows that ran along one side of the living room and dining room, but Pierce didn't care all that much. He knew he'd be spending little time in the apartment anyway.

'It looks nice,' he said. 'Thanks.'

'You're welcome. I hope you like everything. I was just about to leave.'

'Why did you stay?'

She held up her stack of magazines in two hands.

'I wanted to finish a magazine I was reading.'

Pierce wasn't sure why that necessitated her staying at the apartment but he let it go.

'Listen, there's one thing I want to ask you before you leave. Come sit down for a second.'

Monica looked put out by the request. She probably envisioned another phone call impersonating Lilly Quinlan. Nevertheless, she sat down on one of the leather club chairs she'd ordered to go with his couch.

'Okay, what is it?'

Pierce sat on the couch.

'What is your job title at Amedeo Technologies?'

'What do you mean? You know what it is.'

'I want to see if *you* know what it is.'

'Personal assistant to the president. Why?'

'Because I want to make sure you remember that it is *personal* assistant, not just assistant.'

She blinked and looked at his face for a long moment before responding.

'All right, Henry, what's wrong?'

'What's wrong is that I don't appreciate your telling Charlie Condon all about my phone number problems and what I'm trying to do about it.'

She straightened her back and looked aghast but it was a bad act.

'I didn't.'

'That's not what he said. And if you didn't tell him, how did he know everything after he talked to you?'

'Look, okay, all I told him was that you'd gotten this prostitute's old number and you were getting all kinds of calls. I had to tell him something because when he called I didn't recognize his voice and he didn't recognize mine and he said, 'Who's this?' and I kind of snapped at him because I thought he was, you know, calling for Lilly.'

'Uh-huh.'

'And I couldn't make up a lie on the spot. I'm not that good, like some people. Lying, social engineering, whatever you call it. So I told him the truth.'

Pierce almost mentioned that she was pretty good at lying about not telling Charlie at the start of the conversation but he decided not to inflame the situation.

'And that's all you told him, that I had gotten this woman's phone number? You left it at that? You didn't tell him about how you got her address for me and I went to her house?'

'No, I didn't. What's the big deal anyway? You guys are partners, I thought.'

She stood up.

'Can I please go?'

'Monica, sit down here for one more second.'

He pointed to the chair and she reluctantly sat back down.

'The big deal is that loose lips sink ships, you understand that?'

She shrugged her shoulders and wouldn't look at him. She looked down at the stack of magazines in her lap. On the cover of the top one was a photo of Clint Eastwood.

'My actions reflect on the company,' Pierce said. 'Especially right now. Even what I do in private. If what I do is misrepresented or blown out of proportion, it could seriously hurt the company. Right now our company makes zero money, Monica, and we rely on investors to support the research, to pay the rent and the salaries, everything. If investors think we're shaky, then we've got a big problem. If things about me – true or false – get to the wrong people, we could have trouble.'

'I didn't know Charlie was the wrong people,' she said in a sulking voice.

'He's not. He's the right people. That's why I don't mind what you said to him. But what I will mind is if you tell anybody else about what I am doing or what's going on with me. Anyone, Monica. Inside or outside the company.'

He hoped she understood he was talking about Nicole and anybody else she encountered in her daily life.

'I won't. I won't tell a soul. And please don't ask me to get involved in your personal life again. I don't want to baby-sit deliveries or do anything outside of the company again.'

'Fine. I won't ask you to. It was my mistake because I didn't think this would be a problem and you told me you could use the overtime.'

'I can use the overtime but I don't like all of these complications.'

Pierce waited a moment, watching her the whole time.

'Monica, do you even know what we do at Amedeo? I mean, do you know what the project is all about?'

She shrugged.

'Sort of. I know it's about molecular computing. I've read some of the stories on the wall of fame. But the stories are very ... scientific and everything's so secret that I never wanted to ask questions. I just try to do my job.'

'The project isn't secret. The processes we're inventing are. There's a difference.'

He leaned forward and tried to think of the best way to explain it to her without making it confusing or treading into protected areas. He decided to use a tack that Charlie Condon often used with potential investors who might be confused by the science. It was an explanation Charlie had come up with after talking about the project in general once with Cody Zeller. Cody loved movies. And so did Pierce, though he rarely had time to see them in theaters anymore.

'Did you ever see the movie *Pulp Fiction*?'

Monica narrowed her eyes and nodded suspiciously.

'Yes, but what does it – '

'Remember, it's a movie about all these gangsters crossing paths and shooting people and shooting drugs, but at the heart of everything is this briefcase. And they never show what's in the briefcase but everybody sure wants it. And when somebody opens it you can't see what's in it but whatever it is glows like gold. You see that glow. And it's mesmerizing for whoever looks into the briefcase.'

'I remember.'

'Well, that's what we're after at Amedeo. We're after this thing that glows like gold but nobody can see it. We're after it – and a whole bunch of other people are after it – because we all believe it will change the world.'

He waited a moment and she just looked at him, uncomprehending.

'Right now, everywhere in the world, microprocessing chips are made of silicon. It's the standard, right?'

She shrugged again.

'Whatever.'

'What we are trying to do at Amedeo, and what they are trying to do at Bronson Tech and Midas Molecular and the dozens of other companies and universities and governments around the world we are competing with, is create a new generation of computer chips made of molecules. Build an entire computer's circuitry with only organic molecules. A computer that will one day come out of a vat of chemicals, that will assemble itself from the right recipe being put in that vat. We're talking about a computer without silicon or magnetic particles. Tremendously less expensive to build and astronomically more powerful – in which just a teaspoon of molecules could hold more memory than the biggest computer going today.'

She waited to make sure he was done.

'Wow,' she said in an unconvincing tone.

Pierce smiled at her stubbornness. He knew he had probably sounded too much like a salesman. Like Charlie Condon, to be precise. He decided to try again.

'Do you know what computer memory actually is, Monica?'

'Well, yeah, I guess.'

He could tell by her face that she was just covering. Most people in this day and age took things like computers for granted and without explanation.

'I mean how it works,' he said to her. 'It's just ones and zeros in sequence. Every piece of data, every number, every letter, has a specific sequence of ones and zeros. You string the sequences together and you have a word or a number and so on. Forty, fifty years ago it took a computer the size of this room to store basic arithmetic. And now we're down to a silicon chip.'

He held his thumb and finger up, just a half inch apart. Then he squeezed them together.

'But we can go smaller,' he said. 'A lot smaller.'

She nodded but he couldn't tell if she saw the light or was just nodding.

'Molecules,' she said.

He nodded.

'That's right, Monica. And believe me, whoever gets there first is going to change this world. It is conceivable that we could build a whole computer that is smaller than a silicon chip. Take a computer that fills a room now and make it the size of a dime. That's our goal. That's why in the lab we call it "chasing the dime." I'm sure you've heard the saying around the office.'

She shook her head.

'But why would someone want a computer the size of a dime? They couldn't even read it.'

Pierce started laughing but then cut it off. He knew he had to keep this woman quiet and on his side. He shouldn't insult her.

'That's just an example. It's a possibility. The point is, the computing and memory power of this type of technology are limitless. You're right, nobody needs or wants a computer the size of a dime. But think what this advancement would mean for a PalmPilot or a laptop computer. What if you didn't need to carry any of those? What if your computer was in the button of your shirt or the frame of your eyeglasses? What if in your office your desktop wasn't on your desk but in the paint on the walls of your office? What if you talked to the walls and they talked back?'

She shook her head and he could tell she still could not comprehend the possibilities and their applications. She could not break free of the world she currently knew and understood and accepted. He reached into his back pocket and took out his wallet. He removed his American Express card and held it up to her.

'What if this card was a computer? What if it contained a memory chip so powerful that it could record every purchase ever made on this account along with the date, time and location of the purchase? I'm talking about for the lifetime of its user, Monica. A bottomless well of memory in this thin piece of plastic.'

Monica shrugged.

'That would be cool, I guess.'

'We're less than five years away. We have molecular RAM right now. Random access memory. And we're perfecting logic gates. Working circuits. We put them together – logic and memory – and you have integrated circuitry, Monica.'

It still excited him to speak of the possibilities. He slid the credit card back into his wallet and pocketed it. He never took his eyes off her and could tell he still wasn't making a dent. He decided to stop trying to impress her and get to the point.

'Monica, the thing is, we're not alone. It is highly competitive out there. There are a lot of private companies out there just like Amedeo Technologies. A lot of them are bigger and with a lot more money. There's also DARPA, there's UCLA and other universities, there's—'

'What is DARPA?'

'Defense Advanced Research Projects Agency. The government. The agency that keeps its eye on all emerging technologies. It's backing several separate projects in our field. When I started the company I consciously chose not to have the government be my boss. But the point is, most of our competitors are well funded and dug in. We're not. And so to keep going, we need the funding stream to keep flowing. We can't do anything that stops that flow, or we drop out of the race and there is no Amedeo Technologies. Okay?'

'Okay.'

'It would be one thing if this was a car dealership or a business like that. But I happen to think we have a shot at changing the world here. The team I've assembled down in that lab is second to none. We have the—'

'I said okay. But if all this is so important, maybe you ought to think about what you're doing. I just talked about it. You're the one who is out there going to her house and doing things underhanded.'

Anger flared up inside of him and he waited a moment to let it subside.

'Look, I was curious about this and just wanted to make sure the woman was all right. If that is being underhanded, then okay, I was underhanded.

But now I'm done with it. On Monday I want you to get my number changed and hopefully that will be the end of it.'

'Good. Can I go now?'

Pierce nodded. He gave up.

'Yes, you can go. Thanks for waiting for the furniture. I hope you have a good weekend, what's left of it, and I'll see you on Monday.'

He didn't look at her when he said it or when she got up from the chair. She left without another word to him and he remained angry. He decided that once things blew over he would get another personal assistant and Monica could go back to the general pool of assistants at the company.

Pierce sat on the couch for a while but was drawn out of his thinking reverie by the phone. It was another caller for Lilly.

'You're too late,' he said. 'She quit the business and went to USC.'

Then he hung up.

After a while he picked up the phone again and called Information in Venice for the number of James Wainwright. A man answered his next call and Pierce got up and walked to the windows as he spoke.

'I'm looking for Lilly Quinlan's landlord,' he said. 'For the house over on Altair in Venice.'

'That would be me.'

'My name's Pierce. I'm trying to locate Lilly and want to know if you've had any contact with her in the last month or so?'

'Well, first of all, I don't think I know you, Mr. Pierce, and I don't answer questions about my tenants with strangers unless they state their business and convince me I should do otherwise.'

'Fair enough, Mr. Wainwright. I'd be happy to come see you in person if you'd prefer. I'm a friend of the family. Lilly's mother, Vivian, is worried about her daughter because she hasn't heard from her in eight weeks. She asked me to do some checking around. I can give you Vivian's number in Florida if you want to call and check on me.'

It was a risk but Pierce thought it was one worth taking to convince Wainwright to talk. It wasn't too far from the truth, anyway. It was social engineering. Turn the truth just a little bit and make it work for you.

'I have her mother's number on her application. I don't need to call, because I don't have anything that will help you. Lilly Quinlan's paid up through the end of the month. I don't have occasion to see or talk to her unless she has a problem. I have not spoken to or seen her in a couple months, at least.'

'The end of the month? Are you sure?'

Pierce knew that that didn't jibe with the check records he had examined.

'That's right.'

'How did she pay her last rent, check or cash?'

'That's none of your business.'

'Mr. Wainwright, it is my business. Lilly is missing and her mother has asked me to look for her.'

'So you say.'

'Call her.'

'I don't have time to call her. I maintain thirty-two apartments and houses. You think I have – '

'Look, is there somebody who takes care of the lawn that I could talk to?'

'You're already talking to him.'

'So you haven't seen her when you've been over there?'

'Come to think of it, a lot of times she'd come out and say hello when I was there cutting the lawn or working the sprinklers. Or she'd bring me out a Pepsi or a lemonade. One time she gave me a cold beer. But she hasn't been there the last few times I've been there. Her car was gone. I didn't think anything of it. People have lives, you know.'

'What kind of car was it?'

'Gold Lexus. I don't know the model but I know it was a Lexus. Nice car. She took good care of it, too.'

Pierce couldn't think of anything else to ask. Wainwright wasn't much of a help.

'Mr. Wainwright, will you check the application and then call her mother? I need you to call me back about this.'

'Are the police involved? Is there a missing-persons report?'

'Her mother's been talking to the police but she doesn't think they're doing much. That's why she asked me. Do you have something to write with?'

'Sure do.'

Pierce hesitated, realizing that if he gave his home number, Wainwright might recognize it as the same number he had for Lilly. He gave him the direct line to his office at Amedeo instead. He then thanked him and hung up.

He sat there looking at the phone, reviewing the call repeatedly and coming to the same conclusion each time. Wainwright was being evasive. He either knew something or was hiding something, or both.

He opened his backpack and got out the notebook in which he had written down the number for Robin, Lilly's escort partner.

This time when he called he tried to deepen his voice when she answered. His hope was that she would not recognize him from the night before.

'I was wondering if we could get together tonight.'

'Well, I'm open, baby. Have we ever dated? You sound familiar.'

'Uh, no. Not before.'

'Whacha got in mind?'

'Um, maybe dinner and then go to your place. I don't know.'

'Well, honey, I get four hundred an hour. Most guys want to skip the dinner and just come see me. Or I go see them.'

'Then I can just come to you.'

'Okay, fine. What's your name?'

He knew she had caller ID, so he couldn't lie.

'Henry Pierce.'

'And what time were you thinking about?'

He looked at his watch. It was six o'clock.

'How about seven?'

It would give him time to come up with a plan and to get to a cash machine. He knew he had some cash, but not enough. He had a card that could get him $400 maximum on a withdrawal.

'An early-bird special,' she said. 'That's fine with me. Except there ain't a special rate.'

'That's okay. Where do I go?'

'Got a pencil?'

'Right here.'

'I'm sure you have a hard pencil.'

She laughed and then gave him an address of a Smooth Moves shop on Lincoln in Marina del Rey. She told him to go into the shop and get a strawberry blitz and then call her from the pay phone out front at five minutes before seven. When he asked her why she did it this way she said, 'Precautions. I wanna get a look at you before I bring you on up. And I like those little strawberry thingees anyway. That's like bringing me flowers, sugar. Have 'em put some energy powder in it for me, would you? I get a sneaky idea that I'm gonna need it with you.'

She laughed again but it sounded too practiced and hollow to Pierce. It gave him a bad feeling. He said he would get the smoothie and make the call and thanked her, and that was the end of it. As he cradled the phone he felt a wave of trepidation sweep through him. He thought about the speech he had given Monica and how she had correctly turned it right back at him.

'You idiot,' he said to himself.

12

At the appointed time Pierce picked up a pay phone outside of Smooth Moves and called Robin's number. Turning his back to the phone, he saw that across Lincoln was a large apartment complex called the Marina Executive Towers. Only the building didn't really qualify as a tower or towers. It was short and wide – three stories of apartments over a garage. The complex covered half a city block and its length was broken up by color gradations. Its exterior was painted three different pastels – pink, blue, yellow – as it worked its way down the street. A banner hanging off the roofline announced short-term executive rentals and free maid service. Pierce realized it was a perfect place for a prostitute to carry out her business. The place was probably so large and the turnover of renters so high that a steady procession of different men coming in and out would not be noticeable or curious to other residents.

Robin picked up after three rings.

'It's Henry. I called—'

'Hey, baby. Let me get a look at you here.'

Without trying to be too obvious about it, he scanned the windows of the apartment building across the street, looking for someone looking back at him. He didn't see anybody or any curtain movement but he noticed that the windows of several apartments had mirrored glass. He wondered if there was more than one woman like Robin working in the building.

'I see you got my smoothie,' she said. 'You get that energy powder?'

'Yes. They call it a booster rocket. That what you wanted?'

'That's it. Okay, you look all right to me. You're not a cop, are you?'

'No, I'm not.'

'You sure?'

'Yes.'

'Then say it. I'm taping this.'

'I am not a police officer, okay?'

'All right, come on up then. Go across the street to the apartment building and at the main door push apartment two oh three. I'll see you soon.'

'Okay.'

He hung up and crossed the street and followed her instructions. At the door, the button marked 203 had the name Bird after it. *As in robin,* Pierce thought. When he pushed the button, the door lock was buzzed without any further inquiry from Robin over the intercom. Inside, he couldn't find the stairs, so he took the elevator the one flight up. Robin's apartment was two doors from the elevator.

She opened the door before he got a chance to knock. There was a peephole and she apparently had been watching. She took the smoothie from his hand and invited him in.

The place was sparsely furnished and seemed devoid of any personal object. There was just a couch, a chair, a coffee table and a standing lamp. A museum print was framed on the wall. It looked medieval: two angels leading the newly deceased toward the light at the end of a tunnel.

As Pierce stepped in he could see that the glass doors to the balcony had the mirrored film on them. They looked almost directly across to the Smooth Moves shop.

'I could see you but you couldn't see me,' Robin said from behind him. 'I could see you looking.'

He turned to her.

'I was just curious about the setup. You know, how you work this.'

'Well, now you know. Come sit down.'

She moved to a couch and gestured for him to sit next to her. He did. He tried to look around. The place reminded Pierce of a hotel room but he guessed atmosphere wasn't what was important for the business usually conducted within the apartment. He felt her hand take his jaw and turn his face to hers.

'You like what you see?' she asked.

He was pretty sure she was the woman in the photo on the web page. It was hard to be certain because he had not studied it as long and as often as the photo of Lilly. She was barefoot and wore a light blue tank top T-shirt and a pair of red corduroy shorts cut so high that a bathing suit might have been more modest. She was braless and her breasts were huge, most likely the result of implants. Nipples the size of Girl Scout cookies were clearly outlined on the T-shirt. Her blonde hair was parted in the middle and cascaded down the sides of her face in ringlets. She wore no makeup that he could see.

'Yes, I do,' he answered.

'People tell me I have a Meg Ryan thing going.'

Pierce nodded, although he didn't see it. The movie star was older but a lot softer on the eyes.

'Did you bring me something?'

At first he thought she was talking about the smoothie but then he remembered the money.

'Yeah, I've got it here.'

He leaned back on the couch to reach into his pocket. He had the four hundred ready in its own thick fold of twenties fresh from the cash machine. This was the part he had rehearsed. He didn't mind losing the four hundred but he didn't want to give it to her and then be kicked out when he revealed the true reason he was there.

He pulled the money out so she could see it and know it was close and hers for the taking.

'First time, baby?'

'Excuse me?'

'With an escort. First time?'

'How do you know that?'

'Because you're supposed to put that in an envelope for me. Like a gift. It is a gift, isn't it? You're not paying me to do anything.'

'Yes, right. A gift.'

'Thank you.'

'Is that what the G in GFE stands for? Gift?'

She smiled.

'You really are new at this, aren't you? *Girlfriend*, sweetie. Absolutely positive girlfriend experience. It means you get whatever you want, like with your girlfriend before she became your wife.'

'I'm not married.'

'Doesn't matter.'

She reached for the money as she said it but Pierce pulled his hand back.

'Uh, before I give you this ... gift, I have to tell you something.'

All the warning lights on her face fired at once.

'Don't worry, I'm not a cop.'

'Then what, you don't want to use a rubber? Forget it, that's rule number one.'

'No, it's not that. In fact, I don't really want to have sex with you. You're very attractive but all I want is some information.'

Her posture became sharper as she seemed to grow taller, even while sitting down.

'What the fuck are you talking about?'

'I have to find Lilly Quinlan. You can help me.'

'Who is Lilly Quinlan?'

'Come on, you name her on your web page. Double your pleasure? You know who I'm talking about.'

'You're the guy from last night. You called last night.'

He nodded.

'Then get the fuck out of here.'

She quickly stood up and walked toward the door.

'Robin, don't open that door. If you don't talk to me, then you'll talk to the cops. That's my next move.'

She turned around.

'The cops won't give a shit.'

But she didn't open the door. She just stood there, angry and waiting, one hand on the knob.

'Maybe not now but they'll care if I go to them.'

'Why, who are you?'

'I have some juice,' he lied. 'That's all you have to know. If I go to them, they'll come to you. They won't be as nice as me . . . and they won't pay you four hundred dollars for your time.'

He put the money down on the couch where she had been sitting. He watched her eyes go to it.

'Just information, that's all I want. It goes no further than me.'

He waited and after a long moment of silence she came back over to the couch and grabbed the money. She somehow found space for it in her tiny shorts. She folded her arms and remained standing.

'What information? I hardly knew her.'

'You know something. You talk about her in the past tense.'

'I don't know anything. All I know is that she's gone. She just . . . disappeared.'

'When was that?'

'More than a month ago. Suddenly she was just gone.'

'Why do you still have her name on your page if she's been gone that long?'

'You saw her picture. She brings in customers. Sometimes they settle for just me.'

'Okay, how do you know her disappearance was so sudden? Maybe she just packed up and left.'

'I know because one minute we were talking on the phone and the next minute she didn't show up, that's why.'

'Show up for what?'

'We had a gig. A double. She set it up and called me. She told me the time and then she didn't show up. I was there and then the client showed up and he wasn't happy. First of all, there was no place to park and then she wasn't there and I had to scramble around to get another girl to come back over here to my place – and there are no other girls like Lilly, and he really wanted Lilly. It was a fucking fiasco, that's what it was.'

'Where was this?'

'Her place. Her gig pad. She didn't work anywhere else. No outcall. Not even to here. I always had to go to her. Even if they were my clients wanting the double, we had to go to her pad, or it didn't happen.'

'Did you have a key to her place?'

'No. Look, you've gotten your four hundred's worth. It would have been easier just to fuck and forget you. That's it.'

Pierce angrily reached into his pocket and pulled out the rest of his cash. It was $230. He'd counted it in the car. He held it out to her.

'Then take this, because I'm not done. Something happened to her and I'm going to find out what.'

She grabbed the money and it disappeared without her counting it. 'Why do you care?'

'Maybe because nobody else does. Now if you didn't have a key to her place, how do you know she didn't show up that night?'

'Because I knocked for fifteen fucking minutes and then me and the guy waited for another twenty. I'm telling you, she wasn't in there.'

'Do you know if she had something set up before the gig with you?'

Robin thought for a little bit before answering.

'She said she had something to do but I don't know if she was with a client. Because I wanted to do it earlier but she said she was busy with something at the time I wanted. So we set the time she wanted, and so she should have been there but wasn't.'

Pierce tried to imagine what questions a cop would ask her but couldn't guess how the police would approach this. He thought about it as if it were a problem at work, with his usual rigorous approach to problem solving and theory building.

'So before she was to meet with you she had to do something,' he said. 'That something could have been meeting a client. And since you say she worked nowhere else but the apartment, she had to have met this client at the apartment. Nowhere else, right?'

'Right.'

'So when you got there and knocked on the door, she could've been inside with or without this other client but just not answering.'

'I guess so, but she should've been done by then and she would have answered. It was all set up. So maybe it wasn't a client.'

'Or maybe she was not allowed to answer. Maybe she couldn't answer.'

This seemed to give Robin pause, as though she realized how close she might have come to whatever fate befell Lilly.

'Where is this place? Her apartment.'

'It's over in Venice. Off Speedway.'

'What's the exact address?'

'I don't remember. I just know how to get there.'

Pierce nodded. He thought about what else he needed to ask her. He had the feeling he had one shot with her. No second chances.

'How'd you two get together for these, uh, gigs?'

'We linked on the website. If people wanted us both, they'd ask and we'd set it up if we were both available.'

'I mean, how did you two meet in order to have the link? How did you meet in the first place?'

'We met at a shoot and sort of hit it off. It went from there.'

'A shoot? What do you mean?'

'Modeling. It was a girl-girl scene and we met at the studio.'

'You mean, for a magazine?'

'No, a website.'

Pierce thought of the doorway he had opened at Entrepreneurial Concepts.

'Was it for one of the websites Entrepreneurial Concepts operates?'

'Look, it doesn't matter what – '

'What was the name of the site?'

'It was called something like fetish castle dot something or other. I don't know. I don't have a computer. What does it matter?'

'Where was the shoot, at Entrepreneurial Concepts?'

'Yeah. At the studios.'

'So you got the job through L.A. Darlings and Mr. Wentz, right?'

He saw her eyes flare at the mention of the name but she didn't respond.

'What's his first name?'

'I'm not talking to you about him. You can't tell him you got any information from me, you understand?'

He thought he now saw a flash of fear in her eyes.

'I told you, everything you tell me here is private. I promise you that. What's his name?'

'Look, he's got connections and people who work for him who are very mean. *He's* mean. I don't want to talk about him.'

'Just tell me his name and I'll leave it at that, okay?'

'It's Billy. Billy Wentz. Most people call him Billy Wince because he hurts people, okay?'

'Thank you.'

He stood up and looked around the apartment. He walked over to the corner of the living room and looked into a hallway that he guessed led to the bedroom. He was surprised to learn there were two bedrooms with a bathroom in between.

'Why do you have two bedrooms?'

'I share the place with another girl. We each have our own.'

'From the website?'

'Yes.'

'What's her name?'

'Cleo.'

'Billy Wentz put you with her, too.'

'No. Grady did.'

'Who is Grady?'

'He works with Billy. He really runs the place.'

'So why don't you do doubles with Cleo? It'd be more convenient.'

'I probably will. But I told you, I was getting a lot of business with Lilly. There aren't many girls that look like her.'

Pierce nodded.

'You don't live here, do you?'

'No. I work here.'

'Where do you live?'

'I'm not telling you that.'

'You keep any clothes here?'

'What do you mean?'

'You have any clothes besides those? And where are your shoes?'

He gestured to what she was wearing.

'Yes, I changed when I got here. I don't go out like this.'

'Good. Change back and let's go.'

'What are you talking about? Where?'

'I want you to show me where Lilly's place is. Or was.'

'Uh-uh, man. You got your information, that's it.'

Pierce looked at his watch.

'Look, you said four hundred an hour. I've been here twenty minutes, tops. That means I get forty more minutes, or you give me two-thirds of my cash back.'

'That's not how it works.'

'That's how it works today.'

She stared at him angrily for a long moment and then walked silently past him toward the bedroom to change. Pierce walked over to the balcony doors and looked out across Lincoln.

He saw a man standing at the pay phone in front of Smooth Moves, holding a smoothie and looking up at the windows of the building Pierce was in. Another smoothie, another client. He wondered how many women were working in the building. Did they all work for Wentz? Did he own the place? Maybe he even had a piece of the smoothie shop.

He turned around to ask Robin about Wentz and from the angle he was at was able to look down the hallway and through the open bedroom door. Robin was naked and pulling a tight pair of faded blue jeans up over her hips. Her perfectly tanned breasts hung down heavily as she bent over in the process.

When she straightened up to pull the zipper closed over her flat stomach and the small triangle of golden hair below, she looked directly at him through the door. She didn't flinch. Instead, there was a defiant look on her face. She reached over to the bed and picked up a white T-shirt, which she pulled over her head without making any move to turn or hide her nakedness from him.

She came out of the bedroom and slipped her feet into a pair of sandals she pulled from under the coffee table.

'Did you enjoy that?' she asked.

'Yes. I did. I guess I don't have to tell you, you have a beautiful body.'

She walked past him and into the kitchenette. She opened a cabinet over the sink and took out a small black purse.

'Let's go. You've got thirty-five minutes.'

She went to the front door, opened it and stepped out into the hallway. He followed.

'You want your smoothie?'

It was sitting untouched on the breakfast bar.

'No, I hate smoothies. Too fattening. My vice is pizza. Next time bring me a pizza.'

'Then why'd you ask for the smoothie?'

'It was just a way of checking you out, seeing what you would do for me.'

And establishing some control, Pierce thought but didn't say. Control that didn't always last long once the money was paid and the clothes were off.

Pierce stepped into the hallway and looked back into the place where Robin made her living. He felt an uneasiness. A sadness even. He thought about her web page. What was an absolutely positive girlfriend experience and how could it come out of a place like that?

He closed the door, made sure it was locked, and then followed Robin to the elevator.

13

Pierce drove and Robin directed. It was a short trip from the Marina to Speedway in Venice. He tried to make the best use of his time on the way over. But he knew Robin was reluctant to talk.

'So, you're not an independent, are you?'

'What are you talking about?'

'You work for Wentz – the guy who runs the website. He's what I guess you'd call a digital pimp. He sets you girls up in that place, runs your web page. How much does he get? I saw on the site he charges four hundred a month to run your picture but I have a feeling he gets a lot more than that. Guy like that, he probably owns the apartment building and the smoothie shop.'

She didn't say anything.

'He gets a share of that first four hundred I gave you, doesn't he?'

'Look, I'm not talking to you about him. You'll get me killed, too. When we get to her place, that's it. We're done. I'll take a cab.'

'Too?'

She was silent.

'What do you know about what happened to Lilly?'

'Nothing.'

'Then why did you say "too" just then?'

'Look, man, if you knew what was smart for you, you'd leave this thing alone, *too*. Go back to the square world, where it's nice and safe. You don't know these people or what they can do.'

'I have an idea.'

'Yeah? How would you have any fucking idea?'

'I had a sister once . . .'

'And?'

'And you could say she was in your line of work.'

He looked away from the road to Robin. She kept her eyes straight ahead.

'One morning a school bus driver up on Mulholland spotted her body down past the guardrail. I was away at Stanford at the time.'

He looked back at the road.

'It's a funny thing about this city,' he continued after a while. 'She was lying out there in the open like that, naked . . . and the cops said they could tell by the . . . evidence that she had been there at least a couple days. And I always wondered how many people saw her, you know? Saw her and didn't do anything about it. Didn't call anybody. This city can be pretty cold sometimes.'

'Any city can.'

He glanced back at her. He could see the distress in her eyes, like she was looking at a chapter from her own life. A possible final chapter.

'Did they ever catch the guy?' she asked.

'Eventually. But not until after he killed four more.'

She shook her head.

'What are you doing here, Henry? That story has got nothing to do with any of this.'

'I don't know what I'm doing. I'm just . . . following something.'

'Good way to get yourself hurt.'

'Look, nobody's going to know you talked to me. Just tell me, what did you hear about Lilly?'

Silence.

'She wanted to get out, didn't she? She made enough money, she was going to go to school. She wanted to get out of the life.'

'Everybody wants to get out. You think we enjoy it?'

Pierce felt ashamed of the way he was pushing her. The way he had used her hadn't been too different from the rest of her paying customers.

'I'm sorry,' he said.

'No, you're not. You're just like the others. You want something and you're desperate for it. Only I can give you the other thing a lot easier than I can give you what you want.'

He was silent.

'Turn left up here and go down to the end. There's only one parking space for her unit. She used to leave it open for the client.'

He turned off Speedway as instructed and was in an alley behind rows of small apartments on either side. They looked like four-to-six-unit buildings with three-foot-wide walking alleys in between. It was crowded. It was the kind of neighborhood where one barking dog could set everybody on edge.

When he got to the last building, Robin said, 'Somebody took it.'

She pointed to a car parked in a spot below a stairway to an apartment door.

'That's the place up there.'

'Is that her car?'

'No, she had a Lexus.'

Right. He remembered what Wainwright had said. The car in the space was a Volvo wagon. Pierce backed up and squeezed his BMW between two rows of trash cans. It wasn't a legal space but cars could still get past in the alley and he wasn't expecting to be there long.

'You'll have to climb over and get out this side.'

'Great. Thanks.'

They got out, Pierce holding the door as Robin climbed over the seats. As soon as she was out she started heading back down the alley toward Speedway.

'Wait,' Pierce said. 'This way.'

'No, I'm finished. I'm walking back to Speedway and catching a cab.'

Pierce could have argued with her about it but decided to let her go.

'Look, thanks for your help. If I find her, I'll let you know.'

'Who, Lilly or your sister?'

That gave him pause for a moment. From those you least expect it comes insight.

'You going to be all right?' he called after her.

She suddenly stopped, turned and strode back to him, the anger flaring in her eyes again.

'Look, don't pretend you care about me, okay? That phony shit is more disgusting than the men who want to come on my face. At least they're honest about it.'

She turned and walked off again down the alley. Pierce watched her for a few moments to see if she'd look back at him but she didn't. She kept on going, pulling a cell phone out of her purse so she could call a cab.

He walked around the Volvo and noticed that blankets in the back were used to cover the tops of two cardboard boxes and other bulky items he couldn't see. He climbed the stairs to Lilly's apartment. When he got there he saw that the door was ajar. He leaned over the railing and looked up the alley but Robin was almost to Speedway and too far to call to.

He turned back to the door and leaned his head in close to the jamb but he didn't hear anything. With one finger he pushed the door, remaining on the porch as it swung inward. As it opened he could see a sparsely furnished living room with a stairway going up the far wall to a loft. Under the loft was a small kitchen with a pass-through window to the living room. Through the pass-through he could see the torso of a man, moving about and putting liquor bottles into a box on the counter.

Pierce leaned forward and looked in without actually entering the apartment. He saw three cardboard boxes on the floor of the living room but there seemed to be no one else in the apartment except the man in the kitchen. The man appeared to be clearing things out and boxing them all up.

Pierce reached over and knocked on the door and called out, 'Lilly?'

The man in the kitchen was startled and almost dropped a bottle of gin he was holding. He then carefully put the bottle on the counter.

'She's not here anymore,' he called from the kitchen. 'She's moved.'

But he stayed in the kitchen, motionless. Pierce thought that was odd, as if he didn't want his face seen.

'Then who are you?'

'I'm the landlord and I'm busy. You'll have to come back.'

Pierce started putting it together. He stepped into the apartment and moved toward the kitchen. When he got to the doorway he saw a man with long gray hair pulled back into a ponytail. He wore a dirty white T-shirt and dirtier white shorts. He was deeply tanned.

'Why would I come back if she moved away?'

It startled him again.

'What I mean is, you can't come in here. She's gone and I'm working.'

'What's your name?'

'My name doesn't matter. Please leave now.'

'You're Wainwright, aren't you?'

The man looked up at Pierce. The acknowledgment was in his eyes.

'Who are you?'

'I'm Pierce. I talked to you today. I was the one who told you she was gone.'

'Oh. Well, you were right, she's long gone.'

'The money she paid you was for both places. The four grand. You didn't tell me that.'

'You didn't ask.'

'Do you own this building, Mr. Wainwright?'

'I'm not answering your questions, thank you.'

'Or does Billy Wentz own it and you just manage it for him?'

Again, the acknowledgment flickered in the eyes and then went out.

'Okay, leave now. Get out of here.'

Pierce shook his head.

'I'm not leaving yet. If you want to call the cops, go ahead. See what they think about your clearing her stuff out even though you told me she was paid up through the month. Maybe we look under the blankets in the back of your car, too. I'm betting we'd find a plasma TV that used to hang on the wall of the house she rented over on Altair. You probably went by there first, right?'

'She abandoned the place,' Wainwright said testily. 'You should have seen the kitchen in there.'

'I'm sure it must've been just awful. So awful, I guess, you decided to clear the place out and maybe even double-dip on the rent, huh? Housing in Venice is tight. You already got a new tenant lined up? Let me guess, another L.A. darling?'

'Look, you don't try to tell me my business.'

'I wouldn't dream of it.'

'What do you want?'

'To look around. To look at the things you're taking.'

'Then hurry up, because as soon as I'm done in here I'm leaving. And I'm locking the door whether you're still here or not.'

Pierce stepped toward him, entering the kitchen and dropping his gaze down into the box on the counter. It was full of liquor bottles and odd glassware, nothing important. He pulled up one of the brown bottles and saw that it was sixteen-year-old scotch. Good stuff. He dropped the bottle back into the box.

'Hey, easy!' Wainwright protested.

'So, does Billy know you're clearing the place out?'

'I don't know any Billy.'

'So you got the house over on Altair and this place. What other properties are under the wing of Wainwright Properties?'

Wainwright folded his arms and leaned back against the counter. He wasn't talking and Pierce suddenly had the urge to take one of the bottles out of the box and smash it across his face.

'How about the Marina Executive Towers? That one of yours?'

Wainwright reached into one of the front pockets of his pants and took out a package of Camels. He shook out a cigarette and then returned the pack to his pocket. He turned on one of the stove's gas burners and lit the cigarette off the flame, then reached into the box and rooted around in the glassware until he found what he was looking for. He came out with a glass ashtray that he put on the counter and dipped his cigarette into.

Pierce noticed the ashtray had printing on it. He leaned forward slightly to read it.

STOLEN FROM NAT'S DAY OF THE LOCUST BAR
HOLLYWOOD, CA

Pierce had heard of the place. It was a dive that was so low, it was high. It was favored by the black-clad Hollywood night creepers. It was also close to the offices of Entrepreneurial Concepts Unlimited. Was it a clue? He had no idea.

'I'm going to take that look around now,' he said to Wainwright.

'Yeah, you do that. Be quick.'

While he listened to Wainwright clinking glasses and jarring bottles as he packed the box, Pierce went into the living room and crouched in front of the boxes that had already been packed. One contained dishware and other kitchen items. The other two contained things from the loft. Bedroom things. There was a basket of assorted condoms. There were several pairs of high-heel shoes. There were leather straps and whips, a full leather head mask with zippers positioned at the eyes and mouth. On her L. A. Darlings page Lilly did not advertise sadomasochistic services. Pierce wondered if this meant there was another website out there, something darker and with a whole new set of elements to consider in her disappearance.

The last box he checked was full of bras and sheer underwear and negligees and miniskirts on hangers. It was clothing similar to what Pierce had seen in one of the closets of the house on Altair. For a moment he wondered what Wainwright planned to do with the boxes. Sell everything in a bizarre yard sale? Or was he simply going to hold it while he re-rented the apartment and house?

Satisfied with his inventory of the boxes, Pierce decided to check out the loft. As he got up, his eyes came upon the door and he noticed the dead bolt. It was a double-key lock. A key was necessary to open or close the lock from both sides. He now understood Wainwright's threat to lock the door whether Pierce was done with his search or not. If you did not have a key, you could be locked in as well as locked out. Pierce wondered what this meant. Did Lilly lock her clients inside the apartment with her? Perhaps it was a way of ensuring payment for services rendered. Maybe it meant nothing at all.

He moved to the staircase and headed up to the loft. On the landing at the top there was a small window that looked out across the rooftop across the alley to the far edge of the beach and the Pacific. Pierce looked down into the alley and saw his car. His eyes tracked down the alley to Speedway. He caught a glimpse of Robin under a streetlight as she got into a green and yellow cab, closing the door as it took off.

He turned from the window to the loft. It was no more than two hundred square feet on the upper level, including the space of a small bath with a shower. The air up there smelled of an unpleasant mixture of heavy incense and something else that Pierce could not readily place. It was like the spoiled air in a refrigerator that has been turned off. It was there but was overpowered by the incense that held to the room like a ghost.

On the open floor there was a king-size bed with no headboard. It took up most of the available space, leaving room for one small side table and a reading light. On the table was an incense burner that was a Kama Sutra sculpture of a fat man and a thin woman coupling in a rear-entry position. A long ash from a burned down incense stick lapped over the sculpture's bowl and onto the table. Pierce was surprised Wainwright had not taken the piece. He was taking everything else, it seemed.

The bedspread was a light blue and the carpet beige. He went to a small closet and slid open the door. It was empty, the contents now in one of the boxes below.

Pierce looked at the bed. It looked to have been carefully made, the spread tucked tightly under the mattress. But there were no pillows, which he thought was strange. He thought maybe it was one of the rules of the escort business. Robin had said the number one rule was no unprotected sex. Maybe number two was no pillows – too easy to smother you with.

He got down on the carpet and looked underneath the box spring. There was nothing but dust.

But then he saw a dark spot in the beige carpeting. Curious, he straightened up and pushed the bed against the far wall to uncover the spot.

One of the wheels was jammed and he had a difficult time, the bed sliding and bumping on the carpet.

Whatever had spilled or dripped on the carpet was dry. It was a brownish black color and Pierce didn't want to touch it, because he thought it might be blood. He also understood now that it was the source of the odor underlying the smell of incense in the room. He got up and pushed the bed back over the spot.

'What the hell are you doing up there?' Wainwright called up.

Pierce didn't answer. He was consumed with the purpose at hand. He took hold of one corner of the bedspread and pulled it up, revealing the mattress below. No mattress cover or top sheet. No blanket.

He started pulling off the bedspread. He wanted to see the mattress. Sheets and blankets could easily be taken from an apartment and thrown away. Even pillows could be discarded. But a king-size mattress was another matter.

As he pulled the bedspread he questioned the instincts he was blindly following. He didn't understand how he knew what he seemingly knew. But as the bedspread slipped off the mattress, Pierce felt like his intestines had collapsed inside. The center of the mattress was black with something that had congealed and dried and was the color of death. It could only be blood.

'Jesus Christ!' Wainwright said.

He had come up the steps to see what the dragging sounds were all about. He was standing behind Pierce.

'Is that what I think it is?'

Pierce didn't answer. He didn't know what to say. Yesterday he plugged in a new phone. Little more than twenty-four hours later it had led to this ghastly discovery.

'Wrong number,' he said.

'What?' Wainwright asked. 'What are you saying?'

'Never mind. Is there a phone here?'

'No, not that I know of.'

'You have a cell phone?'

'In the car.'

'Go get it.'

14

Pierce looked up when Detective Renner walked in. He tried to keep his anger in check, knowing that the cooler he played this, the faster he would get out and get home. Still, over two hours in an eight-by-eight room with nothing but a five-day-old sports page to read had left him with little patience. He had already given a statement twice. Once to the patrol cops who responded to Wainwright's call, and then to Renner and his partner when they had arrived on the scene. One of the patrol cops had then taken him to the Pacific Division station and locked him in the interview room.

Renner had a file in his hand. He sat down at the table across from Pierce and opened it. Pierce could see some sort of police form with handwriting in all the boxes. Renner stared at the form for an inordinate amount of time and then cleared his throat. He looked like a cop who'd been around more crime scenes than most. Early fifties and still solid, he reminded Pierce of Clyde Vernon in his taciturn way.

'You're thirty-four years old?'

'Yes.'

'Your address is Twenty-eight hundred Ocean Way, apartment twelve oh one.'

'Yes.'

This time exasperation crept into his voice. Renner's eyes came up momentarily to his and then went back to the form.

'But that is not the address on your driver's license.'

'No, I just moved. Ocean is where I live now. Amalfi Drive is where I used to live. Look, it's after midnight. Did you really keep me sitting in here all this time so you could ask me these obvious questions? I already gave you my statement. What else do you want?'

Renner leaned back and looked sternly at Pierce.

'No, Mr. Pierce, I kept you here because we needed to conduct a thorough investigation of what appears to be a crime scene. I am sure you don't begrudge us that.'

'I don't begrudge that. I do begrudge being kept in here like a suspect. I tried that door. It was locked. I knocked and nobody came.'

'I'm sorry about that. There was no one in the detective bureau. It's the middle of the night. But the patrol officer should not have locked the door, because you are not under arrest. If you want to make a personnel complaint against him or me, I'll go get you the necessary forms to fill out.'

'I don't want to make a complaint, okay? No forms. Can we just get on with this so I can get out of here? Is it her blood?'

'What blood?'

'On the bed.'

'How do you know it is blood?'

'I'm assuming. What else could it be?'

'You tell me.'

'What? What is that supposed to mean?'

'It was a question.'

'Wait a minute, you just said I was not a suspect.'

'I said you are not under arrest.'

'So you're saying I am not under arrest but I am a suspect in this?'

'I am not saying anything, Mr. Pierce. I am simply asking questions, trying to figure out what happened in that apartment and what is happening now.'

Pierce pulled back his growing anger. He didn't say anything. Renner referred to his form and spoke without looking up.

'Now in the statement you gave earlier, you say that your new telephone number on Ocean Way belonged at one time to the woman whose apartment you went to this evening.'

'Exactly. That's why I was there. To find out if something happened to her.'

'Do you know this woman, Lilly Quinlan?'

'No, never met her before.'

'Never?'

'Never in my life.'

'Then why did you do this? Go to her apartment, go to the trouble. Why didn't you just change your number? Why did you care?'

'I'll tell you, for the last two hours I've been asking myself the same thing. I mean, you try to check on somebody and maybe do something good and what do you get? Locked in a room for two hours by the cops.'

Renner didn't say anything. He let Pierce rant.

'What does it matter why I cared or whether or not I had a reason to do what I did? Shouldn't *you* care about what happened to her? Why are you asking *me* the questions? Why isn't Billy Wentz sitting in this room instead of me? I told you about him.'

'We'll deal with Billy Wentz, Mr. Pierce. Don't worry. But right now I am talking to you.'

Renner was then quiet a moment while he scratched his forehead with two fingers.

'Tell me again how you knew about that apartment in the first place.'

Pierce's earlier statements had been replete with shadings of the truth designed to cover any illegalities he had committed. But the story he had told about finding the apartment had been a complete lie designed to keep Robin out of the investigation. He had made good on his promise not to reveal her as a source of information. Of everything that he had said over the last four hours, it was the only thing he felt good about.

'As soon as I plugged in my phone I started getting calls from men who wanted Lilly. A few of them were former clients who wanted to see her again. I tried to engage these men in conversation, to see what I could find out about her. One man today told me about the apartment and where it was. So I went over.'

'I see, and what was this former client's name?'

'I don't know. He didn't give it.'

'You have caller ID on your new phone?'

'Yes, but he was calling from a hotel. All it said was that it was coming from the Ritz-Carlton. There are a lot of rooms there. I guess he was in one of them.'

Renner nodded.

'And Mr. Wainwright said you called him earlier today to ask about Miss Quinlan and another property she rented from him.'

'Yes. A house on Altair. She lived there and worked in the apartment off Speedway. The apartment was where she met her clients. Once I told him she was missing, he went and cleared out her property.'

'Had you ever been to that apartment before?'

'No. Never. I told you that.'

'How about the house on Altair? Have you been there?'

Pierce chose his words like he was choosing his steps through a minefield.

'I went there and nobody answered the door. That's why I called Wainwright.'

He hoped Renner wouldn't notice the change in his voice. The detective was asking far more questions than during the initial statement. Pierce knew he was on treacherous ground. The less he said, the better chance he had of getting through unscathed.

'I'm trying to get the chain of events correct,' Renner said. 'You told us you went to this place ECU in Hollywood first. You get the name Lilly Quinlan and address for a mail drop in Santa Monica. You go there and use this thing you call social engagement to—'

'Engineering. Social engineering.'

'Whatever. You *engineer* the address to the house out of the guy at the mail drop, right? You go to the house first, then you call Wainwright, and then you run into him at the apartment. Do I have all of this straight?'

'Yes.'

'Now you have said in both your statements so far tonight that you knocked and found no one home and so you left. That true?'

'Yes, true.'

'Between the time you knocked and found no one home and when you left the premises, did you go into the house on Altair, Mr. Pierce?'

There it was. The question. It required a yes or a no. It required a true answer or a lie which could easily be found out. He had to assume he had left fingerprints in the house. He remembered specifically the knobs on the rolltop desk. The mail he had looked through.

He had given them the Altair address more than two hours ago. For all he knew, they had already been there and already had his fingerprints. The whole question might be a trap set to snare him.

'The door was unlocked,' Pierce said. 'I went in to make sure she wasn't in there. Needing help or something.'

Renner was leaning slightly forward across the table. His eyes came up to Pierce's and held. Pierce could see the line of white below his green irises.

'You were inside that house?'

'That's right.'

'Why didn't you tell us that before?'

'I don't know. I didn't think it was necessary. I was trying to be brief. I didn't want to take up anyone's time, I guess.'

'Well, thanks for thinking of us. Which door was unlocked?'

Pierce hesitated but knew he had to answer.

'The back.'

He said it like a criminal in court pleading guilty. His head was down, his voice low.

'Excuse me?'

'The back door.'

'Is it your custom to go in the back door of the home of a perfect stranger?'

'No, but that was the door that was unlocked. The front wasn't. I told you, I wanted to see if something was wrong.'

'That's right. You wanted to be a rescuer. A hero.'

'It's not that. I just—'

'What did you find in the house?'

'Not a lot. Spoiled food, a giant pile of mail. I could tell she hadn't been there in a long while.'

'Did you take anything?'

'No.'

He said it without hesitation, without blinking.

'What did you touch?'

Pierce shrugged.

'I don't know. Some of the mail. There's a desk. I opened some drawers.'

'Were you expecting to find Miss Quinlan in a desk drawer?'

'No. I just . . .'

He didn't finish. He reminded himself that he was walking on a ledge. He had to keep his answers as short as possible.

Renner changed his posture, leaning back in his seat now, and changed questioning tacks as well.

'Tell me something,' he said. 'How did you know to call Wainwright?'

'Because he's the landlord.'

'Yes, but how did you know that?'

Pierce froze. He knew he could not give an answer that referred in any way to the phone book or mail he had taken from the house. He thought of the phone book hidden behind the stacks of paper in the office's copy room. For the first time he felt a cold sweat forming along his scalp.

'Um, I think . . . no, yeah, it was written down somewhere on the desk in her house. Like a note.'

'You mean like a note that was out in the open?'

'Yeah, I think so. I . . .'

Again he stopped himself before he gave Renner something else with which the detective could club him. Pierce lowered his eyes to the table. He was being walked into a trap and had to figure a way out. Making up the note was a mistake. But now he could not backtrack.

'Mr. Pierce, I just came from that house over on Altair and I looked all through that desk. I didn't see any note.'

Pierce nodded like he agreed, even though he had just said the opposite.

'You know what it was, it was my own note I was picturing. I wrote it after I talked to Vivian. She was the one who told me about Wainwright.'

'Vivian? Who is Vivian?'

'Lilly's mother. In Tampa, Florida. When she asked me to look for Lilly she gave me some names and contacts. I just remembered, that's where I got Wainwright's name.'

Renner's eyebrows peaked halfway up his forehead as he registered his surprise again.

'This is all new information, Mr. Pierce. You are now saying that Lilly Quinlan's mother asked you to look for her daughter?'

'Yes. She said the cops weren't doing anything. She asked me to do what I could.'

Pierce felt good. The answer was true, or at least truer than most of the things he was saying. He thought he might be able to survive this.

'And her mother in Tampa had the name of her daughter's landlord?'

'Well, I think she got a bunch of names and contacts from a private detective she had previously hired to look for Lilly.'

'A private detective.'

Renner looked down at the statement in front of him as if it had personally let him down for not including mention of the private investigator.

'Do you have his name?'

'Philip Glass. I have his number written down in a notebook that is in my car. Take me back to the apartment – my car's there – and I can get it for you.'

'Thank you, but I happen to know Mr. Glass and how to reach him. Have you talked to him?'

'No. I left a message and didn't hear back. But from what Vivian told me, he hadn't had much success in finding Lilly. I wasn't expecting much. I never knew if he was good or just ripping her off, you know?'

It was an opportunity for Renner to tell him what he knew about Glass but the detective didn't take it.

'What about Vivian?' he asked instead.

'I have her number in the car, too. I'll give you everything I've got as soon as I can get out of here.'

'No, I mean what about Vivian in Florida? How did you know to contact her there?'

Pierce coughed. It was like he had been kicked in the gut. Renner had trapped him again. The phone book again. He could not mention it. His respect for the taciturn detective was rising at the same time he felt his mind sagging under the weight of his own lies and obfuscation. He now saw only one way out.

15

Pierce had to give her name. His own lies had left him no other way out. He told himself that Renner would eventually get to her on his own anyway. Lilly Quinlan's site was linked to hers. The connection was inevitable. At least by giving Robin's name now, he might be able to control things. Tell them just enough to get out of there, then he would call her and warn her.

'A girl named Robin,' he said.

Renner shook his head once in an almost unnoticeable way.

'Well, well, another new name,' he said. 'Why doesn't that surprise me, Mr. Pierce? Tell me now, who is Robin?'

'On Lilly Quinlan's web page she mentions the availability of another girl she works with. It says, "Double your pleasure." The other girl's name is Robin. There is a link from Lilly's page to Robin's page. They work together. I went to the page and called Robin's number. She couldn't help me very much. She said she thought Lilly might have gone home to Tampa, where her mother lived. So later on I called Information in Tampa and got phone numbers for people named Quinlan. Eventually, that led me to contacting Vivian.'

Renner nodded.

'Must've been a lot of names. Good Irish name like Quinlan's not too rare.'

'Yes, there were.'

'And Vivian being at the end of the alphabet. You must've called information in Tampa quite a few times.'

'Yes.'

'What's the area code for Tampa, by the way?'

'It's eight one three.'

Pierce felt good about finally being able to answer a question without having to lie and worry about how it would fit with other lies he had told. But then he saw Renner reach into the pocket of his leather bomber jacket and pull out a cell phone. He opened it and punched in the number for 813 information.

Pierce realized he would be caught directly in a lie if Vivian Quinlan's phone number was unlisted.

'What are you doing? It's after three in the morning in Tampa. You'll scare her to death if you—'

Renner held up a hand to silence him and then spoke into the phone. 'Residential listing for Tampa. The name is Vivian Quinlan.'

Renner then waited and Pierce watched his face for reaction. As the seconds passed it felt as though his stomach were being twisted into a double helix formation.

'Okay, thank you,' Renner said.

He closed the phone and returned it to his pocket. He glanced at Pierce for a moment, then withdrew a pen from his shirt pocket and wrote a phone number down on the outside of the file. Pierce could read the number upside down. He recognized it as the number he had gotten out of Lilly Quinlan's phone book.

He exhaled, almost too loudly. He had caught a break.

'I think you are right,' Renner said. 'I think I will check with her at a more reasonable hour.'

'Yes, that might be better.'

'As I think I told you earlier, we don't have Internet access here in the squad, so I haven't seen this website you've mentioned. As soon as I get home I'll check it out. But you say the site is linked to this other woman, Robin.'

'Exactly. They worked together.'

'And you called Robin when you couldn't get ahold of Lilly.'

'Right again.'

'And you talked on the phone and she told you Lilly went off to Tampa to see momma.'

'She said she didn't know. She thought she might have gone there.'

'Did you know Robin previous to this telephone call?'

'No, never.'

'I'm going to take a shot in the dark here, Mr. Pierce, and say I'm betting Robin is a pay-for-play girl. A prostitute. So what you are telling me is that a woman engaged in this sort of business gets a call from a perfect stranger and ends up telling this stranger where she thinks her missing partner in crime went. It just sort of comes out, I guess, huh?'

Pierce almost groaned. Renner would not let it go. He was relentlessly picking at the frayed ends of his statement, threatening to unravel the whole thing. Pierce just wanted to get out, to leave. And he now realized that he needed to say or do anything that would accomplish that. He no longer cared about consequences down the road. He just needed to get out. If he could get to Robin before Renner, then hopefully he could make it work.

'Well . . . I guess I sort of was able to convince her that, you know, I really wanted to find her and make sure everything was all right. Maybe she was worried about her, too.'

'And this was over the telephone?'

'Yes, the telephone.'

'I see. Okay, well, we'll be checking all of this with Robin.'

'Yes, check with her. Can I—'

'And you'd be willing to take a polygraph test, wouldn't you?'

'What?'

'A polygraph. It wouldn't take long. We'd just shoot downtown and get it taken care of.'

'Tonight? Right now?'

'Probably not. I don't think I could get anybody out of bed to give it to you. But we could do it tomorrow morning, first thing.'

'Fine. Set it up for tomorrow. Can I go now?'

'We're almost there, Mr. Pierce.'

His eyes dropped to the statement again. *Surely*, Pierce thought, *we have covered everything on the form. What is left?*

'I don't understand. What else is there to talk about?'

Renner's eyes came to Pierce's without any movement of his head or face.

'Well, your name came up a couple of times on the computer. I thought maybe we'd talk about that.'

Pierce felt his face flush with heat. And anger. The long ago arrest was supposed to have been erased from his record. *Expunged* was the legal term. He had completed the probation and did the 160 hours of public service. That was a long time ago. How did Renner know?

'You're talking about the thing up in Palo Alto?' he asked. 'I was never officially charged. It was diverted. I was suspended from school for a semester. I did public service and probation. That was it.'

'Arrested on suspicion of impersonating a police officer.'

'It was almost fifteen years ago. I was in college.'

'But you see what I'm looking at here. Impersonating an officer then. Running around like some kind of detective now. Maybe you've got a hero complex, Mr. Pierce.'

'No, this is totally different. What that was back then was I was on the phone, trying to get some information. Social engineering – I was soshing out a number. I acted like I was a campus cop so I could get a phone number. That was it. I don't have a hero complex, whatever that is.'

'A phone number for who?'

'A professor. I wanted his home number and it was unlisted. It was nothing.'

'The report says you and your friends used the number to persecute the professor. To pull an elaborate prank on him. Five other students were arrested.'

'It was harmless but they had to make an example of us. It was when hacking was just getting big. We were all suspended and got probation and community service but the punishment was more severe than the crime. What we did was harmless. It was minor.'

'I'm sorry but I don't consider impersonating a police officer to be either harmless or minor.'

Pierce was about to protest further but held his tongue. He knew he would not convince Renner. He waited for the next question and after a moment the detective continued.

'Says in the records you did your community service in a DOJ lab in Sacramento. Were you thinking of becoming a cop then or something?'

'It was after I changed my major to chemistry. I just worked in the blood lab. I did typing and matching, basic work. It was far from cop work.'

'But it must have been interesting, huh? Dealing with cops, putting together the evidence for important cases. Interesting enough for you to stay on after you did your hours.'

'I stayed because they offered me a job and Stanford is expensive. And they didn't give me the important cases. Mostly the cases came to me in FedEx boxes. I did the work and shipped it all back. No big deal. In fact, it was kind of boring.'

Renner moved on without transition.

'Your arrest for impersonating an officer also came a year after your name came up on a crime report down here. It's on the computer.'

Pierce started to shake his head.

'No. I've never been arrested for anything down here. Just that time up at Stanford.'

'I didn't say you were arrested. I said your name's on a crime report. Everything's on computer now. You're a hacker, you know that. You throw in a name and sometimes it's amazing what comes out.'

'I am not a hacker. I don't know the first thing about it anymore. And whatever crime report you are talking about, it must be a different Henry Pierce. I don't remem—'

'I don't think so. Kester Avenue in Sherman Oaks? Did you have a sister named Isabelle Pierce?'

Pierce froze. He was amazed that Renner had made the connection.

'The victim of a homicide, May nineteen eighty-eight.'

All Pierce could do was nod. It was like a secret was being told, or a bandage ripped off an open wound.

'Believed to have been the victim of a killer known as the Dollmaker, later identified as Norman Church. Case closed with the death of Church, September nine, nineteen ninety.'

Case closed, Pierce thought. As if Isabelle were simply a file that could be closed, put in a drawer and forgotten. As if a murder could ever really be solved.

He came out of his thoughts and looked at Renner.

'Yes, my sister. What about it? What's it got to do with this?'

Renner hesitated and then slowly his weary face split into a small smile.

'I suppose it has everything and nothing to do with it.'

'That doesn't make sense.'

'Sure it does. She was older than you, wasn't she?'

'A few years.'

'She was a runaway. You used to go look for her, didn't you? Says so on the computer, so it must be right, right? At night. With your dad. He'd—'

'Stepfather.'

'Stepfather, then. He'd send you into the abandoned buildings to look because you were a kid and the kids in those squats didn't run from another kid. That's what the report says. Says you never found her. Nobody did, until it was too late.'

Pierce folded his arms and leaned across the table.

'Look, is there a point to this? Because I would really like to get out of here, if you don't mind.'

'The point is, you went searching for a lost girl once before, Mr. Pierce. Makes me wonder if you're not trying to make up for something with this girl Lilly. You know what I mean?'

'No,' Pierce said in a voice that sounded very small, even to himself.

Renner nodded.

'Okay, Mr. Pierce, you can go. For now. But let me say for the record that I don't believe for a moment you've told me the whole truth here. It's my job to know when people are lying and I think you're lying or leaving things out, or both. But, you know, I don't feel too bad about it, because things like that catch up with a person. I may move slow, Mr. Pierce. Sure, I kept you waiting in here too long. A fine, upstanding citizen like you. But that's because I am thorough and I'm pretty good at what I do. I'll have the whole picture pretty soon. I guarantee it. And if I find out you crossed any lines in that picture, it's going to be my pleasure, if you know what I mean.'

Renner stood up.

'I'll be in touch about that polygraph. And if I were you, I might want to think about going back to that nice new apartment on Ocean Way and staying there and staying away from this, Mr. Pierce.'

Pierce stood up and walked awkwardly around the table and Renner to the door. He thought of something before leaving.

'Where's my car?'

'Your car? I guess it's wherever you left it. Go to the front desk. They'll call a cab for you.'

'Thanks a lot.'

'Good night, Mr. Pierce. I'll be in touch.'

As he walked through the deserted squad room to the hallway that led to the front desk and the exit, Pierce checked his watch. It was twelve-thirty. He knew he had to get to Robin before Renner did but her number was in the backpack in his car.

And as he approached the front counter he realized he had no money for a cab. He had given every dollar he had on him to Robin. He hesitated for a moment.

'Can I help you, sir?'

It was the cop behind the counter. Pierce realized he was staring at him. 'No, I'm fine.'

He turned and walked out of the police station. On Venice Boulevard he started jogging west toward the beach.

16

As Pierce went down the alley to his car he saw that Lilly Quinlan's apartment was still a nest of police activity. Several cars were clogging the alley and a mobile light had been set up to spray the front of the apartment with illumination.

He noticed Renner standing out front, conversing with his partner, a detective whose name Pierce did not remember. It meant Renner had probably driven right by Pierce on his way back to the crime scene and had not noticed him or had intentionally decided not to offer him a ride. Pierce chose the second possibility. A cop on the street, even at night, would notice a man jogging in full dress. Renner had purposely gone by him.

Standing – or maybe hiding – next to his car while he cooled down from the jog over, Pierce watched for a few minutes and soon Renner and his partner went back inside the apartment. Pierce finally used the keyless remote to unlock the door of the BMW.

He slipped into the car and gently closed the door. He fumbled with the key, trying to find the ignition, and realized the ceiling light was off. He thought it must have burned out because it was set to go on when the door was open. He reached up and tapped the button anyway and nothing happened. He tapped it again and the light came on.

He sat there looking up at the light for a long moment and considering this. He knew the light had a three-setting cycle controlled by pushing the button on the ceiling next to it. The first position was the convenience setting, engaging the light when the door was open. Once the door was closed the light would fade out after about fifteen seconds or the ignition of the car, whichever came first. The second position turned on the light full-time, even if the door was closed. The third position turned the light off with no automatic convenience response.

Pierce knew he always kept the light set on the first position so the interior would be lit when he opened the door. That had not occurred when he had gotten into the car. The light had to have been in the third position of the cycle. He had then pushed the button once – to position one – and the light did not come on, because the door had already been closed. He had pushed it a second time and the light came on in position two.

Opening and closing the door, he went through the cycle until he had confirmed his theory. His conclusion was that someone had been in his car and changed the light setting.

Suddenly panicked by this realization, he reached between the two front seats to the backseat floor. His hand found his backpack. He pulled it forward and made a quick check of its contents. His notebooks were still there. Nothing seemed to be missing.

He opened the glove box and that too seemed undisturbed. Yet he was sure someone had been inside the car.

He knew the most expensive thing in the car was probably the leather backpack itself, yet it had not been taken. This led him to conclude that the car had been searched but not burglarized. That explained why it had been relocked. A car burglar probably wouldn't have bothered to disguise what had happened.

Pierce looked up at the lit doorway of the apartment and knew what had happened. Renner. The police. They had searched his car. He was sure of it.

He considered this and decided there were two possibilities as to how it had happened and how the mistake that led to his tip-off had occurred. The first was that the searcher opened the door – probably with a professional 'slim jim' window channel device – and then hit the light button twice to extinguish the light so as not to be seen in the car.

The second possibility was that the searcher entered the car and closed the door, the overhead light going out on its timer delay. The searcher would have then pushed the overhead button to turn the light back on. When the search was completed he would have then pushed the button again to turn the light off, leaving it in the cycle position Pierce had found it.

His guess was that it was the latter possibility. Not that it mattered. He thought about Renner inside the apartment. He knew then why the detective had not given him a ride. He had wanted to search the car. He beat Pierce back to the scene and searched his car.

The search would have been illegal without his permission but Pierce actually felt the opposite of angry about it. He knew there was nothing in the car that incriminated him in the Lilly Quinlan disappearance or any other crime. He thought about Renner and the disappointment he probably felt when the car turned up clean.

'Fuck you, asshole,' he said out loud.

Just as he was about to finally key the engine he saw the mattress being removed from the apartment. Two people he assumed were crime scene specialists gingerly carried the bulky piece vertically through the door and down the stairs to a van marked LAPD SCIENTIFIC INVESTIGATION DIVISION.

The mattress had been wrapped in thick plastic that was opaque like a shower curtain. The wide and dark blotch at its center clearly showed through. The sight of it being held up in the harsh light immediately depressed Pierce. It was as if they were holding up a billboard that advertised that he had been too late to do anything for Lilly Quinlan.

The mattress was too big and wide to fit in the van. The people from the Scientific Investigation Division hoisted it up onto a rack on top of the vehicle and then secured it with rope. Pierce guessed that the plastic wrapping would secure the integrity of whatever evidence would come from it.

When he looked away from the van he noticed that Renner was standing in the doorway of the apartment, looking at him. Pierce held his stare for a long moment and then started the car. Because of all the official cars clogging the alley, he had to back all the way down to Speedway before being able to turn around and head home.

At his apartment ten minutes later he lifted the phone and immediately got the broken dial tone indicating he had messages. Before checking them he hit the redial button because he knew the last call he had made had been to Robin. The call went to voice mail without a ring, indicating she had turned off the phone or was on a call.

'Listen, Robin, it's me, Henry Pierce. I know you were angry with me but please listen to what I have to say right now. After you left I found the door to Lilly's apartment open. The landlord was in there clearing the place out. We found what looked like blood on the bed and we had to call the cops. I pretty much kept you—'

The beep sounded and he was cut off. He hit redial again, wondering why she had set such a short message window on her phone service. He got a busy signal.

'Damn it!'

He started over and got the busy signal again. Frustrated, he walked out through the bedroom to the balcony. The sea breeze was strong and biting. The Ferris wheel lights were still on, though the amusement park had closed at midnight. He pushed redial again and held the phone to his ear. This time it rang and after one ring was picked up by the real Robin. Her voice was sleepy.

'Robin?'

'Yeah, Henry?'

'Yes, don't hang up. I was just leaving you a message. I—'

'I know. I was just listening to it. Did you get mine?'

'What, a message? No. I just got home. I've been with the cops all night. Listen, I know you're at me but, like I was trying to say on the message, the cops are going to be calling you. I kept you out of it. I didn't say you brought me there or anything else. But when they asked me how I knew Lilly was from Tampa and her mother was there, I told them you told me. It was the only way out. For me, I admit, but I didn't think it would be a problem for you. I mean, your pages are linked. They would have gotten around to talking to you anyway.'

'It's okay.'

He was silent for a moment, surprised by her reaction.

'I told them I convinced you I wanted to find Lilly to make sure she was okay and that you believed me and that's why you told me things about her.'

'You know, you did convince me. That's why I called and left a message. Good thing I have caller ID and had your number. I wanted to tell you I was sorry about what I said in that alley. That was very uncool.'

'Don't worry about it.'

'Thanks.'

They were both silent for a moment.

'Look,' Pierce said. 'The mattress in that place ... There was a lot of blood. I don't know what happened to Lilly but if she was trying to get out of the business to go to school ... I know you're afraid of Billy Wentz but you should be more than that, Robin. Whatever you do, be careful.'

She didn't say anything.

'You have to get away from him and that business. But, listen to me, when you do, don't tell a soul about it. Just disappear without them knowing you're leaving. I think that might have been the mistake Lilly made. She might've told him or told somebody that took it back to him.'

'And you think he did this? She made him money. Why would he—'

'I don't know. I don't know what to think. It could've been the person she was with before she was supposed to meet you. It could've been a lot of things. I saw things in that apartment, whips and masks and things. Who knows what happened to her. But it could have been Wentz sending out the message: Nobody leaves. All I'm saying is that it's a dangerous world you work in, Robin. You should get out of it and you should be damn careful about it when you do.'

She was silent and he knew he wasn't telling her anything she didn't already know. Then he thought he heard her crying but he wasn't sure.

'Are you all right?'

'Yes,' she said. 'It's just that it's not so easy, you know. Quitting. Getting out and going back to the square. I mean, what else do I do? I make a lot of money doing this. More than I'll ever make anywhere else. What should I do, work at a McDonald's? I probably couldn't even get a job there. What do I put on the application, that I've been whoring for the last two years?'

It wasn't the conversation Pierce thought he was going to get into with her. He walked inside from the balcony and back into the living room. He had two new chairs but took his usual spot on the old couch.

'Robin? I don't even know your last name.'

'LaPorte. And my name isn't Robin, either.'

'What is it?'

'It's Lucy.'

'Well, I like that better. Lucy LaPorte. Yeah, I like that. It's got a good sound.'

'I have to give everything else to these men. I decided I'd keep my name.'

She seemed to have stopped crying.

'Well . . . Lucy, if I can call you that. You keep my number. When you're ready to walk away from that life, you call me and I'll do everything I can to help you do it. Money, job, an apartment, whatever you need, just call me and you've got it. I'll do what I can.'

'It's because of your sister that you'd do it, isn't it?'

Pierce thought about this before answering.

'I don't know. Probably.'

'I don't care. Thank you, Henry.'

'Okay, Lucy. I think I'm going to crash now. It's been a long day and I'm tired. I'm sorry I woke you up.'

'Don't worry about it. And don't worry about the cops. I'll handle them.'

'Thanks. Good night.'

He ended the call and then checked his voice mail for messages. He had five. Or rather, Lilly had three and he had two. He erased Lilly's as soon as he determined they were not for him. His first message was from Charlie.

'Just wanted to see how it went in the lab today and to ask if you'd had a chance to review the patent apps yet. If you see any problems, we should know first thing Monday so we have time to fix—'

He erased the message. His plan was to review the patent applications in the morning. He'd call Charlie back after that.

He listened to the entire message from Lucy LaPorte.

'Hey, it's Robin. Look, I just wanted to say I'm sorry about what I said to you at the end. I've just been mad at the whole fucking world lately. But the truth is I can tell you care about Lilly and want to make sure she's okay. Maybe I acted the way I did because I wish there was somebody in the world that cared that way about me. So, anyway, that's it. Give me a call sometime if you want. We can just hang out. And next time I won't make you buy a smoothie. Bye.'

For some reason he saved the message and clicked off. He thought maybe he'd want to listen to it again. He bumped the phone against his chin for a few minutes while he thought about Lucy. There was an underlying sweetness about her that pushed through her harsh mouth and the reality of what she did in order to make her way in the world. He thought about what she had said to him about using the name Robin and keeping the name Lucy for herself.

I have to give everything else to these men. I decided I'd keep my name.

He remembered the police detective sitting in the living room, talking to his mother and stepfather. His father was there, too. He told them that Isabelle had been using another name on the street and with the men she went with to get money. He remembered that the detective said that she used the name Angel.

Pierce knew that Renner had him pegged. What had happened so long ago was always close below the surface. It had bubbled up over the top when the mystery of Lilly Quinlan presented itself. In his desire to find Lilly, to maybe save her, he was finding and saving his own lost sister.

Pierce thought it was an amazing and horrible world out there. What people did to one another but mostly to themselves. He thought maybe this was the reason he shut himself away in the lab for so many hours each day. He shut himself away from the world, from knowing or thinking about bad things. In the lab everything was clear and simple. Quantifiable. Scientific theory was tested and either proved or disproved. No gray areas. No shadows.

He suddenly felt an overwhelming urge to talk to Nicole, to tell her that in the last two days he had learned something he hadn't known before. Something that was hard to put into words but still palpable in his chest. He wanted to tell her that he no longer was going to chase the dime, that as far as he was concerned, it could chase him.

He clicked on the phone and dialed her number. His old number. Amalfi Drive. She picked up the phone after three rings. Her voice was alert but he could tell she had been asleep.

'Nicole, it's me.'

'Henry ... what?'

'I know it's late but I—'

'No ... we talked about this. You told me you weren't going to do this.'

'I know. But I want to talk to you.'

'Have you been drinking?'

'No. I just want to tell you something.'

'It's the middle of the night. You can't do this.'

'Just this one time. I need to tell you something. Let me come over and—'

'No, Henry, no. I was sound asleep. If you want to talk, call me tomorrow. Good-bye now.'

She hung up. He felt his face grow hot with embarrassment. He had just done something that before this night he was sure he would never have done, that he couldn't even imagine himself doing.

He groaned loudly and stood up and went to the windows. Out past the pier to the north he could make out the necklace of lights that marked the Pacific Coast Highway. The mountains rising above it were dark shapes barely discernible below the night sky. He could hear the ocean better than he could see it. The horizon was lost somewhere out there in the darkness.

He felt depressed and tired. His mind drifted from Nicole back to thoughts about Lucy and what he now knew appeared to have been Lilly's fate. As he looked out into the night he promised himself that he would not forget what he had said to Lucy. When she decided she wanted out and was ready to make the move, he would be there, if for no other reason than for himself. Who knows, he thought, it could end up being the best thing he ever did with his life.

Just as he looked at it, the lights of the Ferris wheel went out. He took that as a cue and went back inside the apartment. On the couch he picked up the phone and dialed his voice mail. He listened to the message from Lucy one more time, then went to bed. He had no sheets or blankets or pillows yet. He pulled the sleeping bag up onto the new mattress and climbed inside. He then realized he hadn't eaten anything all day. It was the first time he remembered that ever having happened during a day spent outside the lab. He fell asleep as he was mentally composing a list of things to do when he woke up in the morning.

Soon he was dreaming of a dark hallway with open doors on each side. As he moved down the hallway he would look through each doorway. Each room he looked into was like a hotel room with a bed and a bureau and a TV. And each room was occupied. Mostly by people he didn't recognize and who did not notice him looking. There were couples who were arguing, fucking and crying. Through one doorway he recognized his own parents. His mother and father, not his stepfather, though they were at an age that came after they were divorced. They were getting dressed to go out to a cocktail party.

Pierce moved on down the hallway and in another room saw Detective Renner. He was by himself and was pacing alongside the bed. The sheets and covers were off the bed and there was a large bloodstain on the mattress.

Pierce moved on and in another room Lilly Quinlan was on the bed, as still as a mannequin. The room was dark. She was naked and her eyes were on the television. Though Pierce could not see the screen from his angle of view, the blue glow it threw on Lilly's face made her look dead. He took a step into the room to check on her and she looked up at him. She smiled and he smiled and he turned to close the door, only to find there was no door to the room. When he looked back to her for an explanation, the bed was empty and only the television was on.

17

At exactly noon on Sunday the phone woke up Pierce. A man said, 'Is it too early to speak to Lilly?'

Pierce said, 'No, actually it's too late.'

He hung up and looked at his watch. He thought about the dream he'd had and set to work interpreting it, but then groaned as the first memory of the rest of the night poked into his thoughts. The call he'd made to Nicole in the middle of the night. He climbed out of the sleeping bag and off the bed to take a long, hot shower while he thought about whether to call her again to apologize. But even the stinging hot water couldn't wash away the embarrassment he felt. He decided it would be best not to call her or try to explain himself. He'd try to forget what he had done.

By the time he was dressed his stomach was loudly demanding food but there was nothing in the kitchen, he had no money and his ATM card was tapped out until Monday. He knew he could go to a restaurant or a grocery store and use a credit card but that would take too long. He had come out of the embarrassment of the Nicole call and the baptism of the shower with a desire to put the Lilly Quinlan episode behind him and let the police handle it. He had to get back to work. And he knew that any delay in getting to Amedeo might undermine his resolve.

By one o'clock he was entering the offices. He nodded to the security man behind the front dais but did not address him by name. He was one of Clyde Vernon's new hires and had always acted coolly toward Pierce, who was happy to return the favor.

Pierce kept a coffee mug full of spare change on his desk. Before beginning any work, he dropped his backpack on the desk, grabbed the mug and took the stairs down to the second floor, where snack and soda machines were located in the lunchroom. He almost emptied the mug buying two Cokes, two bags of chips and a package of Oreos. He then checked the lunchroom refrigerator to see if anybody had left anything edible behind but there was nothing to steal. As a rule the janitorial crew emptied the refrigerator out every Friday night.

One bag of chips was empty by the time he got back to the office. Pierce tore into the other and popped one of the Cokes open after sliding behind the desk. He removed the new batch of patent applications from the safe below his desk. Jacob Kaz was an excellent patent attorney but he always needed the scientists to back-read the introductions and summaries of the legal applications. Pierce always had the final sign-off on the patents.

So far, the patents Pierce and Amedeo Technologies had applied for and received over the past six years revolved around protecting proprietary designs of complex biological architectures. The key to the future of nanotechnology was creating the nanostructures that would hold and carry it. This was where Pierce had long ago chosen for Amedeo Tech to make its stand in the arena of molecular computing.

In the lab Pierce and the other members of his team designed and built a wide variety of daisy chains of molecular switches that were delicately strung together to create logic gates, the basic threshold of computing. Most of the patents Pierce and Amedeo held were in this area or the adjunct area of moleculary RAM. A small number of other patents centered on the development of bridging molecules, the latticework of sturdy carbon tubes that would one day connect the hundreds of thousands of nanoswitches that together would make a computer as small as a dime and as powerful as a digital Mack truck.

Before beginning his review of the new group of patents, Pierce leaned back in his chair and looked up at the wall behind his computer monitor. Hanging on the wall was a caricature drawing of Pierce holding up a microscope, his ponytail flying and his eyes wide as if he had just made a fantastic discovery. The caption above it said 'Henry Hears a Who!'

Nicole had given it to him. She'd had an artist on the pier draw it after Pierce had told her the story of his favorite childhood memory, his father reading and telling stories to him and his sister. Before his parents split. Before his father moved to Portland and started a whole new family. Before things started to go wrong for Isabelle.

His favorite book at the time had been Dr. Seuss's *Horton Hears a Who!* It was the story of an elephant who discovers a whole world existing on a speck of dust. A nanoworld long before there was any thought of nanoworlds. Pierce still knew many of the lines from the book by heart. And he thought of them often in the course of his work.

In the story Horton is outcast by a jungle society that doesn't believe his discovery. He is most persecuted by the monkeys – known as the Wickersham gang – but ultimately saves the tiny world on the speck of dust from the monkeys and proves its existence to the rest of society.

Pierce opened the Oreos and ate two of the cookies whole, hoping the sugar charge would help him focus.

He began reviewing the applications with excitement and anticipation. This batch would move Amedeo into a new arena and the science to a new level. Pierce knew it would flat-out rock the world of nanotechnology. And he smiled as he thought about the reaction his competitors would have when their intelligence officers copied the non-proprietary pages of the applications for them or when they read about the Proteus formula in the science journals.

The application package was for protecting a formula for cellular energy conversion. In the layman's terms used in the summary of the first application in the package, Amedeo was seeking patent protection for a 'power supply system' that would energize the biological robots that would one day patrol the bloodstreams of human beings and destroy pathogens threatening their hosts.

They called the formula Proteus in a nod to the movie *Fantastic Voyage*. In the 1966 film a medical team is placed in a submarine called the *Proteus*, then miniaturized with a shrink ray and injected into a man's body to search for and destroy an inoperable blood clot in the brain.

The film was science fiction and it was likely that shrink rays would always remain the purview of the imagination. But the idea of attacking pathogens in the body with biological or cellular robots, not too distant in imagination from the *Proteus*, was on the far horizon of scientific fact.

Since the inception of nanotechnology the potential medical applications had always been the sexiest side of the science. More intriguing than a quantum leap in computing power was the potential for curing cancer, AIDS, any and all diseases. The possibility of patrolling devices in the body that could encounter, identify and eliminate pathogens through chemical reaction was the Holy Grail of the science.

The bottleneck, however – the thing that kept this side of the science theoretical while rafts of researchers pursued molecular RAM and integrated circuits – was the question of a power supply. How to move these molecular submarines through the blood with a power source that was natural and compatible with the body's immune system.

Pierce, along with Larraby, his immunology researcher, had discovered a rudimentary yet highly reliable formula. Using the host's own cells – in this case, Pierce's were harvested and then replicated for research in an incubator – the two researchers developed a combination of proteins that would bind with the cell and draw an electrical stimulus from it. That meant power to drive the nano device could come from within and therefore be compatible with the body's immune system.

The Proteus formula was simple and that was its beauty and value. Pierce imagined all forward nanoresearch in the field being based upon this one discovery. Experimentation, and other discoveries and inventions leading to practical use, formerly seen as two decades or longer out on the horizon might now be half again as close to reality.

The discovery, made just three months earlier while Pierce was in the midst of his difficulties with Nicole, was the single most exciting moment of his life.

'Our buildings, to you, would seem terribly small,' Pierce whispered as he finished his review of the patents. 'But to us, who aren't big, they are wonderfully tall.'

The words of Dr. Seuss.

Pierce was pleased with the package. As usual, Kaz had done an excellent job of blending science-speak and layman's language in the top sheets of each patent. The meat of each application, however, contained the science and the diagrammed segments of the formula. These pages were written by Pierce and Larraby and had been reviewed by both researchers repeatedly.

The application package was good to go, in Pierce's opinion. He was excited. He knew floating such a patent application package into the nanoworld would bring a flood of publicity and a subsequent rise in investor interest. The plan was to show the discovery to Maurice Goddard first and lock down his investment, then submit the applications. If all went well, Goddard would realize he had a short lead and a short window of opportunity and would make a preemptive strike, signing up as the company's main funding source.

Pierce and Charlie Condon had carefully choreographed it. Goddard would be shown the discovery. He would be allowed to check it out for himself in the tunneling electron microscope. He would then have twenty-four hours to make his decision. Pierce wanted a minimum of $18 million over three years. Enough to charge forward faster and further than any competitor. And he was offering 10 percent of the company in exchange.

Pierce wrote a congratulatory note to Jacob Kaz on a yellow Post-it and attached it to the cover sheet of the Proteus application package. He then locked it back in the safe. He'd have it sent by secure transport to Kaz's office in Century City in the morning. No faxes, no e-mails. Pierce might even drive it over himself.

He leaned back, threw another Oreo into his mouth and checked his watch. It was two o'clock. An hour had gone by since he had been in the office but it had seemed like only ten minutes. It felt good to have the feeling again, the vibe. He decided to capitalize on it and move into the lab to do some real work. He grabbed the rest of the cookies and got up.

'Lights.'

Pierce was in the hallway pulling the door closed on the darkened office when the phone rang. It was the distinctive double ring of his private line. Pierce pushed the door back open.

'Lights.'

Few people had his direct office number but one of them was Nicole. Pierce quickly moved around the desk and looked down at the caller ID screen on the phone. It said *private caller* and he knew it wasn't Nicole, because her cell phone and the line from the house on Amalfi were uncloaked. Pierce hesitated but then remembered that Cody Zeller had the number. He picked up the phone.

'Mr. Pierce?'

It wasn't Cody Zeller.

'Yes?'

'It's Philip Glass. You called me yesterday?'

The private investigator. Pierce had forgotten.

'Oh. Yes, yes. Thanks for calling back.'

'I didn't get the message until today. What can I do for you?'

'I want to talk to you about Lilly Quinlan. She's missing. Her mother hired you a few weeks ago. From Florida.'

'Yes, but I am no longer employed on that one.'

Pierce remained standing behind his desk. He put his hand on top of the computer monitor as he spoke.

'I understand that. But I was wondering if I could talk to you about it. I have Vivian Quinlan's permission. You can check with her if you want. You still have her number?'

It took a long while for Glass to respond, so long that Pierce thought he may have quietly hung up.

'Mr. Glass?'

'Yes, I'm here. I'm just thinking. Can you tell me what your interest is in all of this?'

'Well, I want to find her.'

This was met with more silence and Pierce started to understand that he was dealing from a position of weakness. Something was going on with Glass, and Pierce was at a disadvantage for not knowing it. He decided to press his case. He wanted the meeting.

'I'm a friend of the family,' he lied. 'Vivian asked me to see what I could find out.'

'Have you talked to the LAPD?'

Pierce hesitated. Instinctively he knew that Glass's cooperation might be riding on his answer. He thought about the events of the night before and wondered if they could already be known by Glass. Renner had said he knew Glass and he most likely planned to call him. It was Sunday afternoon. Maybe the police detective was waiting until Monday, since Glass seemed to be on the periphery of the case.

'No,' he lied again. 'My understanding from Vivian was that the LAPD wasn't interested in this.'

'Who are you, Mr. Pierce?'

'What? I don't under—'

'Who do you work for?'

'No one. Myself, actually.'

'You're a PI?'

'What's that?'

'Come on.'

'I mean it. I don't under – oh, private investigator. No, I'm not a PI. Like I said, I'm a friend.'

'What do you do for a living?'

'I'm a researcher. I'm a chemist. I don't see what this has to do with—'

'I can see you today. But not at my office. I'm not going in today.'

'Okay, then where? When?'

'One hour from now. Do you know a place in Santa Monica called Cathode Ray's?'

'On Eighteenth, right? I'll be there. How will we know each other?'

'Do you have a hat or something distinctive to wear?'

Pierce leaned down and opened an unlocked desk drawer. He pulled out a baseball cap with blue stitched letters over the brim.

'I'll be wearing a gray baseball cap. It says MOLES in blue stitching above the brim.'

'Moles? As in the small burrowing animal?'

Pierce almost laughed.

'As in molecules. The Fighting Moles was the name of our softball team. Back when we had one. My company sponsored it. It was a long time ago.'

'I'll see you at Cathode Ray's. Please come alone. If I feel you are not alone or it looks like a setup, you won't see me.'

'A setup? What are you—'

Glass hung up and Pierce was listening to dead space.

He put down the phone and put on the hat. He considered the strange questions the private detective had asked and thought about what he had said at the end of the conversation and how he had said it. Pierce realized it was almost as if he had been scared of something.

18

Cathode Ray's was a hangout for the tech generation – usually everybody in the place had a laptop or a PDA on the table next to their double latte. The place was open twenty-four hours a day and provided power and high-speed phone jacks at every table. Connections to local Internet service providers only. It was close to Santa Monica College and the film production and fledgling software districts of the Westside, and it had no corporate affiliations. These combined to make it a popular place with the plugged-in set.

Pierce had been there on many prior occasions, yet he thought it an odd choice by Glass for the meeting. Glass sounded like an older man over the phone, his voice gravelly and tired. If that was the case, then he would stand out in a place like Cathode Ray's. Considering the paranoia that had come over the phone line from him, it seemed strange for him to have picked the coffee shop for the meeting.

At three o'clock Pierce entered Cathode Ray's and took a quick scan around the place for an older man. No one stood out. No one looked at him. He got in line for coffee.

Before leaving the office, he had dumped what change remained in his desk mug into his pocket. He counted it out while waiting and concluded that he had just enough for a basic coffee, medium size, with a little left over for the tip jar.

After hitting the cup with heavy doses of cream and sugar, he moved out to the patio area and selected an empty table in the corner. He sipped his coffee slowly but it was still twenty minutes before he was approached by a short man in black jeans and a black T-shirt. He had a clean-shaven face and dark, hard eyes that were deeply set. He was much younger than Pierce had guessed, maybe late thirties at the most. He had no coffee, he had come straight to the table.

'Mr. Pierce?'

Pierce offered his hand.

'Mr. Glass?'

Glass pulled out the other chair and sat down. He leaned across the table.

'If you don't mind, I'd like to see your ID,' he said.

Pierce put his cup down and started digging in his pocket for his wallet.
'Probably a good idea,' he said. 'Mind if I look at yours?'

After both men had convinced themselves they were sitting with the right party, Pierce leaned back and studied Glass. He seemed to Pierce to be a large man stuck in a small man's body. He exuded intensity. It was as if his skin were stretched too tight over his whole body.

'Do you want to get a coffee before we start to talk?'

'No, I don't use caffeine.'

That seemed to figure.

'Then I guess we should get to it.. What's with all the spook stuff?'

'Excuse me?'

'You know, the "make sure you're alone" and "what do you do for a living" stuff. It all seems to be a little strange.'

Before speaking, Glass nodded as if he agreed.

'What do you know about Lilly Quinlan?'

'I know what she was doing for a living, if that's what you mean.'

'And what was that?'

'She was an escort. She advertised through the Internet. I'm pretty sure she worked for a guy named Billy Wentz. He's sort of a digital pimp. He runs the website where she kept a page. I think he set her up in other things – porno sites, stuff like that. I think she was involved in the S and M scene as well.'

The mention of Wentz seemed to bring a new intensity to Glass's face. He folded his arms on the table and leaned forward.

'Have you spoken to Mr. Wentz yourself?'

Pierce shook his head.

'No, but I tried to. I went to Entrepreneurial Concepts yesterday – that's his umbrella company. I asked to see him but he wasn't there. Why do I feel like I am telling you things you already know? Look, I want to ask questions here, not answer them.'

'There is little I can tell you. I specialize in missing-persons investigations. I was recommended to Vivian Quinlan by someone I know in the LAPD's Missing Persons Unit. It went from there. She paid me for a week's work. I didn't find Lilly or much else about her disappearance.'

Pierce considered this for a long moment. He was an amateur and he had found out quite a bit in less than forty-eight hours. He doubted that Glass was as inept as he was presenting himself to be.

'You did know about the website, right? L.A. Darlings?'

'Yes. I was told she was working as an escort and it was pretty easy to find her. L.A. Darlings is one of the more popular sites, you could say.'

'Did you find her house? Did you talk to her landlord?'

'No and no.'

'What about Lucy LaPorte?'

'Who?'

'She uses the name Robin on the website. Her page is linked to Lilly's.'

'Oh, yes, Robin. Yes, I spoke to her on the phone. It was very brief. She was not cooperative.'

Pierce was suspicious of whether Glass had really called. It seemed to him Lucy would have mentioned that an investigator had already inquired about Lilly. He planned to check with her about the supposed call.

'How long ago was that? The call to Robin.'

Glass shrugged.

'Three weeks. It was at the beginning of my week of work. She was one of the first I called.'

'Did you go see her?'

'No, other things came up. And at the end of the week Mrs. Quinlan was not willing to pay me for further work on the case. That was it for me.'

'What other things came up?'

Glass didn't respond.

'You talked to Wentz, didn't you?'

Glass looked down at his folded arms but didn't reply.

'What did he tell you?'

Glass cleared his throat.

'Listen to me very carefully, Mr. Pierce. You want to stay clear of Billy Wentz.'

'Why?'

'Because he is a dangerous man. Because you are moving in an area that you know nothing about. You could get very seriously hurt if you are not careful.'

'Is that what happened to you. Did you get hurt?'

'We are not talking about me. We are talking about you.'

A man with an iced latte sat down at the table nearest them. Glass looked over and studied him with paranoid eyes. The man took a PalmPilot out of his pocket and opened it. He slid out the stylus and went to work on the device. He paid no mind to Glass or Pierce.

'I want to know what happened when you went to see Wentz,' Pierce said.

Glass unfolded his arms and rubbed his hands together.

'Do you know ... '

He stopped and didn't go on. Pierce had to prompt him.

'Know what?'

'Do you know that so far the only place in which the Internet is significantly profitable is in the adult entertainment sectors?'

'I've heard that. What does—'

'Ten *billion* dollars a year is made off the electronic sex trade in this country. A lot of it is over the net. It's big business, with ties to top-flight corporate America. It's everywhere, available on every computer, on every

TV. Turn on the TV and order hard-core porn courtesy of AT and T. Go online and order a woman like Lilly Quinlan to your door.'

Glass's voice took on a fervor that reminded Pierce of a priest in a pulpit.

'Do you know that Wentz sells franchises across the country? I inquired. Fifty thousand dollars a city. There is now a New York Darlings and a Vegas Darlings. Miami, Seattle, Denver and on and on. Linked to these sites he has porn sites for every imaginable sexual persuasion and fetish. He—'

'I know all of that,' Pierce broke in. 'But what I am interested in is Lilly Quinlan. What does all of that have to do with what happened to her?'

'I don't know,' Glass said. 'But what I am trying to tell you is that there is too much money at stake here. Stay away from Billy Wentz.'

Pierce leaned back and looked at Glass.

'He got to you, didn't he? What did he do, threaten you?'

Glass shook his head. He wasn't going to go there.

'Forget about me. I came here today to try to help you. To warn you about how close you are to the fire. Stay away from Wentz. I can't stress that enough. *Stay away.*'

Pierce could see in his eyes the sincerity of the warning. And the fear. Pierce had no doubt that Wentz had in some way gotten to Glass and scared him off the Quinlan case.

'Okay,' he said. 'I'll keep clear.'

19

Pierce toyed with the idea of going back to the lab after his coffee with Philip Glass but ultimately admitted to himself that the conversation with the private detective had stunted the motivation he had felt only an hour before. Instead, he went to the Lucky Market on Ocean Park Boulevard and filled a shopping cart with food and other basics he would need in the new apartment. He paid with a credit card and loaded the numerous bags into the trunk of his BMW. It wasn't until he was in his parking space in the garage at the Sands that he realized that he would have to make at least three trips up and down the elevator to get all of his purchases into the apartment. He had seen other tenants with small pushcarts, ferrying laundry or groceries up or down the elevator. Now he realized they had the right idea.

On the first trip he took the new plastic laundry basket he had bought and filled it with six bags of groceries, including all of the perishables he wanted to get up and into the apartment refrigerator first.

As he came into the elevator alcove two men were standing by the door that led to the individual storage rooms that came with each apartment. Pierce was reminded that he needed to get a padlock for his storage room and to get the boxes of old records and keepsakes Nicole was still holding for him in the garage at the house on Amalfi. His surfboard, too.

At the elevator one of the men pushed the call button. Pierce exchanged nods with them and guessed that they might be a gay couple. One man was in his forties with a small build and a spreading waist. He wore pointed-toe boots that gave him two extra inches in the heel. The other man was much younger, taller and harder, yet he seemed to defer in body language to his older partner.

When the elevator door opened they allowed Pierce to step on first and then the smaller man asked him what floor he wanted. After the door closed he noticed that the man did not push another button after pressing twelve for him.

'You guys live on twelve?' he asked. 'I just moved in a few days ago.'

'Visitors,' said the smaller one.

Pierce nodded. He turned his attention to the flashing numbers above the door. Maybe it was being so soon after the warning from Glass or the way the smaller man kept stealing glances at the reflection of Pierce in the chrome trim on the door, but as the elevator rose and the numbers got higher, so did his anxiety. He remembered how they had been standing near the storage room door and approached the elevator only when he did. As if they had been waiting there for some reason.

Or for some person.

The elevator finally reached twelve and the door slid open. The men stepped to the side to allow Pierce to step out first. With both hands holding the laundry basket, Pierce nodded forward.

'You guys go ahead,' he said. 'Can you punch the first floor for me? I forgot to get the mail.'

'There is no mail on Sundays,' the smaller man said.

'No, I mean yesterday's. I forgot to get it.'

Nobody moved. The three of them stood there looking at one another until the door started to close and the big man reached out and hit the bumper with a hard forearm. The door shuddered and slowly reopened, as if recovering from a sucker punch. And finally the smaller one spoke.

'Fuck the mail, Henry. You're getting off here. Am I right, Six-Eight?'

Without answering, the man obviously named because of his longitudinal dimensions moved in and grabbed Pierce by the upper arms. He pivoted and hurled Pierce through the open door into the twelfth-floor hallway. His momentum took him across the hall and crashing into a closed door marked ELECTRICAL. Pierce felt his breath blast out of his lungs and the laundry basket slipped from his grasp, landing with a loud thud on the floor.

'Easy now, easy. Keys, Six-Eight.'

Pierce's breath had still not returned. The one named Six-Eight moved toward him and with one hand pressed him back against the door. He slapped Pierce's pants pockets with the other. When he felt the keys he dove his big hand into the pocket and pulled out the key ring. He handed it to the other man.

'Okay.'

With the smaller man leading the way – and knowing the way – Pierce was pushed down the hall toward his apartment. When he got his breath back he started to say something but the bigger man's hand came around from behind and covered his face and his words. The small one held up a finger without looking back.

'Not yet, Bright Boy. Let's get inside so we don't disturb the neighbors more than we have to. You just moved in, after all. You don't want to make a bad impression.'

The smaller one walked with his head down, apparently studying the keys on the ring.

'A Beemer,' he said.

Pierce knew the keyless remote to his car carried the BMW insignia on it.

'I like Beemers. It's the full package; you got power and luxury and a real solid feel. You can't beat that in a car – or a woman.'

He looked back at Pierce and smiled with a raised eyebrow. They got to the door and the smaller man opened it with the second key he tried. Six-Eight pushed Pierce into the apartment and shoved him down onto the couch. He then stepped away and the other man took a position in front of Pierce. He noticed the phone on the arm of the couch and picked it up. Pierce watched him play with the buttons and go through the caller ID directory.

'Been busy here, Henry,' he said as he scrolled the list. 'Philip Glass . . . '

He looked back at Six-Eight, who had stationed himself near the apartment's front hallway, his massive arms folded across his chest. The small man crinkled his eyes in a question.

'Isn't that the guy we had a discussion with a few weeks back?'

Six-Eight nodded. Pierce realized that Glass must have called the apartment before reaching him at Amedeo.

The small man went back to the phone readout and soon his eyes lit on another familiar listing.

'Oh, so now Robin's calling *you*. That's wonderful.'

But Pierce could tell by the man's voice that it wasn't wonderful, that it was going to be anything but wonderful for Lucy LaPorte.

'It's nothing,' Pierce said. 'She just left a message. I can play it for you if you want. I kept it.'

'You falling in love with her, are you?'

'No.'

The smaller guy turned and gave a false smile to Six-Eight. Then suddenly he moved his arm in a quick overhand motion and hit Pierce with the phone on the bridge of his nose, delivering a blow with the full power of the sweeping arc.

Pierce saw a flash of red and black blast across his vision and a searing pain screamed through his head. He couldn't tell if his eyes were closed or he'd gone blind. He instinctively rocked backwards on the couch and turned away from the blow in case another was coming. He vaguely heard the man in front of him yelling but what he was saying wasn't registering. Then strong, large hands clamped around his upper arms again and he was pulled upright and completely off the couch.

He could feel himself being hoisted over Six-Eight's shoulders and then carried. He felt his mouth filling with blood and he struggled to open his eyes but still couldn't do it. He heard the rolling sound of the balcony's sliding door, then the cool air from the ocean touching his skin.

'Wha . . . ,' he managed to say.

Suddenly the hard shoulder that had been in his gut was gone and he started a headfirst free fall. His muscles tightened and his mouth opened to emit the final furious sound of his life. Then, at last, he felt the huge hands grab his ankles and hold. His head and shoulders slammed hard against the rough concrete of the textured exterior of the building.

But at least he was no longer falling.

A few seconds went by. Pierce brought his hands to his face and touched his nose and eyes. His nose was split vertically and horizontally and was bleeding profusely. He managed to wipe his eyes and open them partially. Twelve stories below he could see the green lawn of the beachside park. There were people on blankets down there, most of them homeless. He saw his blood falling in thick drops into the trees directly below. He heard a voice from above him.

'Hello down there. Can you hear me?'

Pierce said nothing and then the hands that held his ankles shook violently, bouncing him off the outside wall again.

'Do I have your attention?'

Pierce spit a mouthful of blood onto the exterior wall and said, 'Yes, I hear you.'

'Good. I suppose by now you know who I am.'

'I think so.'

'Good. No need to mention names then. I just wanted to make sure we're at a point of knowledge and understanding here.'

'What do you want?'

It was hard to talk upside down. Blood was pooling in the back of his throat and on the roof of his mouth.

'What do I want? Well, I first wanted to get a look at you. A guy spends his time sniffing your asshole for two days, you want to see what he looks like, right? There's that. And then I wanted to give you a message. Six-Eight.'

Pierce was suddenly hoisted up. Still upside down, his face had come up to the open bars of the balcony railing. Through the bars he saw that the talker had stooped down so that they were face-to-face, the bars between them.

'What I wanted to say was that not only did you get the wrong number, you got the wrong world, partner. And you got about thirty seconds to decide whether you want to go back to where you came from or you want to go on to the next world. You understand what I am saying to you?'

Pierce nodded and started to cough.

'I . . . unnerstan . . . I'm . . . I'm done.'

'You're damn right you're done. I ought to have my man drop your stupid ass right here and now. But I don't need the heat, so I'm not going to do that. But I have to tell you, Bright Boy, if I catch you sneaking and sniffing around again, you're gonna get dropped. Okay?'

Pierce nodded. The man Pierce was pretty sure was Billy Wentz then reached a hand between the bars and roughly patted Pierce's cheek.

'Be good now.'

He stood up and gave a signal to Six-Eight. Pierce was pulled over the balcony and dropped on the balcony's floor. He broke the fall with his hands and then pushed his way into the corner. He looked up at his two attackers.

'You got a nice view here,' said the smaller man. 'What do you pay?'

Pierce looked out at the ocean. He spit a wad of thick blood onto the floor.

'Three thousand.'

'Jesus Christ! I can get three fucking places for that.'

Now just straddling the edge of consciousness, Pierce wondered how Wentz had intended the word *fucking* to be interpreted. Was he talking about places for fucking or was he just routinely cursing? He tried to shake off the clouds that were encroaching. It occurred to him then that the threat to himself aside, it was important to try to protect Lucy LaPorte.

He spit more blood onto the balcony floor.

'What about Lucy? What are you going to do?'

'Lucy? Who the fuck is Lucy?'

'I mean, Robin.'

'Oh, our little Robin. You know, that's a good question, Henry. 'Cause Robin's a good earner. I have to be prudent. I have to calm myself when it comes to her. Rest assured that whatever we do, we won't leave marks and she'll be back, good as new, in two, three weeks at the most.'

Pierce scrabbled his legs on the concrete in an effort to get up but he was too disoriented and weak.

'Leave her alone,' he said as forcefully as he could. 'I used her and she didn't even know it.'

Wentz's dark eyes seemed to take on a new light. Pierce saw anger work its way into them. He saw Wentz put one hand on the top of the balcony railing as if to brace himself.

'Leave her alone, he says.'

He shook his head again as if to ward off some encroaching power.

'Please,' Pierce said. 'She didn't do anything. It was me. Just leave her alone.'

The small man looked back at Six-Eight and smiled, then shook his head.

'Do you believe this? Telling me like that?'

He turned back toward Pierce, took one step toward him and then swiftly brought his other foot up into a vicious kick. Pierce was expecting it and was able to use his forearm to deflect most of the power but the pointed toe of the boot struck him on the right side of the rib cage. It felt like it took at least two ribs with it.

Pierce slid down into the corner and tried to cover up, expecting more and trying to control the burning pain spreading across his chest. Instead,

Wentz leaned down over him. He yelled at Pierce, spittle raining down on him with the words.

'Don't you fucking dare try to tell me how to run my business. Don't you fucking dare!'

He straightened up and dusted off his hands.

'And one other thing. You tell anybody about our little discussion here today and there will be consequences. Dire consequences. For you. For Robin. For the people you love. Do you understand what I'm telling you?'

Pierce weakly nodded.

'Let me hear you say it.'

'I understand the consequences.'

'Good. Then let's go, Six-Eight.'

And Pierce was left alone, gulping for breath and clarity, trying to stay in the light when he sensed darkness closing in all around.

20

Pierce grabbed a T-shirt out of a box in the bedroom and held it to his face, trying to stop the bleeding. He straightened up and went into the bathroom and saw himself in the mirror. His face was already ballooning and turning color. The swelling of his nose was crowding his vision and widening the wounds on his nose and around his left eye. Most of the bleeding seemed to be internal, a steady stream of thick blood going down the back of his throat. He knew he had to get to a hospital but he had to warn Lucy LaPorte first.

He found the phone on the living room floor. He tried to go to the caller ID directory but the screen remained blank. He tried the on button but couldn't get a dial tone. The phone was broken – either by the impact with his face or when Wentz had thrown it to the floor.

Holding the shirt to his face, involuntary tears streaming out of his eyes, Pierce looked about the apartment for the box holding the earthquake kit he had ordered delivered with the furniture. Monica had showed him a listing of the kit's inventory before ordering it. He knew it contained a first aid kit, flashlights and batteries, two gallons of water, numerous freeze-dried food items and other supplies. It also contained a basic phone that did not use electric current. It simply needed to be jacked into the wall for it to work.

He found the box in the bedroom closet and dripped blood all over it as he desperately used both hands to rip it open. He lost his balance and almost fell over. He realized he was fading. The loss of blood, the depletion of adrenaline. He finally found the phone and took it to the wall jack next to the bed. He got a dial tone. Now all he needed was Robin's number.

He had it written in a notebook but that was in his backpack down in his car. He didn't think he could make it down there without passing out on the way. He wasn't even sure where his keys were. The last he remembered, they had been in the hands of Billy Wentz.

Leaning against the wall, he first called Information for Venice and tried the name Lucy LaPorte, asking the operator to check under various spellings. But there was no number, unlisted or otherwise.

He then slid down the wall to the floor next to the bed. He began to panic. He had to get to her but couldn't – he thought of something and called the lab. But there was no answer. Sundays were sacrosanct with the lab rats. They worked long hours and usually six days a week. But rarely on Sunday. He tried Charlie Condon's office and home but got machines at both numbers.

He thought about Cody Zeller but knew he never answered his phone. The only way to reach him was by page and then he would be at the mercy of waiting for a callback.

He knew what he had to do. He punched in the number and waited. After four rings Nicole answered.

'It's me. I need your help. Can you go to—'

'Who is this?'

'Me, Henry.'

'It doesn't sound like you. What are you—'

'Nicki!' he shouted. 'Listen to me. This is an emergency and I need your help. We can talk about everything after. I can explain after.'

'Okay,' she said in a tone that indicated she wasn't convinced. 'What is the emergency?'

'You still have your computer hooked up?'

'Yes, I don't even have a sign on the house yet. I'm not—'

'Okay, good. Go to your computer. Hurry, go!'

He knew she had a DSL line – he had always been paranoid about it. But now it would get them to the site faster.

When she got to the computer she switched to a headset she kept at the desk.

'Okay, I need you to go to a website. It's L.A. dash darlings dot com.'

'Are you kidding me? Is this some—'

'Just do it! Or somebody might die!'

'Okay, okay. L.A. dash darlings ... '

He waited.

'Okay, I'm there.'

He tried to visualize the website on her screen.

'Okay, double click the Escorts folder and go to Blondes.'

He waited.

'You got it?'

'I'm going as fast as – okay, now what?'

'Scroll through the thumbnails. Click on the one named Robin.'

Again he waited. He realized his breathing was loud, a low whistle coming out of his throat.

'Okay, I've got Robin. Those tits have gotta be fake.'

'Just give me the number.'

She read off the number and Pierce recognized it. It was the right Robin.

'I'll call you back.'

He pressed the plunger on the phone, held it for three seconds, and then let go, getting a new dial tone. He called the number for Robin. He was getting light-headed. What was left of his vision was starting to blur around the edges. After five rings his call went to voice mail.

'Goddamnit!'

He didn't know what to do. He couldn't send the police to her. He didn't even know where her real home was. The message signal beeped after her greeting. As he spoke, his tongue started to feel too big for his mouth.

'Lucy, it's me. It's Henry. Wentz came here. He messed me up and I think he's going to see you next. If you get this message, get out of there. Right now! Just get the hell out of there and call me when you get somewhere safe.'

He added his number to the message and hung up.

He held the bloody shirt back up to his face and leaned against the wall. The flow of adrenaline and endorphins that had flooded his system during the attack from Wentz was ebbing and the deep throb of pain was settling in like winter. It was penetrating his whole body. It seemed as though every muscle and joint ached. His face felt like a neon sign pulsing with rhythmic bursts of searing fire. He didn't feel like moving anymore. He just wanted to pass out and wake up when he was healed and everything was better.

Without moving anything but his arm, he raised the phone off its cradle again and brought it up so he could see the keypad. He thumbed the redial button and waited. The call rang through to Lucy's voice mail again. He wanted to curse out loud but now it would hurt his face to move his mouth. He blindly felt around for the phone cradle and hung up the phone.

It rang while his hand was still on it and he raised it back to his ear.

' 'Lo?'

'It's Nicki. Can you talk? Is everything all right?'

'No.'

'Should I call back?'

'No, I me ehry'ing's nah all ri.'

'What's wrong? Why are you talking funny? Why did you need the number of *that* woman?'

Despite his pain and fear and everything else, he found himself angry at the way she said 'that woman.'

'Lohn story and I cah ... I ... '

He felt himself fading out but as he started to roll off the wall to the floor, the angle of his body sent jabbing pain through his chest and he groaned from somewhere deep inside.

'Henry! Are you hurt! Henry! Can you hear me?'

Pierce slid his hips down along the rug until he could lie flat on his back. Somehow an instinctive warning came through. He knew he might drown in his own blood if he stayed in his current position. Thoughts of rock stars drowning in their own vomit passed through his mind. He had dropped the phone and it was on the carpet next to his head. In his right ear he could hear the tinny sound of a far-off voice calling his name. He thought he recognized the voice and it made him smile. He thought of Jimi Hendrix drowning in his own puke and decided he'd rather drown in his own blood. He tried to sing, his voice a wet whisper.

' 'Suze me why I iss the sy ... '

He couldn't make *k* sounds for some reason. That was strange. But soon it didn't matter. The small voice in his right ear drifted off and soon there was a loud blaring sound in the darkness. And soon even that was gone and there was only darkness all around him. And he liked the darkness.

21

A woman Pierce had never seen before was running her fingers through his hair. She seemed strangely detached and perfunctory for so intimate an action. The woman then leaned in closer to him and he thought she was going to kiss him. But she put her hand on his forehead. She then lifted some sort of tool, a light, and shined it in one eye and then the other. He then heard a man's voice.

'Ribs,' he said. 'Three and four. We might have a puncture.'

'We put a mask over this nose and he'll probably hit the roof,' the woman said.

'I'll give him something.'

Now Pierce saw the man. He moved into view when he raised a hypodermic needle in a gloved hand and squeezed a little spray into the air. Next he felt the jab in his arm and pretty soon warmth and understanding flowed through his body, tickling across his chest. He smiled and almost laughed. Warmth and understanding in a needle. The wonders of chemistry. He had made the right choice.

'Extra straps,' the woman said. 'We're going vertical.'

Whatever that meant. Pierce's eyes were closing. The last thing he saw before escaping into the warmth was a policeman standing over him.

'He going to make it?' he asked.

Pierce didn't hear the answer.

The next time he regained consciousness he was standing. But not really. He opened his eyes and they were all there, crowded close to him. The woman with the light and the man with the needle. And the cop. And Nicole was there, too. She was looking up at him with tears in her dark green eyes. Even so, she was beautiful to him, her skin brown and smooth, her hair pulled back in a ponytail, the blonde highlights shining.

The elevator started to drop and Pierce suddenly thought he might throw up. He tried to get out a warning but couldn't move his jaw. It was like he was tied tightly to the wall. He started to struggle but couldn't move. He couldn't even move his head.

His eyes met Nicole's. She reached up and put her hand on his cheek.

'Hold on, Hewlett,' she said. 'You're going to be all right.'

He noticed how much taller than her he was. He didn't used to be. There was a pinging sound that seemed to echo in his head. Then the elevator door slid open. The man and woman came to either side of him and walked him out. Only he wasn't walking, and he finally realized what 'going vertical' meant.

Once they were out he was lowered and rolled through the lobby. A lot of faces watched as he passed by. The doorman whose name he didn't know looked down at him somberly as he was rolled through the door. He was lifted into an ambulance. He wasn't feeling any pain but he had difficulty breathing. It was more labor-intensive than usual.

After a while he noticed that Nicole was sitting next to him. It looked like she was outright crying now.

He found that in the horizontal position he could move a little bit. He tried to speak but his voice sounded like a muffled echo. The woman, the paramedic, then leaned into his field of vision, looking down at him.

'Don't speak,' she said. 'You've got a mask on.'

No kidding, he thought. *Everybody's got a mask on.* He tried again, this time speaking as loudly as he could. Again it was muffled.

The paramedic leaned in again and lifted the breathing mask.

'Hurry. What is it? You can't take this off.'

He looked past her arm at Nicole.

'Gaw Lucy. Geh 'er ow a dare.'

The mask was put back in place. Nicole leaned close to him and spoke.

'Lucy? Who is Lucy, Henry?'

'I me ... '

The mask was lifted.

'Rahvin. Gaw 'er.'

Nicole nodded. She got it. The mask was put back over his mouth and nose.

'Okay, I will. As soon as we get to the hospital. I brought the number with me.'

'No, now!' he yelled through the mask.

He watched as Nicole opened her purse and took out a cell phone and a small spiral pad. She punched in a number she read from the pad and waited with the phone to her ear. She then reached out with the phone to his ear and he could hear Lucy's voice. It was voice mail. He groaned and tried to shake his head but couldn't.

'Easy,' the paramedic said. 'Easy now. Once we get to the ER we'll take off the straps.'

He closed his eyes. He wanted to go back to the warmth and the darkness. The understanding. Where nobody asked him why. Especially himself.

Pretty soon he was there.

Clarity came and went over the next two hours as he was taken into the

ER, examined by a doctor with a Caesar haircut, treated and then admitted to the hospital. His head finally cleared and he woke up in a white hospital room, startled from sleep by the staccato cough from somebody on the other side of the plastic curtain that was used as a room divider. He looked around and saw Nicole sitting on a chair, her cell phone to her ear. Her hair was loose now and fell around her shoulders. The phone's antenna poked up through its silken smoothness. He watched her until she closed the phone without a word.

'Ni'i,' he said in a hoarse voice. 'Thas ... '

It was still hard to make the *k* sound without pain. She stood up and went to his side.

'Henry. You—'

The cough sounded from the other side of the curtain.

'They're working on getting you a private room,' she whispered. 'Your med plan pays for it.'

'Where am I?'

'St. John's. Henry, what happened? The police got there before I did. They said all these people on the beach called on their cell phones and said two guys were hanging somebody over the balcony. You, Henry. There's blood on the outside wall.'

Pierce looked at her through swollen eyes. The swelling of the bridge of his nose and the gauze on the wound split his vision in half. He remembered what Wentz said right before he left.

'I dohn remember. Wha else did dey say?'

'That's it. They started knocking on doors in the building and when they got to yours it was wide open. You were in the bedroom. I got there when they were taking you out. A detective was here. He wants to talk to you.'

'I don't remember anything.'

He said it with as much force as he could. It was getting easier to talk. All he had to do was practice.

'Henry, what kind of trouble are you in?'

'I don't know.'

'Who is Robin? And Lucy? Who are they?'

He suddenly remembered he needed to warn her.

'How long have I been here?'

'A couple hours.'

'Gi' me your phone. I've got to phone her.'

'I've been calling that number every ten minutes. I was just calling when you woke up. I keep getting voice mail.'

He closed his eyes. He wondered if she had gotten his message and gotten out of there and away from Wentz.

'Le' me see your phone anyway.'

'Let me do it. You probably shouldn't be moving around too much. Who do you want to call?'

He gave her the number for his voice mail and then the pass code number. She didn't seem to attach any significance to it.

'You've got eight messages.'

'Any that are for Lilly just erase. Don't listen.'

That was all of them except for one message which Nicole said he should listen to. She turned up the phone and held it out so he could listen when she replayed it. It was Cody Zeller's voice.

'Hey, Einstein, I've got some stuff for you on that thing you asked about. So give me a buzz and we'll talk. Later, dude.'

Pierce erased the message and handed back the phone.

'Was that Cody?' Nicole asked.

'Yes.'

'I thought so. Why does he still call you that? It's so high school.'

' 'ollege, actually.'

It hurt to say 'college' but not as badly as he thought it would.

'What was he talking about?'

'Nothing. He was doing some online stuff for me.'

He almost started telling her about it and everything else. But before he could put the words together a man in a lab coat came through the door. He had a clipboard. He was in his late fifties with silver hair and a matching beard.

'This is Dr. Hansen,' Nicole said.

'How are you feeling?' the doctor asked.

He leaned over the bed and used his hand on Pierce's jaw to turn his face slightly.

'Only hurts when I breathe. Or talk. Or when somebody does that.'

Hansen let go of his jaw. He used a penlight to study Pierce's pupils.

'Well, you've got some pretty substantial injuries here. You have a grade-two concussion and six stitches in your scalp.'

Pierce hadn't even remembered that injury. It must have come when he hit the outside wall of the building.

'The concussion is the cause of the loginess you may be feeling and any headache discomfort. Let's see, what else? You have a pulmonary contusion, a deep shoulder contusion; you've got two fractured ribs and, of course, the broken nose. The lacerations on your nose and surrounding your eye are going to require plastic surgery to properly close without permanent scarring. I can get somebody in here tonight to do that, depending on the swelling, or if you have a personal surgeon, then you can contact him.'

Pierce shook his head. He knew there were many people in this town who kept personal plastic surgeons on call. But he wasn't one of them.

'Whoever you can get ... '

'Henry,' Nicole said. 'This is your face you're talking about. I think you should get the best possible surgeon you can.'

'I think I can get you a very good one,' Hansen said. 'Let me make some calls and see what I come up with.'

'Thank you.'

He said the words pretty clearly. It seemed as though his speech facility was quickly adapting to the new physical circumstances of his mouth and nasal passages.

'Try to stay as horizontal as possible,' Hansen said. 'I'll be back.'

The doctor nodded and left the room. Pierce looked at Nicole.

'Looks like I'm going to be here awhile. You don't have to stay.'

'I don't mind.'

He smiled and it hurt, but he smiled anyway. He was very happy with her response.

'Why did you call me in the middle of the night, Henry?'

He'd forgotten and the reminder brought the searing embarrassment again. He carefully composed an answer before speaking.

'I don't know. It's a long story. It's been a strange weekend. I wanted to tell you about it. And I wanted to tell you what I had been thinking about.'

'What was that?'

It hurt to talk but he had to tell her.

'I don't know exactly. Just that the things that happened to me somehow made me see your point of view a lot clearer. I know it's probably too little too late. But for some reason I wanted you to know I finally saw the light.'

She shook her head.

'That's good, Henry. But you're lying here with your head and face split open. It appears somebody dangled you off a twelfth-story balcony and the cops say they want to talk to you. It seems like you went to an awful lot of trouble to get my point of view. So excuse me if I don't jump up and embrace the new man you profess yourself to be.'

Pierce knew that if he were up to it, they were heading down the road to familiar territory. But he didn't think he had the stamina for another argument with her.

'Can you try Lucy again?'

Nicole angrily punched the redial button on her cell phone again.

'I ought to just put this on speed dial.'

He watched her eyes and could read that she had reached the voice mail again.

She snapped the phone closed and looked at him.

'Henry, what's going on with you?'

He tried to shake his head but it hurt to do so.

'I got a wrong number,' he said.

22

Pierce came out of a murky dream about free-falling while blindfolded and not knowing how far it was he was falling. When he finally hit the ground he opened his eyes and Detective Renner was there with a lopsided smile on his face.

'You.'

'Yeah, me again. How are you feeling, Mr. Pierce?'

'I'm fine.'

'Looked like a bad dream you were having. You were thrashing around there quite a bit.'

'Maybe I was dreaming about you.'

'Who are the Wickershams?'

'What?'

'You said the name in your sleep. Wickershams.'

'They're monkeys. From the jungle. The non-believers.'

'I don't get it.'

'I know. So never mind. Why are you here? What do you want? It happened – whatever happened – in Santa Monica and I already talked to them. I don't remember what happened. I have a concussion, you know.'

Renner nodded.

'Oh, I know all about your injuries. The nurse told me the plastic surgeon put a hundred and sixty microstitches across your nose and around that eye yesterday morning. Anyway, I'm here on Los Angeles police business. Though it's looking more and more like maybe L.A. and Santa Monica should get together on this one.'

Pierce raised his hand and gently touched the bridge of his nose. There was no gauze. He could feel the zipper of stitches and the puffiness. He tried to remember things. The last thing he could clearly recall was the plastic surgeon hovering over him with a bright light. After that he had been in and out, floating through the darkness.

'What time is it?'

'Three-fifteen.'

There was bright light coming through the window shades. He knew it wasn't the middle of the night. He also realized he was in a private room.

'It's Monday? No, it's Tuesday?'

'That's what it said in the paper today, if you believe what you read in the paper.'

Pierce felt physically strong – he had probably been asleep for more than fifteen straight hours – but was disturbed by the lingering feeling of the dream. And by Renner's presence.

'What do you want?'

'Well, first of all, let me get something out of the way. I'm going to read you your rights real quick here. That way you're protected and so am I.'

The detective pulled the mobile food tray over the bed and placed a microrecorder down on it.

'What do you mean, you're protected? What do you need protection from? That's bullshit, Renner.'

'Not at all. I need to do it to protect the integrity of my investigation. Now I'm going to record everything from here on out.'

He pressed a button on the recorder and a red light came on. He announced his name, the time and date and the location of the interview. He identified Pierce and read him his constitutionally guaranteed rights from a little card he took from his wallet.

'Now, do you understand these rights as I have read them to you?'

'Heard them enough growing up.'

Renner raised an eyebrow.

'In the movies and on TV,' Pierce added.

'Please answer the question and hold off on being clever if you can.'

'Yes, I understand my rights.'

'Good. Now is it all right if I ask you a few questions?'

'Am I a suspect?'

'A suspect in what?'

'I don't know. You tell me.'

'Well, that's the thing, isn't it? Hard to tell what we've got here.'

'But you still think you need to read me my rights. To protect me, of course.'

'That's right.'

'What are your questions? Have you found Lilly Quinlan?'

'We're working on it. You don't know where she is, do you?'

Pierce shook his head and the movement made his head feel a little sloshy. He waited for it to subside before speaking.

'No. I wish I did.'

'Yes, it would kind of clear things up a bit if she just walked through the door, wouldn't it?'

'Yes. Was it her blood on the bed?'

'We're still working on it. Preliminary tests showed that it was human blood. But we have no sample from Lilly Quinlan to compare it with. I think I've got a line on her doctor. We'll see what records and possible samples he has. A woman like that, she probably had her blood checked on a regular basis.'

Pierce assumed Renner was talking about Lilly checking herself for sexually transmitted diseases. Still, confirmation of the seemingly obvious – that it was human blood he had found on the bed – made him feel more depressed. As if the last slim hope he had for Lilly Quinlan was slipping away.

'Let me ask the questions now,' Renner said. 'What about this girl Robin that you mentioned before? Have you seen her?'

'No. I've been here.'

'Talked to her?'

'No. Have you?'

'No, we haven't been able to locate her. We got her number off the website like you said. But all we get is a message. We even tried leaving one where I had a guy in the squad who's good on the phone call up and act like he was, you know, a customer.'

'Social engineering.'

'Yeah, social engineering. But she didn't call back on that one either.'

Pierce felt the bottom completely drop out of his stomach now. Last he remembered, Nicole had tried to reach Lucy repeatedly and was also unsuccessful. Wentz might have gotten to her – or maybe even still had her. He realized he had to make a decision. He could dance around with Renner and continue to hold up a veil of lies in order to protect himself. Or he could try to help Lucy.

'Well, did you trace the number?'

'It's a cell.'

'What about the billing address?'

'The phone's registered to one of her regular clients. He said he does it as a favor. He takes care of the phone for her and the lease on her fuck pad and she gives him a free pop every Sunday afternoon while his wife does the shopping at the Ralph's in the Marina. It's more like Robin's doing the favor, you ask me. The guy's a fat slob. Anyway, she didn't show up Sunday afternoon at the pad – it's a little place in the Marina. We were there. We went with this guy but she didn't show.'

'And he doesn't know where she lives?'

'Nope. She never told him. He just pays for the cell phone and the apartment and shows up every Sunday. He lays the whole thing off on his expense account.'

'Shit.'

He envisioned Lucy in the hands of Wentz and Six-Eight. He reached up and ran his fingers along the seams in his own face. He hoped she got away. He hoped she was just hiding somewhere.

'Yeah, "shit" is exactly what we said. And the thing is, we don't even have her full name – we got her picture from the website, if it is her picture, and the name Robin. That's it, and I get the funny feeling neither one is legit.'

'What about going to the website?'

'I told you, we went—'

'No, the real place. The site office in Hollywood?'

'We did and we caught a lawyer. No cooperation. We need a court order before they'll share client information. And as far as Robin goes, we don't have enough to go talk to a judge about court orders.'

One more time Pierce thought about his choices. Protect himself or help Renner and possibly help Lucy. If it wasn't already too late.

'Turn that off.'

'What, this tape? I can't. This is a formal interview. I told you, I'm taping it.'

'Then it's over. But if you turn that off, I think I can tell you some things that will help you.'

Renner appeared to hesitate while he thought about it but Pierce had the feeling that so far everything had been scripted and was moving in the exact direction the detective had wanted it to go.

The detective clicked a button on the tape recorder and the red record light went off. He slid the device into the right pocket of his jacket.

'Okay, whaddaya got?'

'Her name isn't Robin. She told me her name is Lucy LaPorte. She's from New Orleans. You've got to find her. She's in danger. It might already be too late.'

'In danger from who?'

Pierce didn't answer. He thought about Wentz's threat not to talk to the police. He thought about the warnings from the private investigator, Glass.

'Billy Wentz,' he finally said.

'Wentz again,' Renner said. 'He's the bogeyman in all of this, huh?'

'Look, man, you can believe what I say or not. But just find Robin – I mean, Lucy – and make sure she's okay.'

'That's it? That's all you've got for me?'

'Her website photo is legitimate. I saw her.'

Renner nodded as though he had assumed so the whole time.

'The picture's getting a little clearer here,' he said. 'What else can you tell me about her? When did you see her?'

'Saturday night. She took me to Lilly's apartment. But she left before I went in. She didn't see anything, so I tried to keep her out of it. It was part of the deal I made with her. She was afraid Wentz would find out.'

'That was brilliant. You pay her?'

'Yes, but what does it matter?'

'It matters because money affects motives. How much?'

'About seven hundred dollars.'

'A lot of bread for just a ride through Venice. You get the other kind of ride, too, did you?'

'No, Detective, I didn't.'

'And so if this tale you told me before about Wentz being this big bad digital pimp is right, then her showing you the way to Lilly's apartment sort of puts her in harm's way, doesn't it?'

Pierce nodded. His head didn't go through the fishbowl effect this time. Vertical movement was okay. It was the horizontal moves that caused the problem.

'What else?' Renner said, still pushing.

'She shares that apartment in the Marina with a woman named Cleo. She's supposedly on the same site, though I never checked. Maybe you talk to Cleo and get a line on her.'

'Maybe, maybe not. That it?'

'Last thing, I saw her get into a green and yellow taxi on Speedway on Saturday night. Maybe you can trace it to her place.'

Renner shook his head slightly.

'Works in movies. Not too often in real life. Besides, she probably went back to the fuck pad. Saturdays are busy nights.'

The door to the room opened and Monica Purl stepped in. She saw Renner and stopped in the threshold.

'Oh, sorry. Am I—'

'Yes, you are,' Renner said. 'Police business. Could you wait outside, please?'

'I'll just come back.'

Monica looked at Pierce, her face reacting in horror to what she saw. Pierce tried to smile and raised his left hand and waved.

'I'll call you,' Monica said, and then she went back through the door and was gone.

'Who was that? Another girlfriend?'

'No, my assistant.'

'So you want to talk about what happened on that balcony Sunday? Was it Wentz?'

Pierce didn't say anything for a long time as he thought about the consequences of answering the question. A large part of him wanted to name Wentz and file charges against him. Pierce felt deeply humiliated by what Wentz and his giant had done to him. Even if the surgery on his face was successful and no physical scars were left behind, he knew without a doubt that the attack was going to be hard to live with, always to have in his memory. There would be scars nonetheless.

But still, the threat Wentz had made lodged in his mind as something very real – to himself, to Robin, even to Nicole. If Wentz was able to find him and invade his home so easily, then he would be able to find Nicole.

He finally spoke.

'It's a Santa Monica case, what do you care?'

'It's all one case and you know it.'

'I don't want to talk about it. I don't even remember what happened. I remember I was carrying groceries up to my apartment and then I woke up when the paramedics were working on me.'

'The mind is a tricky thing, isn't it? The way it blocks out the bad things.'

The tone was sarcastic and Pierce could tell by the look on Renner's face that he did not believe his memory loss. The two men stared at each other for a long moment, then the detective reached into his jacket.

'How about this, jog anything loose?'

He pulled out a folded 8 × 10 photo and showed it to Pierce. It was a grainy blowup of the Sands apartment tower taken from a long distance. From the beach. He pulled the photo closer and saw the small images of people on one of the upper balconies. He knew it was the twelfth floor. He knew it was him and Wentz and his muscle man, Six-Eight. Pierce was being held off the balcony by his ankles. The figures in the photo were too small to be recognizable. He handed it back.

'No. Nothing.'

'Right now it's the best we got. But once they put it on the news that we're looking for photos, videos, whatever, we might come up with something decent. A lot of people were out there. Somebody probably got a good shot.'

'Good luck.'

Renner was silent, studying Pierce for a long while before he spoke again.

'Look, if he threatened you, we can protect you.'

'I told you, I don't remember what happened. I don't remember anything at all.'

Renner nodded.

'Sure, sure. Okay, then let's forget the balcony. Let me ask you something else. Tell me, where did you hide Lilly's body?'

Pierce's eyes widened. Renner had used misdirection to hit him with the sucker punch.

'What? Are you—'

'Where is it, Pierce? What did you do with her? And what did you do with Lucy LaPorte?'

A cold feeling of fear began to rise in Pierce's chest. He looked at Renner and knew the detective was deadly serious. And he knew suddenly that he wasn't *a* suspect. He was *the* suspect.

'Are you fucking kidding me? You wouldn't even know about this if I hadn't called you people. I was the only one who cared about it.'

'Yeah, and maybe by calling us and traipsing all over that scene and the house, what you were setting up was a nice little defense. And maybe the job you had Wentz or one of your other pals do on your face was part of the defense. Poor guy gets his nose smashed for sticking it in the wrong place. It doesn't get my sympathy vote, Mr. Pierce.'

Pierce stared at him, speechless. Everything that he had done or that had been done to him was being perceived by Renner from a completely opposite angle.

'Let me tell you a quick little story,' Renner said. 'I used to work up in the Valley and one time we had a missing girl. She was twelve years old, from a good home, and we knew she wasn't a runaway. Sometimes you just know. So we organized the neighbors and volunteers into a search party in the Encino Hills. And lo and behold, one of the neighbor boys finds her. Raped and strangled and stuffed into a culvert. It was a bad one. And you know what, turned out that the boy who found her was the one who did the deed. Took us a while to circle back around to him but we did and he confessed. Being the one who found her like that? That's called the Good Samaritan complex. He who smelled it dealt it. Happens all the time. The doer likes getting close to the cops, likes helping out, makes him feel better than them and better about what he did.'

Pierce was having difficulty even fathoming how everything had turned on him.

'You're wrong,' he said quietly, his voice shaking. 'I didn't do it.'

'Yeah? Am I wrong? Well, let me tell you what I've got. I've got a missing woman and blood on the bed. I've got a bunch of your lies and a bunch of your fingerprints all over the woman's house and fuck pad.'

Pierce closed his eyes. He thought about the apartment off Speedway and the seagull house on Altair. He knew he had touched everything. He'd put his hands on everything. Her perfume, her closets, her mail.

'No ... '

It was all he could think to say.

'No, what?'

'This is all a mistake. All I did ... I mean ... I got her number. I just wanted to see ... I wanted to help her ... You see, it was my fault ... and I thought if I ... '

He didn't finish. The past and present were too close together. They were morphing together, one confusing the other. One moving in front of the other like an eclipse. He opened his eyes and looked at Renner.

'You thought what?' the detective asked.

'What?'

'Finish the line. You thought what?'

'I don't know. I don't want to talk about it.'

'Come on, kid. You started down the road. Finish the ride. It's good to unburden. Good for the soul. It's your fault Lilly's dead. What did you mean by that? It was an accident? Tell me how it happened. Maybe I can live with that and we can go tell the DA together, work something out.'

Pierce felt fear and danger flooding his mind now. He could almost smell it coming off his skin. As if they were chemicals – compound elements sharing common molecules – rising to the surface to escape.

'What are you talking about? Lilly? It's not my fault. I didn't even know her. I tried to help her.'

'By strangling her? Cutting her throat? Or did you do the Jack the Ripper number on her? I think they say the Ripper was a scientist. A doctor or something. You the new Ripper, Pierce? Is that your bag?'

'Get out of here. You're crazy.'

'I don't think I'm the crazy one. Why was it your fault?'

'What?'

'You said she was all your fault. Why? What did she do? Insult your manhood? You got a little pecker, Pierce? Is that it?'

Pierce shook his head emphatically, touching off a bout of dizziness. He closed his eyes.

'I didn't say that. It's not my fault.'

'You said it. I heard it.'

'No. You're putting words into my mouth. It's not my fault. I had nothing to do with it.'

He opened his eyes to see Renner reach into his coat pocket and pull out a tape recorder. The red light was on. Pierce realized that it was a different recorder from the one that had been placed earlier on the food tray and then turned off. The detective had taped the whole conversation.

Renner clicked the rewind button for a few seconds and then jockeyed around with the recording until he found what he wanted and replayed what Pierce had said moments before.

'This is all a mistake. All I did . . . I mean . . . I got her number. I just wanted to see . . . I wanted to help her . . . You see, it was my fault . . . and I thought if I . . . '

The detective clicked off the recorder and looked at Pierce with a smug smile on his face. Renner had him cornered. He had been tricked. All his legal instincts, as limited as they were, told him to not speak another word. But Pierce couldn't stop.

'No,' he said. 'I wasn't talking about her. About Lilly Quinlan. I was talking about my sister. I was—'

'We were talking about Lilly Quinlan and you said, "It was my fault." That is an admission, my friend.'

'No, I told you, I—'

'I know what you told me. It was a nice story.'

'It's no story.'

'Well, you know what? Story, no story, I figure as soon as I find the body I'll have the real story to tell. I'll have you in the bag and be home free.'

Renner leaned over the bed until his face was only inches from Pierce's.

'Where is she, Pierce? You know this is inevitable. We're going to find her. So let's get this over with now. Tell me what you did with her.'

Their eyes were locked. Pierce heard the click of the tape recorder being turned back on.

'Get out.'

'You'd better talk to me. You're running out of time. Once I take this in and it gets to the lawyers, I can't help you anymore. Talk to me, Henry. Come on. Unburden yourself.'

'I said get out. I want a lawyer.'

Renner straightened up and smiled in a knowing way. In an exaggerated fashion he held the tape recorder up and clicked it off.

'Of course you want a lawyer,' he said. 'And you're going to need one. I'm going to the DA, Pierce. I know I've already got you on obstruction and breaking and entering, for starters. Got you there cold. But all of that's bullshit. I want the big one.'

He proffered the tape recorder as though the words he had captured with it were the Holy Grail.

'As soon as that body turns up, it's game over.'

Pierce wasn't really listening anymore. He turned away from Renner and began staring into space, thinking about what was going to happen. All at once he realized he would lose everything. The company – everything. In a split second all the dominoes fell in his imagination, the last one being Goddard pulling out and taking his investment dollars somewhere else, to Bronson Tech or Midas Molecular or one of the other competitors. Goddard would pull out and nobody would be willing to pull in. Not under the glare of a criminal investigation and possible trial. It would be over. He would be out of the race for good.

He looked back at Renner.

'I said I'm not talking to you anymore. I want you to leave. I want a lawyer.'

Renner nodded.

'My advice to you is, make it a good one.'

He reached over to a counter where medical supplies were displayed and picked up a hat Pierce hadn't seen before. It was a brown porkpie hat with the brim cocked down. Pierce thought nobody wore hats like that in L.A. anymore. Nobody. Renner left the room without another word.

23

Pierce sat still for a moment, thinking about his predicament. He wondered how much of what Renner had said about going to the DA had been threat and how much of it was reality. He shook free of the thoughts and looked around to see if the room had a phone. There was nothing on the side table but the bed had side railings with all manner of electronic buttons for positioning the mattress and controlling the television mounted on the opposite wall. He found a phone that snapped out of the right railing. In a plastic pocket next to it he also found a small hand mirror. He held it up and looked at his face for the first time.

He was expecting worse. When he had felt the wound with his fingers in the moments after the assault, it had seemed to him that his face had been split open wide and that wide scarring would be unavoidable. At the time this didn't bother him, because he was happy just to be left alive. Now he was a little more concerned. Looking at his face, he saw the swelling was way down. He was a little puffy around the corners of his eyes and the lower part of his nose. Both nostrils were packed with cotton gauze. Both eyes had dark swatches of purple beneath them. The cornea of his left eye was flooded with blood on one side of the iris. And across his nose were the very fine trails of microstitching.

The stitching formed a K pattern with one line going up the bridge of his nose, and the arms of the K curving below his left eye and above it into his eyebrow. Half of his left eyebrow had been shaved to accommodate the surgery and Pierce thought that might be the oddest thing about the whole face he saw in the mirror.

He put the mirror down and he realized he was smiling. His face was almost destroyed. He had an LAPD cop who was trying to put him in jail for a crime he had uncovered but did not commit. He had a digital pimp with a pet monster out there who was a live and real threat to him and others close to him. Yet he was sitting in bed, smiling.

He didn't understand it but knew it had something to do with what he had seen in the mirror. He had survived and his face showed how close he had come to not making it. In that there was relief and the inappropriate smile.

He picked up the phone and put in a call to Jacob Kaz, the company's patent attorney. His call was put through to the lawyer immediately.

'Henry, are you okay? I heard you were attacked or something. What—'

'It's a long story, Jacob. I'll have to tell you later. What I need from you right now is a name. I need an attorney. A criminal defense attorney. Somebody good but who doesn't like getting his face on TV or his name in the papers.'

Pierce knew that what he was asking for was a rarity in Los Angeles. But containing the situation was going to be as urgent as possibly defending himself against a bogus murder charge. It had to be handled quickly and discreetly, or the falling dominoes Pierce had imagined moments earlier would become the crushing blocks of reality that toppled both him and the company.

Kaz cleared his throat before responding. He gave no indication that Pierce's request was out of the ordinary or anything other than normal in their professional relationship.

'I think I have a name for you,' he said. 'You'll like her.'

24

On Wednesday morning Pierce was on the phone with Charlie Condon when a woman in a gray suit walked into his hospital room. She handed him a card that said JANIS LANGWISER, ATTORNEY AT LAW on it. He cupped his hand over the phone and told her he was wrapping up the call.

'Charlie, I've got to go. My doctor just came in. Just tell him we have to do it over the weekend or next week.'

'Henry, I can't. He wants to see Proteus before we send in the patent. I don't want to delay that and you don't, either. Besides, you've met Maurice. He won't be put off.'

'Just call him again and try to delay it.'

'I will. I'll try. I'll call you back.'

Charlie hung up and Pierce clipped the phone back into the bed's side guard. He tried to smile at Langwiser but his face was sorer than it had been the day before and it hurt to smile. She put out her hand and he shook it.

'Janis Langwiser. Pleased to meet you.'

'Henry Pierce. I can't say the circumstances make it a pleasure to meet you.'

'That's usually the way it is with criminal defense work.'

He had already gotten her pedigree from Jacob Kaz. Langwiser handled the criminal defense work for the small but influential downtown firm of Smith, Levin, Colvin & Enriquez. The firm was so exclusive, according to Kaz, that it wasn't listed in any phone book. Its clients were A-list, but even people on that list still needed criminal defense from time to time. That's where Langwiser came in. She'd been hired away from the district attorney's office a year earlier, after a career that included prosecuting some of Los Angeles's higher-profile cases of recent years. Kaz told Pierce that the firm was taking him as a client as a means of establishing a relationship with him, a relationship that would be mutually beneficial as Amedeo Technologies moved toward going public in years to come. Pierce didn't tell Kaz that there would be no eventual public offering or even an Amedeo Technologies if this situation wasn't handled properly.

After polite inquiries about Pierce's injuries and prognosis, Langwiser asked him why he thought he needed a criminal defense attorney.

'Because there is a police detective out there who believes I'm a killer. He told me he was going to the DA's office to try to charge me with a number of crimes, including murder.'

'An L.A. cop? What's his name?'

'Renner. I don't think he ever told me his first name. Or I don't remember it. I have his card but I never looked at—'

'Robert. I know him. He works out of Pacific Division. He's been around a long time.'

'You know him from a case?'

'Early in my career at the DA I filed cases. I filed a few that he brought in. He seemed like a good cop. I think *thorough* is the word I would use.'

'It's actually the word he uses.'

'He's going to the DA for a murder charge?'

'I'm not sure. There's no body. But he said he was going to charge me with other stuff first. Breaking and entering, he says. Obstruction of justice. I guess he'll try to make a case for the murder after that. I don't know how much is bullshit threats and how much he can do. But I didn't kill anybody, so I need a lawyer.'

She frowned and nodded thoughtfully. She gestured to his face.

'Is this thing with Renner in any way related to your injuries?'

Pierce nodded.

'Why don't we start at the beginning.'

'Do we have an attorney-client relationship at this point?'

'Yes, we do. You can speak freely.'

Pierce nodded. He spent the next thirty minutes telling her the story in as much detail as he could remember. He freely told her about everything he had done, including the crimes he had committed. He left nothing out.

As he talked Langwiser leaned against the equipment counter. She took notes with an expensive-looking pen on a yellow legal pad she took from a black leather bag that was either an oversized purse or an undersized briefcase. Her whole manner exuded expensive confidence. When Pierce was finished telling the story, she went back to the part about what Renner had called an admission from him. She asked several questions, first about the tone of the conversation at that point, what medications Pierce was on at the time and what ill effect from the attack and surgery he was feeling. She then asked specifically what he had meant by saying it was his fault.

'I meant my sister, Isabelle.'

'I don't understand.'

'She died. A long time ago.'

'Come on, Henry, don't make me guess about this. I want to know.'

He shrugged now, and this hurt his shoulder and ribs.

'She ran away from home when we were kids. Then she got killed . . . by some guy who had killed a lot of people. Girls he picked up in Hollywood. Then he got killed by the police and that . . . was it.'

'A serial killer . . . when was this?'

'The eighties. He was called the Dollmaker. They all get names from newspapers, you know? Back then, at least.'

He could see Langwiser reviewing her contemporary history.

'I remember the Dollmaker. I was at UCLA law school back then. I later knew the detective who was the one who shot him. He just retired this year.'

Her thoughts seemed to drift with the memory, then she came back.

'Okay. So how did that get confused with Lilly Quinlan in your conversation with Detective Renner?'

'Well, I've been thinking about my sister a lot lately. Since this thing with Lilly came up. I think it's the reason I did what I did.'

'You mean you think you are responsible for your sister? How can that be, Henry?'

Pierce waited a moment before speaking. He carefully put the story together in his mind. Not the whole story. Just the part he wanted to tell her. He left out the part that he could never tell a stranger.

'My stepfather and I, we used to go down there. We lived in the Valley and we'd go down to Hollywood and look for her. At night. Sometimes during the day, but mostly at night.'

Pierce stared at the blank screen of the television mounted on the wall across the room. He spoke as though he were seeing the story on the screen and repeating it to her.

'I would dress up in old clothes so I would look like them – one of the street kids. My stepfather would send me into the places where the kids hid and slept, where they would have sex for money or do drugs. Whatever . . .'

'Why you? Why didn't your stepfather go in?'

'At the time, he told me that it was because I was a kid and I could fit in and be allowed in. If a man walked into one of those places by himself, everybody might run. Then we'd lose her.'

He stopped talking and Langwiser waited but then had to prompt him.

'You said at the time he told you that was the reason. What did he tell you later?'

Pierce shook his head. She was good. She had picked up the subtleties of his telling of the story.

'Nothing. It's just that . . . I think . . . I mean, she ran away for a reason. The police said she was on drugs but I think that came after. After she was on the street.'

'You think your stepfather was the reason she ran away.'

She said it as a statement and he gave an almost imperceptible nod. He thought about what Lilly Quinlan's mother had said about what her daughter and the woman she knew as Robin had in common.

'What did he do to her?'

'I don't know and it doesn't matter now.'

'Then why would you say to Renner that it was your fault? Why do you think what happened to your sister was your fault?'

'Because I didn't find her. All those nights looking and I never found her. If only . . . '

He said it without conviction or emphasis. It was a lie. The truth he would not tell this woman he had known for only an hour.

Langwiser looked like she wanted to go further with it but also seemed to know she was already stretching a personal boundary with him.

'Okay, Henry. I think it helps explain things – both your actions in regard to Lilly Quinlan's disappearance and your statement to Renner.'

He nodded.

'I am sorry about your sister. In my old job dealing with the families of the victims was the most difficult part. At least you got some closure. The man who did this certainly got what he deserved.'

Pierce tried a sarcastic smile but it hurt too much.

'Yeah, closure. Makes everything better.'

'Is your stepfather alive? Your parents?'

'My stepfather is. Last I heard. I don't talk to him, not in a long time. My mother is not with him anymore. She still lives in the Valley. I haven't talked to her in a long time, either.'

'Where's your father?'

'Oregon. He's got a second family. But we stay in touch. Of all of them, he's the only one I talk to.'

She nodded. She studied her notes for a long period, flipping back the pages on the pad as she reviewed everything he had said from the start of the conversation. She then finally looked up at him.

'Well, I think it's all bullshit.'

Pierce shook his head.

'No, I'm telling you exactly how it hap—'

'No, I mean Renner. I think he's bullshitting. There's nothing there. He's not going to charge you with these lesser crimes. He'd get laughed right out of the DA's office on the B and E. What was your intent? To steal? No, it was to make sure she was okay. They don't know about the mail you took and they can't prove it anyway, because it's gone. As far as the obstruction goes, that's just an idle threat. People lie and hold back with the police all the time. It's expected. To try to charge somebody for it is another matter. I can't even remember the last obstruction case that went to court. At least there were none I remember when I was in the office.'

'What about the tape? I was confused. He said what I said was an admission.'

'He was playing you. Trying to rattle you and see how you'd react, maybe get a more damaging admission out of you. I would have to listen to the statement to get a full take on it, but it sounds as though it is marginal, that your explanation in regard to your sister is certainly legitimate and would be perceived that way by a jury. Add in that I am sure that you were under the influence of a variety of medications and you—'

'This can never go to a jury. If it does, I'm finished. I'm ruined.'

'I understand that. But a jury's view is still the way to look at this because that is how the DA will look at it when considering potential charges. The last thing they will do is go into a case knowing a jury isn't going to buy it.'

'There is nothing to buy. I didn't do it. I just tried to find out if she was all right. That's all.'

Langwiser nodded but didn't seem particularly interested in his protestations of innocence. Pierce had always heard that good defense attorneys were never as interested in the ultimate question of their clients' guilt or innocence as they were in the strategy of defense. They practiced law, not justice. Pierce found this frustrating because he wanted Langwiser to acknowledge his innocence and then go out and fight to defend it.

'First of all,' she said, 'with no body, it is very difficult to make a case against anybody. It is doable but very difficult – especially in this case, when you consider the victim's lifestyle and source of income. I mean, she could be anywhere. And if she is dead, then the suspect list is going to be very long.

'Second, his tying your break-in at one scene to a possible homicide at another scene is not going to work. That's a stretch that I cannot see the DA's office being willing to make. Remember, I worked there and bringing cops down to reality was half the work. I think that unless things change in a big way, you'll be okay, Henry. On all of it.'

'What big way?'

'Like they find the body. Like they find the body and somehow link it to you.'

Pierce shook his head.

'Nothing will link it to me. I never met her.'

'Then good. Then you should be in the clear.'

'Should be?'

'Nothing is ever a hundred percent. Especially in the law. We'll still have to wait and see.'

Langwiser reviewed her notes for a few more moments before speaking again.

'Okay,' she finally said. 'Now, let's call Detective Renner.'

Pierce raised his eyebrows – what was left of them – and it hurt. He winced and said, 'Call him? Why?'

'To put him on notice that you have representation and to see what he has to say for himself.'

She took a cell phone out of her case and opened it.

'I think I have his card in my wallet,' Pierce said. 'It should be in the table drawer.'

'It's all right, I remember the number.'

Her call to the Pacific Division was answered quickly and she asked for Renner. It took a few minutes but she finally got him on the line. While she waited she turned up the volume on the phone and angled it from her ear so Pierce could hear both ends of the conversation. She pointed at him and then put her fingers to her lips, telling him not to enter the conversation.

'Hey, Bob, Janis Langwiser. Remember me?'

After a pause Renner said, 'Sure. I heard you went over to the dark side, though.'

'Very funny. Listen, I'm over here at St. John's. I was visiting with Henry Pierce.'

Another pause.

'Henry Pierce, the Good Samaritan. Longtime rescuer of missing whores and lost pets.'

Pierce felt his face redden.

'You are just full of good humor today, Bob,' Langwiser said dryly. 'That's a new wrinkle with you, isn't it?'

'Henry Pierce is the joker, the stories he tells.'

'Well, that's why I'm calling. No more stories from Henry, Bob. I am representing him and he's no longer talking to you. You blew the chance you had.'

Pierce looked up at Langwiser and she winked at him.

'I didn't blow anything,' Renner protested. 'Anytime he wants to start telling me the complete and true story, I'm here. Otherwise—'

'Look, Detective, you're more interested in busting my guy's chops than figuring out what really happened. That's got to stop. Henry Pierce is now out of your loop. And another thing, you try to take this to court and I'm going to shove that two-tape-recorders trick up your ass.'

'I told him I was recording,' Renner protested. 'I read him his rights and he said he understood them. That is all I'm required to do. I did nothing illegal during his voluntary interview.'

'Maybe not per se, Bob. But judges and juries don't like the cops tricking people. They like a clean game.'

Now there was a long pause from Renner, and Pierce was beginning to think that Langwiser was going too far, that she might push the detective into seeking a charge against him out of pure anger or resentment.

'You really did cross over, didn't you?' Renner finally said. 'I hope you'll be happy over there.'

'Well, if I only get clients like Henry Pierce, people who were just trying to do a good thing, then I will be.'

'A good thing? I wonder if Lucy LaPorte thinks what he did was a good thing.'

'Did he find her?' Pierce blurted out.

Langwiser immediately held her hand up to quiet him.

'Is that Mr. Pierce there? I didn't know we had him listening in, Janis. Speaking of tricks, that was nice of you to tell me.'

'I didn't have to.'

'And I didn't have to tell him about the second recorder once I told him the conversation was being recorded. So shove that up your ass. I gotta go.'

'Wait. Did you find Lucy LaPorte?'

'That's official police business, ma'am. You stay in your loop and I'll stay in mine. Good-bye now.'

Renner hung up and Langwiser closed her phone.

'I told you not to say anything.'

'Sorry. It's just that I've been trying to reach her since Sunday. I wish I could just find out where she is and whether she's okay or needs help. If anything's happened, it's my fault.'

There I go again, he thought. *Finding my own fault in things, offering public admissions of guilt.*

Langwiser didn't seem to notice. She was putting away her phone and notebook.

'I'll make some calls on it. I know some people in Pacific that are a little bit more cooperative than Detective Renner. Like his boss, for example.'

'Will you call me as soon as you find out something?'

'I have your numbers. Meantime, you stay away from all of this. With any luck, that call will scare Renner away for the time being, maybe make him second-guess his moves. You're not out of the woods on this yet, Henry. I think you're almost in the clear but other things could still happen. Keep your head down and stay away from it.'

'Okay, I will.'

'And next time the doctor comes in, get a list of the specific drugs that would have been in your system when Renner recorded you.'

'Okay.'

'Do you know when you are getting out of here yet?'

'Supposed to be anytime now.'

Pierce looked at his watch. He'd been waiting almost two hours for Dr. Hansen to sign him out.

He looked back at Langwiser. She looked ready to go. But she was looking at him like she wanted to ask something but wasn't sure how to ask it.

'What?'

'I don't know. I was just thinking that it was a long jump in your thinking. When you were just a boy, I mean, and you thought your stepfather was the reason your sister left.'

Pierce didn't say anything.

'Anything else you want to tell me about that?'

Pierce looked up at the blank television screen again and saw nothing there. He shook his head.

'No, that's about it.'

He doubted he had gotten the line by her. He assumed that criminal defense lawyers dealt with liars as a matter of course and were as expert at picking up the subtleties of eye movement and body inflection as machines designed for it. But Langwiser simply nodded and let it slide.

'Well, I need to go. I have an arraignment downtown.'

'Okay. Thanks for coming to see me here. That was nice.'

'Part of the service. I'll make some calls while I'm driving in and let you know what I hear about Lucy LaPorte or anything else. But meantime, you really need to stay away from this. Okay? Go back to work.'

Pierce held his hands up in surrender.

'I'm done with it.'

She smiled professionally and left the room.

Pierce detached the phone from the bed's side guard and was punching in Cody Zeller's number when Nicole James stepped into the room. He put the phone back in its place.

Nicole had agreed to come by to drive Pierce home after he was checked out by Dr. Hansen and released. She silently registered pain as she studied Pierce's damaged face. She had visited him often during his hospital stay but it seemed as though she could not get used to seeing the stitch zippers.

Pierce had actually taken her frowns and sympathetic murmurings as a good sign. He would consider it to have been worth all the trouble if it got them back together.

'Poor baby,' she said, lightly patting his cheek. 'How do you feel?'

'Pretty good,' he told her. 'But I'm still waiting on the doctor to sign me out. Almost two hours now.'

'I'll go out and check on things.'

She went back to the door but looked back at Pierce.

'Who was that woman?'

'What woman?'

'Who just left your room.'

'Oh, she's my lawyer. Kaz got her for me.'

'Why do you need her if you have Kaz?'

'She's a criminal defense lawyer.'

She stepped away from the door and went back closer to the bed.

'Criminal defense lawyer? Henry, people who get wrong numbers usually don't need lawyers. What is going on?'

Pierce shrugged his shoulders.

'I don't really know anymore. I got into something and now I'm just trying to get out in one piece. Let me ask you something.'

He got off the bed and walked up to her. His balance was off at first but then he was okay. He lightly touched her forearms with his hands. A suspicious look came across her face.

'What?'

'When we leave here, where are you taking me?'

'Henry, I told you, I'm taking you home. Your home.'

Even with the puffiness and the road map of stitches, his disappointment was visibly evident.

'Henry, we agreed to at least try this. So let's try.'

'I just thought ... '

He didn't finish. He didn't know exactly what he thought or how to put it into words.

'You seem to think that what happened with us all happened so quickly,' she said. 'And that it can be fixed quickly.'

She turned and headed back toward the door.

'And I'm wrong.'

She looked back at him.

'Months, Henry, and you know it. Maybe longer. We hadn't been good together in a long, long time.'

She went through the door to look for the doctor. Pierce sat on the bed and tried to remember the time they were on the Ferris wheel and everything seemed so perfect in the world.

25

Blood was everywhere. A trail of it across the beige rug, on the brand-new bed, on two of the walls and all over the telephone. Pierce stood in the doorway of his bedroom and looked at the mess. He could remember almost none of what had happened after Wentz and his sidekick monster had left.

He stepped into the room and bent down next to the phone. He gingerly lifted the receiver with two fingers and held it a good three inches from his head, just enough to hear the tone and determine if he had any messages.

There were none. He reached over and unplugged the phone and then carried it into the bathroom to attempt to clean it.

Dried blood was splashed across the sink. There were bloody fingerprints on the medicine cabinet door. Pierce had no memory of going into the bathroom after the attack. But the place was a mess. The blood had dried hard and brown and it reminded him of the mattress he had seen the police remove from Lilly Quinlan's apartment.

As he used wet tissues to wipe off the phone as best he could, he had a memory of going to a movie called *Curdled* a few years earlier with Cody Zeller. It was about a woman whose job was to clean up bloody crime scenes after the police were finished with the on-site investigation. He now wondered if there was really such a job and a service he could call. The prospect of cleaning up the bedroom was not attractive to him in the least.

After the phone was reasonably clean he plugged it back into the wall in the bedroom and sat down with it on an unstained edge of the mattress. He checked for messages and again there were none. He thought it unusual. He had not been home for nearly seventy-two hours, yet there were no messages. He thought maybe Lilly Quinlan's page had finally been taken off the L.A. Darlings website. Then he remembered something else. He punched in his number at Amedeo Technologies and waited for the call to ring through to Monica Purl's desk.

'Monica, it's me. Did you change my phone number?'

'Henry? What are—'

'Did you change the number at my apartment?'

'Yes, you told me to. It was supposed to start yesterday.'

'I think it did.'

He knew that when he had been talking Monica into making the call to All American Mail on Saturday that he had told her to change the number on Monday. At the time he guessed he meant it. But now he felt strangely unsettled about losing the number. It was a connection to another world, to Lilly and Lucy.

'Henry? Are you still there?'

'Yes. What's my new number?'

'I have to look it up. Are you out of the hospital?'

'Yes, I'm out. Just look it up, please.'

'I am, I am. I was going to give it to you yesterday but when I went in your room you had that visitor.'

'I understand.'

'Okay, here it is.'

She gave him the number and he grabbed a pen off the bed table and wrote it on his wrist because he didn't have a notebook handy.

'Is there a forwarding on the last number?'

'No, because then I thought all of those guys would be still calling you.'

'Exactly. Good work.'

'Um, Henry, are you coming in today? Charlie was asking about your schedule.'

He thought about this before answering. The day was already half shot. Charlie probably wanted to talk and then overtalk about the Proteus demonstration still scheduled for the next day with Maurice Goddard despite Pierce's urging to delay it.

'I don't know if I'm going to make it in,' Pierce told Monica. 'The doctor wants me to take it easy. If Charlie wants to talk, tell him I'm at home and give him the new number.'

'Okay, Henry.'

'Thank you, Monica. I'll see you later.'

He waited for her to say good-bye but she didn't. He was about to hang up when she spoke.

'Henry, are you all right?'

'I'm fine. I just don't want to come in and scare everybody with this face. Like I scared you yesterday.'

'I wasn't—'

'Yes, you were but that's okay. And thanks for asking how I'm doing, Monica. That was nice. I've gotta go now. Oh, listen, the man who was in my room when you came by?'

'Yes?'

'He's a detective named Renner. From the LAPD. He will probably be calling you to ask about me.'

'About what?'

'About what I had you do for me. You know, making that call as Lilly Quinlan. Things like that.'

There was a short silence and then Monica's voice sounded different, nervous.

'Henry, am I in trouble?'

'Not at all, Monica. He's investigating her disappearance. And he's investigating me. Not you. He's just backtracking on what I did. So if he calls you, just tell him the truth and everything will be fine.'

'Are you sure?'

'Yes, I'm sure. Don't worry about it. I should go now.'

They hung up. Pierce got a fresh dial tone and called Lucy LaPorte's number, knowing it now by heart. Once again he got her voice mail but the greeting was now different. It was her voice but the message was that she was taking a vacation and would not be accepting clients until mid-November.

More than a month, Pierce thought. He felt his insides constrict as he thought about what Renner had intimated and about Wentz and his goon and what they could've done to her. He left a message regardless of what she had said in her greeting.

'Lucy, it's Henry Pierce. It's important. Call me back. I don't care what happened or what they did to you, call me. I can help you. I've got a new number now, so write it down.'

He read the number off his wrist and then hung up. He held the phone on his lap for a few moments, half expecting, half hoping she would immediately call back. She didn't. After a while he got up and left the bedroom.

In the kitchen Pierce found the empty laundry basket on the counter. He remembered he had been using it to carry grocery bags up from the car when he first encountered Wentz and Six-Eight by the elevator. He remembered dropping the laundry basket when he was pushed out of the elevator. Now the basket was here. He opened the refrigerator and looked inside. Everything he had been carrying up – except the eggs, which had probably broken – had been placed inside. He wondered who had done this. Nicole? The police? A neighbor he did not even know?

The question made him think of Detective Renner's statement about the Good Samaritan complex. If such a theory and complex were true, then Pierce felt sorry for all the true do-gooders and volunteers out there in the world. The idea that their efforts might be viewed cynically by members of law enforcement depressed him.

Pierce remembered that he still had several bags of groceries in the trunk of his BMW. He picked up the laundry basket and decided to go get them because he was hungry and the pretzels and sodas and other snacks he had bought were in the trunk.

Still feeling weak from the assault and surgery, he did not overload the basket once he went down to the garage. He decided on two trips and after he got back into the apartment with the second basketful he checked the phone again and learned he had missed a call. He had a message.

Pierce cursed himself for missing the call and then quickly went through the process of setting up a voice mail access code again. Soon he was listening to the message. It was from Lucy LaPorte.

'Help me? You already helped me enough, Henry. They hurt me. I'm all black and blue and nobody can see me like this. I want you to stop calling me and wanting to help me. I'm not talking to you again after this. *Stop calling here, you understand?*'

The message clicked off. Pierce continued to hold the phone to his ear, his mind repeating parts of the message like a scratched old record. *They hurt me. I'm all black and blue.* He felt himself getting light-headed and reached out to the wall for balance. He then turned his back into the wall and slid down until he was sitting on the floor, the phone on his lap again.

He did not move for several seconds and then raised the receiver and started calling her number. Halfway through, he stopped and hung up.

'Okay,' he said out loud.

He closed his eyes. He thought about calling Janis Langwiser to tell her that he had received a message from Lucy, that at the very least she was alive. He could then ask her if she had learned anything new since their meeting at the hospital that morning.

Before he could act on the idea, the phone rang while he was still holding it. He answered immediately. He thought it might be Lucy again – who else had the new number? – and his hello was tinged with a tone of hurried desperation.

But it wasn't Lucy. It was Monica.

'I forgot to tell you, between Monday and Tuesday your friend Cody Zeller left three messages for you on your private line. I guess he really wants you to call him.'

'Thank you, Monica.'

Pierce could not call Zeller back directly. His friend accepted no direct calls. To contact him, Pierce had to call his pager and put in a return number. If Zeller was familiar with the number, he would return the call. Because Pierce had a new number that Zeller would not recognize, he added a prefix of three sevens, which was a code that let Zeller know it was a friend or associate who was attempting to contact him from an unfamiliar number. It was a sometimes cumbersome and always annoying way to conduct life and business but Zeller was a paranoid's paranoid and Pierce had to play it his way.

He settled in to wait for the callback but his page was promptly returned. Unusual for Zeller.

'Jesus, man, when are you going to get a cell phone? I've been trying to reach you for three days.'

'I don't like cell phones. What's up?'

'You can get them with a scramble chip, you know.'

'I know. What's up?'

'What's up is that on Saturday you sure wanted this stuff in a goddamn hurry. Then you don't call me back for three days. I was starting to think you—'

'Code, I've been in the hospital. I just got out.'

'The hospital?'

'I had a little trouble with some guys.'

'Not guys from Entrepreneurial Concepts?'

'I don't know. Did you find out about them?'

'Full scan as requested. These are bad dudes you're dancing with, Hank.'

'I'm getting that idea. You want to tell me about them now?'

'Actually, I'm in the middle of something right now and don't like doing this by phone anyway. But I did drop it all in a FedEx yesterday – when I didn't hear from you. Should've gotten there by this morning. You didn't get it?'

Pierce checked his watch. It was two o'clock. The FedEx run came at about ten every morning. He didn't like the idea of the envelope from Zeller sitting on his desk all this time.

'I haven't been to the office. But I'll go get it now. You have anything else for me?'

'Can't think of anything that's not in the package.'

'Okay, man. I'll call you after I look at everything. Meantime, let me ask you something. I need to track somebody to a location, an address, and all I have is her name and her cell number. But the bill for the cell doesn't go to where she lives and that's what I want.'

'Then it's worthless.'

'Anything else I can do?'

'That's a tough one but it can be done. Is she registered to vote?'

'I kind of doubt it.'

'Well, there are utility hookups and credit cards. How common's her name?'

'Lucy LaPorte of Louisiana.'

Pierce reminded himself that she had told him to stop calling her. She hadn't said anything about not finding her.

'Got that alliteration thing going, huh?' Zeller said. 'Well, I can try some things, see what pops.'

'Thanks, Code.'

'And I suppose you want it yesterday.'

'That's right.'

'Of course.'

'I gotta go.'

Pierce went into the kitchen and looked through the bags he had dumped on the counter for the bread and peanut butter. He quickly made a sandwich and left the apartment, being sure to put on the Moles hat and pull the brim down low on his forehead. He ate the sandwich while waiting for the elevator. The bread tasted stale. It had been in the car trunk since Sunday.

On the ride down to the garage the elevator stopped on six and a woman got on. As was the custom with elevator riders, she avoided looking at Pierce. After they started descending she surreptitiously checked out his reflection in the polished chrome trim on the door. Pierce saw her do a frightened double take.

'Oh my God!' she cried out. 'You're the one everybody's talking about.'

'Excuse me?'

'You're the one who got hung off the balcony, right?'

Pierce looked at her for a long moment. And in that moment he knew that no matter what happened with Nicole, he wouldn't be able to stay in the apartment building. He was moving.

'I don't know what you're talking about.'

'Are you all right? What did they do to you?'

'They didn't do anything. I don't know what you are talking about.'

'You're not the guy who just moved in up on twelve?'

'No. I'm on eight. I'm staying with a friend on eight while I heal.'

'Then what happened?'

'Deviated septum.'

She looked at him suspiciously. The door finally opened on the garage level. Pierce didn't wait for her to get out first. He moved quickly out of the elevator and around the corner toward the door to the building's garage. He glanced back to see the woman staring at him as she came out of the elevator.

Just as he looked forward again he almost walked into the door to the storage area, which had come open as a man and woman were walking their bikes out. Pierce lowered his chin, pulled the brim of his hat down further and held the door and waited until they were out of the way. They both said thank you but didn't mention anything about his being the guy who was hung off the balcony.

The first thing Pierce did when he got inside his car was put on the pair of sunglasses he carried in the glove box.

26

The FedEx envelope was on his desk when Pierce walked into his office. It had been a battle to get there. Almost every step of the way he'd had to fend off looks and inquiries about his face. By the time he got to the office section of the third floor, he was giving one-word answers to all questions – 'Accident.'

'Lights,' he said as he swung around behind his desk.

But the lights didn't come on and Pierce realized that his voice was different because of the swelling of his nasal passages. He got up and turned on the lights manually and then went back to the desk. He took off his sunglasses and put them on top of his computer monitor.

He picked up the envelope and checked the return address. Cody Zeller pulled a painful smile out of him. In the return address Zeller had put the name Eugene Briggs, the Stanford department head the Doomsters had targeted many years before. The prank that had changed their lives.

The smile dropped off his face when Pierce turned over the envelope to open it. The pull tab had already been torn – the envelope was open. He looked inside it and saw a white business envelope. He took this out and found that it had been opened as well. The outside of the envelope said *Henry Pierce, personal and confidential.* There was a folded sheaf of documents inside. He couldn't tell if they had been pulled out or not.

He got up and went out his door to the corral where the assistants had their pods. He went to Monica's desk. He held up the FedEx envelope and the torn envelope that had been inside it.

'Monica, who opened this?'

She looked up at him.

'I did. Why?'

'How come you opened it?'

'I open all your mail. You don't like to deal with it. Remember? I open it so I can tell you what is important and what isn't. If you don't want me to do it that way anymore, just tell me. I won't mind, just less work.'

Pierce calmed. She was right.

'No, that's all right. Did you read this stuff?'

'Not really. I saw the picture of the girl who had your phone number and decided I did *not* want to look at that stuff. Remember what we agreed to on Saturday?'

Pierce nodded.

'Yes, that's good. Thanks.'

He turned to go back to his office.

'Do you want me to tell Charlie you are here?'

'No, I'm only staying a few minutes.'

When he got to the door he looked back at Monica and saw her staring at him with that look of hers. Like she was judging him guilty of something, some crime he knew nothing about.

He closed the door and went behind the desk. He opened the envelope and pulled out the sheaf of printouts from Zeller.

The photo Monica mentioned was not the same photo of Lilly Quinlan from her web page. It was a mug shot taken in Las Vegas three years before, when she had been arrested in a prostitution sting. In the photo she did not look nearly as breathtaking as she did in the website photo. She looked tired and angry and a bit scared all at once.

Zeller's report on Lilly Quinlan was short. He had traced her from Tampa to Dallas to Vegas and then L.A. She was actually twenty-eight years old, not the twenty-three she promised in her web page ad copy. She had a record of two arrests for solicitation in Dallas and the one arrest in Vegas. After each arrest she had spent a few days in jail and was then released for time served. She had come to L.A. three years earlier, according to utilities records. She had avoided arrest and notice of the police until now.

That was it. Pierce looked at the photo again and felt depressed. The mug shot was the reality. The photo he had downloaded from the website and looked at so often over the weekend was the fantasy. Her trail from Tampa to Dallas to Las Vegas to Los Angeles had ended on that bed in the Venice townhouse. There was a killer out there somewhere. And meantime, the cops were focusing on him.

He put the sheaf of printouts down on the desk and picked up the phone. After digging her card out of his wallet, he called Janis Langwiser to check in. He was on hold a good five minutes before she picked up.

'Sorry, I was on the phone with another client. What is happening with you?'

'Me? Nothing. I'm at work. I just wanted to check in and see if you've heard anything new from anybody.'

Meaning, *Is Renner still after me?*

'No, nothing really new. I think we're playing a waiting game here. Renner knows he is on notice and that he's not going to be able to bully you. We have to just see what turns up and go from there.'

Pierce looked at the mug shot on his desk. It could just as well have been a morgue shot for all the harsh lighting and shadows on her face.

'You mean like a body turning up?'

'Not necessarily.'

'Well, I got a call from Lucy LaPorte today.'

'Really? What did she say?'

'It was a message, actually. She said she'd been hurt and she didn't want me to ever contact her again.'

'Well, at least we know she's around. We may need her.'

'Why?'

'If this goes further we could possibly use her as a witness. To your motives and actions.'

'Yeah, well, Renner thinks everything I did with her was part of my plan. You know, being the Good Samaritan and all.'

'That's just his view of it. In a court of law there are always two sides.'

'A court of law? This can't go to—'

'Relax, Henry. I'm just saying that Renner knows that for every piece of supposed evidence that he puts forward, we will have the same opportunity to put forward our side and our view of that evidence. The DA will know that, too.'

'All right. Did you find out from anybody over there what Lucy told him?'

'I know a supervisor in the squad. He told me they haven't found her. They've talked by phone but she hasn't come in. She won't come in.'

Pierce was about to tell her that he had Cody Zeller looking for Lucy when there was a sharp knock on his door and it opened before he could react. Charlie Condon stuck his head in. He was smiling, until he saw Pierce's face.

'Jesus Christ!'

'Who is that?' Langwiser asked.

'My partner. I have to go. Let me know what you hear.'

'When I hear it. Good-bye, Henry.'

Pierce hung up and looked up at Condon's stricken face. He smiled.

'Actually, Jesus Christ is down the hall and to the left. I'm Henry Pierce.'

Condon smiled uneasily and Pierce casually turned over the printouts from the Zeller package. Condon came in and closed the door.

'Man, how do you feel? Are you all right?'

'I'll live.'

'You want to talk about it?'

'No.'

'Henry, I am really sorry I didn't get over to the hospital. But it's been crazy around here getting ready for Maurice.'

'Don't worry about it. So I take it we're still presenting tomorrow.'

Condon nodded.

'He's already in town and waiting on us. No delays. We go tomorrow or he goes – and takes his money with him. I talked to Larraby and Grooms and they said we're—'

'—ready to go. I know. I called them from the hospital. It's not Proteus that's the problem. That's not why I wanted to delay. It's my face. I look like I'm Frankenstein's cousin. And I'm not going to look much better tomorrow.'

'I told him you had a car accident. It's not going to matter what you look like. What matters is Proteus. He wants to see the project and we promised him a first look. Before we send in the patents. Look, Goddard's the type of guy who can write the check on the spot. We need to do this, Henry. Let's get it over with.'

Pierce raised his hands in surrender. Money was always the trump card.

'He's still going to ask a lot of questions when he sees my face.'

'Look,' Condon said. 'It's a dog and pony show. No big deal. You'll be done with him by lunch. If he asks questions, just tell him you went through the windshield and leave it at that. I mean, you haven't even told me what happened. Why should he be any different?'

Pierce saw the momentary look of hurt in his partner's eyes.

'Charlie, I'll tell you when the time is right. I just can't right now.'

'Yes, that's what partners are for, to tell things at the right time.'

'Look, I know I can't win this argument with you, all right? I admit I'm wrong. So let's just leave it alone for now.'

'Sure, Henry, whatever you want. What are you working on now?'

'Nothing. Just some bullshit paperwork.'

'Then you're ready for tomorrow?'

'I'm ready.'

Condon nodded.

'Either way we win,' he said. 'Either we take his money or we put in the patents, go to the press with Proteus and come January there will be a line like fucking *Star Wars* at ETS to talk to us.'

Pierce nodded. But he hated going to Las Vegas for the annual emerging-technologies symposium. It was the most crass clash between science and finance in the world. Full of charlatans and DARPA spies. But a necessary evil just the same. It was where they had first courted one of Maurice Goddard's front men ten months before.

'If we last until January,' Pierce said. 'We need money now.'

'Don't worry about that. My job's finding the money. I think I can come up with a few intermediary fish to hold us until we land another whale.'

Pierce nodded, feeling reassured by his partner. With the situation he was in, thinking forward even a month seemed ridiculous.

'Okay, Charlie.'

'But, hey, it's not going to matter. We're going to land Maurice, right?'

'Right.'

'Good. Then I'll let you get back to work. Tomorrow at nine?'

Pierce leaned back in his chair and groaned. His last protest on the timing.

'I'll be here.'

'Our fearless leader.'

'Yeah, right.'

Charlie knocked sharply on the inside of the door, perhaps some sort of signal of solidarity, and left. Pierce waited a moment and then got up and locked the door. He wanted no more interruptions.

He went back to the printouts. After the short report on Lilly Quinlan came a voluminous report on William Wentz, owner-operator of Entrepreneurial Concepts Unlimited. The report stated that Wentz sat at the top of a burgeoning empire of Internet sleaze, from escort services to porno sites. These sites, though directed from Los Angeles, were operating in twenty cities in fourteen states, and of course reachable by the Internet from around the world.

While the Internet companies Wentz operated might be viewed as sleazy by most, they were still legal. The Internet was a world of largely regulation-free commerce. As long as Wentz did not provide photos of underage models engaged in sex and slapped the proper disclaimers on his escort sites, he operated largely in the clear. If one of his escorts happened to be taken down in a prostitution sting, he could easily distance himself. His site clearly said in a prominent disclaimer that it did not promote prostitution or any sort of trade of sex for money or property. If an escort agreed to take money for sex, then that was her decision and her web page would immediately be eliminated from the site.

Pierce had already gotten a general rundown on Wentz's operations from Philip Glass, the private detective. But Zeller's report was far more detailed and a testimonial to the power and reach of the Internet. Zeller had uncovered Wentz's criminal past in the states of Florida and New York. Contained in the printout package were several more mug shots, these depicting Wentz and another man named Grady Allison, who was listed in California corporate records as the comptroller of ECU. Pierce remembered that Lucy LaPorte had mentioned him. He skipped past the photos and read Zeller's opening summary.

Wentz and Allison appear to be a team. They arrived from Florida within a month of each other six years ago. This after multiple arrests in Orlando probably made things tough for them there. According to intelligence files with the Florida Department of Law Enforcement (FDLE), these men operated a chain of strip joints on the Orange Blossom Trail in Orlando. This was before the Internet made selling sex, real or imagined, so much easier than putting naked chicks on a stage and selling blow jobs on the side. Allison was known as Grade A Allison in Florida because of his skill in recruiting top talent to the stages of the Orange Blossom Trail. Wentz and Allison's clubs were called 'No Strings Attached,' as in full nudity.

IMPORTANT NOTE: The FDLE box connects these guys to one Dominic Silva, 71, Winter Park, FL, who in turn is connected to traditional organized crime in New York and northern New Jersey. BE CAREFUL!

Their pedigree as mobsters didn't surprise Pierce. Not with the way Wentz had been so calculatingly cold and violent when he encountered him in person. What he did find to be an odd fit was the idea that Wentz, the man who could calmly wield a phone as a weapon and wore pointed boots for better bone crunching, could be the man behind a sophisticated Internet empire.

Pierce had seen Wentz in action. His first and lasting impression was that Wentz was muscle first and brains second. He seemed more the caretaker of the operation than the brains behind it.

Pierce thought of the aging mobster mentioned in Zeller's report. Dominic Silva of Winter Park, Florida. Was he the man? The intellect behind the muscle? Pierce intended to find out.

He went to the next page and found a summary listing Wentz's criminal record. Over a five-year period in Florida he had a variety of arrests for pandering and two arrests for something listed as felony GBI. There was also an arrest for manslaughter.

The summaries did not include final disposition of these cases. But reading them – arrest after arrest in five years – Pierce was puzzled as to why Wentz was not in prison.

More of the same questions came up when he went to the next page and reviewed the arrest summaries of Grady 'Grade A' Allison. He, too, seemed to have a recurring pandering pattern. He also topped Wentz in the GBI category with four arrests. He also had an arrest labeled 'sexbat-minor,' which Pierce interpreted to be a charge of having sex with a minor.

Pierce looked at the mug shots of Allison. According to the attendant information, he was forty-six years old, though the photos showed a man who might be older. He had gray-black hair greased back on his head. His ghostly pale face was accented by a nose that looked like it had been broken more than once.

He picked up the phone and called Janis Langwiser again. This time he did not have to wait as long for her to take the call.

'Couple quick questions,' he said. 'Do you know what pandering is, in the legal sense of the word?'

'It's a pimp charge. It means providing a woman for sex in exchange for money or goods. Why?'

'Wait a minute. What about felony GBI? What is GBI?'

'That doesn't sound like anything from the California penal code but usually GBI means "great bodily injury." It would be part of an assault charge.'

Pierce considered this. GBI, as in hitting someone in the face with a phone and then hanging him off a twelfth-story balcony.

'Why, Henry? Have you been talking to Renner?'

He hesitated. He realized he shouldn't have called her, because it might reveal that he was still pursuing the very thing she had told him to stay away from.

'No, nothing like that. I'm just looking at a background check on an employment application. Hard to figure out what all of this means sometimes.'

'Well, it doesn't sound like anybody you would want to have working for you.'

'I think you're right about that. Okay, thanks. Just go ahead and put this on my bill.'

'Don't worry about it.'

After hanging up, he looked at the last page in the report from Zeller. It listed all of the websites that he had been able to link Wentz and ECU to. The single-space listing took up the entire page. The sexual permutations and double entendres contained in the site names and addresses were almost laughable but somehow the sheer volume of it all made it more sickening. This was just one man's operations. It was staggering.

As his eyes scanned down the list they held on one entry – FetishCastle.net – and he realized he knew it. He had heard of it. It took him a few moments and then he remembered Lucy LaPorte telling him that she had first met Lilly Quinlan at a photo shoot for the FetishCastle site.

Swiveling his chair to face the computer, Pierce booted up and went online. In a few minutes he arrived at the FetishCastle home page. The primary image was of an Asian woman wearing black thigh-high boots and little else. She had her hands on her naked hips and had adopted a stern schoolteacher pose. The page promised subscribers that herein were thousands of downloadable fetish photos, streaming videos and links to other sites. All free – with a paid subscription, of course. The coded but easily decipherable list of subject matter contained within included dominants, submissives, switches, water sports, smothering and so on.

Pierce clicked on the JOIN button and jumped to a page with a menu offering several different subscription plans and the promise of immediate approval and access. The going rate was $29.95 a month, chargeable each month to a credit card of your choice. The menu was careful to note in large letters that the billing record would appear on all credit card statements as ECU Enterprises, which would of course be easier than FetishCastle to run by the wife or boss when the bill came in.

There was an introductory offer for $5.95, which allowed access to the site for five days. At the end of that period your credit card would not be charged further if you did not sign up for one of the monthly or yearly plans. This was a one-time offer per credit card.

Pierce pulled out his wallet and used his American Express card to sign up for the introductory offer. Within minutes he had a pass code and user name and he entered the site, coming to a subject tab page with a search window. He went to the window and typed in 'Robin' and hit ENTER. His search returned no hits. He got the same result with a search for 'Lilly' but then had success with 'girl-girl' after remembering that it was how Lucy had described the modeling session with Lilly.

He was connected to a page of thumbnail photos, six rows of six. At the bottom of the page was a prompt that would allow him to go to the next page of thirty-six photos or to skip ahead to any one of forty-eight other pages of girl-girl photos.

Pierce scanned the thumbnails on the first page. They were all photos containing two or more women, no men. The models were engaged in various sex acts and bondage scenes, always a dominant female and her subservient subject. Though the photos were small, he did not want to take the time to click on each and enlarge it. He opened a desk drawer and took out a magnifying glass. He leaned close to the monitor screen and looked for Lucy and Lilly, able to work his way quickly across the grid of photos.

On the fourth screen of thirty-six he came across a series of more than a dozen photos of Lucy and Lilly. In each photo Lilly played the dominant and Lucy the submissive, even though Lucy towered over the diminutive Lilly. Pierce enlarged one of the thumbnails and the photo took over the whole computer screen.

The set had an obviously painted backdrop of a stone castle wall. A dungeon wall, Pierce guessed. There was straw on the floor and candles burning on a nearby table. Lucy was naked and chained to the wall with handcuffs that looked shiny and new rather than medieval. Lilly, dressed in the apparently requisite black leather of a dominatrix, stood in front of her holding a candle, her wrist cocked just enough for the hot wax to drip onto Lucy's breasts. On Lucy's face was a look that Pierce thought was meant to convey agony and ecstasy at the same time. Rapture. On Lilly's face was a look of stern approval and pride.

'Oh, I'm sorry. I thought you were gone.'

Pierce turned to see Monica coming through the door. As his assistant she had the combination to his office door lock because Pierce was often in the lab and she might need access. She started to put a stack of mail down on his desk.

'You told me you were only going to be—'

She stopped when she saw the computer screen. Her mouth opened into a perfect circle. He reached to the screen and killed the monitor. He felt lucky that his face was discolored and scarred. It helped hide his embarrassment.

'Monica, look, I—'

'Is that her? The woman you had me impersonate?'

He nodded.

'I'm just trying to ... '

He didn't know how to explain what he was doing. He wasn't sure what he was doing. He felt even more stupid holding the magnifying glass.

'Dr. Pierce, I like my job here but I'm not sure I want to work directly for you anymore.'

'Monica, don't call me that. And don't start with the job stuff again.'

'Can I please transfer back to the pool?'

Pierce reached up to the monitor for his sunglasses and put them on. A few days ago he wanted to get rid of her, now he couldn't bring himself to look at her disapproving eyes.

'Monica, you can do whatever you want to do,' he said while staring at the blank computer screen. 'But I think you have the wrong idea about me.'

'Thank you. I'll talk to Charlie. And there's your mail.'

And she left, pulling the door closed behind her.

Pierce continued to turn slowly back and forth in his chair, staring at the empty screen through dark glasses. Soon the burn of humiliation dissipated and he started to feel anger. Anger at Monica for not understanding. At his predicament. And mostly at himself.

He reached over and pushed the button and the screen came alive. And there was the photo, Lucy and Lilly together. He studied the wax hardening on Lucy's skin, a frozen drip hanging off one pointed nipple. It had been a job for them, an appointment. They had never met before this captured moment.

He studied the look on each woman's face, the eye contact they shared, and he saw no hint of the act he knew it to be. It looked real in their faces and that was what stirred his own arousal. The castle and everything else was easily fake but not the faces. No, the faces told the viewer a different story. They told who was in control and who was manipulated, who was on top and who was on the bottom.

Pierce looked at the photo for a long time and then looked at every one of the photos in the series before shutting down the computer.

27

Pierce never made it home Wednesday night. Despite the confidence he had portrayed in his office with Charlie Condon, he still felt his days in the hospital had left him behind the curve in the lab. He was also put off by the idea of returning to his apartment, where he knew a bloody mess and cleanup awaited him. Instead, he spent the night in the basement at Amedeo Tech, reviewing the work conducted in his absence by Larraby and Grooms and running his own Proteus experiments. The success of the experiments temporarily energized him, as they always did. But fatigue finally overcame him in the pre-dawn hours and he went into the laser lab to sleep.

The laser lab, where the most delicate measurements were taken, had one-foot-thick concrete walls and was sheathed in copper on the outside and thick foam padding on the inside to eliminate the intrusion of outside vibrations and radio waves that could skew nanoreadings. It was known among the lab rats as the earthquake room because it was probably the safest spot in the building, maybe in all of Santa Monica. The bed-sized pieces of padding were attached to the walls with Velcro straps. It was a common occurrence for an overworked lab rat to go to the laser lab, pull down a pad and sleep on the floor, as long as the lab wasn't being used. In fact, the higher-ranking members of the lab team had specific pads labeled with their names, and over time the pads had taken on the contours of their users' bodies. When in place on the walls, the dented, misshapen pads gave the lab the appearance of having been the site of a tremendous brawl or wrestling match in which bodies had been hurled from wall to wall.

Pierce slept for two hours and woke up refreshed and ready for Maurice Goddard. The second-floor men's locker room had shower facilities and Pierce always kept spare clothes in his locker. They weren't necessarily laundry-fresh but they were fresher than the clothes he had spent the night in. He showered and dressed in blue jeans and a beige shirt with small drawings of sailfish on it. He knew Goddard and Condon and everyone else would be dressed to impress at the presentation but he didn't care. It was the scientist's option to avoid the trappings of the world outside the lab.

In the mirror he noticed that the stitch trails on his face were redder and more pronounced than the day before. He had rubbed his face repeatedly through the night, as the wounds burned and itched. Dr. Hansen had told him this would happen, that the wounds would itch as the skin mended. Hansen had given him a tube of cream to rub on the wounds to help prevent the irritation. But Pierce had left it behind at the apartment.

He leaned closer to the mirror and checked his eyes. The blood had almost completely cleared from the cornea of his left eye. The purple hemorrhage markings beneath each eye were giving way to yellow. He combed his hair back with his fingers and smiled. He decided the zippers gave his face unique character. He then grew embarrassed by his vanity and decided he was happy no one else had been in the locker room to see his fixation at the mirror.

By 9 a.m. he was back in the lab. Larraby and Grooms were there and the other techs were trickling in. There was an electricity in the lab. Everyone was catching the vibe and was excited about the presentation.

Brandon Larraby was a tall and thin researcher who liked the convention of wearing a white lab coat. He was the only one at Amedeo who did. Pierce thought it was a confidence thing: look like a real scientist and you shall do real science. It didn't matter to Pierce what Larraby or anyone else wore as long as they performed. And with Larraby there was no doubt that the immunologist had done so. Larraby was a few years older than Pierce and had come over from the pharmaceutical industry eighteen months before.

Sterling Grooms had been with Pierce and Amedeo Technologies the longest of any full-time employee. He had been Pierce's lab manager through three separate moves, starting at the old warehouse near the airport where Amedeo was born and Pierce had built the first lab completely by himself. Some nights after a long shift in the lab the two men would talk about those 'old days' with a nostalgic reverence. It didn't matter that the old days were less than ten years before. Grooms was just a couple years younger than Pierce. He had signed on after completing his post-doc at UCLA. Twice Grooms was wooed by competitors but Pierce had kept him by giving him points in the company, a seat on the company's board of directors and a piece of the patents.

At 9:20 the word came from Charlie Condon's assistant: Maurice Goddard had arrived. The dog and pony show was about to begin. Pierce hung up the lab phone and looked at Grooms and Larraby.

'Elvis is in the building,' he said. 'Are we ready?'

Both men nodded to him and he nodded back.

'Then let's smash that fly.'

It was a line from a movie that Pierce had liked. He smiled. Cody Zeller would have gotten it but it drew blanks from Grooms and Larraby.

'Never mind. I'll go get them.'

Pierce went through the mantrap and took the elevator up to the administration level. They were in the boardroom. Condon, Goddard and

Goddard's second, a woman named Justine Bechy, whom Charlie privately referred to as Just Bitchy. She was a lawyer who ran interference for Goddard and protected the gates to his investment riches with a lumbering zeal not unlike a 350-pound football lineman protecting his quarterback. Jacob Kaz, the patent attorney, was also seated at the large, long table. Clyde Vernon stood off to the side, an apparent show of security at the ready if needed.

Goddard was saying something about the patent applications when Pierce walked in, announcing his presence with a loud hello which ended conversation and drew their eyes and then their reactions to his damaged face.

'Oh, my gosh,' exclaimed Bechy. 'Oh, Henry!'

Goddard said nothing. He just stared and had what Pierce thought was a small, bemused smile on his face.

'Henry Pierce,' Condon said. 'The man knows how to make an entrance.'

Pierce shook hands with Bechy, Goddard and Kaz and pulled out a chair across the wide, polished table from the visitors. He touched Charlie on the expensively suited arm and looked over at Vernon and nodded. Vernon nodded back but it seemed to cost him something to do so. Pierce just didn't get the guy.

'Thank you so much for seeing us today, Henry,' Bechy said in a tone that suggested he had volunteered to keep the meeting set as scheduled. 'We had no idea your injuries were so serious.'

'Well, it's no problem. And it looks worse than it is. I've been back in the lab and working since yesterday. Though I'm not sure this face and the lab go together too well.'

No one seemed to get his awkward Frankenstein reference. Another swing and a miss for Pierce.

'Good,' Bechy said.

'It was a car accident, we were told,' Goddard said, his first words since Pierce's arrival.

Goddard was in his early fifties with all of his hair and the sharp eyes of a bird that had amassed a quarter billion worms in his day. He wore a crème-colored suit, white shirt and yellow tie and Pierce saw the matching hat on the table next to him. It had been remarked in the office after his first visit that Goddard had adopted the visual persona of the writer Tom Wolfe. The only thing missing was the cane.

'Yes,' Pierce said. 'I hit a wall.'

'When did this happen? Where?'

'Sunday afternoon. Here in Santa Monica.'

Pierce needed to change the subject. He was uncomfortable skirting the truth and he knew Goddard's questioning wasn't casual or concerned conversation. The bird was thinking about ponying up 18 million worms.

His questions were part of the due diligence process. He was finding out what he was possibly getting into.

'Had you been drinking?' Goddard asked bluntly.

Pierce smiled and shook his head.

'No. I wasn't even driving. But I don't drink and drive anyway, Maurice, if that's what you mean.'

'Well, I am glad you are okay. If you get a chance, could you get me a copy of the accident report? For our records, you understand.'

There was a short silence.

'I'm not sure I do. It had nothing to do with Amedeo and what we do here.'

'I understand that. But let's be frank here, Henry. You *are* Amedeo Technologies. It is your creative genius that drives this company. I've met a lot of creative geniuses in my time. Some I would put my last dollar behind. Some I wouldn't give a buck to if I had a hundred.'

He stopped there. And Bechy took over. She was twenty years younger than Goddard, had short dark hair, fair skin and a manner that exuded confidence and one-upsmanship. Even still, Pierce and Condon had agreed previously that she held the position because they believed she had a relationship with the married Goddard that went beyond business.

'What Maurice is saying is that he is considering a sizeable investment in Amedeo Technologies,' she said. 'To be comfortable doing that, he needs to be comfortable with you. He has to know you. He doesn't want to invest in someone who might be a risk taker, who might be reckless with his investment.'

'I thought it was about the science. The project.'

'It is, Henry,' she said. 'But they go hand in hand. The science is no good without the scientist. We want you to be dedicated and obsessed with the science and your projects. But not reckless with your life outside the lab.'

Pierce held her eyes for a long moment. He suddenly wondered if she knew the truth about what happened and about his obsessive investigation of Lilly Quinlan's disappearance.

Condon cleared his throat and cut in, trying to move the meeting forward.

'Justine, Maurice, I am sure that Henry would be happy to cooperate with any kind of personal investigation you would like to conduct. I've known him for a long time and I've worked in the ET field for even longer. He is one of the most levelheaded and focused researchers I've ever come across. That is why I am here. I like the science, I like the project and I'm very comfortable with the man.'

Bechy broke away from Pierce to look at Condon and nod her approval.

'We may take you up on that offer,' she said through a tight smile.

The exchange did little to erode the tension that had quickly enveloped the room. Pierce waited for somebody to say something but there was only silence.

'Um, there's something I should probably tell you then,' he finally said. 'Because you'll find out anyway.'

'Then just tell us,' Bechy said. 'And save us all the time.'

Pierce could almost feel Charlie Condon's muscles seize up under his thousand-dollar suit as he waited for the revelation he knew nothing about.

'Well, the thing is ... I used to have a ponytail. Is that going to be a problem?'

At first the silence prevailed again but then Goddard's stone face cracked into a smile and then laughter came from his mouth. It was followed by Bechy's smile and then everybody was laughing, including Pierce, even though it hurt to do so. The tension was broken. Charlie balled a fist and knocked on the table in an apparent attempt to accentuate the mirth. The response far exceeded the humor in the comment.

'Okay, then,' Condon said. 'You people came to see a show. How about we go down to the lab and see the project that is going to win this comedian here a Nobel Prize?'

He put his hands on the front and back of Pierce's neck and acted as though he were strangling him. Pierce lost his smile and felt his face getting red. Not because of Condon's mock strangulation, but because of the quip about the Nobel. Pierce thought it was uncool to trivialize so serious an honor. Besides, he knew it would never happen. It would never be awarded to the operator of a private lab. The politics were against it.

'One thing before we go downstairs,' Pierce said. 'Jacob, did you bring the nondisclosure forms?'

'Oh, yes, right here,' the lawyer said. 'I almost forgot.'

He pulled his briefcase up from the floor and opened it on the table.

'Is this really necessary?' Condon asked.

It was all part of the choreography. Pierce had insisted that Goddard and Bechy sign nondisclosure forms before entering the lab and viewing the presentation. Condon had disagreed, concerned that it might be insulting to an investor of Goddard's caliber. But Pierce didn't care and would not step back. His lab, his rules. So they settled on a plan in which it would appear to be an annoying routine.

'It's lab policy,' Pierce said. 'I don't think we should deviate. Justine was just talking about how important it is to avoid risks. If we don't—'

'I think it is a perfectly good idea,' Goddard said, interrupting. 'In fact, I would have been concerned if you had not taken such a step.'

Kaz slid two copies of the two-page document across the table to Goddard and Bechy. He took a pen out of his inside suit pocket, twisted it and placed it on the table in front of them.

'It's a pretty standard form,' he said. 'Basically, any and all proprietary processes, procedures and formulas in the lab are protected. Anything you see and hear during your visit must be held in strict confidence.'

Goddard didn't bother reading the document. He left that to Bechy, who took a good five minutes to read it twice. They watched in silence and at the end of her review she silently picked up the pen and signed it. She then gave the pen to Goddard, who signed the form in front of him.

Kaz collected the documents and put them in his briefcase. They all got up from the table then and headed toward the door. Pierce let the others go first. In the hallway as they approached the elevator, Jacob Kaz tapped him on the arm and they delayed for a moment behind the others.

'Everything go okay with Janis?' Kaz whispered.

'Who?'

'Janis Langwiser. Did she call you?'

'Oh. Yeah, she called. Everything's fine. Thank you, Jacob, for the introduction. She seems very capable.'

'Anything else I can do?'

'No. Everything is fine. Thank you.'

The lab elevator opened and they moved toward it.

'Down the rabbit hole, eh, Henry?' Goddard said.

'You got that right,' Pierce replied.

Pierce looked back and saw that Vernon had also held back in the hallway and had apparently been standing right behind Pierce and Kaz as they had spoken privately. This annoyed Pierce but he said nothing about it. Vernon was the last one into the elevator. He put his scramble card into the slot on the control panel and pushed the B button.

'B is for basement,' Condon told the visitors once the door closed. 'If we put L in there for lab, people might think it meant lobby.'

He laughed but no one joined him. It was a nice piece of worthless information he had imparted. But it told Pierce how nervous Condon was about the presentation. For some reason this made Henry smile ever so slightly, not enough to hurt. Condon might lack confidence in the presentation but Pierce certainly didn't. As the elevator descended he felt his energy diametrically rise. He felt his posture straighten and even his vision brighten. The lab was his domain. His stage. The outside world might be dark and in shambles. War and waste. A Hieronymus Bosch painting of chaos. Women selling their bodies to strangers who would take them and hide them, hurt and even kill them. But not in the lab. In the lab there was peace. There was order. And Pierce set that order. It was his world.

He had no doubts about the science or himself in the lab. He knew that in the next hour he would change Maurice Goddard's view of the world. And he would make him a believer. He would believe that his money was not going to be invested so much as it was going to be used to change the world. And he would give it gladly. He would take out his pen and say, Where do I sign, please tell me where to sign.

28

They stood in the lab in a tight semicircle in front of Pierce and Larraby. It was close quarters with the five visitors plus the usual lab crew trying to work. Introductions had already been made and the quick tour of the individual labs given. Now it was time for the show and Pierce was ready. He felt at ease. He never considered himself much of a public speaker but it was a lot easier to talk about the project in the comfort of the lab in which it was born than in a theater at an emerging-technologies symposium or on a college campus.

'I think you are familiar with what has been the main emphasis of the lab work here for the last several years,' he said. 'We talked about that on your first visit. Today we want to talk about a specific offshoot project. Proteus. It is something sort of new in the last year but it is certainly born of the other work. In this world all the research is inter-related, you could say. One idea leads to another. Sort of like dominoes banging into each other. It's a chain reaction. Proteus is part of that chain.'

He described his long-running fascination with the potential medical/biological applications of nanotechnology and his decision almost two years earlier to bring Brandon Larraby on board to be Amedeo's point man on the biological issues of this pursuit.

'Every article you read in every magazine and science journal talks about the biological side of this. It's always the hot point topic. From the elimination of chemical imbalances to possible cures for blood-carried diseases. Well, Proteus does not actually do any of these things. Those things and that day are still a long way off. Not science fiction anymore but still in the distance. Instead, what Proteus is, is a delivery system. It is the battery pack that will allow those future designs and devices to work inside the body. What we have done here is create a formula that will allow cells in the bloodstream to produce the electric impulses that will drive those future inventions.'

'It's really a chicken-and-egg question,' Larraby added. 'What comes first? We decided that the energy source must come first. You build from the bottom up. You start with the engine and to it you add the devices, whatever they might be.'

He stopped and there was silence. This was always expected when a scientist attempted to build a word bridge to the non-scientist. Condon then jumped in, as he had been choreographed to do. He would be the bridge, the interpreter.

'What you are saying is that this formula, this energy source, is the platform which all of this other research and invention will rely upon. Correct?'

'Correct,' Pierce said. 'Once this is established in the science journals and through symposiums and so forth, it will act to foster further research and invention. It will excite the research field. Scientists will now be more attracted to this field because this gateway problem has been solved. We are going to show the way. On Monday morning we will be seeking patent protection for this formula. We will publish our findings soon after. And we will then license it to those who are pursuing this branch of research.'

'To the people who invent and build these bloodstream devices.'

It was Goddard and he had said it as a statement, not a question. It was a good sign. He was joining in. He was getting excited himself.

'Exactly,' Pierce said. 'If you can supply the power, you can do a lot of things. A car without an engine is going nowhere. Well, this is the engine. And it will take a researcher in this field anywhere he wants to go.'

'For example,' Larraby said, 'in this country alone, more than one million people rely on self-administered insulin injections to control diabetes. In fact, I am one of them. It is conceivable in the not too distant future that a cellular device could be built, programmed and placed in the bloodstream and that this device would measure insulin levels and manufacture and release that amount which is needed.'

'Tell them about anthrax,' Condon said.

'Anthrax,' Pierce said. 'We all know from events of the last year how deadly a form of bacteria this is and how difficult it can be to detect when airborne. What this research field is heading toward is a day when, say, all postal employees or maybe members of our armed forces or maybe just all of us will have an implanted biochip that can detect and attack something like anthrax before it is allowed to cultivate and spread in the body.'

'You see,' Larraby said, 'the possibilities are limitless. As I said, the science will be there soon. But how do you power these devices in the body? That's been the bottleneck to the research. It's been a question that has been out there for a long time.'

'And we think the answer is our recipe,' Pierce said. 'Our formula.'

Silence again. He looked at Goddard and knew he had him. The saying is, don't shoot until you see the whites of their eyes. Pierce could see the whites now. Goddard had probably been in the right place at the right time and gotten in on a lot of good things over the years. But nothing like this. Nothing that could make him money down the line – plenty of it – and also make him a hero. Make him feel good about taking that money.

'Can we see the demonstration now?' Bechy asked.

'Absolutely,' Pierce said. 'We have it set up on the SEM.'

He led the group to what they called the imaging lab. It was a room about the size of a bedroom and contained a computerized microscope that was built to the dimensions of an office desk with a twenty-inch viewing monitor on top.

'This is a scanning electron microscope,' Pierce said. 'The experiments we deal with are too small to be seen with most microscopes. So what we do is set up a predetermined reaction with which we can test our project. We put the experiment in the SEM's vault and the results are magnified and viewed on the screen.'

He pointed to the boxlike structure located on a pedestal next to the monitor. He opened a door to the box and removed a tray on which a silicon wafer was displayed.

'I'm not going to get into specifically naming the proteins we are using in the formula but in basic terms what we have on the wafer are human cells and to them we add a combination of certain proteins which bind with the cells. That binding process creates the energy conversion we are talking about. A release of energy that can be harnessed by the molecular devices we were talking about earlier. To test for this conversion, we place the whole experiment in a chemical solution that is sensitive to this electric impulse and responds to it by glowing. Emitting light.'

While Pierce put the experiment tray back in the vault and closed it, Larraby continued the explanation of the process.

'The process converts electrical energy into a biomolecule called ATP, which is the body's energy source. Once created, ATP reacts with leucine – the same molecule that makes fireflies glow. This is called a chemiluminescent process.'

Pierce thought Larraby was getting too technical. He didn't want to lose the audience. He gestured Larraby to the seat in front of the monitor and the immunologist sat down and began working the keyboard. The monitor's screen was black.

'Brandon is now putting the elements together,' Pierce said. 'If you watch the monitor, the results should be pretty quick and pretty obvious.'

He stepped back and ushered Goddard and Bechy forward so they would be able to look over Larraby's shoulders at the monitor. He moved to the back of the room.

'Lights.'

The overheads went off, leaving Pierce happy that his voice had returned enough to normal to fall within the audio receptor's parameters. The blackness was complete in the windowless lab, save for a dull glow from the gray-black screen of the monitor. It was not enough light for Pierce to watch the other faces in the room. He put his hand on the wall and traced it to the hook on which hung a set of heat resonance goggles. He unhooked them and pulled them over his head. He reached to the battery pack on the left side and turned the device on. But then he flipped the lenses up, not ready to use them. He had put the goggles on the hook that morning. They were used in the laser lab but he had wanted them here in imaging because it would allow him to secretly watch Goddard and Bechy and gauge their reactions.

'Okay, here we go,' Larraby said. 'Watch the monitor.'

The screen remained gray-black for almost thirty seconds and then a few pinpoints of light appeared like stars through a cloudy night sky. Then more, and then more, and then the screen looked like the Milky Way.

Everyone was silent. They just watched.

'Go to thermal, Brandon,' Pierce finally said.

Part of the choreography. End with a crescendo. Larraby worked the keyboard, so adept that he did not need any light to see the commands he was typing.

'Going thermal means we'll see colors,' Larraby said. 'Gradations in impulse intensity, from blue on the low end to green, yellow, red and then purple on the high end.'

The monitor screen came alive with waves of color. Yellows and reds mostly, but enough purple to be impressive. The color rippled in a chain reaction across the screen. It undulated like the surface of the ocean at night. It was the Las Vegas strip from thirty thousand feet.

'Aurora borealis,' someone whispered.

Pierce thought it might have been Goddard's voice. He flipped down the lenses and now he was seeing colors, too. Everyone in the room glowed red and yellow in the vision field of the goggles. He focused in on Goddard's face. The gradations of color allowed him to see in the dark. Goddard was intently focused on the computer screen. His mouth was open. His forehead and cheeks were deep red – maroon going to purple – as his face heated with excitement.

The goggles were a form of scientific voyeurism, allowing him to see what people thought they were hiding. He saw Goddard's face break into a wide red smile as he viewed the monitor. And in that moment Pierce knew the deal was done. They had the money, they had secured their future. He looked across the darkened room and saw Charlie Condon leaning against the opposite wall. Charlie was looking back at him, though he didn't have on any goggles. He looked out into the darkness toward where he knew Pierce would be standing. He nodded once, knowing the same thing without needing the goggles.

It was a moment to savor. They were on their way to becoming rich and possibly even famous men. But that wasn't the thing for Pierce. It was something else, something better than money. Something he couldn't put in his pocket but he could put in his head and his heart and it would earn interest measured in pride at staggering rates.

That's what the science gave him. Pride that overcame everything, that took back redemption for everything that had ever gone bad, for every wrong turn he had ever made.

Most of all, for Isabelle.

He slipped off the goggles and hung them back on the hook.

'Aurora borealis,' Pierce whispered quietly to himself.

29

They ran two more experiments on the SEM using new wafers. Both lit up the screen like Christmas and Goddard was satisfied. Pierce then had Grooms go over the other lab projects with him once more just to finish things off. After all, Goddard would be investing in the whole program, not just Proteus. At 12:30 the presentation ended and they broke for lunch in the boardroom. Condon had arranged for the meal to be catered by Joe's, a restaurant on Abbot Kinney that had the rare combination of being a hot place and also having good food.

The conversation was convivial – even Bechy seemed to be enjoying herself. There was a lot of talk about the possibilities of the science. No talk about the money that could be made from it. And at one point Goddard turned to Pierce, who was sitting next to him, and quietly confided, 'I have a daughter with Down's syndrome.'

He said nothing else and didn't have to. Pierce knew he was simply thinking about the timing. The bad timing. A future was coming when such maladies might be eliminated before they occurred.

'But I bet you love her very much,' Pierce said. 'And I bet she knows that.'

Goddard held his eyes for a moment before answering.

'Yes. I do and she does. I often think about her when I make my investments.'

Pierce nodded.

'You have to make sure she is secure.'

'No, not that. She is secure, many times over. What I think about is that no matter how much I make in this world, I won't be able to change her. I won't be able to fix her . . . I guess what I am saying is that . . . the future is out there. This . . . what you are doing . . . '

He looked away, unable to put his thoughts into words.

'I think I know what you mean,' Pierce said.

The quiet moment ended abruptly with a loud outburst of laughter from Bechy, who was sitting across the table and next to Condon. Goddard smiled and nodded as though he had heard whatever it was that had been so funny.

Later, during a dessert of key lime pie, Goddard brought up Nicole.

'You know who I miss?' he said. 'Nicole James. Where is she today? I'd like to at least say hello.'

Pierce and Condon looked at each other. It had been agreed earlier that Charlie would handle any explanations in regard to Nicole.

'Unfortunately, she is no longer with us,' Condon said. 'In fact, last Friday was her last day at Amedeo.'

'Really now? Where did she go?'

'Nowhere at the moment. I think she's just taking some time to think about her next move. But she signed a no-compete contract with us, so we don't have to worry about her showing up at a competitor.'

Goddard frowned and nodded.

'A very sensitive position,' he said.

'It is but it isn't,' Condon replied. 'She was focused outward not inward. She knew just enough about our projects to know what to look for in regard to our competitors. For example, she did not have lab access and she never saw the demonstration you saw this morning.'

That was a lie, only Charlie Condon didn't know it. Just like the lie Pierce had fed Clyde Vernon about how much Nicole knew and had seen. The truth was she had seen it all. Pierce had brought her into the lab on a Sunday night to show her, to light up the SEM screen like the aurora borealis. It was when things were falling apart and he was desperately grasping for a way to keep it together, to hold on to her. He had broken his own rules and taken her to the lab to show her what it was that had drawn him away from her so often. But even showing her the discovery had not worked to stop the momentum of destruction that had enveloped them. Less than a month later Nicole ended the relationship.

Like Goddard, Pierce missed Nicole at that moment, but for different reasons. He grew quiet during the remainder of the meal. Coffee was served and then removed. The plates and utensils were cleared away until all that was left was the polished surface of the table and the reflection of their ghostly images in it.

The caterers cleared out of the room and it was time to get back to business.

'Tell us about the patent,' Bechy said, folding her arms and leaning over the table.

Pierce nodded to Kaz and he took the question.

'It's actually a stepped patent. It's in nine parts, covering all processes related to what you saw today. We think we have thoroughly covered everything. We think it will hold up to any kind of challenge, now or in the future.'

'And when do you go with it?'

'Monday morning. I'll be flying out to Washington tomorrow or

Saturday. The plan is to personally deliver the application to the U.S. Patents and Trademark Office at nine a.m. Monday.'

Since Goddard was sitting next to him, Pierce found it easier and more nonchalant to watch Bechy across from him. She seemed surprised by the speed with which they were moving. This was good. Pierce and Condon wanted to force the issue. Force Goddard to make his move now, or risk losing out by waiting.

'As you know, it's a highly competitive science,' Pierce said. 'We want to make sure we get our formula on the books first. Brandon and I have also completed a paper on this and will be submitting it. We'll send it out tomorrow.'

Pierce raised his wrist and checked his watch. It was almost two.

'In fact,' he said, 'I need to leave you and get back to work now. If anything further comes up that Charlie can't answer, you can reach me in my office or in the lab. If there is no answer down there, that means we have the phone cut off because we're using one of the probes.'

He pushed back his chair and was getting up when Goddard raised his hand and grabbed his upper arm to stop him.

'One moment, Henry, if you don't mind.'

Pierce sat back down. Goddard looked at him and then deliberately cast his glance into every face at the table. Pierce knew what was coming. He could feel it in the tightness of his chest.

'I just want to tell you while we're all here together that I want to invest in your company. I want to be part of this great thing you are doing.'

There was a raucous cheer and a round of clapping. Pierce put out his hand and Goddard shook it vigorously, then took Condon's hand that was stretched across the table.

'Nobody move,' Condon said.

He got up and went to a corner of the room where there was a phone on a small table. He punched in three numbers – an in-house call – and murmured something into the receiver. He then returned to his seat and a few minutes later Monica Purl and Condon's personal assistant, a woman named Holly Kannheiser, came into the boardroom carrying two bottles of Dom Pérignon and a tray of champagne glasses.

Condon popped the bottles and poured. The assistants were asked to stay and take a glass. But both also had throwaway cameras and had to take photos in between sips of champagne.

Condon made the first toast.

'To Maurice Goddard. We're happy to have you with us on this magical ride.'

Then it was Goddard's turn. He raised his glass and simply said, 'To the future!'

He looked at Pierce as he said it. Pierce nodded and raised his almost empty glass. He looked at each face in the room, including Monica's, before speaking. He then said: 'Our buildings, to you, would seem terribly small. But to us, who aren't big, they are wonderfully tall.'

He finished his glass and looked at the others. Nobody seemed to get it.

'It's from a children's book,' he explained. 'Dr. Seuss. It's about believing in the possibilities of other worlds. Worlds the size of a speck of dust.'

'Hear, hear,' Condon said, raising his glass again.

Pierce began moving about the room, shaking hands and sharing words of thanks and encouragement. When he came to Monica she lost her smile and seemed to treat him coldly.

'Thanks for sticking it out, Monica. Did you talk to Charlie yet about your transfer?'

'Not yet. But I will.'

'Okay.'

'Did Mr. Renner call?'

He purposely didn't use the word *detective* in case someone in the room was listening to their conversation.

'Not yet.'

He nodded. He couldn't think of what else to say.

'There are some messages for you on your desk,' she told him. 'One of them, the lawyer, said it was important but I told her I couldn't interrupt your presentation.'

'Okay, thanks.'

As calmly as he could, Pierce went back to Goddard and told him he was being left in Condon's hands to work out the investment deal. He shook his hand again and then backed out of the boardroom and headed down the hallway to his office. He wanted to run but he kept a steady pace.

30

'Lights.'

Pierce slid in behind his desk and picked up the three message slips Monica had left for him. Two were from Janis Langwiser and were marked *urgent*. The message on both was simply 'Please call ASAP.' The other message was from Cody Zeller.

Pierce put the messages back down on his desk and considered them. He didn't see how Langwiser's call could be anything other than bad news. To come from the high of the boardroom to this was almost staggering. He felt himself getting overheated, even claustrophobic. He went over to the window and cranked it open.

He decided to call Zeller back first, thinking that maybe his friend had come up with something new. His page to Zeller was returned in less than a minute.

'Sorry, dude,' Zeller said by way of greeting. 'No can do.'

'What do you mean?'

'On Lucy LaPorte. I can't find her. I got no trace, man. This chick doesn't even have cable.'

'Oh.'

'You're sure that's her legal name?'

'That's what she told me.'

'Is she one of the girls from the website?'

'Yeah.'

'Shit, you should have told me that, dude. They don't use their real names.'

'Lilly Quinlan did.'

'Well, Lucy LaPorte? That sounds like a name somebody dreamed up after watching *A Streetcar Named Desire*. I mean, look at what she does. The chances of her telling the truth about something, even her own name, are probably one in—'

'It was the truth. It was an intimate moment and she told me the truth. I know it.'

'An intimate moment. I thought you told me you didn't—'

'I didn't. It was on the phone. When she told me.'

'Oh, well, phone sex is a whole other ballgame.'

'Never mind, Cody. I have to go.'

'Hey, wait a minute. How'd your thing go with the big money man today?'

'It went fine. Charlie's ringing him up right now.'

'Cool.'

'I have to go, Cody. Thanks for trying on that.'

'Don't worry. I'll be billing you.'

Pierce clicked off and picked up one of the messages from Langwiser. He punched in the number on the phone. A secretary answered and his call was put right through.

'Where have you been?' she began. 'I told your assistant to get the message to you right away.'

'She did what she's supposed to do. I don't like to be interrupted in the lab. What's going on?'

'Well, suffice it to say your attorney is pretty well plugged in. I still have my sources in the police department.'

'And?'

'What I am telling you is highly confidential. It's information I shouldn't have. If it got out, there would be an investigation just on this alone.'

'Okay. What is it?'

'A source told me that Renner spent a good part of his morning at his desk today working on a search warrant application. He then took it to a judge.'

After the urgency of her messages and her warning, Pierce was underwhelmed.

'Okay. And what does that mean?'

'It means he wants to search your property. Your apartment, your car, probably the home where you lived before moving because that was likely your domicile when the crime occurred.'

'You mean the disappearance and supposed murder of Lilly Quinlan.'

'Exactly. But – and this is a big *but* – the application was rejected. The judge told him there wasn't enough. He hadn't presented enough evidence to justify the warrant.'

'So that's good then, right? Does that mean it's over?'

'No, he can go back in anytime he wants. Anytime he gets more. My guess is that he was relying on the tape recording – what he called your admission. So it is good to know that a judge saw through that and said it wasn't enough.'

Pierce contemplated all of this. He was out of his league, unsure what all of the legal maneuverings meant.

'He might now choose to do a little judge shopping,' Langwiser said.

'You mean like taking the application to a different judge?'

'Yes, somebody more accommodating. The thing is, he probably went to the softest sell he knew in the first place. Going somewhere else could cause problems. If a judge finds out a search app has already been rejected by a colleague, it could get testy.'

Trying to follow the legal nuances seemed like a waste of time. Pierce wasn't as unnerved about the news as Langwiser seemed to be. He understood that this was because she could never be completely sure he was innocent of the crime. That margin of doubt raised concerns about what the police would find if they searched his property.

'What if we let him search without a warrant?' he asked.

'No.'

'He wouldn't find anything. I did not do this, Janis. I never even met Lilly Quinlan.'

'It doesn't matter. We don't cooperate. You start cooperating, you start walking into traps.'

'I don't understand. If I'm innocent, what trap could there be?'

'Henry, you want me to advise you, right?'

'Yes.'

'Then listen and take my advice. We make no overtures to the other side. We have put Renner on notice and that is where we keep it.'

'Whatever.'

'Thank you.'

'Will you know if he goes judge shopping or re-applies to the original judge?'

'I have an ear out. We might get a heads up. Either way, you act surprised if he ever shows up with a warrant. I have to protect my source.'

'I will.'

Pierce suddenly thought of something and it put a dagger of fear in his chest.

'What about my office? And the lab? Will he want to search here?'

If that happened, it would be too hard to contain. The story would leak out and into the circles where emerging technologies are discussed. It would certainly get back to Goddard and Bechy.

'I don't know for sure but it would seem unlikely. He will be going for locations likely used in the commission of the crime. It would seem like he might have an even more difficult time if he goes in and tries to convince a judge to let him search a place of business where it was highly unlikely for the crime to have occurred.'

Pierce thought about the phone book he had hidden in the cabinet in the copy room. A direct connection to Lilly Quinlan he had not already acknowledged having. He had to get rid of it somehow.

He then thought of something else.

'You know,' he said, 'they already searched my car. I could tell when I got into it that night outside Lilly's place.'

There was a moment of silence before Langwiser spoke.

'If they did, then it was illegal. We'll never be able to prove it without a witness, though.'

'I didn't see anybody other than cops out there.'

'I'm sure it was just a flashlight search. Quick and dirty. If he gets a warrant approved, they'll do it legally and they'll do more than a once-over. They'll go for hair and fiber evidence, things like that. Things too small to have been seen with a flashlight.'

Pierce thought of the toast he had given less than a half hour before. He realized that a speck of dust might hold his future either way.

'Well, like I said, let them do it,' he said, a note of defiance in his voice. 'Maybe they'll start looking for the real killer once I come up clean.'

'Any ideas on that?'

'Nope.'

'Well, for now, you should worry about yourself. You don't seem to understand the gravity of this situation. With the search warrant, I mean. You think that just because they won't find anything that you're free and clear.'

'Look, Janis, I'm a chemist, not a lawyer. And all I know is that I'm in the middle of this thing but I didn't do it. If I don't understand the gravity of the situation, then tell me exactly what it is you want me to understand.'

It was the first time he had vented his frustration in her direction and he immediately regretted it.

'The reality is that a cop is on your tail and it is unlikely that he is going to be put off by this setback. To Renner, this is only temporary. He is a patient man and he will continue to work this thing until he finds or gets what he needs to get a search warrant signed. You understand?'

'Yes.'

'And then that's only the beginning. Renner is good at what he does. Most of the cops I know that are good are good because they are relentless.'

Pierce felt his body heat rising again. He didn't know what else to say, so he didn't say anything. A long moment of silence went by before Langwiser broke it.

'There's something else. On Saturday night you told them about Lilly Quinlan's home and gave them the address. Well, they went over there and checked it out but they did not formally search the place until Sunday afternoon after Renner got a search warrant. It wasn't clear whether she was dead or alive and it was obvious she was or had been engaged in a profession that likely involved prostitution and other illegalities.'

Pierce nodded. He was beginning to understand how Renner thought.

'So to protect himself, he went and got a warrant,' he said. 'In case they came across something in regard to these other illegal activities. Or if she turned up alive and said, What the hell are you doing in my place?'

'Exactly. But there was another reason as well.'

'To gather evidence against me.'

'Right again.'

'But how can it be evidence *against* me? I told him I went in there. My fingerprints are all over the place because I was looking for her and for what might have happened.'

'That's your story and I believe you. He doesn't. He believes it is a story you made up to cover the fact that you had been in her home.'

'I can't believe this.'

'You'd better. And under the law he had to file what is called a search warrant return within forty-eight hours. It basically is a receipt for anything that was taken by police in the search.'

'Did he?'

'Yes, he filed it and I got a copy. It wasn't sealed – he made a mistake on that. Anyway, it lists personal property that was taken, things like a hairbrush for DNA sampling, on and on. Many items were taken for fingerprint analysis. Pieces of mail, desk drawers, jewelry, perfume bottles, even sexual devices found in drawers.'

Pierce was silent. He remembered the perfume bottle he had picked up while in the house. Could such a simple thing now be used to help convict him? He felt his insides churning, his face felt flush.

'You're not saying anything, Henry.'

'I know. I'm just thinking.'

'Don't tell me you touched these sexual devices.'

Pierce shook his head.

'No, I didn't even see them. I did pick up a perfume bottle, though.'

He heard her exhale.

'What?'

'Why did you pick up a perfume bottle?'

'I don't know. I just did. It reminded me of something, I guess. Of someone. What is the big deal? How does picking up a bottle of perfume equate with murder?'

'It's part of a circumstantial net. You told the police you went into the house to check on her, to see if she was all right.'

'I told them that because that's what I did.'

'Well, did you tell them that you also were picking up her perfume bottles and sniffing them? Were you looking through her underwear drawer, too?'

Pierce didn't respond. He felt like he might throw up. He leaned down and pulled the trash can from under the desk and put it on the floor next to his chair.

'Henry, I'm acting like a prosecutor with you because I need you to see the perilous path you are on. Anything you say or do can be twisted. It can look one way to you and completely different to someone else.'

'Okay, okay. How long before they do the fingerprint stuff?'

'Probably a few days. Without a body, this case is probably not a priority to anyone other than Renner. I heard his own partner is working on other things, that they aren't seeing eye to eye on this and Renner's going it alone.'

'Is the partner your source?'

'I'm not talking to you about my source.'

They were both silent for a while. Pierce had nothing more to say but felt a sense of hope as long as he was connected to Langwiser.

'I'm putting together a list of people we can talk to,' she finally said.

'What do you mean?'

'A list of people associated in some way with the case and questions to ask them. You know, if we need to.'

'I get it.'

He knew she meant if he was arrested and charged. If he was brought to trial.

'So let me work on things for a little while,' Langwiser said. 'I'll call you back if anything else comes up.'

Pierce finally said good-bye and hung up. He then sat without moving in his chair as he thought about the information he had just been given. Renner was making his move. Even without a body. Pierce knew he had to call Nicole and somehow explain that the police believed he was a murderer and the likelihood was that they would be coming to search the home they had shared.

The thought of it sent another wave of sickness through him. He looked down at the trash can. He was about to get up to go get some water or a can of Coke when there was a knock on his door.

31

Charlie Condon poked his head into the office. He was beaming. His smile was as wide and hard as the concrete bed of the L.A. River.

'You did it, man. You fucking did it!'

Pierce swallowed and tried to separate himself from the feelings the phone call had left.

'We all did it,' he said. 'Where is Goddard?'

Condon stepped all the way in and closed the door. Pierce noticed he had loosened his tie after all the champagne.

'He's in my office, talking to his lawyer on the phone.'

'I thought Just Bitchy was his lawyer.'

'She's a lawyer but not a lawyer lawyer, if you know what I mean.'

Pierce was finding it difficult to listen to Condon because thoughts about the call from Langwiser kept intruding.

'You want to hear his opening offer?'

Pierce looked up at Condon and nodded.

'He wants to buy in for twenty over four years. He wants twelve points and he wants to be chairman of the board.'

Pierce forced the image of Renner out of his mind and concentrated on Condon's smiling face. The offer from Goddard was good. Not quite there, but good.

'That's not bad, Charlie.'

'Not bad? It's *great!*'

Condon sounded like Tony the Tiger, accenting the last word too loudly. He'd drunk too much champagne.

'Well, it's only an opener. It's got to get better.'

'I know. It will. I wanted to check with you on a couple things. First, the chair. Do you care about that?'

'Not if you don't.'

Condon was currently the chairman of the company's board of directors. But it wasn't a board with any real power, because Pierce still controlled the company. Condon held 10 percent, they had chipped out another 8 percent to prior investors – no one in the Maurice Goddard class – and employee compensation accounted for another 10. The rest – 72 percent of the company – still belonged to Pierce. So giving Goddard the chair of a largely ceremonial advisory board didn't seem to be giving away much of anything.

'I say give it to him, make him happy,' Condon said. 'Now, what about the points? If I can get him to go to twenty million over *three* years, will you give him the points?'

Pierce shook his head.

'No. The difference between ten and twelve points could end up being a couple hundred million dollars. I'm keeping the points. And if you get the twenty over three years, great. But he's got to give us a minimum of eighteen million over three, or send him back to New York.'

'It's a tall order.'

'Look, we've been over this. Our burn rate right now as we speak is three million a year. If we want to expand and keep ahead of the pack, we're going to need double that. Six million a year is the threshold. Go work it out.'

'You're only giving me the chair to work with.'

'No, I only gave you the invention of the decade to work with. Charlie, did you see that guy's eyes after we put the lights back on? He's not only hooked. He's gutted and already in the frying pan. You're only nailing down details now. So go close the deal and get the first check into escrow. No extra points and get the six a year. We need it to do the work. If he wants to ride with us, that's the price of the ticket.'

'Okay, I'll get it. But you ought to come do it yourself. You're a better closer than me.'

'Not likely.'

Condon left the room then and Pierce was alone with his thoughts again. Once more he reviewed everything Langwiser had told him. Renner was going to search his homes and car. Search the car again. Officially and legally this time. Probably to search for small evidence, evidence likely left behind during the transport of a body.

'Jesus,' he said out loud.

He decided to analyze his situation in the same way he would analyze an experiment in the lab. From the bottom up. Look at it one way and then turn it and look at it another way. Grind it to powder and then look at it under the glass.

Believe nothing about it at the start.

He got out his notebook and wrote down the key elements of his conversation with Langwiser on a fresh page.

Search: apartment
       Amalfi
       Car – second time – material evidence
       Office/Lab?

Search warrant return: fingerprints
Everywhere – perfume

He stared at the page but no answers and no new questions came to him. Finally, he tore the page out, crumpled it and threw it toward the trash can in the corner of the room. He missed.

He leaned back and closed his eyes. He knew he had to call Nicole to prepare her for the inevitable. The police would come and search through everything: hers, his, it didn't matter. Nicole was a very private person. The invasion would be hugely damaging to her and the explanation for it catastrophic to his hopes of reconciliation.

'Oh man,' he said as he got up.

He came around the desk and picked up the crumpled ball of paper. Rather than drop it into the trash can, he took it back with him to his seat. He opened the paper and tried to smooth it out on the desk.

'Believe nothing,' he said.

The words on the wrinkled page defied him. They meant nothing. In a sweeping move of his arm he grabbed the page and balled it in his hand again. He cocked his elbow, ready to make the basket on the retry, when he realized something. He brought his hand down and unwrapped the page again. He looked at one line he had written.

Car – second time – material evidence

Believe nothing. That meant not believing the police had searched the car the first time. A spark of energy exploded inside. He thought he might have something. What if the police had not searched his car? Then who had?

The next jump became obvious. How did he know the car had been searched at all? The truth was he didn't. He only knew one thing: someone had been inside his car while it had been parked in the alley. The dome light had been switched. But had the car actually been searched?

He realized that he had jumped the gun in assuming that the police – in the form of Renner – had searched his car. He actually had no proof or even any indication of this. He only knew one thing: someone had been in the car. This conclusion could support a variety of secondary assumptions. Police search was only one of them. A search by a second party was another. The idea that someone had entered the car to take something was also another.

And the idea that someone had entered the car to put something in it was yet another.

Pierce got up and quickly left his office. In the hallway he punched the elevator button but immediately decided not to wait. He charged into the stairwell and quickly took the steps to the first floor. He went through the lobby without acknowledging the security man and into the adjoining parking garage.

He started with the trunk of the BMW. He pulled up the lining, looked under the spare, opened the disc changer and the tool pouch. He noticed nothing added, nothing taken. He moved to the passenger compartment, spending nearly ten minutes conducting the same kind of search and inventory. Nothing added, nothing taken.

The engine compartment was last and quickest. Nothing added, nothing taken.

That left his backpack. He relocked the car and returned to the Amedeo building, choosing the stairs again over a wait for an elevator. As he passed by Monica's desk on his way back to his office he noticed her looking at him strangely.

'What?'

'Nothing. You're just acting ... weird.'

'It's not an act.'

He closed and locked his office door. The backpack was on his desk. Still standing, he grabbed it and started unzipping and looking through its many compartments. It had a cushioned storage section for a laptop computer, a divided section for paperwork and files, and three different zippered compartments for carrying smaller items such as pens and notebooks and cell phone or PDA.

Pierce found nothing out of order until he reached the front section, which contained a compartment within a compartment. It was a small zippered pouch big enough to hold a passport and possibly a fold of currency. It wasn't a secret compartment but it could easily be hidden behind a book or a folded newspaper while traveling. He opened the zipper and reached in.

His fingers touched what felt like a credit card. He thought maybe it was an old one, a card he had put in the pocket while traveling and then forgotten about. But when he pulled it out he was looking at a black plastic scramble card. There was a magnetic strip on one side. On the other side it had a company logo that said U-STORE-IT. Pierce was sure he had never seen it before. It was not his.

He put the card down on his desk and stared at it for a long moment. He knew that U-Store-It was a nationwide company that rented trucks and storage spaces in warehouses normally siding freeways. He could think of two U-Store-It locations visible from the 405 Freeway in L.A. alone.

A foreboding sense of dread fell over him. Whoever had been in his car on Saturday night had planted the scramble card in his backpack. Pierce knew he was in the middle of something he was not controlling. He was being used, set up for something he knew nothing about.

He tried to shake it off. He knew fear bred inertia and he could not afford to be standing still. He had to move. He had to do something.

He reached down to the cabinet beneath the computer monitor and pulled up the heavy Yellow Pages. He opened it and quickly found the pages offering listings and advertisements for self-storage facilities. U-Store-It had a half-page ad that listed eight different facilities in the Los Angeles area. Pierce started with the location closest to Santa Monica. He picked up the phone and called the U-Store-It location in Culver City. The call was answered by a young man's voice. Pierce envisioned Curt, the acne-scarred kid from All American Mail.

'This is going to sound strange,' Pierce said. 'But I think I rented a storage unit there but I can't remember. I know it was U-Store-It but now I can't remember which place it was I rented it at.'

'Name?'

The kid acted like it was a routine call and request.

'Henry Pierce.'

He heard the information tapped onto a keyboard.

'Nope, not here.'

'Does that connect with your other locations? Can you tell where – '

'No, just here. We're not connected. It's a franchise.'

Pierce did not see why that would disqualify a centrally connected computer network but didn't bother asking. He thanked the voice, hung up and called the next geographically closest franchise listed in the Yellow Pages.

He got a computer hit on his third call. The U-Store-It franchise in Van Nuys. The woman who answered his call told him he had rented a twelve-by-ten storage room at the Victory Boulevard facility six weeks earlier. She told him the room was climate-controlled, had electric power and was alarm-protected. He had twenty-four-hour-a-day access to it.

'What address do you have for me on your records?'

'I can't give that out, sir. If you want to give me your address, I can check it against the computer.'

Six weeks earlier Pierce had not even begun the apartment search that would eventually put him into the Sands. So he gave the Amalfi Drive address.

'That's it.'

Pierce said nothing. He stared at the black plastic card on the desk.

'What is the unit number?' he finally asked.

'I can only give you that if I see a photo ID, sir. Come in before six and show me your driver's license and I can remind you what space you have.'

'I don't understand. I thought you said I had twenty-four-hour service.'

'You do. But the office is only open nine till six.'

'Oh, okay.'

He tried to think of what else he should ask but he drew a blank. He thanked the woman and hung up.

He sat still, then slowly he picked up the scramble card and slid it into his shirt pocket. He put his hand on the phone again but didn't lift it.

Pierce knew he could call Langwiser but he didn't need her cool and calm professional manner, and he didn't want to hear her tell him to leave it alone. He knew he could call Nicole but that would only lead to raised voices and an argument. He knew he would get that anyway when he told her about the impending police search.

And he knew he could call Cody Zeller but didn't think he could take the sarcasm.

For a fleeting moment the thought of calling Lucy LaPorte entered his mind. He quickly dismissed the idea but not the thought of what it said about him. Here he was, in the most desperate situation of his life, and who could he call for help and advice?

The answer was no one. And the answer made him feel cold from the inside out.

32

With his sunglasses and hat on, Pierce entered the office at the U-Store-It in Van Nuys and went to the counter, his driver's license in his hand. A young woman in a green golf shirt and tan pants was sitting there reading a book called *Hell to Pay*. It seemed to be a struggle for her to take her eyes from it and bring them up to Pierce. When she did her chin dropped, as she was startled by the ugly stitch zipper that wandered down Pierce's nose from beneath his sunglasses.

She tried to quickly cover up like she hadn't noticed anything unusual.

'That's okay,' Pierce said. 'I'm getting that a lot.'

He slid his license across the counter.

'I called a little while ago about the storage space I rented. I can't remember the number.'

She picked up the license and looked at it and then back up at his face, studying it. Pierce took off his hat but not the sunglasses.

'It's me.'

'Sorry, I just had to be sure.'

She used her legs to kick backwards, rolling and spinning on her chair until she came to the computer that was on a table on the other side of the office.

The screen was too far away for Pierce to read. He watched her type in his name. In a few moments a data screen appeared and she started checking information from his driver's license against the screen. He knew his license still had the Amalfi Drive address, which she had earlier informed him was on the rental record for the storage unit.

Satisfied, she scrolled down and read something. Running her finger across the screen.

'Three three one,' she said.

She kicked off the opposite wall and came rolling and spinning back to the counter. She slapped the driver's license down on the surface and Pierce took it back.

'Just take the elevator up, right?'

'You remember the code?'

'No. Sorry. I guess I'm pretty useless today.'

'Four five four plus the last four digits of your license number.'

He nodded his thanks and started to turn from the counter. He looked back at her.

'Do I owe you any money?'

'Excuse me?'

'I can't remember how I paid for the unit. I was wondering if I have a bill coming.'

'Oh.'

She kicked her chair back across the floor to the computer. Pierce liked the way she did it. One smooth, turning move.

His information was still on the screen. She scrolled down and then said without looking back at him, 'No, you're fine. You paid six months up front in cash. You still have a while.'

'Okay. Great. Thank you.'

He stepped out of the office and over to the elevator area. After punching in the call code, he rode up to the third floor and stepped out into a deserted hallway as long as a football field with roll-down doors running along both sides. The walls were gray and the floor a matching linoleum that had been scuffed a million times by the black wheels of movers' dollies. He walked down the hall until he came to a roll-down door marked 331.

The door was a rusty brown color. There were no other markings on it but the numbers, painted in yellow with a stencil. To the right of the door was a scramble card reader with a glowing red light next to the reader. But at the bottom of the door was a hasp with a padlock holding the door secure. Pierce realized that the scramble card he had found in his backpack was only an alarm card. It would not open the door.

He pulled the U-Store-It card from his pocket and slid it through the reader. The light turned green – the unit's alarm was off. He then squatted down and took hold of the lock. He pulled it but it was secure. He couldn't open the door.

After a long moment of weighing his next move, he stood up and headed back toward the elevator. He decided he would go to the car and check the backpack again. The key to the padlock must be there. Why plant the scramble card and not the key? If it was not there, then he would return to the U-Store-It office. The woman behind the counter would surely have a lock cutter he could borrow after explaining he had forgotten his key.

In the parking lot Pierce raised his electronic key and unlocked his car. The moment he heard the snap of the locks disengaging he stopped in his tracks and looked down at his raised hand. A memory vision played through his mind. Wentz walking in front of him, moving down the hallway to his apartment door. Pierce reheard the sound of his keys in the little man's hands, the comment on the craftsmanship of the BMW.

One by one Pierce turned the keys on the ring, identifying them and the locks they corresponded to: apartment, garage, gym, Amalfi Drive front and back, office backup, desk, lab backup, computer room. He also had a key to the house he had grown up in, though it had long ago been passed from his family. He'd always kept it. It was a last connection to that time and place, to his sister. He realized he had a habit of keeping keys to places where he no longer lived.

He identified all keys on the ring but two. The strangers were stainless steel and small, not door locks. One was slightly larger than the other. Stamped on both along the circumference of the tab was the word MASTER.

His scalp seemed to draw tight on his skull as he looked at it. Instinctively he knew that one of the keys would open the lock on the storage room door.

Wentz. The little man was the one. He had slipped the keys on the ring as they had moved down the hall. Or maybe afterward, while Pierce had been dangled off the balcony. When he had returned from the hospital he had to be let into his apartment by building security. He found his keys on the living room floor. He knew Wentz had had plenty of time to slip the keys on the ring.

Pierce couldn't fathom it. Why? What was going on? Though he had no answers, he did know where he would find them – or begin to find them. He turned and headed back to the elevator.

Three minutes later Pierce slid the larger of the two stranger keys into the padlock at the bottom of the door to storage unit 331. He turned it and the lock snapped open with tooled precision. He pulled it out of the hasp and dropped it on the floor. He then gripped the door handle and began to raise it.

As the door rolled up it made a loud metallic screech that echoed right through Pierce and all the way down the hallway. The door banged loudly when it reached the top. Pierce stood with his arm raised, his hand still attached to the handle.

The space was twelve by ten and dark. But the corridor threw light in over his shoulder. Standing at center in the room was a large white box. There was a low humming sound coming from the room. Pierce stepped in and his eyes registered the white string of a pull cord for the overhead light. He pulled it and the room filled with light.

The white box was a freezer. A chest freezer with a top door that was held closed with a small padlock that Pierce knew he would be able to open with the second stranger key.

He didn't have to open the freezer to know what was in it but he opened it anyway. He felt compelled, possibly by a dream that it might be empty and that this was all part of an elaborate hoax. More likely it was simply because he knew he had to see with his own eyes, so that there would be no doubts and no going back.

He raised the second stranger key, the smaller one, and opened the padlock. He removed it and flipped up the latch. He then lifted the top of the freezer, the air lock breaking and the rubber seal making a *snik* sound as he raised it. He felt cold air puff out of the box and a damp, fetid smell invaded his nose.

With one arm he held the lid open. He looked down through the mist that was rising up out of the box like a ghost. And he saw the form of a body at the bottom of the freezer. A woman naked and crumpled in the fetal position, her neck a terrible mess of blood and damage. She lay on her right side. Blood was pooled and frozen black at the bottom of the freezer. White frost had crusted on her dark hair and upturned hip. Hair had fallen across her face but did not totally obscure it. He readily recognized the face. He had seen it only in photos but he recognized it.

It was Lilly Quinlan.

'Ah, Jesus . . .'

He said it quietly. Not in surprise but in horrible confirmation. He let go of the lid and it slammed closed with a heavy thump that was louder than he had expected. It scared him, but not enough to obscure the complete sense of dread that had engulfed him. He turned and slid down the front of the freezer until he was sitting on the floor, elbows on his knees, hands gathering the hair at the back of his head.

He closed his eyes and heard a rising pounding sound like someone running toward him down the hallway. He then realized it was internal, blood pounding in his ears as he grew light-headed. He thought he might pass out but realized he had to hold on and stay alert. *What if I pass out? What if I am found here?*

Pierce shook it off, reached for the top of the freezer and pulled himself up. He fought for his balance and to hold back the nausea creeping into his stomach. He pulled himself across the freezer and hugged it, putting his cheek down on the cold white top. He breathed in deeply and after a few moments it all passed and his mind was clear. He stood up straight and stepped back from the freezer. He studied it, listened to its quiet hum. He knew it was time for more AE work. Analyze and evaluate. When the unknown or unexpected came up in the lab you stopped and went into AE mode. What do you see? What do you know? What does it mean?

Pierce was standing there, looking at a freezer sitting in the middle of a storage room that he – according to the office records – had rented. The freezer contained the body of a woman he had never met before but for whose death he would certainly now be blamed.

What Pierce knew was that he had been carefully and convincingly set up. Wentz was behind it, or at least part of it. What he didn't know was why.

He decided not to be distracted by the why. Not yet. He needed more information to get to that. Instead, he decided on more AE. If he could disassemble the setup and study all the moving parts, then it might give him a chance at figuring out what – and who – was behind it.

Pacing in the small space in front of the freezer, he began with the things that had led him to discover the setup. The scramble card and the padlock keys. They had been hidden, or at least camouflaged. Had it been meant for him to find them? After stopping his pacing and contemplating this for a long moment, he decided no. It had been luck that he had noticed that his car had been entered. A plan of this magnitude and complication could not rely on such luck.

So he now concluded that he had an edge. He knew what he was not supposed to know. He knew about the body and the freezer and the storage unit. He knew the location of the trap before it had been sprung.

Next question. What if he had not found the scramble card and had not been led to the body? He considered this. Langwiser had warned him of an impending police search. Surely, Renner and his fellow searchers would leave no stone unturned. They would find the scramble card and be led to the storage space. They would check his key ring for keys to the padlocks and they would find the body. End of story. Pierce would be left to defend himself against a seemingly perfect frame.

He felt his scalp grow warm as he realized how narrowly he had escaped that – if only for the time being. And in the same moment he felt a full understanding of how complete and careful the setup had been. It was reliant on the police investigation. It relied on Renner making the moves he was making.

It also relied on Pierce. And as he came to understand this he felt the sweat start to bead in his hair. He grew hot beneath his shirt. He needed air-conditioning. The confusion and sorrow that had gripped him – maybe even the awe in which he viewed the careful plan – were now turning to anger, being forged into steel-point rage.

He now understood that the setup – his setup – had counted on his own moves. Every one of them. The setup was reliant on his own history and the likelihood of his moves based on that history. Like chemicals on a silicon wafer, elements that could be relied upon to act in a predictable manner, to bond in expected patterns.

He stepped forward and opened the freezer again. He had to. He needed to look again so the shock of it all would hit him in the face like cold water. He had to move. He had to act in an unpredictable pattern. He needed a plan and needed a clear head to come up with it.

The body obviously hadn't moved. Pierce held the top of the freezer open with one hand and clasped the other over his mouth. In her final repose Lilly Quinlan seemed tiny. Like a child. He tried to remember the height and weight dimensions she so dutifully advertised on her web page but it seemed so long since the day he first read it that he couldn't remember.

He shifted his own weight on his feet and the movement changed the light from overhead into the freezer. A glint from her hair caught his eye and he bent down into the box.

With his free hand Pierce attempted to pull back the hair from her face.

It was frozen and individual strands broke as he moved them. He uncovered her upturned ear and there attached to the lobe was an earring. A silver cup holding a drop of amber with a silver feather below. He turned his hand so that the amber caught more of the light leaking into the box. It was then that he could see it. A tiny bug of some kind frozen in the amber, long ago drawn to sweetness and sustenance but caught in one of nature's deadly traps.

Pierce thought about that bug's fate and knew what he had to do. He, too, had to hide her. Hide Lilly. Move her. Keep her from discovery. From Renner. From everyone.

A sigh escaped through his mouth as he considered this. The moment was surreal, even bizarre. He was contemplating how to hide a frozen body, how to hide it in such a way as to hold no immediate connection to him. It was a task fraught with impossibility.

He quickly closed and relocked the freezer, as if it were a measure that would stop its contents from ever coming out and haunting him.

But the simple action broke the inertia in his mind. He started thinking.

He knew he had to move the freezer. No choice. Renner was coming. It was possible that he would find the storage unit even without the clues of keys and scramble card. Whoever had set this up could just make an anonymous call. He could count on nothing. He had to move her. If Renner found the freezer, then everything ended. Amedeo Tech, Proteus, his life, everything. He would be a bug in amber after that.

Pierce leaned down and placed his hands on the front corners of the freezer. He applied pressure to see if it was movable. The freezer slid the last remaining six inches to the rear wall of the storage unit without much resistance. It had rollers. It was movable. The question now was, movable to where?

A quick fix was needed, something that at a minimum would work safely in the short run while he figured out a plan for the long run. He left the storage unit and moved quickly down the corridor, his eyes sweeping back and forth from door to door as he searched for an unlocked, unrented unit.

He passed by the elevator and was halfway down the other wing before he found a door with no lock through the hasp. The door was marked 307. The light on the card reader to the right of the door glowed neither green nor red. The alarm appeared to be inactive, probably left so until the unit was rented. Pierce reached down, flipped the hasp and pulled up the door. The space was dark. No alarm sounded. He found and flipped on the light switch and saw that the space was identical to the unit rented under his own name. He checked the rear wall and saw the electric socket.

He ran down the corridor back to unit 331. He moved behind the freezer and yanked out the plug. He heard the hum of the freezer's electric heart go silent. He threw the cord over the top of the appliance and then leaned his weight into it. The freezer rolled toward the hallway with relative ease. In a few seconds he had it out of the storage room and into the corridor.

The freezer's rollers were set in line, designed to make it convenient to move the appliance backwards and forward in tight spaces, and to provide access for service. Pierce had to bend down and put his full strength into pushing it into the turn into the hallway. The rollers scraped loudly on the floor. Once he had it pointed in the right direction, he pushed harder and got the heavy box moving with momentum. He wasn't quite halfway to unit 307 when he heard the sound of the elevator moving. He dropped into a crouch to put more power into his pushing. But it seemed that no matter how much strength he expended, he could not pick up speed. The rollers were small and not built for speed.

Pierce crossed in front of the elevator just as the humming from the shaft silenced. He turned his face away and kept pushing, listening for the door of one of the cars to open.

It didn't happen. The elevator had apparently stopped on another floor. He blew out his breath in relief and exhaustion. And just as he got to the open door of unit 307 the stairwell door at the end of the hallway nearest him banged open and a man stepped into the hallway. Pierce jumped and nearly cursed out loud.

The man, wearing painter's whites, his hair and skin flecked with white paint, approached. He seemed winded by his climb up the stairs.

'You the one holding up the elevator?' he asked good-naturedly.

'No,' Pierce said, too defensively. 'I've been up here.'

'Just asking. You need a hand with that?'

'No, I'm fine. I'm just . . .'

The painter ignored his response and came up next to Pierce. He put his hands on the back of the freezer and nodded toward the open door of the storage room.

'In there?'

'Yeah. Thanks.'

Together they pushed and the freezer moved quickly into the turn and then into the storage room.

'There,' the painter said, seemingly winded again. He then stuck out his right hand. 'Frank Aiello.'

Pierce shook his hand. Aiello's left hand went into the pocket of his shirt and came out with a business card. He handed it to Pierce.

'You need any work, give me a call.'

'Okay.'

The painter looked down at the freezer, seemingly noticing for the first time what it was he had helped move into the storage area.

'That thing's a bear. What do you have in there, a frozen body?'

Pierce faked a small guffaw and shook his head, keeping his chin down the whole time.

'Actually, it's empty. I'm just storing it.'

Aiello reached over and flicked the padlock on the freezer.

'Making sure nobody steals the air in there, huh?'

'No, I . . . it's just that with the way kids get into things, I've always kept it locked.'

'Probably a good idea.'

Pierce had turned and the light was on his face. The painter noticed the stitch zipper running down his nose.

'That looks like it hurt.'

Pierce nodded.

'It's a long story.'

'Not the kind I want to hear. Remember what I said.'

'What do you mean?'

'You need a painter, you call.'

'Oh. Yeah. I've got your card.'

He nodded and watched as Aiello walked out of the room, his footsteps moving down the hallway. Pierce thought about the comment about a body being in the freezer. Was it a lucky guess, or was Aiello not what he appeared to be?

Pierce heard a set of keys jangling out in the hallway and then the metallic snap of a lock. It was followed by the screeching of an overhead door being lifted. He guessed that Aiello might be getting equipment from his storage space. He waited and after a few minutes he heard the door being pulled down and closed. Soon the hum of the elevator followed. Aiello was going to take it down instead of the stairs.

As soon as he was sure he was alone on the floor again he plugged the freezer in and waited until he heard the compressor begin working.

He then pulled his shirt out of his pants and used the tail to wipe every surface on the freezer and electrical cord that he could have conceivably touched. When he was sure he had covered his tracks he backed out of the space and pulled the door down. He locked it with the padlock from the other unit and wiped the lock and door with his shirttail.

As he moved away from the unit and toward the elevator alcove a terrible guilt and fear swept over him. He knew that this was because he had been operating for the last half hour on instincts and adrenaline. He hadn't been thinking out his moves as much as just making them. Now the adrenaline tank's needle was on empty and there was nothing left but his thoughts to contend with.

He knew he was far from harm's way. Moving the freezer was like putting a Band-Aid on a bullet hole. He needed to know what was happening to him and why. He needed to come up with a plan that would save his life.

33

The immediate urge was to curl up on the floor in the same position as the body in the freezer, but Pierce knew that to collapse under the pressure of the moment would be to ensure his demise. He unlocked the door and went into his apartment, shaking with fear and anger and the true knowledge that he was the only one he could rely on to find his way out of this dark tunnel. He promised himself that he would rise up off the floor. And he would get up fighting.

As if to underscore this avowal, he balled a fist and took a swing at the five-day-old standing lamp Monica Purl had ordered and then positioned next to the couch. His punch sent it crashing into the wall, where its delicate beige shade collapsed and the bulb shattered. The lamp slid down the wall to the floor like a punch-drunk boxer.

'There, goddamnit!'

He sat down on the couch but then immediately stood up. All his pistons were firing. He had just moved and hidden a body – a murder victim. Somehow sitting down seemed like the least wise thing to do.

Yet he knew he had to. He had to sit down and look at this. He had to think like a scientist, not a detective. Detectives move on a linear plane. They move from clue to clue and then put together the picture. But sometimes the clues added up to the wrong picture.

Pierce was a scientist. He knew he had to go with what had always worked for him. He had to approach this the way he had approached and solved the question of the car search. From the bottom. Find the logic gateways, the places where the wires crossed. Take apart the frame and study the design, the architecture. Throw out linear thinking and approach the subject from all new angles. Look at the subject matter and then turn it and look at it again. Grind it down to a powder and look at it under the glass. Life was an experiment conducted under uncontrolled conditions. It was one long chemical reaction that was as unpredictable as it was vibrant. But this setup was different. It had occurred under controlled circumstances. The reactions were predicted and expected. In that he knew was the key. That meant it was something that could be taken apart.

He sat back down and from his backpack he pulled his notebook. He was ready to write, ready to attack. The first object of his scrutiny was Wentz. A man he did not know and had never met before the day he was assaulted. A man that in the initial view was the linchpin of the frame. The question was, Why would Wentz choose Pierce to hang a murder on?

After a few minutes of turning it and grinding it and looking at it from opposite angles, Pierce came to some basic case logic.

Conclusion 1: Wentz had not chosen Pierce. There was no logical connection or link that would allow for this. While animosities existed now, the two men had never met before the setup was already in play. Pierce was sure of it. And so this conclusion led in turn to the supposition that Pierce therefore had to have been chosen for Wentz by someone other than Wentz.

Conclusion 2: There was a third party in the setup. Wentz and the muscle man he called Six-Eight were only tools. They were cogs in the wheels of the setup. Someone else's hand was behind this.

The third party.

Now Pierce considered this. What did the third party need to build the frame? The setup was complex and relied on Pierce's predictable movements in a fluid environment. He knew that under controlled circumstances the movement of molecules could be relied upon. What about himself? He turned the question and looked at it again. He then came to a basic realization about himself and the third party.

Conclusion 3: Isabelle. His sister. The setup was orchestrated by a third party with knowledge of his personal history, which led to an understanding of how he would most likely react under certain controlled circumstances. The customer phone calls to Lilly were the inciting element of the experiment. The third party understood how Pierce would likely react, that he would investigate and pursue. That he would chase his sister's ghost. Therefore, the third party knew about his ghosts. The third party knew about Isabelle.

Conclusion 4: The wrong number was the right number. He had not been randomly assigned Lilly Quinlan's old number. It was intentional. It was part of the setup.

Conclusion 5: Monica Purl. She was part of it. She had set up his phone service. She had to have specifically requested the phone number that would trip the chase.

Pierce got up and started pacing. This last conclusion changed everything. If the setup was tied to Monica, then it was tied to Amedeo. It meant the frame was part of a conspiracy of a higher order. It wasn't about hanging a murder on Pierce. It was about something else. In this respect Lilly Quinlan was like Wentz. A tool in the setup, a cog in the wheel. Her murder was simply a way to get to Pierce.

Putting the horror of this aside for the moment, he sat back down and considered the most basic question. The one for which the answer would explain all. Why?

Why was Pierce the target of the frame? What did they want?

He turned it and looked at it from another angle. What would happen if the setup succeeded? In the long run he would be arrested, tried and possibly – likely – convicted. He would be imprisoned, possibly even put to death. In the short run there would be media focus and scandal, disgrace. Maurice Goddard and his money would go away. Amedeo Technologies would crash and burn.

He turned it again and the question became one of means to an end. Why go to the trouble? Why the elaborate plot? Why kill Lilly Quinlan and set up a vast scheme that could fall apart at any step along the way? Why not simply target Pierce? Kill Pierce instead of Lilly and achieve the same end with much simpler means. He would be out of the picture again, Goddard still walks and Amedeo still crashes and burns.

Conclusion 6: The target is different. It is not Pierce and it is not Amedeo. It is something else.

As a scientist Pierce enjoyed most the moments of clarity in the vision field of a microscope, the moment things came together, when molecules combined in a natural order, in a way he knew they would. It was the magic he found in his daily life.

A moment of similar clarity struck him then as he stared out at the ocean. It was a moment in which he glimpsed the big picture and knew the natural order of things.

'Proteus,' he whispered.

They wanted Proteus.

Conclusion 7: The setup was designed to push Pierce so hard into a corner that he would have no choice but to give up what they wanted. The Proteus project. He would trade Proteus for his freedom, for the return of his life.

Pierce backed up. He had to be sure. He ran it all through his mind again and once more came up with Proteus. He leaned forward and ran his fingers through his hair. He felt sick to his stomach. Not because of his conclusion that Proteus was the ultimate target. But because he had jumped quickly ahead of that. He had ridden the wave of clarity all the way into shore. He had put it together. He finally had the big picture and in the middle of it stood the third party. She was smiling at him, her eyes bright and beautiful.

Conclusion 8: Nicole.

She was the link. She was the one who connected all the dots. She had secret knowledge of the Proteus project because he had given it to her – he had goddamn demonstrated it to her! And she knew his most secret history, the true and full story about Isabelle he had never told anyone but her.

Pierce shook his head. He couldn't believe it, yet he did. He knew it worked. He figured she had gone to Elliot Bronson or maybe Gil Franks, head man at Midas Molecular. Maybe she had gone to DARPA. It didn't matter. What was clear was that she had sold him out, told of the project, agreed to steal it or maybe just delay it enough until it could be replicated and taken to the patent office by a competitor first.

He folded his arms tightly across his chest and the moment of nausea passed.

He knew he needed a plan. He needed to test his conclusions somehow and then react to the findings. It was time for some AE, time to experiment.

There was only one way to do that, he decided. He would go see her, confront her, get the truth.

He remembered his vow to fight. He decided to take his first shot. He picked up the phone and called Jacob Kaz's office. It was late in the day but the patent lawyer was still there and picked up the transfer quickly.

'Henry, you were fantastic today,' he said by way of greeting.

'You were pretty good yourself, Jacob.'

'Thank you. What can I do for you?'

'Is the package ready to go?'

'Yep. It has been. I finished with it last night. Only thing left to do is file it. I'm going to fly out Saturday, visit my brother in southern Maryland, maybe some friends I have in Baileys Crossroads in Virginia, and then be there first thing Monday morning to file. Like I told Maurice today. That's still the plan.'

Pierce cleared his throat.

'We have to change the plan.'

'Really? How so?'

'Jacob, I want you to take a red-eye tonight. I want you to file it first thing tomorrow morning. As soon as they open.'

'Henry, I really think . . . that's going to be a bit expensive to get a flight tonight on such short notice. I usually fly business class and that's—'

'I don't care what it costs. I don't care where you sit. I want you on a plane tonight. In the morning call me as soon as it's filed.'

'Is something wrong, Henry? You seem a bit—'

'Yes, something's wrong, Jacob, that's why I'm sending you tonight.'

'Well, do you want to talk about it? Maybe I can help.'

'You can help by getting on that plane and getting it filed first thing tomorrow. Other than that, I can't talk about it yet. But just get over there and get the thing filed and then call me. I don't care how early it is out here. Call me.'

'Okay, Henry, I will. I'll make the arrangements right now.'

'When does the filing office open?'

'Nine.'

'Okay, then I will talk to you shortly after six my time. And Jacob?'

'Yes, Henry?'

'Don't tell anyone other than your wife and kids that you're going tonight. Okay?'

'Uh ... what about Charlie? He said today that he might call me tonight to go over last-minute—'

'If Charlie calls you, don't tell him you're going tonight. If he calls after you leave, tell your wife to tell him you had to go out with another client. An emergency or something.'

Kaz was silent for a long moment.

'Are you all right with this, Jacob? I'm not saying anything about Charlie. It's just that at the moment I can't trust anybody. You understand?'

'Yes, I understand.'

'Okay, I'll let you go so you can call the airline. Thank you, Jacob. Call me from D.C.'

Pierce clicked off. He felt bad about possibly impugning Charlie Condon in Kaz's eyes. But Pierce knew he could take no chances. He opened a fresh line and called Condon's direct line. He was still there.

'It's Henry.'

'I just went down to your office to look for you.'

'I'm at home. What's up?'

'I thought maybe you'd want to say good-bye to Maurice. But you missed him. He left. He heads back to New York tomorrow but said he wants to talk to you before he leaves. He'll call in the morning.'

'Fine. Did you make the deal?'

'We came to an agreement in principle. We'll have contracts the end of next week.'

'How did it come out?'

'I got the twenty, but over three years. The breakdown is a two-million bump on the front end and then one million bimonthly. He becomes the chairman of the board and gets his ten points. The points will vest on a schedule. He gets a point for the up-front payment and then a point every four months. If something happens and he bails early, he leaves with the points he's accumulated only. We retain the option to buy them back within one year at eighty percent.'

'Okay.'

'Just okay? Aren't you happy?'

'It's a good deal, Charlie. For us and him.'

'I'm very happy. So is he.'

'When do we get the up-front money?'

'The escrow period is thirty days. One month, then everybody gets a raise, right?'

'Yeah, right.'

Pierce knew Condon was looking for excitement if not jocularity over the deal. But he couldn't give it. He wondered if he'd even be around at the end of a month.

'So where did you disappear to?' Condon asked.

'Uh, home.'

'Home? Why? I thought we'd—'

'I had things to do. Listen, did Maurice or Justine ask you anything about me? Anything more about the accident?'

There was a silence while Condon evidently thought about this. 'No. In fact, I thought they might bring up that thing about wanting the accident report again but they didn't. I think they were so blown away by what they saw in the lab that they don't care anymore about what happened to your face.'

Pierce remembered the blood red color of Goddard's face in the vision field of the heat resonance goggles.

'I hope so.'

'You ever going to tell me what happened to you?'

Pierce hesitated. He was feeling guilty over hiding things from Condon. But he had to remain cautious.

'Not right now, Charlie. The time's not right.'

This put a pause in Condon's reply, and in the silence Pierce could feel the injury he was inflicting on their relationship. If there was only a way for him to be sure about Condon. If there was a question he could ask. His social engineering skills had deserted him and that left only silence.

'Well,' Condon said. 'I'm going to go. Congratulations, Henry. Today was a good day.'

'Congratulations, Charlie.'

After hanging up, Pierce pulled out his key ring to check for something. Not the padlock keys. He had left them behind at the storage facility, hidden on the top of an exit sign on the third floor. He checked the ring once more to make sure he still had the key to the house on Amalfi Drive. If Nicole wasn't home, he was going to go in anyway. And he would wait for her.

34

Pierce took the California Incline down to the Coast Highway and then north to the mouth of Santa Monica Canyon. He turned right on Channel and parked at the first meter he found open. He then got out of the BMW and walked back toward the beach, looking over his shoulder and about him every ten yards for followers. When he got to the corner he looked around once more and then quickly went down the stairs into the pedestrian tunnel that went under the highway to the beach.

The walls of the tunnel were a collage of graffiti, some of it recognized by Pierce even though it had been at least a year since he had walked through the tunnel. During happier times with Nicole it had been their routine to get the paper and coffee on Sunday mornings and take it all down to the beach. But over the last year Pierce had been working on Proteus most Sundays and didn't have time for the beach.

On the other side the tunnel branched into two separate staircases leading up. He knew the further staircase came up on the sand right next to the drainage channel that emptied surface water runoff from the canyon into the ocean. He chose this stairway and came up into the sunlight to find the beach deserted. He saw the yellow lifeguard stand where he and Nicole would have their coffee and read the paper. It looked as abandoned as their Sunday ritual had become. He just wanted to see it, to remember it, before he went up the hill to her. After a while he turned back to the mouth of the tunnel and went back down the stairs.

A quarter of the way back through the sixty-yard tunnel Pierce saw a man coming down the opposite staircase. Because of the light from above him, the man was in silhouette. Pierce was suddenly stricken with the thought of a confrontation with Renner in the tunnel. The cop had followed him and was here to arrest him.

The man approached, moving swiftly and still unidentifiable. He now seemed big. Or at least bulky. Pierce slowed his step but knew that their meeting was inevitable. To turn and run would be a ridiculous show of guilt.

When they were twenty feet apart the approaching man cleared his throat. A few feet later he came into view and Pierce saw that it wasn't

Renner. It was no one that he knew. The man was in his early twenties and looked like a burned-out surfer. He incongruously wore a heavy ski jacket that was unzipped and open to reveal he had no shirt on underneath. His chest was smooth and tan and hairless.

'Hey, you looking for some – what happened to your face, man?'

Pierce kept moving past him, picking up his stride, not answering. On prior occasions he had been solicited in the tunnel. There were two gay bars on Channel and it came with the territory.

Pulling away from the curb a few minutes later, Pierce checked the mirrors of the BMW and saw no followers. The tightness in his chest began to relax. Just a little. He knew he still had Nicole to confront.

At the intersection where the canyon elementary school was located, he turned left on Entrada and took it down to Amalfi Drive. He turned left and Amalfi climbed up the north bank of the canyon, winding in a hairpin pattern. As he went by his old home he glanced down the driveway and saw Nicole's old Speedster in the carport. It appeared she was home. He yanked the wheel and came to a stop next to the curb. He sat still for a moment, pulling his thoughts and courage together. Ahead of him he saw a beat-up old Volkswagen idling in a driveway, blue smoke pumping out of the twin exhaust pipes, a Domino's Pizza sign on the roof. It reminded him that he was hungry. He had only picked at his catered lunch because he had been too keyed up from the presentation and the anticipation of making a deal with Goddard.

But food right now had to wait. He got out of the car.

Pierce stepped into the entry alcove and knocked on the door. It was a single-light French door, so Nicole would know it was him the moment she stepped into the hallway. But the glass worked both ways. He saw her the moment she saw him. She hesitated but knew she couldn't get away with acting like she wasn't home. She stepped forward and unlocked and opened the door.

But then she stood in the opening, not giving him passage. She was wearing washed-out jeans and a lightweight navy blue sweater. The sweater was cut to show off her flat and tanned stomach and the gold ring that pierced her navel. She was barefoot and Pierce imagined that her favorite clogs were somewhere nearby.

'Henry. What are you doing here?'

'I need to talk to you. Can I come in?'

'Well, I'm expecting some calls. Can you—'

'From who, Billy Wentz?'

This gave her pause. A puzzled look entered her eyes.

'Who?'

'You know who. How about Elliot Bronson or Gil Franks?'

She shook her head like she felt sorry for him.

'Look, Henry, if this is some kind of jealous ex-boyfriend scene, you can save it. I don't know any Billy Wentz and I am not trying to get a job with Elliot Bronson or with Gil Franks. I signed a no-compete clause, remember?'

That put a chink in his armor. She had deftly deflected his first attack so smoothly and naturally that Pierce felt a tremor in his resolve. All his turning and grinding and looking of an hour before was suddenly becoming suspect.

'Look, can I come in or not? I don't want to do this out here.'

She hesitated again but then moved back and motioned him in. They walked into the living room, which was to the right off the hallway. It was a large dark room with cherrywood floors and sixteen-foot ceilings. There was an empty spot where his leather couch had been – the only piece of furniture he had taken. Otherwise, the room was still the same. One wall was a vast floor-to-ceiling bookcase with double-depth shelves. Most of the shelves were filled with her books, two layers on each. She put only books she had read on these shelves, and she had read a lot. One of the things Pierce had loved most about her was that she would rather spend an evening on the couch reading a book and eating peanut butter and jelly sandwiches than go to a movie and Chinois for dinner. It was also one of the things he knew he had taken advantage of. She didn't need him to read a book, which made it easier to stay in the lab that extra hour. Or those extra hours, as it more often was.

'Are you feeling all right?' she said, trying for a level of cordiality. 'You look a lot better.'

'I'm fine.'

'How did it go with Maurice Goddard today?'

'It went fine. How did you know about it?'

Her face adopted a put-out expression.

'Because I was working there until Friday and the presentation was already scheduled. Remember?'

He nodded. She was right. Nothing suspicious there.

'I forgot.'

'Is he coming on board?'

'It looks like it.'

She didn't sit down. She stood in the middle of the living room and faced him. The shelves of books rose fortress-like behind her, dwarfing her, all of them silent condemnations of him, each one a night he didn't come home to her. They intimidated him and yet he knew he had to keep his anger sharp for this confrontation.

'Okay, Henry, you're here. I'm here. What is it?'

He nodded. Now was the time. It dawned on him that he really had no plan at this point. He was improvising.

'Well, what it is, is that it probably doesn't matter anymore in the scheme of things but I want to know for myself so maybe I can live with it a little easier. Just tell me, Nicki, did somebody get to you, did they pressure you, threaten you? Or did you just flat-out sell me out?'

Her mouth formed a perfect circle. Pierce had lived with her for three years and believed he knew all her facial expressions. He doubted she could put a look on her face that he hadn't seen before. And that perfect circle of a mouth he had seen before. But it was not the shock of being found out. It was confusion.

'Henry, what are you talking about?'

It was too late. He had to go with it.

'You know what I'm talking about. You set me up. And I want to know why and I want to know for who. Bronson? Midas? Who? And did you know they were going to kill her, Nicole? Don't tell me you knew that.'

Her eyes started to get the violet sparks that he knew signaled her anger. Or her tears. Or both.

'I have no idea what you are talking about. Set you up for what? Kill who?'

'Come on, Nicole. Are they here? Hey, is Elliot hiding in the house? When do I get the presentation from them? When do we make the trade? My life back for Proteus.'

'Henry, I think something's happened to you. When they held you over the balcony and you hit the wall. I think—'

'Bullshit! You were the only one who knew the story about Isabelle. You were the only one I ever told. And then you used it to do this. How could you do that? For money? Or was it just to get back at me for messing things up so bad?'

He could see her starting to tremble, to weaken. Maybe he was cracking through. She raised her hands, fingers splayed, and backed away. She was moving back toward the hallway.

'Get out of here, Henry. You're crazy. If it wasn't hitting that wall, then it was too many hours in the lab. It finally made you snap. You better go check into a—'

'You're not getting it,' he said calmly. 'You're not getting Proteus. Before you even wake up tomorrow it will be registered. You understand that?'

'No, Henry, I don't.'

'What I'd like to know is, who killed her? Was it you, or did you have Wentz do it for you? He took care of all the dirty work, didn't he?'

That stopped her. She turned and almost shrieked at him.

'*What?* What are you saying? Killed who? Can you even listen to yourself?'

He paused, hoping she would calm down. This wasn't going the way he had thought or hoped it would. He needed an admission from her. Instead, she was starting to cry.

'Nicole, I loved you. I don't know what is wrong with me, because, fuck it, I still do.'

She composed herself, wiped her cheeks and folded her arms across her chest.

'Okay, will you do me one favor, Henry?' she asked quietly.

'Haven't you gotten enough from me? What more do you want?'

'Would you please sit down on that chair there and I'll sit over here.'

She directed him to the chair and then she moved behind the one where she would sit.

'Just sit down and do me this favor. Tell me what has happened. Tell me as though I didn't know anything about it. I know you don't believe that but I want you to tell me like you do. Tell me it like a story. You can say whatever you want to say about me in the story, any bad thing, but just tell it. From the start. Okay, Henry?'

Pierce slowly sat down on the chair she had pointed him to. He stared at her the whole time, watched her eyes. When she stepped over and sat down across from him he began to tell the story.

'I guess you could say this started twenty years ago. On the night I found my sister in Hollywood. And I didn't tell my stepfather about it.'

35

An hour later Pierce stood in the bedroom and saw that nothing had changed. Right down to the stack of books on the floor next to her side of the bed, nothing seemed different. He stepped over to look at the book that was opened and left on the pillow where he used to sleep. It was called *Iguana Love* and he wondered what it was about.

She came up behind him and lightly touched his shoulders with her fingers. He turned into her and she brought up her hands to hold his face while she studied the scars running across his nose to his eye.

'I'm sorry, baby,' she said.

'I'm sorry for that downstairs. That I doubted you. I'm sorry for everything about this past year. I thought I could keep you and still work like—'

Her hands went behind his neck and she pulled him down into a kiss. He turned her and gently pushed her down onto the edge of the bed in a sitting position. He then slid down to his knees on the floor in front of her. With his hands he gently spread her knees and moved forward between them. He then leaned further into her and they kissed again. This time longer and harder. It seemed so long since he had felt the contours of her lips with his own.

He reached down to her hips and pulled her toward him. He didn't do it gently. Soon he felt one of her hands on the back of his neck and the other working the buttons of his shirt. They struggled with each other's clothing until finally they broke apart to work on their own clothes. Both knew without saying anything that it would be faster.

They worked with gathering momentum. When he pulled his shirt off she grimaced at the sight of the bruising on his chest and side. But then she leaned forward and kissed him there. And when they were finally naked they moved onto the bed and pulled each other together in an embrace that was fueled by equal parts carnal lust and tender longing. He realized that all the while he had missed her, missed her sense and the emotional makeup of their relationship, he had also missed her body. He had a flat-out craving for the touch and taste of her body.

He pushed his face down to her breasts and then slowly moved further down, pressing his nose into her skin, holding the gold ring that pierced her skin between his teeth for a moment and tugging it before moving down further. She had her neck back and her throat exposed and vulnerable. Her eyes were closed and the back of one hand was against her mouth, the knuckle of one finger between her teeth.

When she was ready and he was ready he moved up over her body and took her hand and brought it to his center so she could guide him. It had always been their way, their routine. She moved slowly, taking him to her place, her legs coming up his sides and crossing behind him. He opened his eyes to look down on her face. One time he had brought the goggles home and they had taken turns wearing them. He knew at this moment her face would register a wonderfully velvety purple on the vision field.

She stopped and opened her own eyes. He felt her let go of him.

'What?' he said.

She sighed.

'What?' he asked again.

'I can't.'

'Can't what?'

'Henry, I am so sorry but I can't do this.'

She unhooked her legs and dropped them to the bed. She then brought both her hands up to his chest and started to push him off. He resisted.

'Get off me, please.'

'You're kidding, right?'

'No. Get off!'

He rolled onto his side, next to her. She immediately sat up on the edge of the bed, her back to him. She folded her arms and leaned over, as if huddling with herself, the points of her spine creating a beautiful ridge on her naked back. Pierce reached up and lightly touched her neck and then ran his thumb down her spine like he was moving it across the keys of a piano.

'What is it, Nicki? What's the matter?'

'I thought after what we talked about downstairs that this would be good. That it was something we needed. But it's not. We can't do this, Henry. It's not right. We're not together anymore and if we do this – I don't know. I just can't. I'm sorry.'

Pierce smiled, though she could not see this with her back to him. He reached over and touched the tattoo on her right hip. It was small enough to go unseen most of the time. He only discovered it the first night they had made love. It intrigued him and turned him on in the same way the belly button ring had. She called it a kanji. It was *fu*, the Chinese character pictogram that meant 'happiness.' She had told him that it was a reminder that happiness came from within, not material things.

She turned and looked at him.

'Why are you smiling? I would think you'd be upset. Any other man would be.'

He shrugged.

'I don't know. I guess I understand.'

But slowly it dawned on her. What he had done. She stood up from the bed and turned to him. She reached over for a pillow and held it up in front of her, to cover herself. The message was clear. She no longer wanted to be naked with him.

'What?'

'You bastard.'

'What are you talking about?'

He saw the sparks in her eyes but this time she wasn't crying.

'This was a test, wasn't it? Some sort of perverted test. You knew if I fucked you, then everything downstairs was a lie.'

'Nicki, I don't think—'

'Get out.'

'Nicole . . .'

'You and your goddamned tests and experiments. I said, Get out!'

Embarrassed now by what he had done, he stood up and started putting on his clothes, pulling on his underwear and jeans at the same time.

'Can I say something?'

'No. I don't want to hear you.'

She turned and walked to the bathroom. She dropped the pillow and walked casually, showing him the back side of her body as if taunting him with it. Letting him understand that he would never see it again.

'I'm sorry, Nicole. I thought that—'

She closed the bathroom door loudly. She never looked back at him.

'Go,' he heard her say from within.

Then he heard the shower come on and he knew she was washing away his touch for the final time.

Pierce finished dressing and went down the stairs. He sat on the bottom step and put on his shoes. He wondered how had he been so desperately wrong about her.

Before leaving, he went back into the living room and stood before her bookcase. The shelves were crowded. Hardcover books only. It was an altar to knowledge and experience and adventure. He remembered one time walking into the living room and finding her on the couch. She wasn't reading. She was just looking up at her books.

One of the shelves was completely dedicated to books about tattoos and graphic design. He stepped over and let his finger tick along the spines of the books until he found the one he knew was there and pulled it out. It was a book about Chinese pictograms, the book from which she had chosen her tattoo. He turned the pages until he found *fu* and read the copy. It quoted Confucius.

With coarse rice to eat, with only water to drink, and my bended arm for a pillow, I am happy.

He should have known. Pierce knew he should have known it wasn't her. The logic was wrong. The science was wrong. It had led him to doubt the one thing he should have been sure of.

He turned the pages of the book until he came to *shu*, the symbol of forgiveness.

' "Forgiveness is the action of the heart," ' he read out loud.

He took the book to the coffee table and placed it down still open to the page displaying *shu*. He knew she would find it soon.

Locking the door, he pulled it closed behind him and went to his car. He sat behind the wheel thinking about what he had done, about his sins. He knew he got what he deserved. Most people did.

He slid the key in and turned over the engine. The random access memory of his mind produced the image of the pizza delivery car he had seen earlier. A reminder that he was hungry.

And in that moment atoms smashed together to create a new element. He had an idea. A good one. He turned off the engine and got back out.

Nicole was either still in the shower or not answering the door. But he didn't care, because he still had a key. He unlocked the door and walked down the hallway toward the kitchen.

'Nicole,' he called. 'It's me. I just need to use the phone.'

There was no response and he thought he could hear the sound of water running far off in the house. She was still in the shower.

On the kitchen phone he dialed Information for Venice and asked for the number for Domino's Pizza. There were two locations and he took both numbers, writing them down on a pad Nicole kept by the phone. He dialed the first number and while he waited he opened the cabinet above the phone and pulled out the Yellow Pages. He knew if Domino's didn't work, he would have to call every pizza delivery service in Venice to run out the idea.

'Domino's Pizza, can I help you?'

'I want to order a pizza.'

'Phone number?'

From memory Pierce gave Lucy LaPorte's cell number. He heard it being typed into a computer. He waited and then the man on the other end said, 'What is your address?'

'You mean I'm not on there?'

'No, sir.'

'Sorry, I called the wrong one.'

He hung up and called the second Domino's and went through the same routine, giving Lucy's number to the woman on the other end of the line.

'Nine oh nine Breeze?'

'Excuse me?'

'Is your address Nine oh nine Breeze? Name, LaPorte?'

'Uh, yeah, that's it.'

He wrote the address down, feeling the spark of adrenaline dumping into his blood. It made his writing on the pad tight and jagged.

'What would you like?'

'Um, does your computer say what we got last time?'

'Regular size, onion, peppers and mushrooms.'

'That's good. Same thing.'

'Anything to drink? Garlic bread?'

'No, just the pizza.'

'Okay, thirty minutes.'

She hung up without saying good-bye or giving him the chance to say it. Pierce hung up the phone and turned to head to the door.

Nicole was standing there. Her hair was wet and she wore a white terrycloth robe. It had been his. She gave it to him as a present on their first Christmas together but he never wore it because he wasn't a bathrobe guy. She appropriated it and it was too big on her, and that made her look very sexy in it. She knew what seeing her in the robe did to him and she used it like a flag she would hang out. When she showered and put on the robe, it meant they were going to make love.

But not this time. No more. The look on her face was anything but provocative or sexy. She glanced down at the Yellow Pages, open to the ads for pizza delivery.

'I can't believe you, Henry. After what just happened and what you did, you just come on down and order a pizza like it's nothing. I used to think you had a conscience.'

She walked over to the refrigerator and opened it.

'I asked you to leave.'

'I am. But it's not what you think, Nicole. I'm trying to find somebody and this is the only way.'

She took a bottle of water from the refrigerator and started unscrewing the cap.

'I asked you to leave,' she said again.

'All right, I'm leaving.'

He made a move to squeeze between her and the kitchen's center island. But suddenly he changed course and moved into her. He grabbed her by the shoulders and pulled her toward him. He kissed her on the mouth. She quickly pushed him back, spilling water on both of them.

'Good-bye,' he said before she could speak. 'I still love you.'

As he walked toward the door he slid the key to the house off his key ring. He dropped it on the small entry table under the mirror by the door. He turned and looked back at her as he opened the door. And she turned away.

36

Breeze was one of the Venice walk streets, which meant Pierce would have to get out of his car to get close to it. In several neighborhoods near the beach the small bungalows were built facing each other, with only a sidewalk between them. No streets. Narrow alleys ran behind the houses so owners had access to their garages. But the fronts of the homes bordered the shared sidewalk. It was a distinct plan in Venice, a design to promote neighborliness and at the same time put more homes on smaller parcels of land. Walk street houses were highly prized.

Pierce found a parking space at the curb on Ocean near the hand-painted war memorial and walked down to Breeze. It was nearly seven o'clock and the sky was beginning to acquire the burnt-orange color of a smoggy sunset. The address he had gotten from Domino's was halfway down the block. Pierce strolled along the sidewalk like he was on his way to the beach for the sunset. As he passed 909 he nonchalantly took a look. It was a yellow bungalow, smaller than most of the others on the block, with a wide front porch with an old glider seat on it. Like most of the houses on the block, it had a white picket fence out front with a gate.

The curtains behind the front windows were drawn. The light on the ceiling over the porch was on and he took this as a bad sign. It was too early for the light to be on and he guessed that it had to have been on since the night before. He began to worry, now that he had finally found the place that neither Detective Renner nor Cody Zeller had been able to find, that Lucy LaPorte would be gone.

He continued his walk to where Breeze ended at Speedway and there was a beach parking lot. He thought about going back to his car and bringing it over to the lot, but then figured it wasn't worth the time. He loitered in the lot and watched the sun drop toward the horizon for another ten minutes. He then started back down Breeze.

This time he walked even more slowly and his eyes scanned all the homes for signs of activity. It was a quiet night on Breeze. He saw no one. He heard no one, not even a television voice. He passed 909 again and saw no indication that the tiny house was currently inhabited.

As he got to the end of Breeze a blue pickup truck pulled up and stopped at the mouth of the sidewalk. It had the familiar Domino's sign on the top. A small man of Mexican descent jumped out with a red insulated pizza carrier and quickly headed down the sidewalk. Pierce let him get a good lead and then followed. He could smell the pizza despite the insulation. It smelled good. He was hungry. When the man walked across the porch to the front door of 909, Pierce slowed to a stop and used a red bougainvillea tree in the next-door neighbor's yard as a blind.

The pizza man knocked twice – louder the second time – and looked like he was about to give up when the door was opened. Pierce realized he had chosen a poor location to watch from because the angle of view prevented him from seeing into the house. But then he heard a voice and knew it was Lucy LaPorte who had answered the door.

'I didn't order that.'

'Are you sure? I have Nine oh nine Breeze.'

The pizza man opened the side of his carrier and pulled out a flat box. He read something off the side.

'LaPorte, regular with onion, pepper and mushroom.'

She giggled.

'Well, that's me and that's what I usually get but I didn't order that one tonight. Maybe it was like a computer glitch or something and the order came in again.'

The man looked down at the pizza and sadly shook his head.

'Well, okay then. I tell them.'

He shoved the box back into the carrier and turned from the door. As he came down off the porch the door to the house was closed behind him. Pierce was waiting for him by the bougainvillea tree with a twenty-dollar bill.

'Hey, if she doesn't want it, I'll take it.'

The pizza man's face brightened.

'Okay, fine with me.'

Pierce exchanged the twenty for the pizza.

'Keep the change.'

The pizza man's face brightened further. He had turned a delivery disaster into a large tip.

'Thank you! Have a good night.'

'I'll try.'

Without hesitation Pierce carried the pizza to 909, went through the front gate and up onto the porch. He knocked on the door and was thankful there was no peephole – at least that he could see. It took only a few seconds for her to answer the door this time. Her eyes were cast down – to the expected level of the small pizza man. When she raised them and saw Pierce and registered the damage to his face, the shock contorted her own unbruised, undamaged face.

'Hey, Lucy. You said next time bring you a pizza. Remember?'

'What are you doing here? You're not supposed to be here. I told you not to bother me.'

'You told me not to call you. I didn't.'

She tried to close the door but he was expecting it. He shot his hand out and stiff-armed the door. He held it open while she tried to push it closed. But the pressure was weak. She either wasn't really trying or she just didn't have the juice. He was able to keep the door open with one hand and hold the pizza up like a waiter with the other.

'We have to talk.'

'Not now. You have to go.'

'Now.'

She relented and stopped what little pressure she was putting on the door. He kept his hand on it just in case it was a trick.

'Okay, what do you want?'

'First of all, I want to come in. I don't like standing out here.'

She backed away from the door and he stepped in. The living room was small, with barely enough room for a couch, a stuffed chair and a coffee table. There was a TV on a stand and it was tuned to one of the Hollywood news and entertainment shows. There was a small fireplace but it didn't look like it had seen a fire in a few years.

Pierce closed the door. He stepped further into the room and put the pizza box down on the coffee table and picked up the TV remote. He killed the tube and tossed the remote back onto the table, which was crowded with entertainment magazines and gossip rags and an ashtray overburdened with butts.

'I was watching that,' Lucy said.

She stood near the fireplace.

'I know,' Pierce said. 'Why don't you sit down, have a piece of pizza.'

'I don't want pizza. If I wanted it, I would have bought it from that guy. Is that how you found me?'

She was wearing cutoff blue jeans and a green sleeveless T-shirt. No shoes. She looked very tired to Pierce and he thought maybe she had been wearing makeup after all on the night they had first met.

'Yeah, they had your address.'

'I ought to sue them.'

'Forget them, Lucy, and talk to me. You lied to me. You said they hurt you, that you were too black and blue to be seen.'

'I didn't lie.'

'Well, you sure heal up fast then. I'd like to know the secret to –'

She pulled her shirt up, exposing her stomach and chest. She had deep purple bruising on the left side along the line where her ribs crested beneath her skin. Her right breast was misshapen. There were small and distinctly separate bruises on it that Pierce knew came from fingers.

'Jesus,' he whispered.

She dropped her shirt.

'I wasn't lying. I'm hurt. He wrecked my implant, too. It might even be leaking but I can't get in to the doctor until tomorrow.'

Pierce studied her face. It was clear that she was in pain and that she was scared and alone. He slowly sat down on the couch. Whatever designs he had on the pizza were now long gone. He felt like grabbing it, opening the door and flinging it out onto the sidewalk. His mind was clogged with images of Lucy being held by Six-Eight while Wentz hurt her. He clearly saw the joy on Wentz's face. He had seen it before.

'Lucy, I'm sorry.'

'So am I. I am sorry I ever got involved with you. That's why you have to leave. If they know you came here, they'll come back and it will be a lot worse for me.'

'Yeah, okay. I'll leave.'

But he made no move to get up.

'I don't know,' he said. 'I'm batting zero tonight. I came here because I thought you were part of it. I came to find out who was setting me up.'

'Setting you up for what?'

'For Lilly Quinlan. Her murder.'

Lucy slowly lowered herself into the stuffed chair.

'She's dead for sure?'

He looked at her and then down at the pizza box. He thought of what he had seen in the freezer and nodded his head.

'The police think I did it. They're trying to make a case.'

'The detective who I talked to?'

'Yeah, Renner.'

'I'll tell him that you were just trying to find her, to make sure she was okay.'

'Thank you. But it won't matter. He says that was part of my plan. I used you and others, I called the cops, all to cover that I did it. He says the killer often disguises himself as the Good Samaritan.'

It was her turn but she didn't speak for a long while. Pierce studied the headlines of an old issue of the *National Enquirer* that was on the table. He realized he was far out of touch with the world. He didn't recognize a single name or photo of a celebrity on the front page.

'I could tell him that I was told to lead you to her place,' Lucy said quietly.

Pierce looked up at her.

'Is that true?'

She nodded.

'But I swear to God, I didn't know he was setting you up, Henry.'

'Who is "he"?'

'Billy.'

'What did he tell you to do?'

'He just told me that I would be getting a call from you, Henry Pierce, and that I should set up a date and lead you to Lilly's place. He said to make it seem like it was your idea to go there. That was all I was to do and that's all I knew. I didn't know, Henry.'

He nodded.

'That's okay. I understand. I am not mad at you, Lucy. You had to do what he told you to do.'

He thought about this, turning it and trying to see if this was significant information. It seemed to him that it was definitely evidence of the setup, though at the same time he had to acknowledge that the source of this evidence would not rate highly with cops, lawyers and juries. He then remembered the money he had paid Lucy on the night they had met. He knew little about criminal law but enough to know that the money would be a problem. It might taint or even disqualify Lucy as a witness.

'I could tell the detective that,' Lucy said. 'Then he would know it was part of a plan.'

Pierce shook his head and all at once realized he had been thinking selfishly, contemplating solely how this woman could help or hurt him, not for once considering her situation.

'No, Lucy. That would put you in danger from Wentz. Besides . . .'

He almost said that a prostitute's word would not count for much with the police.

'Besides what?'

'I don't know. I just don't think it would be enough to change the way Renner's looking at this. Plus he knows I paid you money. He'd turn that into something it's not.'

He thought of something and changed tack.

'Lucy, if that's all Wentz told you to do with me, and then you did it, why did they come here? Why did they hurt you?'

'To scare me. They knew the cops would want to talk to me. They told me exactly what to say. It was a script I had to follow. Then they just wanted me to drop out of sight for a while. They said in a couple weeks everything will be normal again.'

A couple weeks, Pierce thought. *By then the play will be over.*

'So I guess everything you told me about Lilly was part of the script.'

'No. There was no script for that. What stuff?'

'Like about the day you went to her apartment but she didn't show up. That was just made up so I'd want to go there, right?'

'No, that part was the truth. Actually, all of it was true. I didn't lie to you, Henry. I just led you. I used the truth to lead you where he wanted you to go. And you wanted to go. The client, the car, all that trouble, it was all true.'

'What do you mean, the car?'

'I told you before. The parking space was taken and that was supposed to be left open for the client. My client. It was a pain in the ass because we had to go park and then walk back and he was getting sweaty. I hate sweaty guys. Then we get there and there's no answer. It was fucked up.'

It came back to Pierce. He had missed it in the first go-round because he didn't know what to ask. He didn't know what was important. Lilly Quinlan didn't answer the door that day because she was dead inside the apartment. But she might not have been alone. There was a car.

'Was it her car in the space?'

'No, like I said, she always left it for the client.'

'Do you remember the car that was there?'

'Yeah, I remember because they left the top down and I wouldn't leave a car like that with the top down in that neighborhood. Too close to all the dregs that hang out at the beach.'

'What kind of car was it?'

'It was a black Jag.'

'With the top down.'

'Yeah. That's what I said.'

'A two-seater?'

'Yeah, the sports car.'

Pierce stared at her without speaking for a long time. For a moment he felt light-headed and thought he might fall over on the couch, go face first into the pizza box. Everything came rushing into his mind at once. He saw it all, lit up and shining, and everything seemed to fit.

'Aurora borealis.'

He whispered it just under his breath.

'What?' Lucy asked.

Pierce pulled himself up from the couch.

'I have to go now.'

'Are you all right?'

'I am now.'

He walked toward the door but stopped suddenly and turned back to look at Lucy.

'Grady Allison.'

'What about him?'

'Could it have been his car?'

'I don't know. I've never seen his car.'

'What does he look like?'

Pierce envisioned the mug shot photo of Allison that Zeller had sent him. A pale, broken-nose thug with greased-back hair.

'Um, sort of young, kind of leathery from too much sun.'

'Like a surfer?'

'Uh-huh.'

'He has a ponytail, right?'

'Sometimes.'

Pierce nodded and turned back to the door.

'Do you want to take your pizza?'

Pierce shook his head.

'I don't think I could eat it.'

37

It was two hours before Cody Zeller finally showed up at Amedeo Technologies. Because Pierce needed his own time to prepare things, he hadn't even made the call to his friend until midnight. He then told Zeller that he had to come in, that there had been a breach in the computer system. Zeller had protested that he was with someone and couldn't get away until morning. Pierce said that the morning would be too late. He said that he would accept no excuse, that he needed him, that it was an emergency. Pierce made it clear without saying so that attendance was required if Zeller wanted to keep the Amedeo account and their friendship intact. It was hard to keep his voice under control because at that moment the friendship was beyond sundered.

Two hours after that call Pierce was in the lab, waiting and watching the security cameras on the computer station monitor. It was a multiplex system that allowed him to track Zeller as he parked his black Jaguar in the garage and came through the main entrance doors to the security dais, where the lone security man on duty gave him a scramble card and instructions to meet Pierce in the lab. Pierce watched Zeller ride the elevator down and move into the mantrap. At that point he switched off the security cams and started the computer's dictation program. He adjusted the microphone on the top of the monitor and then killed the screen.

'All right,' he said. 'Here we go. Time to smash that fly.'

Zeller could only get into the mantrap with the scramble card. The second door had a keypad lock. Of course, Pierce had no doubt that Zeller knew the entry combination, as it was changed every month and the new number sent to the lab staff by e-mail. But when Zeller came through the trap to the interior stop he simply pounded on the copper-sheathed door.

Pierce got up and let him in. Zeller entered the lab throwing off the demeanor of a man who was seriously put out by the circumstances he was in.

'All right, Hank, I'm here. What's the big crisis? You know, I was right in the middle of knocking off a piece when you called.'

Pierce went back to his seat at the computer station and sat down. He swiveled the seat around so he was looking at Zeller.

'Well, it took you long enough to get here. So don't tell me you stopped because of me.'

'How wrong you are, my friend. I took so long only because being the perfect gentleman that I am, I had to get her back to the Valley and goddamn if there wasn't a frigging slide again in Malibu Canyon. So then I had to go turn around and go all the way down to Topanga. I still got here as fast as I could. What's that smell anyway?'

Zeller was speaking very fast. Pierce thought he might be drunk or high or both. He didn't know how this would affect the experiment. It was adding a new element to the settings.

'Carbon,' he said. 'I figured I'd bake a batch of wires while I waited on you.'

Pierce nodded toward the closed door of the wire lab. Zeller snapped his fingers repeatedly as he attempted to draw something from memory.

'That smell . . . it reminds me of when I was a kid . . . and I'd set my little plastic cars on fire. Yeah, my model cars. Like you made from a kit with glue.'

'That's a nice memory. Go in the lab there. It's worse. Take a deep breath and maybe you'll have the whole flashback.'

'No thanks. I think I'll pass on that for the time being. Okay. So I'm here. What's the rumpus?'

Pierce identified the question as a line from the Coen brothers' film *Miller's Crossing*, a Zeller favorite and dialogue bank from which he often made a withdrawal. But Pierce didn't acknowledge knowing the line. He wasn't going to play that game with Zeller this night. He was concentrating on the play, the experiment he was conducting under controlled conditions.

'I told you, we've been breached,' he said. 'Your supposedly impregnable security system is for shit, Code. Somebody's been stealing all our secrets.'

The accusation made Zeller immediately become agitated. His hands came together in front of his chest, the fingers seemingly fighting with one another.

'Whoa, whoa, first of all, how do you know somebody's stealing secrets?'

'I just know.'

'All right, you just know. I guess I am supposed to accept that. Okay, then how do you know it's through the data system and not just somebody's big mouth leaking it or selling it? What about Charlie Condon? I've had a few drinks with him. He likes to talk, that guy.'

'It's his job to talk. But I'm talking about secrets Charlie doesn't even know. That only I and a few others know. People in the lab. And I'm talking about this.'

He opened a drawer in the computer station and pulled out a small device that looked like a relay switch box. It had an AC/DC plug and a small wire antenna attached. From one end of it stretched a six-inch cable attached to a computer slot card. He put it down on the top of the desk.

'I got suspicious and went into the maintenance files and looked around but didn't find anything. So I then went and looked at the hardware on the mainframe and found this little slot attachment. It's got a wireless modem. I believe it's what you guys call a sniffer.'

Zeller stepped closer to the desk and picked up the device.

'Us guys? Do you mean corporate computer security specialists?'

He turned the device in his hands. It was a data catcher. Programmed and attached to a mainframe, it would intercept and collect all e-mail traffic in the computer system and ship it out over the wireless modem to a predetermined location. In the lingo of the hacking world it was called a sniffer because it collected everything and the thief was then free to sniff through all the data for the gems.

Zeller's face showed a deep concern. It was a very good act, Pierce thought.

'Homemade,' Zeller said as he examined the device.

'Aren't they all?' Pierce asked. 'It's not like you can bop into a Radio Shack and pick up a sniffer.'

Zeller ignored the comment. His voice had a deep quaver in it when he spoke.

'How the hell did that get on there, and why didn't your system maintenance guy see it?'

Pierce leaned back and tried to play it as cool as he could.

'Why don't you quit bullshitting and tell me, Cody?'

Zeller looked from the device in his hands to Pierce. He looked surprised and hurt.

'How would I know? I built your system but I didn't build this.'

'Yeah, you built the system. And this was built into the mainframe. Maintenance didn't see it because they were either bought off by you or it was too well hidden. I found it only because I was looking for it.'

'Look, anybody with a scramble card has access to that computer room and could've put this on there. I told you when we designed the place you should've put it down here in the lab. For the security.'

Pierce shook his head, revisiting the three-year-old debate and confirming his decision.

'Too much interference from the mainframe on the experiments. You know that. But that's beside the point. That's your sniffer. I may have diverted from computer science to chemistry at Stanford but I still know a thing or two. I put the modem card in my laptop and used it on my dial-up. It's programmed. It connected with a data dump site registered as DoomstersInk.'

He waited for the reaction and got a barely noticeable eye movement from Zeller.

'One word, *ink* like the stuff in a pen,' Pierce said. 'But you already know that. It's been a pretty active site, I would imagine. My guess is that you installed the sniffer when we moved in here. For three years you've been watching, listening, stealing. Whatever you want to call it.'

Zeller shook his head and placed the device back down on the desk. He kept his eyes down as Pierce continued.

'A year or so ago – after I'd hired Larraby – you started seeing e-mail back and forth between us about a project called Proteus. Then there was e-mail back and forth with Charlie on it and then my patent lawyer. I checked, man. I keep all my e-mail. Paranoid that way. I checked and you could've put together what was happening from the e-mail. Not the formula itself, we weren't that stupid. But enough for you to know we had it and what we were going to do with it.'

'All right, so what if I did? So I listened in, big deal.'

'The big deal is you sold us out. You used what you got to cut a deal with somebody.'

Zeller shook his head sadly.

'Tell you what, Henry, I'm gonna go. I think you've been spending too much time in here. You know, when I used to melt those plastic cars I'd get a really bad headache from that smell. I mean, it can't be good for you. And here you are . . .'

He gestured toward the wire lab door.

Pierce stood up. His anger felt like a rock the size of a fist stuck in his throat.

'You set me up. I don't know what the play is, but you set me up.'

'You're fucked up, man. I don't know anything about a setup. Yeah, sure, I've been sniffing around. It was the hacker instinct in me. Once in the blood, you know about that. Yes, I put it on there when I set up the system. Tell you the truth, I mostly forgot about it, the stuff I was seeing at first was so boring. I quit checking that site a couple years ago at least. So that's it, man. I don't know anything about a setup.'

Pierce was undaunted.

'I can guess the connection to Wentz. You probably set up the security on his systems. I mean, I doubt the subject matter would have bothered you. Business is business, right?'

Zeller didn't answer and Pierce wasn't expecting him to. He forged ahead.

'You're Grady Allison.'

Zeller's face showed slight surprise but then he covered it.

'Yeah, I got the mug shots and mob connections. It was all phony, all part of the play.'

Again Zeller was silent and not even looking at Pierce. But Pierce could tell he had his complete attention.

'And the phone number. The number was the key. At first I thought it had to be my assistant, that she had to have requested the number for the scheme to begin. But then I realized it was the other way around. You got my number in the e-mail I sent out. You then turned around and put it on the site. On Lilly's web page. And then it all began. Some of the calls were probably from people you put up to it. The rest were probably legit – just icing on the cake. But that was why I found no phone records at her house. And no phone. Because she never *had* the number. She operated like Robin – with just a cell phone.'

Again he waited for a response and got none.

'But the part I'm having trouble with is my sister. She was part of this. You had to know about her, about the time I found her and let her go. It had to be part of the planning, part of the profile. You had to know that this time I wouldn't let it go. That I would look for Lilly and walk right into the setup.'

Zeller didn't respond. He turned and moved to the door. He turned the knob but the door wouldn't open. The combination had to be entered to come in or go out.

'Open the door, Henry. I want to leave.'

'You're not leaving until I know what the play is. Who are you doing this for? How much are they paying you?'

'All right, fine. I'll do it myself.'

Zeller punched in the combination and sprang the door lock. He pulled the door open and looked back at Pierce.

'*Vaya con dios*, dude.'

'How'd you know the combination?'

That put a pause in Zeller's step and Pierce almost smiled. His knowing and using the combination was an admission. Not a big one, but it counted.

'Come on. How'd you know the combo? We change it every month – your idea, in fact. We put it out on e-mail to all the lab rats but you said you haven't checked the sniffer in two years. So how'd you know the combo?'

Pierce turned and gestured to the sniffer. Zeller's eyes followed and landed on the device. Then the focus of his eyes moved slightly and Pierce saw him register something. He stepped back into the lab and let the mantrap door close behind him with a loud *fump*.

'Henry, why do you have the monitor off? I see you've got the tower on but the monitor's off.'

Zeller didn't wait for an answer and Pierce didn't give one anyway. Zeller stepped over to the computer station and reached down and pushed the monitor's on/off button.

The screen activated and Zeller bent down, both hands on the desk, to look at it. On the screen was the transcription of their conversation, the last line reading, 'Henry, why do you have the monitor off? I see you've got the tower on but the monitor's off.'

It was a good program, a third-generation high resonance voice-recognition system from SacredSoftware. The researchers in the lab used it routinely to dictate notes from experiments or to describe tests as they were conducted.

Pierce watched as Zeller pulled out the keyboard drawer and typed in commands to kill the program. He then erased the file.

'It will still be recoverable,' Pierce said. 'You know that.'

'That's why I'm taking the drive.'

He squatted down in front of the computer tower and slid it around so he could get to the screws that held the shell in place. He took a folding knife out of his pocket and snapped open a Phillips bit. He pulled out the power cord and began to work on the top screw on the shell.

But then he stopped. He had noticed the phone line jacked into the back of the computer. He unplugged it and held the line in his hand.

'Now Henry that's unlike you. A paranoid like you. Why would you have the computer jacked?'

'Because I was online. Because I wanted that file you just killed to be sent out as you said the words. It's a SacredSoft program. You recommended it, remember? Each voice receives a recognition code. I set up a file for you. It's as good as a tape recording. If I have to, I'll be able to match your voice to those words.'

Zeller reached up from his crouched position and slapped his tool down hard on the desk. His back to Pierce, the angle of his head rose, as if he were looking up at the dime taped to the wall behind the computer station.

Slowly he stood up, going into one of his pockets again. He turned around while opening a silver cell phone.

'Well, I know you don't have a computer at home, Henry,' he said. 'Too paranoid. So I'm guessing Nicki. I'm going to have somebody go by and pick up her drive too, if you don't mind.'

A moment of fear seized Pierce but he calmed himself. The threat to Nicole wasn't counted on but it wasn't totally unexpected, either. But the truth was the phone jack was just part of the play. The dictation file had not been sent anywhere.

Zeller waited for his call to go through, but it didn't. He took his phone away from his ear and looked at it as if it had betrayed him.

'Goddamn phone.'

'There's copper in the walls. Remember? Nothing gets in but nothing gets out either.'

'Fine, then I'll be right with you.'

Zeller punched in the door combination again and moved into the man-trap. As soon as the door closed Pierce went over to the computer station. He picked up Zeller's tool and unfolded a blade. He knelt down by the computer tower and picked up the phone line, looped it in his hand and then sliced through it with the knife.

He stood up and put the tool back on the desk along with the cut piece of phone line just as Zeller came back through the mantrap. Zeller was holding the scramble card in one hand and his phone in the other.

'Sorry about that,' Pierce said. 'I had them give you a card that would let you in but not out. You can program them that way.'

Zeller nodded his head and saw the cut phone line on the desk.

'And that was the only line into the lab,' he said.

'That's right.'

Zeller flicked the scramble card at Pierce like he was flipping a baseball card against the curb. It bounced off Pierce's chest and fell to the floor.

'Where's your card?'

'I left it in my car. I had to have the guard bring me down here. We're stuck, Code. No phones, no cameras, no one coming. Nobody's coming down here to let us out for at least five or six hours, until the lab rats start rolling in. So you might as well make yourself comfortable. You might as well sit down and tell me the story.'

38

Cody Zeller looked around the lab, at the ceiling, at the desks, at the framed Dr. Seuss illustrations on the walls, anywhere but at Pierce. He caught an idea and abruptly started pacing through the lab with a renewed vigor, his head swiveling as he began a search for a specific target.

Pierce knew what he was doing.

'There is a fire alarm. But it's a direct system. You pull it and fire and police come. You want them coming? You want to explain it to them?'

'I don't care. You can explain it.'

Zeller saw the red emergency pull on the wall next to the door to the wire lab. He walked over and without hesitation pulled it down. He turned back to Pierce with a clever smile on his face.

But then nothing happened. Zeller's smile broke. His eyes turned into question marks and Pierce nodded as if to say, *Yes, I disconnected the system.*

Dejected by the failure of his efforts, Zeller walked over to the probe station furthest from Pierce in the lab, pulled out the desk chair and dropped heavily into it. He closed his eyes, folded his arms and put his feet up on the table, just inches from a $250,000 scanning tunneling microscope.

Pierce waited. He had all night if he needed it. Zeller had masterfully played him. Now it was time to reverse the field. Pierce would play him. Fifteen years before, when the campus police had rounded up the Doomsters, they had separated them and waited them out. The cops had nothing. Zeller was the one who broke, who told everything. Not out of fear, not out of being worn down. Out of wanting to talk, out of a need to share his genius.

Pierce was counting on that need now.

Almost five minutes went by. When Zeller finally spoke, it was while in the same posture, his eyes still closed.

'It was when you came back after the funeral.'

That was all he said and a long moment went by. Pierce waited, unsure how to dislodge the rest. Finally, he went with the direct approach.

'What are you talking about? Whose funeral?'

'Your sister's. When you came back up to Palo Alto you wouldn't talk about it. You kept it in. Then one night it all came out. We got drunk one night and I had some stuff left over from Christmas break in Maui. We smoked that up and, man, then you couldn't stop talking about it.'

Pierce didn't remember this. He did, of course, remember drinking heavily and ingesting a variety of drugs in the days and months after Isabelle's death. He just didn't remember talking about it with Zeller or anyone else.

'You said that one time when you were out cruising around with your stepfather that you did actually find her. She was sleeping in this abandoned hotel where all the runaways had taken over the rooms. You found her and you were going to rescue her and bring her out, bring her back home. But she convinced you not to do it and not to tell your stepdad. She told you he had done things to her, raped her or whatever, and that's why she ran away. You said she convinced you she was better off on the street than at home with him.'

Now Pierce closed his eyes. Remembering the moment of the story, if not remembering the drunken confession of it to a college roommate.

'So you left her and you lied to the old man. You said she wasn't there. Then for a whole 'nother year you two kept going out at night, looking for her. Only you were really avoiding her and he didn't know it.'

Pierce remembered his plan. To get older, get out and then come back for her, to find and rescue her then. But she was dead before he got the chance. And all his life since then he knew she would be alive if he had not listened and believed her.

'You never mentioned it again after that night,' Zeller said. 'But I remembered it.'

Pierce was seeing the eventual confrontation with his stepfather. It was years later. He had been handcuffed, unable to tell his mother what he knew because to reveal it would be to reveal his own complicity in Isabelle's death, that one night he had found her but then let her go and lied about it.

But, finally, the burden grew until it outweighed the damage the revelation could cause him. The confrontation was in the kitchen, where the confrontations always were in that house. Denials, threats, recriminations. His mother didn't believe him, and in not believing him, she was denying her lost daughter as well. Pierce had not spoken to her since.

Pierce opened his eyes, relieved to leave the haunting memory for the present nightmare.

'You remembered,' he said to Zeller. 'You remembered and you held it tight and you kept it for the right time. This time.'

'It wasn't like that. Something just came up and what I knew fit in. It helped.'

'Nice penetration, Cody. You have a picture of me up on the wall with all the logos now?'

'It's not like that, Hank.'

'Don't call me that. That's what my stepfather called me. Don't ever call me that again.'

'Whatever you want, Henry.'

Zeller pulled his folded arms tighter against his body.

'So what's the setup?' Pierce asked. 'My guess is you have to deliver the formula to keep your end of the deal. Who gets it?'

Zeller turned his head and looked at him, challenge or defiance in his eyes. Pierce wasn't sure which way to read it.

'I don't know why we're playing this game. The walls are about to come down on you, man, and you don't even know it.'

'What walls? Are you talking about Lilly Quinlan?'

'You know I am. There are people who will be contacting you. Soon. You make the deal with them and everything else goes away. You don't make the deal, then God help you. Everything will come down on you like a ton of bricks. So my advice is, play it cool, make the deal and walk away alive, happy and rich.'

'What is the deal?'

'Simple. You give up Proteus. You hand over the patent. You go back to building your molecular memory and computers and make lots of money that way. Stay away from the biologicals.'

Pierce nodded. Now he understood. The pharmaceutical industry. One of Zeller's other clients was somehow threatened by Proteus.

'Are you serious?' he said. 'A pharmaceutical is behind this? What did you tell them? Don't you know that Proteus will help them? It's a delivery system. What will it deliver? Drug therapy. This could be the biggest development in that industry since it began.'

'Exactly. It will change everything and they're not ready for it.'

'Doesn't matter. There's time. Proteus is just a start – we're a minimum ten years away from any kind of practical application.'

'Yeah, ten years. That's still fifteen years closer than it was before Proteus. The formula will excite the research, to use a phrase from one of your own e-mails. It will kick start it. Maybe you are ten years away and maybe you're five. Maybe you're four. Three. Doesn't matter. You are a threat, man. To a major industrial complex.'

Zeller shook his head in disgust.

'You scientists think the fucking world is your oyster and you can make your discoveries and change whatever you want and everybody will be happy about it. Well, there's a world order and if you think the giants of industry are going to let a little worker ant like you cut them down to size, then you are living in a goddamn dream.'

He unfolded his arms and gestured toward one of the framed pages from *Horton Hears a Who!* Pierce's eyes followed and he saw it was the page that showed Horton being persecuted by the other jungle animals. He could recite the words in his head. *Through the high jungle tree tops, the news quickly spread. He talks to a dust speck. He's out of his head!*

'I am *helping* you by doing this, Einstein. You understand? This is your dose of reality. Because don't expect the semiconductor people to sit around while you cut them down, either. Consider this a fucking heads up.'

Pierce almost laughed but it was too pathetic.

'My heads up? Man, that's great. Thank you, Cody Zeller, for setting me straight in the world.'

'Don't mention it.'

'And what do you get for this great gesture?'

'Me? I get money. Lots of it.'

Pierce nodded. Money. The ultimate motivation. The ultimate way of keeping score.

'So what happens?' he asked quietly. 'I make the deal and what happens?'

Zeller sat quietly for a moment while he fashioned an answer.

'Do you remember that urban legend about the garage workshop inventor who came up with a form of rubber that was so strong, it would never wear out? It was a fluke. He was trying to invent one thing but came up with this rubber instead.'

'He sold it to a tire company so the world would have tires that would never wear out.'

'Yeah, that's right. That's the story. The name of the tire company was different depending on who told the story. But the story and the end were always the same. The tire company took the formula and put it in a safe.'

'They never made the tires.'

'They never made the tires because if they did that, they wouldn't make very many tires anymore, would they? Planned obsolescence, Einstein. It's what makes the world go around. Let me ask you this: How do you know that story is urban legend? I mean, how do you really know it didn't happen?'

Pierce nodded before he spoke.

'They'll bury Proteus. They won't license it. It will never see the light of day.'

'Do you know that the pharmaceutical industry invents and studies and tests several hundred different new drugs for every one that eventually comes to market after the FDA is through with it? Do you understand the costs involved? It's a big, huge machine, Henry, and it's got energy and momentum and you can't stop it. They won't let you.'

Zeller raised a hand and made some kind of gesture and then dropped it to the armrest of the chair. They both sat silently for a long moment.

'They are going to come to me and take away Proteus.'

'They're going to pay you for it. Pay you well. The offer's actually already on the table.'

Pierce sprang forward in his seat, the pose of calm completely disappearing. He looked over at Zeller, who was not looking back.

'Are you telling me it's Goddard? Goddard is behind this?'

'Goddard is only the emissary. The front. He calls you tomorrow and you make the deal with him. You give him Proteus. You don't need to know who is behind him. You don't ever need to know that.'

'He takes Proteus from me, then holds ten percent of the company and sits as chairman of my fucking board.'

'I think they want to make sure you steer clear of internal medicine. They also know a good investment when they see it. They know you're the leader in the field.'

Zeller smiled, as if he were throwing in a bonus. Pierce thought about Goddard and the things he had said – confided – during the celebration. About his daughter. About the future. He wondered if it was all sham. If it had all been part of the play.

'What if I don't do it?' Pierce asked. 'What if I go ahead and file the patent and say fuck you to them?'

'Then you won't get the chance to file it. And you won't get the chance to work another day in this lab.'

'What are they going to do, kill me?'

'If they have to, but they don't have to. Come on, man, you know what's going on. The cops are this close behind you.'

Zeller held up his right hand, his thumb and forefinger an inch apart.

'Lilly Quinlan,' Pierce said.

Zeller nodded.

'Darling Lilly. They're missing only one thing. They find it and you're history. You do as you're told here and that will all go away. I guarantee it will be taken care of.'

'I didn't do it and you know it.'

'Doesn't matter. They find the body and it points to you, then it doesn't matter.'

'So Lilly is dead.'

Zeller nodded.

'Oh, yeah. She's dead.'

There was a smile in his voice, if not on his face, when he said it. Pierce looked down. He put his elbows on his knees and put his face in his hands.

'All because of me. Because of Proteus.'

He didn't move for a long moment. He knew if Zeller were to make the ultimate mistake, he would do it now.

'Actually . . .'

Nothing. That was it. Pierce looked up from his hands.

'Actually what?'

'I was going to say, Don't beat yourself up too badly about that. Lilly . . . you could say circumstances dictated she be folded into the plan.'

'I don't – what do you mean?'

'I mean, look at it this way. Lilly would be dead whether you were involved in this or not. But she's dead. And we used all available resources to make this deal happen.'

Pierce stood up and walked to the back of the lab where Zeller sat, his legs still up on the probe station table.

'You son of a bitch. You know all about it. You killed her, didn't you? You killed her and set the frame around me.'

Zeller didn't move an inch. But his eyes rose to Pierce's and then a strange look came over his face. The change was subtle but Pierce could see it. It was the incongruous mixture of pride and embarrassment and self-loathing.

'I had known Lilly since she first came to L.A. You could say she was part of my compensation package for L.A. Darlings. And by the way, don't insult me with that thing about me doing the work for Wentz. Wentz works for me, you understand? They all do.'

Pierce nodded to himself. He should have expected as much. Zeller continued unbidden.

'Man, she was a choice piece. Darling Lilly. But she got to know too much about me. You don't want anyone to know all your secrets. At least not those kinds of secrets. So I worked her into the assignment I had. The Proteus Plan, I called it.'

His eyes were far off now. He was watching a movie inside and liking it. He and Lilly, maybe the final meeting in the townhouse off Speedway. It prompted Pierce to draw another line from *Miller's Crossing*.

'Nobody knows nobody, not that well.'

'*Miller's Crossing*,' Zeller said, smiling and nodding. 'I guess that means you got my "what's the rumpus" coming in.'

'Yeah, I got it, Cody.'

After a pause he continued quietly.

'You killed her, didn't you? You did it and then you were ready, if necessary, to put it on me.'

Zeller didn't answer at first. Pierce studied his face and could tell he wanted to talk, wanted to tell him every detail of his ingenious plan. It was in his nature to tell it. But common sense told him not to, told him to be safe.

'Put it this way. Lilly served her purpose for me. And then she served her purpose for me again. I'll never admit more than that.'

'It's all right. You just did.'

Pierce hadn't said it. It was a new voice. Both men turned at the sound and saw Detective Robert Renner standing in the open doorway of the wire lab. He held a gun loosely down at his side.

'Who the fuck are you?' Zeller asked as he dropped his feet to the floor and came up out of the chair.

'LAPD,' Renner said.

He moved from the lab doorway toward Zeller, reaching behind his back as he came.

'You're under arrest for murder. That's for starters. We'll worry about the rest later.'

His hand came back around his body, holding a pair of handcuffs. He moved in on Zeller, twirled him around and bent him over the probe station. He holstered his weapon and then pulled Zeller's arms behind his back and started cuffing them. He worked with the professionalism and practice of a man who had done it a thousand times or more. In the process he pushed Zeller's face into the hard steel cowling of the microscope.

'Careful,' Pierce said. 'That microscope is very sensitive – and expensive. You might damage it.'

'Wouldn't want to do that,' Renner said. 'Not with all these important discoveries you're making in here.'

He then glanced over at Pierce with what probably passed for him as a full-fledged smile.

39

Zeller didn't say anything as he was being cuffed. He just turned and stared at Pierce, who threw it right back at him. Once Zeller was secured Renner started searching him. When the detective patted down the right leg he came up with something. He lifted the cuff of Zeller's pants and pulled a small pistol out of an ankle holster. He displayed it to Pierce, then put it down on the table.

'That's for protection,' Zeller protested. 'This whole thing is bullshit. It will never stand up.'

'Is that right?' Renner asked good-naturedly.

He pulled Zeller back off the table and then roughly sat him back down in the seat.

'Stay there.'

He stepped over to Pierce and nodded toward his chest.

'Open up.'

Pierce started to unbutton his shirt, revealing the battery pack and transmitter taped across his left ribs.

'How did it come through?' he asked.

'Perfect. Got every word.'

'You motherfucker,' Zeller said with a steel-hard hiss in his voice.

Pierce looked at him.

'Oh, so I'm the motherfucker for wearing a wire. You set me up for a murder and *you* get upset that I'm wired. Cody, you can go—'

'All right, all right, break it up,' Renner said. 'Both of you shut it down.'

As if to accentuate the point, he tore the tape securing the audio surveillance equipment off Pierce's body with one hard tug. Pierce almost let out a scream but was able to reduce it to a 'goddamn, that hurt!'

'Good. Sit down over there, Mr. Righteous. It will start to feel better in a minute.'

He turned back to Zeller.

'Before I take you out of here, I'm going to read you your rights. So shut up and listen.'

He reached into one of the inside pockets of his bomber jacket and pulled out a stack of cards. He shuffled through them, finding the scramble card Pierce had given him earlier. He reached over and handed it to Pierce.

'You lead the way. Open the door.'

Pierce took the card but didn't get up. His side was still burning. Renner found the rights card he was looking for and started reading it to Zeller.

'You have the right to—'

There was a loud metallic clack as the mantrap door's lock was sprung. The door swung open and Pierce saw the security guard from the front dais standing there. His eyes looked dulled and his hair was uncombed. He had one hand behind his back as though hiding something.

In his peripheral vision Pierce saw Renner tense. He dropped the card he was reading from and his hand started inside his jacket for his holster.

'It's my security guy,' Pierce blurted out.

In the same moment he said it he saw the security man suddenly propelled into the lab by an unseen force from behind. The guard, a man named Rudolpho Gonsalves, crashed into the computer station and toppled over it, landing on the floor, with the monitor then falling onto his chest. Then the familiar image of Six-Eight followed through the door, the big man ducking as he crossed the threshold.

Billy Wentz stepped in behind him. He held a large black gun in his right hand and his eyes sharpened when he saw the three men on the other side of the lab.

'What's taking so—'

'Cops!' Zeller yelled. 'He's a cop!'

Renner was already pulling his gun from his holster but Wentz had the advantage. With the utmost economy of movement, the little gangster pointed his weapon across the lab and started firing. He stepped forward as he fired, moving the barrel of the gun in a two-inch-wide back and forth arc. The sound was deafening.

Pierce didn't see it but he knew Renner had started returning fire. He heard the sound of gunfire to his right and instinctively dove to his left. He rolled and turned to see the detective going down, a spray of fat drops of blood hitting the wall behind him. He turned the other way to see Wentz still advancing. He was trapped. Wentz was squarely between him and the mantrap door.

'Lights!'

The lab dropped into darkness. Two flashes of light accompanied the last two shots from Wentz and then complete blackness set in. Pierce immediately rolled to his right again so he would not be in the same position Wentz had last remembered him to be. On his hands and knees he held perfectly still, trying to control his breathing. He listened for any sound that was not his own.

There was a low guttural sound to his right and behind him. It was either

Renner or Zeller. Hurt. Pierce knew he could not call out to Renner, because it could help Wentz focus his next shot.

'Lights!'

It was Wentz but the voice reader was set to receive and identify only the top tier of the lab team. Wentz's voice would not do it.

'Lights!'

Still nothing.

'Six-Eight? There's gotta be a switch. Find the light switch.'

There was no reply or sound of movement.

'Six-Eight?'

Nothing.

'Six-Eight, goddamnit!'

Again, no reply. Then Pierce heard a banging sound ahead of him and to the right. Wentz had walked into something. He judged by the sound that it was at least twenty feet away. Wentz was probably near the mantrap, searching for his backup man or the light switch. He knew it did not give him a lot of time. The light switch was not next to the mantrap door but it was only five or six feet away, by the electric control panel.

Pierce turned and crawled silently but quickly back toward the probe station. He remembered the gun Renner had found on Zeller.

When he got to the table he reached up and ran his hand along the top surface. His fingers dragged through something thick and wet and then they touched what he clearly identified as someone's nose and lips. At first he was repelled, then he reached back and let his fingers follow the face up, over the crown of the head until they found the knot of hair at the back. It was Zeller. And it appeared that he was dead.

After a moment's pause he continued the search, his hand finally clasping around the small pistol. He turned back in the direction of the mantrap entrance. As he made the maneuver his ankle clipped a steel trash can that was under the table and it went over in a loud clatter.

Pierce ducked and rolled as two more shots echoed through the lab and he saw two microsecond flashes of Wentz's face in the darkness. Pierce did not return fire, he was too busy moving out of Wentz's aim. He heard the distinct *thwap thwap* sound of the bullets meant for him hitting the copper sheeting on the outside wall of the laser lab at the end of the room.

Pierce tucked the gun into the pocket of his jeans so he could crawl more quickly and efficiently. He once more concentrated on calming himself and his breathing and then started crawling forward and to his left.

He reached out one hand until he touched the wall and gathered his bearings. He then crawled silently forward, using the wall as a guide. He passed the threshold to the wire room – he could tell by the concentrated smell of burned carbon – and moved to the next room down, the imaging lab.

He slowly stood up, his ears primed for the sound of any close movement. There was only silence and then a metallic snapping sound from the other side of the room. Pierce identified it as the sound of a bullet clip being ejected from a gun. He did not have a lot of experience with guns but the sound seemed to fit with what he was imagining in his head: Wentz reloading or checking the number of bullets he had left in his clip.

'Hey, Bright Boy,' Wentz called out then, his voice splitting the darkness like lightning. 'It's just you and me now. Better get ready because I'm coming for you. And I'm gonna do more than make you put the lights back on.'

Wentz cackled loudly in the darkness.

Pierce slowly turned the handle on the imaging lab door and opened it without a sound. He stepped in and closed the door. He worked from memory. He took two steps toward the back of the room and then three to his right. He put his hand out and in another step touched the wall. With fingers spread wide on each hand he swept the wall – his hands making figure eight motions – until his left hand hit the hook on which hung the heat resonance goggles he had used during the presentation to Goddard that morning.

Pierce turned on the goggles, pulled the top piece over his head and adjusted the eyepieces. The room came up blue-black except for the yellow and red glow of the electron microscope's computer terminal and monitor. He reached into his pocket and pulled out the gun. He looked down at it. It too showed blue in the vision field. He put a red finger through the guard and pulled it in close to the trigger.

As he quietly pulled the lab door open Pierce saw a variety of colors in the central lab. To his left he saw the large body of Six-Eight sprawled near the mantrap door. His torso was a collage of reds and yellows tapering in his extremities to blue. He was dead and turning cold.

There was a bright red and yellow image of a man huddled against the wall to the right of the main computer station. Pierce raised the gun and aimed but then stopped himself when he remembered Rudolpho Gonsalves. The huddled man was the security guard Wentz had used to gain entrance to the lab.

He swept right and saw two more still figures, one slumped over the probe station and turning blue in the extremities. Cody Zeller. The other body was on the floor. It was red and yellow in the vision field. Renner. Alive. It looked like he had turtled backward into the kneehole of a desk. Pierce noted a high-heat demarcation on the detective's left shoulder. It was a drip pattern. The purple was warm blood leaking from a wound.

He swept left and then right. There were no other readings, save for yellow reactions off the screens of the monitors in the room and the overhead lights.

Wentz was gone.

But that was impossible. Pierce realized that Wentz must have moved into one of the side labs. Perhaps looking for a window or some sort of illumination or a place from which he could attack in ambush.

He took one step through the doorway and then suddenly hands were upon him, grabbing his throat. He was slammed backward into the wall and held there.

The vision field filled with the blaring red forehead and otherworldly eyes of Billy Wentz. The warm barrel of a gun was pressed harshly into the softness under Pierce's chin.

'Okay, Bright Boy, this is it.'

Pierce closed his eyes and prepared for the bullet the best he could.

But it didn't come.

'Turn the fucking lights on and open the door.'

Pierce didn't move. He realized Wentz needed his help before he could kill him. In that moment he also realized that Wentz probably wasn't expecting that he would have a gun in his hand.

The hand that gripped his shirt and throat shook him violently.

'The lights, I said.'

'Okay, okay. Lights.'

As he said the words he brought the gun up to Wentz's temple and pulled the trigger twice. There was no other way, no other choice. The blasts were almost simultaneous and came instantaneously to the lights in the lab suite coming on. The vision field went black and Pierce reached his other hand up and shoved the goggles off. They fell to the ground ahead of Wentz, who somehow maintained his balance for a few seconds, despite his left eye and temple having been torn away by the bullets Pierce had fired. Wentz still held the gun pointed up but it was no longer under Pierce's chin. Pierce reached out and pushed the gun back, until its aim was no longer a danger. The push also sent Wentz on his way. He fell backwards onto the floor and lay still, dead.

Pierce looked down at him for ten seconds before taking his first breath. He then collected himself and looked around. Gonsalves was getting up slowly, using the far wall to hold himself steady.

'Rudolpho, okay?'

'Yes, sir.'

Pierce swung his view to the desk beneath which Renner had crawled. He could see the cop's eyes, open and alert. He was breathing heavily, the left shoulder and chest of his shirt soaked in blood.

'Rudolpho, get upstairs to a phone. Call paramedics and tell them we have a cop down. Gunshot wound.'

'Yes, sir.'

'Then call the police and tell them the same thing. Then call Clyde Vernon and get him in here.'

The guard hustled to the mantrap door. He had to lean over Six-Eight's body to reach the combo lock. He then had to step widely over the big man's body to go through the door. Pierce saw a bullet hole in the center of the monster's throat. Renner had hit him squarely and he had gone down right in his tracks. Pierce realized he had never heard the big man speak a single word.

He moved to Renner and helped the injured detective crawl out from beneath the desk. His breathing was raspy but Pierce saw no blood on his lips. This meant his lungs were likely still intact.

'Where are you hit?'

'Shoulder.'

He groaned with the movement.

'Don't move. Just wait. Help is coming.'

'Hit my shooting arm. And I'm useless at distance with a gun in my right hand. I figured the best I could do was hide.'

He pulled himself into a sitting position and leaned back against the desk. He gestured with his right hand toward Cody Zeller, handcuffed and slumped forward over the probe table.

'That's not going to look too good.'

Pierce studied his former friend's body for a long moment. He then broke away and looked back at Renner.

'Don't worry. Ballistics will show it came from Wentz.'

'Hope so. Help me up. I want to walk.'

'No, man, you shouldn't. You're hurt.'

'Help me up.'

Pierce did as he was instructed. As he lifted Renner by the right arm he could tell the smell of carbon had permeated the man's clothes.

'What are you smiling at?' Renner asked.

'I think our plan ruined your clothes, even before the bullet. I didn't think you'd be stuck in there with the furnace so long.'

'I'm not worried about it. Zeller was right, though. It does give you a headache.'

'I know.'

Renner pushed him away with his right hand and then walked by himself over to where Wentz's body was lying. He looked down silently for a long moment.

'Doesn't look so tough right now, does he?'

'No,' Pierce said.

'You did good, Pierce. Real good. Nice trick with the lights.'

'I'll have to thank my partner, Charlie. The lights were his idea.'

Pierce silently promised never to complain about the gadgetry again. It reminded him of how he had held things back from Charlie, how he had been suspicious. He knew he would have to make up for it in some way.

'Speaking of partners, mine's going to shit himself when he finds out what he missed,' Renner said. 'And I guess I'll be headed to the shitter myself for doing this on my own.'

He sat down on the edge of one of the desks and looked glumly at the bodies. Pierce realized that the detective had possibly jeopardized his career.

'Look,' he said. 'Nobody could have seen all of this coming. Whatever you need me to do or say, just let me know.'

'Yeah, thanks. What I might need is a job.'

'Well, then you've got it.'

Renner moved from the desk and lowered himself into a chair. His face was screwed up from the pain. Pierce wished he could do something.

'Look, man, stop moving around, stop talking. Just wait for the paramedics.'

But Renner ignored him.

'You know that stuff Zeller was talking about? About when you were a kid and you found your sister but didn't tell anybody?'

Pierce nodded.

'Don't beat yourself up on that anymore. People make their own choices. They decide what path to take. You understand?'

Pierce nodded again.

'Okay.'

The door to the mantrap snapped loudly, making Pierce but not Renner jump. Gonsalves came through the door.

'They're on the way. Everybody. ETA on the ambulance is about four minutes.'

Renner nodded and looked up at Pierce.

'I'll make it.'

'I'm glad.'

Pierce looked back at Gonsalves.

'You call Vernon?'

'Yes, he's coming.'

'Okay. Wait upstairs for everybody and then bring them down.'

After the security man was gone Pierce thought about how Clyde Vernon was going to react to what had happened in the laboratory he was charged with protecting. He knew that the former FBI man was going to implode with anger. He would have to deal with it. They both would.

Pierce walked over to the desk where Cody Zeller's body was sprawled. He looked down upon the man he had known for so long but now understood he hadn't really known at all. A sense of grief started to fill him. He wondered when his friend had turned in the wrong direction. Was it back at Palo Alto, when they had both made choices about the future? Or was it more recently? He had said that money was the motivation but Pierce wasn't sure the reason was as complete and definable as that. He knew it would be something that he would think about and consider for a long time to come.

He turned and looked over at Renner, who seemed to be weakening. He was leaning forward, hunched over on himself. His face was very pale.

'Are you okay? Maybe you should lie down on the floor.'

The detective ignored the question and the suggestion. His mind was still working the case.

'I guess the shame of it is, they're all dead,' he said. 'Now we may never find Lilly Quinlan. Her body, I mean.'

Pierce stepped over to him and leaned back against a desk.

'Uh, there's a few things I didn't tell you before.'

Renner held his gaze for a long moment.

'I figured as much. Give.'

'I know where the body is.'

Renner looked at him for a long moment and then nodded.

'I should have known. How long?'

'Not long. Just today. I couldn't tell you until I was sure you would help me.'

Renner shook his head in annoyance.

'This better be good. Start talking.'

40

Pierce was sitting in his office on the third floor, waiting to face the detectives again. It was six-thirty Friday morning. The investigators from the county coroner's office were still down in the lab. The detectives were waiting for the all-clear signal to go down and were spending their time grilling him on the moment-by-moment details of what had happened in the basement of the building.

After an hour of that Pierce said he needed a break. He retreated from the boardroom, where the interviews were being conducted, to his office. He got no more than five minutes by himself before Charlie Condon stuck his head through the door. He had been roused from sleep by Clyde Vernon, who had of course been roused from sleep by Rudolpho Gonsalves.

'Henry, can I come in?'

'Sure. Close the door.'

Condon came in and looked at him with a slight shake of his head, almost like a tremor.

'Wow!'

'Yeah. It's "wow" all right.'

'Anybody told you what's going on with Goddard?'

'Not really. They wanted to know where he and Bechy were staying and I told them. I think they were going to go over there and arrest them as co-conspirators or something.'

'You still don't know who they worked for?'

'No. Cody didn't say. One of his clients, I assume. They'll find out, either from Goddard or when they get into Zeller's place.'

Condon sat down on the couch to the side of Pierce's desk. He was not wearing his usual suit and tie and Pierce realized how much younger he looked in knockabout clothes.

'We have to start over,' Pierce said. 'Find a new investor.'

Condon looked incredulous.

'Are you kidding? After this? Who would—'

'We're still in business, Charlie. The science is still the thing. The patent. There will be investors out there who will know this. You have to go out and do the Ahab thing. Find another great white whale.'

'Easier said than done.'

'Everything in this world is easier said than done. What happened to me last night and in the last week is easier said than done. But it's done. I made it through and it's given me a hotter fire than ever.'

Condon nodded.

'Nobody stops us now,' he said.

'That's right. We're going to take a media firestorm today and probably over the next few weeks. But we have to figure out the way to turn it to our advantage, to pull investors in, not scare them away. I'm not talking about the daily news. I'm talking about the journals, the industry.'

'I'll get on it. But you know where we're going to be totally screwed?'

'Where?'

'Nicki. She was our spokesperson. We need her. She knew these people, the reporters. Who is going to handle the media on this? They'll be all over this for the next few days, at least, or until the next big thing happens to draw them away.'

Pierce considered this for a few moments. He looked up at the framed poster showing the *Proteus* submarine moving through a sea of many different colors. The human sea.

'Call her up and hire her back. She can keep the severance. All she has to do is come back.'

Condon paused before replying.

'Henry, how is that going to work with you two? I doubt she'll consider it.'

Pierce suddenly got excited about the idea. He would tell her that the rehire was strictly professional, that they would have no other relationship outside of work. He then would show her how he had changed. How the dime chased him now, not the other way around.

He thought of the book of Chinese characters he had left open on the coffee table. Forgiveness. He decided that he could make it work. He would win her back and he would make it work.

'If you want, I'll call her. I'll get—'

His direct line rang and he immediately answered it.

'Henry, it's Jacob. It's so early there. I thought I was going to get your voice mail.'

'No, I've been here all night. Did you file it?'

'I filed it twenty minutes ago. Proteus is protected. You are protected, Henry.'

'Thank you, Jacob. I'm glad you went last night.'

'Is everything okay back there?'

'Everything except we lost Goddard.'

'Oh my gosh! What happened?'

'It's a long story. When are you coming back?'

'I'm going to go visit my brother and his family down in Owings in southern Maryland. I'll fly back Sunday.'

'Do they have cable down in Owings?'

'Yes. I'm pretty sure they do.'

'Keep your eye on CNN. I have a feeling we're going to light it up.'

'Is there—'

'Jacob, I'm in the middle of something. I have to go. Go see your brother and get some sleep. I hate red-eye flights.'

Kaz agreed and then they hung up. Pierce looked at Condon.

'We're in. He filed the package.'

Condon's face lit up.

'How?'

'I sent him last night. They can't touch us now, Charlie.'

Condon thought about this for a few moments and then nodded his head.

'Why didn't you tell me you were sending him?'

Pierce just looked at him. He could see the realization in Condon's face, that Pierce had not trusted him.

'I didn't know, Charlie. I couldn't talk to anybody until I knew.'

Condon nodded but the hurt remained on his face.

'Must be hard. Living with all that suspicion. Must be hard to be so alone.'

Now it was Pierce's turn to just nod. Condon said he was going to get some coffee and left him alone in the office.

For a few moments Pierce didn't move. He thought about Condon and what he had said. He knew his partner's words were cutting but true. He knew it was time to change all of that.

It was still early in the day but Pierce didn't want to wait to begin. He picked up the phone and called the house on Amalfi Drive.

ACKNOWLEDGMENTS

This book could not have been written without the help of Dr. James Heath, professor of chemistry, University of California, Los Angeles, and Carolyn Chriss, researcher extraordinaire. This story is fiction. However, the science contained within it is real. The race to build the first molecular computer is real. Any errors or unintended exaggerations within the story are solely the responsibility of the author.

For their help and advice the author is also indebted to Terrill Lee Lankford, Larry Bernard, Jane Davis, Robert Connelly, Paul Connelly, John Houghton, Mary Lavelle, Linda Connelly, Philip Spitzer and Joel Gotler.

Many thanks also go to Michael Pietsch and Jane Wood for going beyond the call of duty as editors with this manuscript, and as well to Stephen Lamont for the excellent copyediting.